SHADES
OF
PERCEPTION

BOOK 1

BOOK 1

FiniteVoid

Podium

Cover design by Creadfectus

ISBN: 978-1-0394-7104-7

Published in 2024 by Podium Publishing
www.podiumaudio.com

SHADES
OF
PERCEPTION

BOOK 1

Chapter 1

OBSERVATION

Someone was following him.

No matter the time of the day, whether he was surrounded by a bustling crowd out in the boroughs or alone in his lodging at night, someone was watching him, observing all his actions. Somewhere very close, yet just out of sight.

If Vern had to trace back this odd feeling, it would have started right after he had gotten off the train and set foot in the city three days ago. But why would anyone care about his visit to Elmhurst? Hundreds of researchers and more than a couple savants like him gathered here daily from all over the empire for the upcoming annual conference at the Symposium.

He had yet to do his duty as a civilian and involve the Kingsmen, but he didn't have any solid evidence to back up his claims, and being locked away in some room under the name of protection wasn't his idea of a paid vacation.

Driven by the suspicion that maybe all the savants were targets of this surveillance, Vern had reached out to his colleagues, subtly inquiring about the matter in his letters. In response, they had either completely missed the hints or implicitly denied any such happenings.

Shaking his head, Vern cleared his mind and focused on navigating the streets. Now wasn't the time to reflect on his fruitless investigations. Elmhurst had its own charms that needed exploring, like the famous toast at this coffeehouse by the cathedral. He wouldn't miss out on it, even if someone was fulfilling their voyeuristic tendencies at his expense.

The morning sun rose above the myriad towering spires, casting a golden glow over the shorter buildings that lined the streets of this borough. The architecture of the buildings was grand and imposing, boasting intricate details and ornate facades complemented by high ceilings and grand entrances.

As the morning rush began, the streets quickly filled with people hurrying to their various destinations. Men in top hats and long coats made their way to offices and businesses, while women in proper dresses and bonnets hurried along the sidewalks on their way to shops or social calls. The droning of the steam carriages and calls of street vendors added to the bustle and noise of the city.

Despite the crowds, however, an air of formality and decorum permeated the scene, with people moving with a sense of purpose as they went about their lives.

Vern dressed to match the city's aesthetics in a crisp white shirt with a high collar, neatly tucked into his charcoal gray trousers tailored to fit. Draped over the shirt was an unbuttoned black single-breasted coat with six pockets, its smooth fabric accentuating his lean figure. To rid himself of monochrome tones, he also wore a gold chain that extended from the button of his shirt to a pocket watch resting in his trousers.

Blending right into the crowd, he advanced toward his noble objective, turning onto Carmen Street—and he felt it. Swiveling to the left, he looked straight at a window on the second floor of a house across the street.

Something shuffled in the dim ambiance of the room before the blinds clamped shut. He stood there, staring at the now-closed window, blocking the people behind him on the walkway.

Feeling chilled, he buttoned his coat and exited the scene with quick strides. Having made some distance from the place, he pulled out his notebook and pencil from the pockets and made another entry in the long list of his suspected sightings. Details about all the times he had been able to notice the stares.

They weren't much to go on, and most were as vague as this encounter, occurrences he would have generally passed off as mere coincidence if they didn't happen so damn often. A simple count of entries spoke of a trend. The unwelcome trackers were either getting bolder by the day, or he had gotten better at noticing them.

But, well, the cathedral was right around the corner, and his deductions could wait until he had something in his stomach. Not like this was the first time it had happened to him anyway.

Weaving through the crowd, he got closer to the aroma of freshly baked bread that wafted from all around, and that's when he saw it. Another one in such a short interval!

In the mirror of a store window a few paces behind him, someone was looking straight at him, barely visible in the sea of heads and hats.

A chance!

He had never been able to notice one of them so closely, and there was no way he was going to miss this opportunity. Vern maneuvered through the crowd to mask himself from the line of sight of his supposed stalker and, with only a few steps, slipped into an alleyway.

This alleyway, like most others, was just a backstreet that connected two parallel ones. Keeping a clear vision of the flowing crowd, he backpedaled. It was a chance to get a good look at his perpetrator and finally involve the Kingsmen with solid evidence.

A few seconds passed in wild anticipation as the throng of people moved forward without the man crossing the small opening. Until he did, moving right past the entrance and drowning in the horde of people. *Not very perceptive, are we?*

He was a thin man with a pale face, wearing shabby clothes that were too big for him. There was a fair share of destitute beggars in the city, and nothing about him struck Vern as odd. But whatever the case, he was sure that someone had had his eyes glued on him ever since he left his place, and this guy was probably the culprit.

If not by a direct confrontation, Vern could always have a better day with one less creep eyeing him. Hell, even better, he could circle around and stalk the stalker from a little distance to give him a taste of his own medicine while confirming his suspicions.

It wasn't every day you got to play with fire while having insurance to not have your house burn down. Elmhurst was a haven during the conference month and likely the reason he had yet to faint from his nerves at this whole ordeal.

In every borough he'd been to, Kingsmen dotted the roofs, staring down like executioners with their gleaming gear and sharp eyes. Just yesterday, from his balcony, he saw one of these punishers swoop down with their ropecaster and sever the arm of some trigger-happy individual in the blink of an eye. Efficient and accurate.

Shaping up the exact details of his spontaneous plan, he turned around with a grin—and instantly froze up. A towering figure stood right in front of him draped in black from head to toe. The top hat's brim obscured the stranger's forehead while a mask that covered his entire face, including the eyes, hid his countenance.

Vern backed up a little and looked the figure straight in its eyes. *Wow, I fucked up. Did they get mad that I escaped them for a second? They have never confronted me like this. What's changed?*

"I've got a whole crew on my back, eh?" asked Vern without delay in a calm tone while his heart was anything but that, drumming like crazy. "Care to shed some light on why I'm so popular?" he followed up, making sure his voice didn't waver.

No way they will attack me in broad daylight with hundreds of people just a few steps away. Should I shout for help?

He bit down hard and suppressed his impulsiveness as he waited for an answer. *There must be a reason for this.* They've had far better opportunities than this to get rid of him quietly.

A few seconds passed before the figure moved, and Vern watched his movements with rapt attention, ready to retreat at a moment's notice.

The person in black pulled out a paper from their pocket and shoved it onto Vern's chest before turning around and walking away at a brisk pace.

Vern was dumbfounded but wasn't ready to let the man go just yet. He stored the paper in his pocket and chased after the figure, shouting, "At least tell me who you work for."

The figure exited the alley without a response and made for the right. Vern pursued posthaste, and when his vision opened to the bright street outside, a somewhat crowded walkway greeted him with no signs of the figure in black.

Scary bastards!

It was frustrating, to say the least. All he had to do was shout that this man was a thief, and someone on the street would have gladly played the hero.

But doing so ran the risk of harming Vern's relations with their organization. And there was no guarantee that the figure would divulge anything useful, even if he managed to stop him. His unwanted observers had finally initiated an interaction after three days, and he didn't want to burn the bridge without first understanding their angle on the situation.

Vern went around the back of the cathedral to Carmen Street, then sauntered to his original destination. Entering the coffeehouse, he beelined to a corner table and ordered the toast he was so eager to try not so long ago. Without further ado, he retrieved the paper and scanned its contents with a frown.

CLC-307-23. Mayst thou accept the gracious gift of eyes, ere the hour of reckoning befalls thee. ~Yharl Ballin

Vern knew a library book identification number when he saw one. It was simply the author's initials, section, and shelf number. But the message and name after that? Yeah, he had no clue.

What is this? A team of highly coordinated specialists monitored me twenty-four seven, all in an elaborate plan to scare me and deliver this threat? Gift? Is this their version of a stick and a carrot? If I don't get this gift of eyes within some time, reckoning will befall me? As in, they will simply kill me if I don't comply and accept this gift?

He had somehow managed to underestimate and overestimate the severity of this situation simultaneously.

After a few minutes, a waiter dropped his plate of baked bread straight from the oven, lightly toasted to golden brown with butter melting over the slices in excess as fragrant steam rose from the plate. Vern took off his black gauntlet gloves and made quick work of the toasts.

Having sated his appetite, he took out his notepad and added the key points of the latest development to his entries. It helped him get his mental gears grinding.

The motivation of his invasive followers was still unclear, but involving Kingsmen right away didn't seem like the smartest idea. He had already reduced the possibility of his murder being their motive to under 10 percent. They wanted something from him, and if reading a book could help him make an informed decision, he wasn't averse to the idea.

What if they were some invasive assholes that ruined the start of his vacation? If the scale of balance between benefit and comfort was tipped toward the benefit, he wouldn't mind entertaining their proposal.

However, he wouldn't work on something illegal. He already had a clear path to success with his apprenticeship and was on the cusp of plucking the fruits of his labor.

That aside, the amount of information he had gathered in three days was pathetic, and little could be concluded from it. He did have a clear course of action though. *I can check out the book today, but for the name, I will have to ask around or send an inquiry to Master. I can't involve Ari in this affair, after all.*

However, the message had quite a peculiar word choice, suggesting that reading this book would give him a gift of eyes. As in opening his eyes to something significant? Vern had a hard time believing that.

As one of the youngest savants recognized by the coven for his significant contributions to the advancement of civilization, there was little that could shake him anymore. But knowledge was not to be denied, and his stalkers deserved the benefit of the doubt for all their effort.

A long day in the library sounded tempting regardless, and he didn't have much else to do before the conference other than touring around the city anyway.

His next steps planned, Vern didn't dally any further, paid his well-spent three crowns, and left the establishment. There wasn't much contest as to where this book was located.

Elmhurst had a library to which one shouldn't miss paying a visit, even if they didn't fancy books. The building's beauty and architecture were praised by many as a symbol of the coven's superior aesthetics. Not that Vern cared much about that himself.

Eleonora's archive was one of the grandest in the whole empire, and Vern had been looking for excuses to go there.

He retrieved a city map from another of his coat's pockets and planned a route to the archive. Looking at it, he'd need to do a lot of walking in rush hour and get directions from locals multiple times to get there. *Or I could just get a carriage.*

Vern stood at the sidewalk's edge and raised his arm, making eye contact with all the drivers passing by. His arm got sore in no time, and before he got bored enough to bring out and continue reading the analysis of this state-of-the-art force multiplication gearbox he'd been fascinated with, a hissing sound intensified and died down with a sputter as a carriage stopped by.

"Where to, good sir?"

"To Eleonora's archive, please."

"I can drop you by the bridge across the scholar's place if that's okay with you. It's just a few minutes' walk from there. You see, I can't cross the bridge without paying a full day's toll," said the scrawny yet well-dressed man with an obsequious smile.

"Sure. How much is the ride?"

"Three crowns, eight pence. The usual for this distance."

Vern nodded and boarded the carriage, settling on the corner seat across from an elderly couple. In but a few seconds, the scenery outside the windows started receding, changing from packed streets to broader roads, passing by what seemed like a craft market, then onto narrower roads with housing squares, and at last, one of those bridges that the city was so famous for.

This one, just like the others he'd seen before, was a feat of engineering. A myriad of thin cables ran above, and massive pillars taller than the thirty-meter gorge below stood underneath. The whole thing was somehow wide enough to have four carriages pass side by side from one bank to the other, more spacious than most streets.

Vern still felt awed every time he saw one of these. It wasn't that these bridges had cutting-edge technology or anything, but they were impressive because they were built about seven hundred years ago.

Why did he know this? Because anyone who didn't know about Elmhurst's bridges might as well be living under a rock. Whatever these bridges were made of was strong. So strong, in fact, that even a team of chaos fundamentalists failed to scrape more than a handful of dust from the bridges.

The vista outside the window ceased to retreat as the carriage screeched to a halt. He deboarded without much elegance and shelled out four crowns. Handing them to the driver with a nod, he turned around and walked across the metallic relic toward the archive.

Fancy balustrades carved in the sights of old gods lined the railings, and queer symbols ran along the wires, stretching all the way to the top if he saw correctly.

Vern took out his notepad and started penning down these oddities like any other enthusiastic citizen.

Once the patterns began repeating themselves, he got bored of them and asked himself the real question. *Is someone still following me?* He didn't know.

Over the last three days, Vern had developed the habit of glancing back every so often, but he had yet to register those dark shadows lurking around.

Not like he was always able to notice them, and more often than not, it was just his paranoia and hypersensitivity scaring him of dark shadows, which this city inexplicably had an abundance of.

Also, there was no way his followers got left behind in the dust from a simple carriage ride. He had taken quite a few of those since he arrived in the city, yet he never managed to really lose them.

However, this whole chain of events was perplexing. *Do they really just mean to deliver this note to me? Why wait three days? Do they have some condition set for delivery based on some performance metric for which they monitor me?*

How hard could it have been to set up a meeting and talk like refined gentlemen? Even interviewing him was on the table if they wanted to test him or something. He'd have agreed in exchange for some compensation anyway.

But there's got to be more than what meets the eye. It wouldn't do me any good to underestimate this situation any longer. He did not have the information needed to understand their perspective or why they were doing all this. So, for now, he would take it a step at a time and handle things as they came.

Then, before he fell into another cycle of recursive thoughts, the colossal archive was upon him.

As grand as the largest cathedral he'd seen, the library spanned what seemed to be a whole residential block. Its steep-pitched roof that towered high above was studded with spires, each reaching for the sky. Complex corbellings jutted out of the structure's intricate brickwork decorated by arched windows and numerous balconies.

A purple hue radiated from the windows and terrace, most likely emitted by flameless lighting, the recent invention of Sterling Rupert, already ubiquitous in most rich establishments.

Hopefully, he will clarify the technicalities of his subpar paper on cyclical condensation during his lecture at the conference. We could have had so many derivations in the market if only they understood whatever the hell he's talking about in the paper.

Vern's steps grew quicker, halting at the entrance. Five Kingsmen stood guard—two women and three men—their gear shimmering in the sunlight. Doing his best to form an amiable smile, Vern unhooked the coven badge from the pocket watch's chain and passed it over to the only one with an hourglass emblem etched on his uniform.

The man scrutinized the badge with the same symbol as his own and spoke after a bit. "This is good. However, before you go in, and excuse me for asking, but do you happen to have anything highly flammable on your person? If so, I'm afraid I'll have to ask you to deposit it here for safekeeping until you're ready to leave. Hiding or smuggling any such materials is strictly prohibited under the coven's laws and could result in heavy penalties."

Knowing this was the procedure of all the coven's libraries, Vern just shook his head and retrieved the items from the myriad pockets of his coat and spread them out on the table by the representative. "Nothing of the sort. Please feel free to shake me down."

The coven's representative motioned toward Vern, and one of the Kingsmen grunted before giving Vern a thorough pat down. With a nod, he returned to his position, and the representative gave his emblem back, waving him in.

Vern latched his emblem back on, shoved all his belongings back into their respective dwellings, and walked by a narrow corridor alongside a few clerks before his sight opened to a vast reading hall.

Rows upon rows of shelves lined the colossal hall, each stacked with literary promises to another world or a voyage to a time bygone. A throng of scholars drifted around in their institutes' uniforms, their heads glued to the graying books in a numbing silence disturbed only by the clock's ticking.

Chandeliers adorned the ceiling, while every pillar was studded with tiny circular chunks of glass that reflected the omnipresent lavender radiance. Murals of Lennian scholars dyed the pristine white walls, portraying their major inventions in gorgeous strokes.

On the ceiling hung small spherical flameless lanterns, suffusing the environment with their rich amethyst glow. Another wonder derived from some obscure Lennian fundamental by Rupert. Two small compartments were conjoined in a connection that somehow emitted this beautiful light.

It's pretty and all, but purple light isn't really the best for reading. Though it's quite bright and probably better than not being able to read past sundown or burning the library while doing so.

Vern squinted at the little devilish contraptions. He had inquired about purchasing them in all kinds of places with nothing to show for it. Petitioning to buy one from the library's management was an option he considered, but the queue of petitions was already a few months long. So, he could always borrow one, right? No doubt he would reassemble it and return it to its rightful place. *Yeah, I should grab one from somewhere less crowded.*

Making up his mind on that front, Vern approached a clerk and asked for directions to section 307 in a hushed tone. According to the clerk, section 307, being on the second floor instead of the third, made perfect sense. Shaking his head, he made his way over to one of the staircases and climbed the spiral to the second floor.

This floor seemed like a sprawling maze, packed with more shelves than scholars. Another set of Lennian murals dyed the walls in crimson strokes. Arches and pillars were adorned with the same flameless spherical lanterns and mirrors, their glow overshadowed by the blazing sun pouring in from the floor-to-ceiling windows.

Vern skipped past many aisles to zero in on this section 307, his steps quick and a little haphazard. It'd be a lie to say that the prior events hadn't fazed him.

Getting chased around by shadowy figures for no apparent reason had done more than a number on his mental state. It was one thing to not feel threatened because of the city's protective measures, but it was another to be in a situation where he had no control over the outcome.

He was playing right into the hands of the perpetrator by reading this book. Pursuing this might get him some answers, but it might mean getting further embroiled in whatever his stalkers or this Yharl Ballin was cooking up.

Passing another section, he finally reached 307. Just another set of big old shelves that were arranged in ascending order. So getting to shelf 23 wasn't an ordeal. Loaded with thick tomes, the shelf seemed dedicated to older books with a knack for lengthy extents and poor binding.

Finding no interesting titles at first glance, he did another sweep of the shelf while focusing on the authors' names on the spines and found the culprit in no time—a thin one in this thick bunch. *Observation Record of Subjectivity* by Cyrus L. Cartwright. Retrieving it without hesitation, Vern found himself a quiet table in a corner by one of the massive windows and settled down.

It looked ancient, bound in faded leather and containing decrepit and yellowing pages, but an intricate embossing, barely visible, was etched into its surface. Vern flipped open the book and was greeted by the distinct scent of old parchment and ink alongside a peculiar introduction.

The pursuit of objectivity is a prerequisite in determining the facts about our cosmos. However, the acquisition of these facts is dependent upon the act of observation, but to observe is to shade reality with one's perception, thereby rendering the concept of objectivity somewhat elusive.

It is, therefore, pertinent to explore the question of what constitutes objectivity within the context of observation. This text, however, doesn't intend to ambitiously define objectivity but instead aims to enable one to perceive the subjectivity of reality. A path to enlightenment, to be regarded as a quantifiable entity, an observer.

His brows furrowed as he read on. Intrigued, he zoned out the noise and immersed himself in the arcane words.

Chapter 2

SUBJECTIVITY

Vern stood out on the terrace, his coat buttoned up all the way to combat the chill. A frown creased his brows as he held the worn book in his hand and leaned against the railing. A sprawling city encompassed his vision, multiple disjointing boroughs connected to each other via metal bridges. Bridges that spanned the meandering rivers, which cut through the metropolis, gave these tiny disparate landmasses a semblance of unity.

Six chimes reverberated throughout the city as the short hand of the clockface on the tallest tower in Fulham borough pointed straight down. An enormity, peeking through the shimmering rays of the setting sun, visible all the way here, three bridges away.

This is wrong. It just doesn't make any logical sense. Vern had gone over the book, and the fundamentalist within him couldn't seem to come to terms with the situation. He would have no doubt passed it off as mere fiction with great attention to detail if it wasn't for that diagram.

The information within wasn't just significant, as he'd hoped. It was borderline heretical, if that could be a thing in the context of mechanical arts. It presented the idea of viewing reality through a unique perspective. At first glance, there was nothing remarkable about that, right? Everyone already had a unique viewpoint, after all. Wrong.

This was something deeper, more primal. It was about the laws that governed reality itself, and the idea was that one could see these very laws in their own unique interpretation as their subjective observer. This alone, if real, would send every fundamentalist on Prima into a maddening frenzy.

The ability to form new schools of thought, grounded in a core concept, would no doubt usher the whole civilization into a new era and bring about revolutionary changes. It was subversive to the point it made Vern contemplate existence. Lennian fundamentalism defined reality, but no one had ever found something like subjective observation in them.

The story, however, didn't end there. From reading between the lines and extrapolating from context, it was all but written in bold that it was possible to change the very laws of reality itself with subjective observers of one mind in enough quantity. Vern didn't even want to think of the disaster that could spell.

A simple thought experiment, however, was necessary despite his unease. Assuming there were enough subjective observers that decided to observe the laws of gravity, and they concluded that it should only exert half its current force.

Then the entire reality would be thrown into a state of low-gravity chaos. Buildings and infrastructures not built to withstand such conditions might crumble or float away, their foundational assumptions literally upended.

Objects would weigh half as much as they used to, disrupting a myriad of daily activities from the mundane act of walking to the critical task of cooking. Even more concerning, trees would struggle to draw water from the ground, birds would have to relearn flight, and the tides of the oceans would dramatically shift, possibly leading to a widespread ecological disaster.

The very atmosphere of Prima might start to escape into the ether due to the reduced gravitational pull, threatening all life as we know it. This and billions of other changes he couldn't even begin to fathom would come simply on the whims of a group of people.

The thought sent shivers down his spine, and the frown in his brows only grew deeper. The very act of touching this delicate balance of current laws could grind civilization to a halt in no time or even annihilate it completely. All this was bizarre enough as ideas, but what made him panic was the diagram he encountered a few pages into the book.

Ascension from an objective to a subjective observer didn't include some sacrificial ritual like one would expect. It was apparently as simple as comprehending the abstract diagram in the book. It appeared to be nothing more than a picture printed onto some textured paper, but looking at it was like hallucinating.

The intricate patterns moved and reformed on the piece of paper! Just this mechanical art of moving lines on paper without an apparent energy source could pique the curiosity of all Lennian fundamentalists. Though he doubted it worked like that.

What borderline made him consider visiting a psychiatrist was the nature of the diagram itself. If he focused hard enough, the lines would rearrange themselves into sentences that only got more concise as time passed by, becoming more rudimentary as links formed between them in some mesmerizing pattern. Vern had spent more than five hours straight gazing at differing variations of that diagram.

The final nail in the coffin that made him close the book for good was when Vern felt something form within himself. A feeling of being on the verge of understanding and comprehension, perceiving that fleeting insight that would change everything, lingered in his mind.

And that is where Vern had to draw the line. A balanced and stable mind-set was the key to long-term progression. This feeling of imminent comprehension was compulsive and made him anxious.

It was one thing to make an informed decision and receive enlightenment from his own will, but completely another to be compelled by stalkers and a book to delve outside the realm of Lennian fundamentalism and possibly lose his head due to naive stupidity and haste.

The book didn't have specifics on the risks and aftereffects that would follow this enlightenment, and Vern never made it a habit to gamble unless necessary.

If he had to generalize this idea of enlightenment from the given information, it was probably as simple as acknowledging and comprehending that the world around one can be subjective and exist in a state of superposition, all possibilities existing at the same time.

The diagram was simply a catalyst or example to guide the perception. But something was missing. If it was that simple, someone could post this paper in the city square and forcibly enlighten everyone that saw it. It would spread faster than a plague, and there was no way something with such a low barrier of entry could have stayed under wraps for so long.

However, the book was too short. The diagram was only a few pages in, and everything else after that was just blank pages. Inferring from what he knew about observation, he even suspected that they weren't really blank, but he had to be a subjective observer to read them.

This would need proper consideration and auxiliary research before I—

His thoughts were cut short as two arms clasped around his chest from behind, passing on their warmth to his cold self.

"Big brother, please go to hell!" a feminine voice exclaimed in a hushed tone.

Chapter 3

SISTER

Uh?! Shit. Vern pocketed the decrepit book in his coat in a swift motion and turned around in the loose embrace. His eyes reflected a petite girl whom he promptly hugged back. The perpetual frown that hung on his face melted away, and a radiant smile bloomed in its place. He lifted her off the ground a little and squeezed her tight.

She wore a long, loose green coat that was draped over a white vest, paired with matching two-tone earrings. Her pitch-black hair was worn in a half up messy style that shimmered under the twilight, and her oval face had a soft glow to it beset by her eyes, which shone with a cheery gleam.

"How've you been, Ariane?" asked Vern as he put her down, ignoring her lovely greeting.

"I see, I see. Willful, intentional neglect. You don't care anymore. I heard you arrived here three days ago. Three whole days, and you didn't even come say hi? Yes, please just go find a new sister," replied Ariane in a matter-of-fact tone as she struggled out of his embrace.

"Didn't your last letter mention that you had exams this week? So, I was really just trying to be considerate and not distract you until you were done."

Ariane's gaze turned dejected as she squirmed out from the embrace and hung her head low.

"Not like I study all the time. It would've only taken you a few minutes to come by. I see. Now that you are successful, you don't need a sister anymore. He doesn't need me. He doesn't love me. He doesn't need me. He doesn't love me," she kept repeating in a voice that lowered by the second.

"Uh, umm . . . Ari. Calm down, it's nothing like that. Please listen to me—" He closed in on her, and his shaky voice paused as a smirk peeked through between her repeated murmurs.

Cheat! "Actually, you're right. I should find a new sister. This one's defective. Your gods forgot to install a brain up there, which people use to logically think through situations and not jump to conclusions," uttered Vern in an apathetic voice as he turned around and waved his hand.

She rushed up to him and yanked his arm. "You can actually say that? How rude! I'll write to your master, citing your lacking ethics and mistreatment of your adorable little sister."

"Hmph. Can't even play victim correctly," said Vern with a sneer.

Ariane nodded slowly, "I see. Never mind me." She unclipped a fountain pen from her vest pocket and started waving it in the air, "Mm-hmm . . . Mm-hmm.

Dear Master-in-law, your apprentice's behavior leaves a lot to be desired. He lacks the manners and grace expected of a gentleman, showing little regard for honor or respect for his peers. He is a loathsome sociopath with nothing but apathy for those around him. A stain on this beautiful society—"

"Okay, okay, milady Ariane, please calm down. I meant well. I was really gonna visit you tomorrow. I knew you'd be done with exams by today. Also, I had this situation where involving you could have been unfavorable."

His original plan was to send her a letter, blaming work for his inability to visit and avoiding any complications. No way he was going to get her involved with these stalkers if he didn't already have an inkling about their intentions. She did catch him off guard though.

"Don't believe you."

She was right not to. He could only blame himself for having to lie to his sister like that.

Vern took a step back and held a nonexistent top hat before executing a full bow. "I apologize for the neglect. Dear Master's-apprentice's-sister, I brought a few souvenirs from my master's personal library that you might fancy. I was hoping to give them to you at my earliest convenience, but your rejection to accommodate my schedule has broken my heart. I might have to line up for quacks and get it remedied bef—"

"UGH! Stop, stop! Just pay for this month's expenses on top of the books, and I'll forgive you."

". . ."

"I have to save my paychecks for something important."

". . ."

"I swear on Lady's name that it isn't wasteful! Pretty please . . ." She grabbed hold of both his palms and looked up with watery eyes.

". . ."

". . ." She tilted her face a notch higher.

"Ugh, whatever, just this time then."

"Great! Then let's eat these desserts I got for us! You're paying for them too, obviously."

Ariane pointed at the creamy white pastries sitting atop one of the tables with a cheeky grin.

". . ."

Vern shook his head, retreated from the edge, and grabbed himself a chair by the table. The terrace was there to relax on anyway. The usual restrictions of being discreet and quiet didn't apply out here. He was getting a little hungry admittedly. Ariane sat next to him and helped herself to the desserts.

"How'd you know I was here?" asked Vern as he gobbled down the creamy dessert.

"Oh, that? A friend of mine saw you here and informed me."

"Huh. How do they even know what I look like?"

Ariane looked from side to side and murmured, "It might or might not have something to do with me bragging about being your sister. You're somewhat famous, you know. Anyway, never mind that. How long are you planning on staying in Elmhurst this time?"

Vern didn't comment on the pathetic change of topic. "I plan to leave three days after the conference ends, so about ten more days."

"So soon? It's too short. How would I leech . . . I mean, be a good host if you're gone so soon?"

"Well, I can't be running off from my apprenticeship without a recommendation to at least a duke's house . . . or maybe even a count. Also, I need to go back to my lab and apply the feedback and comments I'll receive after my research presentation at the conference."

"Hmph, nerd. Also, what did you mean earlier when you said involving me could have been unfavorable?"

Vern turned silent and thought about the consequences of sharing his recent experiences and promptly dismissed any such notion. It would only be a disservice to her without adding any value, possibly even getting her added to the list of person-ages to be stalked. So Vern shook his head and said, "I can't talk about it."

"Huh? Why is that?"

"Top secret."

"PLEASE!"

"Yeah, that trick only works once a week."

Ariane looked at him with a pout and stared daggers at him.

"So, what are you presenting at the conference?"

"Huh. Are you actually interested or something?"

"I can always brag about it to my friends."

Vern spread his arms wide. "Well, if you're dying to know, then I can't not tell you. It's about event ratios and phenomenon replication. It's largely hypotheti-cal right now, and figuring out an equilibrium for even an isolated event is a tedious—"

"Aghh, Aghh, I am dying, I am deaf . . . I can't hear anything."

" . . . "

"Whatever you just recited sounds sooo boring. I would have probably deigned to listen to your ramblings if you researched something about stars. But this? Yeah, no. Do something more interesting next time, okay?"

"That wasn't even half the thesis . . . Is your attention span getting worse? Are you secretly a goldfish?"

"A goddess, you said? How charming. Yes, yes, let me tell you how this goddess became the leader of the astronomy club in an epic political maneuver."

Caretakers ignited the flameless hearths, just larger versions of Rupert's spheres, illuminating the library's interior a bright violet. The glow blended with the moon-light into something of a lighter shade out on the balcony.

Vern also set off the spherical lamp on his table by thrusting the little mechanism attached to its sides, triggering some reaction as it instantly radiated a beautiful purple. The marvelous yet slightly inefficient cycle of combustion and condensation within the lamps did nothing to ward away the chill but slowly suffused the sur-roundings with a woody scent.

An acceptable companion for the upcoming conversation, and even possibly a souvenir for his lab if he could unscrew it without anyone noticing.

Nine chimes hummed their metallic rhythm as he looked around yet again. It wasn't the stalkers, but something was wrong. That feeling of urgency and being on the precipice that he'd been suppressing with his strict mental control and distracting conversation only grew wilder and wilder. *I shouldn't have inspected that diagram for so long. If only I was more cautious.*

"Vee. Vee. Vee?" A hand waved in front of him, and only then did he register Ari's figure.

"Vee, are you okay? Are you really thinking about another experiment instead of listening to my magnificent feat of banishing that fat mouse from my room?"

"Mouse? No, you were trying to gloss over how you failed your history test again."

"What do you mean, again!? It's the first time this year. And don't change the topic, please. Is everything okay? You seem . . . distracted. Way more distracted than usual." She took his palm in her hands and looked him straight in the eye.

Vern dodged the stare and looked up at the sky in silence. The words in his stalkers' message implied limited time, and the incessant urging of his own curious mind had him going crazy sitting here and doing nothing.

But he knew this was the best course of action. What did it even mean that he could see the laws? Would he lose his basic sight and only see these laws? That would be a disaster while away from his own city and filled with unknown.

If necessary, he could sleep it off tonight with some medicine and take a train straight back to Nvoria to his master's workshop first thing in the morning. He needed another opinion because ignoring this issue wasn't really working, and his brain actually didn't want to, as knowledge was one thing he couldn't resist.

A few more seconds passed by before he replied, "I am sorry, Ari. I can't tell you everything, but I have this great opportunity in front of me. However, there are too many unknowns around it, and the indecision is making me anxious and jittery."

The grip on his hands grew tighter, and she spoke after a soft sigh. "I understand. Take your time."

There wasn't anything else to read about enlightenment or subjectivity. All the pages after the diagram were empty, and he had already checked the other books in the same section. They were just random books with nothing of interest. As of now, he felt like he had exhausted most of his circumstantial information and needed to go off of tangents to gather something new. *Wait, I actually didn't pursue that at all.*

"Ari, do you know someone named Yharl Ballin?"

She tilted her head and responded after a few breaths, "Do you mean Administrator Yharl?"

"Administrator Yharl?"

"Yeah, he's the leader of the Ascendant Council. A group of fanatics of history, no less. It's quite a famous religion in the city, mainly because they worship Lady Lennix and derive their philosophy from the fundamentals as well."

"Hmm, then where does the administrator prefix come from? That's a political title, not religious. "

"Umm, I don't really know. He may be related to a noble or something. I only know what I do because they've been in the newspaper quite recently."

When he was about to follow up with more questions, a bunch of people streamed onto the balcony and started arguing while pointing at the sky.

He withdrew his hands, signaled Ariane to pause, and followed the gaze of the masses. Everyone had their necks craned, looking at the moon, which was somehow becoming increasingly darker. Their surroundings were losing their ambiance as the pale glow faded by the second.

"Ari?" She would know more than him about whatever was going on up in the sky. She was smart like that.

"Hmm, this is so odd. The sky is as clear as it gets, but the moon is losing light. This shouldn't be happening at this time of the year," said Ariane as she squinted hard at the sky.

"So, not an eclipse?"

"Mm-hmm, the next one is about three months from now."

Everyone gawked at the display with rapt attention, including Vern and Ariane.

"Any idea what's going on?

She tapped her fingers on the table and spoke after a pause, "This is definitely not normal. I'll need to use proper tools and observe the positions of other celestial bodies and calculate their trajectories to reach a conclusion. Something must have changed drastically to cause this."

People visible down in the streets began clamoring as they noticed the oddity themselves. A few stopped to marvel at the scene, while others continued their business like it didn't matter, while some went completely ballistic and knelt right where they stood and began reciting their prayers in a frenzy.

The whole scene made Vern uneasy, and it didn't help that the conjectures of scholars around him were only becoming more unbridled and distressing by the second.

"Is this the reckoning? Goddess is displaying her rage at the heresy we've all committed by stealing her fundamentals."

"NO! This is a celestial phenomenon. It's a planetary collision. We're all gonna die. It's the end. It's the end. There's no other explanation! I need to pray!"

"It could just be an eclipse, you all. Why are we overreacting?"

"Don't interrupt if you're not well-versed in the field, young one. There *is* no eclipse this month, and that is why I need to record this. This is a momentous event, and its every detail needs to go down in the annals of history."

"My compass is telling me the magnetic fields are in disarray. This will mess up all my experiments. Someone needs to stop this. The coven needs to do something. What are they doing? Why didn't they predict this?"

Things were getting just as heated beyond the terrace. Three Kingsmen dropped down to the street as people began to get restless. They unsheathed their blades from the scabbards on their backs, leaving steam in their wake, igniting the very air around them. The effect was instant as the mob stilled, and a stifling calm settled down in the surroundings.

Vern didn't have time to guess at the fundamentals used to build the scabbards that held and overheated those blades before screams and gasps echoed all around. People started running indoors, pointing at the fading mass of white yet again. Vern finally looked back up, and his heart raced as blood surged through his body with intense thumping.

On the still somewhat bright moon's perimeter appeared tendrils of dark that grew at a breakneck pace, like a crack forming through the celestial body itself.

Chapter 4

INEXISTENCE

More dark tendrils materialized on the moon's perimeter, blanketing the glow behind them in waves of darkness.

Simultaneously, something just as bizarre was going on elsewhere in the sky. Starting from the bridge in the east, the glow of twinkling stars faded in an absurd transition toward the west over by the clock tower. It was as if a curtain was being draped over the very atmosphere itself.

In this nonsensical situation, a blaring siren screamed from the clock tower. All the Kingsmen around halted in their tracks and took out something from their pockets before crushing it in their palms.

Steam rose all around them as they each knelt on one knee and closed their eyes. The steam didn't touch a single hair on their head yet incessantly streamed out from their closed fists, scalding anything that got too close.

With everything happening all at once, the chaos on the streets grew destructive as people began running into nearby buildings. The stampede didn't last for long as the streets cleared out in no time, leaving only victims of the mass and the kneeling Kingsmen, still completely unharmed.

Vern himself didn't know what to make of this situation, but he realized something was going very wrong, and then things started to click in his mind. He now understood why he received the letter today and why the urgency. Even with these questions answered, many more still lingered, but now wasn't the time for hesitation.

He retrieved the book from his pocket and flipped it open to the exact page. The plexus of twisting lines began to churn and morph into curves that transitioned into words in no time. The light in his peripheral vision got dimmer and dimmer until nothing remained. He waited for his eyes to adjust to the low purple light. They didn't.

The unusually bright purple glow of the lamp on his table eluded his sight, and all that remained was an inky abyss. It was as if he had been swallowed by a starless night devoid of even the faintest glimmer of light, which might as well be what was happening. There was no distinction between his opened and closed eyes. Uniform darkness consumed him no matter what.

"Brother! I— It's dark. It's, it's not coming back. Brother, I can't see. Vee, it's not . . ."

Mirroring her earlier actions, Vern grabbed hold of both her hands and rubbed them gently. "It's okay, Ari. Breathe. I can't see either, and it's probably not just us hearing how everyone around is panicking. Just take deep breaths and calm down."

Worse than before, the crowd up here was becoming more frenzied by the second. It was clear from the noise that many were fumbling around frantically in their newfound darkness, only adding to the chaos.

He didn't know what to feel about this sudden change. If only he had accepted the enlightenment earlier, he'd have many more options available to deal with this situation. However, it wasn't his style to mope around and regret his mistakes in the heat of the moment. There would be time for reflection later. Now was the time to analyze the current situation and plan his course of action.

"W-What should we do, Vern? This . . . This . . . is this really it?"

"Ari, there's no point in trying to answer that question. If we die in this, there's really not much we can do, but I doubt this is the end." His stalkers already knew about this happening as mentioned in the letter. So why would they go to the whole trouble of surveilling him and giving him a chance at enlightenment if the planet was going to be some cosmic debris by the end of the day? It wasn't the most convincing argument, but it was logical.

"Whatever's going on seems more ephemeral and less physical. Especially the lack of eyesight is peculiar. I can still smell the scent emanating from the lamp. So the cyclical condensation hasn't stopped, and it's still generating light."

"So, what exactly should we do?"

"I am trying something, but like I said, what can we do? Running around blind with this mob is one quick way to get injured and lose our way. We know exactly where we are, and I remember the way out. We can try and leave once things get a little calmer."

All Vern heard were Ariane's hum of confirmation mixed with her quick breaths and his own thumping heart as he zoned out the surroundings. *In hindsight, I made the right decision of not enlightening myself, but I didn't expect—this. Whatever this situation is. Is it still possible to comprehend the diagram?*

Vern glided his free hand over the coarse page, looking for changes—something, anything. In another pass, he grazed it and, in the next one, pressed hard onto it. Sensing nothing at all, he closed in and put his left ear on the paper, only to feel its coarse warmth. *Yeah, this isn't working.*

Not discouraged, Vern moved on to the mental version of the diagram he had. It wouldn't be as dynamic as the real thing, but introspection was better than nothing. But that's when it hit him. A sense of incongruity gave him a pause, and he replayed what he felt just a few seconds ago. *No. That can't be.*

His hand left the book unattended and moved toward the center of the table. *It is actually happening.* His hands touched a warm metallic surface with intricate grooves, and he thrust his hand upward along the surface—it jolted back reflexively. *Fuck!*

"Ari, we need to leave. Now!" he whispered, and his linked hand tugged upward before he even finished his sentence.

"What— What happened? You just said it was better to wait."

"This place will soon go up in flames. We need to get out of here," he whispered again as he moved toward what he considered to be the direction back to the reading room, pulling Ariane's hand with him.

"Fire in a coven's library? How could that be? Is it— Is it related to this whole thing? What exactly are you talking about?" She didn't resist, even amid her complaints.

"It burned with heat! That lamp back at the table was burning with heat. Did you notice the cold slipping away as we sat by the table? If this is happening to all these lights, what happens to the big hearth blazing inside?"

He did have a conjecture about what was going on. The rules related to inine, the chemical fueling these lamps, or the very light itself, were changed to generate heat.

"By my lady! How could this be?" she gasped, horror apparent in her voice. "Vee, we should let everyone know right now!"

"Ari, wait, no. Don't do it! The moment we do that, the mob will rush us, and we will completely lose our sense of direction and probably even get trampled underneath their feet."

Vern felt a jerk on his hand and was forced to stop as Ariane refused to budge.

"Vee, no! You're pretty much condemning everyone here to death."

"Ari, please. We don't have time for moral debates right now."

She didn't reply. Mere seconds of silence in this raucous environment felt like they stretched for half an eternity. He didn't see any way to ensure their safety with the whole crowd of these delirious scholars panicking even harder to scramble out of here.

"Ari, we're running out of time. I don't mind dying in an inevitable apocalypse, but sacrificing ourselves for the greater good is just not how I plan to go out."

"Vern, this isn't right. I really don't want to go against you right after we've finally caught up in so long. But could you please just go ahead by yourself? I'll catch up."

"Ari, this isn't a game! Don't do this right now, please. I'll explain later, and you can blame me if you want. We are losing precious time by doing this."

"You don't know for sure that your scenario will play out. Since we would be the ones to warn them about the fire, we could also take control of the situation and lead everyone out of the building more harmoniously. It will be better than going by ourselves, and we can continue to stick together if something else comes up after this."

She had yet to start shouting and attracting attention, so there was still a chance for persuasion. "Ari, it's not that simple when no one can see each other, and I've heard some of these people; they are too paranoid. The second you say anything about a fire, they will go crazy. Neither of us has the charisma to pull it off so quickly without it posing a big risk."

"..."

"Let's take a step back and find a realistic balance, okay? We shout and let everyone know once we are downstairs. Now please, let's just go!"

Not giving her a chance to argue, he rushed her forward and didn't encounter much resistance. He walked a few paces and slowly waved his hand around to feel for the door's casing. Inching forward bit by bit, his hand struck a wooden construct, and he grabbed hold of it, propelling himself forward.

"If I remember correctly, there should be a bookshelf right ahead of us, and then from its opposite end, if we skip two cabinets toward the right, we should end up next to a staircase."

"Mm-hmm."

Sounds of tumbling and cries of agony echoed all around them, drowned by the piercing boom of the clock tower siren. Focusing on isolating the sounds in close vicinity, he trudged forward cautiously, hand in hand with Ari, sweeping away the crunching glass and books on the floor with his legs. Someone had already toppled over some shelves and decorations.

His mental image of the library was still quite vivid, and it wasn't too hard to navigate, but this whole situation didn't look too good. He wasn't panicking like those outside, but whatever was happening was just too detached from reality. *One step at a time.*

Slowly walking atop what seemed to be a fallen shelf, he measured the height of his every step before committing. He made slow progress and finally got off the heightened shelf in a stable step. "Watch your step for height. We will turn here, and then—"

The annoying siren faded into silence as all sounds he'd been relying on stopped registering. The subtle hum of life, the taps of his shoes, the chaotic chatter, and the frantic cadence of his own breathing all slipped into an eerie hush. His ears, straining for the ghost of a sound, were met with nothing but the unsettling quietude.

Everything felt muted. The feedback of his legs touching the environment was dampened, and his whole body felt light, almost as if underwater.

Ariane's hand was also just barely perceptible from the little heat he felt in his hands. But now wasn't the time to stop. The fire wouldn't care if they couldn't see or hear or feel.

He had this little conjecture, which predicted survival if they managed to keep their physical bodies safe for the time being. His idea was that any changes to the rules weren't permanent. That something had to give, and there were limitations to these bizarre happenings around and within him. So, not dying by fire and waiting out these sensory disruptions could very well be the key to persevering in this nightmare.

Tightening his grip further, which gave him little feedback, he started moving again slowly but firmly within this solitary confinement of his senses. But it wasn't going according to the plans.

It felt like he was hammered, and what he assumed were firm steps didn't give him the reaction he expected, and hence came the fall. Or not? He didn't know. Everything was dulling by the second.

Then before he could make another attempt, an unsettling calm pervaded this sensory void, leaving him with nothing but the haunting echo of his own thoughts.

CHAPTER 5

OBJECTIVITY

He'd failed. It was one thing to die from his own stupidity, but he also got Ariane mixed up in the whole mess. If he hadn't been in the library, had turned her away, or had simply checked out the book and returned to his room, Ariane would never have stayed there or even visited the library. From all these valid possibilities, he'd somehow fucked up everything perfectly to get both of them ensnared in this deathtrap.

If he had accepted the enlightenment on time, things could have been very different. Maybe he would have noticed everything before it took place by peeking at the laws and making better decisions. Or even better, it was possible he could outright ignore the deprivation as a subjective observer.

So many things he could have done differently, but he still couldn't find a consistent logic that would have led him to make any of these decisions. Not just in hindsight, but even in the long term, the decisions he'd made were quite rational and grounded in solid reasoning.

If he had to pick something that could have led to a better outcome without violating his fundamental personality, it would've been not to have underestimated the message in the note.

The note clearly signified a limited time, but he had attributed that as a personal threat against himself from the stalkers, undermining the circumstantial information at hand.

The primary mistake, therefore, was misjudging the severity and context of the situation. It was actually quite foolish of him. Why would a world-shattering secret like subjectivity be shared with him unless it was deemed necessary? *A set of miscalculations I probably can't fix. Ever.*

A simple estimation accounting for the locations of the fire's sources and all the dry fuel in the library gave him despairing numbers. Fire would engulf every corner of the library in less than fifteen minutes.

This sensory deprivation had been going on for a while already, so seven or eight minutes at best before it would reach him and Ari near the center of the library. *It is hopeless.*

Suddenly, however, something changed. He failed to put his finger on it for a second, but then he felt it. Amid this numbing silence—an unsettling presence wormed within his psyche. The sensation crawled through his mind like an insect, asserting that he was no longer alone in his own thoughts. A disturbing dread washed over him, amplified by the nothingness.

Yet even that didn't last for long. His surroundings seemed to change as if unknown formless entities caressed his body. Every instinct screamed at him to flee, but his body refused to obey. *What the hell?*

Then abruptly, a flood of sensations came rushing in.

An unidentifiable odor, rich and foul, assaulted his nostrils, pungent like rotting vegetation and something far more sinister. The scent was invasive, filling his lungs with each tremulous breath, a stark contrast against the sterile void he'd been trapped in. He nearly threw up, but his body denied him even that simple relief.

An orchestra of disturbing sounds shattered the silence that oppressed him just a minute ago. Soft skittering noises echoed all around him, a symphony of tiny, unseen feet on a hard surface.

Occasionally, low, guttural growls punctuated these chilling noises permeating his very bones. It was a sound so primal and terrifying he felt a scream rise within him, one he couldn't release.

His skin, which was barely perceptive not long ago, turned extremely sensitive. The charged air throbbed against him, and whenever the unseen entities brushed past, his heart threatened to explode.

Intermingling with these were the faintest whispers, words indistinguishable and foreign, uttered in a voice that slithered in his ears. Their haunting timbre rose and fell in a rhythm that was almost hypnotic, each syllable seeming to gouge out the thoughts running through his head.

His inability to move only made worse. Why could he feel all of it so vividly when his body was still petrified? He wasn't one to believe in the supernatural, but this? This was worse than a nightmare.

Something continued to worm its way into his thoughts, and the slightest incongruency within them sent ripples of panic coursing through him. After all, his mind was supposed to be his greatest asset. If even that was snatched away, what was the point?

These macabre senses, so alien and yet so horrifyingly real, held him hostage. Each noise—even his own heart's, amplified by his fear, transformed the world into a soundscape of terror.

And in the backdrop of this sensory onslaught, he was acutely aware of the horrifying promise. That opening his eyes would unveil a reality far more terrifying than the one painted by all his other senses combined.

It was a twisted invitation. He couldn't control any of his limbs, yet his eyelids felt light as ever, awaiting his command to unveil a sight that was guaranteed to traumatize him forever.

So, he sat there, a prisoner in his own body. Unable to act, unable to escape, and far too terrified to dare look upon the unseen horror that lurked just beyond his eyelids.

The thought of what would happen if he allowed his sense of sight to join this macabre experience sent a deep, unsettling chill coursing through him.

This can't go on! Forget opening his eyes; just the screeches and whispers were taking a toll on his mind. The moment he tried relaxing, his thoughts slurred, slipping away in an incoherent noise.

There was a maddening compulsion within these foreign thoughts. They instilled notions in his mind that he would generally never consider entertaining.

In one moment, they fostered in him a need to sway side to side. Another wanted him to shriek, while the next ingrained within him a desire to squeeze his hand out through his stomach. But it was all wrong. The impulses these thoughts infused in him were not meant for a human body. He just didn't have the organs needed to fulfill any of these uncanny notions. Not that he was going to anyway.

This can't go on! I need to focus. A common denominator among all savants was their ability to isolate their thoughts.

Vern did precisely that and brought up the diagram in an attempt to zone out his surroundings. His usual reflection of fundamentals wouldn't give him any valuable insight in this situation. The diagram might.

It was usually a simple thing, but his mind kept going back to what brought about this situation. *Why am I here? What is this place?* His innate curiosity only led to even more questions that he dared not even ask. It went against all his notions of reality. So he had to focus.

The diagram. The lines. The rotting smell. The curves. The curves. The curves. The words. That thing he should see. The curves. The words. The words.

The diagram was a thing of immense complexity. It was one thing to look at it and comprehend its nuances but another to replicate the changes and further disseminate its intricacies.

The base concept seemed simple to him. Subjective observation allowed one to first recognize the possibilities of reality around them and then scrutinize them in a specific light. The diagram assisted in doing just that.

However, a mental model only gave him further insight into the nature of the diagram itself. He couldn't simulate the feedback that the diagram was generating based on his thoughts. He was missing the crucial aspect of it.

Despite such being the case, he kept reminding himself of all the changes it held. He already knew that the diagram could facilitate enlightenment due to its innate subjective nature. But what did that say about the process of enlightenment itself? Didn't that just mean that someone who's used to living in a fake objective reality must realize the sham?

Then, by the extension of that logic, another method of enlightenment would be to observe something innately objective. But what exactly did objectivity entail when everything was subjective? Did something inherently objective even exist? What about that being outside?

Aghh!

The mere idea shattered his focus, and the entity beyond the eyelids occupied all his thoughts. The silence he'd cultivated ended up like the world holding its breath before a storm.

Just as his mind started to trick him into a false sense of relief, a chilling high-pitched shriek pierced the silence, bouncing off unseen walls to echo and seep into his consciousness, a cruel reminder of his horrifying reality.

His heartbeat stopped in fearful anticipation of comeuppance, and his imagination conjured scenarios that threatened to devour his waning mental defenses. Yet nothing happened other than the omnipresent parasitic thoughts slurring his cognition further. As seconds ticked by, he slowly calmed down.

This was doable. The entity seemed not to care about him specifically, which actually made sense. He wasn't the target, probably nothing more than some collateral damage in the grand scheme of this entity.

If he could just hold the perennial infiltration of these madness-inducing thoughts at bay. He had a chance.

A chance at enlightenment.

The plan took shape in his head in no time. He was sure that the real danger of the situation came from the infiltration of his psyche. His theory was that everything around him, including all the sounds and senses, was actually conjured by these mind-bending thoughts. If he could only keep them at bay, the process would be simplified.

So, it was back to the diagram. *The lines. The curves. The curves. The curves. The words.* His thoughts shifted from one to the next in a logically consistent fashion on their own.

His already thumping heart accelerated in anticipation and fear, yet the model of the diagram didn't waver as his thoughts continued their cascade. When he felt detached enough from everything around him, he was ready.

Was it foolish? He didn't know. Something had to change to survive the fire out there, assuming this horrorscape wasn't the new reality. This was the necessary gamble to induce that deviation. To find objectiveness in this insanity. Summoning a courage born of desperation, he did it.

He opened his eyes.

For a fraction of a second, his vision flickered to life, and fog covered the terrain. Hundreds of tendrils dropped down from the sky, barely discernable in the fog only due to the red sheen reflecting off their writhing mass and unnatural curves. Silhouettes lurked in the fog, shaking with an eerie cadence.

He tried to turn his eyes away from this alarming spectacle, but then it registered.

Past the chaotic flurries of darkness towered a shadow. No, it wasn't a mere shadow. It was an entity.

An entity that loomed even higher than the writhing appendages, standing in a sea of . . . blood? No, that didn't seem right either. Three outlines extended out of the enormous thing, gripping the head of these appendages, their black mass shining with that same red.

Vern feasted his eyes upon this chilling sight. The appendages exploded into more tendrils, one of their two ends rushing towards the silhouettes within the fog, while the other—

Aghhhh!!

A sudden, searing pain exploded in his eyes. It was as if they had been subjected to unbearable pressure, a force too much for them to handle. His psyche, already teetering on the edge of oblivion, shattered into a thousand fragments, each with an inkling of the entity beyond, each more horrifying than the last.

There was no way to cope with what he'd seen, but his subconscious had done him good. Killed itself before it could process all that he'd seen. The entity was objective. Indeed, there couldn't be more than one definition of such a thing.

The formless beings stopped whispering in his ears. All sounds and smells vanished, taking away the sickeningly pervasive thoughts with them. Still, something far more bizarre now lingered in his memories, and pain overwhelmed him, becoming more and more prominent as the horrorscape faded from all his senses.

At the same time, the irate feeling of standing on a precipice was gone, melted down into a sense of pure bliss, filling his mind with thousands of ideas. In this intermix of contradictory senses, the ideas came together, and their mental images sought each other.

The thoughts merged, growing larger and larger into a single compound, a compound that compressed into a dot.

A dot that floated in the sea of darkness, emitting a blue hue that fluctuated like a dying ember. Tiny scant cinders whirled around it. Its subtle glow, calming aura, and very existence pulled him in.

Vern stared at the glowing beacon with an empty gaze for a few moments before his eyes regained focus. And when they did, the twinkling particles around the dot faded, and a quartz-like sphere revealed itself. Tendrils of light manifested out of thin air and began etching themselves onto the orb.

The shiny threads weaved and sewed the globe with their ethereal light, and a radiant pattern emerged on its surface. It had some order to it, yet just as much was chaos.

When another one of these strings of light got into its place for the umpteenth time, the pattern shook and disintegrated into thin streams of light that spread within the bounds of the glassy construct. Light swam through the glass like some viscous liquid, this time settling in no apparent pattern.

Before he could inspect the object any further, the threads of light dematerialized with rippling waves of cyan. The scattered darkness gushed to claim back its estate. Visible in the ebbing luster of ripples, a crack ran down from the very center of the sphere as it split into two even pieces. Their gleams shone dimly . . . and they disappeared.

ARGHHHHHH!

Vern's mind shuddered as a searing sensation crept through his very being. It felt like a hole burned through his eyes, the pain pushing him past the barrier of his divested senses. With no energy to conjure stray thoughts to occlude his mind, he felt every bit of what was happening within his eyes. So much so he knew when his sclera evaporated and when his corneas were blazed, and something was plastered on top of his singed irises.

Lacking any practical method to vent his agony, he barely hung on to lucidity. Every second, it felt like a hot sigil branded his eyes and his very being, changing something within him.

The torment slowly eased out as a profound sense of exhaustion hit him in waves. In a sluggish tussle between delusional fatigue and survival, Vern forced his eyes open bit by bit, going against his primal instincts.

There was a peculiar transition, and it wasn't dark anymore. Flames of purple and vermillion blazed all around him.

Chapter 6

PERCEPTION

The flames encroached from both ends of the floor. The two-toned fire ate through everything in its path. Flesh, books, glass—whatever came in its wake only served to fuel this ghastly sight.

In a blurry glimpse of this macabre scene, his sluggish mind snapped to wakefulness in an instant. People were lying limp everywhere in this maze of shelves. Some lay there in odd postures, while others had their faces to the ground, probably from having taken bad falls.

Then, there were the unfortunate ones—serene expressions hung on their faces as flames engulfed them bit by bit, scorching their flesh and melting their skin.

Rows upon rows of shelves were torched as years of history turned into smoke, threatening to cover the hall in a fatal deluge of poisonous soot. Curiously, a few people around him had their eyes open, blankly staring ahead, while the rest seemed unconscious as they fueled the fire, their bodies melting away with a terrible stench.

Vern took a shallow breath, repressing the disgust and terror that came from this sight and turned around to where Ariane was supposed to be. She was right there next to him, lying atop a fallen shelf with her eyes closed, breathing in a serene rhythm. He scanned her body and heaved a sigh at her mostly unharmed state.

One wave of fire was moving closer than the other. Despite all the resulting smoke, it still looked like the situation was bearable due to the sky-high ceiling and the natural ventilation in place.

Shaking his head, he focused on the task at hand. *I can probably save a few more people if I am quick.* He turned to Ariane and squatted down, reaching for her head and knees.

And his hands passed right through her.

He stared in disbelief at where his hands should be. As if right on cue, a prickling sensation crept up, starting at his palms that he felt were inside her head and knee. His hands were definitely there. He could wave them around, make fists, and even clasp them together, but he could not see them.

He looked down and saw his clothes lying on the ground in the outline of a man, and it clicked.

Repercussions of enlightenment? No. That can't be right. Yharl Ballin, as suggested by Ari's description, was a man of flesh and blood. Unless I am mistaken in assuming that Yharl himself is an observer, this shouldn't be their standard form.

Then it must be some sort of special transitional state. It must be. But I— She doesn't have time. I don't fucking have time for this! The sight of the melting husks of these unknown scholars was bearable, but he didn't even want to imagine Ari getting engulfed by the flames as he stood there, helpless.

No. I still have options, but I need more information before I can model this.

He could barely keep his eyes open as it was, so he would need to fall back to his usual approach to the problem as a fundamentalist. Analyze the variables, look for patterns, build a hypothesis, and then figure out how to use these patterns and properties to nudge the result in an intended direction.

If he considered the conflagration as a test environment and himself as the subject, it might be easier to fall into the usual habits and zone out the prospects of failing in this reality.

Vern stepped back a bit and reached for his coat on the floor. His hand passed right through the coat's collar and tingled as it did. He went for it again, but this time, he stopped his hand when it was within the collar and concentrated on the sensation.

The tingling returned and soon turned into an odd burning impression. Vern retracted his hand and closed his eyes to concentrate on the feeling. It felt like frostbite, numbing and freezing for the most part.

The more I focus on picking up the coat, the worse it gets. In a general case, that would mean if I try to interact with corporeal objects, it puts a strain of some kind on this form.

But that can't be the full equation. How can I firmly stand on the floor? If the focus is the only factor, I should have plunged straight down to Prima's core.

Tapping his invisible foot on the floor, he stretched his leg into the coat, and it went right through the fabric without any resistance as he shivered from the chill. Then he stepped on a book nearby, and a prickling sensation arose from his feet touching the solid floor.

Retreating from the book, Vern ran his hand through his hair and snapped off a piece. He pulled that invisible strand on opposite ends with both hands, stretching it taut. He positioned his hands so that the strand passed through the collar, but its ends were held tight.

A few seconds passed by, and nothing happened. Rising back up, he walked toward the fire and didn't even think twice before he plunged his hand right into the inferno.

Not even a prickle.

He furrowed his brows and walked into the flames. As expected, nothing happened again. His theory had the right direction. It had something to do with his subconscious's desire to interact, but some absolute limits restricted and penalized it.

Done with his experiments, he retreated to Ariane. The conclusion was simple yet distressful.

There was no quick way to make his body interact with corporeal objects at will. He speculated that if he could somehow trick his mind into thinking that Ariane was just some flooring, it'd be possible, but he had no clue how to go about doing that. Observation might work, but if he knew how to make proper use of it, why would he go to all this trouble and not just straight up solve the fire itself?

His conjectures may not be grounded in proper logic, but he just did not have the time to experiment properly and gain any worthwhile insight.

All the while, the fire only got closer. *Three minutes, maybe four, before it devours Ari. This is beyond sense. Why the fuck is nothing ever straightforward?! Why now? This will not work.*

The very plausible mental image of Ariane consumed by the inferno, fire searing through her flesh, singeing her into a charred lifeless husk as he stood there doing nothing, was a torment that sliced through him sharper than any physical blade ever could.

Not now. Not right now. It just wasn't the time to wallow in self-pity. He had yet to try and leverage whatever was inciting this tortuous pain in his eyes. Still, this very pain gave him the confidence to stay somewhat calm in this whole disaster.

Under the assumption that it would be comparatively faster to figure out this temporary form instead of the whole subjective observation business, he had done all these silly tests. But as usual with everything else today, he'd been wrong.

FOCUS!

Something had very literally been melded with his eyes, and he felt the difference. It was as if there were another set of ethereal eyelids that closed him off from the world, but they weren't there to impede light or something so simple.

One leg inside his coat, Vern braced himself, took a deep breath, and opened his elusive eyes.

Illeana closed her eyes to focus on all the new sensations that stemmed from her true perception. She had just witnessed the most terrifying thing that could exist, yet she was disappointed in herself. The fact that it had riled up her emotions to such a degree, knowing full well it wouldn't be fatal to someone of her caliber, was just shameful.

But this wasn't the time to reflect on her loss of control. She had barely made it back in time.

Within her true perception, even without cutting off the incomprehensible aspects of it, she felt a wave of vibrations heading toward her at a leisurely pace. Those calm vibrations were just so obvious when everyone else was struggling to hold on to their sanity from that being.

It is just how Father said it would be. The world she saw with her true perception was unlike any composition she had ever experienced. Alas, she didn't have the time to marvel at the breathtaking symphony.

She quickly singled out the truth she sought from the thrumming tapestry and instantly felt exposed. Something caressed her thoughts with a gentle touch, and the noise faded away as out came the oscillations.

The fluctuation of the very world itself pulsed in her mind, the vibrations weaving a choral symphony. Inanimate objects around her seemed to have found their own voices, each one ready to sing out its story.

The paintings spoke of pride, while the walls told of age and weariness. The crackling of fire whispered of warmth and comfort as the chandeliers articulated their radiance.

The rhythm and cadence were her means to peer into the window of emotion that resided in everything.

Or at least that's how she saw it.

However, amid this orchestra of serene vibrations were howls and shrieks, the shuffling of tiny footsteps, and the mad ravings of things unknown, leaking from the fluctuations of her royal guards outside and maids that took care of the mansion. In this passive and tense cacophony was one set of calm vibrations, becoming louder by the second.

Illeana jolted out of her reverie, and her thoughts raced. She could finally hear the emotions, and it was just as exciting as she'd hoped. All that was left now was to become familiar with it.

She stood up from her bed and opened her eyes. There was no need to be as tensed and focused now that the hard part of enlightenment was over. Her beautiful chamber, adorned with paintings of the most renowned musicians, was jam-packed with many instruments.

In the corner of the darkened room, a grand piano rested elegantly by the tall window, its polished black surface reflecting the flames from the hearth. A mandolin hung next to it, a gift from her father. A harp and a violin had their own stations too, as did many other musical apparatuses.

Playing them and learning their unique cadences had always soothed her mind and calmed her nerves. But tonight, their sight broke her heart.

She knew that staying here in her own kingdom was an impossibility. Without her father around, there were too many strong characters vying for the throne, and she didn't have the strength needed to rightfully succeed him. Yet.

And she couldn't take anything with her, not while she was still in free representation. It allowed her great insight into the truth and unknown, yet it came with the small cost of making one intangible.

She had heard little about free representation from her father, and many aspects of it were just bizarre. If she tried, she would phase right through the piano, yet the walls and windows would act like usual bounds. Not trying to make sense of the insensible, she focused on the task at hand.

She had two options. One was to run away right now to save some time and possibly engage her pursuer in an unknown environment once they caught up with her. Another was to stay right here on her personal stage and compose a satisfying piece.

She obviously chose the latter. If all she wanted was safety, she could very well have hidden away long before all this began. Father was gone, and she had to take things into her own hands. Gather her own information, make her own decisions, and send her own message to those looking forward to her death.

Regulating and assessing her emotions in a life-and-death situation sounded like a perfect opportunity for her debut as an observer anyway. If she managed to die with all the advantages at hand, she only had herself to blame.

Though it did miff her that she didn't have her clothes on. Made her lose a little bit of that self-confidence. However, it didn't matter much. The most anyone could perceive someone within free representation was as a silhouette, so her noble image wasn't really being tarnished.

While she waited for the culprit to arrive, she took the time to get familiar with the observation. Recalling all the teachings her father had crammed into her in the last few days, she tested the pulses and the emotions attached to them.

No amount of training could have helped her grasp these concepts beforehand, and all theories needed practice for proper implementation. However, she had a precise awareness of what would work and what wouldn't. It was another one of those parting gifts from Father.

She didn't like the tone of the soul seer, but according to her father, it was the only observation record that was closely related to her own viewpoint and didn't come with catastrophic repercussions.

It included insights from those who had walked a similar path and taught her how to weaponize emotions in an effective manner, even though it came along with nonsense about souls. She didn't plan on following the record religiously. One's viewpoint had to be unique, or they were destined for mediocrity.

She remembered her father's words. *To shade reality with your perception is a matter of intuition. It is to use your understanding and comprehension of your viewpoint to manipulate the truth and bring forth the change.*

It sounded like some enigmatic and complex process back when she was learning the theory from Father and the book. But in free representation, she felt like anything was possible, which was actually the case.

Free representation was the time for an observer to gauge the extent of a viewpoint, its harmony with their method of isolation, and assess their compatibility. Maybe there was more to it, but she didn't know or need to know.

She listened to the rhythm of fire and hummed a counter to it along with her will, and the room turned pitch black. Noticing the dark, she was reminded of the dim vista outside the window. It was a bright morning before all hell broke loose.

Her guards had jumped right in and demanded she evacuate. Illeana had to assure them of her safety multiple times before she got fed up and ordered them in the name of the princess herself.

Shaking her head, she mimicked the earlier rhythm of fire with a low whistle. The melody of fire came back alive in an instant, joining the passive ensemble as wood burned with great vigor.

A little too much there.

Now, for her next test, the windows had to go. She didn't have the heart to break anything else in the room for the sake of experimentation.

The world itself was helping her achieve her visions. So it was as simple as imagining the tones of the glass reaching an emotional crescendo to converge, followed by releasing the tension in a sudden plunge as the glass shards cried out in agony, flying all around her, through her.

A lightless dark vista of her city greeted her, filled with eerie quiet and impassive vibrations as her eyes stung with newfound intensity. To avoid overloading herself with the myriad pulses and sounds from everything outside, she limited her perception, which alleviated some of the pain. It was so dark, her normal vision couldn't even resolve the trees in her garden.

Minutes passed by as she kept trying new things, all to build up enough proficiency to finally play the piano without breaking its keys.

She converged some of the ubiquitous muted emotions around her into a cylinder and willed it forward as it struck the key. Suddenly, the vibrations and their tone grew noisy, and she crouched down right where she stood next to the piano. A beam of utter darkness coursed through the air, annihilating everything in its path.

The wall, the piano, and a painting had gaping holes burned through them as the ray died out, disintegrating even the ashes. An offbeat note reverberated in the room with a lingering dissonance as Illeana looked at the piano with a quiver before she turned to the door. *It is time for a live performance.*

"Greetings, princess."

CHAPTER 7

SOUL SEER

A man donning a gray coat and a bowler hat opened the door, which disintegrated into purple ash at his touch. With a rhythmic tap of his cane, he entered the room and stopped beside her violin, his noble visage marked by a meticulously groomed beard. In the dark room lit only by the fire in the hearth, his hawklike eyes shone like beacons with an eerie purple hue.

Illeana's gaze pierced through the dim ambiance, her eyes narrowing into icy slits as they fixed upon his towering figure. "Duke Nathaniel, it's not very gentlemanly of you to come into a lady's room uninvited, much less the princess's."

The duke looked around where she stood, then at the bed where her white dress lay, before he chuckled. "Augustus finally let you become an observer? Here I thought our princess was a dimwit with no aptitude or enough coherent thoughts to form a viewpoint."

"I see the dog has learned to bark. Weren't you just some lowly landlord before the royal father decided to take pity on you?"

Duke held his bowler hat with one hand as he guffawed, his body shaking with laughter. "Our princess is indeed as funny as they said. Do you not see the irony in this situation? This lowly landlord now wields power over the destiny of the high and mighty princess."

Illeana scoffed. "Indeed, calling you a dog is disrespectful to their species. At least they're loyal to their masters. You, on the other hand, have come to bite the very hand that feeds you."

"Let's not insult each other's intelligence, princess. This has nothing to do with my loyalty. I was the staunchest supporter of the king and still would be if he had decided not to be irresponsible and foolhardy. I am just looking out for myself in these troubling times. You see—"

"What audacity! How dare you mock the royal father? What gives you the gall to not kneel, grovel, and beg for mercy after such a flagrant display of insolence toward the throne?" The performance was about to begin, so it was time to set the stage.

The duke nodded. "I didn't expect to miss that one. But who can blame me? No one would have thought that you would have overcome the unseen one's influence in such a short time. Not just that, can you even see my vision?"

The duke stopped, his expression turning thoughtful for a second before he gasped. "Ahh, I understand. It must be one of Augustus's famous trinkets. Yes, yes. It only makes sense. As for the gall?" He pointed at his eyes and blinked.

Thousands of new screaming fluctuations emerged in her perception, and a purple smog burned around him that chipped away at everything it touched. He tapped his cane hard at the floor, and a big chunk of the planks dissolved. Furniture and instruments fell to the floor below in disarrayed and fractured melodies as the purple mass droned in the air.

"You better watch your fucking tone! A mere sightless that received enlightenment moments ago dares to question me? Your title of a princess is nothing but a mere construct in front of the truth. But what would you know?

"The rash king is going against the unseen one, ignoring his duty to the kingdom, while his foolish daughter is courting death before an entity who, to her, might as well be a god. Bear witness, for you're in the presence of a shadow artificer with three shades, and it will be my pleasure to consign you to the grave."

Ignoring most of the speech of the narcissist, she tiptoed to the right, avoiding the screaming ray of darkness that manifested beneath her feet.

This is good. He is agitated already. I might be able to pull off the silence of soul-strings. It was the only greater vision requiring four shades that she had learned with all her heart from the observation record. The reasoning behind doing so was simple. It was a vision that purely manipulated emotions and had nothing to do with souls other than in name.

Ever since Father had explained all about the observation and viewpoint, it didn't take her long to decide how she wanted to observe the reality. Emotions were the root of everything in society, and she firmly believed that the ability to perceive the exact state of someone's mind might as well be the same as being omniscient.

It would take her a long time to get there in reality, but the current empowerment of free representation was nothing short of that fabled omniscience. She could feel the melody of every emotion coming from the duke, so it was high time she began her performance.

The core idea behind this vision was simple. One had to guide the emotions of their foe in a manner such that one specific timbre never repeated until the vision was complete. Then at each of these steps, she had to influence the vibrations of Duke Nathaniel to match her own. There was much more to it than that, but she trusted her intuition and the world to help with the rest.

For starters, she had to manipulate his agitated fluctuations to match her own. Concealing the minor vibrations needed to insinuate the change within her words, she spoke with amusement clear in her voice. "Having trouble reaching a mere sightless, oh great shadow artificer?"

"Ha ha, you little whore. You really don't understand the situation, eh?"
Annoyed.

Before she could send another veiled alteration his way, savage vibrations gathered around the duke's hand as he raised his fingers. She swiveled to the right with immaculate grace, and a dark beam whizzed past her shoulders, dissolving everything in its wake.

"Some god you are," she chuckled, her words disguising the subtle guiding tones.
Irate. It changed too fast—she had just barely managed the last one.

"You really thought royal father would leave me helpless, knowing full well what was to come?" Not missing a chance to tighten the noose farther, she attuned this new emotion to match her own rhythm as well. Veiled as just another intonation of her discourse.

Doubtful now, are we? But this is almost changing too rapidly! The observation record had said that new emotions permeated a soul in a gradual fashion. Even if a person's outward emotions changed in the blink of an eye, the soul was supposed to take its time. *As expected, this whole concept of a soul is just sub-standard nonsense.*

Nevertheless, she hummed a tone with notes that belied somberness, caressing the symbol on her invisible forearm with low vibrations. Seizing this opportunity to also employ her fine-tuned melody, she dampened his rhythm to align with hers.

Then, just like Father promised, hundreds of green motes of light materialized around her and condensed into a pocket watch within an instant.

The playful smile that hung on the duke's face disappeared in a moment, and his eyes blazed a bright purple as he snapped his fingers. Many patches of darkness appeared all around Illeana, shrieks and droning screeches blasting within her perception.

Not wasting any time, she clicked the knob of her pocket watch, and a green haze enveloped her with a suddenness that mirrored the rapidness of the screaming patches.

The darkness that had vaporized everything in its path until now entered the haze and lost all its momentum, collating into a dark globule within the green mist as more and more of it poured in from the dark wells outside. Anything that reached the haze was stopped dead in its tracks, moving slower than a mournful violin melody played with delicate vibrato.

Astonished. Just one more phase. The duke had yet to notice any of her manipulations, so his true perceptions must be blind to truths regarding vibrations, emotions, or even the soul.

The duke shot rapid-fire small beams at her before clapping his hands together. The whole room turned pitch black for a second, and everything disintegrated except Illeana standing within her haze. The entire mansion crumbled as chunks and pieces of debris fell around her, some stopping within her haze.

Her vision turned moist as she envisioned another set of counter tones, fusing them within her words. "Pathetic!"

The duke glared at her, blood leaking from his eyes. With a rough jerk of his hand, he reached for his bowler hat, and his form began to darken.

Hatred. This is it.

Then, like a conductor guiding the ensemble of emotion to the climax, she raised her hand high, and a wave of muted emotions congregated all around the duke, surging forth like a tsunami with him in the center.

"Must be fun hiding behind your daddy's little trinkets, pretending to be all high and mighty. Can't do anything by yourself, even as an observer? Then you're better off dying anyway!"

Ignoring his words, she focused on controlling the orchestra of passive emotions with shifts of her hand complemented by her vision. Now it was all or nothing.

"I, Illeana Maximillian, second princess of the Kingdom of Karthain." Her veins bulged as she felt the blood pumping through her eyes with wild abandon.

Duke Nathaniel pushed his right hand through the bowler hat, which sank right into it. Before she could do something else, a hand appeared within her sphere, grabbing at her pocket watch—but it was already too late.

The seemingly harmless yet all-encompassing vibrations crashed into the duke, past his burning smog, constricting him.

The duke's innate pulses of emotions blanked out, replaced by a passive hum, ready to billow or plunge at her beck and call.

"I command you . . . to die!" Then, like an executioner delivering the sentence, she chopped down in a swift motion, and the veins around her eyes burst, blood pouring out from them in invisible gushes.

The man let go of his bowler hat, which fell to the ground, and the hand disappeared from her haze. Resting it on his chest, his eyes glowed purple. In a flash of darkness, there was a gaping hole in his chest, the building's ruin visible through it. The body lost the force keeping it afloat, falling into the crater like a rag doll.

It was over. She had done it.

Taking a deep breath, she twisted the watch's knob backward with a sharp motion. The forces of the planet remembered to apply to the green mass, and she glided down in a smooth motion, landing in the crater across from the lifeless husk.

She fell on her knees as soon as the force holding her afloat disappeared, holding her illusory palms over her eyes as blood seeped through them. She took deep breaths and regulated her breathing, kneeling on the ruined pavement.

Minutes passed by before she gathered herself and hummed an upbeat tune. The green motes, alongside all the dark energy and debris within it, dematerialized into shimmering dots that returned to the pattern on her invisible forearm.

Tucking the loose strands of her hair behind her ears, she stood up and looked at the aftermath of her first battle of perspectives. This man had obliterated her mansion, including all her instruments and guards. It hurt. It hurt losing everything, but losing control of her emotions would hurt even more.

She took a deep breath and reflected. *This is indeed the right path for me.* Other than the situation at the end, she had handled it well.

It's not like she would have lost the watch, as it was bound to her. But even a second outside its protection would have been enough to silence her forever. Didn't matter if she was in free representation—a single touch from that thing could have reduced her to mere notes on a page, never to be heard again.

But the duke had misjudged the situation and underestimated her. Even if she had just finished her enlightenment, it didn't mean she was as weak as others at this stage. Her enlightenment was orders above most.

The vision she had just employed was something she could only emulate as an observer without a single shade due to free representation. With this experience, she felt confident enough in her understanding of the concept to shade her perception with it maybe twice, but that was about it.

Who knew how long it would take her to reach four shades and silence someone's soulstrings another time? And that was assuming she wouldn't find a more suitable observation record in the meantime.

She looked a final time at the barely visible crater polluted with messy and jumbled fluctuations of broken laws and walked away.

She was leaving as an orphaned princess, but there would come a day when she would play her favorite piece here as the queen of Karthain.

CHAPTER 8

BALANCE (I)

Vern had some ideas of what to expect, and to say that he was surprised would be underselling it. It was absolute chaos.

The image of a burning library in his mind was thrown to the back as hundreds of different phases of reality fluttered past in the blink of an eye.

Everything was changing, represented as seemingly random things, and it was captivating. There was an order to this chaos.

Every shelf, human, air particle, and concept took the form of one singular nature before it quickly transmuted into something utterly unique. Everything blended into an uncanny fusion of colors, textures, shapes, sounds, and incomprehensible things.

He focused hard, ready to glean as much as he could about one of these scenarios in the short fraction of a second they appeared for. However, the flickering chaos stabilized into one vision as he focused, albeit a little abruptly.

Everything around him turned into something like glass. Each object in the room was slightly distinct from the next in how opaque or transparent it was. The shelf right next to him looked diaphanous, sitting on a translucent floor as contents from the ground floor peeked through it in a similar refractive fashion.

The fire itself was a crystalline wall of glittering white, prohibiting all other light from passing as it surged with shimmering rays. The human bodies, on the other hand, seemed to be a little reflective.

Not knowing what to make of all this, he lost concentration, and the glassy world disappeared, replaced by the flickering cycle of unreal states.

Hmm. So I can inspect these scenarios at will with a little focus?

He concentrated on another sight from the chaotic backdrop, and hundreds of dots populated his vision that moved in straight lines. Some went faster, while others went slower. A few completely left the plane and moved in a straight line in a third dimension.

This one did make some sense to him. It was some sort of a graphical representation of objects and their coordinates in a specific system that he didn't have the time to figure out.

He needed more. There was clearly a pattern to all this, so it was something that could be modeled. Bracing for the jarring change to his vision, he zeroed in on another one.

This time, the surroundings took on a vibrant hue. Each human body around him turned a fiery orange, while everything else emerged as saturated green. It looked more like a badly colored picture than a representation of reality.

Then, that must mean . . .

He was close. He had zeroed in on one of the variables, but there was more. Understanding this was the key to finding a solution to his current predicament. The pieces had almost fallen into place, but something was missing to make it all fit together.

For the following few seconds, he simply looked on at the fleeting chaos, and what struck him as odd was that some of the scenarios repeated.

The next time he saw the glassy environment, he felt a sense of incongruity. He doubled down and immersed himself in it. And as expected, something was different.

The opacity of all the crystalline objects was unlike the last time. The wall of fire, which was shining earlier, was gone, replaced by transparent fragments, whereas the books, which looked as clear as water in the first vision, were completely opaque now.

Could it be?

He blinked and allowed the frenzied scape of colors, textures, and vibrations to overwhelm him before he finally found himself in another glassy scape, and he locked it down with intense focus.

This time, again, his surroundings turned to glass, but their transparencies were assigned in a completely different manner.

I see what is going on!

To confirm his hypothesis, he quickly cycled through a few more repeated variations of sights other than glass, and it was just like he had theorized.

These scenarios were all the possible combinations of laws and their interpretations.

This answered one of the questions he had asked himself when reading the *Observation Record of Subjectivity*.

The text said that observers could see the very laws in their own interpretation. How exactly did these observers choose the law they wanted to see? What did it mean when it said they would see these laws in their own interpretation?

It all became clear. In the first glassy scenario, everything was being interpreted as glass, and an object's opacity represented the intensity of the observed law at that location.

Following this logic, Vern believed that the first vision he had focused on observed the laws of heat. The glass crystals around the fire were shimmering with great intensity, whereas everything else was transparent. So, the hotter the area, the shinier and higher the opacity.

When the glassy scenario repeated itself, the interpretation remained the same, but the law changed. That is to say, the one to change would still be the opacity of the glasses, but the criteria which determined the exact translucency would be something else.

So, fire being transparent and books being opaque could mean the law being observed had to do with something like knowledge. As in books had more coherent knowledge than fire.

He might be wrong about the small details, but that didn't matter as he had confirmed a similar pattern with other scenarios too.

So what did this mean for him?

A chance!

The text he'd read in the book suggested that observers, in enough quantity, could change the laws of the world itself. Then didn't that mean that a single observer could change the laws in a smaller space all by themselves?

It was a logical conclusion, but it assumed too much about the situation. Still, something was better than nothing in this situation.

Lost in analyzing the changes, his heart lurched when, even in this ever-changing canvas, something moved forward relentlessly. The shimmering tide of glasses got closer as the representation of bodies in its wake disappeared. The green space shrank, and shapes became smaller. The sounds turned discordant, and the figures grew longer. All a not-so-gentle reminder of the fire extending its gaping maw.

But it was okay. He could focus. He had to. Nothing else would help right now. He had managed not to get distracted for hours on end while comprehending the projection of Lennian fundamentals. This was nothing. This was nothing. It was okay. It was okay.

Gritting his teeth so hard they almost felt like they would crack, he continued his earlier train of thought. This canvas allowed him to peek at the fundamentals of anything.

Infinite possibilities, but this led to a dilemma. What should he choose to observe that could help him rescue Ariane right now but also not be so limiting that it would haunt him for the rest of his life?

This was probably a decision that would stick with him moving forward. So it needed some thought even in this dire situation. *I need to find a balance between my current practical necessity but also my own perspective.*

Before jumping to conclusions, however, he gave himself a limit of ten seconds to ensure the decision was actually in his hands. Who said that it was a choice? He wouldn't know until he tried.

He occupied his thoughts with the intricacies of the glassy scape, and then before he could do something else, his sight was filled with shimmering lights that rapidly flew around in an organic pattern.

Looking closely, the opacities and reflectance of the glass were jumping around every instant. These were all scenarios when interpreted as glass. This meant he could consciously choose the interpretation.

But he didn't want to risk choosing the law and an interpretation at the same time. What if he was locked out of options once he consciously picked both the law and how he wanted to interpret it?

He had no interest in looking at everything as glass for the rest of his life. On top of that, opacity, glimmer, and reflection seemed like crude and impractical methods to perceive reality anyway.

He dismissed the thought of glass, and as if on cue, the world followed his command and began cycling through the myriad scenarios again. Not wasting any more time, he recalled his study of heat in Lennian fundamentals: how objects transmuted from one to another once they came in contact with heat, how they evaporated at certain thresholds, and how there was a consistent logic to all of it.

The scenery changed, and there was no doubt that everything barraging his senses right now was somehow representing heat. In one of them, the entire world turned black, filled with red spheres, creating blazing fireballs from beyond the floors and walls like they didn't even exist, giving him an illusion of floating in space surrounded by burning planets.

In another, a network of veins overlaid the original scene—the vibrant lines snaked across the shelves and pillars, casting an eerie glow across the floor. The veins interlinked with one another, connecting into the shape of an entity.

Vern closed his eyes and calmed himself. His heart wanted to see more, but every second counted, and he needed to make a decision. He had gathered all the information he could in the limited time he had, and spending any more time would only be harmful.

However, now came the real question. What law and interpretation would work best for him and this situation?

The options were nearly limitless, and this subjective observation allowed him to look at the world from any possible perspective. But he realized after a few seconds of thought that it wasn't so simple.

Not all interpretations or laws were equal. A few combinations were definitely more practical and useful than the rest.

A simple mental simulation of the combinations suggested that some interpretations would have perfect synergy with one law while being a logical fallacy for another. Few interpretations could make a seemingly useless law a valid choice, whereas others would waste the potential of even the most complex laws.

It was relatively easy to come up with a useless combination. What if someone interpreted everything as black? How would you make use of any law at all if everything was just black and unchangeable? What information could one glean from that?

On the other end of this spectrum, what if he thought up something absurd like interpreting the laws of energy as a canvas that could be painted upon?

Would he be able to simply paint away all mass and energy around himself as black and destroy the very matter itself? If things so absurd could exist, there was no way their current society would've survived for so long.

Since that was the case, there were some limitations on what one could achieve; he just didn't know what they were yet. That actually made his decision easier.

He would just follow his usual ideology of balance, which only made sense given a choice was all about his perspective. He liked to find balance in everything within his life, so it was only natural that he tried peeking at the world through that lens. The idea was enticing and might even be the best option for him in the long and short terms.

Making up his mind, he thought of this fragile concept of balance. The world in itself, as depicted by the Lennian fundamentalists, was a balance of matter with different properties. Then there was the cosmic balance of heat and cold on Prima due to its distance from the sun.

If one looked for it, they would find some kind of balance in everything around them. The laws of society tried to balance freedom and restrictions, while the scale of resource distribution in civilization tended to tip toward the wealthier nobles.

These equilibriums may or may not be the most optimal or compassionate, but similar ones existed in each construct of the society. That is to say, things weren't black or white—instead, they rested somewhere in the shades of gray when balanced around two ideas.

Vern kept on linking his thoughts together, and the flickering world came to a halt, settling down into a vista of monochrome gradients.

Some overlapped others, while a few just extended far beyond any walls. Some shades emerged from nowhere, whereas others abruptly disintegrated into nothingness. A couple were changing their contrast every second, while another bunch morphed into odd shapes with jarring boundaries.

Blood rushed through his eyes, pumping so fast it almost seemed to scorch his veins. It felt as if his eyes were twin steam engines that were pushed too hard.

But he didn't waver. This seemed like a crucial step, and it was too fascinating to just close his eyes.

After what seemed like a second or two, a shiver ran through him, filing through his thoughts and picking them apart in a rugged fashion before putting them back together.

Instead of feeling repulsed at this pervasive intrusion, the experience was more akin to rejuvenation. *What is this sensation? It's like my ideas are far more consolidated. The s—*

His mind blanked, and he noticed the sensation, or absence of it. The tingling that had been coming from his leg from standing on his coat had disappeared at some point in time. He jolted out of the reverie, and his blood ran cold.

The fire from the right end of the hall was already here, burning away his outfit on the ground, just seconds away from torching Ariane's hand.

But how can this be? There should have been at least another two minutes or so before the fire reached them. How had this happened?

He had been keeping a very close eye on the fire even among all his bizarre experiences and deductions. Something had gone wrong with him, and he hadn't even realized it.

From the other side of the hall, one of the shelves had burned its base and toppled over, leading to a domino effect of burning wooden racks that overturned their neighbors, sharing their warmth with the unkindled ones.

Luckily, they had walked a little outside the rows of shelves, or this would've already been over before he came to. He would've lost Ariane because he couldn't fucking keep track of the time.

He had to do something right now or— *There is no or. I have to do this!*

C H A P T E R 9

BALANCE (II)

Setting aside all his thoughts, Vern focused on his ethereal eyes yet again. The monochrome world of myriad gradients had disappeared, replaced by this all-encompassing conflagration, supplemented by the putrid smell of burning flesh and sounds of the crackling fire.

He was pretty sure that all he had to do was think and follow the same process as before, and the changes would manifest in the world around him. But what exactly were the laws of balance?

He didn't know what this piece of glass plastered on his eyes considered balance, but Vern's study of Lennian fundamentals had given him strong opinions about it. *Balance is a simplified framework that one can use to study relations of other concepts and their conditions.*

Like Temperature. Then, in a flash, the world around him turned dark. The red fire shone a cloudy gray, while purple morphed into a saturated white. Burning cabinets turned a shade darker while pillars, walls, and their occlusion tinted themselves a barely noticeable shadowy gray.

Humans lying around him diffused to a dark gray shade that fluctuated a little over time, and all of it faded into pitch black about seven or eight meters away.

It was clear what was happening. This was the representation of the balance of temperature in his surroundings. *So, does that mean I could change the balance of heat around me?* It sure looked like it.

Not wasting any time, he came up with multiple hypotheses on how the manipulation part of observation worked.

The first one was simple. He willed for the fire to not exist—nothing happened. Other than wasting a few seconds, that is. Next, he thought in terms of balance. The idea was to tip the balance of temperature toward cold. A quiver ran through his eyes, but nothing happened again.

His heart, which he had just calmed down from the earlier shock, began to race again as he noticed the long coat that stretched all the way to her shoes caught fire the moment a wisp landed on it.

The monochrome vision shattered, flinging him back to reality. Ariane's face, which used to have a healthy sheen to it, was now teeming with drops of sweat, her rosy cheeks reflecting the oversaturated violet.

His instincts screamed at him to do something. Stomp on the flames, get some water, wave the fire away, anything. Something dripped through his hands, and he finally noticed how hard he'd been clenching his fist. But it didn't matter. Nothing he'd done had mattered since this day started.

NO! The vision works. I am just missing something simple to make it work fully. His mind whirled faster than it ever did, and he had another idea.

Vern took a deep breath and relaxed his eyes. Everything went out of focus, and he imagined a grayscale hall with silhouettes of books strewn haphazardly, carcasses of men and women littered the floor, dimly lit by the orbs in front of some. He augmented every detail—it was almost a spitting image of the sight he'd just witnessed but without any bright spots. The incandescent fire didn't latch on to the mahogany shelves, books didn't turn to ash, and bodies weren't melting anymore. Ariane's coat only had a little patch burned off it.

It was the library's second floor but without the burning menace.

As he refocused his eyes, Vern willed for this vision to superimpose on the world around him. The moment he did so—

"AAAGHHHHH!"

He let out a piercing scream and fell on his knees as a throbbing pain wrecked his eyes. Clutching his eyes that felt ready to burst, he peered through the gaps, not ready to give up just yet—and froze in his tracks.

Something extraordinary was happening around him. It was like a sphere a few meters wide was carved out in the flaming inferno with Ariane in the center. The drops of sweat on her face disappeared like they never had existed, and many cabinets that fueled the fire crumbled in an instant from the sudden change of temperature.

He had done it—just in the nick of time. A little too close for comfort, but he had done it. He let go of his tense body, which fell straight back on the floor as he looked at the smoke-filled ceiling.

So the idea was to imagine in shades of gray. To modify what I see in the vision instead of manipulating the reality itself. He closed his eyes to rest them, but when he blinked out of habit, his breath caught in his throat, and he bounced right back up.

The flames hadn't stopped! The sphere of tranquility had deformed, and fire naturally began filling in the void.

Fuck! He had been naive. He assumed that whatever he envisioned would become permanent, but it only made sense that it didn't.

He had only been able to see that vision for a fraction of a second before the excruciating pain forced his eyes shut. So it was no surprise that the fire didn't stay put and resumed its relentless invasion once the vision was gone.

I need another solution right now. My current method isn't sustainable. All I did there was buy myself a few seconds. But what exactly? He had done something right since it worked, but something had gone just as wrong. There was no way he could keep doing the earlier stunt every few seconds.

Another thing to note was the sphere. He had imagined the entirety of the hall, but only a small area within the sphere was affected. *It could be a limit on observation, personal or otherwise.*

Could he maintain a smaller area without any fire for long? Maybe, but he felt there was a better solution to this. What other way was there to keep the fire at bay? The answer was simple, but he didn't want to risk it on the whole room this time in case he needed to repeat the earlier stunt.

Some sort of resource must be actively depleting in order to facilitate this, and he wouldn't needlessly gamble on it being endless.

Air. The pain from his earlier recklessness didn't stop, but everything around him glowed a brilliant white while human carcasses created subtle patches of darkness. Borders of all structures appeared dark as some of them slowly dissolved into white.

Without wasting any more time, he envisioned a little black sphere amid the sea of white. This time, he didn't fill in every detail. The sphere simply covered the nose of the silhouette of a person near the stairs. Then he attempted to superimpose this slight modification to reality as he willed in his mind for it to be so.

The grayscale disappeared like smoke, and color slipped back into the blurry figures. Lightheaded, he observed the fuzzy figure of a man by the stairs.

After blinking a few times, his sight cleared up. The man had involuntarily begun breathing with his mouth as if his nostrils were blocked.

It can work! The increase in stress on his eyes from this wasn't unacceptable, and the effect could be maintained, though it was quite taxing on his brain to do so. The moment he took his eyes away, the man's chest fell back down, returning to the usual rhythm of relaxed breathing.

The wooden aisle next to them breathed its last, blowing out a deluge of dark smoke as a shimmering lilac maw peeked through the cloud, pouncing forward to swallow it whole.

Air!

Vern hurriedly visualized a hollow spherical film of darkness that draped around them, passing through the cabinet and floor amid the dazzling white that painted his sight. Willing for it to occur, his vision swam with another bout of pain, and he fell back on the floor, gazing up at the ceiling.

Another abnormal sight played out around him. Flames, red and purple, drowned the entirety of the hall. The floor, shelves, people, books—everything was being torched into blazing luminance. However, in this infernal chaos, was a recess.

A gaping hole doused any flame that dared enter its perimeter. It was unnerving, yet just as fantastic to experience. Outside the invisible barrier, the tongues of fire leapt toward it with great intensity only to disappear without a trace once they crossed that invisible threshold.

He had done the best in the little time available to him. He envisioned this barrier to be hollow so Ariane wouldn't suffocate in an airless environment. Another consideration was to reduce any potential cost associated with this vision. The changes he had augmented this time were nowhere near as significant as the earlier stunt.

Vern sighed and gazed around himself, checking to see if he had forgotten something crucial yet again.

It was actually better than expected. Even though his luck had been rough lately, at least a few things were working in his favor.

The floor of the library wasn't made of wood, so he didn't have to fear it collapsing on him, and the ceilings were so tall the smoke had yet to become a problem.

He finally sighed and felt his nervousness fizzle away. As he regulated his erratic breathing, the all-consuming pangs drumming at his eyes began to dwindle, leaving behind a dull heaviness at his eyelids. It had only been around fifteen minutes since the start of everything, but too much had happened, and he needed time to process it.

He slowly turned his head toward Ariane, making sure the curtain of vacuum didn't have any problems as he did so. He guessed it wasn't the eye contact that held the vision together but his mental focus on the task.

Ariane's eyes were still closed with no visible signs of change other than her half-burned long olive-colored coat and a thin layer of soot on her face.

She's good. But what is going on? Why did everyone get pulled into that space? Just where did all this come from? What exactly is this observation?

Which reminded him. Vern looked down at his coat and noticed that most of it was gone. There was a pile of ashes on the ground, including the pocket where he had kept the ancient book.

So reading the rest of that book, which would have hopefully been visible to him as an observer, wasn't on the list of options anymore.

Rolling over to one side, he pushed himself up with his invisible arm and sat up. The disconnect between his touch and sight baffled him still. It was like the vicarious experiences he'd heard of from psyche fundamentalists. Yet very real and very terrifying.

His short experiment with the form had given him a clear sign that it wasn't to be messed with lightly. It would need a considerably larger and rigorous set of tests and trials before Vern could tease out its potential.

Minutes passed by as his thoughts whirled, generating more questions than answers.

Outside their little haven, red flames with an eerie purple edge to them blazed the architecture in plumes of smoke. The likening of scholars turned to ash, the statues melting into formless monsters.

No screams escaped the mouths of scholars as tissues melted off their serene faces, bodies shriveling under the assault of the chemical fire. It was a sight right out of hell. Nauseated, Vern looked away.

Focus. He couldn't have the vision fade even for a second. He'd managed to keep her unharmed under one of the most stressful circumstances of his life. Letting up at this point, even for a bit, would be truly pathetic.

A few more minutes passed by, and his eyes only got better over time, making it increasingly easier to keep the vision running smoothly. The fire, on the other hand, didn't show any signs of letting up. It had too much fuel, and the hearths were probably still churning out more heat.

He had gotten a chance to clear his mind, but this whole situation still baffled him.

Vision and subjectivity were deeply unsettling. He had been a fundamentalist for quite a while, and that meant he had an extensive understanding of the civilization's limits and its advancements. Never had fundamentals revealed anything so . . . disruptive. But these concepts did exist, and he was using them himself. So, did he have to accept that Lennian fundamentals were not universal and comprehensive in nature? Or had people just failed to discover this in the fundamentals as yet?

Shaking his head, he slowly stood up, his torso crossing the short hemisphere of tranquility out into the fiery expanse. It whizzed right through him, not fazing him one bit. Also, he could now completely look away and maintain his vision without a problem. So, visions had all to do with his thoughts and less with his line of sight.

His plan was to inspect the streets and see what was happening to everyone outside. While at it, he would also check out the structural integrity of the library from the balcony. He started backpedaling with short and measured steps as if sneaking away. The haven remained tranquil as he continued the retreat toward the balcony's edge, but then came a point where the farther edge of the hemisphere began receding.

Vern stopped right there, close to the burning entrance of the balcony, and he estimated the distance between himself and the farthest point of the vacuum pocket. It was around twelve meters, which was odd given how, when he first performed the stunt of manipulating the temperature itself, the sphere spanned only around five meters in diameter while the monochrome sight was also only around seven to eight meters.

Remembering all these numbers for future reference, Vern slowly turned around where he stood—his neck craned back to ensure the airless compartment stayed tight.

Swiveling back, before he could take a gander at the barely visible streets, his eyes snapped toward it, up in the sky. A gasp escaped his lips, and before he got too engrossed, he snapped his eyes shut. The simple action jolted him out of his reverie.

Flustered, he cast a nervous look back toward Ariane and sighed in relief. At least he hadn't interrupted the vision in his moment of distraction. Then before turning back to face the spectacle one more time, he took a deep breath and reminded himself not to get too lost.

A colossal chasm loomed high in the starless sky, stretching across the unlit expanse like an unhealed wound.

C H A P T E R 10

HOLLOWBROOK

Orange and blue sparks lined the fringe of the sky's chasm, flickering in and out at unpredictable frequencies. Shimmering rays of light peeked from this incongruous breach in the sky, their subdued radiance illuminating the world beneath.

Vern simply stared wide-eyed at the grand display. Had this tear always existed but he had just never seen it as someone without subjective eyes? *No, that doesn't add up.*

Stars were twinkling through the veil—this dimly lit ambiance of the world a sum of all their parts. *This must be what covered the atmosphere at the start of all this.*

But he didn't remember seeing the tear before everyone was pulled into that nightmare. What exactly had happened that such a massive incision opened up in the sky? What was going on with the world?

It had been just another day. Whenever a phenomenon on such a large scale happens, there are signs. Things change, and people notice. In the Calidian Empire, there were more than a few organizations that closely monitored Prima for all sorts of things to predict natural disasters.

Verdant order looked out for floods and wildfires, while earth wardens warned about earthquakes, landslides, and eruptions. Then there was the Royal Aethereology Society, which usually announced eclipses, solar flares, and the like.

None of them had noticed anything? Even with subjectivity and observation in the equation, it didn't add up. According to the age of that book, the concept of observation had existed for at least a few hundred years. It'd be more than a stretch to attribute this anomaly to subjectivity.

Peeking another glance at Ariane to ensure her well-being, his eyes involuntarily drifted off to the scholars lying on the stairs—on the brink of being reduced to cinders. He thought of possible outcomes of attempting to help them and came up with more than a few detrimental ones. In simpler terms, he wouldn't risk it.

If assisting them meant putting Ariane at risk, he just would not take the chance. What if he initiated another monochrome vision to form a vacuum pocket for these people, but it replaced Ariane's?

He liked to test and experiment, but that didn't mean he would play with his sister's life for the sake of some random people he'd never met. They were just too far down on his priority list compared to her.

However, this brought his attention to something peculiar. One of the women who was about to meet the flames had her eyes open, and this reminded him of something. When he came to, more than a few people were blankly staring wide-eyed ahead. *So, these people with open eyes tried to glance at that entity too?*

What differentiated his case from theirs? If it was as simple as mustering the courage to look at the thing, he doubted he would have been the first in the lot to do so. A reasonable guess would be to attribute it to the diagram or the fundamentals. Being a savant, his grasp of fundamentals was leagues ahead of these scholars, but he didn't see how that could have impacted anything in this particular situation.

The diagram, on the other hand, was clearly meant for enlightenment. Could it be that prior exposure to the subjectivity of the diagram allowed him to look at the entity longer than others? But was that alone sufficient? It seemed like a probable conclusion but not the full picture.

His list of assumptions, conjectures, and hunches was only growing longer by the second. The lack of a notepad to write down all of it gnawed at him. He liked to put things on paper because memory was a frail thing, and hedging too much on it was a fool's errand.

Shaking off the distractions, he looked back at the streets. Many people that had hid inside buildings at the start were back on the streets, probably after panicking from their newfound blindness. Hundreds were lying on the streets in poor shape. Many were bruised and battered, while few were quickly losing blood from their hard falls. A couple of really unfortunate ones, however, ended up too close to the steam and met gruesome fates, their bodies scalded beyond recognition.

Puffs of steam endlessly churned out from the closed hands of the Kingsmen, who had joined the ranks of everyone else, lying prone on the solid ground. Just like commoners, albeit a little more gracefully—perhaps due to their previous kneeling postures. *At least there is no all-consuming fire out there.*

As for his other objective of checking the library's exterior? There was no way to achieve such a simple assessment. He couldn't walk an inch farther, or he ran the risk of dispelling the vacuum. There were no mirrors that just happened to be in the position to catch a glimpse at the state of the building from outside either.

So he just stopped and stared at the gloomy city. After all, the archive's second floor was higher than most residences.

It was disastrous. He knew the adrenaline was keeping his mind too active to feel it, and he had yet to come to terms with the whole situation, but the sheer horror and scale of this event was catastrophic. Just how many could escape the clutches of that being before this ended? Would it even end?

This appeared like a worldwide phenomenon, and its effects would be much more than some incapacitated people getting bruised from falling on the pavement. Anything that needed active monitoring would fail. Trains would collide, ships would sink, factories would explode . . . *No. This is downright tragic.*

His conjectures only hammered home the severity of this situation. Who knew how long he would have lasted within that world of terror, but he wouldn't bet on being able to hold on for more than an hour. He was convinced that with every passing minute, millions were succumbing to that thing. Losing their rationality forever.

More than a few hundred were already taking their last breaths in this very library. Scholars he would have listened to and argued against in only a few days' time at the conference. The whole fundamentalism movement would lose so many bright talents, all human evolution halting in its place.

The world as he knew it was gone.

His colleagues and friends back at Nvoria, whom he had spent his last four years debating and learning with, might never see the light of day again. His master could probably handle it for quite a while, but what about the fate of his wife and son? That man would break if anything happened to his family.

He didn't know if he should feel lucky about not having to worry about any other family members in this tragedy.

Vern heaved a long sigh and settled down in a spot amid the raging inferno, its flickering light casting a forlorn glow onto his sharp features. Drawing his knees toward his chest, he wrapped his arms around his body and stared into the gaping void that hung high in the sky. Every blink seemed to linger for a fraction longer than the last as the fire burned away.

Rowan finally looked away from the newly formed crack in the heavens and focused back on the goddess in white that floated above the church. Her radiance was too dazzling. He felt like it was easier to look at the sun than stare at her majesty. But that was just how it was meant to be. After all, she was the servant of Lady Lennix herself.

He had never seen a deity before today, but in his heart, he had always believed that his faith was not in vain. That there would come a day when his devotion would not go unnoticed. That Tailor Bismile had always chided him for being too superstitious, yet there he was, shaking like a leaf as he knelt among everyone else.

The whole town had gathered in front of the church to receive the words of the goddess. Then suddenly, she made a move. It was as if the light falling off the great chasm in the sky bent to her will. Her shake of a finger made changes his brain couldn't comprehend. Why would he be able to comprehend? This was divine. Not for mere mortals like him to understand.

After the world finally settled back down from her short movement, the priest spoke with great fervor.

"My children, due to the descent of an indomitable evil, the rest of the world has embarked into an epoch of abyssal darkness. Yet, our city stands as the sole bastion that still bathes in the celestial radiance of our lady. Praise be to Lady!"

"Praise be to Lady!"

"Praise be to Lady!"

The whole crowd around Rowan, including himself, thundered back with great vigor as they maintained their kneeling postures. Some were shaking with joy, barely able to look at the white goddess, while others began chanting the verses from the Luminous Litany. This was the holiest his town had ever been.

Praise be to Lady, for she's just and fair. She knew her faithful ones and decided to reward them for their belief.

Their town of Hollowbrook was the only place that did not lose the light of the heavens beyond, while those heretics would live on in eternal darkness. The great gash must have only been opened for the townsfolk to bask in the glory of the lady herself.

Rowan didn't know exactly what had happened to the world, nor did he care. Those making use of the sinister devices made by the blasphemers didn't deserve his pity anyway. What he did know, however, was that Lady had shown her grace. So her servant, this goddess in white, must have come with a task for us faithful ones.

And he was right. In another of her enigmatic movements, the world changed, and motes of lights fell from the sky. No, no, no. It was holier than that. These were divine. These lights took the shape of white lotus flowers as they slowly fell from the sky.

Rowan jumped and grabbed himself the first of these divine blessings before everyone joined in, frantically grabbing at the radiant flowers. *Heh. These fake devotees don't even understand what the goddess wants.*

One of the women who didn't manage to find herself a flower prostrated and began striking her forehead on the ground. *Incompetent fool!*

But that thought threw him for a loop. No. Maybe he was the incompetent one for only grabbing one flower.

He should find himself another. Snatch it from these insincere bastards. If he did that, the goddess might show more grace to him. *Yes! Yes! Goddess will like it.*

However, before he could perform this magnificent demonstration of faith, the priest bellowed, "Goddess has spoken. Everyone must pray for the light. Pray for the light."

"Pray for the light."

"Pray for the light."

Then before Rowan could resume his portrayal of dedication, the goddess disappeared. A beam of light streaked down south toward the river, leaving behind a dazzling trail that faded by the second.

But she had yet to see his sublime display of deep faith. *Why did she leave like that?* But it didn't matter either; he would get himself more flowers and then find the goddess. She must know. She must receive his expression of unwavering conviction.

Rowan didn't have his tools from the shop, but that didn't matter. As he sincerely prayed for light with the glowing lotus flower in one hand, he grabbed a sharp rock from the ground with the other. Not delaying his grand gesture of faith, he jammed the sharp edge of that rock in Bismile's head.

Bismile looked at him with an unfocused gaze and was about to commit the blasphemy of letting the flower drop to the ground, but Rowan caught it with his other hand. He now had two flowers. Would goddess praise him now? *She will. No doubt she will.*

He looked around and noticed the woman fervently pummeling her head into the ground. *She must be a heretic.* Her dirty blood flowed in the grooves of the pavement, staining these holy grounds.

How dare she?! Then before Rowan could set things straight, the priest, the only other real believer, did it for him. He crushed her head to a pulp in a powerful downward blow of his staff.

Rowan wanted to sing his praises, but he couldn't stop praying for the light. That would be utterly unacceptable. There were a few other fervent ones that removed these pests and took their flowers, but Rowan would be the first one to get to the goddess and gain her favor.

So he walked out of this irreverent crowd, but something tried stealing his flower. That grocer Herman's kid had stabbed a piece of broken glass in his thigh, reaching out to steal his flower. Rowan kicked the thing to the ground and smashed the thing's head into a broken mess in a few seconds.

No one would interrupt his expression of loyalty. NO ONE! Chanting the prayer of light with two flowers in hand, he ran toward the river. Goddess was definitely still here. Her glow was evident by the river. There was no chance in heaven she would leave without rewarding him for his efforts.

So, he ran. Ran toward the river. Not once did he stop running, and not once did he stop chanting. He was devout like that. So when he reached the verdant foliage that bordered the riverbank, his footsteps only grew firmer. Her beaming radiance lit the shadowy trees, and when he finally saw her outline, he slowed down.

Slowly walking toward the shimmering rays that peeked through the shades of these trees, his mind whirled. He didn't understand. What? What had happened? Why?

But why had he . . . ? No, he had to show his loyalty. But why had he done that? Bismile was like his brother. But why had Bismile not given the flower to him? Rowan didn't understand. His mind felt heavy, and he needed light. *I shouldn't have ventured into the shade. The heaven's light doesn't reach here.* But then he wouldn't be able to show his loyalty to the goddess.

Before he could make sense of his jumbled memories, it came into view. The goddess was standing at the bank of the river under the torn sky—her arms wide apart, reaching for the heavens. Hundreds of motes of light slowly manifested all around her as the flowers in Rowan's hand turned into streaks of light, disappearing from his grip.

The motes of light grew more prominent and material. Some of them changed form, turning into the familiar shape of lamps. Some turned into candles, some resembled the moon, and some mirrored lanterns.

Few were those steam machinery, while the rest must be something made by those heretic fundamentalists. All these things surrounded the goddess in their spectral white glow. These glowing apparatuses occupied more than two plots' worth of land.

Rowan wanted to go up to her and explain how he had managed to find himself two flowers, but he didn't want to interrupt her. However, why did he want to express his loyalty with flowers? Before Rowan could come to a decision or realization, the radiance of the world shifted.

The spectral devices turned blazing white, but even in this saturated vista, she remained brighter. Just like every time she moved, the light itself bent for her, and she gently united her palms, creating a whisper of a clap.

The world turned white, and he heard her voice, which resounded like ethereal melodies, stirring the very depths of his soul. "I see you all."

And then the world turned black.

Chapter 11

EXPERIMENTATION

Vern sat there motionless as minutes passed by. Then there was a flash.

Did that just happen? His tired mind snapped back to wakefulness in an instant. Was it just his new eyes playing pranks on him? Not knowing what to believe, Vern rose and performed a few quick jumps to shake away the lethargy. *It's getting worse.*

He had gotten the hang of keeping the vision active even when he wasn't focusing too hard, but his body felt more tired by the second. He wasn't lacking sleep for the day, so it was quite unnatural for him to be so drowsy.

There was an obvious probable reason for this—the whole enlightenment process. Getting up right after seeing that thing was an ordeal in itself, and it was only getting worse. But it was still within realms of plausibility for now.

Following his earlier train of thought, it was simple. The actual process of observation was too simple. He had a rough time at the start because he had to work against the clock. But otherwise, it was too simple to break any Lennian fundamentals with this.

It's like there's really no limit to this power. This vision had been going on for about half an hour. Instead of feeling any deficiency or loss of some resource, his eyesight was becoming sharper. *Unless, getting sleepier is the cost. Because if it is, I am willing to go to bed six times a day.*

The pain in his eyes had completely subsided, and the vacuum pocket he had created almost didn't strain him at all. It was too good. His earlier conjecture of being unable to destroy reality by painting it black held less and less weight by the second.

If not for the possibility of the vacuum being dismissed, he would have tried so many things to tease the constraints of observation. There was some limit on the range, sure. He had already hit that threshold when he had tried to change the balance of temperature to coldness. But that seemed to have more to do with his method than ability, as the range wasn't always constant.

It was quite hard for him to suppress the temptation to experiment with the possibilities. But he wouldn't have to do so for much longer.

The relentless fire had devoured countless pages of narrative and knowledge, their ashes slowly falling like dark snow, escaping the shrinking cloud of soot and darkness. The previously vibrant mahogany shelves had long surrendered to heat, their polished surfaces now charred and cracked—the final vestige of their proud structure collapsing in defeat.

The fire itself was beginning to show signs of fatigue. What just a few minutes ago had been mighty, hungry flames were now reduced to lethargic licks of fire that clung to the more resilient materials, struggling to keep their essence alive.

Just in time too. Vern calculated that the air within the bubble would get dangerous to breathe very soon. Ariane had been breathing from that enclosed hemisphere without a new supply of fresh air. Based on the breathing rate of an average human and the size of that bubble, the fresh air would, at most, last for another ten minutes.

To that end, he didn't have to worry much. The fire had almost completely died out close to the center of the library. From what he could make out at the edges of the floor from here, the hearths had already burned away their combustion chambers—not meant to handle the heat, nullifying the cycle. So there wasn't a proper source of heat anymore.

What sickened him, however, was the stench. If not for this ethereal form and its unusual suppression of his senses, he doubted he would have managed to sit here without throwing up. It was a gruesome scene, more so now that the fire was gone.

The bodies, once human, were now reduced to grotesque forms—blackened, charred, and partially incinerated. The fire had eaten away at their clothes, and the skin beneath was blistered and cracked open in several places.

Limbs lay at unnatural angles, stiffened from death, some grotesquely exposed where the flesh had been cooked away. The faces, recently filled with animated expressions, were now horrific masks, their flesh seared away, revealing skeletal grins.

Vern took repeated short breaths, somehow managing not to lose his balance as he walked over. *There's nothing I could have done.* But was that the truth? What if he had accepted the enlightenment earlier? *No. I already made my peace with the fact that I made a mistake in judging the severity of the situation. Nothing would have changed my decision without prior knowledge.*

He had done all he could, barely making it out alive before being forced to adapt and understand observation in the direst circumstances he'd ever found himself. So it wasn't really worth weighing down his conscience over. He would live with the decisions he had made.

After another silent minute, the remaining flames around Ariane were gone. The air would still be poisonous, but it would be better than whatever had become of the air inside the vacuum. He had a few plans about taking care of that too. He sighed in relief and closed his eyes. The falling ash that had subtly skirted around an invisible barrier fell right through and began to blanket Ariane.

It would be a lie to say that Vern wasn't growing more anxious. *Ariane is courageous and strong-willed, but how much longer can she hold on against that thing?* He didn't even know where to begin and try to help her in this situation. *Join her in that nightmare? How? Help her? Just how?*

Well, now that I can try out observation in more suitable conditions, I might just figure out something.

The first order of business was to figure out what was possible and what wasn't and see if there was some way to purify the air around Ariane. He might have chosen to observe balance, but it was such a vague concept, even he didn't know what to expect. So he would go through some of the test scenarios he'd thought of while moping.

Vern followed the previous method to bring up the monochrome scape and attempted to think of factors that make up the balance of poison.

A shiver ran down the intricate network of veins in his eyes, yet nothing changed. *A failure. So there are indeed some limits.* But what was the general trend?

Steadying himself, Vern thought of the situation more logically. What exactly would it mean to have the balance of poison? What even counted as poison? It wasn't really Vern's field of expertise, but didn't that in itself mean something? It definitely did.

Balance of evolution. Nothing changed.

Temperature. A vision akin to his first attempt covered his eyes. Everything with some heat to it was a little gray, while the flames were straight-up white. But he was trying something else right now; this vision was just to make sure he could still see the balance.

Lennian fundamentals. Another failure.

Mortality. Funnily enough, the earlier vision shattered, and the whole world turned pitch black except for a silhouette of a woman glowing brightly right beneath him. *What!?* He had thought to observe this mostly as a joke.

Am I to believe this would unambiguously give me control over the balance of life and death? No. Something was wrong here. The world did not work like that. He might just be overreacting. It was also quite easy for him to observe the balance of temperature, but manipulating it had nearly snapped the springs in his brain.

Not one to give up so easily, he looked at where one of those grotesque bodies lay, currently nothing more than black mesh against an even darker backdrop. Not being an idiot like before, he imagined the indistinct silhouette to turn just a shade brighter, nothing drastic.

Ready this time, he took the fall gracefully. It didn't send blood rushing out of his eyes, sure. But it was an unsavory experience, nonetheless. This failure, however, made Vern happy. He didn't like the idea of observers being able to play with life and death at a whim. Because if he can do it, then there's got to be others who can also do it.

Vern liked balanced frameworks. This one had an inkling of being of that nature.

But he had veered too far off his original goal. Dismissing the morbid vision of utter darkness, he found himself a more comfortable position. Vern extended his legs in front of him with his hands placed firmly behind his upper body.

It was back to more experiments. He still didn't know how to purify the air around Ariane. The whole thing was a little mind-bending to think about. When looking for the balance of the air, was he looking for its existence? That seemed to be what he was doing. Otherwise, how had he removed the air to create the vacuum?

But balance wasn't supposed to be as simple of a thing. If the earlier balance was acting upon the presence and absence of air in an area, then could he observe another kind of balance within the air? Like the balance of how each individual type of gas is distributed?

Right as he finished the thought, the scenery changed. A noise of black and white dots dominated his perception. Like tiny ants crawling all over, the motion was unfathomable. The whole vista was utterly random, and in but a few seconds, his eyes started to throb.

Discarding the sight, he leaned over to one side and massaged his forehead. It probably wasn't as easy as he made it out to be. Everything did take some toll. *However, if peering into the essence of reality is this cheap, I'll gladly keep doing this whenever I get a chance.*

All these unrelated assessments were quite insightful. He might even have figured out how to finally solve the air purity problem.

The observation seemed to do better on concepts that he had some understanding of himself. On top of that, the right amount of vagueness and clarity in what to observe was necessary. Too clear, and it'd show the core concepts that he could not make any practical use of. Too vague, and nothing would happen at all.

Breathable air.

So this time, a white smog that looked like polluted smoke churning out of a factory's chimney appeared. However, that impression couldn't be further from reality.

At long last, he had finally found the keywords needed to manipulate this balance. *Hopefully it won't be an impossible task like fire and mortality.*

Ready for any backlash, he envisioned a small sphere of lighter smog in the vicinity of Ariane. He wouldn't make the same mistake of trying to tip the balance to the limit in one direction by imagining a completely white sphere, and possibly getting another eye-bleed.

A quick stab of pain coursed through his eyes, but nothing he couldn't handle. However, he wasn't done yet.

Vern was intent on not making life harder for Ariane due to his ignorance. Not waiting another second, he discarded the current monochrome vista representing balance depicting breathable air.

Instead, he conjured the vision representing the simple balance between the presence and absence of just air like the one he used to abate the fire.

Visualizing a thin hollow sphere of black around Ariane once again, he was done at last. He had first envisioned the air in that sphere to be breathable, then locked it in position using the same vacuum bubble.

Vern had the choice between either the purification of air or the vacuum persisting. To him, keeping the vacuum made more sense due to the familiarity and ease of maintaining it.

However, there was another essential test he wanted to perform before he would call it a day. *Can I maintain two visions at once?*

The idea sounded simple, but it implied focusing on two things at the same time. According to his thousands of hours spent deciphering fundamentals, it was impossible. The closest one could come to mastering the notion was by rapidly switching between two tasks. That's what he was attempting.

While trying to keep the veil of vacuum intact, he conceived the existence of breathable air around him—and the vision instantly shattered.

Not wasting any precious time, he discarded the thoughts of breathable air and simply conjured another veil of vacuum right back up.

It is indeed infeasible. He might be able to make some progress if he could skip some steps before every conjuration or figure out the difference between maintaining and persisting the vision. Until then, it was just a pipe dream.

Or maybe, I can just use brute force and keep practicing until it's muscle memory. He didn't have the time for that. And his time would be better spent doing something else with this omnipotent vision rather than repeating the same task.

Left with nothing else to do but watch Ariane once again, he buried himself in his thoughts.

Why was she not waking up? She had yet to stop breathing, so that was a relief, but what was taking so long? It had been more than fifty minutes since the whole ordeal began.

Fifty minutes under that pressure. Even if she survived this, he couldn't imagine the trauma this would cause. *Will she ever be able to recover from this?* Could his observation deal with her trauma? But was it even possible to isolate trauma to such a degree?

What if he messed with her personality on a fundamental level and broke something? It may indeed be a possibility to scrutinize humans through the lens of balance, but he didn't feel nearly confident or knowledgeable enough to know the implications of such a thing. *There could be as much as a million balances within—*

A dull echo of words resounded in his ears. "Oh, Mistress, forgive me. Oh, radiant empress, forgive me."

C H A P T E R 12

CONTRADICTION

Oh empress, why would you show me light when I will forget it all?"

Words? Words. Words! Someone's here.

Vern snapped out of his reverie, and his mind failed to catch up. Someone other than himself was awake, and they were approaching his location. The dull echo of the voice was getting louder.

"Oh, Mistress, how could you? I will forget. I will forget! I will forget your grace!"

Can this be that man in black? Vern perked up at the thought. Even if his stalkers weren't the most courteous of the people, they had helped him out one way or the other. *They might even lend me a hand in getting Ariane out of here and give me some context about this scenario.*

However, as he got up, his languid brain turned for the better, and the incongruency of the situation reared its head. *The behavior doesn't match up at all. My stalker has never even said a word much less rambled like a madman.*

Not just that. Why would they wait until now if they are always following me? Has something changed?

But just the fact that this person is awake and functioning during this nightmare must mean they're an observer.

"How can you be so cruel, oh empress?"

The voice is getting clearer as moments pass. They are definitely moving toward me. If they're not my stalkers, it doesn't make any sense. Why would anyone come here? For me? But how would they even know I am here?

"I waited. I waited. I waited ALL THIS TIME!"

Vern's hair stood on end as the possibility crossed his mind, further exacerbated by the shrill shout. *They're here to silence me.*

If someone other than his stalkers knew exactly where he was, then they had some transcendent observation method he couldn't even imagine pinpointing him. But what did that say about their motive? The world of observation had been so well-hidden that it wouldn't be surprising if they simply killed anyone and everyone that came in contact with it.

I should plan for the worst case.

Then the first order of business is to get away from Ariane. Vern of a few hours ago wouldn't consider this necessary. However, his reflections pointed out a clear flaw in his mode of operations. He'd been too passive.

The balance between his proactiveness and reactiveness was tipping far too much toward the latter. But this situation demanded the former. He always knew what the worst case entailed, but he had allowed them to come to pass.

Not anymore.

In his pursuit to become a savant and comprehend as many fundamentals as possible, he had gone through more literature than most coven leaders. But the study of fundamentals needed a balanced mind-set. Too much focused knowledge was as good as overfilling a train's engine with coal—it could, in his master's words, *cloud the view, weigh down the journey, and risk causing more problems than it solves.*

So, the master's solution to that was to add fundamentals dictating relationships within society into Vern's already exaggerated curriculum. The loathing he felt for the first few months at being forced to study sociology, psychology, economics, and the like instead of mechanical arts was still vivid in his mind.

He never managed to become a savant in the realm of relationships, but it had served him well in his desired path of mechanical arts. Better than he was ever willing to credit it. He didn't want to go back to those days of endless social anxiety.

That mind-set gave him an edge of its own, but he still rather preferred being a functioning member of the civilization. *A now-ruined civilization.*

So this situation's worst case entailed possible harm to Ariane by association. *No way am I implicating Ari once again.* She had survived the worst of it and might even wake up soon. Letting her breathe some poisonous air was still better than getting her killed as collateral damage just because some madman decided she was linked to him.

"ALL THIS TIME, and you decide to do this to me when you know I will forget?"

Making up his mind, Vern took a deep breath and walked toward the stairs, descending one step at a time, feeling just the solid touch of the steps. No texture. No heat.

It is better to confront the man before he ascends to this floor and avoid having Ariane acknowledged at all.

The thought of just running away also crossed his mind. Given his ethereal form, he might not incur many injuries from jumping from the balcony. But if they can pinpoint his location anyway, what would be the point of doing that? Also, there was the possibility that this person was friendly. However minuscule, it was still a possibility.

"I will forget. I will forget!"

Halfway down the stairs, he saw him. A man of great fashion with a hint of fantastical flair entered the reading hall, walking straight through the fire and smoke. His indigo velvet frock coat billowed gracefully with his every step, its edges adorned with golden embroidery. A design that embellished his black top hat too. A sleek jaw and sharp features paired with a twisted smile and a resounding voice added a touch of insanity to his sophisticated profile.

Vern continued his descent, scrutinizing the changes in the fire around the man. It was bizarre. Every time a flame would leap for him, it would pass right through as if he didn't exist. But that meant the man could choose what to interact with, because his clothes didn't fall off him like they did for Vern.

Or was it inherently different for him and was related to his viewpoint? It seemed just like Vern's own form but visible to the eyes.

Does that mean this ethereal form is not temporary but is the standard for all the observers, and I just don't know how to control it yet? Or does this person's viewpoint allow him to manipulate himself like that?

"Oh mistre—" The man abruptly halted beside a fallen chandelier, twisted his head sideways, and peered straight at the staircase, his gaze landing right on Vern.

He can see me.

It was somewhat expected. If a novice like Vern could look through walls, what was a little smoke and awkward invisibility to an actual observer?

He turned around to face Vern and adjusted the rim of his hat. "Mistress was correct as always!"

Then out of nowhere, a coin appeared in his palm, which he flipped without a wasted second. Not knowing what to make of it, Vern maintained his composure and sensed for changes around himself.

Huh?!

Out of thin air, a cluster of sharp-edged golden crystals flourished right in the middle of where Vern's chest should be. It was shining with a malignant glimmer, its razor-sharp ends expanding and rapidly shrinking with a grating noise.

The sight sent a shiver down his spine, and his heart thumped so fast it seemed ready to burst out of his chest any second. The cluster of crystals would have absolutely punctured a thousand holes in his heart if it wasn't for his presently immaterial form.

Vern resumed his descent, taking one measured step after another and sometimes stepping right through the bones of corpses. Ensuring he didn't stumble from his nerves was the priority. Distance didn't mean much to his foe, but his only chance at retaliation had range limits that he would need to comply with by getting up close.

Clap. Clap. Clap. The sound reverberated among the ambient noise of billowing smoke. Vern involuntarily glanced at the elegant man and his exaggerated clapping. "My guess was right on the fucking money! You're as subjective as one could get in enlightenment. Not even a single wisp of representation is leaking out."

Abruptly, the man stopped clapping, and the world went quiet. Then he spoke in a scathing tone. "Now, before I shatter your conscious for the sheer audacity of going against the empress's decree, tell me—which visionary fostered your viewpoint? Because I don't remember our empress exempting anyone from that in Elmhurst."

Vern clung to the railing as if his life depended on it. His mind was sent in disarray from the simple string of words. Contradicting thoughts filled his mind—to flee and to huddle in a corner, to cry and to laugh, to jump and to lie prone. Hundreds of such thoughts flashed through his mind, their sheer contrast stretching his mind at the seams.

But the words soon ended, their nerve-racking deviation gone as quickly as they had arrived. Vern took a deep breath and employed his typical method of avoiding faux pas—he replied in an impassive tone, using it as a crutch to gain some semblance of control in the conversation.

"I apologize for my ignorance, but I have yet to learn from anyone with the title of a visionary. Nor do I know of the decree sent down by the empress. I came into contact with this whole facet of reality just this morning, and that was due to events orchestrated by someone named Yharl Ballin."

"Heh. So you're saying that you're just some random fucker who got roped into the observer society by another random fucker? Then you just happened to break all your shackles of subjectivity, and you don't even know about the empress's decree or what a visionary is? And I am supposed to believe all that?" He paused, and his eyes turned a deep shade of indigo visible all the way to Vern on the stairs when they shone like a beacon.

Everything began vibrating.

"I am to believe that you just happened to have a perfectly realized viewpoint and that it's okay for you alone to remember while the world will forget? I, HENSEN VEHEN WILL FORGET? FORGET HER GRACE! WHILE YOU REMEMBER EVERYTHING?" screamed the man.

The world followed his pace. The fire blew sideways, turning into . . . water? The smoke grew white, plunging to the ground with urgency. The debris and ashes flew in the air haphazardly, creating a tempest of shimmering sparks that rotated into incalculable directions.

Some of the furniture went up but reappeared back at its original place a second later. Things disappeared. The water met the sparks and created an orchestra of lighting in one of the most harrowing abuses of reality Vern had ever seen.

What was even more bizarre was the fact that this phenomenon had a sharp boundary. The sparks that went out of this threshold just disappeared—the smoke reaching the boundary never made it outside. From the looks of it, the boundary was roughly everything within the line of sight of Hensen.

Vern had conjectured during his enlightenment that something this absurd would be impossible. But apparently, he had been wrong. More than just wrong. The sight made his knees feel weak. What was he to do in front of this godlike display?

What would he do even if he reached within the activation range of his own vision?

But it'd be the most passive choice not to try and find a solution. The first order was to—

"I swear in the name of Lady Lennix herself. May her fundamentals forsake me if there was a shred of falsehood in my previous words," yelled Vern, trying to get his words across in this calamitous wreckage.

He waited with bated breath for a change. A response—none came.

In this rampage of uncanny interactions, the figure was obscured by the rapidly shifting aspects of reality. But then Vern got a glimpse.

Hensen's eyes were glazed over, staring off into the distance as something went awry with his left hand. The previously smooth arm was morphing, losing its mass— turning into things Vern couldn't comprehend. One second it was a hand. Next, it became a blistered mass. Another second, and it turned pure white like a corpse's before its shape started stretching out unnaturally.

Just looking at it gave Vern a feeling of dissociation, as if his limbs were being chopped off, and he averted his gaze without any hesitation.

Fuck! This is getting out of hand. It's just not something I should be dealing with. This whole situation is way above my pay grade.

FUCK! But he knew. Now wasn't the time to start moping again. Something was wrong with the man, and this was Vern's only shot at getting closer without being subjected to tens of other ungodly visions, potentially dying in the process.

At least I don't have to go against this chaotic mess using my own visions. He left caution to the wind and began leaping over the stairs.

But the world didn't want it.

Seconds passed by, but the floor never inched closer. He kept jumping down the stairs only to make another leap and get nowhere. It was as if the staircase had infinite steps. He never made it from the twenty-fourth step to the twenty-third.

CHAPTER 13

HENSEN VEHEN

Something is wrong with the stairs.

However, this was okay. Vern didn't panic. He wasn't just an ordinary fundamentalist anymore. It wasn't his first instinct, but the idea of observing the balance came to him quite naturally after realizing the problem.

He looked at the stairs and considered the *balance of the height.*

As expected, something had gone more than just wrong. One would predict that a balance of height would start with black on top, with every step getting lighter depending on how close it was to the ground. It didn't.

What he saw instead was that each step was actually a short, shaded cylinder with the whole staircase being a tunnel made of these small pieces. What was worse, however, was that when he stepped down, all he actually did was walk along the inner surface of these cylinders.

Vern ignored the grand anomaly around him and tried to wrap his head around this mind-bending vision of cylindrical grayscale.

Instead of stepping down to the next stair, he tried walking side to side. This did give him some modicum of progress within the vision toward white, but there wasn't nearly enough space. So he charted a route within the gradient that went from black to white in a linear fashion. But it would be a stretch to call it a route.

When contrasted with his general sight, the path looked like it wanted him to go headfirst into the railing and then just walk through the air. It didn't make sense at all. Still, he knew something was amiss with his general perception of space, and this path in the air was very likely the real way down.

Not hesitating or double guessing too much, he jumped the railing and found solid footing in the air. He wasn't keen on giving his perception more contradictory feedback, so he closed his fleshly eyes and trudged on.

It would be a lie to say that he wasn't confounded by the whole experience. But this scenario of trusting logic instead of his own senses was somewhat of a staple as a Lennian fundamentalist.

Just a few months ago, he had to muddle his way through incomplete depictions when he delved too deep into the upper projection of the northeastern octant of the insight sphere. Most of the memories of experiences within fizzled away as soon as he roused back from the projection, but he remembered that his sight was more than just wrong in extrapolating the fundamentals. Any progress he made in there came from following the previous logic of that depiction. It was quite an unnatural encounter, much like this one.

Vern's unicolor vision guided him to travel in a spiral through the strange tunnel, and he trudged on without any challenges. The laws of gravity were not acting as they should in the spiral. But again, what was acting normal today, anyway? In just a few seconds, he was already at the mouth of the tunnel.

He opened his fleshly eyes and stepped outside the tunnel. In his real vision, he was halfway inside a pillar, rotated awkwardly. However, when he blinked again, the peculiar sight was no more, and he found himself teetering off-balance at the foot of the staircase.

Stabilizing himself, he continued walking. Now that he was on the solid floor, hopefully the path itself wasn't warped. The balance of height wouldn't help him chart his way through this one.

However, his worries were unfounded, as he managed to reduce the distance between himself and Hensen without any more anomalies rearing their heads—except the constant storm of sparks, water, and debris that phased right through him.

In no time, he was just a few meters away from Hensen, whose eyes looked hollow, staring at Lady knows what. *But what should I do?* How was he to use something like balance to confront this transcendent observer? Hensen was still standing mostly unharmed, the tempest raging on in front of him. He had his arm stretched out, still morphing into a thousand different things, and Vern didn't dare look too closely.

A few seconds passed by as Vern stood there, not knowing what to do. Until he remembered the situation he had been in mere moments ago, and it gave him an idea.

Gravity.

The whole library disappeared, and past the boundary of this anomalous storm, everything below him was a dark, unfathomable void, whereas the sky above faded into a murky gray. It was like he was standing on a cliffside next to an abyss.

He also realized that he could see either of the two realities—the vibrant realistic one or the monochrome nihilistic one—as he desired. All he had to do was focus hard enough, and the grayscale completely dominated his sight, eliminating the need to physically close his eyelids to ignore reality.

Besides that, this small section where he stood was chaos beyond imagination. It was like that etheric dance of skylights that the fundamentalists from the Northern Senn Empire talked about, except they weren't in the recorded shades of green and blue.

The grayscale balance of gravity was flowing like liquid, twisting and turning into patterns that didn't make sense. Probably one of the reasons everything around him was churning like a storm.

Still, something was a little different than usual with the balanced sight. This time, the scope of the gravity being perceived by his eyes was too much.

Usually, everything was limited to the room or even the stairs. If, in his earlier sight, the scope of height was on a scale as grand as this, then the staircase's top and bottom both would've been similar shades of gray. Because, from the perspective of the whole planet, the height of both ends of the staircase wasn't very different.

But Vern didn't have the time to glean anything about this obscure fundamental of gravity from this view. Every fraction of a second that passed by put an enormous strain on his eyes.

So he did what anyone would have done in this situation. He imagined a somewhat dark shape that would have covered the figure of Hensen in his real sight and turned the world around Hensen a shade lighter.

Taking a deep breath, he braced himself and superimposed this modification onto his real sight.

It didn't burst his eyes. Heck, the pain was even milder than when he had been experimenting with the air. *Can it be related to gravity already being in a mess? But then why is it so taxing to just look at it?*

However, the effect of the vision wasn't as gentle. The chandelier, debris, shelves, flames, smoke, and things from even beyond the hall began hurling toward Hensen, accelerating as they reached him—and passed right through him.

Except his ever-changing arm. Wreckage stuck to whatever extended out of his shoulder and concentrated all around it, brutalizing the blob of mass every second.

"Aaaagh!"

Vern involuntarily jerked back in response to the sudden scream, and the vision shattered. *Fuck.* Why was it so hard to maintain focus? It was already an ordeal to keep the vision active—this little disturbance ended up being the pin that jammed his gears.

"Aaaagh!" The flowing water turned back into sparks that fell all around them.

"Hah." Debris fell right back down with loud thumps.

"Ha ha. Ha ha. Hah." Smoke regressed back to its former darkness.

"Ha ha ha ha ha . . ."

"Listen here, you scrapshit." Hensen flung his arm, and the debris collating around it dispersed in all directions. But then his laughter died down as he noticed the state of his hand, and a horrified look briefly flashed past his eyes.

Vern was already backing away, trying to get out of Hensen's sight. *The hell do I do now?* What other balance could he manipulate that wouldn't knock the wind out of his sails and actually do something to this madman?

But before he could turn around, that sense of contradiction filled every inch of his body, and he stood there, rooted on the spot. Hensen started walking toward Vern, ignoring his now static yet mangled hand.

A sinister smile was etched on his face as he said, "You just happen to know how to use that vision on me, right? But you said today's the first time you learned about subjectivity. I let myself lament for a bit, and any random fucker thinks they can walk all over me. But no matter, the empress knows the truth." He raised his unharmed palm and spread it open, fingers representing the number five.

"You may not forget, but you have to live to remember, right? Let's see how many contradictions you can handle before you give up." Then with a chuckle, he tucked in the thumb.

An endless surge of contradicting thoughts suddenly rose in Vern's mind. *To cry. Laugh. LaughCry. Fuck. No. No. NoCry. Laugh.* Tears trickled down Vern's cheeks as he began laughing uproariously. "Hahhahhah it hahhah is hahh." It was annoying to feel his body escape his control. This was exactly like that situation in that horrorscape before, but swift and more potent.

So the solution wouldn't be too far off from the last time—simply focus on something else entirely. *But I shouldn't jump the gun just yet.* Hensen was already pissed for unknown reasons, and if Vern displayed that he could disregard his vision, things might take a turn for the worse.

"Hahhah it is hhhah my eyes haahhhahah, right? Hahhah take aghhh take them. Aghh," said Vern forcefully amid his fits of laughter and groans, tears continuously leaking from his eyes.

"Are you trying to fuck with me, or do you really not know?" said Hensen with narrowed eyes.

"I do hahagh not hahhaghh. I only look hhaahhaah for a aghh peaceful resolution."

"Wrong answer." Hensen dropped his index finger, leaving only three fingers upright.

Vern walked forward, but his upper body jerked backward. His eyelids began blinking rapidly, shutting only once every few seconds. It was as if blinking and keeping his eyes open were inversed. Pushing his right hand led to his left hand being pulled. The coordination of his body was an utter mess.

It gave the impression of a marionette controlling a puppet with jumbled strings. The more Vern tried out his body's functions, the worse he realized it operated.

This really was getting to be too much. What the hell was wrong with this guy? He wasn't willing to believe anything Vern said and made nothing but assumptions without giving him a chance to explain. What didn't bode well for Vern was that this madman's observation was bizarre. Bizarre and formidable.

Vern could maybe ignore a few of these commands, but this was starting to overwhelm him. He had always had a calm mind, but it was physically becoming impossible to stay in control. *This is terrible. What the hell does he want?*

"Does that make you wanna talk straight, or you got more shit to say? If eyes worked like that, I would have long ago gouged your pair out even if I had to hide from the visionary behind you for a couple decades."

So eyes can't be transferred? Fuck that. Should I just make up the name of some visionary? Would that get him off my back? But what if Hensen knows all the visionaries? He already came to the conclusion that Yharl Ballin wasn't a visionary, calling him some random fucker.

One wrong word and Hensen might step up the torture, leaving him unable to recover. From Hensen's words, it was obvious—more than a little obvious—that Vern was going to remember whatever was about to happen, but not him. Was that because of his ethereal form? But didn't Hensen have something just like him too? However, that wasn't important right now. He saw a chance here.

Rejecting many subpar choices, Vern finally landed on a simple yet viable one. *It might actually work.* Making up his mind, he spoke, "HahhAGHHH hahha I—"

The world shook, and Vern lost his footing, plunging to the ground and landing on his back, blinking like a lunatic. He looked around, mirroring Hensen, who seemed just as perplexed.

The carcasses of scholars that littered the ground began glowing a crimson before a shiny scarlet thread seeped out of each of them. A thread that became thicker and taller by the second, flowing like a liquid toward the ceiling.

Hundreds of streams of what almost seemed like blood soared all around them, boring holes through the thick ceiling and spire beyond it without any hindrance.

Before Vern could restrain his laughter and tears enough to get a word out, Hensen spoke, "Well, we're out of time. I don't know whatever the fuck this is, but the Monarch of Karthain is about to turn back the clock. Since you refuse to identify your affiliation, your visionary will have to take issue with the empress once the dusk has fallen."

"Because if I have to forget, you don't deserve to remember either!" And he folded his middle finger.

C H A P T E R 14

BEYOND TIME

Vern's mind instantly grew lightheaded, and his limbs felt heavy. His heart began racing faster than a high-pressure steam engine at full tilt, but the pangs in his chest only became more pronounced. It seemed as though his blood had turned far more viscous, jamming and coagulating in his veins.

But his heart didn't care about any of that and only pumped faster and faster, giving the impression that it would burst from the sheer pressure it bore to pump such dense blood.

This was the moment. He was feeling it. If he didn't do anything right now, he wouldn't even know when it all stopped. His consciousness would just fizzle away, never to generate thoughts again.

All his ambitions of embarking on his own path of fundamentals would die, rendering him nothing but another cog that fell out of the machinery called life without even a clank.

So it was time for his last ditch effort.

Gravity.

Not wasting any time in taking in the vast abyss, he envisioned a black hole at Hensen's mangled hand and a line of white that connected it directly to a sharp shard of glass by the chandelier.

Whoosh.

The moment he overlayed this change onto reality, blood flew through the air alongside a severed arm. At the same time, Vern found himself free of the uncanny afflictions of blood, tears, and disarrayed coordination.

However, he was only halfway done.

Greed.

Seizing every instant, Vern rapidly processed the new distribution of shades of gray around him and cranked the shade of greed in Hensen to be far whiter than whatever it was."

"Aghhh. You FUCKING—"

"I WILL REMEMBER FOR YOU!" yelled Vern at the top of his lungs, cutting him off.

"If the time is turning back, I will find you and remind you of everything you want to remember. You do not have to kill me. This does not need to end like this," said Vern, clutching his eyes from the immense pain caused by that last vision.

Hensen cradled his stump with his other hand and looked at Vern with unfocused eyes. "I will remember? You really don't have an imprint of a visionary on you? You will truly remind me?"

"That's right. That's right. Why would they leave such a versatile viewpoint unprotected if you had one."

"Aah, Mistress! Empress! So cruel, so fucking cruel. You really want me to forget your blessings. How can you be so selfish!

"Come, come. Since you don't really have an affiliation, you only have one option: become my slave and remind me of Her Majesty after the duskfall. Acquiesce to the thoughts within your mind, and it shall be done. Or die!"

Vern closely inspected Hensen's expression through the gap between the fingers and saw the mad fervor in his eyes. *Crack my fucking cogs! This is the result of greed as well.*

Pay homage, reverently kneel, serve the liege, lower myself, follow the words, serve forever, bend the knee, offer obeisance.

Similar phrases of offering allegiance and words conveying acceptance of servitude filled every corner of his mind, beseeching him to do the same. Vern promptly disregarded any such notions and closed off his mind, focusing elsewhere.

He hadn't even thought of the possibility that the crazy would want to enslave him. This was a big mistake that could've been just as bad as dying. But it looked like some kind of consent was necessary for this to work.

Trusting his instincts, he chose to gamble. A necessary gamble. He would rather die than serve someone as insane and maniacal as this. The visions Hensen had at his disposal were too unconventional, and the power imbalance was too much.

Vern stood back up and shook his head. "If you try to force me into any kind of servitude, I will kill myself right here and now, or you can do it yourself. Then, your selfishness and greed will be the reason your future self will be deprived of the empress's majesty."

Hensen's sharp gaze pierced Vern, and a shiver ran down his spine. Hensen fumed at the words and seemed ready to pounce at any moment. The world vibrated, and surrounding reality was abused once again. Debris and fire churned into aberrant directions like before.

But after a few seconds, it all died down, fizzling away into a quiet hum.

Hensen took numerous sharp, deep breaths, and a hateful look marred his visage as he spoke. "Remember. Remember with all your fucking brain. Because there is a cost to threatening Hensen Vehen. There will come a day when I will make you suffer through the eternal paradox of your vile existence!

"If it was any other circumstance, I would have ruined you and everything you held dear, razing it from the very fabric of reality for fucking with my emotions. You think I can't see your petty little tricks?

"But it's okay. It's okay. For Mistress. FOR MISTRESS, I will bear it. If you won't accept a mental suggestion of servitude, then I will give you one last option."

Hensen paused and took a deep breath as if trying to suppress his overwhelming rage. "Carve this within your mind and accept the burden of the Cryptic Constructor." He waved his hand, and a bunch of wreckage floated around him to form a symbol. It started with a rough shape but quickly became far more intricate and complex as the small pieces of debris crunched farther and farther to perfect the outline.

"What do you mean carve it in my mind? And what is this burden?" The hell did he mean by that?

"Really an illiterate fucking sightless. Heh. I said what I said. CARVE IT IN YOUR MIND!" He began shouting.

"Make up a fucking vision that looks like this and shove it in your mind. You have ten seconds before I change my mind and burst you like a blood sac."

This guy is batshit fucking crazy.

But Vern knew he couldn't push his luck further. This lunatic wasn't going to reason with him any longer.

Reluctantly doing as told, Vern envisioned the exact shape by recreating every detail: the curves, the engravings, the edges. The shape looked similar to two inverted triangles but with sharp edges, intricate grooves, and out-of-place lines that extended from the triangles. Vern imagined this as a white shape in a world of black, without any specific balance in mind.

Something happened. He felt it. The vision shattered on its own, and something definitely happened. Vern couldn't pinpoint—

"At least the fucker knows how to do what he's told. All right, now that you have the burden, here's how this is going to work. I have had the same burden in my mind since forever, but yours is a derivative of mine. Every time you make use of this burden, I will sense it."

"And I know myself. Before or after the duskfall—one way or the other—I will end up looking for a leech that is stealing my representation. He-he, I will take care of everything after that. Even if you don't use it, once the Cryptic Constructor descends, I will sense it anyway."

He knew it. *This is a fucking trap.* But what could he do? Instead of sulking, he asked, "What do I need to remember? And does it really have to end with me suffering setbacks or dying? I haven't really done anything to offend either Mistress or you. Everything was either a coincidence or just me trying to defend myself."

"Oh, that will depend on whether Mistress figures out that I couldn't silence you in time. If she does, too bad for you, I couldn't care less. I would lose my chance to remember, but this is a gamble, after all. As for how you'll remind me? The content is really only for me to know. So you will have to forget this little story I am about to tell you until we meet again."

"So the lady showed—"

"Wait—"

"—a second."

His vision flickered, and it was already done. *FUCK THIS.*

Vern quickly realized that a few minutes had passed, and he remembered none of it. The thick streams of blood that gravitated toward the ceiling and beyond were already gone—just like their source. All the macabre half-burned bodies around him were gone, even their ashes a lost cause.

No. It has already started.

Yes, it had started. That reversal of the clock that Hensen was talking about. Maybe this was even the reason he was back in control of himself. Hensen stood right there—still like a mannequin. The whole world seemed like it was waiting for something.

But it was terrible. His brain felt like a mess, and he just wanted to pass out. It was finally getting too much for him to bear. He was just another human for the love of all his gears. He just wanted to sleep.

Ticktock . . . Ticktock . . . Ticktock . . .

His groggy mind found a second wind from these ear-shattering ticking sounds, and he sat back up. The loud booms banged in his head, but soon he didn't have the time to care about that.

It was just as bizarre as he imagined it would be. When Hensen said the clock would turn back, he did imagine something like this happening. But this was the worst-case scenario.

Like a music box that had its gears keyed in the wrong direction, the world began its grand performance.

The violent dance of the flames ceased their forward motion, shrinking down as the army of fiery serpents retreated. The light and heat found its way back from the charred wood and paper, their scorched edges mending themselves. Smoke, once rising to form a smothering cloak of darkness overhead, began to swirl in a cyclonic dance, plunging downward back into the books from whence it came.

The charred garments and accessories that lay on the floor began floating in the air as if their owners had donned their possessions again. But that was the uncanny part of it. Everything was taking the same course that it had in the past, except that stream of blood and all the bodies.

The holes in the ceiling started repairing themselves, but where was that stream of blood? Why were these humans the only ones that did not reform? It was as if the reversal of time recorded everything that happened down to the turn of some random cog and undid it, but it forgot about the humans.

But it only forgot about the dead humans, as Hensen was walking back and performing random gestures with his bloody stump, gibberish coming from his mouth.

The fragments and shards of glass began finding their way back to the chandelier, its radiance and glow being restored at a moderate pace. No. The pace was changing. Hensen's steps grew quicker and quicker alongside his reversed words—

Wait! Can I glean something about my missing memories from his speech?

"Evahstxn ymothtsp dht emdewolsth shtwrtu htem fglotehs.

"Eno keve evasot aive yr dd svwdn a tubnoallebqrnton siviht drlowqht evdsotsihtgnssodzlaew."

Vern focused hard.

But it wasn't meant to be. His brain was just too dull right now, and the gibberish was getting faster, turning into a slurry of words. He tried. He tried his darndest hard, but his mind just couldn't process it. He wasn't in any condition to use any visions either. Everything was just so heavy.

Still, some words were just too obvious not to be deciphered, like—*shattered, duskfall, save, shades, isolation, viewpoint, visionary, Mistress . . . Livia?* However, there wasn't any context around them. He couldn't figure out what meaning each of them held.

Before he knew it, the opportunity was gone. The chopped arm flew back and attached itself to Hensen's stump. The abnormal tempest raged once again in reverse, and in another few seconds, Hensen was already backpedaling out of the library.

Vern would've loved to follow the man back to wherever he came from, but he could barely even move, let alone follow someone that was retreating faster than a steam engine.

Well. Since this was the case, he would go back upstairs and see what was happening to Ariane. Pulling his weary and exhausted body up, he limped his way back to the staircase.

Clinging on to the tangible handrails, he towed himself upward—one step after another. The burned clothes of the men and women on the staircase looked like balloons filled with air, their upper layers pretending to have something in their hollow shells. Necklaces and earrings were floating in apparent positions where someone would've worn them.

TicktockTicktockTicktock.

The omnipresent ticking sounds grew louder and faster by the second—their cadence almost resembling thunderous rain.

On the verge of falling back after each step, he somehow held on and managed, collapsing on the floor the moment he reached the end of the stairs.

Ariane was right there.

It almost looked like she was the only person moving forward in this bizarre world with its hourglass reversed. But it was just a trick of his eyes. Figuratively and literally—she always had a bubble surrounding her, after all.

A few more seconds passed until the fire started receding from the stairs, shelves materialized out of thin air, books flew back to their dwellings, and Vern's coat revived from the ashes. Another beat of his heart, and his outfit turned into a balloon, an empty husk where his body should've been.

Then began the most bizarre puppet show he had ever seen in his life.

Hundreds of unsullied yet hollow outfits stood back up and began playing human. Ariane arose from her fall as his empty three-piece suit began to walk back with her past the now-pristine shelves filled with unscathed tomes of knowledge.

TckockTkTikTokTicTicIckTococOTock.

The absurd sound of ticking turned into a mishmash that was too fast to resemble any real clock, and then when he blinked again, a dead silence encompassed the world.

With the last strength in his body, he crawled a little to the right and managed to get a clear view of Ariane sitting outside on the balcony, surrounded by tens of hollow outfits.

Dinggggg.

Then with a booming sound, the silence was shattered. Instantly, the facades of the humanoid outfits that speckled in the immaculate and beautiful archive fell apart. Unoccupied clothes and accessories plunged to the ground in a cacophony of rustling sounds.

Then Ari reached toward Vern's sinking clothes, and a shrill shout escaped her mouth. "Vee!"

She moved. She moved. Ari moved. She survived. That's all he needed to know before his mind gave up. Content, an endless void of fatigue consumed him.

CHAPTER 15

VON INDUSTRIES INTERVIEW

All Cera wanted to do was get back home and bury her face in the pillow. Was her glee apparent on her face? If it really was, that would be so unprofessional of her. What if Madam Helena got a bad impression of her because of that?

She couldn't have that happening when she was so close! She was almost done and had managed to somehow not crash and burn on her first big assignment. The compensation just for going around factories and coming for this interview was twenty crowns! More than two weeks' worth of her usual salary.

Maybe she could even pay to get some steam at the house for the next couple of weeks. *Verdant order posted that it would snow heavily this fortnight, and Mum was already a little out of sorts. It will definitely make her feel better—*

"Miss Cera?" a voice registered in her mind, and she snapped out of her daydream, quickly schooling her expression back to the stoic one she had cultivated after so much practice.

"Yes?" said Cera to the secretary that came out of Madam's workroom.

"I apologize for the long delay. Please come in. Madam is waiting for you."

"Thanks. Please lead the way."

This whole situation was a windfall she had never even expected. Cera was picked by the boss to tour the many factories of Von Industries, and now she was to meet the famous, or infamous, Helena Von Arden. If she didn't muck it up, there was even a chance that she could be chosen to become a contracted scribe for Von Industries.

If that happened, Mum and Dad wouldn't have any other excuses not to move out of that shabby house. But she didn't know what she had done to deserve this. What was she going to be judged on once she was inside? Would it be some kind of test? Her writing skills? Her boss hadn't given her any clues for what to expect.

Now that it was the time to actually go in, her heart was racing faster than the chains of that sawing machine she had seen today. What if she gave Madam Helena a bad first impression? What if she was as scary as people said? *What if I commit some faux pas, and she complains about it to the agency?*

She shook her head and got up. Madam wasn't going to wait for her to feel confident, or she would be waiting forever. Cera took off her ragged coat and fixed her outfit one final time. She was in her best attire for this meeting, saved for special occasions like this. Even if it had a few touches of dust from the rough day in the factories, it was still presentable.

Her high-collared cotton blouse was warm ivory and tucked into a thick woolen skirt dyed a rich cobalt blue, which clung to her in folds of warmth and comfort. As if that wasn't excessive enough, she even had her favorite black cotton stockings on, which didn't quite match her outfit but looked great with her sturdy boots—or so she hoped.

"Please follow me," said the secretary as she pushed open the ornate door.

Chucking that annoying bang out of her face, she lifted her shoulder-length hair a little to give it a tad more volume, which Mum said made her look more imposing. She quickly closed her eyes and prayed, *"Oh, Benevolent Ephram, the Great Conductor of fate, grant me the confidence, open all gates."*

Grant me the confidence, open all gates. Mum would be so mad if Cera told her she almost forgot to pray before going in.

Then she hung the satchel containing her essentials on her shoulders and hurried behind the secretary into the workroom, leaving her thick shaggy coat and scarf in the corridor outside.

The now-familiar smell of metal filled her nose again as a luxurious chamber entered her vision, its golden opulence more than just dazzling. Every inch of it was filled with gadgets and contraptions that showed off the mechanical advancement of Von Industries. Some of whose manufacturing processes she had seen just today.

On the ceiling was an enormous chandelier made of those devices, which rubbed some precious crystal to produce golden light. Then there was an over-the-top table, which had a smooth metal top and legs that looked like pistons. Sprockets and cogs wrapped around each of them, somehow allowing one to change the height and width of the table by pulling a lever. She had seen it happen twice and still didn't know what sorcery was going on in those cogs.

The walls were decorated with different variations of firearms. Some were clearly made for large animals living beyond the bridges, while the rest were designed to handle the outlaws of the city.

All three generations of Kingsmen's ignition blades adorned the alcoves in each of the walls, reminding her of the many times she had seen these blades resolve situations in the city—mostly resulting with someone dead or disabled. Apparently, the latest ones could even melt bullets, working both as a defensive and offensive weapon.

Finally, there was the giant clock that hung behind the madam's seat, encased in glass and showing off all its intricate and sophisticated clockwork in full glory. Every tick, a section of hundreds of cogs turned in unison, perfectly shifting the long second hand over to its next destination.

Having done everything to distract herself from the nervousness that was building up, she finally took in the sight of Madam Helena by the window and found herself dumbstruck.

"Ma'am, this is Miss Cera Thorne from *Sharlam Daily*. She just returned from the tour and is here for the marketing scribe interview."

The tall woman turned around, her long burgundy hair following her whims, falling over her shoulder in silky waves. She wore an exquisite beige day dress, and draped over it was a thin red robe extending all the way to her feet. The robe had designs of cogs and machinery embroidered onto it, which helped blend her charm into this *fantastique* atmosphere.

She had soft features that contrasted with her vibrant hair and sharp eyes. But how was this someone in their late thirties? *Isn't she supposed to be this ruthless, sinister woman that laid waste to most other rivaling manufacturers in the city, leading Von Industries to its current height?* But this was a gorgeous woman with nigh-infinite charm.

"Yes, I remember. Please have a seat, Miss Cera," said Madam in a silken tone, gesturing toward the piston table.

Cera's brain had yet to completely process the sight, but her body knew what to do. She pulled the edges of her skirt to either side and curtsied in an exaggerated manner. "It is a pleasure to meet you, Ma'am Helena."

Madam simply nodded and walked toward her chair, which was just as complex as most of the other contraptions in the room.

Cera hurried to one of the two seats across from Madam and settled down, nimbly retrieving her writing tools and some papers from the satchel in case she was to write something. *Let's not be dumb. It's very simple. She isn't even scary. She's just another person.*

"How did you like the tour of our factories? I hope you didn't have a hard time getting around to all of them since some are a few bridges apart," said Madam as she nonchalantly grabbed a pencil and started drawing something, not even looking at Cera.

"Oh, please don't worry about me. It was really an eye-opening experience, and I didn't expect that so much goes into making these machines I see every day. Also, the snow has yet to clog the roads, so carriages were aplenty and the journey was beautiful." Obviously, it had been a marvelous experience. Everything was paid for by her newspaper agency, after all.

"Well, that sounds wonderful. In that case, I won't dillydally any further. You've already seen the whole slew of new devices we're working on."

Madam looked back up for a second, meeting Cera's eyes, her pupils a dazzling golden color. "So, Miss Cera, please honestly tell me. What do you think will be the effect of these inventions on society moving forward?" The sounds of her pencil scratching across the paper never stopped.

As expected, she is going straight to the point. Cera didn't have the luxury to care about Madam's drawing. Her brain was churning through hundreds of ideas on how to articulate her response.

Was this the test? If so, she could do it. Mum had always said she was good at worrying about the future. No. No. That just meant she was good at thinking about the future.

"Ah, I see. In that case, I will go one by one." Sitting upright, Cera wet her lips and started speaking. "According to me, the one with the most influence over the city would be the wind-up lanterns. Especially in boroughs inhabited by people from the working class like myself.

"Most people I know in my neighborhood simply end their day at sundown because it's too expensive to burn oil or gas for the lamp. Not a cost worth paying just for some extra light. But according to the fundamentalist I met at the factory, these lanterns only need to be wound up once every other hour, and that only takes a few minutes of physical work to do so. So, if the price is right, the fact that one lantern has a lifetime of three years makes it a very appealing purchase.

"Kids would have more time to study because no parent wants their child to sit under a streetlamp in the biting cold right now. Together with wind-up stations for anyone that can't wind the lamps themselves and bigger machines using the same pollution-free mechanical art, this will be very beneficial for society."

It almost made her wonder why it had taken those fundamentalists so long to come up with this. They've been thriving for over a decade now, after all.

Stopping for a few seconds, she thought hard and came up with the next part of her answer. "Hmm, another one that would bring about an evident change to the society would be by making snow much more manageable with a . . . uh—" She flipped her notes in panic, trying to remember the name of that specific device.

"Frost furnace," completed Madam Helena, leaning in farther to her drawing as locks of those ruby hairs fell to either side of the paper.

"Ah, yes. The frost furnace." *Ughh!* How had she forgotten the name when she just reasoned so much about its uses? But she had to keep going.

Picking back up her train of thought, she said, "That's going to be such a convenient tool in the winter. A poll conducted by our newspaper last year showed that more than seventy percent of the people in Westerleigh borough loathe the snow because of how it prohibits their travel plans.

"So if it works as intended, it will become a cakewalk to clean the streets of snow and keep the city well-connected even after snowstorms. Roads won't be blocked for too long, emergency funds spent by the Crown to cope with unexpected storms will be reduced, and establishments could lower the buffer of stock they have to keep. Its effects will be wide and far-reaching." But in reality, Cera didn't like the invention. It wasn't all as sunny as she had made it sound.

Another brief pause, and Cera knew what to say. "Next would be—"

"Stop." The scribbles halted abruptly, and Madam looked at Cera with a frown.

Oh no! I've done it. I've definitely done something wrong. Was it the stumble? Did I say something inaccurate? Or maybe it was my speech intonation? What should I do now?

Madam Helena's resplendent golden eyes bore through Cera as she spoke in an impassive tone. "Miss Cera, I asked you to speak honestly, didn't I? Did you know that you're the third person Sharlam has sent to me that has done this?"

It was over. She was even being told that she would be sent back like others. Others she didn't even know about. Why hadn't boss Sharlam told her about any of this? "Um, no, Ma'am. I didn't mean to. I just—"

"Please let me finish, Miss Cera. I said I wanted your honest personal opinion, not one tailored to please me.

"I do think Sharlam has chosen well this time, but please don't mock my intelligence like this. I don't really seek to hire incompetent employees that can't even follow orders properly."

Every word that came out of Madam's mouth felt like a boulder dropping onto Cera's heart, sinking it deeper and deeper.

I have offended one of the most powerful people in the city without even knowing or intending to! How did she even realize I wasn't speaking my mind?

What was this situation? Was her career over already? What would she say to Mum?

No. Madam had yet to kick her out. If she was fast enough, this might still be salvageable.

Cera took a deep breath and made up her mind. Apologizing didn't seem like the right idea at this moment, so a different approach was necessary. If Madam wanted honesty, then that's what she was gonna get.

"Then please pardon my rude words, but most of the gadgets in production right now are a double-edged sword. They will bring about the deaths of thousands of citizens just this winter, and who knows how many in coming years." She closely examined Madam's expression and continued when she didn't show any signs of interrupting.

"A lot of people in my neighborhood alone are regularly contracted by the Bureau of Public Affairs to carry out the task of snow removal. But with this frost furnace in the picture, the arduous task of shoveling, transporting, and depositing snow that takes dozens of men could be done by just one."

Her father had worked these miscellaneous jobs for years on end, but their family still had to skip meals every other day to barely manage tuition for her studies. How many other families like hers were still there?

"I understand that the evolution of mechanical arts has always meant the displacement of jobs, but these people are illiterate due to the last emperor's prejudiced policies. So that means they wouldn't be able to find alternative jobs this winter.

"They are barely surviving by doing these odd jobs in this harsh weather, and taking that away means they won't have food on their table for the night. On top of that—may Benevolent Ephram protect me—but Emperor Aldric wouldn't care one whit if it meant a better outcome for the city as a whole," finished Cera all in one breath.

Madam had gone back to scribbling more lines, but the frown that creased her brow was no more, and her lips seemed to be upturned a little by the corners. *Is that maybe a smile?* Did that mean it wasn't over just yet, and she could go back and give Mum some happy news?

Her confidence growing, Cera continued, "However, I am not just talking about the frost furnace. Von Industries has already mechanized a lot of work in the factories, and some of your new devices will certainly aid other industries in doing the same. That's going to change the lives of more than a fifth of the whole population of Elmhurst that currently works in these fact— Aggghhh!"

A shriek escaped Cera's mouth as her eyes widened in horror. The secretary . . . just disappeared.

A healthy woman had just disappeared in front of her eyes! The elegant woman that stood beside Madam Helena since the start of this conversation was now nowhere to be seen. All that was left were her luxurious clothes that fell on the floor with a rustle.

Chapter 16

CITY AFTER DUSKFALL

Madam Helena stood up with so much force her seat rolled back and banged into the wall. Her eyebrows knitted into a deep frown as she first looked at the garments and then all around before closing her eyes as if to sense something.

Cera didn't even dare look at the clothes. Her mind was still reeling in shock at the sheer wrongness of the events. Just how could someone disappear like that? This was unnatural. This was not correct. This wasn't happening. She must be hallucinating.

Oh, Benevolent Ephram, grace my soul, let your light within me console. Oh, Benevolent Ephram, grace my soul, let your wisdom in my heart unfold.

She repeated the prayer a few more times before her heart finally calmed down and her brain started working again. Was it really the time to be like this? What if this unnatural reaper came for her next? Or maybe Madam Helena?

"Ma'am, I— Uh— What just happened? Should we hide? Is this an assassin?"

"No." That's all she said before striding toward the window, her eyes still closed.

A few seconds passed, and Madam simply stood there, clutching the curtains.

Feeling too timid to ask another question but too jittery to just stay put, Cera got up and joined Madam by the window.

She looked outside . . . and what she saw made her lightheaded. The world blurred before her eyes, and she swayed, disoriented by a sudden rush of vertigo.

Madam suddenly gripped Cera's shoulder, helping her avoid an embarrassing fall.

Cera took a few deep breaths before she finally got a hold of herself and her brain processed the scene her eyes had just taken in.

"What in the name of the Benevolent One is going on out there?!"

It was horrible outside. Carriages were running amok, not stopping for the flabbergasted pedestrians on the crossing. One charged headlong into a building, while two others left a horrific tableau in their wake, reducing unsuspecting pedestrians to a gruesome mess.

Many people stood there looking lost. Some held clothes in their arms, while others just gaped at the empty garments lying beside them.

"Oh, Benevolent Ephram, grace my soul, let your light within me console. Oh, Benevolent Ephram, grace my soul, and let this dream go untold.

"Oh, Benevolent Ephram, grace my soul, let your light within me console. Oh, Benevolent Ephram, grace my soul, and let this dream go untold."

Cera chanted audibly, not minding Madam's presence. This was crazy. The world had gone crazy. She knew it must've been a dream. There was no way she first had such a great windfall and then this. Whatever this was.

"Oh, Benevolent One, please help me wake up. Let this dream go untold. Let this dream go untold. Let this dream go untold—"

"Miss Cera. Please get a hold of yourself!" Madam's sharp voice cut through her prayers as the grip on her shoulders hardened considerably.

"This is not a time to play damsel in distress. The dusk has fallen, and it's worse than what anyone would have guessed."

"I don't have the time to babysit you, so get yourself some air and make your way home. I'll send someone over to inform you what happens going forward. If you're still willing to work for Von Industries, that is."

After saying that, Madam walked to her table and opened a drawer. From within, she grabbed what looked like a sketchbook and strode out of the room, not even glancing at Cera or the secretary's last vestige before leaving.

What did she mean by dusk has fallen? Cera stood there dumbfounded, not knowing what to do or believe. Was this really not a dream? Was she really supposed to accept that?

But nothing had happened. No sound, no world-shattering natural disaster, no evil organization. This didn't make one whit of sense to her.

But she had to do something. Sitting here would accomplish nothing.

Still out of sorts, she walked back to her seat and noticed the drawing Madam had been scribbling. Just like the current situation, it didn't make sense either. There were hundreds of dots connected to one another with lines. Lines that seemed completely random to her.

Further spooked, Cera left the drawing untouched, packed her items back into her satchel, and left the room. Donning the coat and wrapping her scarf around her neck, she absent-mindedly trudged through the corridor until she reached a staircase, which she drolly descended before finally exiting the grand metallic building.

Outside was more of a nightmare than she had realized from upstairs. The smell of blood and gas permeated the air as panicked civilians scrambled frantically.

"Help. Help. By the gods, save my son! Someone took him away. Someone save my son!"

"Where did she go?! WHERE IS SHE?"

"Aaaaaaghhhh! What is happening?"

Cries of agony and mourning flooded her ears as people scrambled around to find their loved ones, clothes clutched in their hands.

Most carriages had already found their destinations. Some upended the lampposts, while others smashed open holes in buildings—gas and water leaking from the broken pipes. Then there were a few regular-looking carriages parked neatly by the side of the road, their drivers fleshly humans instead of piles of clothes. They were also looking around, flabbergasted.

It just didn't make any sense. Not everyone had disappeared, but many had.

Cera left the Von Industries head station with haste. Madam was actually right. She should go home. What if Mum and Dad were worrying too much about her? Running around outside, given the state of his back, wouldn't exactly speed along Dad's recovery.

At every intersection she had crossed, the unrest in the surroundings had only grown worse. People ran out of their houses, shouting and begging for help. No one looked in their right mind as tears marred their faces, their voices already hoarse from shouting the names of their loved ones.

Some people huddled together in groups, trying to make sense of the situation, while others went down on their knees and asked for divine intervention. Then there were those demanding answers from the emperor and his reapers high above.

The deadly peacemakers that used to dot the boroughs—dropping down from the skies at the first hint of disturbance, firmly ignored any and all pleas as they jumped from one roof to the next. All of them hurried toward the clamorous siren that originated in Ferrovane Heights—the borough that housed the royals and the castle of Emperor Aldric.

But she sped up her strides to a jog. Kingsmen wouldn't help her get home faster anyway. She had a lot of distance to cover, and the whole atmosphere gave her chills. She was two bridges away still, and the conjectures in her mind were only getting worse by the second.

NO! Nothing would happen to Mum or Dad. The Benevolent One wouldn't let that happen. It just couldn't be. She just had to make her way back home, and everything would be all right.

In just a few minutes, her lungs felt like they were on fire, so she slowed down and leaned on the railing of the bridge between Mosaic Miles and Fulham borough.

But that was when a man approached her and exclaimed with great vigor, "Rinni. Rinni! I knew you were all right. I knew nothing had happened to you. Why did you scare me like that, Rinni?"

It was a man wearing gentleman clothes, definitely of noble upbringing, but something wasn't right with him. He wasn't even looking at Cera as he spoke. Before Cera could figure out what was going on, the man took hold of her arm and pulled her forward gently.

"Rinni, the city has gone crazy. We need to get out of here, Rinni, but don't run around alone, okay? Do you know how scared I was? I thought I lost you. You . . . you just disappeared. How did you— No. You're here. We just have to run, okay? Just don't leave me alone again, please."

Cera quickly realized what was going on. The man had mistaken her for someone else. But no. She didn't have the time to play pretend for someone this unhinged. Her heart, which was already racing due to the jog, only quickened its pace, apprehension and fear overtaking her thoughts.

No. Not today.

Cera stopped dead in her tracks, forcefully extricating her arm from his grasp as she said, "Excuse me, sir, but I am not this Rinni you're talking about. I have somewhere I urgently need to be, so I must take my leave."

Not waiting for his response, she started running. She had dealt with more than her fair share of creeps. If she gave him a chance, he might try to overpower her physically. She didn't have the mind to deal with any of that right now. So she ran.

But before she could get far, she realized the man wasn't even trying to catch up. Cera glanced back and heard, "You're . . . You're . . . You're not Rinni either? I am sorry. I am really, really sorry. I didn't mean to. You just looked so much like her. I am sorry." The man dropped on his knees as his voice cracked with every syllable.

Tears started streaming down his face as he murmured, "Is she . . . Is she really gone?" Cera didn't know how to react to this situation. May Ephram bless the poor soul. He seemed hurt. But she already had so much on her mind, and she really had to get back to Mum and Dad.

However, before she could make up her mind, the man pulled something out from his waist, and her legs came to a halt instantly, terrified of what he might do.

"I am sorry. I am sorry. I am really sorry. I am really sorry. Rinni, I am sorry, but I-I can't take this."

Cera then realized his intentions and reached back for the man, yelling at the top of her lungs, "NOOOO!"

Bang!

The body fell limp on the bridge, a hole in its head as Cera looked on, her hand outstretched as if that would've stopped the man.

She closed her eyes and turned away, not having the heart to look at the gruesome aftermath. This wasn't meant to be. Why did it turn out like this? *Oh, Benevolent One.*

Oh, Benevolent One. Oh, Benevolent Ephram. May his soul rest in your eternal embrace.

Cera walked on in a distracted haze as she navigated Fulham borough. Was it her fault that he had died? Maybe not all of it, but she could have done something, right?

Soon, however, the gravity of the situation descended on her once again. Getting back home was the priority. Her conscience wasn't of concern right now.

I can blame myself later. She strengthened her resolve and started running again.

No handlers arrived to rescue the injured—neither did the earth wardens as more people ran out from burning buildings while carrying piles of clothes with them. Some broke down in tears while others lay dejected. Some cursed the gods, the rest damned the emperor.

The city square, which was always a bustling hub of activity, seemed lifeless. The clock tower high above continued to tick away, but only empty stalls lined the streets. Many people were wandering around, calling out names, their voices growing hoarser by the second.

However, even in this somber environment, a few took the chance to swipe the contraptions and goods from the stalls, going as far as to ransack all the accessories from the now empty husks.

Kids cried out incessantly, calling for their parents, but no one moved to help them. Cera didn't either and kept running. She had to get back home. She couldn't stop to support that woman with a fracture or help that old man who had asked her to look for his sister. She had to get back to Mum and Dad. Nothing had happened to her, and she would show that to Mum and Dad. Similarly, nothing happened to them!

She loathed every second of this journey. Never had crossing two boroughs been so nerve-racking and distressing.

Finally, she was close to home and was crossing the bridge from Fulham borough to Tannery district.

This can't be real. Is this the divine retribution? None of it makes any sense. What will happen to— But then abruptly in the periphery of her vision, an orange glow appeared where there should be just darkness.

Boooom!

A thundering explosion resounded, which swallowed even her frantic heartbeat. She lost her footing and tumbled violently on the sidewalk, skidding across the gravel.

Chapter 17

COLD

Her hand hurt, and her calf was bleeding, but all she could think of was to stand back up and get home quickly. She gasped for air, which turned into a fit of coughing in no time.

Resting her hand on her heart, she took rapid, deep breaths and slowly calmed down. In the process, her eyes involuntarily turned toward that amber light.

A massive fireball blossomed from the direction of the Ironhart district, flaring like a monstrous sun that had been birthed in the heart of the city. The world was bathed in its eerily beautiful light, a stark contrast to the typical dark that permeated the city.

She sat there, stunned and rooted to the cobblestone as the echo of the explosion faded away and the grand inferno shrank, leaving an ominous column of smoke and fire to snake its way into the heavens.

Cera coughed several times, her lungs heavy as if weighed down by lead. She had exerted herself too much in the run, but Mum and Dad couldn't wait. She slowly pushed herself up amid fits of dry coughing and began a slow jog. Maintaining that pace, she only got a few more steps in when—

Boom!

This explosion was much milder compared to the last one, but she knew that was a lie. It was just farther away, but its intensity was definitely superior, as the mini-sun that bloomed in the distance was a magnitude larger than the one in Ironhart. Apparently, world-shattering explosions were becoming the norm.

Not having lost her footing this time, she resumed her trot only to be interrupted by another explosion. This one was very close to the first one. Maybe the fire had spread and did something?

Was this it? Was the world ending? Only more reason to get back home and be with Mum and Dad. *At least we'll be together.*

So she resumed her march, this time not caring about any subsequent noises—no matter how dull or thunderous. She walked past tens of boulevards, ignored all the helpless crying, and reached her neighborhood.

It was . . . missing something. The bustle of children, the boisterous overcrowded streets—all of that was absent. What greeted her instead were sparsely filled streets where most people hid in their homes, not daring to come out. The absence of liveliness here hit her harder than in any of the boroughs she had just dashed through.

"Praise the night! Cera, you are well! Mother Asea heard my prayers and saved your soul. You should really come with me. The world is becoming very dangerous, and everyone is dying—"

She ignored the voice of that bastard Percival, who tried to annoy her with his flowery words yet again and ran right past him. A few other older women tried to get her to stay and talk about what was happening, but she was having none of it.

Finally, she stopped in front of a quaint little house. It was one among the many others in a monotonous array of uniform dwellings, cloaked in a drab exterior of brickwork and weathered timber, identical to its neighbors.

She had been saving up for quite a while now to finally get Mum and Dad out of this shithole.

Cera didn't bother knocking and used the key, which she had retrieved from her satchel. The door opened, and the smell of clean laundry filled her nose—a much-needed respite from all the smog and metal out in the city.

She quickly closed the door behind her and yelled, "Mum! Dad! Are you guys feeling all right? Did you see what's happening outside?"

She waited for a response, taking this time to catch her breath, but none came.

The inside of the house was dark as usual. She had just recently managed to convince Dad to stop reading the newspaper at night. His eyes could barely see anything as it was.

"Mum? Dad? Mummy?!"

She felt cold.

In no time, her eyes adjusted to the deep darkness. Alongside her familiarity with the layout, she easily made her way to the small kitchen. After throwing her hands around the right corner of the counter, she found the lamp.

She reeled back the string, which acted as a flint, and the gas lit up. Light breathed into her surroundings as the flickering blue flame of the lamp facilitated the furniture to cast eerie shadows on the wall.

Cera walked back out into the drawing room, which looked exactly like it had that morning. A soot-covered hearth with wooden logs nailed onto it to reduce the cold air from seeping in from the chimney. A wooden sofa, three chairs around a small table with leftovers on it, and a cupboard huddled close together. Finally, there was the ladder in the corner that led to her room in the attic.

"Mum!"

Not finding any signs of Mum or Dad, she walked toward their room. After rapping on the door thrice, she opened it. "Dad?"

No.

Unfolded laundry littered the room, but there was no sign of Mum or Dad in the small space. Her eyes lingered on the ground for a second before she slammed the door shut and climbed the creaky ladder up to her room, lantern in hand.

She bent her back a little and craned her neck to the side to not hit the ceiling. A short, small bed, a table, a chair, and a compact closet inhabited the floor alongside the numerous newspaper cuttings that were plastered onto the wall—a reminder of simpler times. But none of it mattered right now.

She put the lamp by the table, slipped out of her boots, and slumped onto the bed. Closing her eyes, she murmured.

"Oh, Benevolent Ephram, grace my soul, let this dream go untold.

"Oh, Benevolent Ephram, grace my soul, let this dream go untold."

Gradually, she began to withdraw into herself. Arms clasped around her knees, she pressed herself into the smallest space she could manage, her frail silhouette shivering gently.

Her voice was a mere whisper, hollow and haunting.

It was cold.

Who knew how many times she had chanted before her hoarse whispers died down and a dead silence pervaded the room.

Why was it so cold? Why was no one listening? The Benevolent One wasn't listening. The dream never ended. Why was Mum not back already? Where did Dad go at a time like this?

She slowly sat up, disheveled hair covering her face. Not like it mattered. The gas lamp had long run out, and the only light in the room came from the window, which wasn't much at all.

Getting off the bed, she descended the ladder barefoot and beelined to the door of the house. Opening it, she sat on the single stair by the door and stared off into the distance.

It was so cold.

The moon still hung high in the sky, its glow barely adding any color to the empty, damp, and dark streets.

She waited.

But nothing changed.

No one came. Not Mum. Not Dad.

Her eyes felt very heavy.

Everything was so cold.

Then the silence was disturbed as someone walked by—a haunted look in their eyes hardly apparent in this dim ambiance. It was a young boy making his way down the road with sluggish steps, a gown held tightly in his hand.

He walked from the left field of her vision all the way to her right before he halted.

"Aagghhh! AGHHH!" He screamed hoarsely as he began crying.

Cera's vision grew cloudy, so she clamped her eyes shut. But the cries only got louder and louder.

She got up and rushed back inside, slamming the door behind her. She stood there silently for a while, but it wasn't working anymore.

It just wasn't working.

Her feet moved again, heading straight for the bedroom. She entered the room and stood beside the plain bed. On it were dozens of items of clothing.

She fell on her knees and grabbed at a shirt, pair of pants, and a gown before clutching them so hard as if wanting to absorb them into herself.

And she broke.

"UWAHHHHH!"

Tears started streaming down her face as her frail body shuddered under the force of her silent sobs. The room seemed to close in, reality pressing down on her like a physical entity, merciless and unforgiving.

She couldn't deny it anymore. They were gone.

The stark absence of their laughter, their words, their scolding, their love—it all felt like a gaping wound, raw and tender.

IT WAS COLD.

With each rivulet of tear that traced the contours of her face, she seemed to whisper their names. The world around her blurred into a haze of mournful grays, its vibrance nothing more than a mockery of life itself.

IT HURT!

She yearned for it all to simply halt, for this nightmare to cease, and to awaken into yesterday's reality. But it seemed the world was deaf to her pleas, as even her own tears refused to heed her call. Her throat was utterly parched, but the sobs only grew louder, permeating the room already thick with grief and sorrow.

In this sheer agony and pain, seconds turned into minutes and sobs turned into whimpers. The well of tears never fully dried up, but her mind surrendered. Blacks turned blacker, and darkness consumed her.

Knock. Knock. Knock.

Mum.

Knock. Knock.

Mummy.

Knock. Knock. Knock.

"Mum, could you please check who's on the door?" But her voice shattered the fragile peace she had cultivated, reminding her of the unfair reality.

Knock. Knock. Knock.

The knocking only grew louder, but Cera didn't feel like opening her eyes, much less getting up and checking who was at the door.

It was still cold, after all.

Knock. Knock. Knock.

She was leaning on the side of the plain bed, cradling the pair of clothes. She opened her bleary eyes and was greeted by sunlight that shone right in her face.

Her eyes were swollen, and her face was a mess. Alongside was an atrocious headache that felt like someone was smacking a baton on her forehead without mercy.

Who cares?

A loud thump sounded, followed by the creaking of the door.

I didn't close the door last night!

All sorts of thoughts filled her mind, but the world was still spinning around her. She hadn't had food or water for who knew how long, and every little movement and thought felt like she had to go against the laws of nature itself.

Not having the energy to lift herself up, she haphazardly pushed herself into a corner with her feet.

Before she could do anything else, someone entered the room. It was a man, not the tallest, since he could walk through the doorframe without having to crane his neck to one side like Dad.

He wore a long black robe with red lining, his head covered by its hood. A riveted black mask, which curved to match the shape of his jaw and was pulled up all the way to his nose, hid most of his features. Vibrant ruby hairs peeked through the hood in shiny layers, blending with the hem of his robe.

Yet, the most prominent aspect of his attire was the red strap that went across his outfit on the front and holstered a large crimson-hued rifle on his back. The rifle was so long it peeked over from behind his shoulders, its intricate pipes, valves, and machinery on full display.

"Oh, my lady. What a mess," spoke the man in a gruff voice as he face-palmed.

"I am not doing this. I need to get out of here." He shoved his hand in the pockets of his robe and flung a book toward Cera.

The small book swiveled a few times in the air before landing right next to her. Cera involuntarily recoiled from the book, huddling farther into the corner.

The man looked on with a pitiful gaze and massaged his temples. "Hey, listen. Madam has assigned you a few tasks that she expects you to complete soon. Get yourself together, eh?

"The world has changed too much, and if you stay like this, you're not gonna survive for long. Madam is giving you a great chance. Don't throw it away due to what's already happened."

Cera kept looking at him, an uneasy expression on her face.

"Man, I shouldn't have come. I knew it'd be something like this," he said, massaging his temples.

"Okay, listen. Read the book. It'll do you good, understand? Madam's orders are in there too."

Cera glanced at the book and then back at him, not knowing what to make of any of this.

"Ah, man. I need to get out of here! I am really not meant to handle this."

He turned around and started walking away, his rifle bobbing up and down with his motions.

But right as he was about to exit the house, he stopped.

"Fuck this. Why is it always like this?!" He turned around and pushed his robe away from the seams at the side. His belt peeked through the gap, and he pulled out a golden revolver filled with similar small pipes and minute dials.

Cera clamped inward even farther, holding her hands in front of her like some shield as she shivered.

"Not trying to kill you, I swear."

Clack.

Something cold hit her on the leg, and she jolted back. Peeking from the gap in between her hands, she noticed it was the revolver.

"By my lady. How did Madam hire someone like you? Get a grip."

"Ah, I am not helping. I am done here. Use it if you have to."

The taps of his shoes retreated, and the door closed with a bang. Once it was silent again, Cera felt all her energy fizzle as her arms slumped to her sides.

That was pathetic of her.

Chapter 18

INVESTIGATION

Cera stared at the tombstones in front of her, on which crudely carved were the names ALIYAH THORNE and JEREMY THORNE.

The wind picked up, and the sun shifted its gaze, but she stood there, blankly looking at her parents' gravestones. However, she had tried this before. Standing still and doing nothing for hours on end numbed the pain, but it didn't bring back Mum or Dad.

She had endlessly hoped that things would go back to the way they were. That their empty clothes would have magic breathed into them, and whatever god or devil had whisked them away would return them to her. That they would come back and scold her for not taking care of herself.

But reality was cruel. Crueler than it had any right to be.

If it was going to be so heartless—not just to her but also to half the city—then why not just end it all? Why have those explosions stop? Wouldn't it have been better if they covered the whole city and turned everything to ash? Why leave the frail and vulnerable to fend for themselves in this unforgiving world?

Cera had seen it all in the past three days. Kingsmen had retreated to the districts closest to the royals, leaving the grief-stricken at the mercy of lordlings with bigger fists or firearms. It was as if these deviants were just waiting for the world to burn, reveling in the prospect of chaos and disorder.

They had been just like any other person at the start—grieving the loss of their loved ones. She even used to call some of them uncles or friends. But soon, they didn't see the sorrow or distress in the eyes of the rest. They saw opportunity.

An opportunity to turn their miserable lives around.

There was no one to enforce the law, and endless riches were sitting there unclaimed. Shops were looted, men were killed, women were raped, and young orphans were nabbed to fulfill untold desires.

Everything had gradually spiraled into a nightmare of anarchy.

The water pipes stopped working on the very first day, which probably had something to do with the explosions in the Ironhart district, where most of the city's pipes originated from. So when her body had finally refused to survive without food and water, she had ventured out, lining up for water at the hand pump, which was on the other end of the Tannery district.

It had been gloomy yet serene at noontime. Everyone, already dead inside, filled their vessels with water and left in peace. But later that same day, Percival, that scoundrel, had set up a perimeter around the hand pump with his gang of miscreants, who had all somehow survived the culling.

When Cera went out once again in the evening to get more water, they were brutally pummeling to death any man that got near the hand pump. Those not occupied with manslaughter harassed the women who ventured nearby, oblivious of what fates awaited them.

Cera had tried arguing with him only to be "generously" asked by that bastard to follow him back to his new dwelling in Crescent Bay, where most facilities had yet to be cut off.

Cera was obviously having none of it and had brandished her gun for the first time, escaping the scene with three other women. But what did that achieve? That bastard was still there, and people needed water. The river water was too poisonous to drink since the wells had been out of commission for a decade. Some chose to walk to other districts, but who knew if that was completely safe?

Kingsmen denied entry to any strangers seeking refuge in the safer boroughs, prepared to eliminate trespassers at the drop of a hat.

In the last two days, it had only gotten worse. More and more gave in to their base desires, preying on those weaker than themselves. Those faint of heart remained cloistered in their houses, surviving off whatever they had hoarded before duskfall, as it was now called.

Many tried rising against the scoundrels only to be swiftly put down. Somehow, the rogues were cooperating better than everyone else. Again, what exactly could Cera do in this whole situation? Yes, she had a gun, but she wouldn't count on being a real markswoman if it came down to it. She had never even held a gun before, much less knew how to aim properly.

She might manage if the target stood still a few meters away. But anything else like ten tall men closing in on her—she was better off running away. Just getting around a few blocks required her to brandish the gun every few paces. But who knew how long that would work?

Every time she brought it out, her nervousness was apparent on her face—she knew it. So she solved this by sewing a holster into her outfit.

Cera wore Mum's black dress, which Dad had bought for her for their twentieth anniversary. It had a high-neck black vest with elbow-length sleeves and clung tightly to her body. Its intricate floral embroidery of even deeper black roses mimicked the regalia of Empress Sinatra of the last era.

A skirt as black as a raven's wing swirled gently around her, a ghostly wisp of despair worn above the high boots that encased her black stockings. A garter holster wrapped around her thigh, holding that majestic revolver, while her hands, sheathed in inky gloves, were clasped tightly on her lap.

It had become much easier for her to maintain the facade of control when the revolver wasn't in her hand but was still visible to the miscreants from under her skirt.

She wondered whether it was even right to call this weapon a revolver. Probably not.

Von Industries had never commercialized this weapon, and its manufacturing process wasn't included in the tour. It might even be a secret, given how many options and modes it had compared to any other firearm she had seen in the market.

The dials had a legend marking overcharge, heated, concussive, and normal. She obviously hadn't tried any of them. She had only used the gun to deter others as yet and hoped that would continue to be the case. Who knew how much ammunition was left in there, and what if she ran out? The small thing had so many dials and levers that she didn't trust herself to open the ammunition compartment without breaking something.

But all this reminded her that she had to get going. She had finally managed to escape the cycle of self-destructive thoughts, and it would be a very horrible idea to waste any more time standing here. Mum was gone, and Dad was gone. There was no denying it at this point.

So she picked up her satchel from the ground, looked at the tombstones one final time, and turned away, walking through the empty cemetery. Winds gently blew her hair in front of her eyes as she walked the land of dead, crossing hundreds of headstones with her steps.

It is time for change.

She had been given the revelations of Benevolent Ephram himself. The book that the redheaded man had given her was . . . eye-opening, to say the least. She had avoided opening it that first day, but when her tears ran out, she wanted a distraction. She needed it.

So she read the book.

Cera sought to deny the drivel within, but after what had happened in the world, she realized it wasn't that far-fetched. It introduced her to the concept of observation and the path of a conductor. The possibility that one could view the interactions and relations of objects as tangible ideas just blew her mind.

But as she kept reading, it all started to click. These were the revelations of Ephram himself, the Benevolent One, the Great Conductor. However, right as she got to the crucial part, the book came to an abrupt end, followed by myriad warnings and a letter from Madam Helena.

Cera was indeed wondering why Madam had given her so many opportunities, one after another. It was all but obvious in the light of new information. One's personality and thoughts had to resonate with what the book preached, or becoming an observer of that domain would be an uphill battle.

However, Madam wasn't a charitable person and had many conditions that Cera needed to fulfill before she would be graced with a real observation record. Her letter, which Cera remembered verbatim for she had read it tens of times, said:

Miss Cera, in light of our brief talk yesterday, I see great potential in you to become a conductor that guides this new society. However, your reaction to the unexpected yesterday leaves a lot to be desired.

Observers aren't allowed to be faint of heart, for the whispers from beyond are a constant, and feeble-minded are better off never recognizing the reality.

Von Industries doesn't intend to foster anyone who would undoubtedly lose themselves before shading their perception even once. So I expect you to find an opportunity to enlighten yourself. This will either strengthen your resolve, or you will find yourself lost to the whispers.

The book will give you enough insights into Ephram's domain to get your viewpoint started on the right track, but the rest is up to you.

A few locations and events that could give you this opportunity will be attached as another letter to this book by Alistair. However, keep in mind that these are novel anomalies that our intelligence network has got wind of in the past few hours. We do not know the extent of the dangers they pose and do not have the manpower to explore either.

So if you manage to learn something valuable or enlighten yourself, you can report it to Alistair at the Von Industries head station, and he will reward you appropriately. These rewards could be future excerpts of the observation record or something else to your liking.

Proceed with caution, and hopefully, the next time we meet, I will have a new conductor under my fold. ~Helena Von Arden.

She still didn't know what to feel about the letter. Madam was a pragmatist that wasn't willing to squander her resources on someone like Cera. And Cera was only thankful for that decision.

Yes, she was good at predicting things, but did that really give her any right to demand something from others? What if she failed and wasn't as good as Madam hoped? She would much rather delve into this new world by herself and figure things out one by one.

Did she really understand all of it? No. But that didn't matter because it was a path. It was a path to immense power, as described in the book, and if she followed it to the end, there was a chance.

A chance to fulfill that wish, which she didn't dare voice into words just yet. But it gave her hope, so she would work for it. She wouldn't pick the coward's path like the man on the bridge. Mum hadn't raised her like that. Not when there was hope. Not when there was a new world waiting for her with its arms wide open.

Walking across the pavement that was akin to a path in a sea of dead, Cera retrieved a piece of paper from her vest's pocket. It had a short list of locations with a brief description beneath each.

These were the locations that could supposedly trigger enlightenment. She had long disregarded the ones that sounded onerous.

Yes, she was feeling bolder with that revolver stuck to her thigh, but she wouldn't walk into the wreckage of an underground factory that had exploded not long ago.

Nor did she have any plans of exploring that banquet hall of vanished in Westerleigh borough. According to the description, more than a thousand people of great renown had disappeared in that hall alone. That is to say, most nobles that attended the marriage of Duke Armen were lost to the wind.

So the only viable option was the steamscript relay hub in Starfall Heights. The description only mentioned that the relay pipes were behaving abnormally. She didn't know what that meant, but it sounded harmless enough compared to everything else.

But she wouldn't go in unprepared. The world had changed, and just the fact that this location was on this list meant something was wrong with it. So she would first figure out what to expect in there.

She knew the hub relayed messages to other cities, but she didn't have the first clue on how it worked. Where did the pipes come in? What did it mean for them to behave anomalously? So her plan was simple. She would first figure out everything about steamscripts, and only then would she dare venture into the hub.

The obvious place to find more about the contraptions of fundamentalists was the Symposium. However, the attendees were elitist snobs that didn't give commoners a second of their day even before things turned south. Who knew how they would react to her showing up to ask for information during a situation like this? And forcing the coven was not even an option. She wasn't the only one with a gun.

Then the only sensible option was a library. So that was her next destination.

Eleonora's archive was in the Silverthread district, which was three bridges away if she cut through the Tannery district and exited from its north bridge. But she didn't want to run into that Percival bastard once again. So she would first go to Fulham borough and then cross three more bridges to get there.

As she finally reached the gate to the land of living and exited the cemetery, many eyes turned to her. However, they retreated just as quickly, noticing the golden sheen peeking through her skirt. Not many had firearms in the Tannery district, after all.

It was going to be a long walk.

Eleonora's archive reminded her of all the history classes and research she was forced to do on the city's legacy. As far as she knew, the archive was built during the reign of Empress Sinatra and was named in honor of her first daughter, who was said to be a genius scholar of her era.

Then later, when covens rose to power due to their newly found fundamentals, they quickly took over most scholarly organizations. A very welcome change to the society.

The knowledge, which had been previously hoarded by noble families to maintain their edge on the masses, became obsolete in no time when fundamentalists worldwide worked together to solve society's problems. They were arrogant bastards, yes. But some of them deserved to be.

Cera dismissed her idle thoughts and focused back on the majestic structure.

But something was amiss.

She had expected there to be at least a few people in there. But at first glance, it seemed utterly devoid of life. Not just devoid of readers, mind you. But its grandeur and opulence. It was as if termites had flooded the place, leaving behind a desolate expanse stripped of its life and vitality. The grand door was missing and so were most of the decorations.

She entered through the open doorway and found herself in a naturally lit hall that looked ransacked. All the golden-framed paintings, chandeliers, and trinkets which she saw last time were gone. Left were the books, unadorned furniture, and hundreds of drab-looking outfits that littered the floor.

Does no one fear the coven anymore? It's only been three days, for Ephram's sake.

Shaking her head, she got back to the task at hand. It was afternoon already, and it would take her at least a few hours to find something about the steamscript relay without anyone around to point her to the correct section. Hopefully, she would have something to go on before evening.

Apparently, the first floor only housed texts on social studies and had nothing about a single gear, much less something complex like steamscript relay. She didn't go through every book, but she noticed early on that most sections had similar books, and glancing at one's name was enough to get an idea of the whole section.

So she marched up the stairs. It was as destitute as the ground floor. The lamp holders were empty, and all the gold that was inlaid into the cabinets had been scraped off.

Is gold even worth anything in a society like this?

Nonetheless, when she looked to her right, something entered her vision, and she recoiled, her heart racing with intense thumping as she clamped her eyes shut.

"AGHH—"

But she quickly covered her mouth and muffled her scream. She had to do better. She had to stop reacting to these situations naively. Madam would really toss her to the side if she couldn't even handle a dead body.

So she took a few deep breaths and opened her eyes.

It was the severed body of a handsome young man lying on the ground. His bare back and torso looked unharmed, but he had nothing beyond his waist.

Huh? Where is the blood? The organs?

No. She was seeing things. This couldn't be right. Was he actually . . . growing legs?

Chapter 19

WHISPERS

The room was shrouded in a cold mechanical glow, and an almost palpable chill settled over Vern's body. He found himself standing before a massive contraption of cogs, wheels, and levers, each interlocking part buzzing with an odd, hypnotic rhythm.

In the surreal ambiance, he noticed a curious phenomenon—from the chaos of rotating gears, a beautiful and intricate pattern took form every few seconds before shrinking away, only to reappear after an interval. It was a mesmerizing dance of order born out of disorder.

As he watched, he could feel the rhythm of the gears, the constant shift from chaos to order and back again. It was as if he was witnessing the very heartbeat of existence.

Then suddenly, a cog fell out of pace, bending unrecognizably as it broke off from the contraption. The pattern disappeared alongside it, and a voice emerged. "What is going on?"

The mechanical voice continued to speak, "How could this happen?

"Ah! Why is he naked!?"

But then, suddenly, the whole contraption began falling apart. Cogs came loose and buried him alive as the world faded into nothingness.

"Can you hear me?

"Don't move one inch, and tell me exactly what is going on."

Vern finally opened his eyes, and a dark brown floor filled his vision. His mind felt very clear, and things started coming back to him.

He was probably still in the library.

Wait. Wasn't that just now one of my explorations of the insight sphere? Which octant was it? Why did it end so abruptly? I need to write it down. I need to write it down!

He pushed himself up, but his head hit something cylindrical and cold, and a chill crept up his spine.

"I told you not to move! If you do, in the name of Ephram, I will really shoot!"

What the hell was this situation?

Vern let his body fall back down and tried to figure out his circumstances. Someone was threatening him at gunpoint. But wasn't this the voice of that contraption? Or was that just the voice of this lady bleeding into his dream?

Anyway, he had to de-escalate first. His heart hadn't even had the time to start beating regularly before it was pushed into a frenzy right after he woke up.

From her earlier words, it seemed like the lady herself didn't know what was happening and was as shocked as him.

The assurance that if things really got out of hand, he could always try something fancy with his observation allowed him to ignore his thumping heart and consider his responses.

"I understand, miss. I will not move. Can you please stay your hand?" Addressing any woman as being a young miss would only do him a favor in this situation. She sounded young anyway.

"Tell me what is going on right this instant. Who are you?"

"Miss, I am as lost as you are. I am Vern Lockwood, a fundamentalist and member of the Coven of Truth. I recently came to Elmhurst for the annual conference at the Symposium."

"Then why are you here? And why were you . . . uh . . . invisible?" she asked, her voice stumbling at the end.

Invisible, huh? It must be related to that ethereal form after enlightenment. But she can see me right now. Heck, I can see myself right now. He internally sighed in relief. He wasn't really looking forward to roaming around like a ghost anyway.

"Like I just told you, miss, I am not a local. So I wanted to witness the majesty of the famous Eleonora's archive with my own eyes. But that was when chaos ensued, and I lost consciousness. I have no clue what happened after that."

Crack his cogs, but he wasn't going to babble all about his experiences to some random lady who was ready to punch a hole in his head. She had no reason to suspect his words anyway. Not when it was obvious that she didn't know what she was talking about.

"You were here in the library when dusk fell?"

A puzzled look spread across his face as he replied, "Dusk? No. The phenomenon happened around late evening. As far as I remember, the clock tower had just chimed nine times."

"Uh, I mean when people disappeared."

People disappeared? I guess that's how it would have looked like to everyone after the clock was turned back. But is she saying people outside the library disappeared as well? But then, how did she survive? What was the criteria?

"Yes, I was here when that happened, but like I said, I wasn't conscious for very long. So, I don't know what happened to me or anyone else. However, please pardon me for asking, but why did you connect that event to dusk falling?"

"That . . . that was because Madam Helena referred to the event as duskfall."

She actually answered that? It might not have to get ugly. She seems reasonable.

"Madam Helena?"

"Helena Von Arden—head of Von Industries and Arden noble family."

"Oh, her?" How was any of this related to that unimaginably rich monopolist? A few years ago, she had bought more than three institutes of fundamentalists in a single day, restricting access to all their findings.

"Anyway, don't try to change the topic," she asserted, pressing down the barrel harder on his head. "You won't fool me. I know you are some kind of observer. You must be. There is no way you can turn invisible like that as some ordinary fundamentalist. Tell me exactly what happened here."

Vern's mind reeled in shock at her words. *Why does she know about observation? Is she an observer herself?*

But she doesn't sound confident in her words. Did observation become common knowledge in one night?

Fuck! Who said it's only been one night? How long has it been? If some random person knew about observation, then months could've passed, and he wouldn't have known better.

But if she knows so much, I can't let this situation go on.

His element of surprise wouldn't be worth a cog if he didn't do something about it right away. *I need to take control. I can always answer her questions once I have the gun.*

So he imagined the balance of the most useful concept he had figured out as of yet.

Gravity.

Before his vision could fully take the expected shades, he envisioned the hand of the woman that must be right above him to be connected with a dark thread that stuck to the floor. This would jerk her hand with such force that she wouldn't be able to react, and in this brief moment of confusion, Vern would get up and snatch the gun.

So he overlaid the vision onto reality—

"Argh!"

He felt like his innards were being pulled down, and his body felt heavy. Immeasurably heavy. His vision distorted, and the world curled and bent. Then what seemed like a cold hand reached inside his skull, whispering, "Vorptex slythium noll grinxel prathon zelth."

Another voice joined in, quietly murmuring, "Lethrosh zyvren opthaleon qyrth ubroxis drath."

They wormed their way into his mind, their whispering static threatening to drown out his sense of self. More and more voices chimed in, whispering their sweet promises in his mind, growing prominent by the second.

"Ephrodis vrang oplinthian molux strintholum tervex."

"Quinzorflar plorvix ulmexthar spheridox zythralan."

"Azulianthra triloxthor zephyrianth malanthro."

"Loximorphis xyrinthar galaxtris phantosynx."

They sheared his thoughts the moment they formed, tearing them into tiny notions that quickly scattered into the ether. But even in this turbid collage of senses, the whispers conveyed one idea.

To see everything as everything.

Vern clutched at his head and writhed around. He was losing it. There were no two ways about it. He was losing it.

But on further thought, it wasn't worth defying.

This was his calling—his duty—to become part of something higher than himself. And why shouldn't he heed these calls? It was knowledge. Something he yearned for day and night. He couldn't deny that—not in his right mind.

So he followed the lead and let the whispers guide him. "Frothnix velk orblinthus zarth yxilothran phex."

The fog squirmed, and the shadows lengthened. The ground seemed to breathe, and a metallic taste filled his mouth.

Whispers said first was the existence, second was the creation, next came the preservation, fourth was—

Snap!

A shudder went through him, and everything ceased. It was as if a thread of knowledge, taut with immeasurable tension, was snapped in half as the whispers abruptly died off, turning into a noisy buzz. Then, in his distorted senses appeared two inverted triangles in every form—as sounds, as shapes, as feelings, as things he couldn't even put a name to.

The symbol suddenly shone, buzzed, cried, and a wave of searing heat razed his consciousness, all stray thoughts evaporating in its wake like shadows under blue light—and he jolted awake.

"Haaaah."

Like a drowning man that had just reached the surface, he gasped for air, flailing his hands. His heart, which had almost stopped, began to beat again, and warmth spread in his body.

He didn't know how much time had passed before his thoughts churned and ideas began forming in his mind. The library took shape, and his sight cleared up.

A graceful lady, dressed in all blacks, was sitting on her knees to his side as he lay there, unnerved. Her ungloved hand rested on his forehead as raven locks fell to either side of her rosy face. Eyebrows drawn together and lips pressed into a thin line, her abyssal eyes gazed at him with intense focus.

However, before he knew it, the warmth abruptly disappeared from his forehead as she said in a fluster, "I was just checking your temperature. You were as cold as a block of ice. Are you okay?"

Still feeling hazy, he shook his head and managed to utter, "Please give me a few minutes."

A lot had just happened. He had failed his observation miserably and almost . . . lost himself? But what was that? What were those sounds? What was that pull? Those thoughts? It was indisputable that he would have lost himself if not for that burden of the Cryptic Constructor.

It hasn't even been a minute since I woke up, and I have already triggered the trap that Hensen set for me. But he was thankful. If not for that symbol, it wouldn't have been pretty. It was better to be alive than feel ecstatic about those self-destructive notions as he slowly lost himself to the whispers.

There was a lot to be unpacked here, but he needed time. Too many things were happening, and he needed a blasted notepad to jot it down.

However, one thing he didn't need any notepad to remember was to not fuck around with observation. Not until he understood more about it. He would bet all his coven badges that this lady in front of him knew more about observation than himself.

Yes, he had used it without any restraints last he remembered, but something had changed. And it was such a radical change that it almost got him killed for who knows what.

It looked like his previous assumption of there being some cost to the process of observation was right. Still, it wasn't as straightforward as he imagined it to be.

The lady rummaged through her bag and pulled out a small water canteen. Opening the lid, she extended it toward Vern.

Using both his hands, he somehow succeeded in bringing the canteen to his mouth and drank it all.

That was rude of him. Really rude of him, given how he had wanted to snatch her gun and threaten her not long ago.

He closed his eyes and organized his thoughts before speaking. "Thank you, miss. I apologize for my earlier actions."

A puzzled look appeared on her face before it quickly turned into one of realization. "I knew it. I see what all those warnings were about. You really are an observer. You were thrashing around because you tried to observe something you don't comprehend, right?"

Something I don't comprehend? That was peculiar.

However, her expressions were like readings on a pressure gauge, shifting radically every second. This time it turned into one of indignance.

"You were going to use that vision on me?" She took out a gun-like contraption from a holster on her thigh and aimed it right at him.

Vern shook his head. "I can only beg your pardon. Please consider my situation. I lost consciousness during that mess, and the second I woke up, someone had their gun cocked and aimed at my head. How am I supposed to react to all this?"

But after saying that, a cheeky grin appeared on his face, and he pressed his head against the chamber of the gun. "However, I doubt you can actually do something to me with this."

Her dynamic expression, which was just starting to soften, turned grave in an instant. "You really have gone mad. I should've ended you when you were wriggling like the vermin you are. It's really my fault for hoping you fundamentalists might actually be humans. You think I can't shoot? One more word, and I will not hesitate to pull the trigger."

Vern pulled his hands back and chuckled. "I jest. I jest. I say that because you haven't ignited the vapor chamber of this gun of yours. It won't shoot anything, even if you pulled the trigger."

He might not have seen this exact prototype, but he very well knew how it worked—and how it didn't.

She looked at him skeptically with a tinge of hesitation before she used her other hand to support the dud firearm and stabilize herself. "Sorry, but some naked barbarian can't tell me what I can and can't do."

CHAPTER 20

CONVERSATION

It was like a thunderclap went off in Vern's mind, and his thoughts came to a screeching halt. He was . . . what? He almost screamed in horror when he noticed the chill on his body and revisited his memories of the last few minutes.

He was naked!

But after he looked down, he heaved a long sigh. It wasn't as bad as he had thought. A bluish-black blazer covered his privates, and he wasn't really flashing in front of this beautiful lady.

But this wasn't here when I lost consciousness.

The implication made his face heat up, and he dropped his head in his palms. It was over. His prestige was no more. What sort of gentleman displayed this kind of behavior? Why wasn't there some method to remove these memories from her brain?

"Pffft." She snickered, but he didn't dare look back up as she said, "What happened to the oh-so-smart fundamentalist now?"

"Miss, could you please give me a moment of privacy to grab myself some clothes?" He wanted to bury his head in the ground.

"Not until you tell me how to ignite that chamber or whatever," she replied flatly.

" . . . "

She wasn't budging at all.

"Even though it obviously uses a vapor chamber, it's not a model I've ever used before. Single shots can usually work as long as you have any measure of steam in the chamber."

He paused and mustered more courage from within before resuming. "There's probably a dial or button on the gun that would first trigger vaporization, priming the gun for proper use." Giving her a few seconds to process his words, he repeated, "Now, can you please leave me be?"

Sounds of metal being abused played in his ears before she said, "I, um, can't find it. Can you look at it and tell me what needs to be pressed?"

When Vern didn't reply, she added, "Please?"

This was the most embarrassed he had been in a long while. Did she really need that gun to shoot before he found himself some clothes?

"Umm . . . if it's any consolation, I covered you up long before your lower body was visible. Even though it was like some sort of invisibility being reversed, it seemed as if legs were growing out of your waist. I have no interest in watching any of that."

That . . . helped. He reluctantly lifted his head and noticed her confused expression and steady pose as she tried to fiddle with the gun.

He needed to be done with it quickly, or he would really die of embarrassment. So he asked, "Can you turn it to the side?"

He waited. "No. The other side . . . Yes, now flip it upside down."

"So, you simply need to pull that third lever on the side, and it should be ready to go. Now please?" he asked, clapping his hands together in prayer.

She got up and descended the stairs, having performed the actions he'd just suggested on the firearm. *At least she didn't wait until it was primed to shoot me in the head.*

Anyway, he got up and quickly found himself some clothes that fit him. There were just too many options lying all around. He wasn't going to be picky about having to wear the unwashed clothes of some bloke. *Some bloke that didn't survive that fire . . . or duskfall?*

He shook his head and focused on the attire. Black pants, a white shirt, that blue blazer, and a pair of dusty black boots. Reflexively, he looked around the balcony, but obviously there were no signs of Ariane ever having been there. *How is she doing? Did she read—*

His thoughts were interrupted as a shout came from downstairs. "Mr. Vern, uh, How do I turn this off? It's not stopping—it looks like it's going to burst. What do I do?"

"I'll be right there!"

Vern rapidly descended the stairs and snatched the gun from her hands. She was juggling it between both her hands anyway. He turned one of the dials on the contraption in the opposite direction, and the vapor chamber released plumes of steam, ejecting all the excess within.

Once it was cold enough, he handed it back to the lady and asked, "Have you never used this weapon before? Did you . . . uh . . . get your hands on it by unconventional means? Not that I am judging you, of course. I am just curious why you are using such a complicated weapon without understanding its nuances. You should have opened this valve right here before pulling the trigger. If you shoot without doing so, the vacuum within will make it impossible for steam to release, and the projectile will cook inside the revolver. Maybe even explode if left unchecked."

Like a cog that found its place in the clockwork, a look of realization dawned on her face before she said, embarrassed, "It was . . . a gift. But I didn't get a chance to learn its intricacies."

"I see," he said with a blank expression that didn't betray his suspicions.

Then, remembering his manners, he rested his hand on his chest and bowed a little as he said, "That aside, please accept my formal apology for my previous misconduct. I was just a little spooked by all these absurd happenings. Also, thank you for being understanding during that . . . episode."

She looked slightly flustered as she responded, "Mr. Vern, please don't be sorry. I took things too far as well. I shouldn't have threatened you with a gun to your head as soon as you woke up. I-I just didn't know what else to do when you suddenly started shifting around. You are an observer, after all."

Vern looked thoughtful as he remarked, "You could have just left me alone."

"I had my reasons," she muttered before sliding the gun back into the holster under her dress.

"Hope you don't mind my asking, but I never caught your name. You are Miss . . . ?"

She looked taken aback before curtsying slightly as she declared, "Cera, Cera Thorne." Then with a sudden frown and shake of her head, she turned around and walked back upstairs.

"Sorry, but I have already wasted enough time as it is. I really need to get back to my original task."

As he watched her march upstairs, Vern felt like he should stop her. There were many things that had to be done, but the most vital one was to figure out more about observation and why he had almost died in the process just before.

The activation of that burden of the Cryptic Constructor didn't really help either. Who knew how long he had before that lunatic Hensen caught up to him once again. He had to seize every opportunity available to him.

Miss Cera wasn't as simpleminded as he had first assumed. She was handling this situation with great caution. She also had that revolver, which would be hard to come by, even for himself. But the final nail in the coffin was her response to his episode. She had said something about warnings and observing without comprehension. What did that mean?

What if others outside didn't really know scrapshit about observation? There was a source of information right in front of him, and it would be stupid of him to squander such an opportunity.

So he had to find a reason to stick around.

"Miss Cera, is there anything I can do to help you out?" he asked as he trailed her steps.

She kept walking and replied, "Yes, you can tell me how you enlightened yourself."

Well, he shot himself in the foot with that one.

"Um . . . isn't there anything else I can do to be of service? It's not that I can't tell you. I just don't think you can or should follow the method I used." He didn't really want to talk about his experiences without knowing the extent of this situation.

What if talking about it caused some kind of paradox or got him noticed by the perpetrator or something? It might not be as serious as that, but he didn't feel like tempting fate twice on the same day.

Also, this confirms that she isn't an observer herself. Then, why does she know so much about observation but not enlightenment?

Miss Cera moved toward the shelves on the left and kept walking as she said, "And why exactly do you want to help me again? Just because I didn't shoot you? That's a low bar for sure."

Funny.

"Miss Cera, I'll be honest with you. I don't know what is going on in the world. I have no clue how many months have passed or how much has changed. But I need to know what to expect going outside. Given how destitute a library under the coven has become, I doubt that people out there are going to be as reasonable as you are."

He was sure that straight up asking about observation would backfire, and he had to understand the changes anyway.

She chuckled. "Months? No. It's only been three days. But I hear you. Elmhurst has changed a lot. Much more than I would have liked," she murmured at the end as she entered one of the aisles lined with shelves.

"Anyway, I see your point. You're a fundamentalist, aren't you? Would you happen to know anything about steamscript relays?" she said, picking out a book from the shelf and extending it toward him.

He'd be a fraud if he didn't.

"Yes, obviously. Do you need to send a letter to someone abroad? But is the relay hub in the city still working?" said Vern as he accepted the book and opened it.

"No. I just want to know how they work," she said, folding her arms as she leaned on the shelf.

Vern continued flipping the pages, primarily hunting for some diagrams and images. They made it easier to explain.

"Your wish is my command." He then found one diagram to his liking and turned the book around to show it to Miss Cera.

Pointing at the images, he explained, "The high-level gist is that it's a typewriter attached to a complex mechanism, which converts each letter you type into a very specific sound. That sound is then played by those giant steam whistles atop the hubs."

Flipping over to the next page, he continued, "They set the whistle's trajectory and modulation to perfectly reach the next relay hub. This is why all letters can only be delivered at midnight and why the hubs have to be built on high ground."

Even though he wanted to dig deep into the fundamentals of it, he stopped and waited for a response. One of his completely unrelated discoveries had been implemented by the fundamentalists behind steamscript relays to better balance the modulation sound for farther transmission.

"That's it?" she asked skeptically as the rays of the afternoon sun lit her face.

Yes! Just what he wanted to hear.

"I can go into much more detail if you'd like. First, there's the typewriter, which is quite similar to the one used for writing, but instead of a typebar, which is laden with ink, this one uses—"

"No, wait. That's not what I want to know. It's more about understanding the sounds," she said, interrupting him.

Vern was mystified by the question. "Why do you want to understand the sounds yourself? There's usually a scribe that reads the text from the script plotter for you. If the relay hub is closed or nonfunctional, no one would be sending or receiving messages anyway."

Standing there, she looked unsure for a while but eventually gave up and said, "It's complicated. Never mind that. Please tell me. What would you like to know?"

Finally.

"Can you describe the changes that have taken place in the city while I was out cold? In as many details as you can, please?"

This was disastrous. Vern had already predicted that it was bound to be dire, but this was . . . too much. Miss Cera didn't know any statistics, but when he asked her to remember the number of clothes compared to humans when people had disappeared, she told him around thirty people had been standing next to maybe twenty sets of clothing.

So if he extrapolated based on just that, there was a possibility that two-fifths of the population was wiped off the face of the planet. Obviously, it was a very crude estimation, and it assumed that disappearances were distributed uniformly around the planet and that there weren't any criteria deciding who survived.

But there is a criterion!

He hadn't seen it with his own two eyes, but his hunch was that everyone that managed to endure the mental assault of that horrifying presence until the clock wound back survived, while the rest were scattered to the wind.

No. It wasn't the wind. He squinted hard and recalled that scene when Hensen had stopped playing around and bodies all around him turned into that blood-like liquid that rushed toward the skies.

But this wasn't the full equation either. He struggled to believe that if someone as, uh, unlearned as Miss Cera could survive the mental invasion, then why hadn't even a single scholar in this vast library managed to do the same?

So it was to say that anyone that was already dead—be that a mental death or physical death—was turned into that bloody liquid and excluded from the reversal of time.

So he had really done great work keeping Ariane out of harm's way. But on that note, where was Ariane?

It's been three days—

"Mr. Vern? Is something wrong with my face?" Miss Cera asked, her cheeks red.

Oops. He had been staring right at her all this time. "Ah, sorry. I was just a little lost, trying to process the implications," he responded in his signature faux calmness. There was no need for unnecessary misunderstandings.

Miss Cera had told him a lot, but she had glossed over just as much. Her account jumped from one place to another without a coherent link between them, and a lot of it still didn't make sense to him.

Why was she with Helena Von Arden? Why did this Madam Helena call the event duskfall? Did she already know about it? Why does Miss Cera know about observation at all?

From the looks of it, she appeared to be someone from a noble family, which could explain her link with the head of Von Industries, but her etiquette and manners could use a little more polish. Not shoving a gun barrel into people's faces would be a start.

She had already given him a lot of information, but there was one question that had puzzled him to no end, and he couldn't stop himself from asking, "Your actions confound me, Miss Cera. The whole world is in turmoil, but you're out here looking to learn more about steamscript relays."

Her embarrassment quickly faded, and a serious expression took its place. Vern continued, not minding the change, "I don't believe you're looking to start learning fundamentals in these grim times. Then am I right to assume it has something to do with your search for a path to enlightenment?"

Chapter 21

BACK TO THE LIGHT

She looked down, and Vern couldn't decipher her studious expressions anymore. More than a couple seconds passed by in silence before she replied in a quiet voice, "You're right."

Steeling her expression, she continued, "Yes, I have to become an observer as soon as I can, and my sources tell me that one such opportunity might be available at the steamscript relay."

Vern nodded. It only made sense. But he had more questions, so he inquired, "You didn't specifically talk about this, but is observation something like an open secret now? Was it announced to the masses to quell the panic?"

Miss Cera shook her head. "Nothing of the sort." But she didn't elaborate further and sealed her lips.

Vern wasn't ready to back down just yet, so he pressed on, "Then if you don't mind my asking, why do you know about observation?"

She narrowed her eyes and replied in that flat tone, "I don't see how that is any of your concern. I don't remember us being close enough to share secrets—not when you don't like to divulge your own."

Damn. He overdid it. She was right. They were just being polite to each other and hadn't really shared anything of value. It wasn't fair of him to expect any more from her.

The somewhat cheerful atmosphere that had built up shattered as she went back to browsing the books on the shelves.

Seconds passed by as he racked his brain to find some middle ground.

And he quickly had an idea. It was time for a compromise.

He started again, "I fear I've overstepped my boundaries. So let me put it this way." He paused and adjusted his cuffs as Miss Cera looked back with puzzlement.

He extended his arm in a graceful gesture and said, "How do you feel about the prospect of an exchange? Your knowledge of observation could prove invaluable to me, and in return, I'm willing to assist you in your quest for enlightenment."

Seconds passed without a response as he stood there with his hand outstretched. Just before he began feeling like a savant in the fundamental of awkwardness, her eyes seemed to focus, and she replied, "I can only share general insights and warnings. I won't be able to help you out with anything specific to a viewpoint."

That was exactly what he needed! He didn't even understand what she meant by information specific to a viewpoint anyway. How could one even write down their viewpoint?

So, he responded in an affirmative tone, "That's music to my ears. I wouldn't dare ask for more. I, for one, don't mind following along with you to the steamscript relay hub. As a savant in mechanical arts and an observer myself, I will do my best to aid you in your enlightenment."

He reached out his hand even farther and asked, "So can I consider this a deal?"

Cera hesitated for a few more breaths before extending her arm. Her gloved fingers grasped his wrist, and he followed suit. This was the common gesture of affirming friendships and new relations in the continent of Quartzford.

In usual circumstances, people would bless any trinkets worn on each other's wrists, but Miss Cera seemed minimalistic with her gloves, while Vern was lucky to even have cufflinks.

After what felt like ages, Vern finally left the library and returned to civilization—however devastated it was. He had also grabbed himself a beret and scarf to hide that naturally affable face of his.

There was a lot that had to be done. First, he needed to get his wares from his lodging. His clothing, money, and other vital possessions were still there, after all.

Does money even matter anymore? That was a question he would have to figure out himself. Miss Cera's account was somehow jaded, with little information on how exactly the economy of the city fared. However, it would be reasonable to assume that as long as the royal lineage remained strong, the currency would come in handy at some point in time.

Miss Cera said Kingsmen were still doing their jobs, just in a smaller radius. That should mean at least the throne was stable, but who was sitting on it was a different matter. *Not that he cared about it as long as someone was up there and doing their job.*

On that note, Miss Cera was still in the library. She was reading up on the sounds made by the typebar. Probably her way of preparing for the oncoming excursion to the relay hub.

She wanted to go tomorrow, but Vern needed more time. So they came to an agreement to meet at the library two days later, around four in the afternoon. She said it was easy to get to Starfall Heights from the library.

He would have liked to have gotten more information out of her, but she was only becoming more and more unresponsive as minutes went by. She seemed to like her alone time, and Vern wasn't going to intrude on that by needlessly idling around.

He had too many things to do. Like find a way to meet Ariane. It had been three days, and who knew what had gone through her mind as she saw him disappear in front of her eyes?

If she hadn't changed her residence from the last time he received her letter, she must still be living in the Athenaeum district. The same one where he had ridden the carriage from before the world went to hell.

He would have rushed to her place right away, but according to Miss Cera, that district was under Kingsmen protection. He would need a better understanding of the situation to worm his way in there without getting his head chopped off.

So before he could plan any of that, he had to walk quite a distance to get back to his room, assuming it hadn't burned down or been subjected to a thorough looting.

Outside was as he had expected. The cobblestone road was flanked by a parade of towering buildings, the archive being the grandest of them. Flags, boards, clocks, and signboards artistically showcasing shop names hung above the storefronts, jutting out from them like perches in a mechanical jungle.

However, the usual bustle of boroughs like this was nowhere to be seen. The salons, apothecary, cane emporium, hat boutique, and many other shops were shuttered. Some were broken into, while the rest looked hardly disturbed.

Maybe thieves have no interest in wearing hats? Vern lampooned as he walked on the sidewalks, retrieving a map from his pocket. It was a new one he had taken from the library alongside a pencil and a notepad from the foyer, just like any other thief.

He had already jotted down his earlier dream and a few other details, but he would fill up the rest of the pages when he was by himself.

He wasn't going to pretend that he was some noble scion of righteousness, but he understood the difference between swiping some stationery from the coven with nigh-infinite wealth compared to looting the livelihood of honest men.

And he hadn't seen it for himself, but if "only" two-fifths of the population had disappeared, then the society would start rebuilding sooner or later. People were too afraid and hesitant to come out right now, but some kind of order would be achieved. It would be one thing if a larger fraction of lives had been eradicated, but this was definitely in the realm of plausibility for recovery.

That was to say, anyone losing their merchandise or shops was going to have a harder time getting back on their feet once society started rebuilding.

However, it won't be exactly the way it was before. How did observers fit in this situation? This needed more than just a secondary thought.

Five chimes resounded from the clock tower, the sound giving him a general direction to move toward since his lodging was right next to it in Fulham borough. But there were no carriages this time around.

So he charted a route that skirted the edges of both the boroughs in between. It wouldn't be very smart of him to walk through neighborhoods where he could be surrounded easily. Unlike a certain lady he knew, he didn't have a four-state vapor blaster that could act as a potent deterrent against robbers.

According to Miss Cera, it was a lawless land out there, and rogues could jump him at any moment.

He doubted that circumstances would prove as dire for him. She was a beautiful lady, so it only made sense that she attracted much more attention than a man. Just by the nature of her being a woman, many would assume her to be an easy target and take action.

However, it would be stupid to not take any precautions. So he put the map back into his pocket and picked up a broken pipe from one of the wrecked stores as he started his long march. Something was better than nothing.

Crossing the bridge, which was just as majestic but much more desolate than before, he exited Silverthread district.

In no time, he was greeted with the sight of humans, which was in line with reason. From what he had read, Silverthread district was more of a market than a residential district, so people weren't commuting to their workplaces in this situation. This borough, however, was called Seraphim's Square. According to the map, it was dotted with places of worship and was the spiritual center of the city.

People walked around in groups, sparsely filling the winding thoroughfares and quaint lanes branching off them. In just his sight, he saw a few groups. The one in front of Vern was an odd bunch. They were comprised of three women and four men, but that wasn't the peculiarity. Four of them held makeshift weapons, just like Vern, but the rest looked quite sickly.

He didn't see any flesh wounds on them from altercations, so it had to be internal or chronic ailments. But why would they be moving around if they weren't feeling well? The healthy ones could get rations by themselves. What was the need for all of them to move? *Were they chased out of their living quarters?*

One would think space was something that would be in abundance right now. *I guess the greed of men knows no bounds.*

But he shook his head and minded his own business. Vern kept his distance from them while walking along the riverside, and they did the same.

Minutes passed as he traversed the waterfront in the ambient beauty of the city before he noticed another group of people exiting from an alley ahead of him. He slowed down to ensure he wouldn't be too close to them.

But then he noticed that two men in this group had parchment in their hands. This threw him for a loop until he realized where this sense of déjà vu was coming from.

He shifted his gaze and, as anticipated, someone in the first group was clutching a paper too. The sickly woman who was supported by the other one was holding on to a yellow paper with all her strength.

Not just that, now that he had become aware of it, he saw it everywhere. On the doors of the houses, on the lampposts, on the derelict carriage that had smashed into a mailbox. The poster stuck to everything.

His eyes weren't good enough to read the tiny text at the bottom, but the title was clear. "Mother Asea's Tears: The Miracle of Healing." Then he squinted harder and discerned the subtitle, "5:00 P.M. at Plaza of Existence." There was more, but he didn't want to break the status quo with the other groups just to get a better look.

Are all these people going to check out this miracle of healing? That's gullible of them—

Vern paused mid-thought. *Wait, that's not right. What if observation is added to the equation?* That's got to be it. Observation can be used for healing? Were they going to do that in front of a whole crowd? Didn't that run against their idea of staying hidden? Why was observation popping up everywhere now that the world had gone through that disaster? It didn't make sense.

After thinking about it for a few seconds, he made up his mind. He was going to follow them.

He would go and see what this miracle was all about. It might have already begun since the poster mentioned a five o'clock starting time, and it was a little past that. But any information or interaction with observation was more than welcome in his books.

As the road began to widen, many lanes merged into this road as more and more groups joined him in his walk along the riverside. Some were smaller groups of two or three, while most were at least five people.

I guess being late doesn't matter much.

In another few minutes, the road became wider than ever as the actual cobble-stone street curved into a path to the bridge southward toward Edison Enclave. To his right, however, his sight opened to a huge plaza where stood a towering statue of a graceful woman under the sky.

Far behind the bronze sculpture was a majestic arched edifice, hundreds of colossal pillars propping up its ceiling, while in front of it was a wooden stage on which stood a few people.

However, what made him furrow his eyebrows was the crowd gathered around the platform. From a single glance, it looked like more than a few hundred people were gathered, and more were joining every second. That's when he heard a booming voice amid this raucous crowd.

"Blessed by the eternal grace of Mother Asea, another soul has triumphed over their frailties, rejuvenated through the nurturing warmth of the Mother's tears!" proclaimed an imposing man on the stage as he supported a healthy man, who looked giddy.

"All praise her everlasting gaze!" yelled the imposing man, thrusting his fist up in the air.

The crowd thundered back, "Under her watch, we stand!"

"Beneath her gaze, across the land!"

"Under her watch, we stand!"

C H A P T E R **22**

MIRACLE OF TEARS

Many who had yet to merge with the grand assembly joined in the shouting and roared loudly. Vern pulled his beret farther down and followed the groups to join the masses.

Was it the atmosphere? The faith? All these people that had been suspicious of everything a short while ago were rushing to get closer to each other. They collectively dropped their guards as if this was some haven. *Strength of religion, I guess.*

The metallic sculpture only seemed more and more majestic as he got closer. It was the likening of a graceful woman who cradled a sphere in her palms. Her gaze studied it, penetrating the veil that draped across her face. On her right hand ran what seemed like a vine with leaves that then wrapped around the sphere.

He took his eyes off the sophisticated statue and focused on the people on the stage. At the center of the podium stood a man who looked divine in his own right. Sharp, well-defined features graced his face. A prominent nose and chiseled jawline framed a pair of lucid, sapphire blue eyes that seemed to hold wisdom beyond the ordinary. With his unblemished white robe, long blond hair bunched into a neat ponytail, and powerful arms, he signaled an exuberant man in drab garb down the stairs of the podium.

Then he motioned for the crowd to calm down, and the clamor died off in an instant. After a bit, he began speaking into a contraption that projected and amplified his voice through the myriad pipes on its other end. "Oh, cherished offspring of our grieving Mother! You have gazed upon the divine visage of her sanctity, witnessed her celestial might with your own mortal eyes. This is a miraculous manifestation wrought from her own torment, her own anguish!"

He paused long enough to let the crowd churn again before he resumed. "While the pantheon of gods indulged in the perverse delight of subjecting humanity to harsh tribulations, she wept!"

"As her beloved sons and daughters across this vast world fell under the oppressive shadow of the duskfall, she, our Mother, lamented in profound despair."

His voice reached a higher octave with each sentence. He exclaimed, "Her sacred tears flowed like rivulets of divine sorrow, streaming down her celestial face as she valiantly contended with the gods, striving to put an end to this divine trial!

"But alas, she was too late."

A mournful look adorned his face as he spread his hands apart and cried out in indignation, "Many of our brothers and sisters were lost forever. We, the chosen ones, have sustained losses so profound they surpass the bounds of verbal expression. But know that Mother watches over you."

He paused and turned sideways, pointing at the statue as he thundered, "Mother watches over you! For this miraculous manifestation of tears is her divine decree. In her infinite benevolence, she yearns to soothe the torment of her surviving children, those who have endured the duskfall of sorrows."

His voice became faster with every word, and he yelled, "So come, children! Come and soothe your pains. Shed away your afflictions as you bask in the tender warmth of her tears, for they hold the power to breathe life even into those teetering on the precipice of demise. Know that this is her love, that this is her gift."

Then he paused and screamed as his voice boomed throughout the plaza, "ALL PRAISE HER EVERLASTING GAZE!"

The crowd erupted without delay, their echoes threatening to deafen Vern with their sheer vigor. "Under her watch, we stand! Beneath her gaze, across the land!"

Many men in white robes walked up to the stage with goblets in their hands as they knelt beneath the sculpture. Then in a bizarre turn of events, two thin trails of discoloration spread beneath the bronze statue's veil as if from its eyes, and a liquid began swirling in the goblets underneath, appearing out of thin air.

Many in the crowd gasped at the display while the rest continued their chanting. Vern, on the other hand, was more than a little unnerved by the whole thing.

A divine trial? Is this how they're explaining the disappearances? It was straight-up scrapshit, and he knew it. That was no fucking trial. That was corruption. Corruption of mind and body.

But it was indeed an explanation worthy of these religious fanatics' approval. They even found ways to discredit other religions while at it, blaming the calamity on other gods. *Can they even get away with it?*

Also, where did the name duskfall even come from? They actually extended it, calling it duskfall of sorrows. *It fits the situation, but why was there a consensus between Helena Von Arden and these fanatics? Why do they both call it by the same name?*

However, that wasn't what he was here for.

The real question was *How are they doing this?* He didn't believe that the discoloration or liquid appearing in the goblets was some divine decree of their goddess. It was somehow being orchestrated, but it was done so flawlessly he couldn't see the hand behind the trick.

Before he could ponder any further, the men in robes got up, and the guards standing at the bottom of the stage allowed some in the audience to ascend. One had only one leg, while another seemed to have burn marks all over his body. Some seemed dazed, while others needed help to get up on the stage.

Then as if in a knighting ceremony, the believers knelt with or without help, and all the white-robed men stepped forward. As if on cue, they each dipped a finger into the goblet, closing their eyes as they prayed one more time.

Afterward, they took their fingers and held them over the commoners on the stage. The whole crowd turned silent once again, and then a droplet slid down each finger, one by one.

"It's so bright! Oh, Mother Asea, I can see you again! I can . . . uwahhhh." The shouts of a woman on the stage turned into sobs, which were soon drowned out by the exclamations of the crowd, clamoring uproariously. Many looked like they couldn't believe their eyes, and others simply knelt out of reverence among the crowd.

"All praise her everlasting gaze!"

"All praise her everlasting gaze!"

Vern stood there dumbfounded. The earlier show of filling the goblets seemed like a trick, but this was . . . beyond comprehension. This was too out of the norm.

From the amputee's stump, a bone sprouted seemingly out of thin air, growing slowly yet steadily. Meanwhile, on the other man's body, the burn marks began to scab over at a pace discernible to the naked eye. Similar phenomena repeated to some degree with all the other sickly ones on the stage.

What was this? Just what kind of viewpoint was this? How was this working? Who was doing this? *There's bound to be some observer around here that's doing this, right?*

If not, just what was going on behind the scenes? Could objects like this liquid be imbued with properties of a viewpoint? If so, what were the conditions? What was the whole process?

Millions of questions ran through his mind as he got closer to the stage, weaving through the thick crowd that was filled with ardor. He had to figure out the cause and effect of this whole situation.

Up close, he saw every detail. In no time, the skin began growing around the incomplete bone of that amputee as if clay were being coated over it.

But then, it suddenly stopped, and the skin closed around the wounds as the whole process halted midway.

The man who was looking at his recovering leg with unadulterated ecstasy seemed to be taken aback as he gasped in abject horror. So without wasting any time, he begged, "Lord! Can I get another drop? Just one more, my lord. In the name of Mother Asea. Am I not a devout believer? Please, Lord!"

The imposing man who made the earlier speech and looked like the leader of the white-robed men stepped up to the amputee. "Brother, let patience and gratitude guide you. Remember, even though the Mother's tears possess divine healing, they are not limitless. You surely wouldn't wish for your fellow brethren to depart from this sanctuary unaided, would you?"

The amputee wanted to say something, but the leader rested his arms on the amputee's shoulder and helped him up from the kneeling posture. Then with a soothing voice, he continued, "Yet despair not, for the Mother's love is boundless, and she would never abandon any of her cherished offspring to languish in suffering."

While keeping the amputee propped up, the leader turned back to the amplifying contraption as he addressed the crowd. "My brethren. Know that the Mother loves you. She loves you even if you fail to cast aside your ailments today. She loves even those who couldn't join us in her expression of love."

"So I, deacon of the eternal, fervently beckon all children of her vast creation to partake in the sanctifying healing of the divine tears within the hallowed confines of the Cathedral of the Eternal."

Then with a serious tone, he continued, "Understand this, my siblings, though the trial may have passed, her children wander aimlessly, bereft of guidance, bereft of a beacon! As her chosen progeny, we bear the responsibility to shepherd our brethren and sistren back onto the illuminated path."

"So, prepare your hearts, for the Mother may select a few among you to be that radiant guide for those shrouded in darkness, to lead the wayward back into her comforting clasp. I trust that when the Mother extends her call, her children will not turn away."

A fervent echo of assent surged around Vern as everyone chanted in unison, "We won't turn away! We heed the Mother's call!" Their voices swelled into a zealous chorus that shook the very air.

Many hands shot toward the sky, their fingers outstretched as if to touch the divine. Other believers bowed their heads in solemn pledges, murmuring sacred promises. The atmosphere around him bristled with collective resolve, their faith so palpable, so tangible, it charged the air.

Good grief. Do they really not see the trap? They are tempting people to rely on these "Mother's tears." Was it bordering on supernatural with its capabilities? Yes. But did that automagically make it safe to use? No.

What were the adverse effects of this one? Every medicine had to be rigorously tested for hundreds of different criteria before they were allowed to be used en masse.

Was it possible that this liquid had no side effects because some observer made it? Maybe. *But all these people don't know about observation and should be skeptical of anything so potent. It seems like this . . . duskfall of sorrows really got to their heads.* Vern wanted to shake his head in disappointment, but he wouldn't underestimate this bunch of fanatics. In such an atmosphere, any hint of disrespect could very well incite the mob to maul him to death.

So he simply looked on at the proceedings, trying to figure out something about the logic behind it. One group of ecstatic people descended the platform as another went up and received the baptism of tears.

The cycle repeated, and he stood there with his notepad in his hands—neither moving to line up for the tears nor going back to his room—jotting down any notable remarks.

He had recorded the exact process of healing and would revisit it later to look for some pattern because he couldn't figure out the slightest bit of how any of this worked right now. And he wasn't mad enough to try it out on himself.

The sun had set, and it was growing increasingly difficult to write in such dim lighting. So he finally shoved the notepad back into his pocket and stretched his body, ready to leave. He had seen enough.

But then he reflexively looked up, and his heart dropped instantly. He was mid-step, teetering on the brink of losing his footing, but before the situation could deteriorate, a kind soul from the crowd extended a helping hand.

"Are you holding up well, young man? Keep your spirits aloft, yes? We might not get the opportunity to be purified in Mother's tears today, but morrow always brings another chance. Don't lose heart," said a short, burly man with a curly mustache as he propped Vern up.

Vern steadied himself and went along with the man's story. "Ah . . . yes, thank you. I was just a little disheartened, but I guess I can always go to the cathedral in the morning."

Then he paused for a second and looked back up before he asked, "Good sir, do you see that thing up in the sky?" Vern pointed at that horrifying rift in the sky, making sure not to specifically mention what he was indicating.

He had completely forgotten all about it due to the situations he'd found himself in ever since he woke up. But it was right there, like a wound in the sky, orange and blue sparks pulsating all around it. He hadn't seen any signs of it just a while ago when the sun was up.

"Indeed, young man. Indeed. I see that treacherous moon goddess who took my Iffy away from me. Young man, I tell you, anytime you see those worshippers of the moon, give them hell. They worthin' deserve it." The man spat to the side as he advised Vern, loathing evident on his face.

Vern ignored the latter part of his assertion and instead focused on the former. *So he can't see it.* Kind of what he expected. Everyone would be shouting and running around by now if they could see it.

However, something was different about it from the last time. The moon was right there. As were the stars, but the radiance seeping in from that gash still seemed too dazzling compared to the ambient light in the sky.

It was like both the abnormality and normality overlapped each other.

Well, he would make sense of it when he was in his hotel room. Too many questions were piling up, and he had to sit down and untangle this mess.

So he bowed to the burly man, thanked him again, and left the crowd, heading straight for the bridge. He needed food and some time alone with his thoughts.

CHAPTER 23

HOTEL INKWELL

Vern navigated the intersection of Timekeeper Lane and Primrose Boulevard, where the clock tower stood tall in all its mechanical glory. He was still making his way to Hotel Inkwell, which was located east of the clock tower at the intersection of Timekeeper Lane and Willowby Street.

It had taken him much longer than anticipated to get back here. He might have underestimated Miss Cera's warning a bit. Some of the locals were indeed a little too unrestrained right now. He had to sneak past many hubs of unrest and make multiple detours to get back here in one piece.

He was a little out of sorts because of a short sprint a few minutes ago. Some asshole had noticed Vern looking at them as they were raiding a Kingsmen barracks, instantly alarming everyone around him. However, he had the distance advantage in the chase, and for some reason, they didn't dare follow him past a certain neighborhood.

It's like they've marked their own territories.

There was a religious gathering going on in the Fulham borough as well, but it didn't seem as interesting as the earlier one, so he ignored it in a bid to get back to the hotel faster.

But none of this was a major concern for him right now. The real problem was food. Hopefully, the hotel wasn't already looted to the point of ruin. Because then he'd have to look for some empty house to squat in until he could get his bearings and reach out to some of his contacts in the city—assuming they were still alive, of course.

So he continued, still somehow not having traversed the width of the clock tower. It was another relic of this city, built in the same era as the bridges. At least, that's what the books said. The leaked schematics of the clock tower he'd seen last year painted a different picture.

Shaking his head, Vern escaped his idle thoughts and hastened toward the hotel. The lights of the moon and rift from the sky winked in and out of his vision as he walked under the awnings of many stores. Usually, they would be retracted at the end of the day, but that day has yet to end for a lot of people.

There were people in some of these buildings who eyed Vern with suspicion, but he ignored them and continued on his way.

In no time, he was standing in front of the Hotel Inkwell, which was a landmark in its own right. The hotel exuded an air of grandeur, its imposing facade constructed of time-weathered sandstone, which was gracefully nestled beneath sections of a cobalt blue bell-cast roof.

Rows upon rows of large, symmetrical windows imprisoned within grilles punctuated its exterior walls, their glass panes gleaming and reflecting the soft glow of the moon's shine. Yet there were a few windows that shimmered with the warm, inviting glow of the gas lamps from within.

Vern let out a sigh of relief when he saw that. *That is reassuring.*

The hotel's entrance was imposing, defined by a heavy oak double door painted navy blue. Flanking the entrance was a pair of marble pillars embellished with finely carved motifs that supported a canopy that had an intricately carved wooden sign proudly declaring the hotel's name, which was etched in gold lettering. On the pillars were two wrought iron gas lamps that cast dancing shadows on the cobblestones underneath.

Looking at this familiar door being in such excellent shape, a lot of his anxieties fizzled. Squatting in some random house wasn't his idea of a conducive environment, nor was it his dream to loot supplies from others.

He lightly exerted himself and pushed the towering door, but it remained immobile. It was locked shut.

So he held the golden door knocker and rapped it thrice. Taps of footsteps approached from within, and a deep voice boomed, "Hotel Inkwell is not accepting reservations from new customers right now. If you're not a current guest, please move along. May Lady watch over you."

Vern remembered this voice. It was the hotel's butler. So he perked up and responded, "I am indeed a current guest of the hotel. I have a suite reserved under the name Vern Lockwood. I checked in six days ago, and if I am not mistaken, I should have another week before my reservation runs out."

It was odd that the hotel management still cared about reservations and such, but he didn't mind as long as it meant he had a place to stay.

The butler didn't reply.

Clack.

The sound of a latch being unlocked played in his ears as the door opened just a hint. An old butler in his immaculate black-and-white suit greeted Vern with a deep bow.

"Welcome back, Mr. Vern. I had assumed you met the same fate as many of our other guests. But it seems that I was wrong, happily so. Please come in."

Vern nodded at the butler and squeezed in. "Who knows how I survived these past three days? So you weren't exactly wrong in assuming the worst."

The entrance was still quite neat, if not as opulent as it was before the duskfall. *Heh. Even I call it duskfall now.* It was indeed convenient to call it that instead of whatever that bunch of events was.

The foyer wasn't in the state of ruin that he was expecting it to be. What greeted him instead was a neat hall with a reception desk to the right, a drinks bar to the left, and a wide staircase in the middle. The chandelier hanging from the ceiling wasn't lit, so most of the illumination came from the windows and a couple of dim lamps that were still ablaze. Butler Beaumont and whatever was left of the staff had done a great job in these trying times. Before Vern could complement Beaumont for his effort and perseverance, the butler said, "Mr. Vern, as you may already know, these are precarious times, so we have implemented a few changes to ensure we can continue serving our guests without having to force any evictions." The old man closed the door behind him, locking it shut.

"First, the food will only be served twice a day until our supply chain is restored. Second, all guests will have to help ensure the smooth running of the hotel's amenities however they can. Third, no one is allowed to leave or enter between the hours of midnight and seven in the morning. Fourth, guests cannot bring outsiders with them. Fifth, the cost of the suite has been tripled, so you'll have to pay the overdue amount as soon as possible. Any questions?" finished the butler with an indifferent expression, the wrinkles on his face following suit.

Obviously, Vern had many questions. What was that second term? But he didn't want to argue about any of that right now. It wasn't completely unreasonable anyway, and he needed food and time alone. So he skipped the formalities and simply nodded. "No problem. Please send dinner to my room as soon as possible. I will come down in the morning to pay the due, and then we can talk."

The butler stepped aside and extended his arm toward the staircase as if to truly welcome him this time. Vern nodded one final time and left Beaumont to his own devices.

The management's response to this whole situation was quite peculiar, and understanding the rationale behind it might give him some idea about his own plans. Vern would thoroughly shake down this butler for all the information he could. Just not right now.

His suite was on the third floor, so he didn't even bother with the elevator. Beaumont probably wouldn't let him use it, so they could save on steam anyway. So after another quick unintended workout, he reached the third floor.

The carpeted floor of the long corridor on either side of the staircase was dimly lit, with only a few lamps barely illuminating the doors and room numbers on them. He strode toward room 307 on the left side and started turning the circular knobs on the four corners of the lock to match his secret sequence, which he had set up at check-in.

These mechanical locks weren't the safest on the market, but they struck a good balance in value and security. It wasn't worth waiting two days and paying triple the cost to get a new door installed just for a better lock. He would know. His master was paranoid and always fussed about the locks in even his temporary residences.

With a click, the cogs fit perfectly, and the lock came loose. He entered the room, and luckily it looked undisturbed. Moonlight illuminated the rolltop desk, which was littered with papers, tools, and some contraptions he'd been fiddling with before he had left that day.

He flipped the switch for heat and light, and the outline of a lavish couch, chair, hearth, table, wall clock, and curtains were filled with their respective textures and yellow haze as he took in his room.

Locking the door behind him, he made straight for the desk next to the window and pulled open the top drawer. A crystal clear glassy sphere with thin golden lines on its surface rolled around in it, and he let out another sigh of relief.

Phew. *At least the insight sphere is still intact.* It had taken him years to save up for one of his own, and he would have raised hell if someone had stolen it.

He made for the wooden chair in front of the desk and plopped down on it, his energy ebbing as his mind finally relaxed.

He closed his eyes and kneaded his forehead, clearing his mind of stray thoughts. A few minutes passed as the room heated up and he sat there, his eyes closed.

Then when the clock tower started its chimes for the next hour, his eyes snapped open, and he sat back up straight. A clear and sharp edge returned to his eyes as he picked up a pen, retrieved the notepad, and threw his blazer aside.

It was time to figure this out.

So he was able to observe and manipulate reality just fine when he was in that ethereal form. But as soon as he woke up, he had failed his observation and lost that form. He struck out one of his earlier hypotheses and rewrote it with this new information. *Observers aren't always in the ethereal form. Confirmed to be a temporary state.*

So whatever Hensen was doing by walking through fire indeed had something to do with his viewpoint, not that ethereal form.

Also, he had only faced serious repercussions for observation when he was in his natural state of a material human being. He had experienced eye bleeds and vertigo back in the burning library, but nothing like those . . . voices.

When he had first experimented with the balance, he had also wondered at the time why observation was so easy. And now it started making sense. It wasn't that observation was easy. It was that ethereal form that made it a breeze. Now that it was gone, there must be some other limitations and rules as to how observation worked.

That's what he had to figure out.

He jotted down the exact process of many events that had happened to him, and he noticed a problem.

When he planned to snatch that gun from Cera, he had completely skipped the part of taking in the shades of gray in the environment from his perception and had simply simulated what it would look like while envisioning changes to it to hasten the process.

This is definitely a problem. He furrowed his brows, repeatedly circling the terms *observation* and *envision*.

Did he almost get himself killed because he didn't follow the proper sequence? He had skipped the observation part and went straight to envisioning.

This might indeed be one of the factors behind that catastrophic failure. A supporting argument to this conjecture was the fact that he could only cause changes to reality when he envisioned what the shades of gray would look like after the change. Simply envisioning a different reality hadn't worked.

This got him thinking further. What would happen if he tried to envision a state of grays that was drastically different from the original distribution of grays? It would be like he tried to envision a revolver in front of him to be lighter than it was, but in reality, there was a carriage in front of him, not the assumed revolver.

There just wasn't any realistic way to have that vision come to fruition.

But he very precisely remembered what that monochrome vista of gravity looked like, and it was simple to extrapolate it for the second floor of the library. That was what he had done back then. He was sure that even if he was a little off in his imagination during that attempt, there was no way it was significantly dissimilar to what he would have perceived from the grays.

Unless . . . *Fuck. Yes, that might be it!*

He would need to try it out to confirm his new hypothesis. *But what if I am wrong, and I trigger those voices again?*

A few more minutes passed as Vern tried to figure out any loopholes in his argument.

Even Miss Cera had said something about observing without comprehension. Did that hint at the fact that he failed because he didn't really understand gravity? Maybe yes. But was that to say he could only observe things he understood? *But then what would be the point of observation in itself if it's just a representation of how I believe things to be?*

Then it hit him: *to be able to envision changes to it!*

Yes. That did make more and more sense by the second. If those shades of gray were just a representation of what he believed them to be, what would be the point of them at all, if not to make it easier for him to envision changes to it and manipulate reality?

Indeed, that was logical. So now he really had to try out observation to confirm his hypothesis on what initially went wrong. If he was right, then he might be able to make it work again.

Vern made up his mind, got off the chair, and went straight to his bed, lying down on it. He didn't want to fall off the chair and injure himself in case he had another one of those episodes.

He risked triggering the burden of the Cryptic Constructor once again if things went south, but his conjectures gave him a high enough chance of success, which warranted taking the risk.

So he settled down comfortably and let go of his inhibitions. Not going for something overly complicated like gravity, he focused on the simple balance of brightness and darkness around him.

It should be just a black-and-white version of his current sight but with a different level of detail. So he thought about it with the intention of observing it as shades.

His perception, which was nothing but a transparent veil, suddenly turned black. Pitch black. Just like he had expected.

C H A P T E R 24

CANVAS OF THOUGHT

Instead of a world that should have been tinted black and white, Vern was greeted with a pitch-black vista as if there was nothing to be perceived.

Something to rejoice about was that neither those alluring inhuman voices beckoned him, nor did that symbol of the Cryptic Constructor raze his mind. This was in line with his conjectures.

This black perception confirmed his hypothesis.

So the issue back then wasn't that he had envisioned the changes to reality inaccurately. The problem was that the base state of his perception was completely black. That is to say, it didn't perceive anything at all.

So, that ethereal form was helping me perceive the shades of gray for any concept of my choice.

But now that the form was gone, he had lost all those advantages and was left with nothing.

Vern closed off his perception, got off the bed, and went back to his chair. This was a great start! If there wasn't a risk in simply observing, then he could continue his experiments with an assurance that he wouldn't unknowingly surrender his mind to some unnatural voices.

Penning the new events into his notebook, he reorganized his thoughts. The current situation entailed that he had a completely blank perception. This time, he had an inkling of how to proceed.

Miss Cera had given him a big hint with just a few words. He believed it was about comprehension. So the better he comprehended the concept he observed, the more detailed his perception would be.

But this argument had a few flaws of its own. Primarily, why was everything completely black? He knew enough about light to not have an entirely empty perception of it. Maybe just knowing wasn't enough, and he had to actively think about it?

Not hesitating this time, he opened his perception once again to that black canvas. Ensuring that no voices were seeping into his thoughts, he attempted to figure out the lightness of the environment around him.

To start, he gazed with his natural sight at the lamp that stuck to a column by the wall and directed his thoughts to discern its lightness. He considered how the lamp emitted light and illuminated everything around it and how the light generated from within was reflected by its metal frame. How—

Suddenly, it changed. He was caught off guard as something appeared in his perception. A bright sheen in the endless black overlaid the lamp. *I knew it—*

However, before he could rejoice, the brightness was gone. The spark that had quickly appeared from nowhere in the deep darkness of his perception disappeared just as swiftly.

Obviously. Nothing can be this straightforward.

Shaking his head, he focused again and directed his thoughts to dissect how exactly that lamp interacted with its surroundings. Its radiance, its effect of light in his room, the shadows it helped create, its reflection off the walls, and many other factors. Before he got too far, a small wick of white appeared in his perception yet again.

This time, however, he didn't let the change disturb his concentration, and he kept going and mapped more and more effects of the light on the surroundings. The dark canvas with a sole blaze began to populate itself with a few more outlines of different gradations of white.

Minutes passed, and sweat trickled down his face as he persisted in recreating the surroundings within his perception. He guided his thoughts to assess how exactly light reacted and what caused one spot to be brighter than the other.

Vern even contrasted different sources of light with one another, comparing their nature and how their position made an obvious difference in their illumination radius.

It was a taxing task. His mind was already starting to feel the pinch. But he didn't want to let up.

However, something wasn't right. A lot of his speculations and deliberations on the nature of light didn't do anything. Just now, he had even gone for over half a minute without inducing any change in the perception at all.

I am doing something wrong.

However, he persevered, and another couple of minutes passed by in silence as nothing changed in the canvas of black that was speckled with odd grays. He was starting to feel lightheaded, and the process was draining his mental capacity.

Damn.

So he stopped analyzing the light and its ramifications. There was no need to rush it. He would have continued if the situation called for it, but a balanced approach was always better during experimentation.

He relaxed his mind and looked at his ethereal perception, which had a few wicks of flame, odd shades for the cage of the lamps, and a couple specular highlights where objects should be.

Vern scrutinized it with fascination when he realized something. It was changing. No. It was fading. *Crack my fucking cogs!*

It was fading away like before. All the progress he had made was being erased like it never had existed. He had an impulsive thought to start inspecting light again and somehow stop the grays in his perception from dissipating. But he sighed and let it be.

It wouldn't really be sustainable for him to use observation like this. He wouldn't have five minutes in real life to first sit down and analyze the world and then anxiously maintain his perception—always fearful of losing the grays.

So he instead tried to determine the underlying logic of this phenomenon. A few things struck him as odd. The first was the fact that a lot of his thoughts didn't incite any shift in the perception of the grays. Second was this whole business of his perception just fading away.

There was no way Hensen was repeatedly doing all this while envisioning those mind-boggling changes to the environment. So Vern must be missing something.

He waited until his perception became pitch black for a third time before inscribing the peculiarities on the notepad. Wiping away the sweat, he rested his forehead on the edge of the desk. That was more draining than he'd have thought. His empty stomach didn't help either.

Time moved on like this as he relaxed his mind. Then hearing the subtle chime of the thirty-minute mark from the clock tower, he sat up straight once again.

He had to change his strategy. He was doing something wrong. What other information did he have that could give him some clarity on observation? The burden of the Cryptic Constructor sounded like one such avenue, but he wouldn't go near it if he had a choice.

He was on the right track since he was able to shade his perception to an extent, but the problem was that it was temporary and too inefficient.

Hmm.

He tried to remember the words from the *Observation Record of Subjectivity*. Its primary idea was to view the world through a unique perspective. But he was already doing that, right?

Actually. He might not have been doing that. Just now, he had tried to rationalize the lighting of the room like he would fundamentals. Logically following the effect and cause to comprehend it further. But was it really done subjectively?

That might be it! He had neglected to think about the matter more subjectively. That would mean he should have used his insights of balance to analyze the concept.

Well, that sounded like a solid plan. So he tried to think what balance would even mean in such a situation.

In a moment, he already had an idea. Steering his thoughts to consider the lightness and darkness, he looked at the darkest corner of the room and chose it to be one end of the spectrum. Then he shifted his gaze to the lamp and elected it to be the other end of the spectrum.

A white wick appeared in his perception once again, but this wasn't all he had thought up. Looking at the notepad in front of him, he mentally compared its brightness to the lamp and the dark corner and assigned it a shade of gray based on where it sat in terms of brightness on the spectrum.

To his surprise and delight, a gray rectangular outline appeared in his perception. One that was much more well-defined than his last try. Not letting this little victory go to his head, he kept going. Primed to repeat the success, he looked at the bright part of the couch and mentally assigned it a cloudy color based on how it fared relative to that same lamp and the corner. As if on cue, a soft cloudy patch appeared in his perception.

He repeated this process for other items one by one, and new shades started populating the black canvas every few seconds. Every time he assigned a shade to another object, he had to make sure that the gray that he chose was logical and precise—because his perception wasn't correcting any of his mistakes.

In his fatigue, he had erroneously assigned a darker balance to the bright clock, and his perception represented it as it was. That is to say, this was akin to a canvas that he could paint however he liked. But he was sure that incorrectly perceiving the world around him wouldn't do him any favors. It might actually be detrimental instead since what he perceived wouldn't be consistent with reality, and this would devolve into the same situation as in the library.

Shaking his head, he focused back on the exhausting task of assigning a balance to the hearth.

A few more shapes took color in his perception, which became increasingly more detailed. His head was feeling heavier by the second, and this continuous cycle of comparing luminescence was becoming tough to keep up. Assigning balance to even one more object seemed impossible.

Ugh!

But this wasn't enough to make him give up. He hadn't reached his tipping point just yet.

His perception was much more comprehensive compared to the last time. Though it wasn't even close to what he had experienced during enlightenment. It was like a black painting with some blotches of grays painted by some amateur, but he felt like it was a masterpiece that just needed more work.

So he looked at the top of a vase in the room and asserted that it should be a slate gray since it was far from the lamp and was mainly lit by the moonlight from the window.

But nothing happened.

Huh?

Why didn't that work? He was sure that he had done exactly what he'd been doing so far. Even if it was taxing, he had done it correctly. So he concentrated on the vase once again and assigned it a similar balance.

Not a single thing changed.

What the hell is this now?

Not ready to give up just yet, he shifted his gaze to another lamp in the room and tried assigning it a balance close to the bright extreme of the spectrum.

Nope. Nothing's working!

This was the same situation as his previous attempt when he wasn't thinking about it subjectively. He kept trying, but no new balances materialized. Every gray he tried to perceive didn't manifest, and his perception became completely static.

No. It wasn't static. The grays were actually losing their brightness by the second.

Not again! He involuntarily crumpled the page of the notepad as his perception began to lose all its details rapidly.

Knock knock knock.

A sudden knocking echoed in his ears, and Vern jerked back as he inadvertently let go of the pen, which fell on the desk with a clang. The dark space with gray speckles that overlaid his natural sight was gone without a trace as he lost all concentration.

"Hotel service here with your dinner, sir."

Fuck. That blew all the steam out of me!

"Yes, give me one second."

Smoothing out the crumpled page, he closed the notepad and got up. Making his way to the door, he opened it and was greeted by the sight of Beaumont, who was standing next to a lavish multitiered food cart that didn't have as many dishes on it to justify its use. This wasn't the person who usually delivered his meals.

Vern didn't say anything, but as if understanding his questioning gaze, Beaumont admitted with a bitter tone, "We're indeed quite short-staffed right now. Three of us are cooking, and two are fixing the leaks while the rest are in the basement, pumping the furnace. Can't have the guests sleep in the cold, can we?"

He seemed to not expect any response as he pushed the cart into the room without a pause.

Vern comforted the old man. "I wouldn't really know where to go if not for the hotel. Your services are very much appreciated in these trying times."

The butler tersely nodded and stopped the cart next to the dining table in the room. Two silver cloches rested on the top shelf of the magnificent bronze cart, hiding something sumptuous within. A subdued smile appeared on Beaumont's face as he lifted both the lids just a tad and swirled them around the dishes beneath before uncovering them wholly in a swift motion.

Vern forgot all about his problems as the aroma filled the room, and his stomach reminded him of its existence, delivering intense pangs of hunger, which he had been disregarding for quite a while. The plate on the left had potatoes and a bowl of leek soup while an elegantly prepared roasted guinea fowl rested on the right one, all in judicious portions.

He didn't wait for Beaumont to explain as he walked toward the food, only to be interrupted abruptly.

"FUCK! Stop knockin'! What in the name of four hells is wrong with ye fuckers? I said I don't need nothin'!" A muffled shout seeped in from the room next door.

Beaumont, who was transferring the plates to the table, halted midway and stood up straight while holding one of the dishes palm-up, looking to where the noise originated. Vern was just as taken aback as he turned around and focused on the sound.

"I tell ye. If ye don't fuckin' stop right now, I'll shoot ye right in the head. Yer hotel be damned!"

Vern glanced back at Beaumont, and their gazes met in confusion. *What knocking is this guy yelling about?* No one was knocking. He would've heard it quite a while ago if it was as annoying as he insinuated.

Beaumont elegantly placed the remaining platter on the table and walked toward the door, and Vern followed close behind him.

"All right! I see. Ye won't see the coffin until ye're nailed. Then let me clip yer head with some iron."

However, before Vern could even reach the door, a multitude of sounds resounded in his ears.

"AAAAAHHHH!"

Bang.

Chapter 25

CRYPTIC DEATHS

Vern heard a guttural scream followed by a gunshot.

Beaumont dashed out the door in a hurry, almost running into the wall of the corridor due to the momentum. When Vern followed him out, the shadowy hall was empty except for the two of them.

The door to room 308 was ajar and hoarse screams alongside a disgusting smell wafted out of it unceasingly. Beaumont didn't pay it any mind and tackled the door, charging into the room. Vern, however, halted right outside. There was a gun involved in the situation, and running in without disarming the user wouldn't be anything less than suicidal.

"AAAHH! EEEEHHHHH!"

The man continued to scream, and Vern peered into the room from the cover of the wall. A lanky man with sunken eyes dressed in a shirt with red blotches was splayed on the ground, his legs stretched out in front of him. His hands were planted behind him as he crawled back haphazardly, screaming incoherently at the top of his lungs.

Then, in his peripheral vision, Vern noticed a thin stream of smoke, which he followed to the source, and he sighed in relief. The gun was dropped on the floor a little to his left inside the room. Vern took two steps and swiftly picked it up, tucking it under his waistband. Pulling out his shirt to conceal the weapon, he refocused.

No way in hell was he going to leave a gun unattended.

"AAAAAAAAAAAAAAAAHHH!"

The man swung his head side to side so fervently that it was a surprise he hadn't cracked a bone already. His eyes, however, were glued to the space in front of him, aimed at something even in those frantic oscillations. In no time, he had backed himself against the wall, cutting his retreat. The already foul musk in the room had another mixed into it as a wet patch appeared at the man's crotch.

Having secured the gun, Vern was much more composed, but the actions of the man and the state of this room sent a chill down his spine.

There was nothing in front of the man but a depraved room that told a gruesome story. The yellow light of the lamp illuminated a bloody carpet, on which lay the torso of a human, blood still flowing out of the choppy wound on its neck.

Trails of blood were everywhere, and in the center of the room was an altar. When Vern's mind registered what was on the altar, his blood ran cold, and a shiver ran down his spine. The head of a woman was placed on the altar, her eyes gouged out. What seemed like tears of blood ran down her eye sockets, seeping onto the altar.

Vern took a deep breath and repressed the disgust welling up inside him. Luckily, he hadn't had anything to eat yet.

Beaumont seemed to be just as flabbergasted at the state of the room.

"EEEAAAAAAH! AAAH! AHHHHH!"

But the man's screams turned shriller. Beaumont finally seemed to recover from his stupor, for he dropped to the ground and grabbed hold of the man's shoulder, speaking to him like a child. "Calm down. Mr. Garfield, calm down. There's nothing here. Calm down."

Garfield, however, continued to shriek incoherently, curling into himself as he pointed in front of him.

Vern made to move closer to Garfield as well, but then he noticed it. A yellow parchment was lying right next to the altar, the blood from the head dripping onto it. But what gave him pause was the symbol at the top. Drawn in red were two inverted triangles—one within the other.

The symbol of the Cryptic Constructor.

Vern's mind reeled in shock as his brain processed the implications. His first instinct was to stay as far away as possible, but that would be stupid of him. Surely the parchment has something related to the Cryptic Constructor on it.

But he didn't have the time to think about it for long. Footsteps were rushing toward the room from all over—other guests of the hotel were about to arrive. He had to make a decision quickly.

So Vern made up his mind and rushed toward the altar while Beaumont was still trying to soothe the screaming Garfield.

In a few steps, he was already next to the altar. Before Beaumont could sense anything amiss, Vern snatched the parchment from the floor. Hurriedly folding it, he thrust it into his pocket.

But before he could back away from the altar, a few people stormed in.

"EEEHHH!" A woman that had come running in screamed at the sight and retreated to the corridor in a fluster. Other than her, a tall and stout man dressed in a neat suit entered the room, holding on to his top hat, which barely covered his bald head, unperturbed. The man seemed to squint as he took in the vile scenery.

A few others arrived as well, but none of them dared to enter. Vern had luckily managed to grab the parchment before anyone else came in. Otherwise, he risked having to give up on it or get labeled as a vile cultist like Garfield. This room wasn't really a good look on anyone associated with it.

But he was still quite perplexed at this whole situation. What was Garfield so afraid of? Vern didn't see or feel anything. If something subjective was in the room, he should be able to see it too, right?

Then out of the blue, the room suddenly turned silent, and the shrill screaming stopped grating on his ears. Everyone, including Vern, who had been looking at the newcomers, turned their gaze back to Garfield, who suddenly went limp.

Beaumont seemed unsure of what to do. But then he yelled, "Is anyone here a doctor? Also, can someone grab the medicine pouch from the reception?" Beaumont then lifted Garfield's shirt, checking for bleeding or injuries. However, the skin beneath the patches of blood on his shirt was unblemished and smooth with not a hint of injury.

Before Beaumont could conjure a response to this baffling situation, the bald man strode farther into the room and said, "Kindly step aside, dear butler. Let the deceased rest. He was a rather unpleasant character who has faced the consequences of his actions. Let's not waste our sympathies on him. He is beyond the aid of any physician now."

Just as Beaumont made to say something, he was interrupted yet again. Someone from the crowd exclaimed, "Good heavens above! What in the name of propriety is transpiring within this hotel? Butler, do explain yourself! How could you permit such unspeakable occurrences to unfold under your watch? And that woman there. Mercy on my soul! Was she not one of our fellow boarders in this hotel? Are your eyes all painted on, or do you see this abhorrent spectacle?"

More people chimed in with their own opinions.

"Murderer. Sinner. What a vile creature! He got what he deserved."

"None of that matters right now. Who killed him?! Butler, is the killer still among us?"

"Burn this room. It's a den of sin. I thought the city outside was a land of death, but this hotel is worse. Those fucking Kingsmen, never here when you need them."

"The butler must have killed him, I tell you. The man was well and good this morning when I talked to him. It must be the butler."

Clap!

A loud clap rang in the room, and the bald man demanded, "Everyone, please give me a moment of your time." The chatter died down in an instant as the crowd looked at him with rapt attention.

The bald man took a deep breath as if to make up his mind and started again. "I implore you all to maintain your composure. This is decidedly not the moment for panic." His voice seemed to have a soothing effect, as the crowd visibly relaxed. He continued, "There have been a series of regrettable fatalities within the confines of this venerable hotel. It would serve us all well to allow these memories to fade into oblivion, ensuring our continued safety. Shall we agree on this, ladies and gentlemen?"

Vern snapped his gaze back to the bald man and looked at him incredulously. *What did he say?*

However, what was even more bizarre was that no one called him out over this illogical assertion. Instead, a few people seemed to agree with him, offering nods, while the rest seemed confused.

The corner of the bald man's lips turned up, and he continued, "Would it not be in our collective interest to concur that this unfortunate incident has been nothing more than a figment of our imaginations? The decapitated figure over there was once a vibrant individual, much like the esteemed company present here. Would you genuinely wish to shoulder the unsettling knowledge that you, too, could face such a fate?"

Vern felt a little lightheaded as the words started to make more and more sense to him. *The man does have a point.*

"Observe that bloody eye he holds in his hands if you will. Such sights are not the sort we wish to ponder as we retire for the evening, are they? Let's put such distasteful thoughts aside for the sake of our peaceful slumber."

Right. Garfield was indeed clutching a spherical object in one of his hands, blood dripping out of it. Yeah, why would Vern want to think about that during his sleep? But no. This wasn't right. This wasn't right.

This is bad! Something was off with this man's words.

But the moment Vern realized the incongruity, it was as if a haze that was starting to fog his mind was lifted. The bald man's sentences seemed to feel illogical once again. Vern frowned, and a possibility crossed his mind. *This has to be some kind of observation.*

He was doing something to everyone's thought processes. And Vern had no plans of falling for it—not when it was nowhere near as influential or imposing as Hensen's methods. So he kept reminding himself of the fallacies in the bald man's words, who rambled these illogical sentences nonstop. What if those strange emotions returned if he allowed his thoughts to relax?

The man surveyed everyone closely, and he asked, "Do we all find harmony in the perspective I've proposed?"

Before Vern could stop his own deluge of negations to keep his thoughts pure, the ramblings had already come to an end, and the bald man was looking at Vern with a scowl.

Vern's heart raced as a feeling of impending doom filled him. *Shit! Did he notice?* In a bid to keep his thoughts stable, he had completely forgotten about his frowning expression.

Is it too late to change it now? But if I suddenly start nodding, he might realize that I am faking my reaction. Vern was still caught in the dilemma when the man squinted at him and said, "You are also in agreement with me. Is that right, good sir?"

Vern felt a little woozy, but nothing he couldn't handle. However, he didn't miss this heaven-sent chance that had dropped on his lap and played along. Following in the footsteps of the others, he relaxed his eyes and nodded languidly.

The man smiled and said, "Great! Now that we have come to a consensus, I propose we return to our rooms and resume our earlier endeavors. May your evening be filled with peace and pleasant dreams."

As he said this, people started to disperse. He couldn't fuck this up. Who knew what this man might do to him if he realized Vern wasn't really swayed by his words.

Vern did have the gun on him, but was it really a good idea to shoot this guy right now? If everyone suddenly became lucid again, they would witness Vern shooting the man. He doubted he could explain himself out of that one. Luckily, the man just wanted everyone to forget and be on their way.

He could do that. He could pretend like he hadn't seen anything. So Vern started walking in lazy steps to exit the room. But suddenly, he noticed someone moving against the crowd. A man was walking opposite the crowd and straight into the room. Vern didn't manage to catch his face properly due to the obstruction from other guests. On top of that, he couldn't even turn around to get a better look lest the bald man notice.

"I presented you with an opportunity, and see how that unfolded. Are you still reluctant to join my cause? With the correct insight, you could have preserved that lady's life. And with correct guidance, you could do so much more. It's your unyielding stubbornness that led to her unfortunate demise," said the bald man in a hushed tone.

"Will you still not join me in my cause?"

Then after a few seconds, a hoarse voice replied, "I-I agree." But then the door clicked shut, and rest wasn't audible.

Who was that just now? What does any of that mean?

However, now wasn't the time to answer those questions. Who knew what kind of observation skills those men had? So Vern maintained the same pace and walked to his own room, following Beaumont, who was heading in the same direction.

At the door of 307, Beaumont entered the room, and Vern followed.

Then after Beaumont walked back to the food cart, he looked around in confusion before he gracefully picked the second platter from the cart and placed it on the table.

"Please indulge, Mr. Vern."

Vern didn't flinch at Beaumont's reaction and replied with a smile, "Thank you, Beaumont. Have a good night."

"May Lady bless your dreams too." Then with a shallow bow, he wheeled the cart out of Vern's room and closed the door behind him.

But I can't stop. He just had to be so unlucky as to be in the room next to those two men. That was to say, he might still be within a radius where they could observe him. Who knew what kind of tricks they had up their sleeves. If their observation allowed them some method to see through walls, then he would have to be very careful.

Any odd behavior, like trying to listen in on their conversation or even taking out the parchment or gun from his pocket, might raise suspicions. *Fuck me.* So Vern had to play it cool until they were gone because even leaving the room might warrant some unwanted reaction.

C H A P T E R 26

PLAYING PRETEND

Vern sat in front of the polished wooden table, its edges lined with bronze, and its corners adorned with fancy patterns. Every few seconds, he scooped a bit of leek soup onto his spoon and sipped it. It had gone cold long ago, but to Vern, this might as well be one of the fanciest dishes he had ever eaten.

His body was finally getting the nourishment it was owed, and Vern got to play pretend without having to do anything unusual. Once in a while, a sound came from the other room, and Vern grew more annoyed.

The hell are they doing in there? Please leave already.

He was dying to review the parchment with the Cryptic Constructor's symbol on it. What could be in there? He had to find a way to get rid of this burden in his mind. But before that, he'd first need to figure out exactly who or what this Cryptic Constructor was.

Vern had given it some thought during his walk back from the library. The first idea was that it either had to be some powerful observer or a god.

For quite a while in his life, he had taken the stance that gods didn't exist. At least not the way they were portrayed in all the legends. They were good for symbolism, but other than that, they were just glorified scapegoats and a means of self-justification.

He himself liked to call upon the name of Lady, but it was more of a habit that he'd built up over his childhood than some personal belief. Did Lady Lennix ever exist the way she was depicted in the Luminous Litany? Just a few days ago, he would have replied with a half shrug and a *maybe*. Getting into debates over such abstract topics with no concrete facts was always exhausting.

But now, with all this fresh knowledge, he was more inclined to believe that she might actually be the creator of insight spheres, just like the primal fundamentalists preached since the day they found those orbs with infinite knowledge.

But that was getting off the topic. Even if the Cryptic Constructor was some god, they didn't seem the virtuous type from the impression he had gotten from Hensen and his neighborhood cultist.

This gave Vern another reason to read that steaming piece of paper in his pocket. He wanted to know what the fuck that Garfield was doing. Why would he go and decapitate a woman in cold blood? Was it due to the content of that parchment? *If only these men would get out of my face.*

Shaking his head, Vern wiped his mouth with the handkerchief and piled up all the dishes, setting them aside.

What to do? He was feeling miserable right about now. There were too many gaps in his knowledge about the observation. It was possible that he was being too paranoid, but really, who was to say that these observers next door weren't looking at him right now, waiting for him to make a mistake?

He just didn't know anything clearly. What was the range of a person's observation? Can all observers see through walls? Was there any way to tell if someone was an observer? Would they realize that Vern was an observer if he went back to his prior experiments with the shades of gray? What exactly was possible? And what wasn't?

Just how did any of this work?

UGH! If only I still had that copy of the observation record of subjectivity.

The Ariane he knew would have taken his outfit with her no matter what. Then there was a good chance that she ended up reading the unorthodox book. However, she was going to have a hard time getting through it. Text-heavy books like that one didn't really grind her gears. She would still finish it though. He was sure of that.

The corners of his lips lifted in a subtle smile. *I can only be thankful it turned out like that.*

She would be safer as an observer, right? If only he could make his way to the inner districts somehow. But he had no clue how to get past the Kingsmen who stood guard on the bridges.

But then an obvious thought hit him, and he face-palmed. *I can just go to the Ascendant Council and ask them for another book.* Hopefully, they would be located in one of the outer districts.

If they could put a book like that in the library just for him, then there had to be more where that came from, right? They must have had some goodwill toward him since they allowed him to read that book.

On top of that, they should've survived the duskfall just fine. After all, they would have already known something was about to go wrong with the world.

This was obviously assuming that their head station wasn't in some inner district guarded by Kingsmen.

Ariane had told him she read something about Yharl Ballin in the newspapers. So he simply had to ask around where their main station was. *Well. I should have thought of this sooner.* He could've straight up walked to their station instead of coming back to the hotel. Surely Eleonora's archive must've had something about them.

Hmm. Not really. He contradicted himself in no time. He remembered how he had gullibly walked into that burden because he ended up in a situation with too big of a power imbalance.

Yes, Yharl Ballin seemed to have some goodwill toward him, but he had no clue about the organization as a whole. So it was indeed a better choice to come back to the hotel and sort things out.

This is why I hate this. He didn't know how cautious was being too cautious. He just didn't have the information needed to strike a proper balance between being reactive and proactive.

But, well, this was a direction. He would ask about this Ascendant Council first thing in the morning. Hopefully, other guests would be amenable to the idea, thanks to that third-rate psychiatrist still doing Lady knows what in the next room.

Finally fed up, Vern stood and walked to his desk by the window. First, he wrote a little about this situation in the notepad in tiny handwriting, hoping these men weren't as omniscient to be able to figure out what he was penning. Then he pushed his notepad aside and cleared the desk.

No one would find it odd if a fundamentalist delved into fundamentals in his own room, right? So he opened the top drawer again and retrieved the insight sphere.

The transparent glassy orb had four golden lines that ran down its curved surface from top to bottom, dividing the whole sphere into four equal sections. Then there was a thicker horizontal line that ran through all the vertical ones like an equator, serving as a demarcating border that further partitioned each of the vertical segments into two.

This made for eight octants in the whole sphere.

Octants were how the fundamentalists categorized their findings. If they figured out a new phenomenon by studying the projection emerging from the southwestern octant in the lower hemisphere, their finding would then loosely be classified under chaos fundamentals.

The Coven of Truth that Vern belonged to—assuming a good chunk of its members hadn't been lost to the duskfall—usually worked on fundamentals found in the upper northeastern and northwestern octants. No clear-cut name existed for these two octants. Fundamentalists never managed to come to a consensus on the proper name for most of the octants, after all.

So Vern also retrieved the sphere's stand and a lumenscope from the second drawer. The insight sphere was like a treasure trove that had its own peculiar method of exploration. He put the sphere on its stand, steadily fastening into its thin clamps. Then he settled the lumenscope beside the sphere, which was a somewhat heavy if small yet long cylindrical contraption that tapered off at one end.

It was one of the most sophisticated pieces of machinery he had the pleasure of owning. The glassy cylinder had three compartments and a short conical beam emitter at the front, each more sophisticated than the last. The whole device was reinforced by an intricate lattice of polished brass, creating beautiful curvy patterns that seemed to be there for nothing else but visual appeal.

The compartment on the back featured a miniature winding assembly—a mesmerizing spectacle of gears and spindles, providing the much-needed rotational force to the middle chamber that housed the two radiant stones as a pair of compact circular disks, which were arranged horizontally, one after the other. Then finally there was the mirror assembly which—

Thud.

Vern instantly halted his ruminations on the intricacies of the lumenscope, focusing instead on the muffled sound. If he had heard it right, the sound had come from the room next door.

They're finally leaving! Thank Lady.

Vern didn't betray his excitement and began winding the lumenscope, using its circular crank at the back as if to prime it for projection.

Tap. Tap.

The faint sounds of footsteps approached but then suddenly stopped. Vern's heart, which had been beating out of excitement, shifted gears, sending blood surging through his body as a sense of unease spread in his mind. The footsteps stopped outside his room.

Vern slowly and covertly reached for the gun at his waist, ready to brandish it at a moment's notice. Seconds passed as he remained tightly strung, waiting for a change.

Knock. Knock. Knock.

FUCK! Why?

He forced himself to stand. Not answering would only be worse. It would make it look like he had something to hide. Assuming they already knew he was sitting at his desk, he couldn't even play it off as being asleep and having missed their knock.

Calm down. If it really comes down to it, we'll just have to see who can shoot better at a hand's distance. But they were two people. His odds weren't the best.

Taking a deep breath, he leisurely dangled his arms to his side—within a second's reach of the revolver. From what he remembered, there should still be at least three bullets inside the chamber. That should be enough.

Then instead of opening the door, he bent forward and looked through the peephole. As his eye focused, a jolt of cold terror shot through his veins.

A red pupil was staring back at him from the other side, enveloping his sight.

"AAAH—"

A shriek escaped his mouth, and his blood ran cold. He recoiled, somehow managing to not lose his marbles as he reached for the gun.

"WHAT THE FUC—"

But before Vern could do anything else, the world turned dark, and all he managed was to not fall headfirst.

Ticktock. Ticktock. Ticktock.

The ticking of the clock in the otherwise silent ambiance seeped into his mind, awakening his senses. He opened his eyes only to be greeted by the wooden floor.

Again.

What?

A few moments passed as he groggily tried to process the situation.

I was still working on figuring out the shades. What happened?

He pushed himself off the ground and used the doorknob to hoist himself up. Then he looked around, and nothing was where it should be. Why was the insight sphere out on the desk? Why were there plates on the dining table? Why wasn't he hungry? Why was it eleven o'clock already?

He left the support of the door only to find himself keeling over, almost losing balance. Somehow managing to not tumble ungainly, he navigated back to the desk and settled down on the chair in front of it.

His eyes appraised the beautiful orb as he tried to recall the details. He was still working on assigning grays to his perception.

Oh, yes. Someone had knocked on the door, disturbing his speculative trance of those beautiful grays depicting light.

But after that . . .

What happened after that?

Minutes passed by as he sat there in silence. Nothing was coming to him. Was he just too exhausted?

No, that didn't make sense. He had already experienced something similar hundreds of times in his life, and once even recently, under the hands of Hensen.

However, fundamentals never fogged his prior memories. The insight sphere was out on the table, which meant that he might have peeked at the projection and lost some of his memories during the process. But usually, it only took around a minute before one became lucid after emerging from the projection of fundamentals.

This was the whole reason he had first started keeping a notepad with him—to be able to quickly jot down his experiences right after waking up from each trance. But it was different this time. He didn't remember anything before or after. It was somewhat similar to that situation with Hensen. But completely unexplained.

He slid the chair forward, and while doing so, he felt something on his waist. He frowned and lifted his shirttail only to see the handle and chamber of what looked like a revolver.

His frown only deepened as he pulled out the bronze revolver and placed it on the desk. Its warm hue was accentuated by intricate engravings and filigree patterns that adorned its surface. Not the most beautiful work he'd seen, but nothing too shabby either.

It's not like someone else could have tucked a revolver on his waist, right? Then something had definitely gone wrong with his memories.

Could something have happened to fundamentals after the duskfall? He remembered a few cases of amnesia had propped up among the fundamentalists. If it was something like that, it might be a one-off thing.

But that still didn't explain this revolver. Where did it come from? He didn't believe himself to be a frolicker that would run around stealing guns. Unless someone gave it to him, he didn't see why he would have it. Yes, he wanted to get his hands on a firearm after having to run around sneakily this morning, but this wasn't how he planned on getting it.

Shoving the lumenscope to one side, he retrieved his notepad. It was better to write this down and then figure things out from there. Hopefully, whoever he had stolen this gun from wasn't hot on his tail or something.

Skipping the first few pages filled with crude sketches of men—drawn by the previous owner of this notepad—he reached the last page. And before he could pick up his pen to write about these new happenings, something caught his eye.

There were some new words written in a small font, barely legible.

CHAPTER 27

CRYPTIC CONSTRUCTOR

He read on, and a chill ran down his spine. Apparently, some cultist had died in the room next door. But that wasn't the real problem. It was those two men. From the chain of events, it seemed that the incident had taken place around nine o'clock.

So more than two hours had passed already. But what happened at the end? His notes ended with *I am still waiting for them to leave.* So that meant the men had done something to him before departing.

But they neither had entered the room nor did they take away his gun or the . . . parchment. The parchment that was still in his pocket. Didn't this mean that either they didn't realize or didn't care about these things? Because if they did, why would they just leave him be after forcing him into such a vulnerable state?

He still wasn't fully sure what had transpired, but it was enough for him to know that he had a clue about the Cryptic Constructor in his pocket and that those men had given him a break. Even if they hadn't, the scale was tipping far too much toward cautiousness, and it wouldn't do him any good to pretend anymore.

He had already lost his memory to some randoms. What was next? He needed to use every tool available to him and prepare for the worse. For being vulnerable could very well mean death.

So he cleared up some space on the table and withdrew the crumpled paper from his pocket. The yellow parchment was littered with drops of red that smelled of metal—or actually blood. Not minding any of that, he unfolded the parchment and laid it flat on the desk. It was almost as big as a page from those huge church tomes.

As written in his notes, two inverted triangles were drawn on the top with red ink. Upon a closer look, however, what seemed like artistic detailing on the edges of the triangle were actually blotches of blood that had long since dried.

Vern quickly moved on. Cultists wouldn't be cultists if they didn't do creepy scrapshit like that. He already noticed a few choice words that made his heart leap with excitement.

> *Etchings of Existence: First Edifice*
> *Under the shadowed mantle of the Cryptic Constructor—the Unseen Architect—truths of the cosmos unfold in hushed whispers, meant only for those worthy of hearing them. He is the silent weaver of order, the divine draftsman, etching unbroken lines into the fabric of existence.*
> *His truths are not for the uninitiated but for those who decipher the world through the sacred prism. Each sees a different facet, a unique fragment of the grand design etched in the cosmos by the Immutable Shaper.*

His blessing is the unveiling, a divine act that transcends mere sight, to perceive the very bones of reality. It begets the ability to manipulate the world, to bend it to the will of the chosen ones, altering the course of what is and what shall be.

By the grace of the Constructor, his disciples are bestowed with the dark visions. These are not mere spells, but the manifestation of their thoughts, potent enough to rewrite the laws of reality itself. These visions spring forth from the Aetheric Void, an expanse that grows with each insight, each revelation about the grand scheme.

That was . . . a little bit of new information mixed with a rehash of things he already knew. Who would've thought that fanatics under the Cryptic Constructor liked to make simple concepts sound more . . . cryptic?

That aside, he was right to assume that the Cryptic Constructor was some kind of god that people worshipped. But there was much more here than just that. *Sacred prism?* That sounded very much like that lens that had fused onto his eyes after enlightenment. Then there was that line, *the Aetheric Void, an expanse that grows with each insight.*

This was interesting, however it didn't make sense without more context, so he continued reading.

To peer into the elusive depth of reality, to bear witness to the unobserved facets of reality, one must be ready to offer a sacrifice. An offering not of material wealth or mundane possession, but of eyes. A piece of existence, surrendered unto the unseeable forces, a token to placate the Architect's ineffable attendants.

These unseen servants, known to us as the silent schemers, respond to the call of sacrifice. They are the sacred harbingers of our divine patron, poised to grant a miraculous insight to those brave and devoted enough.

When your sacrifice rings true, the silent schemers will bestow upon you a divine revelation—a glimpse into the heart of reality. This miracle is neither for the faint of heart nor for those of narrow vision. It is an enlightening terror, an awe-inspiring spectacle, a testament to the boundless complexity of the cosmos.

So stand firm, acolyte. Cast your offering into the void and be ready to behold the unseeable. This is but the first fragment of your journey, the initial step into the realm of the Architect of Abstractions. Proceed with reverence and caution, for this path is treacherous, yet it is the one to true enlightenment.

This . . . ritual had to be what that madman was conducting in his room. It was unfortunate that he didn't actually remember all the details, but his notes definitely spoke of a similar event.

This might also explain the weird reaction Garfield had according to Vern's notes—he was looking at the air in front of him with horror. He probably saw an enlightening terror after the sacrifice rang true. *Hmm, but that still doesn't explain the involvement of those two men and the knocking Garfield was blabbering about.*

Also, it seemed like the diagram from the *Objective Record of Subjectivity* wasn't a famous method of enlightenment. Vern wondered why anyone would sacrifice eyes to unknown entities if they could simply comprehend a diagram and be done with it.

Hmm, I don't really have a reference as to how difficult it is to comprehend that diagram. What if it is much more challenging for others to grasp its nature? Also, he didn't know the amount of effort or cost that went into making that diagram.

Did the observer society also have resource limitations? The thought made him chuckle. No matter how grim the contents of this parchment were, there was no reason for him to feel despondent over it. This was study material, after all.

Flipping the page over, he skipped the first two paragraphs that detailed how to prepare the sacrifice because there was something far more interesting right beneath it. It was written in the same red ink that was used for the symbol, completely distinct from the rest of the text.

First vision: instability inducement

In the realm of existence, all structures bear the mark of the Cryptic Constructor, from the sturdiest fortress to the sharpest blade. Each object, each creation, carries within it a silent resonance, a harmony of order and purpose.

Yet, within this cohesive resonance, an underlying instability lurks. A minute, whispering inconsistency that yearns to be unveiled. This is the flaw, the hidden imperfection, the seed of potential entropy that resides in all things.

Seek first the comprehension of this instability. Delve into the arcane depths of the artifact's essence, the silent whisper of its narrative, the story it tells of its own creation. Understand its pattern, its consistency, its continuity.

This understanding is your key.

Now, disciples, extend thy perception into the Aetheric Void. Draw upon the essence of your thoughts, and allow this inscrutable wisdom to permeate your mind, your senses, your very being.

Let the hidden flaws pulse within the Aetheric Void. Accentuate their rifts, highlight their edges, quicken their divergence. The subtle fissure will grow to a chasm, the minor fracture to a shattering split.

The flaw will reveal itself, growing, spreading, until the edifice is undermined, the structure compromised, the fortress crumbled, or the blade shattered.

Such is the power of the Cryptic Constructor, and such is the power bestowed upon you, his chosen disciples.

Seek the flaws. Understand them. Exploit them.

This is but the beginning, the first edifice in the composition of reality. So it is written. So it shall be.

Vern's heart pounded with exhilaration as he clutched the ends of the parchment, reflexively leaning in closer to get a better look at each word. It was as if every word was a passage of its own, loaded with boundless intent.

The words created connections in his mind that hadn't existed, giving him insights into how the world was composited, how they transmuted from one to the others—it was just like fundamentals.

Every insight that came to his mind was a fleeting thought. Each entered his mind and gave him a vague idea before another one reared its head without a pause. It was like someone told him the answer to a tricky question they had just asked, but before he could understand the logic behind it, another person came in and asked him their question and answered right after. Then this cycle repeated.

It gave him the sense that his thoughts were growing, expanding. But they felt . . . foreign. Like that text you memorized but didn't understand. Except, something concrete was also taking shape in his mind. It was like a path was being etched amid the plexus of his thoughts.

Every moment that unfolded, the path grew distinct as the foreign notions gravitated toward it, assimilating into its edges.

He couldn't discern the passage of time as he sat there in a trance.

His forehead was teeming with sweat, and his head throbbed with intense pulsations. It was the feeling he used to have when he crammed too much, and every thought made him anxious that he would forget something.

What the hell was that?

He sat back up straight and wiped the sweat with his sleeve before massaging his temples.

Quarter-hour bells chimed from the clock tower yet again, and he finally looked back up at the clock that hung on the wall. Its shortest hand was about to reach two, while the minute hand was past three-quarters.

He didn't even feel like being surprised anymore. Every time he encountered something related to observation, the time became less and less perceivable.

But this is exciting! A vision!

The words definitely had some kind of subjectivity to them, just like that diagram in *Observation Record of Subjectivity*.

Its effects were clear from the words, and the whole concept seemed very fitting for Vern's viewpoint. Except, he didn't know how to translate the ideas mentioned into a construct of balance.

Still, some of the ideas mentioned could easily be mapped one to one from his own viewpoint.

Though he still wasn't sure how to perform the actual manipulation part. *Let the hidden flaws pulse within the Aetheric Void. Accentuate their rifts, highlight their edges, quicken their divergence. The subtle fissure will grow to a chasm, the minor fracture to a shattering split.* These words were surely describing the envisioning part, but the line about the Aetheric Void stumped him yet again.

This description made it seem like the Aetheric Void was just a fancy term for his perception. But the first few lines in the parchment used the same word in a completely different context . . .

One step at a time.

However, this brief shift in thinking reminded him of the burden, and his mood dampened instantly. How would this knowledge interact with that burden? Would it make it easier for Hensen to find him? The parchment was definitely very useful, but it didn't offer any clue on what to do about this burden.

Oh well. Not something I can do much about. I really need this edge, no matter what. Just in half a day, someone has already erased my memories once. Who knows what else is waiting out there? If he didn't have a habit of writing down events, he would still be perplexed over what the hell happened to him during that lapse in his memories.

So he shook his head, got up, and stretched his lethargic body for a while.

When he felt a little more energized, he sat back down and opened his perception. It was time to see what had changed.

At first, it was obviously completely black since he hadn't chosen what to observe. So he gave it a thought and settled on a keyword that was the essence of that whole vision described in the parchment.

Composition.

He didn't believe that *flaw* was the proper keyword since flaws only existed within compositions. What flaw existed by itself? Just thinking about it gave him a headache.

But nothing changed. His perception remained as dark as ever.

Disappointing, but it's only to be expected. It would have been nice if all those new insights filled his perception by themselves, like back in the library.

Well, no matter. He would have to determine how to assign shades of gray to an intangible concept like composition.

It wouldn't work to just think about the outline of an object, like heat or height. If he was observing heat, he could simply assign hotter objects as whiter and darken the shades of grays as things turned colder.

Similarly, he could assign height just like he saw for the staircase back in the library, with the ceiling being white and the floor being dark. But how was one supposed to think about composition in terms of balance?

Feeling foolish for jumping into observing something that he didn't know how to rationalize, he closed his perception and brainstormed.

Many minutes passed as he sat there in silence, contemplating the myriad theories he had learned throughout his life, retrofitting those ideas to suit the scenario.

The melodious bells did their eternal duty, reminding him of the passage of time, even so deep in the night. And after a few more minutes, he finally found a solution.

The first thing he decided was not to try and assign shades to the whole room. That was something he had realized he had been doing unnecessarily. Why perceive the whole room if he just had to manipulate laws for one small object?

So, since he needed to look for the composition, he chose an object with multiple tiers of it. The lumenscope sat there on his desk still shoved to one side of it.

His idea was to view composition as a balance of complexity instead.

C H A P T E R **28**

INSTABILITY INDUCEMENT

Composition was a more abstract concept that couldn't have two well-defined ends to strike a balance between. But complexity, on the other hand, was something that could be balanced while also incorporating the notions of the composition of an object.

So anything that was complex, he would set to be dark, while everything that was relatively simpler would be assigned brighter shades. This way, he was still observing the composition of an object in a sense, but now it could be balanced.

That was a hard one. Can observers that aren't fundamentalists or researchers of some kind really solve problems like this?

Shaking his head, he focused again. He had only figured out the theory. Now was the time to put it into practice.

Complexity.

For starters, he assigned the mirror assembly on the left to be a bright white in his empty perception. After all, it was a very simple setup—they were just a few mirrors rotated in predefined angles.

Next, he looked at the middle compartment that housed both the gemstones that provided the light for projection. This had a few spokes and gears that rotated the mini-enclosure, which held said gems. So he allocated a slate gray to the compartment as a whole, but he wasn't too sure about the gems.

In the sense of artificial complexity, the only refinement done to the gems was grinding them to fit the shape of the compartments, so maybe a silver-white would do them justice?

But he didn't go into too much detail after this, or he would have to assign a different shade to every little component in the whole contraption. He remembered from his experiments back in the library that being too precise while observing wasn't really the best idea, nor was it great to leave things too vague. *Strike a balance. Like usual.*

It delighted him every time he identified the concept of balance in random things.

Nevertheless, he moved on to the rightmost compartment and assigned it a heavy dark. Relative to the whole device, this had to be the most sophisticated aspect of it. Hundreds of different gears of various sizes came together in a plexus of force distribution network that effectively wound the three springs—made of the ever-twisting alloy aptly named cranksteel.

But this threw him for a loop.

Wasn't everything black when he started as well? That was to say, the whole room was also black in his perception, but did that really mean that they were as complex as that winding mechanism? *No way.*

That would make this whole methodology a bust. So he tried to focus just on the lumenscope, hoping to ignore the rest of the room.

And the ambient and omnipresent black was gone like it never existed.

Perfect. It seems like it's more of a representation of nothingness than being really black. That worked out flawlessly for him. A welcome change amid his pervasive setbacks as an observer.

On the note of successes, another factor of observation that was panning out better than he had expected was the assignment of grays themselves. Just a few hours ago—when he was trying to assign grays to represent the light in his room—every gradation that he designated was a monumental task in and of itself. This time, however, it was as easy as a walk in the park.

Hmm, there could be two reasons behind this ease. One could be that I have a better understanding of the concept of complexity than light, while the other possibility is that it has something to do with the thoughts that filled my mind after reading that first vision on the parchment.

Or it could be both. Who knew?

But this is good. Now the real question is, How do I manipulate this and make it worth all the effort?

The Cryptic Constructor's vision was called instability inducement, and it also mentioned that one had to find the flaws in the composition and then expand them.

What was the flaw in this lumenscope? There were many.

Yes, the springs used were called ever-twisting, but if they were displaced from their enclosure even a little bit—with all that force, they would launch the whole gearbox out of the contraption at a breakneck pace, shattering more than a few vital components and collapsing the whole device internally.

Cranksteel was a great alloy, but it was just as deadly. A small over-coiled crank-steel, if used without its safety measures, could throw a four-person carriage around like a rock.

Another flaw in the lumenscope was the fact that the contact edges between gears and cogs were prone to wear and tear. If something went wrong with them, it would stop the whole mechanism from functioning, and one wouldn't even know what went wrong unless they dismantled it.

But as he thought about all these flaws, an inkling appeared in his mind. A notion. Focusing on where the spring would be located inside that glassy contraption made the notion even more significant.

A notion with which if he engaged would lead to something . . . something greater.

And he wanted to know.

So he guided his thoughts to perceive that notion.

His mind flitted through a series of ideas, and a gap appeared around the back end of that shaded lumenscope.

Crack.

"NO!"

He was jolted out of his reverie as he lost all focus, and he cried out—albeit a little too late.

A dozen broken gears and cogs launched out of the top of the winding chamber of the lumenscope, blasting a hole open in the device. A crack ran down the circumference of the contraption around the housing of the cranksteel.

More gears, bearings, and tiny flywheels spilled out of the cylinder as Vern looked on in horror.

"Crack my fucking cogs! That cost more than ten regalias!" he yelled, slamming his fist on the desk, which sent more sprockets and springs from within the shell tumbling down to the floor.

Vern took a deep breath and stood there for more than a minute, his eyes closed.

How the hell was he going to peer into fundamentals without a lumenscope? Who the hell would be selling one in this situation? Even if someone was, he wouldn't have the regalias to pay them. That thing cost him half a fortune when he bought it.

Taking deep breaths, he walked to the dining table and poured himself some water from the jug. Chugging two glasses, one after the other, he finally heaved a long sigh.

Time to look at the bright side, I guess.

He had just used a vision! And he didn't trigger any horrifying voices, which would have forcefully activated the burden! On top of all that, it wasn't even a simple vision. It needed a lot of sophisticated thinking and deep knowledge. Nothing like the free lunch he had eaten back at the library.

This was supernatural! No human could do that with just his thoughts. Yes, fundamentals enabled men to do feats that were deemed impossible just a few decades ago. But their results were external and didn't belong to the user. The wonders born from fundamentals made use of what already existed in reality, nudging them to do their bidding.

But this was changing the fundamentals themselves!

Vern looked around the room and thought to repeat his success. But this time, he wouldn't dare observe something so expensive. He didn't know that perceiving that notion would trigger and destabilize the flaws instantly.

I should have predicted it! I was observing the lumenscope, after all.

After a short while, his breathing calmed and he reconsidered the situation.

He wasn't a control freak, and beating himself over something that was unintentional would be pushing it too hard, especially when it was just a contraption, not something irreplaceable.

Or unfixable.

He probably didn't have the exact components that broke off or were chipped away, but he could always try some spares and slightly modify the whole design. This model was a few years old, so there were more than a few blueprints of it floating around among fundamentalists, which he could use for reference. But that was for when he got in touch with the coven.

It was just like his master said, *A balanced mind is the key to stable progression.* He might not be able to anticipate everything that would go wrong, but as long as he learned from it and did his best not to muck it up, he should be fine.

So yeah. Never try new visions on personal equipment.

Finally, working toward peace with himself, he surveyed the room for things to induce instability into. He first discarded observing the gun or the insight sphere.

He had had enough losses for the day. He didn't want to mess with chairs or books because he had no clue what their faults were in terms of complexity.

He could maybe half-ass something, but it might take him another hour or so to ponder. Except, he was getting sleepy, and there was a lot to do tomorrow like find some way to get into the inner districts and surprise Ari.

A mischievous smile played on his face as he turned to the quiet ticking coming from the other side of the room. *Hmm, that wall clock looks quite complex.*

Nodding, he gave its flaws a quick thought. The clock had a common flaw with the lumenscope. If even one of the cogs or gear was abrased, the whole thing would stop working.

Complexity.

He couldn't see through the face of the clock to peer into the mechanism behind it, but he had fixed more than his fair share of clocks in the name of training. So even if he didn't have the exact image in his mind for this specific variant, he could hazard a few guesses on the complexity of it.

Also, being too exact would only make it impossible for him to find flaws in the whole structure.

So he shaded the dials and the face of the clock a bright white due to their simplicity, but then he paused. *The mechanism is physically behind the face. I can't exactly see it.*

After a short bout of contemplation, he realized it was another one of those thought-provoking questions that was better solved with simplistic logic and vague reasoning.

He was shading his perception, not sight. So he just perceived the complex mechanism to be beyond the face of the clock.

And as expected, he could feel every change he made to his perception, not just with his eyes but through his thoughts.

So he rapidly assigned a stormy gray to all the gears he assumed alongside a pitch-black shade to the small winding mechanism that used a simpler spring than cranksteel.

This time, however, he didn't want to break the clock or have its gears boring a hole into the wall. So when that guiding notion appeared in his mind once again, he focused on the flaw that the gears created in that complex mechanism, not on the springs.

Then like a compass, it steered his thoughts through the sophisticated composition of the clock. A gap opened in his perception, and like a tram, it pulled his thoughts on its track.

Then the gap became a proverbial fissure, and the second hand of the clock stopped its relentless march. However, the clock was still ticking since the sound came from the wheel train, not the hand. That was to say, some gear between the wheel train and the second hand was slipping, preventing the gears from turning.

"Yes!" He shot his fist in the air and cheered himself on.

This was finally going somewhere. He could only praise his forgotten self for grabbing that parchment before anyone had noticed. This could be a lifesaving trick up his sleeve that would help him in navigating this new treacherous reality.

He settled down and sat on the chair.

This was the most relaxed he'd felt since he first arrived in Elmhurst. Every moment he'd spent in the city had been filled with some kind of trouble or anxiety. Anxieties that he was good at managing. But they still occupied his thoughts and made him paranoid. This, however, gave him some confidence.

Observation was indeed something he could personally harness and not some abstract concept that could only be dreamt of. There were still many things that weighed on his mind, but it was good to have the balance of his life shifted back toward control—even if just a little.

Looking at the clock that had stopped, he noticed it was past three already. *I really should call it a day . . . or night.*

In a jovial mood, he cleaned up the mess made by his lumenscope. Piling all the little components in one drawer, he freshened up and turned off the lamps.

Once done, he walked toward the window and looked up at the eerily beautiful sky. The bright moon and the gaping rift hung high, complementing each other's radiance.

Taking in the sight once more, he softly closed the curtains and retired to his bed.

One day. One day, he would uncover it all.

CHAPTER 29

A SIMPLE MORNING

Vern sat on his bed, leaning against the wall with a screwdriver in his hands and the wall clock in his lap. A couple of gears were littered around him, waiting for their turn to be put back in the right place. It would be no good to have a defective clock in a fundamentalist's room. That would be worse than a blacksmith keeping broken weapons.

When he dismantled the simple machine, he noticed that more than a few gears were abrased, breaking off contact from their successor, leading to a disrupted gear train.

It was quite peculiar how instability inducement had done its job. He didn't explicitly choose these gears or something when creating the flaw. He just had an abstract idea of what could go wrong, then his thoughts—guided by that notion— had done the rest.

It was obviously due to the special words which explained vision on that parchment, incepting this peculiar notion in his mind. *But it's a different method than the one I was using back in the library.* It was like his mind was steered to perform the necessary tasks by the notion—he wasn't the one in control.

Though it's only a fraction of a second. And he was still the one that had to figure out the flaw in composition and shade his perception with it, so it wasn't exactly brainless either. However, that was to say, it wasn't the same thing he was doing back in the library. Both of them seemed like two different methods of executing visions.

One was guided by foreign insights, while the other was a completely conscious effort on the observer's part.

But that's the problem. Trying to envision things myself is what led those other-worldly voices to ring in my head, beckoning me to surrender to Lady knows what.

Was it just that one was a proper method while the other was incorrect? Then why was he able to use it in the library at all? There was something going on here, but he couldn't pinpoint it. It was probably about the underlying principles of how both worked, but he didn't have enough to go on.

Hopefully, the Ascendant Council will have something for me.

Finally done putting back all the gears while replacing the chipped ones with some from his own kit, the second hand started revolving in its orbit yet again.

After a few minutes, the clock tower chimed eleven times, and Vern quickly set the clock in his hand to start from there. Hanging the clock back to a nail jutting out of the wall, he turned off the heat and made for the shower.

Once the lukewarm water pelted his body, he had a thought.

Where is all the water, steam, and gas coming from? Miss Cera had said that a major plant that supplied essentials to the city had exploded. *Water and steam could be explained by a personal water pump for the hotel that extracts water from the ground, but what about the gas?*

Similar random questions whirled around in his mind as he dried himself off before stepping out of the bathroom.

Grabbing some choice clothes from his suitcase underneath the bed, he meticulously donned the maroon striped vest over a white shirt whose narrow collar tapered into pointy ends, perfectly matching the angle of the vest's V-shaped neckline. Pulling up narrow pitch-black trousers checkered with thin lines, he hooked on his graphite pocket watch to it. Then over all this, he put on a long smoky black trench coat, which would make for an easier time out in the city compared to a tight formal jacket.

Then to complete the ensemble, he combed his unruly wet hair to one side and put on a top hat with a red satin band matching the hue of his vest.

Fashion was the language of the society, one he had come to enjoy speaking himself.

Checking the chamber of the revolver one more time, he put it in his trench coat pocket. There were four bullets in the gun, and he might be able to secure a few more from Beaumont. He had used firearms a few times before in his life, but it was mostly for testing purposes.

So he'd need to find some way to practice his shots because even though instability inducement was a card up his sleeve, it wasn't exactly the offensive kind by nature. It seemed versatile, but he had felt it last night. Even though he had only used it twice, it drained his mental faculties and made him lethargic.

And this was when he found faults in simple compositions. What would happen if he tried something grander?

Shaking his head, he looked at the room one final time.

He had already hidden the parchment after wasting a quarter hour looking at it to no avail. No new insights came to him, nor did any fuzzy notions. And there wasn't anything else on that parchment. It hinted at more excerpts, but this one ended right after the explanation of the first vision.

The lumenscope was still sitting in a drawer of its own, waiting to be fixed. Maybe when Vern found some time and a proper schema.

The insight sphere was back in his suitcase, which had a lock that was far more secure. However, if a thief wanted it anyway, they could just take his whole suitcase.

Ugh. His brain was starting to hurt thinking about all these mundane problems that didn't exist in a civilized society. *This is good enough for now.*

Stepping out the door, he randomly rotated the knobs on the four corners of the lock as it clicked shut.

The corridor was still as empty as before, but sunlight shone in from the window at its end, casting shadows on the iron bars which encased the window. Room 308 looked completely serene. Nothing out of the ordinary. No revolting smells, no screams. Just a normal room in the hotel.

He brushed it off and left it behind, making his way to the grand staircase, which was shining from all the light seeping into the building from its glass roof. A few people stood at the landing of each floor, chatting in groups. Vern descended the flight of stairs, gliding his hand across the masterfully carved handrails.

". . . grace, I do declare, I'm quite set on attending this spectacle! Those ruffians will at last receive their just deserts."

"If only they had done this sooner. The poor souls outside wouldn't have had to suffer in silence these last three days."

Vern had joined the conversation in the middle of it, but he was already quite intrigued by whatever they were talking about. So he slowed down his descent and made his way toward the group.

It was two men and a woman. The two on the right looked like a middle-aged couple, while the last man seemed a little too enthusiastic this late in the morning.

They noticed him approaching and turned toward him with askance gazes. Vern didn't make them wait and tipped his top hat as he spoke. "Good morning, milady and gentlemen. I couldn't help but overhear what you were talking about. Could you shed some light on this spectacle you were just mentioning a moment ago?"

The man on the right chortled and said, "A late morning to you as well, young man. Well, you see, since you spent the wee hours of the morning in a hearty sleep, you missed the correspondence we had here—"

But the lady at his side waved her hand in front of him and stated, "Don't be rude, Benedict. He's such a polite lad." Then with a smile, the lady, who was dressed in a seaweed-colored high skirt and a khaki long-sleeved bodice, faced Vern and replied politely, "It's good news, young man. Duke Neagan has started his quest to reclaim the lost boroughs under the orders of our emperor. A messenger carriage escorted by a troop of guards from the duke's estate announced that the quest to reclaim Fulham borough will begin in three days."

The third man also jumped in, "Yes. Yes, I tell you. They did that to scare those outlaws into hiding. No one would fight against the might of the weapons of those guards. I work for the Bureau, and I know where they came from. Just last week, the duke's palace applied for funding from the treasury to stock up on an arsenal of weapons from Von Industries."

Von industries, huh? Is it really a coincidence that this Duke Neagan just happened to stock up right before things went downhill?

"They have some of the most advanced weapons known to man. I tell you, when the duke starts his conquest, a mere glance at those formidable weapons will be enough to make those criminals lose control of their bladders. I was telling everyone that the emperor was just biding his time. I was right! We can finally go back to our previous lives."

"Not so fast, Wilfred. Not so fast," interjected the lady once again. "If it was that simple to conquer lost land, the empire wouldn't be getting its boundaries pushed every other year. On top of that, what makes you think the criminals don't have their own channels for weapons in these new times?"

"Right. Right," agreed Benedict. "There's much more to the city than what your delusional colleagues and bosses tell you. All that red tape has muddled your head. We are not going back to the time before. Who knows how my men who handled the supply line for my tobacco business fared after the purge? We were lucky enough to survive the culling. Expecting any more miracles would be to our folly."

"But such is the way of things, young man. Care to spare two pence for your thoughts on this whole matter?" asked the lady with an interested gaze.

Vern played along with their idea, reciprocating with some information of his own. "I wholeheartedly agree with what the madam and sir have to say. Things are not as simple as they seem, and it'd be foolhardy to undermine what lurks in the shadows. That reminds me, there are a few religious zealots out in the city, which you intelligent people would do well to keep your distance from."

"Oh, why is that?" asked the enthusiastic man.

"Followers of Mother Asea are distributing some miracle liquid that supposedly heals any wound."

"Any wound?" asked the man on the left while the rest looked back at Vern with astonishment.

"Indeed. I saw it with my own eyes yesterday. Though, personally, I would recommend against considering it until it's proved to be harmless in the long run."

"Oh, what did you see?"

"That can't be right. It must be some product of fundamentalism."

But this turned into another meandering conversation in no time.

After responding to a few queries perfunctorily, Vern asked a question of his own, "By the way, would any of you lovely people happen to remember hearing a shout or commotion last night?"

"No. I didn—"

"Oh yes, there was one, wasn't there?" interrupted the lady yet another time. "Do you not remember that guy on the ground floor who started shouting at everyone, acting like he'd drunk twelve of those cheap Barley Bishops?"

Hmm. So they really don't remember.

"Really a stain on what's left of the society."

"Yes, indeed. I tell you, they wouldn't stop there. Last month, a drunkard came to my office and . . ."

Then the group began another tangential discussion, and Vern felt like he was fourth-wheeling them. So when an appropriate lull appeared in their discussion, Vern interjected, "It was a pleasure talking to you lovely folks, but I must head out, for the day is bright and there are tasks I must attend to."

"Indeed, we shouldn't hold you, young man. Tell us more about that miracle liquid next time. For now, go get your breakfast before the butler packs it away."

Finally free of their winding ramblings, he quickly descended the stairs and walked toward the bar to the right. Beaumont stood there, wiping clean one of the glasses in his immaculate suit with not even a trace of blood that must have spilled on it during the event last night.

Did he clean it? Or he's just wearing a new outfit?

"Good morning, Mr. Vern. Would you like me to serve your breakfast?"

"Yes, please, and thank you for your effort, as always," said Vern, making his way to one of the stools in front of the mahogany counter.

With a nod, Beaumont left the bar unattended and entered the door to what seemed like the kitchen.

After a while, he came back out with a plate—three steaming pancakes on it, cooked to golden brown and served alongside a toast with some butter on it. The sight made Vern gulp as he received the plates without any more courtesy. Grabbing the fork and knife, he started.

Beaumont wiped the counter on the other side when Vern asked, a piece of pancake skewered onto his fork, ready to be devoured, "Beaumont, do you happen to know anything about Administrator Yharl Ballin?"

Beaumont paused and stood. "Administrator Yharl Ballin? There are a few administrators in the city, but none of them are named Yharl Ballin. Are you sure you haven't gotten the name wrong?"

Vern knitted his eyebrows as he savored the flavor of the pancake. Stabbing his fork in the heart of the steaming disk once again, he pulled out another chunk and replied, "I am talking about the leader of the Ascendant Council. Yharl Ballin. Is he not an administrator?"

"Hmm, you might be confusing things, Mr. Vern. The leader of the Ascendant Council is indeed an administrator, but he isn't named Yharl Ballin. It is the brother-in-law of Duke Armen, Administrator Hoist."

Vern frowned at the implications. *This can't be right.*

C H A P T E R 30

ASCENDANT COUNCIL

Did Ari mistake the administrator's name? Or does Beaumont not know enough about this topic?

The butler looked back at Vern with a quizzical look, waiting for a response.

"Are you sure, Beaumont? My sister told me Administrator Yharl and the Ascendant Council were in the newspaper just a few weeks ago."

He nodded. "You are right that the Ascendant Council was all over the newspapers in the second week of this month, but it had nothing about this Yharl Ballin you keep mentioning."

"I can grab you the exact publications of that day if you'd like."

"That would be very kind of you."

So the butler nodded and stooped under the counter before he began piling newspapers from different agencies one after another in front of Vern. All of them were dated for the tenth of this month. Seventeen days ago.

Vern began rifling through the papers with one hand as he continued to chow down the rest of his meal.

Everything indeed mentioned an Administrator Hoist, not Administrator Yharl. But the news was a bunch of political nonsense along with flowery words that didn't explain what was happening at all. It was just a lot of meandering arguments and "expert" opinions . . .

"Hmm, it says they became . . . radical out of nowhere. Could you elaborate more on that? I don't really know much about the Ascendant Council at all, and there's too much censoring going on here in the news reports."

The butler continued to portion drinks from one bottle to another as he said, "As you wish, Mr. Vern, I will give you a little more background. The Ascendant Council is a group of people that failed to become fundamentalists. Administrator Hoist was one such person himself."

"Apparently, there was a time when he invited a few coven leaders to mentor him. But it wasn't meant to be. He was as untalented as they come, scraping the bottom of the barrel when it came to peering into the fundamentals of his own volition. I still don't understand half of what peering into anything has to do with talent. But my daughter always tried to explain it to me, yet I—" The man suddenly halted as he looked down at the ground.

However, before Vern could ask about it, Beaumont continued, "So administrator Hoist created a club for people like himself who couldn't peer into fundamentals. Their goal was to look at the history of our society to learn more about Lady Lennix. To learn the source of it all. To figure out where the fundamentals came from. Their club gained traction as more people joined in, frustrated by the lack of their own talent or to get closer to the relative of a duke. The perks of being in that club, which became a council in no time weren't too shabby either."

"They always loathed all fundamentalists, but it was never to the point of what happened this time. Since the start of this month, the newspaper has run at least one column about the death of a fundamentalist in each issue. Some died in their houses, while the rest were found dead out on the streets. This became a big mystery until someone from the Symposium came out with proof that these killings were orchestrated by the Ascendant Council."

That's . . .

A chill crept up his spine when he connected the dots and considered his own experiences after entering the city.

Could I have been one of the targets in this chain of deaths?

Vern continued his inquiry, "Was there any resolution to this whole situation?"

Beaumont shook his head. "Not that I know of. Administrator Hoist does what he pleases. As you can see in the news itself, no one dared to clearly write that the murders had something to do with the Ascendant Council. The killings didn't stop even until the day everything went to hell. Not many could stop that man in this city. Not before he became the head of the Ascendant Council, much less after that."

There was a trace of bitterness in those last words. Vern didn't know what that meant in this situation, so he tactfully asked, "If you're comfortable discussing it, did you also suffer at the hands of that man?"

Beaumont continued staring at the ground for a while before he shook his head and answered, "Nothing of matter anymore. We've all lost too much, and I'd rather not talk about it."

Vern nodded and ate in silence, reading the different newspapers in more detail.

When he was done, he asked, "So, Beaumont, how much more do I have to pay for the rent?"

The butler, who was busy stocking items, didn't even look at him and replied, "Five sovereigns and eighteen crowns."

"And how much does it go up if I want a box of rounds for a third-generation ironsong?"

"That would be another sovereign and seventy-five crowns per box," came the response without hesitation.

Vern had seen a similar transaction take place at this counter before, and he was flabbergasted. He wouldn't even have guessed that that was something one could buy in hotels. At least hotels back at Nvoria didn't sell bullet rounds at a drink counter.

Hmm, if I remember correctly, 175 crowns isn't too bad compared to the market price of bullets back in Nvoria. However, Elmhurst was supposed to have much lower costs for weapons and ammunition in general. *But then, a lot has happened.*

He didn't argue much about it and pulled out seven sovereign notes from the inner pocket of his coat. Sliding them across the counter, he said, "I will take one box for now."

Beaumont grabbed the notes from the counter and went back into the kitchen. When he returned, he had a small box in his hands, which he placed on the counter alongside seven crowns. "Anything else, Mr. Vern?"

Vern had more questions, but a lot of them didn't make any sense. Asking too much would just confuse them both, so he refrained from talking about the council for now.

He also wanted to ask about last night. But his query upstairs already had been risky enough. What if those two men were still somewhere in the hotel? It wouldn't be funny if they got wind of him not having lost his memories just because he was being unnecessarily nosy.

That would be foolish of him.

So he instead asked, "Yes, one last question. Do you know where the base of operations for the Ascendant Council is located?"

"That would be in Westerleigh Borough, right across from the estate of Duke Armen."

Damn! That's one of the boroughs under the Kingsmen's protection.

Vern got up from the stool and replied, "Thank you."

"Then I'll take my leave."

Beaumont left with a shallow bow and headed toward the reception.

He was only waiting here for me. Or the rent.

Well, that didn't matter. There was a lot more going on here. Why was the Ascendant Council killing the fundamentalists? Was he also one of the targets of those killings, but he had managed to survive due to some criteria? That note given by the man in black didn't seem to show any contempt for the fundamentalists like Beaumont had mentioned.

And then there was the biggest incongruity of all. Who was Administrator Yharl Ballin? All the newspapers only had one name linked to the Ascendant Council, and that was Hoist Thornfield. There was not even a trace of someone named Yharl.

Did Ari really get it wrong? I could always ask again when I meet later. But that didn't seem right. She liked to fool around but never on such serious matters.

Ughh. He sighed.

Every answer came with fifteen strings attached, each ending in a question of its own.

I guess it's about time I try and find a way into the inner districts.

Opening the box in front of him, he pulled out two cartridges from the assortment of fifty. Looking around and finding nobody paying him attention, he swiftly loaded the bullets into the chamber of the ironsong. It was the simplest six-bullet chamber with none of the goodness of steam or newer mechanical arts. *But it's better than nothing.*

Leaving the newspapers and cutlery on the counter, he shoved the ammo box into his coat, placed his top hat on his head, and made for the exit.

As Vern got close to the door, another member of the hotel staff ran toward him and then looked out the peephole before unlocking the complicated lock and pulling open the heavy door just a tad. "Have a safe day out, sir."

Vern thanked the man and exited onto the streets of Fulham borough. The domineering clock tower stood tall among the dwarves that were the rest of these establishments. It was gloomy outside. Clouds obscured the sky, banishing the sun's shine while dry air nipped at Vern's skin, escorted by a chilly wind.

However, the streets had a few new additions today.

A large group of around twenty people in clean clothes were following a carriage in some formation, which seemed to be loaded with grains. In front of that was a man in a clean gray robe, and everyone nearby seemed to look at him reverently.

After a while, the procession stopped in front of a building. The moment it did, a few people came running out of the building and prostrated in front of the man. He then waved his hand as two from the formation moved and unloaded a bag from the carriage, placing it within the building.

Religious leaders actually have consciences?

But other than this procession, the long-stretching Timekeeper Lane was mostly deserted, giving the illusion that no one resided in all these buildings of great beauty that lined the edges of the road.

Vern shook his head and started moving westward. He was going to survey the bridge, which connected this borough to Mosaic Miles—the same place from where Miss Cera had narrated her experience of the duskfall.

But as Vern quickened his strides, a man turned onto Timekeeper Lane from the next intersection, trudging forward with his back stooped, carrying a heavy stone tablet in his hands and an axe tucked under his arm. Vern looked at the man intently as he muddled his way through the walkway, still littered with ragged knickknacks, trinkets, and clothes.

After a while, the man stopped on the walkway in front of a bench and laid down the heavy slab with a thud. Grabbing the pickaxe from under his arms, he started swinging at the cobblestone footpath. With each powerful strike, bricks were loosened, their edges chipping away rapidly.

As Vern got closer to the bench, dirt and broken bricks were piled around a small hole. Then the man hoisted the slab a little off the ground and planted it into the cavity.

After staring at it for a little while, he shoveled back some of the dislodged mud and debris, stabilizing the slab. As Vern passed him by, he caught a glimpse of some words that looked like a name. A name he couldn't read, for the man placed his forehead on the gravestone and began shaking violently.

Muffled sobs echoed in Vern's ears as he continued his westward march.

Before Vern got close to the bridge, he could still make out a few details. He had been asking himself, Just how did the Kingsmen manage to keep people locked outside of the inner districts? And the answer was simpler than he'd thought.

They just blockaded the bridges and stood guard.

This bridge curved upward over the not-so-wide river. At intervals, rusted lampposts stretched out like skeletal arms, their glassy eyes vacant. Upturned carriages lay scattered at its mouth, their wooden bones splintered and entwined. The ground was a canvas of chaos, painted with the scattered remains of abandoned wares.

But more to the point, the restrictions were as strict and brutal as he had thought. The only Kingsman on the bridge was picking up a body that had its head sliced off neatly, carrying it over to the edge of the bridge. Who knew how many such corpses were already sinking beneath that stream of water?

However, just as all this was happening, a man ran out of an alleyway and broke into a dash toward the bridge. He crossed half of it before that Kingsman even managed to drop the corpse down the river.

But the moment the body plopped in the gushing water, two strings of metal, barely visible from so far away, launched out of the Kingsman's ropecaster. They stuck to the other end of the bridge, pulling the Kingsman toward the running man with great momentum as he unsheathed the steaming blades from his back in a swift motion.

Then before Vern could blink, another head flew off in the air as the tall man flicked his blade, and any blood that hadn't evaporated off its seething edge flew away in a grim trail.

Well, this isn't looking very hopeful.

CHAPTER 31

KINGSMAN

This Kingsman, like all others, donned a worn thick leather trench coat held closed by a series of crisscrossed leather strings. It was tarnished with many a scratch, but its frayed hem and ornate stitching only seemed to boast the countless battles it had weathered.

Billowing from the man's shoulders was a capelet of dark gray, which swayed with the gusts of wind. A wide-brimmed tricorn hat sat on his head, crafted from the same darkened leather, which cast a concealing shadow over his face hidden under the neckcloth, which was pulled up like a mask.

Matching leather trousers, mottled with patches of wear, clung to the man's legs, and attached to his hips was a thick brassy belt and a holster. The belt was actually a contraption of immense complexity made by the labor of hundreds of fundamentalists.

Vern knew it as a ropecaster long before it had become a staple among law enforcement and took different names throughout the empire. His master had worked on its initial prototype alongside many other fundamentalists to produce this deadly beauty originally meant to allow men to defy gravity and navigate the otherwise unscalable cliffs of Ashen Heights to extract cranksteel.

However, it was quickly adapted by others to suit their specific needs. This model right here was a masterpiece from the Coven of Truth that blended the cutting-edge advancements of steam core with gear assemblies that provided an unprecedented level of control and precision. It had a well-designed modular mechanism that could cling to any terrain due to its swappable hooks and controlled release and braking capabilities. It even had an arm attachment through which the strand could be redirected for a better aim or to quickly swap the hook.

What made it deadly, however, was its synergy with the overall combat style of Kingsmen and their unmatched skills with the device. They could run circles around their enemies, get the drop on them from uncanny angles, dodge attacks, and never touch ground—all with a single contraption.

It was as lightweight as it came and used the same power source as the ember edge. Those sheaths could heat the blades in a second. Something he would hopefully get his hands on at some point. He had just learned their technical names from the newspaper today. Thin pipes ran down from the steam core in the sheaths, providing the ropecaster—or whatever the Kingsmen called it—with all the energy needed to coil and uncoil the steel strand within for those bursts of speed.

But he quickly forced himself out of his fascinated ruminations. He was here to survey the security, not to drool over all the state-of-the-art contraptions equipped by these death gods. He would need to assess the risks and rewards of trying to get past them. No point antagonizing the city's law enforcers without any hope of success.

He also planned to figure out the limitations of his ability while at it. Vern still remembered all the seemingly random distances he was able to use in his visions from back in the library. But to make a proper, consistent system out of it, he'd either need to use those same visions again or collect new data of his own.

Since the first option would most likely start and end with inhuman murmurings that'd wrench his psyche, he didn't even consider it a valid choice. That was to say, he would have to figure out the range limitations of both his perception and instability inducement.

He had been locked in his room ever since he figured out that vision and hadn't found a chance to determine just how far this metaphysical vision worked.

Vern found himself a nice spot with a clear view of the bridge and leaned onto the rear of a toppled carriage. Taking off his top hat, he opened his perception.

Complexity.

For starters, he focused on another carriage that had its doors ripped apart, lying there overturned about three meters away from him.

Since he didn't plan on manipulating it or inducing any instability in it, he assigned a vague bright shade to one of its wheels. And it turned out to be as easy as shading the wall clock last night.

So he moved on and looked at a suitcase on the ground close to the intersection between Timekeeper Lane and the riverside walkway. *Should be about fifteen to twenty meters.*

He could barely make out the sophisticated lock on it, which he attempted to assign a slate gray.

It came to pass in no time as Vern nodded. *A little taxing but entirely manageable.*

So he upped the ante and looked right at the ropecaster of the Kingsman—barely a hazy shade of gold on the man garbed in black leather within his conventional sight.

But Vern knew exactly what it was supposed to look like. Since perception was more about thoughts than vision, he augmented a greater number of details than what his eyes could resolve. He assigned a pitch-black shade around the back of the man's waist, taking the form of intricate shapes that wound around the interior of the contraption. Alongside this, he also imagined a cloudy white shade for the chamber, which held the coiled steel strand.

The moment he augmented these thoughts onto his perception, he flinched and lost the shades on the carriage door and the suitcase. But the desired shades followed the movement of the Kingsman's waist. *Hmm. So, the greater the distance, the fewer the objects I can have in my perception?*

He clamped his free hand against one of his eyes, which proved to be futile in alleviating the throbbing ache that began pulsating in his head.

But it works!

Even though he could barely keep it up and had inadvertently lost the closer objects from his perception, this was still highly practical.

Not having reached his limits just yet, he looked at the other end of the bridge and quickly found another carriage.

Let's see how far before my eyes—

But Vern's ruminations were rudely interrupted by a group of four men who covered his vision as they exited the riverside walkway onto Timekeeper Lane, right in between Vern and the Kingsman.

Then the tall one on the right spoke with his hand on his holster, "All right, folks. We've already seen enough. We now know how this one operates. It's about time we claim one of these sets for ourselves. Number Three, you will have to distract him by running onto the bridge like that fool earlier. Do NOT start until I signal.

"This one has a habit of hooking his gear at a few choice locations on the bridge. Number Five up on the roof will shoot his hook the moment it latches on to one of those positions, throwing him completely off-kilter.

"However, that won't be the end of things because our rifle is a bolt action. So Five will need time to bolt it again before he can kill this Crown's lackey, while I will need to be closer to make my shot count. So, Three, you will run in and try to hold down the fucker while Two and I will rush in there to help you right away. As long as you can do that—Five or I will deliver the coup de grace. Finally, One, you will keep watch and make sure those infidels from Asea's Church don't come and fuck with us."

All the men grunted. From the looks of it, Two was the one with a hatchet in his hands, while Three was the scrawny one with nothing in the name of muscles, and Four wore aviator goggles that made him look smarter than the rest.

"Hey, One, some fucker is already listening in. What should we do about him?" the guy with the goggles asked in a gruff voice.

"Off with his head if he tries anything funny. Otherwise, we'll take care of him afterward. We can't waste this opportunity for some sissy boy. The Crown's lackeys are rarely alone—it is now or never!"

Hearing their words, Vern backed up and hid behind the carriage as he put his free hand in his trench coat's pocket—his finger resting on the revolver's trigger.

This is troublesome.

Should I escape while they're busy? If he didn't leave right now, there might not be a chance after this.

But this was an interesting situation in its own right. This group of people was planning to steal the gear of a Kingsman. A Kingsman! With just a gun and more numbers. That was . . . stupid.

They might have a chance if they sniped him, but this plan was beyond dumb.

Hmm, now that I'm thinking about it, if they have a rifle, why don't they just snipe him? If their shooter can target a hook, they can obviously aim for the head as well, right? That was indeed very odd.

This actually made him want to stick around. As long as he didn't aid this group in any form, there was little reason for the Kingsman to come after him.

This chaos might actually just be the chance he needed. So he relaxed and surveyed the situation.

During this time, the Kingsman was repeating his previous actions, now carrying the headless corpse on his shoulders toward the edge of the bridge.

All four of the men got into position behind carriages and towers of the bridge as the one that looked like their leader turned back and nodded toward the roof of the building next to Vern, raising five fingers in a signal.

Then after a moment, he tucked in the thumb.

Four.

Three.

Two.

One . . .

"YOU BASTARDS! You can't stop me from going back to my family!" yelled scrawny Three as he burst into a sprint toward the other end of the bridge.

Then as if ready for it this time, the Kingsman turned around with lightning-fast reflexes. Before the headless body that he had shrugged could hit the ground with a thud, steam released from around him as scorching blades appeared in his hands. Two steel strands launched out of his waist and latched on to one of the trusses of the bridge. Exactly like the last time, just on the opposite side of the bridge.

Bang.

A thunderous roar echoed from somewhere above Vern's head as he winced inadvertently.

Then before Kingsman could repeat history and send another head flying across the air, one of his steel strands snapped, and he rolled midair, losing balance as he was pulled in a skewed fashion by one of his strands. Three bolted toward the disoriented Kingsman with even faster speed as the leader and the one with the hatchet sprang forth from the towers of the bridge, sprinting toward the Kingsman in haste.

But there wasn't even a hint of panic in the Kingsman as he took his own burning blade and slashed the other wire, severing it with a single touch.

Bang.

This time, the leader had stopped and shot his revolver. Everything was happening too quickly.

All Vern saw was that the man in leather, who was still rotated awkwardly in the air, was suddenly covered by a glowing redness. And with a flip, he landed stably on his legs. Not a scratch on his body, much less a bullet wound.

Not wasting any time, the Kingsman took the metal wire that was dangling off his ropecaster and redirected it to a contraption through his hands. Then something bizarre happened.

The man reversed his grip on his blades and charged toward his adversaries. Then in this lean rush, with a flourish of his hand, a hook flew from his palms toward the scrawny man at meteoric speed.

"AGHHHHHHHHH!"

Blood spurted out of Three's chest as the hook passed through his heart, and the latch extended, widening the hole. With another flick of his hand, the Kingsman reeled it back and connected the second dangling wire to the attachment on his other palm. His hand shot up in the air as an axe and hacked away at the location he was just standing at a moment ago.

Bang.

Another gunshot resounded, and this time Vern saw it. From the sides of the ember edge was released a haze, a heat so scorching it created a heat wave in its surroundings and instantly melted the small projectile that flew toward it.

That's why they didn't try to snipe him! This is genius! He couldn't believe someone had managed to create a conduction system so efficient that it could release heat in this manner. But the fight wasn't over, and Vern knew now wasn't the time to let his fascination get the best of him. This was a one-sided battle, but it might just be his chance.

Opening his perception again, he found that some aspects of that ropecaster were still shaded. So he started shading them again as the harbinger of death began his dance on the bridge.

It was surreal. He ran on the thin beam of the bridge and suddenly dropped down with a descending strike of his blazing blade, while his other hand shot a delayed steel strand that whirled him back up in the air. The man with the axe didn't even get to scream before his body fell on the ground, a sizzling slanted chop across his head—the wound cauterizing visibly.

Vern's heart beat frantically. This had to be the most unrestrained he'd ever seen a Kingsman. They've never been given such free rein to kill. He had seen more than his fair share of deaths, but this was unreal.

But his chance was getting closer. *Black to the complex pipes and mechanism in the back and gray to the front.* He reinforced the shades in his perception as a throbbing headache began wrecking his mind.

"DEMON! HELP!" yelled the leader, who was halfway across the bridge, his arm bleeding profusely. Turning around, he catapulted himself toward the river and jumped right off the railing.

Kingsmen weren't called the gods of death for no reason. Standing upon a beam on the bridge, the hunter in black leather began his sprint and leapt toward the river, his cape surging around him like the mantle of a reaper. Twirling to one side, he launched his right hand's steel strand onto the edge of the bridge's tower and swung around, perfectly intercepting the leader's trajectory—chopping the man in half.

A torso and legs fell in the water as the reaper ended up perched laterally onto the tower. Then he suddenly kicked against the wall—*bang*—and launched himself high up on the bridge as a bullet created a gaping hole right where he had been perched a second ago, a spiderweb of cracks extending from the point of impact.

But Vern focused. He was about to get his chance!

C H A P T E R 32

OPPORTUNISTIC

Though man with goggles, who was supposed to be a lookout, had started running away the moment their leader missed the shot. So the only troublesome factors left in this whole equation were the sharpshooter on the roof and the Kingsman himself.

Vern still hadn't mixed himself up in the situation, so there was no reason for the Kingsman to come for him. But he had to cross the bridge, and he doubted that he would just happen to run into such a perfect situation anywhere else.

That leader said it is hard to isolate the Kingsmen. Other bridges might have more than one of these reapers waiting, and there's no running past that. So, if he missed such an opportunity, who knew how long it would be before he could get into the inner districts? There was a lot to be done in there.

And just what are they trying to achieve by doing this? Wouldn't it be sufficient to police the inner districts and be done with it? Why stop people from coming in?

Not like they could really stop everyone. All the districts were surrounded by water, after all. A little time underwater with proper gear could allow one to cross any of these rivers. The currents were fast but not enough to be insurmountable for the dedicated.

Ah, Do I really need to come up with all these random conjectures right now? Later.

His eyes were glued to the building with the sharpshooter while the Kingsman jumped from one beam to another, rapidly closing in. Vern started taking measured steps toward the bridge, trying to stay in the shadows as much as possible and avoiding the Kingsman's line of sight.

Vern's heart, just like his head, began thumping. If he didn't get the timing right and ended up killing the Kingsman in a fall or some accident—not only would it weigh on his conscience, but the shooter on the roof would become a real problem. Who was to say that the marksman wouldn't shoot him down when he tried to cross the bridge?

But not taking care of the Kingsman wasn't an option either.

Damn. He focused on the road for one second, and some of the shades from the ropecaster began fading mercilessly, punishing him for losing focus even for a second.

So Vern hid behind the next carriage and peeked over, trying to seem as small as possible, working extra hard to keep that ropecaster in his perception. The reaper was already at the front of the bridge on the closest tower.

Bang.

The man seemed to hold his blades harder. A fiery haze covered him for a second, and he soon walked out of it unscathed. Then with another flick of his hand, a steel strand darted across Vern's peripheral above him. It bolted into a high window of the house beside him as it cracked the glass before entering and latching on to something.

Then the reaper jumped and pressed some triggers on his hands as he began propelling toward the building next to Vern in a rapid arc.

Should I do it now?!

Vern barely contained himself. There was quite some distance between the bridge's tower and any other building. This grapple alone wasn't going to be enough to get him all the way to the shooter. If he destabilized the ropecaster now, it would only backfire.

Before Vern knew it, the man flew above his head and stabbed his right blade into the brickwork of the building, using it as a ledge to launch himself higher. Abandoning the impaled blade mid-jump, he sent another steel strand flying from his left hand toward the railing of the roof.

Almost.

Vern focused on one of the flaws of the ropecaster. At the highest level, it had release and retraction mechanisms. If he could simply get either one of those to stop working, he should be fine since the man wouldn't be able to catch up to him.

These flaws actually did physical damage to the device, so he didn't even have to maintain the vision. He just needed to sneakily destabilize the ropecaster and get as much ground on the man as possible before he could come running after him. Descending this tall building would be no joke, not when the man would have to follow the laws of gravity like a good little human for once and maybe find some stairs.

Bang.

The next shot, however, hit right on the hook, and the strand that had just latched on to the railing recoiled and went limp, throwing the Kingsman off-balance. But the reaper, with his lightning-fast reflexes, plunged his other blade into the building and found footing on the wall. But not for long, as he suddenly pulled it out with both hands and leapt away.

The shadow looming over Vern's head grew larger as the reaper seemed to be coming for him with that seething blade. Vern dodged to the side, and his heart lurched to a halt. *What?!*

But the man already had his right hand outstretched as another swinging strand sent him hurling back into the sky toward the roof at a wide angle.

Fuck! Giving me a scare for nothing.

But this wasn't the time to slowly soothe his heart. There was no way he could predict how the Kingsman would move once he was out of sight, and his perception would be assigned grays incorrectly. Who knew if he could still perform the vision in such a situation?

So the moment the Kingsman gripped the edge of the roof—

Now!

Vern concentrated on the releasing mechanism of the contraption and sought that destructive notion. A crack appeared in his perception, which widened farther until . . .

Thump.

He involuntarily punched the carriage as his top hat fell from his embrace. He wanted to scream, but it would draw unnecessary attention.

That was painful. More painful than he expected it to be. The man wasn't even too far away at this point. Why did it drain him so much? His other hand still clutched his head as the veins around his eyes surged with overwhelming pulsations.

But the vision had done its job. Sparks flew from the Kingsman's waist from the intense grinding and screeching. Still, the reaper didn't pay any mind. He vaulted over the railing and landed on the roof.

Vern pressed harder on his head, picked up the top hat, and made a break for it. He bolted past the carriages, the debris, and all the wreckage that littered the roads.

Bang.

Once on the bridge, he glanced back and saw a red aura in front of the sharp-shooter on the roof of the building. It was a foregone conclusion. He had tried to use the long rifle like a staff to crack open the reaper's head, but the rifle was quickly sliced in half along with his head.

It was fine. Vern easily should be able to find himself some hiding spot by the time the Kingsman could get down from the roof. That's assuming the other end of the bridge was unguarded. If it wasn't—he was done for.

Here's hoping.

He ran down the cobblestone bridge, his coat billowing behind him. His boots thudded loudly, drowned by the gushing of water underneath. His breaths came in ragged gasps, sweat dripping from his brow as he pushed himself harder, faster, one hand still clutching his eyes.

He quickly reached the halfway mark after crossing the three corpses—one headless, one with half a head, and the last one with an intact skull but a gaping hole in his chest. The sight made him shudder, but he kept up the pace. Arriving at the inner boroughs even half a day earlier meant that much less unwarranted grief for Ari.

Luckily, this side of the bridge was as barren as the other. Nothing but vestiges of a once-bustling city littered the bridge—strollers, trinkets, carriages, clothes—just like everywhere else. No more Kingsmen, at least not in his field of vision.

Vern shot a glance behind him, and his pupils constricted.

The Kingsman was hanging on the edge of the wall, making his way down by . . . stabbing through the building and using his blade as a ledge. After gaining some distance, he extracted it and jumped for his earlier blade that was still jutting out of the wall next to the window, completely cold.

But the moment he put his hand on it, he stabbed his other blade next to it and sheathed the first one before pulling it out again in the wake of more steam. Then like some mountaineer, he scaled down the building at breakneck speed with the two seething blades.

Blast it all! These fuckers are crazy! Nothing was normal in this city. Why can't someone just stay within the calculations for once?

Vern accelerated, already at the other end of the bridge. He just had to blend in before the man could catch up.

Sidestepping the many books, canes, and hats that littered the streets, he glanced one more time before a carriage blocked his sight—the reaper was already halfway across the bridge.

Vern's heart wanted to leap out of his chest for this foolish game he had just played, but it would be worth it if he could just get inside one of the buildings.

After breaking his line of sight, he quickly turned into an alleyway and twisted and turned in different directions to confuse his pursuer.

"Do you need some help, my friend?"

Huh? Vern turned in the direction of the voice to see a man running beside him in somewhat shabby clothes.

Vern wanted to stop and ask just what the hell was going on, but this wasn't the Kingsman, and the reaper was probably still hot on his tail. So he took a shallow breath as he squeezed through a narrow gap and replied, "How do you plan on helping me?"

The man ducked just like Vern to avoid hitting his head on the short entrance of the alleyway and responded, "By deflecting your chaser, my friend."

Yeah, Vern didn't know what the hell he meant by that, and nor would he want anyone to fight that monster for him.

"Let's not, and just keep running. He shouldn't be able to locate us."

The man seemed to take that response in stride as he nodded and simply kept up, following all the random directions Vern moved in.

After what seemed to be another minute, Vern ended up on some kind of major street once again and saw a large establishment with a crowd gathered in front of it—plaques and signs in their hands. Vern didn't waste any time and rushed into the crowd, followed by the shabby man, who stopped right beside him.

Passing many people somewhere close to the center, he settled down and again donned his top hat, perfectly blending in with others in the crowd. But not even after a few seconds, he saw a red glow through the tapestry of heads and hats. Someone was walking out of the same street from where he just came.

Sweat trickled down his brow as he took deep breaths—a hard task in and of itself. His body wasn't in quite the shape he would have liked.

Looking at the red aura that seemed to not move around, he thought, *I really am not worth pursuing. Please leave me.*

He looked with his peripheral vision, pulling his hat farther down. Then the red aura seemed to disappear as the faintly discernible shape sheathed his blades.

Yes. You can't have more people slipping into the inner district just to pursue a random nobody like me.

After a tense few minutes, Vern heaved a sigh of relief as the shape finally turned back and entered the alleyway from where it came.

That was a little too close for comfort. It would have been game over—

"So, my friend, how did you do it?"

Vern glanced back at the man, a sharp glint in his eyes. "How did I do . . . what?"

"You orchestrated that, right, my friend?"

Vern turned around and took in the sight of the man among this crowd. He had a scraggy beard, long frayed hair, and a crumpled hat that mostly hid his foreign visage. Draped over his thin frame was a rustic tunic covered by a brown coat that was in tatters. A grimy bandage wrapped his arm from his elbow all the way to his fingers, and his neck was enswathed by a ragged scarf.

But in contrast to his outfit were his sharp eyes under the shadow of his hat and the scabbard that hung on his waist above his balloon pants and tall boots. The man still had one of his hands resting on the ornate handle of the sword as if ready to draw it at a moment's notice.

This threw Vern for a loop. This man didn't look like anyone from the empire, much less a Kingsman. So what was this situation? This question? But Vern still replied to the scraggy swordsman. "I am not sure what you mean."

"Oh, did you really not do it, my friend? I sensed a ripple around you," he said, his accent surprisingly minor.

Since the man wasn't keen on being clear about what he meant, Vern wasn't going to oust himself to some random swordsman for the sake of it. So he feigned innocence. "I just saw a chance and made a run for it, good sir. I don't understand what you're trying to say."

The swordsman looked to be in deep thought, pausing for a while before he replied, "Could you be a mystic that doesn't know about his own gifts?"

CHAPTER 33

INNER DISTRICTS

I am thoroughly confused by your words now," replied Vern to the swordsman, continuing his charade of ignorance.

The man leaned in and whispered next to Vern's ear, "Do you not have a spirit sight, my friend? Do you not see the world in colors of your own?"

Yeah, he knows. So Vern tried to probe him for more information in a quiet voice of his own. "I don't have this spirit sight you speak of, but even if I did, I don't see how that's any of your concern."

The man withdrew and tapped his temple with his index and middle fingers before moving on to his throat, then chest, and finally, the wrist of his sword hand as he enunciated each word clearly, "My friend, know that the gift of gods mustn't be wasted. For those chosen by the gods shall come together to banish evil and keep the innocent out of harm's way."

What had he gotten himself into? Was this another effort at converting him?

Vern stared at the man and his sword, contemplating his next course of action. It might not be in his best interest to share everything, but if a little pretending could get him more information about this so-called 'spirit sight,' why should he say no? Calming down his still-thumping heart, he continued, "I am indeed an avid believer of Lady Lennix. Can you explain more about this spirit sight?"

"For one blessed by the goddess, you sure know very little, my friend. Come, walk with me back to our head station. Someone there can determine your blessing. If it is not from an evil god, I shall explain everything to you."

Determine my blessing? What even was a blessing, anyway? His observation wasn't a gift from some god. It wasn't, right?

Vern sank into contemplation yet again. Did the burden of the Cryptic Constructor count as the blessing of an evil god? But the swordsman had been using the word *blessing* in the context of a chance to observe or something along those lines.

Well. That's sad. What will they do if they learn about my evil blessing? Better not find out. Miss Cera will help me out anyway.

But when Vern focused back to reply, the swordsman's eyes were closed, and his body seemed tense.

"Mister, I don't think—"

The man waved his arm, interrupting Vern.

After a while, he said rapidly, "I must leave now, my friend, for evil is rearing its head once again! But know that the Vigil of Duskfall is embracing the newly blessed in its fold. Show this to anyone at the station and tell them I gave it to you. They won't ignore you like some commoner."

Dropping a silver badge that resembled an eye in Vern's hands, the man pulled his crumpled hat down, nodded, and turned around. "May the clarity guide your path, my friend."

Vern stood dumbfounded with his hand outstretched as the man exited the crowd with uncanny grace, somehow not coming in contact with anyone in the process.

That was . . . so random. He didn't even tell me his name. He came out of nowhere, and then disappeared just as arbitrarily. Where was this station he talked about? What was the Vigil of Duskfall?

Vern frowned as the shouts of the crowd started registering in his mind again. He looked up at the massive letters carved atop the grand building, which read like the name of some bank, and pondered more about this whole situation. It was one thing after another.

Is this swordsman going to be a problem? Hopefully not. The man seemed friendly, understanding, and . . . inviting. But what if they really found out about his burden? How was he going to explain that to anyone? One Hensen was already enough. Another group of people chasing him with pitchforks and swords to banish him like some evil's spawn didn't sound very enticing.

Hmm, I should be able to make a more informed decision after I read more of that observation record in Ari's hands. He pulled out the map and quickly charted a route to Ariane's room.

He would find some time to visit the Ascendant Council and this Vigil of Duskfall later. Ari came first.

Done planning the route, he assessed his surroundings. It looked like some kind of protest.

"—es tell us! Give me back my money!"

"Where is my money?!"

"I can't feed my child. Please!"

"All my savings—"

Similar yells echoed around him as the protesters tried to force their way into the building. *Seems like something has gone wrong with the money flow in the city.* In all honesty, it was a miracle that people could use currency at all. Past large-scale fatalities didn't just lead to the collapse of a fiat currency—they ended up bringing down the whole societal structure. This was far better than the worst possible outcome.

Not having anything to do with this protest, Vern pocketed the badge and weaved through the crowd, exiting it from a different direction than the one he had entered from.

As he navigated the streets, he noticed that the walkways in here were . . . crammed. Not with people, mind you. There were a few lost souls here and there, moving around despondently, but the real noteworthy addition was all the tombstones that were arrayed helter-skelter, close to the inner rim of the walkways.

A group of men were actually working on the task wholesale. A few embedded more tombstones, some dug up new holes, while the rest carved names on them. *I see. They are entombing people right where they disappeared.* That sounded . . . fitting. That man outside Hotel Inkwell might've left the inner district just to pay respect to the ones he had lost.

Vern didn't know what to feel about this. So in this sorrowful atmosphere, he walked all the way to the Athenaeum district. This time, the bridge was in use by civilians, and no reaper stood guard to behead any trespassers.

The lack of bustle alongside those hundreds of tombstones hit him harder when he compared this scenery to his last memories of that carriage ride. Several buildings were in disrepair, their residents nowhere to be seen. Entrances to all the institutions, which used to be bustling with scholars, were devoid of any such activity.

It was like civilization had lost its brightness. Just what he expected, but it hit harder than he would've hoped. Was this going to be the new reality? Lifeless institutions, empty houses, unattended shops, and everything just a husk of its former self?

His brooding continued until he finally stopped outside an ordinary-looking residence on Hartley Street. This was Ari's dormitory. He had never been here in person, but all the letters were relayed under this address.

He was doing well financially for the past few years due to all the royalties, but since earlier this year, he'd been getting a lot more side projects because of his newly earned reputation as a savant. However, even with all this, he was far from being rich, and his master had finally started taking a bigger cut of his earnings—a cut he fully deserved.

With his income, he'd been able to pay for Ari's tuition just fine, but she insisted on earning her daily expenses alongside the rent for the dormitory. That grubby-looking Ari back in the library was nothing more than a facade.

This gave him an idea, and a mischievous smile played on his lips. Quietly laughing to himself, he entered the building.

Dim sunlight illuminated the foyer, and each side of the thin hall had a few doors with numbered wooden plaques next to them. Making his way to the stairs at the back, he ascended to the only other floor, ambling over to room 202. He fixed his clothes, which were a little out of sorts due to all the walking and running, and—

Knock. Knock. Knock.

After rapping thrice, he spoke in an artificially high-pitched voice. "Water meter check! Payment is due, please."

Stepping aside, he hid from the view of the peephole. *He-he. Can't miss this reaction for the life of me.*

Seconds passed by, but there was no response.

Is she not home?

Vern frowned and knocked again, shouting louder. "Water meter!"

Nothing.

He scowled harder and knocked repeatedly. Not in the mood for jokes anymore, he yelled, "Ari. It's Vern. Open the door."

"Ariane!"

Finally, out of patience, he turned the knob out of frustration.

Clack.

Surprisingly, the door opened right up, the lock not performing its intended job. *What?!* Vern's train of thought derailed as many unwieldy scenarios ran through his mind. Pulling out the revolver from his coat, he readied himself and fully pushed open the door.

A dark room with its curtains drawn greeted him as he cautiously walked in, surveying all the corners. It wasn't too big, and everything was visible in a single glance. A table had an astrolabe sitting atop it along with a miniature planetary orrery, crumpled papers, and dozens of books, which were stacked haphazardly.

Next to the window stood a telescope, its viewing mirror primed for stargazing. Then there was a beauty mirror hung on the wall beside a closet, which had its doors ajar. Finally, there was the bed, a plethora of papers littered across it.

But where is Ari?

Heading over to the table, he assessed the star-shaped lamp for a second before he found its string. After he yanked it, the room lit up in a blue glow, and he surveyed it again for things he'd missed.

Checking under the table and finding nothing but dust, he put the revolver back in its holster and sat down on the bed. Furrowing his brows, he looked at all the papers in puzzlement. There was nothing wrong with the room. It was just like she had gone out and had yet to be back. But then, why would she leave the door unlocked?

He wouldn't put it past her that she just forgot to lock it in haste, and that would deserve a scolding. But something didn't feel right.

However, he kept his paranoia in check and waited, reading the notes splayed on the bed. *She might be back soon.*

Vern placed his top hat on the table and hung his coat around the chair. He paced the room, glowering at the telescope.

Why is she always making me worry?

Where was she? This didn't feel right. Why was she not back yet? But then, there could be a million reasons. She might have gone to some friends' place. Or maybe she was out learning more about observation. Or she might have stepped out to buy something. Or . . .

Nothing in the room hinted at anything. The notes were mostly a bunch of jargon about stars and constellations, and the books were more of the same.

He shook his head. *Might as well ask around.* Surely someone else in all these rooms must have an idea, right? This was a dormitory, after all. They might be her friends.

So he strode out of the empty room and stopped in front of the room next door—201. Not feeling any shame at disturbing people out of the blue, he knocked.

No one replied. Repeating his earlier actions, he rapped again, only to be met with silence. So he moved over to 203.

Knock. Knock. Knock.

Footsteps echoed, followed by a woman's voice from within. "Can't anyone let me get some rest? Get the fuck away from my room!"

Vern didn't react and simply asked, "Ma'am, would you happen to know the whereabouts of your neighbor in 202?"

"Yeah, I don't care about pretty bitches. Go away! This is the last warning."

Vern closed his eyes, took a deep breath, and simply moved on. This person wouldn't have told him much anyway.

After four more fruitless attempts, he circled around and reached the door in front of Ari's room. Surprisingly, someone came out. It was a girl with curly brown hair and soft eyes, dressed modestly. Before Vern could say something himself, she cried out in amazement, "Could you be . . . Ariane's brother? That savant?"

CHAPTER 34

COUNCIL IN THE BOROUGH

Vern sighed internally. *This person has to know something, right?*

So he answered with a nod and said, "Yes, that would be me. Sorry for disturbing you like this, but would you happen to know where Ariane might be?"

She seemed excited a moment ago, but after his question, she calmed down.

"I-I don't really. She hasn't been talking to me since . . . uh . . . you know—since everyone disappeared. I tried to chat with her like we used to, but she remained cooped up in her room all day. Our group . . . or what's left of it, wanted to check out what's happening at the academy, but she never opened the door," said the girl.

"She can be . . . difficult at times. Did you notice anything out of place?"

"Yes!"

Vern waited for her as she collected herself and continued, "Some men in white robes were pestering her every few hours."

"She never gave any of us a reaction, but when those men came, she always yelled very loudly. It was always something along the lines of *Please leave me alone.*

"I-I tried asking her about that too. But she just wouldn't talk to me, no matter what. Since it was becoming fruitless, I didn't even come to the door to check yesterday when it last happened."

"Yesterday? Do you remember when exactly?"

"Umm, early morning, I guess?"

"I . . . see. Anything else that you noticed? What did these men look like? Were there any signs or symbols on their robes? Did they say anything?"

"Um . . . not really. I was only ever looking at their backs through the peephole, and their robes were pure white. I never heard them say anything at all. They just knocked and stood there for a while before leaving."

"Did something happen to her?" she murmured, clutching at the hem of her day dress.

"The door was unlocked, and she hasn't returned in the past two hours."

The girl seemed surprised as she stuck out her neck, looking past Vern, and murmured, "Did they really take her away?"

The same worries were running through Vern's mind as he tried to think of who these men in white robes could be. Someone from the Ascendant Council? Asea's church? But if they were coming here repeatedly, then that's to say they didn't use force for the first . . . uh . . . ?

"Sorry, but can you recall how many times these white-robed men came?"

"I heard it about seven or eight times, including the one yesterday."

So, at least the first eight times, they didn't use any force and just asked for her cooperation? Did they want something from her? That observation record? But how would they ever know that Ari had it on her person? Was it something else?

"I-Is she going to be all right? Is there anything I can do to help?"

"You've already helped quite a bit, miss. Thank you very much," said Vern with a shallow bow.

She seemed disappointed as she replied, "Hope you find her safe and sound. Please tell her to come chat with me. There's a lot to talk about."

The girl curtsied and seemed to want to say something. Her eyes lingered on his face, but she eventually closed the gate.

Not minding the awkward farewell, he went back into Ari's room and donned his hat and coat. Grabbing a notepad from her desk, he penned a short note. *Ari, this is Vern. Please wait here tonight if you're reading this, I will explain everything when I am back.*

Shoving all the clutter on her bed to one side, he left the pad with that note in a conspicuous position. Closing the door, he left her room.

His next destination was the Ascendant Council. It was about time he paid them a visit. Repercussions be damned. Someone was messing with Ari, and he wasn't going to sit around and wait for bad news.

Westerleigh borough lay beneath a solemn, amber evening sky, a veritable forest of gothic mansions that loomed over the winding cobblestone streets. Each edifice was a brooding silhouette of formidable architecture, punctuated with pointed arches and intricate stonework. Their tall metal gates supported by sprawling fences housed massive gardens, austere in their dark elegance.

Steam released from the vapor spire of the carriage as it came to a halt. Vern stepped out, one hand on his top hat as he paid fifteen crowns to the man. Carriage ride prices were becoming exorbitant. Then with another plume of steam, the carriage sputtered away as he stood there, his eyes closed, waiting for his vision to clear.

This design with sideways exhaust is just atrocious.

Heaving a sigh, he looked at the map again. The driver said he wasn't allowed to drive all the way to Duke's residence. But it was only a few minutes' walk from here.

So he started his march up the inclined road as carriages drove down the hill— some with unique designs, others exhibiting the symbols of noble families. This indeed had to be the place for the aristocracy with all those unnecessary and inefficient design choices.

Passing by gardens that seemed to be forests and bungalows that looked to be millennia old, he reached a mansion that would do better to be called a castle with all those flying buttresses, spires taller than the highest surrounding hills, and labyrinthine design.

But Vern wasn't here to admire the grounds. This was Duke Armen's manor.

So he tore his eyes away from the grandiose architecture and looked to his right instead. Under the sky that was growing more amber by the second stood another baroque mansion, its design a touch . . . eerier.

Nowhere near as grand as that castle, but large in its own right, it was built of some obsidian stone with sharp corners and tall, narrow windows. The roof was steep and angular, with towering chimneys and wrought iron detailing. Ivy clung to the sides of the building, crawling up toward the roof and adding a haunting touch. The outer entrance was grand, with large double doors flanked by stone statues and a fence bounding the whole place.

But those weren't the only statues. Dozens of other sculptures lined the courtyard, leaving nothing but a path that went from the outer entrance to the mansion's door. When Vern looked closely, some were figurines of . . . Lady Lennix? But many other unknown statues crowded around them. Some had their faces melted off, while others had hollows for eyes.

How could rock statues melt unless it was intentional? Just why the hell would you have such sculptures in a religious gathering location, for steam's sake? And next to Lady's likening at that? Not that it looked religious at all. It was more than a little chilling.

Shaking his head, he pushed open the grand door, which, surprisingly or unsurprisingly, was neither guarded nor locked.

Walking past bronze statues of differing heights and forms, he looked to his right beyond the statues. The section wasn't visible from outside due to the fence, but it really started giving him the creeps.

Why the hell were there tombstones in here? Why were some of them even larger than the freaking statues? If not for that signage by the inner entrance boldly proclaiming *Ascendant Council* in elegant fonts, he would have assumed he was in the wrong place.

Well. If they can be in the news and have so much fame and members, it might as well be their trademark. This whole architecture seems like one of those millennia-old ones, anyway. Maybe they just never refurbished it.

Not ready to shy away from the spooky atmosphere, he crossed the statues and stood in front of the gate.

Knock. Knock. Knock.

No one responded, and a feeling of déjà vu arose in him. Not even bothering to knock another time, he simply turned the knob, and this time logic prevailed—the door opened. It wasn't very surprising though. Clubs were supposed to be free to enter, after all. It's the engagement with other members and perks that warrants the membership fee.

However, they were supposed to be lit and well-maintained. This . . . was neither. Faint light entered from the narrow, tinted windows and illuminated some of the articles by the entrance. A reception desk stood in front of two spiraling staircases that met each other on the second-floor landing—splitting again until they met at the next one.

To both sides of the landing were long halls—silver patterns on the interior doors shimmering even in this dim vista. But even with everything shrouded in darkness, the opulence of the club was clear to his eyes. Extravagant woodwork was a staple in every element of his surroundings: the balustrades of the staircase, the thick pillars that supported the ceiling, bookcases, chairs, and couches.

All of this wasn't in the style of this era at all. Only a few contraptions existed in here, like that water clock or that ancient steam-powered piano whose notes would boom through the whole building. The room and its contents were made in the traditional designs from the time before fundamentals were discovered.

It was to the point that even the chandelier, which wasn't currently ignited, was one that used kerosene, something that caretakers would have to refuel every night. No pipes ran to the ceiling, which had long ago mechanized such tedious processes. *Now I doubt they even have gas pipes coming in from the city. It is just like those backwater towns that refuse to adopt devices crafted using insights from fundamentals.*

But Vern shrugged and moved on. He wasn't here to comment on their distaste for fundamentals. As long as they could help him with observation, they could live in huts like wandering hermits for all he cared.

However, the noise of the club was notable.

Clack.

Thud.

Angh.

A myriad of low sounds registered in his ears as if coming from far away . . . or perhaps muffled by the doors. Footsteps coming from the ceiling also shuffled around above him.

So Vern hollered, "Hello! Is anyone here?" All the sounds disappeared, the room falling into a pin-drop silence. But after another few seconds, the hushed noises resumed their earlier cadence around him.

Vern didn't walk inside the building completely and remained outside, one hand keeping the door propped open. This wasn't the most inviting environment. He had expected quite a lot of things coming up here, but this wasn't one of them.

The Ascendant Council was supposed to be a group of politickers and motivated individuals that worked toward shared goals. They were meant to be these highly enlightened individuals that had their own perspectives regarding fundamentalism and observation.

Not this . . . creepy mansion with people hiding in the shadows. This helped him make up his mind about a purchase. It was about time he started carrying a pocket illuminator on him—maybe even a winding one so it wouldn't run out at the most inopportune times. It would help him feel less anxious navigating Elmhurst, where any place could become dark out of nowhere.

Vern stood there and waited, focusing on all the muffled sounds.

Thump. Thump.

See. See. See.

Anghh. Anghh.

Eyesabovehelpgoddownseemehelplife . . .

Hungh. Hungh.

Secret I tell come.

It was all so bizarre. Faint echoes of laughter, shouts, unintelligible whispers, and anguished cries came from far-off rooms, softened and distorted by the mansion's many walls and corridors. They seemed to come from everywhere and nowhere all at once, permeating the whole mansion. Apart from that were the rattling and creaking of doors overlaid by some sounds that didn't make any sense to him.

But in this amalgamation of garbled voices was a special one, coming from one direction in particular. *Yes. Seems like it's from the first door down the right hall.* It said, "Secret, I tell. Come. Come." Vern concentrated on it further. "You. Yes. You. I got secrets. Give it to me, and I give secrets."

Not sure what to make of it, he just waited there, not making any move to walk in. The whole thing was giving him the creeps. He had read enough fiction to know not to jump headfirst into situations like this.

Minutes passed, but nothing happened. The ambient noises continued their course, except for the voice that uttered new sentences every few seconds. "Come. I show secret. Secret of the sphere. Come, I give secret, you give back."

Sphere? Insight sphere?

C H A P T E R 35

TRAP

*I*s he saying he knows some secret about insight spheres? *Was that even possible? Weren't these people blind to the fundamentals?*

Nonetheless, anything new regarding fundamentals had to be explored. This wasn't what he had come for, but the gloomy sun was setting in the west, losing its vigor by the second. Standing here and listening to all these noises wasn't doing him any favors.

What should I do? Go in and try to converse with the nutcase, or just come back tomorrow in the morning? But there's no guarantee that it would be any different tomorrow. He stood there, unsure of what course of action to pursue. But when all those turbulent clouds up in the sky began taking a purple hue, he finally made up his mind.

He first moved back out of the mansion and looked closely at the door's lock. It was a traditional key lock mechanism that was at least a few decades old—though its bolt was quite hefty. If it came down to it, his revolver might not be able to break through it in a hurry.

Yes, he was planning his escape before going in. Call this paranoia, but he wouldn't put it past these jerks to try to entrap a fundamentalist. He had thought this was just another organization that loathed his kind. But the more he looked at the interior design, the more he realized that things weren't so simple.

On top of that, he had no idea just how many of these people were in there. He believed as long as he had a clear path back outside, he should be fine.

Done with his basic analysis, he hoisted over one of the statues from the corridor and propped open the door with it. Then with a deep breath, he gripped the ironsong properly and walked in.

With slow steps, he passed pillar after pillar and his heartbeat rose proportionally as the noises became clearer. Some of them were cries, some were growls, but barring that, the man behind the first door spoke with a higher and faster pitch. "Yes! Yes! Give me, I give back. Secret of sphere."

Moving in this heavy darkness, barely avoiding all the obstacles, he treaded lightly toward the right hall. But then his heart lurched to a halt—

Shuffle. Shuffle.

Something moved behind him. With a swift jerk, he glanced back only to notice a shadow flitting past on the second floor.

Fuck. I really shouldn't be doing this. I am really not moving an inch next time without a light. This is unnecessarily tense. Glancing at the wide open main door, he felt some semblance of control and inhaled deeply, taking measured strides toward the right hall.

"Yes! Faster. Take my secret."

When he walked past the staircase, a dark corridor stared back at him, eerie noises playing from some of the rooms within. The thought of where these sounds originated from sent a shiver down his spine.

Suppressing the dread boiling up within him, he stood a few paces away from that door, the ironsong aimed at the silver patterns around the glassy insets on the gate. It was ready to be unloaded if something tried to come for him abruptly. Fuck the empire's laws—this was necessary for survival.

Then with a low voice, Vern asked, "I am here. Tell me the secret."

"Yes, yes. Give it to me, I tell the secret," replied the voice from within, no doubt addressing Vern. The high pitch of that shrill voice made his hairs stand on end, but he still negotiated.

"First tell me the secret. I will give it to you after." Vern had no clue what the man wanted, but it was obviously not going to be good. Since he planned on escaping anyway, what did it matter? What was a fair exchange when one party was not right in the head?

He could ask about this secret and make a run for it. He didn't like the idea of wasting his evening and fifteen crowns. Something fruitful should come out of his long-awaited excursion to the Ascendant Council. If he couldn't procure a copy of the *Observation Record of Subjectivity*, it'd do to learn some secrets about the insight sphere and fundamentals.

"You will give it to me, right?" asked the voice. Suddenly, light radiated out from the dull glass insets on the door. A silhouette could barely be made out from the disjointed glassy embedment.

Vern slowly approached and replied, "Yes."

But before Vern could get a better look, the voice uttered, "Okay! Then give it to me after. I tell secret."

"The sphere can preserve your thoughts. Ha-ha. I can't see, but I can preserve."

However, the voice had nothing else to add except some heavy breathing. So Vern inquired further, "That's it? Can you explain a little more? That's not enough for me to give it to you."

"EEHAHHH! I give secret already. EHAHHH! EAHHAHH!"

"Okay, just tell me how you found out about it? You can't even peer into an insight sphere, right?" he asked, hoping to get something more legible out of this conversation.

"The whispers told me. They told me I can gather my thoughts and unleash them later. To look at them. The fundamentals. Yes, I will be able to see them. Now give it to me."

"What whispers?"

But he shrieked and banged on the door. "GIVE IT TO ME!"

"I will give it to you. But how do I believe that you're telling the truth? What if you lied to me? Prove to me that you're speaking the truth." Vern rambled whatever came to his mind, trying to pry more out of the lunatic.

The voice suddenly quieted down, and out came the sounds of rummaging as falling metals clanked on the floor followed by the creak of the door opening. "Here.

My thoughts in there. See . . ." said the guttural voice as a pale hand stretched from behind the door, an insight sphere resting atop his palm.

That's the real deal!

Vern wasn't a miser or anything, but the sight of another insight sphere fueled his greed. Forget everything else, this sphere alone would be worth it. So, with slow steps, he steadily crept toward the hand—his revolver aimed right where the chest connected to this arm should be. He didn't aim for the head because it would be harder to predict even with those glassy insets and their distorted glimpse inside. There was no chance of missing on the chest.

"GIVE IT! I SHOW! I ALREADY SHOW! GIVE IT!"

The pale hand seemed to shake in the murky darkness, but the insight sphere atop it breathed some light into the environment. "Okay, let me check what's in there. I will give it back to you," said Vern as he extended his hand toward the top of the sphere, ready to wrench it from the grasp of the pale hand.

But the moment his palm touched the smooth glassy surface, something gripped his wrist.

FUCK! Vern's heart seemed to jump out of his chest as he let go of all his inhibitions and pulled the trigger.

Bang!

"AAAAAAHHHHHHHHHHHHH!"

FUCK! FUCK! FUCK! He fucking shot a person! The thought rampaged in his mind as he barely managed to keep the revolver from jumping due to the recoil.

But the moment the grip on his arm loosened, he yanked the sphere free from the clutches of that thing. Not wasting even a moment, he turned around . . . and it all went dark.

Thump.

With a loud clack, the front door clicked shut. The fucking door, which had a heavier-than-rock statue propping it open, had closed shut!

What in the name of seven steams is this bullshit? Someone just moved that thing from behind me, and I didn't even hear a thing? This is bad!

There was that madman behind him inside the room, and now there was someone in front of him by the door as well. He was pinched between two unknown enemies. This was exactly what he had hoped to avoid with his vigilance. Vigilance that ended up being inadequate.

Where to? Running upstairs wasn't an option. Going from two to twenty enemies would be foolish beyond comprehension. The windows were too narrow and high up. A single shot would only break a small section, and even after that, he'd need to be able to jump high enough to reach them.

He had also analyzed the lock on the door, but he wasn't sure if he could use instability inducement on it. It was worth a shot, though. So in his short burst of motion, he hadn't even looked back to assess the damage of the bullet, but instead began shading the lock on the door within his perception.

But this was such a weird problem. The lock wasn't complex. It was quite a simple device. It had a crevasse for the key to go in, which when turned, would push a long heavy latch out that would bolt it with the other door. There wasn't much in the name of gears or anything.

Ugh!

This boggled his mind, but he still shaded the key's aperture to be a slate gray and the bolt a cloudy white. But that notion, which usually guided his thoughts, didn't emerge.

"AHJHHJHHGGHH!"

A shriek resounded behind him, sounding like the squeal of a dying pig, quickly followed by a shrill shout.

"GIVE IT TO MEEEE! GIVE ME YOUR EYES! AAAAAAJJGHH!"

Vern's breath caught in his throat, but he shoved the insight sphere into his coat and jumped over the couch, sidestepping the pillars in a frenzied run. Luckily, his memory was clear enough to remember exactly where all these obstacles were arranged on the ground. His eyes could barely see anything.

It was hard to focus on shading something right in front of his eyes, much less the door. But he had to do it.

As he concentrated on shading with more details and looked for that flaw, he could barely focus on his surroundings. But then his pupils constricted as a sheen appeared in his eyes, high up in the air. A sheen that was rising higher and stretching farther back as if getting set to cleave back down with overwhelming might.

This has to be the person that closed the door!

Not second-guessing himself, he grabbed one of the pillars and transferred his momentum to the side in a short spin when the glint came smashing down like a meteor.

Crrackk.

Wood splinters flew all around Vern as an axe impaled the ground next to him. A huge shadow seemed to loom right behind the handle of that huge axe. He wanted to scream, but—*damn*—if that pulled more of these suckers down, he would only have himself to blame.

Now a little off course, he bolted toward the door as fast as he could while he tried to think of a fucking flaw in that lock. Just what was a complexity-related flaw in that lock? Maybe the aperture? The movement of the latch? He flitted through many ideas, and slowly a notion began forming in his mind.

YES!

It was very faint, but he let it guide his thoughts, and a crack appeared in his perception. A very small crack, which grew wider by the second, but even when he was almost upon the door, the crack didn't even cover half his vision. Then suddenly, the notion concluded its guidance, and all the shades disappeared as he braced for the impact and rushed at the door with all his might.

Thud.

His shoulder hurt like a bitch, and he found himself recoiling from the large door, which didn't budge at all.

Fuck me! This . . .

He tried turning the knob, but nothing worked. The heck was he supposed to do now? It was really dumb of him. *Obviously, someone can just move the statue away—the same as how I put it there. Why did that make me feel safe? But who the hell would expect axe-wielding psychos in a public club?* He was already feeling too paranoid for having done what he did.

But now really wasn't the time to cry about all this. If it wasn't working, he would just have to try something else. So he turned around and shot another bullet at the looming shadow behind him.

Bang!

It seemed like it should've hit the thing, but Vern didn't wait around to find out and ran toward the left hall as another piece of furniture was hacked to pieces right behind him.

"EYES! GIVE ME YOUR EYESS! I WILL SEE THE FUNDAMENTALS!"

Immediately, a humanoid shape lunged for him, raving madly. Vern didn't get an opportunity to retaliate as he was swept up in the momentum, falling sideways with a thud—that thing still on top of him. He didn't even get a chance to aim his revolver before the hollows above and beneath his eye socket were met with an unbearable pressure as bony fingers squeezed in a bid to pull his eye out.

"AGHHHHH!" Vern screamed as the monster above him clenched his eye with intense fervor. Still, he just shoved his pistol wherever he felt some skin, and he shot it point-blank.

Bang!

As anticipated, the grip on his eye loosened. Not missing the chance, he kicked the thing hard in its stomach and backed away, haphazardly getting back on his feet. His vision was hazy, so he closed his right eye and continued to take long strides toward the left hall.

"EYES! I GIVE SECRET! GIVE ME EYES!"

In this nerve-racking chase, he noticed that one of the doors was ajar. It didn't look like someone was behind it. Skipping any further contemplation, he entered the room and slammed the door behind him, turning the lock as it clicked shut.

At least there was no one in the room. Finding another crazy might have been the end of the line for him. Also, the room actually had a window, but he soon saw it was fucking encased within iron bars!

Crack.

"AGH!"

An intense pain shot through his shoulder as blood spurted out of it. Vern muffled his scream and moved away from the door. That axe from before had just come smashing through the door. But luckily, it had lost most of its momentum before it hit his shoulder, or he would have already lost his arm. If that axe had landed even a little to the side, he wouldn't be thinking right now.

His mistakes were quickly piling up.

Fuck. Fuck. Fuck. Fuck. Why aren't they dead yet?

Chapter 36

INSIGHTS

I need to calm down.

He squeezed his eyes shut, took a deep breath, and sat down on the bed—completely ignoring the door that was buckling under the forceful blows, splintering crevices opening all over it.

Zoning out his surroundings, he considered his options. *I have about twenty seconds before that door gets hacked to bits.*

Okay. So, I was able to find some flaw in the lock outside, but either it wasn't large enough, or complexity is just not the right outlook to find flaws in something as simple as a lock. But then what else could work? I don't have another hour to sit here and muddle through my options.

This was all because he had wanted to know that fucking secret. What secret? That one can gather and unleash thoughts using an insight sphere? What in the name of mighty cogs did that even mean?

But there must be something to it. The madman outside even said something about his thoughts being in there. With furrowed brows, Vern pulled out the glassy sphere from his pocket. It looked nothing out of the ordinary—four vertical lines and one horizontal that divided it into eight octants. But what was he to do with it? He didn't have a lumenscope with him to peer into fundamentals.

However, this reminded him. He had never tried to perceive an insight sphere with his viewpoint.

Not wasting any time unproductively, he tried to assign a pitch-black shade to the thing, recalling its immense complexity. But then, something unexpected happened. The tones assigned to it . . . just disappeared.

Frowning harder, he repeated his action of assigning it shades, and it was as if his thoughts were swallowed by the sphere. His mind went adrift, and a sense of loss filled him. *This . . . Is this what he meant by the secret? That insight spheres can preserve thoughts?*

Then can there be any way to release those thoughts and use them to my benefit?

Instead of trying to find complexity in the sphere, he simply sensed it within his perception without meaning to shade it—and a feeling arose in him. A feeling that he had been longing for. It was like he was within a projection of an insight sphere, peering at fundamentals.

Just detecting it within his perception gave him the same sensation as when he started his sessions with a lumenscope. He was right at the core of the sphere—at the void of initiation—in that empty black space where ideas were born from nothing. As usual, he got the feeling that logically comprehending the happenings in one direction would allow him to make progress. But there was more here, exceeding the norm.

Typically, the sense of direction within projections came from the kind of logic one encountered as they followed an insight. For example, if every new insight he came across had to be comprehended using ideas related to destruction, then that would mean he was moving toward the lower southwestern octant, the domain of the chaos fundamentalists.

And based on similar loose concepts, one could reorient themself to the direction they want to further explore in the domain of their choice. But something was different this time. He felt his own thoughts of complexity that had just vanished coming from one specific direction.

However, that wasn't the end of it. There was more. Two other directions held some different kinds of thoughts. Thoughts that weren't his own. One was diametrically opposite to his, while the other was somewhere in a direction between them both.

But will any of this really help me resolve this situation? Wouldn't I be better off just shooting them through the door while reloading in safety?

However, he quickly realized that these options weren't exactly mutually exclusive. He could still shoot blindly if this didn't work.

But traversing those thoughts of complexity, which he had just instilled in the sphere, wouldn't give him any edge.

A change was necessary to escape this dire predicament. So, he picked the direction that was in the middle of the two opposing thoughts and began traversing the fundamentals. Navigating the early sections of fundamentals was easy.

The void of initiation was the genesis ground where concepts bloomed from nothing. As long as one continued comprehending the next idea based on assumptions from prior sections, one could build up on those insights and continue progressing in fundamentals—even come across something unknown by mankind.

For Vern, he had more than mastered the first few hours of insights in five of the octants. And luckily, the one he was moving toward happened to be in the lower northwestern octant. If it had been an octant he had no clue about, it'd have taken him over three hours to reach those hidden thoughts. He didn't have three minutes, much less three hours.

But one could traverse fundamentals at the speed of thought if one used their previous insight—and he did just that. The usual ideas of this octant filled his senses as his mind swam through the fundamentals, thoughts cascading in a logical fashion.

From nothingness, particles coalesce. Particles form matter. Matter, by nature, adheres to conservation. Conservation invokes protection. Protection cultivates maintenance. Maintenance implies durability. Durability suggests endurance. Endurance births resilience. Resilience favors adaptation. Adaptation breeds transformation. Transformation holds essence, an echo of inheritance. Inheritance implies perpetuity. Perpetuity intertwines with preservation. Preservation is a dance eternally enshrined within existence.

Veering from a simple cluster to a symphony of preservation, he moved, traversing the fundamental to the profound. And before he knew it, he approached what he'd like to call a cloud of foreign ideas. They were quite consolidated and seemed less abstract than fundamentals.

Boom.

The moment his thoughts nearly reached that cloud, it was as if an explosion went off in his mind—ideas flitted past his perception, and his brain, which was fatigued and scared, had a surge of vigor imbued in it. Thoughts generated in his mind at an unreal pace, flooding him like a whirlwind.

It was like those fabled moments of infinite insight that primal fundamentalists talked about, where each second allowed him profound insights to whatever he set his mind on.

Crackk.

Drunk with pleasure, he almost let himself think through all his unanswered questions, when reality came knocking. The axe tore big chunks out of the door before its gleaming head fully appeared in his sight. The wielder then turned it sideways and began wrenching as the wood came apart in patches.

Damn! Almost fucked myself over.

His heart, which had quickened out of excitement, calmed down, and he found himself back in control. Instead of solving random problems, he needed to find some way to overcome this situation. Fight or escape were the only two options available to him. But he had to figure out the exact details of what to do.

Not even a moment passed by in this state of unparalleled clarity as millions of combinations ran through his mind, and he found the answer.

This is transcendent! Just what kind of thoughts are stored within this insight sphere?

But these were not to be wasted like this. So he exited this trance—abandoning his progress of fundamentals—and dropped the sphere back into his pocket.

Finally, with a plan in mind, Vern got up from the bed and sought to use his new idea on the door in front of him. Opening his right eye, which still gave him a hazy view of the world, he conjured a perception.

Integrity.

A simple word. But the number of thoughts he had gone through to come to this conclusion couldn't have taken less than a few hours of brainstorming with his notepad. It was one of those things that seemed obvious once you knew about it, but until then, you were left trying to retrofit hundreds of variables to suit specific needs. In this case, it was to adapt the idea of composition to balance but in a broader sense than complexity.

But that transcendent state had its own limitations. He had hoped to find some way to outright eliminate his opponents, yet he came up with nothing. He couldn't think of any valid flaws within the bodies of his enemies that would trigger that notion of instability in his mind.

It was as if his thoughts were accelerated—but that was it. He was still limited by the information available to him. No outlandishly smart ideas came to him to eradicate his enemies.

However, this should be enough to get out of this immediate predicament. Integrity utilized an even simpler method than complexity in looking for flaws. It was vaguer in nature and could apply to a wider range of objects. Though it would probably come along with worse efficiency.

So without lingering any further, he shaded the lock of the door in front of him. In terms of flaws, there were a few odd scratches on the latch and a bend in the metal that it had developed from all that pushing. He shaded the latch closer to black while giving the rest of it a white to depict its greater integrity. Then he focused hard on the bend and considered how it could be the flaw.

And as expected, that notion appeared in his mind—not as faint as before. So he guided his thoughts toward that notion, and a crack appeared in his perception. A crack that grew wider by the second and . . .

Smash.

The axe-wielder and the other madman who had been scratching the door with his nails came crashing down as the door swung open. Ready for this, Vern didn't give them a chance to reorient themselves and jumped over the two men, exiting the room. One was a burly man with unclear features, while the other had two large holes in his pale face that bled black blood in small quantities.

"EYES!"

The smaller man tried to grab at his ankles but failed due to his awkward position, and Vern passed right over them, bolting toward the main door. Already clear on what to do, he repeated his earlier actions and used instability inducement on this main door with integrity in mind.

Clack.

A short sound resounded from the door, and Vern raced toward it with all his dexterity, avoiding the obstacles to the best of his capabilities while maintaining speed.

However, right when he was at the foot of the staircase, something appeared in his peripheral vision, and he felt his eyes drawn toward it.

A silhouette was descending the stairs, short highlights of light from the window drawing an outline of a woman. Two glowing red orbs floated in place of her eyes, which seemed to radiate blood. Inadvertently, when he peered into them, a chill went down his spine, and the hall of era-old wooden furniture became covered with blood and gore.

His heart disagreed, but his brain, which was still, knew now wasn't the time to stop.

Completely ignoring this feedback from his eyes, he tore his gaze away from those uncaring pupils and rammed his shoulder into the pair of gaping maws that took the place of that large door. This time, he didn't bounce back and instead felt the door swing wide open, barely catching his footing on the steps outside.

Not daring to take another glance back inside, he charged through the path of sculptures, which now looked like bleeding cadavers, and cut right through them. Shoving open the huge iron doors dripping with blood, he felt his vision return to normal as the dark sky greeted him, illuminating Duke Armen's castle.

Nothing stopped him, not even himself, as he continued to make distance from that building, dashing downhill.

He only stopped when his lungs felt like bursting, right next to the bridge back to Mosaic Miles.

What the fuck was that? Those pupils . . . That sight. Just who the heck was that?

Taking mouthfuls of air, one after another, he regulated his heart, which was miraculously still pumping blood and hadn't failed him just yet. Dropping down on the ground, he leaned onto the tower of the bridge and sat there as the passersby looked at him suspiciously.

CHAPTER 37

HEIGHT OF THE SKY

Vern sat on the bed by the window next to the telescope as he slowly cleaned away the blood from his shoulder with cotton and some purge tincture. *Ugh.*

It hurt. It steaming hurt. Never in his life had Vern gotten himself a wound like this. He'd had a few new experiences recently, but they were all more or less psychological or under conditions where he was numbed. The worst he'd had was a broken bone as a kid, but even that didn't hurt as much.

Luckily, the wound was shallow, and he hadn't broken any bones, or it would have been a nightmare to deal with.

Crack my cogs. Just what the hell did I get myself into?

He still couldn't come to terms with whatever had happened at the Ascendant Council. Why were his bullets useless on that pale man? Why did those monsters instinctively want to either gouge his eyes out or hack him to pieces? Then there was that woman. Just what was that macabre sight he experienced after briefly peering into her red eyes?

Moreover, his previous questions remained completely unanswered. Where was the stalker who gave him that note? Who and where was Yharl Ballin? What about that Hoist guy? All that the Ascendant Council had in store for him was a bunch of psychos, out for blood.

Still, he was able to confirm a few things from this trip.

First was that those people in white robes who took Ari did not belong to the council. There was no conclusive proof of this, but there was no way a proper organization was running in that haunted manor. That atmosphere wasn't conducive to disciplined ranks and structure. Also, dwellers of the council seemed to not want to come out of their burrow since they didn't chase him outside.

It is already past nine. Ari had yet to be back, so it was possible that those white robes had somehow managed to get her to join them or something along those lines.

Then there was the thing about Hoist and Yharl. Who was the real leader of the Ascendant Council? And just what had the leader done to turn its members into . . . that? Definitely something had gone wrong after duskfall, and figuring out more about that might lead him closer to Yharl Ballin.

But on the bright side, he got himself another insight sphere. He had used up a big chunk of those invigorating thoughts in the lower northwestern octant, but there was still some leftover. And then there was another set of unknown thoughts floating directly opposite to his own regarding complexity. One he would try and explore once he felt a little better.

His mind was exhausted right now, and doing anything related to observation was out of the picture for the night.

Putting the sphere back, he wrapped a bandage around his shoulder and used his teeth to tie a sloppy knot. Once done, he took the earlier note he had penned for Ari and placed it on the bed again.

Careful not to scrape his bandage, he donned his coat, which now had a tear on its shoulder, and left the room—regrettably, without his top hat. He had lost it at some point during that haphazard chase at the Ascendant Council. *It was a matching one too.*

Shaking his head, he descended the dormitory stairs. He was in dire need of some food and materials. Food to survive, and materials to make himself a portable lamp because he wasn't going into any more of these dark places without some form of contraption to illuminate his surroundings.

Buying a premade lamp was also an option, but he doubted that top-notch contraptions were sold on the streets in times like this.

Exiting the building, he looked up at the rift complementing the waning moon. But as he was about to shrug it off, a wild thought crossed his mind. *What if I calculate the height of this rift?*

He stood there rooted in place, trying to figure out how to go about doing this. Who cared if the information would be useful or not? The idea sounded fun, and it might just ease his mind to know exactly how high up this thing was in the atmosphere. Better to rationalize it than leave it as some unknown cosmic phenomenon.

Right now, it looked like the rift was in front of the moon because of how some of the cracks spilled over and covered some of the moon's glow. This simple experiment would make it obvious. So he pulled out the map and looked at the scale on its corner. It said that every column and row which divided the map into cells was about four hundred meters.

Hmm, I should be able to get a reasonable accuracy if I walk about two kilometers. So he picked two points on the map, exactly five cells away from each other and in a straight line. To keep it easy for himself, he set one endpoint to be the bridge that connected this district to the Silverthread district. He wasn't an astral fundamentalist, but he knew enough about parallax distance measurement to get a rough estimate.

He would first find a parallax angle at one point in the district, then at another and compile the information to get the height of the rift. Running back up into Ari's room, he grabbed the astrolabe, walked back outside, and made his way toward the other point he'd marked on the map. It was just a few hundred meters south of Hartley Street.

Some men were still toiling away, digging the walkways, entombing new graves, while the soft rustling noises on the roof marked the presence of Kingsmen in the area. He had no reason to disturb any of them.

Once at the spot, Vern positioned himself strategically under the expanse of dark sky as he intently peered upward through the small lens of the astrolabe. The motion of lifting his shoulder made him groan in pain, although it was already noticeably better than before. Focusing on the top left corner of the rift, he traced an invisible line from his eyes to the blue-red fissure and then straight down to the cobblestones underfoot.

Bending down, he grabbed a stone from the walkway and put it at the imaginary line from the rift to the ground, and then by keeping the astrolabe flat on his hands, he found the angle between his position and the stone.

He duplicated the same efforts for the moon to have another reference.

During all this, the tombstone workers stopped and looked at Vern with amusement, but he simply jotted down the measurement of the angle in his notepad. Without explaining himself, he began his march toward the other end of the district, leaving the diggers to their own devices.

Crossing one empty street after another, he passed by dozens of closed shops before finally finding himself a diner with lights on. Going in, he ordered an overpriced dinner and waited for his meal. There was no need to hurry to the bridge.

It didn't seem like this rift revolved around their planet, so he should be fine even if he waited an hour between taking both his measurements.

He needed some semblance of normalcy in his routine. It would be impractical to worry about the million other things that weighed on his mind—especially sustenance. He was doing his best to make progress toward solving this tangled mess. Any more mental strain would just be priming his mind to become a pressure engine on the verge of exploding.

During the wait, he noticed the small lamps that hung around the interior and addressed the diner's only server—an older man wearing a flat cap, a cheap-looking cigar in his mouth. He asked, "Mister, would you be willing to sell one of these lamps?"

Blowing a puff of thin smoke out of his mouth, the man glanced at Vern and replied in a husky voice, "I don't see why not. But that's such a peculiar demand. Tell me, night farer, what fancies you in such a mundane thing?"

The man stood up, poured more leaves into the front of his pipe, and took another puff as he waited for an answer.

"I simply need a small lamp frame that I can carry with myself."

"You say that, but this one can't even handle a shake, much less be carried on your person easily. You didn't know that, did ya? You'd be much better off going to the mechanist market at the dawn and getting something more fitting for the task."

"Hah. Please don't worry about that. I just need the frame; I'll fix the rest of it myself."

"Oh, we've got a tinkerer, have we? That mechanist market I just told ya bout used to have many more like ya. I heard many were lost to the duskfall. The blessed ones that survived took over the shops and items of the dead—may Lady rest their soul. But tell me night farer, why do you think we survived the culling? One such as me deserved a one-way charter to the River Styx if I say so myself."

Stumped by such a profound question out of the blue, Vern ruminated for a while, before he chuckled with a bitter expression. "We just got lucky, is all."

"Ha ha ha. I hear you, night farer. I hear you. That really must be the case. Otherwise, so many kind souls wouldn't be lost to the winds. Besides that, night farer, what kind of tinkering—"

The tedious question the man was about to ask was interrupted by a shout from the kitchen, and he left promptly. When he came back out with food, Vern didn't waste much time chatting and asked a few perfunctory questions before the man left him alone.

After paying fifteen crowns total for the meal and the lamp, he exited the small diner.

And as expected, the rift seemed to stay in position while the moon had drifted apart from it.

Confident in his calculations, he made his way to the bridge in this deep night, a small lamp in his hands, its frail wick about to be snuffed any moment by the wind. It was indeed a chore to keep it burning, but he would fix it tomorrow.

He lampooned about random things until he finally reached the other point he had marked for himself on the map—right next to the bridge. Standing in a somewhat open area, he placed the lamp on the ground and took out the astrolabe again before focusing on exactly the same top left corner of the rift.

Repeating the earlier actions, he found himself another angle. Then putting the lamp on the railing of the bridge, he started his calculations on his notepad under the dim orange illumination.

Having traversed a reasonable distance across the city and noted the positions of both the moon and the rift, he now held the basic components for a parallax calculation. Two angles and a base distance—it was a simple ratio analysis problem. But the result was proving to be anything but.

The angle between the rift and the moon, measured from the two different locations, should have shown some difference. But the two angles were virtually identical. He frowned and traced the lines of his drawings, the moon's position moving, but the rift's . . .

He shook his head in disbelief, scrubbing a gloved hand through his hair. It was as if the rift were so far away that his change in perspective hadn't altered its position at all. But that would mean the rift was . . . it was . . .

His calculations halted; the numbers too outrageous to believe. He glanced back at the rift, the implications making his stomach churn with unease. His mind swirled with confusion and a growing sense of fear. He knew it wasn't something ordinary because normal citizens couldn't perceive it. But this . . . ?

His calculations were saying this rift was more than a billion kilometers away from the planet's surface. Then how could it appear in front of the moon?

Chapter 38

SEEKING TRUTH

Vern shook his head and closed the notepad. His calculations couldn't be right unless the rift was not a physical phenomenon at all.

Frowning, he dragged himself all the way back to his starting point by Hartley Street to double-check his measurements. This time, the gravediggers had already moved quite a distance away from his chosen spot, giving him space to work in peace.

But obviously, he hadn't been wrong. The values were exactly the same as before.

This was quite peculiar and required further investigation. So he closed the notepad and marched back to Ari's room. She had a telescope there.

Surely, it would enable him to scrutinize this cosmic phenomenon with more acuity. Again, he wasn't an astral fundamentalist, but one didn't need to be a savant to understand basic examination in that fundamental.

Strolling back to the well-maintained dormitory, he beelined to her room and opened the curtain, uncovering the primary mirror of the telescope. He hadn't used one before, but the idea was simple enough—point it in the right direction, rotate a few dials, and ensure that the reflection was crisp.

There were a lot more control levers on the thing, but he didn't need to know how to use all of them. After fiddling with it for a few minutes, he figured out which dial affected which aspect and got to it. Groaning a little, he bent over and looked through the eyepiece.

After dozens of more minor adjustments to the position, aperture, focus, and magnification, he finally had the rift in sight—crisp and clear.

It was gorgeous.

It was a colossal chasm, its edges lined with blue and orange sparks that churned with too much energy. It was a significantly sharper view than the one he got from his naked eyes. He hadn't dared to look at that thing through his perception and completely buried all such notions after finding out its supposed immense distance.

Fascinated, Vern gradually shifted the telescope and began to survey the edges of the fissure. He was no astronomer and didn't know what to make of this, but it was so enthralling he didn't want to tear his eyes away from the sight.

Then his hands moved instinctively and adjusted the tube to peer at what was inside the rift. Initially, all he could resolve were some stars that peeked from beyond—radiating more light than the moon.

But it was too beautiful. How could something so magnificent be hidden from everyone else's eyes?

Involuntarily, he turned the dial for magnification, and his other hand moved to rotate the focus wheel to match its new position. As if the world had nothing else in it, he focused on the sources of light. They were . . .

No. Must be.

It was the light. The disturbing energy. It spoke to him.

Triloxthor.

The rift, oh, the rift—it sang to him in an insane harmony. His eye glued to the Zeldranth, glued, stuck, ensnared. There were patterns in the chaos. Patterns! Whirling, swirling, twirling. Shapes no man should see, should ever see.

Xanthura. Eryndor. Qylxian.

Felt the shapes coursing, coursing, and racing like a deranged heartbeat. His Yphyrxan were a runaway steam engine, no brakes, no control, hurtling toward . . . toward what? Alethrae? Revelation? The line was blurring. Reality was blurring. Rift and mind, mind and rift. Dancing. Together. Faster. Faster.

Teladrax. Yhylum. Zephontrax. Eldryxan. Theldron. Xalimyr.

Senses spiraling, spiraling into the vortex of his own cognition. His Vernathian was a wild vortex, unrestrained, no tether, plunging into . . . into where? Oblivion? Xalimyr? The boundary was dissolving. Perception was dissolving. Rift and soul, soul and rift. Whirling. Entwined. Quicker. Quicker.

But then, two triangles appeared in his mind, sparkling with brilliant luminance. The moment they did, his mind jolted awake, and he closed his eyes, recoiling from the telescope. A shrill scream escaped his mouth. His heart ramped up with intense thumping as he looked at the telescope with wide eyes, his arms shivering uncontrollably.

It was those sounds again! I-I couldn't control myself.

Resting a shaking hand on his pounding heart, he sifted through his memories and quickly realized he had lost agency the moment he turned the scope away from the fringes and moved it toward the center of the rift. His hands had begun moving on their own. It was as if his eye was stuck to the eyepiece, unable to tear away from the breathtaking vista.

He took deep breaths and backed up to the bed, leaning on its frame, odd whispers still ringing in his mind. *It seems as if that burden of the Cryptic Constructor didn't fully activate.* Which was a good thing since it wouldn't alert Hensen, but it also meant that he'd have to deal with the residual influence of those sounds by himself.

Pinching his glabella, he mused, *My curiosity isn't doing me many favors. It is one snag after another. I really need to relax a little.*

But it was quite hard to focus at the moment, and his thoughts were being interrupted by unusual noises. So he gave up on any further ruminations and simply worked on gathering his thoughts.

After spending what felt like an hour with a splitting headache, he finally stood up and made his way outside the room to the shared bathroom at the end of the hallway. After washing his face with freezing water that came in a trickle from the tap, a cold serenity washed over his mind.

That was no joke. Early fundamentalists also had one accident after another due to their recklessness, but such was the cost of exploration. Yet, all the knowledge in the world would be of little use if he couldn't stay alive long enough to reap its benefits.

As a seeker of truth himself, it'd be contemptuous of him to give up after such a small setback, but it would also be stupid to not have fail-safes for situations like this.

Just like many other risky experimental settings, a proper protocol and general set of steps should be implemented to minimize the risk. Contingencies should be set, and safety measures should be designed. It would have been significantly more straightforward if he was back in Nvoria. He could have worked alongside his master to delve into these mysteries more safely.

Ahh. But then I'd have been anxious about Ari day and night.

It was foolish to think of the what-ifs. So he ambled back to Ari's room, locked the door from inside, and sat on the chair as he jotted down his new experiences like some experimental report.

Then not even bothering to turn off the lamp, he flopped on the bed, and sleep claimed him instantly.

Sunlight illuminated the room as Vern latched the small metallic lamp to his pocket watch's chain. With this design, his hands would be unfettered, free to wield the ironsong or any other weapon he saw fit. And should he need to wrestle the darkness into submission with more finesse, the arrangement permitted him to unhook the contraption at a moment's notice.

He had to dismantle Ari's star-shaped lamp and scrounge some of its parts to craft this masterpiece. It wasn't a winding machine like he'd hoped, but this would do. There was a clear indication of the amount of fuel left, and he had optimized its efficiency with some of the latest mechanical arts.

The actual fire was completely isolated from the outside environment, and along with the remodeled fuel chamber, it was effectively a portable lamp that wouldn't die even if the whole thing was turned upside down. Remembering another important task, he picked up the ironsong, removed the used shells, and reloaded it with more bullets.

Nodding with satisfaction, he placed the note addressed to Ari on the bed. This time, it had a few more lines asking her to come to Hotel Inkwell if she saw the note. Who knew if he could find a way back into the inner districts so easily again?

It was time to meet Miss Cera and finally shed some light on this concept of observation.

Thud.

"Good afternoon, Mr. Vern."

Ahh?

He turned around and noticed that Ari's friend was coming up the stairs, her chestnut hair falling to either side of her face in silky waves.

"A lovely noon to you as well, Miss . . . ?"

"Selena. Not the same spelling as in the Saint Salena Cathedral—just Selena with two *e*'s. Um—did you find out anything about Ariane? Did she come back?"

Vern shook his head with a bitter expression.

"I see. I was actually just meeting up with some of our common friends. I had asked about Ariane, but none of them had talked to her since that event," she said with a sullen look.

"Please don't worry too much, Miss Selena. It'd be great if you could find some clues, but if not, don't push yourself too hard. Ari is an adult, and if she went with those people willingly, there must be some reason behind it. Just make sure to let her know that Vern wants to talk to her if you end up encountering her."

Selena seemed a little surprised but nodded and began unlocking her room.

But then Vern remembered something. "Actually, I have another question. Do Kingsmen have any problem with people exiting the inner districts?"

"Mr. Vern, you want to go to the outer districts? It's not a good idea. My friends told me it's lawless out there. Bandits and looters roam around en masse and can jump you anywhere. One of my friend's uncles died there before Kingsmen had fortified these boroughs. Bless Emperor for his quick actions."

Well, that was a valid take, but it wasn't as bad as the rumors made it sound. At least not yet. "I do understand the stakes, Miss Selena, but it's necessary for me to go there. Would you happen to know if it's legal to do so?"

She seemed conflicted for a while before she sighed. "It isn't the going out that's a problem. It's the coming back in. Kingsmen don't care about people going out, but that's because almost no one does. Mainly because once you're out, there's no coming back. Not unless you're some kind of nobility."

That will do. Vern reached his hand toward his head to tip his hat but quickly realized it wasn't there. So he nodded back and bid her farewell. "Just what I wanted to hear. I will be off then, Miss Selena. Please take care of yourself."

"Ah. You too."

Leaving the dormitory with one final glance, he traced the same path he walked last night. Eleonora's archive was in the Silverthread district, after all.

It was finally time to figure out what was up with this steamscript relay. He still wasn't sure what to expect in there—it was just an establishment with some machinery in it. But the fact that Miss Cera seemed to believe that it could somehow trigger enlightenment must mean that something had gone wrong there.

However, given her knowledge and sources, why would she take on something so risky? She had channels that were out of his reach. Maybe it was her aristocratic relations or something to do with Helena Von Arden.

"Halt right there."

Vern was jerked out of his thoughts as a piercing voice resounded above him. He complied, for the blade on the man's back was shining under the bright sun.

At another glance, he noticed two more men garbed in a similar fashion. One was perched on the parapet of the bridge, another was sharpening his blades with an edge grinder. The Kingsman above Vern stood on a ledge, his capelet flowing in the cold wind.

"State your purpose, fellow. You look like someone with a brain. Why come here? Did you not hear the emperor's decree?"

Vern was reminded of yesterday when the Kingsman had chased him like a death god with blazing blades in both his hands. There were three of them now. But he was on the side of the law this time.

Inhaling deeply, Vern steeled his expression and spoke solemnly, "My apologies, my lordship. But I'd like to cross the bridge to the districts outside. A close friend of mine lives in the outer districts, and I must check up on him."

He didn't even turn around but simply shook his head. "Another one trying to play the hero? Not that I will stop you. Do as you please but know that there's no coming back. Not until the emperor issues an edict."

"Thank you, my lordship." Not trying to overstay his welcome, he made a short bow toward the three men and crossed the bridge that was marred with trails of blood. Spreading his arms wide apart in a nonthreatening gesture, he passed the other two Kingsmen. They didn't even glance at him, and he quickly reached the Silverthread district.

Traces of fights could be spotted everywhere. But having already seen enough of the same, he ignored them and wielded the ironsong to intimidate the annoying pests that were already boring their predatory gazes on him from beyond the corners and alleyways.

They're waiting here in ambush, hoping to rob people the moment they arrive. Well, that was abominable. But they quickly turned their gazes away the second he pulled out the revolver.

Smart too. I doubt it's worth looting someone with a gun when easier targets pass by every few hours. Not letting these random jerks stop him, he made for Eleonora's archive. Having already looked at the map innumerable times, he was getting familiar with the cardinal directions and could more or less guess the general route to his destinations.

Crossing one deserted intersection after another, he passed darkened windows that once glittered with the allure of gleaming contraptions, artisan tea shops now devoid of their fragrant brews, and desolate boutiques where opulent gowns hung like spectral memories of grand balls and brighter days. Each silent storefront a poignant sonnet to the grandeur that once was.

He finally reached the archive. A burned-down archive.

CHAPTER 39

REVELATIONS

Vern stood there dumbfounded as he looked at the charred ruins of the library. It was as if time had never reversed its course. This is what the library would've looked like if the fire during the duskfall had continued its blazing onslaught.

He paused, maintaining a respectful distance from the grandeur now marred by disaster. The cathedral-like library, once an architectural masterpiece adorned with spires and ornate brickwork, now stood desolate and scorched. The roof that had towered into the sky was partially caved in, its high-reaching spires reduced to blackened stubs.

The purple hue that had once spilled from its numerous arched windows and balconies was replaced with the bleakness of charred timbers and smoky, darkened glass. Where elaborate corbellings once graced the structure's exterior, only jagged remnants clung stubbornly to the blackened facade.

This didn't make any sense. What had gone wrong? It had only been two days, for steam's sake!

Before he could approach the scene, he noticed someone sitting on the bench across the ruin. She wore a white shirt beneath a short black jacket that had an emblem of Von Industries—a cog pierced by a straight blade—prominently displayed on both her shoulders.

Over her shirt and under her jacket, she wore a raven cravat tied neatly around her neck. The lower half of her outfit was comprised of black breeches tucked into tall charcoal leather boots. A gray belt encircled her slim waist, and a golden four-state vapor blaster was tucked into a holster.

That looks like some standard uniform. She's got to be more than just superficially associated with Von Industries.

But the moment he noticed her, she shifted her eyes from the crumbled wreckage and met his gaze. She quickly got up and walked toward him with graceful steps.

Cursing the lack of his top hat yet again, he moved to meet her in the middle. At an appropriate distance, he bowed in an elaborate gesture to give a better first impression than last time.

"Hello, Miss Cera. Glad to see you're all right."

"Good evening, Vern."

But before anything else, he had a burning question—pun intended—that had to be asked. "Miss, do you know what happened here? This . . . wasn't how I left the archive just a couple days ago."

"Certain individuals set it on fire yesterday," she said without hesitation.

Perhaps noticing his perplexed expression, she carried on, "I came back here prior morning to read up on a few more things, but then a trio came in and urged me to withdraw with haste." Shifted a little and looked at him with narrowed eyes. "They said there was an anomaly surrounding the archive that had led to the death of everyone in the library, and it's better to cleanse this place as soon as possible."

Vern became speechless.

They were indeed right. A disproportionate number of people had disappeared from the library compared to everywhere else. He knew it was because of the fire that engulfed the place, burning all scholars before they could be extricated from the jaws of that entity—somehow being omitted during the reversal of time. But anyone without this knowledge would indeed think of this as some anomaly.

After a while, he spoke, ignoring the questioning look in her eyes. "Who was it? The Kingsmen?"

Her tresses waved back and forth as she shook her head. "They called themselves vigilantes of Duskfall."

Oh? That was unexpected. The same organization that the swordsman tried to recruit him into? Their name was quite telling in and of itself, but he didn't anticipate they would do something like this.

It must be quite an organization to have members working both in the inner and outer districts. They are either working in tandem with the Kingsmen or have some way to traverse the barricaded bridges. Nonetheless, how had they even realized something had gone wrong in the library?

Miss Cera remained silent, gazing at the ruins, just like him.

Unwilling to waste any more time, he finally shrugged. "Well, it's unfortunate, but there's not much we can do about it. Anyway, I hope I didn't make you wait longer than necessary."

She shook her head gently. "I was done with my other matters a little earlier, so I ended up waiting here. But time is of the essence; we should get going."

Vern nodded and turned around, leading the way to Starfall Heights in the west. Then he heard her say, "Still, we should first iron out the finer details of our strategy. Could you . . . um clarify exactly how you're planning to help?"

"For me to answer that, you'll first have to elaborate on what's expected of me. What's waiting for us in the steamscript relay? What are your plans regarding your enlightenment?"

Following his steps, she nodded before speaking. "According to the information I have, the relay station is incessantly ringing with peculiar noises, but the eccentricity there is that the factories that supplied gas and steam to the station were reduced to ashes during the duskfall. Where is the energy required by the pipes to produce these sounds coming from?"

"Hmm, is it really such a big deal? The station could just have its own vapor engines, no?"

"I have already examined the architectural blueprints of the station I found in privileged sections of the archive, and such is not the case. The amount of energy needed to operate the station is massive, and there are no on-site engines that produce that much steam."

"There has been no news of any deaths in the vicinity, and it's one of the most harmless options I could have picked. My plan is to simply observe the anomaly from as far as possible and trigger enlightenment. Then we leave the moment I am done forming my viewpoint."

Vern's countenance tensed, but luckily she was behind him and couldn't notice the changes. *What does she mean by leave as soon as she's done? It took me three days! I can't wait there for three days.*

But he didn't want to ask her such a simple question. He didn't know what was normal, and it would only arouse suspicions about his own enlightenment. What if he had an irregular experience, and asking about this ousted that fact? She was already suspicious of him now that those vigilantes burned down the archive. He had no plans of divulging whatever happened in the library—not even indirectly.

So he started with a different question. "Hmm, then, Miss Cera, how long do you think it would take you to form your viewpoint?"

"I-I don't know."

Hmm.

"Do you know the average time it takes to do so?"

She turned silent for a beat before she said, "For those who religiously study their observation records prior to their enlightenment, it could take anywhere from a few minutes to half an hour."

That's it? His scowled unknowingly but still replied in a natural tone. "So I simply have to protect you during that period?"

"If you can, yes. But that's my question. What visions can you employ other than that invisibility? It might be a useful skill, but I don't see how that would come in handy in this situation—unless you can use that vision on me . . . ?" she said, catching up to him and matching him step for step as they made their way toward the tall bridge in the distance.

Huh? What? She thinks that's a vision I can use?

But it only made sense. She just said it only takes a few minutes to form a viewpoint. Naturally, she wouldn't assume that he was invisible for three days due to enlightenment. It seemed like the process of enlightenment generally didn't include going invisible. It was all but obvious that his experience was atypical.

But now that she was right next to him, he quickly schooled his expression to one of indifference, hiding his panic underneath as he rambled, "Uh, that vision has some uncanny limitations, and I can only use it very sparingly."

"Oh . . ." A soft sigh escaped her lips, her shoulders slumping a little.

Damn.

She was losing confidence in him. He must prevent that from happening. She had already indirectly given him more information than he had figured out by himself in the past few days. He had to somehow keep her invested.

So he said, "But I can do something else."

He looked around and promptly noticed a familiar target just a few paces away. It was a clock that hung on a ledge, jutting out of some office. Going for the theatrics this time, he quickly perceived it based on complexity and focused on the flaw that came from the spring in the winding mechanism.

The speed at which he shaded familiar objects had been improving by the day. So, it didn't even take a second before that notion appeared in his mind—one he followed without hesitation, inducing an instability within the device.

Crack.

Crunch.

"AAH—"

Miss Cera stopped in her tracks as she muffled her scream. Shards of glass burst forth alongside a bunch of gears and sprockets that spilled from the clock and scattered on the cobblestone underneath.

She gasped in amazement, looking back and forth between Vern and the fragments of broken clockwork. "That— That was you?"

Vern simply smiled back, feeling a little smug. *This should assuage her worries for the time being.*

"Ephram. Is this really the power of observers?" she mumbled to herself as she rapidly closed the distance between Vern and herself again.

But something struck him as odd. *Has she not seen other observers in action?*

"It is very impressive that you can do something like this just with your eyes. If you were capable of this, I wonder why you almost succumbed to the whispers back in the library."

She calls those voices whispers, eh? Didn't that madman at the Ascendant Council also ramble something about learning the secret from the whispers? But that wasn't the point right now. He needed an excuse.

"I . . . wasn't in the best state of mind."

To this, Miss Cera stared at the ground in deep thought, and a few boulevards went by as they walked on wordlessly. Then out of the blue, she looked back up, pointed at her revolver, and asked, "I wonder how you'd match up against a gun like this? Can observers really surpass the might of these firearms?"

"Uh, let's not discuss malevolent schemes of violence against little harmless me, okay? I just wanted to show that I am not completely lost. I have been an observer for a while and just need some ideas on how to formally progress my viewpoint."

She tilted her head to one side, and one of her eyebrows quirked in puzzlement. "Do you not have an observation record of your own?"

I knew it! There are multiple observation records, and not everyone learns from those bloody parchments. Ah, but this meant he needed more justification. After a quick thought, he settled on this story.

"I-I lost it . . ."

"You lost it? But you were able to read about visions and enlightenment? Um, did you not even read the preamble before becoming an observer? That sounds very . . . foolish?"

"I agree. But my circumstances were quite peculiar when I first got my hands on the record." Then he suddenly turned sideways and peered into her dark eyes—one of them hiding behind her locks. "And this is why I lack basic knowledge about observation."

Hoping to change this topic and reduce his missteps while being a touch franker, he appealed, "Anything that you can tell me before we venture into the relay station will benefit us both. You don't need to divulge anything significant, but even a basic insight might just prove to be of vital consequence."

She blinked, her movements pausing as if momentarily derailed before she turned thoughtful and inquired back, "Then, do you know about the shades of perception?"

Chapter 40

THOUGHT SPACE

Cera's question puzzled Vern. Was she talking about how he shaded his perception with tones of grays? Didn't every viewpoint have its own different representation? She shouldn't know about that. Assuming it must be a general term, he replied, "Shades of perception? Yes, I shade it every time I want to use my visions."

"Huh? No. That's not what I meant. Shading your perception is the act of imprinting a vision onto your thought space. I still don't understand everything since I haven't even enlightened myself, much less shaded my perception, but it isn't something you do every time you employ a vision."

That sounded a little like what happened with instability inducement. It wouldn't be too far off to say he had imprinted it into his thoughts. But was that really it? He had shaded his perception without even knowing about it?

They reached the tall bridge connecting this district to Starfall Heights with minimal disturbance. Perhaps noticing his lack of response, she continued, "I don't know everything, but if you have shaded your perception, you should have some kind of blessing that aids you in your observation."

"Blessing?" This was only getting increasingly confusing. He was pretty sure that the burden of the Cryptic Constructor didn't count as a blessing. It had helped him, yes. But something far more nefarious was going on behind the scenes, he was sure of it. And he had no other blessings.

He retrieved his notepad from his coat pocket and flipped it open to the page that had lines from the parchment of the Cryptic Constructor. A relevant line read, *Constructor's blessing is the unveiling, a divine act that transcends mere sight, to perceive the very bones of reality.*

"Yes. The vision with which you shade your perception determines the kind of blessing you receive. I can't share the effects of the vision I plan to shade my perception with. But I can tell you the blessing I will supposedly receive. Since I will be following a record of Ephram, the Great Conductor, I ought to be able to subtly perceive the resonance between people, ideas, and objects."

This sounds useful. I wonder what the limitations are of such a thing. But this changes a lot of my previous theories. Was that swordsman talking about blessings in this context? This was quite peculiar. Then what would be considered an evil blessing?

But this also threw him back to the same question he had at the start of this conversation. Since he didn't have a blessing or anything of the sort, did that mean he hadn't shaded his perception? Then, what exactly did it mean to imprint a vision? What were the steps?

"I see. Then I don't think I have any such blessings."

"That . . ." She stared at the ground, lost in thought as they walked alongside each other.

Vern also tried to wrap his mind around this whole thing. So there was something called thought space where one had to imprint visions. And instability inducement had yet to be imprinted, or he would have had a blessing that sounded like things that would unveil the bones of reality? That would be welcome.

On the other hand, the blessing that Miss Cera will get comes from Ephram, which allows her to perceive resonance between disparate concepts.

It's quite a departure from the technical terminology used in the Observation Record of Subjectivity, *but they seem to be encompassing the same concepts. Very intriguing indeed.*

Four chimes resounded from the faraway clock tower when she finally looked back up at him and asked, "But this makes no sense. How can you use such potent visions without shading your perception? Given your unstable thought space which has zero shades, you shouldn't be able to use anything so practical."

Zero shades? Is that to say perception can be shaded multiple times?

He furrowed his brows and responded, "Is it not possible to envision anything useful until one has shaded their perception?"

"Mm-hmm. As I said, it shouldn't be possible to imprint a profound chain of ideas in an unstable thought space. Taking the ideas that make up your desired vision and intentionally imprinting them into your thought space is how you shade your perception. That is what makes a thought space stable."

That was a lot of information. Retrieving the pen from his pocket, he rested the notepad on the hand that gripped the ironsong and began writing. After a few quick scribbles, he asked, "Can you tell me more about this thought space you keep mentioning?"

She first looked at him with one of her eyebrows raised, then lapsed in a moment of quietude before speaking. "Yes, but that will be the last thing I explain. I have already spoken too much for having received nothing in return." Then she cleared her throat and continued, "In simpler terms, thought space is where insights regarding your viewpoint congregate. Think of it as a more permanent form of the world you perceive during observation."

Then a look of realization dawned on her face. "I see now. I think this is what you meant when you said you have to shade your perception again and again. If you had a stable thought space, you wouldn't have to interpret the world around you every time you wanted to use a vision."

"But then again, just the fact that you can use those visions is a problem. I don't know." She sighed. "I really need to feel all these constructs and ideas for myself. So much theory without getting a practical hands-on experience is making it hard for me to wrap my mind around everything."

She seemed as confused as he was about a lot of the details, and it only made sense. There's only so much one could comprehend as a non-observer. He still wasn't sure how to shade his perception because he didn't know how to access the thought space. But he wasn't about to pester her for more answers just yet. She had given him more than he deserved, and as a gentleman, he would respect the boundary she had set.

He wasn't some power-hungry freak looking to become the most influential observer on the planet. But the very nature of observation called to him. Those sights he had seen back in the library—he longed for them. But more than that, it was about balance.

He would love to sit in one place and experiment with instability inducement until he couldn't anymore—to figure out everything about it. But an equilibrium had to be achieved between his proactiveness and reactiveness regarding the unknown threats that lurked around him.

There was that sacrifice in the hotel, those two men, the rift, the whispers, Hensen, the Ascendant Council, Kingsmen, the swordsman, men in white robes, Ariane, and new abnormalities were being added to the list almost every day. All these curiosities were now a part of his life, but he didn't understand them. Not one bit. Didn't know what their deals were.

And that lack of knowledge irked him. Remaining passive and holed up in his room wouldn't give him insight into any of these peculiarities.

But then he noticed the change in the architecture style and the presence of more people on the streets, courtesy of being the residential district for middle-class citizens. Shaking his head, he finally exited his meandering ruminations, and replied, "That's indeed insightful, Miss Cera. Thank you. I will try my best to ensure you succeed in your endeavor."

Moving a little ahead of him, she gracefully adjusted her stance, and with a gentle inclination of her head, she said, "Then can I ask you something?"

Vern nodded, not wanting to be ungrateful.

"Can you tell me more about your enlightenment? You don't have to talk about your specific experience, but what exactly are the criteria that trigger enlightenment? In the record, it suggests observing anomalies. But what kind of anomaly? Would any sort of anomaly elicit a response from beyond and enlighten me? It's all just so vague."

Huh? Anomaly? I guess one could call subjective occurrences anomalies. But this quickly threw him for a loop. What exactly were subjective occurrences? The diagram in the *Observation Record of Subjectivity* was one. But what else was a subjective phenomenon?

Miss Cera waited patiently as he kept walking and pondered the matter.

He hadn't given it much thought before, but it was perplexing for sure. He had executed a vision in front of her, but it didn't instigate any changes. Didn't enlighten her.

His conjecture back in the library was that enlightenment was triggered by looking and comprehending something that was either inherently subjective or objective.

Is that rift subjective in nature? But it doesn't matter because even if it is, average people can't see it. Well, this was complicated.

"Hmm, I don't know if I can put it into words because of its elusive nature. But does that mean you're not sure what will trigger enlightenment in the steamscript relay station? Whoever gave you this information didn't tell you what you're supposed to do in there?"

As if caught in some lie, she flinched. "I—I only know that there's an anomaly in there. They suggested a few locations to me, and I decided on the hub."

That was understandable. If subjective phenomena were like fruits on a tree, the world would have been in far more chaos.

"So, it's possible that there might be nothing in there that can trigger your enlightenment?"

The glow of the sun reflected off her face as she bit her lip and nodded slightly.

"That's fair. In that case, all I can tell you is that you have to observe something that is out of the norm. Something that doesn't comply with our notion of reality."

She sank into another bout of contemplation. Vern saw a pattern in her behavior and readied himself for another involved question as he went through his notes one more time.

He had learned a lot, but this was all still a puzzle. A puzzle for which he only had a few pieces. He was still missing many critical points needed to extrapolate the details and find a consistent logic for the system. But it was a start. He could—

"It doesn't make sense. When you were invisible back in the archive, it blew my mind and had me doubting my sight and senses for quite a while. Was that not far enough from my notion of reality?"

Yep. She loves making these odd connections too.

He shrugged with a shake of his head. "I really do not know the answer to that. It should have been the case, but we wouldn't be having this conversation if you were an observer already."

Deflating instantly, she slumped her shoulders and said, "Well . . . then I have more questions. Is it unbearable when the lens of perception intertwines with one's eyes?"

Lens of perception? She must be talking about that lenslike thing that melded with my irises.

He nodded gravely. "It wasn't a great experience. I cannot speak for others, but the feeling of having your sclera singed away and cornea evaporated isn't a pleasant one."

Surprisingly, she didn't even flinch at his words and nodded. "But I do not see anything wrong with your eyes. They look perfectly fine to me. They don't even glow like Madam Helena's."

"So Madam Helena is an observer?"

She gasped and brought a palm to her mouth as she stuttered, "Uh Um . . . Ah y-yes? I don't know if I was supposed to say that."

Vern chuckled. "Don't worry. I don't plan on sharing anything about what we've discussed so far with anyone. And it might not be such a big deal anyway."

Her expressions, which clearly expressed everything about her state of mind, conveyed relief as she sighed. "Ah, thank you. I just can't forget that moment. I thought my eyes were playing tricks on me. There was this time when I was talking to her, and I am sure I saw her golden eyes shine like a beacon. Back then, I chalked it up to nervousness, but I know better now. They were glowing for sure."

"Hmm, I haven't noticed any physical differences with my eyes. Maybe it's something that only occurs once you've shaded your perception? Sounds quite inconvenient and exposing to me."

"Spoken like a lackluster fundamentalist with no knack for fashion. I would take shining eyes over dull and dark ones any day," she said with a snicker.

Huh! Was she questioning his sense of fashion? This couldn't go unaddressed. "I—"

"Ah, please forget about that. Now that you have a better understanding of our situation, can you tell me how you can help me out?"

Exhaling deeply, Vern reminded himself not to feel affronted by stray remarks of the inexperienced. He said, "Let's see. As a savant of the Coven of Truth, I have been working on contraptions like the ones in the steamscript relay since forever. If something's gone wrong with the energy source, as you mentioned, I can quickly figure out the root of the problem. Then there were the pipes—"

But then a voice made its way to his ears from in front of them, interrupting his attempt at conversation. "Heh, ain't that somethin', fellas? Playin' sweethearts while the world's burnin' itself to cinders."

Chapter 41

SURROUNDED

A man that seemed like he was about to walk past them suddenly halted, pushed his hat up with the tip of his umbrella, and spoke with a wide grin. "All right, spill it. Which one of you's keen to toss over their shiny baubles first? Or perhaps the lady might offer something a bit more . . . enticing?"

"Hahhahhah."

"Hahhahhahhah."

"Fresh meat on the block, boss. You got eagle eyes, catchin' 'em from a mile away."

"Heh, ain't no protection for them outsiders, boss. Today, we're gonna eat good."

Laughter echoed around them as a few more individuals garbed in dark overalls walked out of the alleyway.

Windows of the buildings around them quickly clamped shut, and people retreated into their houses. The bystanders made a run for it—some stormed into alleyways while others backed away and looked on in interest.

"What do you guys think you're doing?!"

Miss Cera brandished her gun without hesitation, pointing it in the general direction of the boss. He was a man of average build, his face marred with deep lines and hollowed cheeks. He wore a tattered oil-stained tailcoat that harmonized with his top hat, its rim frayed and color faded.

"Hey, boss. We ought to be afraid, okay? Little missy has a gun, and so does the boy toy."

"Hahhahah."

"Hahhahhah."

Vern held himself back, discretely shelving the notepad in his coat. A few men had already surrounded them, and acting rashly in such situations was never to one's benefit. It would be one thing if he had seen them coming and had some plan. But right now, he knew nothing about them, and reacting violently would be too risky.

From the voices, he surmised that there should be about five people around them, including the boss in the front. This wasn't looking too good. Since they were mocking his and Cera's firearms, it was obvious that they came prepared and had some sort of countermeasure.

It seems like people in Starfall Heights have more gall or better measures to contend against firearms. But damn, was it too late to figure that out? If he had had an inkling of the situation being like that in this district, he wouldn't have been so immersed in his conversation with Cera. He had become too lax since everyone actively had avoided them in previous districts.

It wasn't the first time he had found himself in a perilous situation out of nowhere, but damn, did his heart not want to keep pace, ramping up its beating with great intensity. But this was okay. The men seemed to want to shake them down instead of outright killing them. Maybe it was their twisted method of asserting dominance.

Shaping up a plan in his mind, he first said in a low voice, "Miss Cera, please calm down." But when he turned his gaze to her, he noticed her outstretched arms shaking intensely.

This was bad. She was already panicking hard. If these people noticed it, they would only make the coming conversation all the more unbearable. These men usually had a knack for detecting fear in their victims.

"Oy, look-a-here, the missus got her blaster aimed. Should I start shaking in me boots, eh? Keep yer cool, ya blasted wench. I'm keepin' it civil for now. Y'don't wanna see me ruffled."

Clack.

Click.

The moment he said that, sounds of guns cocking filled the space around them. Then someone from behind chortled. "You can always try your luck, you know. Try out if these guns won't riddle you with holes before you get one shot out."

"Hahhahhah."

Peals of laughter echoed all around them as the other men seemed to enjoy the situation.

Still, this didn't make sense. Was the boss really not afraid of being shot? Even if his underlings unloaded a volley of shots after that, what would be the point?

But that's when Vern saw the abnormality as the boss flung his arm. In the right hand of the greasy man was what looked like a short bronze umbrella. An umbrella that quickly opened its canopy. The man held it over himself as if to catch some shade from the sun.

But Vern wasn't fooled so easily. That thing had two tops, hundreds of gears clearly visible underneath the canopy. He didn't have to think too hard before a few possibilities crossed his mind.

He wasn't sure, but it was possible that when fully opened, the upper layer of the dual-layered canopy would rotate. Generally, such a design would be nothing more than a flashy contraption used to amuse kids.

But obviously, he wouldn't be using an umbrella to wow us at such a time.

Just as he was thinking about it, the man took the umbrella and pointed it at Vern, the canopy of the contraption covering most of his body as if to shield him.

But then Vern's pupils constricted, and his hair stood on end when he saw the peak of that canopy. It was a muzzle aimed at him directly. This umbrella was actually a gun!

However, he bit his tongue and stood his ground, not making any rash movements. Pulling a trigger took less than a fraction of a second. He wasn't foolish enough to think himself faster than fingers. But he quickly needed to confirm his plan of action. It still wasn't clear what these men wanted from them.

"Listen up, you two. This turf? It belongs to Bishop Garmen. Can't just waltz in 'ere all high 'n' mighty without payin' the price. As the bishop's loyal man, it's me job to ensure everyone pays their fair share. So, you ready to cough up, or do we have to have ourselves a little . . . amusement?"

Great. This wasn't going to turn bloody before he had a chance. There was time to set things up. Fighting with guns might not be his forte, but a little use of his brain and tongue wasn't a challenge. He had to assess his surroundings and make a proper plan.

Vern let his revolver swivel downward in his fingers in a gesture of surrender. Raising his arms, he spoke sheepishly, "My sincerest apologies, esteemed sir. Working under the banner of someone as renowned as Bishop Garmen, I can only imagine your stature. We seem to have blundered into a place where we don't quite belong. We mean no disruption to the bishop's peace. Quite the contrary, we want to ensure we're on the right side of things."

Then with a fawning voice, he continued, "I must admit, your strong presence and the respect you command is truly admirable. As newcomers, we could surely benefit from your wisdom. Would you be so kind as to clarify what you'd like from us?"

Miss Cera looked at him with puzzlement, her aim completely off-kilter. He seemed to hear her whisper under her breath, "Vern, what are you doing?"

Not changing his expression one bit, he simply ignored her. Five men had their eyes glued on them, and he didn't have the time to explain anything or even give her a signal. They were all looking at him with rapt attention, and any misstep would cause them to raise their guards.

"Hahhahhah. You see this, boss? The boy toy actually understands the gravity of his mistake."

Flashing an obsequious smile at the one who spoke, Vern glanced back and took this chance to survey the surroundings. There were two men at his three and four o'clocks, slowly moving closer, a carbine and a pipe in their respective hands. Then there was the one at his six o'clock, the closest one, holding a double-barrel. The fifth was around his nine o'clock in the direction of Miss Cera, holding a simple revolver.

All right, I got this.

Complexity.

A sharp glint appeared in his eyes as the world around him began turning into shades of gray. Integrity was easier than complexity, yes. But he believed that integrity came with its own set of repercussions that he didn't want to test right now. He knew what complexity entailed, and he was going to stick to it.

Also, it was harder to think of specific flaws of such complex machines in terms of integrity except for maybe cracking the barrels, which could or couldn't work.

Chuckling, the boss rubbed his bearded chin with his other hand, lowering the umbrella a little bit. "Heh, look at 'cha. Ain't you a sharpshooter in the head."

His eyes scanned Vern and Cera, sizing them up. "Now, since you've gotten the lay of the land, let's make things easy. Drop those fancy toys you're holdin', and you might get a chance. For the lassie, if she knows 'ow to keep a man entertained, there might be a spot for her among us. But for you, lad, we ain't got room for pretty faces unless they've got somethin' worth our while. Just knowin' to blabber honeyed words ain't gonna cut it. So, whatcha—"

"This is enough!" Miss Cera interrupted. "I work for Helena Von Arden. If you think you can get away with this, think twice. And do you really believe I won't shoot you? Your men might pepper me with bullets right after, but you won't survive to see any of that—"

The boss abruptly shifted the tip of his umbrella toward Miss Cera, and before Vern could react. *No!*

Bang!

"SHUT UP!"

Smoke rose from the cobblestones next to Miss Cera's feet as she stood there unharmed, the color from her face drained completely.

Vern internally heaved a sigh of relief and increased the pace of perceiving and internalizing the flaws of weapons around him. Miss Cera didn't know about his plans, and if he didn't do something quick, she would really try something foolish.

And he couldn't exactly blame her. From the flow of the conversation, these men were scum, and she would be the one to bear the brunt of their depravity. Top that with Vern's obsequious response and neglect of her opinion, she was obviously distrusting of him. He could maybe try to hold her back with some choice words, but he didn't want to.

These men deserved it. So it was time to focus.

He had seen every one of these guns at some point in his life except the umbrella that the boss held. He should be able to figure out some kind of flaw in each one of them.

Given that the boss was fearless in front of Miss Cera's blaster, it was possible that his umbrella was not just a gun. If Vern had to guess, the canopy could rotate at a breakneck pace, somehow defending the holder by grinding the bullet away.

But other than that, he didn't have a clue how the projectile mechanism of the thing worked. Still, he might just be able to find a flaw in his defense. Churning up multiple ideas about defects and flaws in all these weapons, he quickly began assigning complexities to the different sections of weapons that surrounded him.

Amid his rapid thoughts, the boss continued his rant, "Push me one more bloody time, and your head'll be meetin' my next round. You're only standing 'cause of that pretty mug, got it? As for this Helena lass, I couldn't give a damn. She's got beef, she can take it up with the bishop. But don't think you can cross me, bitch!"

Even now, Miss Cera's arms were shaking, but a determined expression quickly overtook her face as her aim stilled. She was about to do something. Vern ramped up his pace and ignored the boss completely.

The double-barrel had two synchronized hammers. If one could be delayed even a little, it could imbalance the discharge and damage the gun itself. Not the most surefire flaw, but other ideas that he ran through didn't lead to the emergence of that notion of instability in his mind.

Then for the carbine, it was easier because they have rifled barrels. Messing with the spiral grooves within even a little bit would send the bullet way off the mark. No matter how the shooter corrected its course, it'd be hard to predict and error correct without an aligner.

The revolver was even more straightforward. It relies on the rotating cylinder to align the next bullet in the gun. If he homed in on the rotating mechanism, it would jam the cylinder.

Again, he didn't know about the barrel of the umbrella, but blocking the rotation itself by shifting the balance of complexity of some of the gears toward crudeness should be simple.

"DROP THE GUN OR FUCKIN' DIE!"

"Lady, I suggest you drop that gun to the side like your boy toy. I would rather not have to undress a corpse, you know."

"Hahhahhah."

"Hahhahhah."

This seemed to flip a switch in Miss Cera, and her chest heaved with every breath. Her knuckles turned white from the force of her grip on the vapor blaster.

Even Vern's expression faltered at this comment, and an icy glint crossed his eyes. He couldn't care less about being called boy toy or whatever—their opinion of him was their personal purview and not his business. But the insinuations they were making were going a little too far.

It was about balance. Even if it was with an ulterior motive, he had tried to be polite with them. He understood that might is right when there's no one to enforce the law, but that didn't mean one had to revert to the baseness of barbarians. Power imbalance always existed in society, but that doesn't mean it had to manifest this nastily.

There were probably other solutions to this situation, but first they provoked both of them one-sidedly and now they were crossing the line. These people were pushing it too far, and they deserved whatever was coming to them. Pretense of humanity be damned.

Any inhibitions he had regarding harming these people were thrown out of the window as he closed his eyes and felt all four notions that emerged in his mind.

It was time to tip the balance of control back in his favor.

Chapter 42

SHOWDOWN

All the flaws whirled in his mind, and it was time to surprise these wretches.

The boss held up three fingers and shouted, looking at Miss Cera with a lecherous grin, "Ain't got all day, ya bloody wench! Three ticks o' the clock, and that's all ya get. THREE!"

This fucker.

Nevertheless, Vern disregarded his dissatisfaction instantly. Now wasn't the time.

He couldn't exactly follow all the flaws in an instant, but he had an order in mind. In his perception, he first pursued the notion that hovered over the man with a double-barrel.

When the crack on the gun widened to its zenith, a very muted sound of clacking played in his mind. But it was negligible, and the man wouldn't suspect a thing without shooting the gun.

The process took less than an instant, and his veins began to throb intensely. He knew it was done, so he quickly moved on to the cloudy figurine of a carbine's muzzle that was floating in his mind.

"TWO!"

The spiral grooves etched in the barrel were made to be of a dark shade due to their complexity, while the outer edge of the muzzle was toned a brilliant white for its simplicity.

Unhesitatingly, he pursued the notion, and this crack also began to widen before quickly becoming so large it tore away the muzzle from his cognition. This one didn't generate any sound, as the changes were so insignificant.

The intricate network of his eyes pulsed with intense fervor, but he ignored them and moved on to the revolver, whose chamber's rotational gears were shaded a slate black, its muzzle and triggers relatively bright.

And he unhesitatingly induced another instability. His brain seemed to grow dull, and the pain in his eyes made him want to scream.

Just one more. Just one more.

"ONE!"

Vern could hear Miss Cera's breathing grow heavy and rapid. Her footsteps shifted as she turned away, and a sudden quiet in her voice told him she was focused elsewhere. Must have been disappointed by his lack of action and scared demeanor.

Fuck! Just one more.

The umbrella had hundreds of gears to efficiently transfer the rotational energy from multiple sections. He chose two of them and grabbed hold of their basic flaws with desperate precision.

Allowing his lightheaded thoughts to follow this one to the end as well, a crack appeared, which drowned his perception, shattering the world of grays.

Then the universe seemed to hold its breath, and Vern managed to stay stable on his feet, shaking away the side effects of his visions before he roared, "Miss Cera, fire!"

"ZERO. KILL THE BITCH!"

Bang!

Bang!

Boom!

"AAAAAHHHH!"

"AAHH! FUCK!"

Bang!

"I'll kill you! You bitch!"

A whirlwind of events unfolded simultaneously. Vern had already stepped to one side, forcing his bleary eyes open to get a better view of everything that had transpired.

When the man shot his double-barrel, it had caused a jarring recoil that threw his aim wildly off target. The pellets sprayed in disparate directions, some embedding themselves in the wall, others clattering harmlessly on the floor. This left the man staggering, trying to regain control.

For the carbine, it was a similar story. When the trigger was pulled, the bullet veered inexplicably off course as if some unseen force had nudged it at the last moment. The shot went wide, missing its intended target and striking the glass of a window instead. The shooter looked at his weapon in disbelief, bewildered by the sudden deviation in its performance.

At the same time, the man with a revolver, who had a sinister glint in his eyes, pulled the trigger, and a horrifying explosion replaced the expected bang of the shot. The cylinder had jammed, and the bullet, trapped in its confined space, exploded within the gun itself.

A flash of fire and smoke erupted from the weapon, and the man screamed in pain as shards of metal tore into his hand. The revolver's barrel split open like a flower, its twisted remains dropping on the paved ground.

"Help! AGHGAAGHHH!"

Yet, all this was merely a distraction. The boss was the one who held Vern's unwavering attention. The moment he was done counting, he had already turtled behind the umbrella, flourishing it in a manner that covered most of his body.

As expected, the top began to rotate in a whirlwind, but soon the gears began to screech, and sparks flew everywhere. The gyrating top came to an abrupt halt, the gears whirling and grinding helplessly, falling out of their places.

And then, before anything else could happen, a black dot streaked across Vern's vision, piercing a hole in the brassy contraption and shattering its defense, which was followed by the squeal of what seemed like a dying pig.

"AHHHH! THIS BITCH!"

Miss Cera's shot had connected! Not fatally, but it had made an impact. She had either understood what Vern was doing or had just shot out of spite.

However, the cause held little significance; she had done her part, and there was more to do. This situation wasn't wrapped up just yet.

Vern swiveled back and aimed at the man, who was bolting toward Miss Cera—a pipe in his hand.

Bang!

The bullet went quite off mark, grazing the man's shoulders.

FUCK ME!

The man was moving too damn fast. Vern didn't have any clue how to aim at such a target. He would probably need to do some course correction alongside leading the shot a little—all of which was easier said than done.

"Vern! I will handle this guy. Please take care of that umbrella," yelled Miss Cera with a steely gaze as she turned around and did something to her revolver.

It looked like she knew what she was doing, and Vern was only happy to be given a chance to go after the only stable gun in the hands of his enemies.

She didn't need his protection, and he had to quickly double down on their advantage—the surprise factor wouldn't last for long. The guys with the carbine and double-barrel were still unharmed, after all.

So Vern ignored the man that was charging toward them and raced to the boss. He was lying collapsed on the ground, blood flowing from his leg. Clutching the umbrella in his trembling arm, he yelled, "BLAST IT, you worthless sacks of slop! What's the use of ya? ATTACK 'EM, NOW!"

The one with the shotgun yelled at the top of his lungs, "It's a rigged play, boss! These fuckin' guns are all bunged up! Ain't nothin' workin' right!"

Vern crisscrossed the street, trying to throw off the boss, who had closed the canopy of the umbrella and was attempting to aim its tip at him.

Bang!

A bullet streaked by his legs and hit the wall of a house, fizzling uselessly. Apparently, Vern wasn't the only one who had a hard time aiming at moving targets.

Bang!

Another bullet went quite off mark as Vern ran right past the boss, who was now sprawled on the road. The man tried to haphazardly direct the umbrella toward Vern, ignoring the river of blood that surged from his leg, but he wasn't quick enough.

This was why Vern had circled behind him. The boss would have to turn around to zero in on him. Using the brief respite from the fire of that umbrella, Vern gripped his ironsong and steadied his thundering heart with a deep breath.

With that vile face locked in his focus, marked by hollowed cheeks and sinister lines, he pulled the trigger.

Bang!

"AAHHHHHH." A final moan escaped the man's lips as his sunken eyes lost their luster—his body hitting the ground with a thud. The bronze contraption slipped from his fingers and rolled on the ground.

It turned out that aiming at the head of a stationary target just a meter away wasn't as difficult as one might think. Vern took no pleasure in the sight and shifted his gaze back to his surroundings.

"You've really stepped in it now, ya morons! Bishop Garmen ain't gonna let this slide. You're done for!"

Sizzle.

"AAH! MY HAND!"

Another shriek came from Miss Cera's vicinity, but Vern sped toward the umbrella, snatching it from the ground.

He heard Miss Cera say, "If either of you try anything funny, your fate won't be any different from these three." Looking up, Miss Cera had her gun aimed at the man with the carbine, who had been rapidly bolting it for another shot.

Bang!

"Why the fuck is this junk not shooting right? I just used it in the morning. What the hell happened."

"Fuck! Silo. Someone's messed with our weapons. It's time to—"

The moment their eyes met, it was as if they shared a single plan. Without hesitation, they rushed toward the nearest alleyway, fleeing with a breakneck urgency.

Vern wasn't ready to give up just yet, and neither was Miss Cera.

Bang!

Bang!

Bang!

Bang!

Bang!

Shot after shot, he emptied his whole chamber while Miss Cera shot a few of her own. All of them missed.

FUCK! I really need to practice my shots.

Vern even aimed the umbrella in their direction and pulled a trigger-like mechanism protruding out of its shaft.

Bang!

A waste. This one had even worse accuracy at long range. The round had completely missed the mark.

Miss Cera sidestepped the man who was holding his blistered arm and hastened toward the alleyway where those two had fled.

"They're too fast, Vern. Should we cut them off at the other exit?"

Adrenaline still pumping hard in his body, he scampered toward her and grabbed hold of her arm that was shaking wildly. "Miss Cera. It's enough. We need to get the hell out of here. They might have reinforcements nearby."

She seemed to break out of a reverie as the gun almost slipped out of her hand. Barely managing to not drop it, she followed Vern's lead.

There were two options in front of him right now. One was to run back to the Silverthread district and retreat somewhere safe. But the greedy aspect of him wanted them to head toward the steamscript relay instead.

Yes, they had triggered the men of this Bishop Garmen, but his experience with Fulham borough told him that there should be multiple territories in this district, each controlled by a different group.

The relay station was quite a distance away from here, so it wouldn't be wrong to assume that they'd cross more than one territory in the meantime. Also, they were a bit too careless this time around, letting themselves get surrounded. However, it was easy to avoid such a situation as long as they were vigilant.

Having rationalized his choice, Vern pulled Miss Cera along. She was looking at their surroundings with a horrified gaze, her eyes glued to the man who was crying in agony, bones visible on his singed hand. Probably a result of a different mode of her vapor blaster.

Vern, however, didn't have one shred of remorse for any of them. This man was the thug that was passing all those nasty remarks not so long ago. If one practiced a strong-eat-weak ideology, then if the tables were turned, one must also be ready to face the consequences of their own philosophy.

Speeding past them, they crossed the other man, who was trying to seem as small as possible, attempting to pull shards of metal out of his palm to stop the bleeding.

Then trampling right next to the corpse of the boss, they ran deeper into Starfall Heights. A few bystanders that had been looking on with interest backed away in panic, trying to stay away from them.

"Oh, Mother Asea. They killed the bishop's men."

"You go help that one. He seems alive. Bishop might reward you."

"No, get the hell away from here. Do you think I want to be interrogated by whoever comes after this mess? They'll flay me for all the information. I am getting the fuck outta here—"

Similar hushed exchanges entered his ears as his steps matched the pace of his heart, still thumping wildly.

After a while, he saw another group of men far in the distance, so he dragged Miss Cera over to one of the alleyways.

Passing through one narrow passage after another, his sense of direction began to muddle. So he exited over to the closest large street he found and reoriented himself.

Surprisingly, Miss Cera had been keeping up with him even in such a distraught state.

"Just a little farther, and we should be safe."

"Mm-hmm," she assented amid rapid breaths.

Assessing his options, he noticed a theater a dozen houses to the north. But there were a bunch of people in the streets. He didn't want anyone noticing them heading in there.

It was a simple problem to solve in this city, which had back alleys that branched more than a carpus tree.

Diving back into the alleys, Vern followed one of them north and quickly reached the back entrance of the theater.

It looked completely lifeless, which was a good thing. Turning over the knob of the small decrepit door, he pushed it.

And it opened, just like that.

He was fully expecting to waste more than a few minutes trying to get the lock sorted out, but apparently, it had been left open. Not exactly the most impossible happening in this city where everything had been looted to some extent.

Vern let go of Miss Cera's hand and entered the building while she did the same, closing the door behind her and locking it shut.

"PHEW." He slumped against a wall and took deep breaths, turning the knob of his lamp as an orange glow illuminated the surroundings.

This should be good enough for now.

Chapter 43

RESPITE

The orange glow of the lamp illuminated his surroundings, and a musty smell permeated the long yet thin corridor that led to two sections of the building. One was a short set of wooden stairs, while the other extended farther into the same floor—a thin layer of dust all over it.

Vern paid it little mind and instead focused on regulating his breathing, and Miss Cera seemed to do the same. Her short hair clung to her face that had managed to conjure drops of sweat in such chilly weather.

Clank.

The gun slipped from her palms and came crashing down, landing on the ground with a sharp metallic clank. She closed her eyes and covered her face with her hands as her back collapsed against the door.

Her body slowly lost all strength as she sagged down, crumbling on the floor. Her knees closed the gap between her palms, which rested against her eyes as low sniffles pervaded the air.

Vern looked at the frail girl and held himself back. She had to process what she had done by herself. This was the harsh reality—yesterday's crime was today's survival tactic.

She didn't need his soothing. Not yet.

So he instead took more deep breaths and processed some recent events of his own.

He had shot someone in the head.

Killed someone.

Willingly.

Yes, there were excuses like it had been a tense situation and that if he hadn't killed the boss, he wouldn't be alive right now, and whatnot. But he had reduced the already low count of humans on the planet for selfish reasons.

Objectively, it was quite a justified action. From society's perspective, a man such as that criminal was better off dead than alive. He would have destroyed so many lives if he had lived.

But everyone negatively impacted the lives of others to some extent by simply existing. If skilled people didn't live, then the unskilled would have it easier. If beautiful people weren't around, plain-looking individuals would be in demand.

Yes, from what he'd seen, this person had a much higher negative impact on the world than most, but who was Vern to decide that his balance of positive-to-negative impact on society was enough to warrant death?

Who decided the threshold where it was justified to grant death? Was there even a threshold? Is any such threshold objectively correct?

Vern sighed and shook his head.

These were all rhetorical questions with no real answers. As always, these philosophical thoughts were futile. They were good to reorient one's moral compass, but they almost always ignored the practicality of the real world.

For now, he'd have to accept the fact that the man had crossed Vern's subjective threshold of negative impact on his life.

He might have had a more vehement reaction to his first murder if the world was a tinge saner. But the repercussions of this were going to be fueled by vendetta and how he'd managed to affront the authority of some bishop rather than going against the morality of human society.

This was a shit show.

He had considered this topic beforehand. What would he do if he ever had to commit such a crime? None of that was coming in handy right now because the base assumptions of the world didn't quite match up.

AAH! I need to let it go. What's done is done.

It was indeed time for reflection, but this was going nowhere. He'd need to sit down in a more serene environment and contemplate to arrive at a more complete answer.

So he pushed off the ground and stood up. His eyes and head were still heavy, but his heart had calmed down.

Unhooking the lamp from his waist, he held it higher and shone it at the corridor. Thick ropes were extending from a couple pulley systems—the strands snaked upward, fading into the darkness.

There was also a short set of wooden stairs that led to a raised platform. He didn't even need to go up to realize it was the stage. This building was a theater, after all.

A minimal amount of space was wasted in here. The stage was just a meter away from the outer wall of the building.

Well, real estate used to be quite expensive, so such decisions only make sense. Not anymore though. It might even be the cheapest commodity nowadays.

A few cupboards and cabinets also lined the other end of the long thin hall, probably housing dresses and props for stage performances.

This seemed to be an old type of theater where actual humans performed. Film had sensationalized drama at the start of this decade. But nobles believed that real humans performing for them was far superior to the fake drama of films—killing the industry in its infancy.

So, it was only logical that the middle class tried to emulate the aristocracy. It was apparent that it used to be quite a busy theater because even though the air in here was stale, the contraptions and pulleys seemed well-maintained.

Another few minutes passed by as he silently took in his surroundings.

"Mum, this— I . . . you. Ephram, I . . ."

A faint whisper entered his ears, half its content too low for him to hear. She was sitting there, leaning on the door, hugging her knees, holding herself tightly.

It was hard to watch.

He decided to give her a little more time.

Moving farther into the thin corridor, he scrutinized the pulleys and the ropes. He even ventured up the short stairs of the stage to check out what was going on there.

Seemed like a good way to distract himself. Thinking too much about those events made him want to retch. In the last five days, he'd had experienced a bit too much gore for his liking. Recalling it wasn't going to do him any favors in keeping his lunch in his stomach.

So, yeah. He quickly found out that those ropes were there to draw and undraw huge curtains that covered the stage from the audience.

His curiosity sated, he walked back down and opened a trunk surrounded by a bunch of props on the other side of the building. As expected, it was costumes and dresses.

After wasting what seemed like a quarter of an hour, he walked back to the door with two masks in hand. They would make them look conspicuous in their own right, but it should be good enough for them to move about the district at night without being recognized quickly.

Miss Cera sat there, her face resting on her knees—eyes distant and swollen.

It should be fine to talk now, right?

Vern walked to her side and turned around before sitting next to her. He put the lamp in between them, the masks on his lap. He played with the masks for a while before he spoke softly. "Would you like to talk?"

She simply stared into nothingness for a while before she whispered, her voice cracking, "Please don't do that again . . . I was scared."

"I couldn't risk them figuring it out before I was ready."

"I . . . know. I was just, just scared."

" . . . "

"Have you done this before? You seem so . . . unfazed," she said, turning to face him. The soft orange glow drew highlights on her exquisite visage marred by tearstains.

He lightly shook his head, resting it on the wall and looking at the ceiling. "I might have a good poker face. But you were quite unfazed during the situation yourself."

"It . . . It was necessary. At least I believed that."

"You don't believe it anymore?"

"I . . . don't know. We killed them, Vern. We killed them."

Vern shook his head again, this time with more vigor. Even though his own argument didn't convince him, it was still solid.

"If we hadn't done what we did, you'd be underneath some random man, while I might have just been another corpse floating in the river."

A twinge of unease prickled in his gut because the words didn't sound as harsh in his mind as they did in the air.

" . . . Yes. I just . . ."

She lapsed into another bout of silence. Her black locks tried to hide it, but her eyes were growing moist again.

After a while, she uttered, "Just what happened to everyone, Vern? People were unpleasant before duskfall, but this is too much. Why did it have to turn out like this? I understand the logic, but why did this happen? Just why did it happen?"

Her voice, which was a whisper, began to tremble, taking on a higher, shaky tone as she struggled to contain her emotions. "Just why did so many people disappear?"

Vern focused back on her, the intensity in her words making him question it himself. What was the impetus?

Blinking rapidly, she wailed, "Just where did they go?"

Were they really dead?

"Just where did Mum go?"

He didn't know.

"Just why did things turn out this way?!"

Only if he understood it himself.

Tears slipped past her fingers and rolled off her cheeks.

"Just why can't things go back to how they were?"

It was . . .

"Just why does everything feel so overwhelming?"

It was hard . . .

This outburst wasn't just about what had happened at the bridge. It ran deeper than that.

And it was hard to watch.

He closed his own eyes for a moment, holding back his roiling emotions. He'd rather not fall into her pace and recall the anxieties he'd been keeping in check.

With slow, deliberate movements, he shifted his weight to one side, turning his body toward her. Sliding closer to her on the floor, his eyes locked onto hers for a brief second before something in her expression made him want to reach out.

"Just why is the world—" Her next words were caught in her mouth as Vern did something that didn't match his usual demeanor.

With a gentleness he hadn't known he possessed, he wrapped his arms around her, feeling her slight frame tremble under his touch. It was clear that words weren't enough, but perhaps this simple act of compassion could give her the solace she needed.

And himself.

Her body stiffened for just a moment at his touch, but then she relaxed, leaning into his embrace. Her breathing was ragged, and he could feel her tears dampening his shoulder.

He said nothing, simply holding her as the silent sobs took their toll on her.

Minutes passed in silence as her warmth became a comforting distraction from his own worries.

He tried to remember the last time he had hugged someone other than Ariane. Nothing came to mind except those formal conferences and parties where it was an obligation rather than a choice.

But hopefully, this helped her release some of her bottled emotions. She seemed to be a person who tended to do that.

Finally, she pulled away slightly. Wiping her eyes, she looked at him with a mix of gratitude and uncertainty. "Thank you. I am . . ." She sniffled. "I am sorry."

"Please don't worry. Just keep yourself mentally well because this new world isn't very forgiving. Repressing your emotions will wear you down one day or the other."

". . . Yes."

After wiping away her tears with her sleeves, she ran her fingers through her dark hair and smoothed them. Meeting his gaze with those beautiful eyes, she said, "I apologize for doubting you back at the bridge."

Shaking his head yet again, he replied, "It was the right thing to do. Please don't worry about it." But then he remembered his manners and continued, "Thank you as well for quickly adapting to my plans. If you hadn't taken the shot at the boss, all my smartness and discreteness would have been nothing more than arrogant foolishness."

She hummed, and her lips stretched toward a smile. But shaking her head, she crawled forward a little and reached for the gun that was lying on the ground before holstering it quickly.

Finally looking like her prim and proper self, she stood up and spoke with a little more vigor, her sweet voice still cracking. "We should go. I've wasted enough of our time."

Nodding, Vern extended his arm and offered her one of the masks.

"Let's go."

Chapter 44

WHISPERS

Starfall Heights had its own distinct flair in terms of architectural style, but the inspiration was clear. Streets were mostly comprised of one- or two-story buildings, which had narrow facades adorned with intricate carvings and decorative wrought iron railings.

Each building boasted unique brass fittings and mechanical adornments, from brass door knockers shaped like gears to tiny chimneys,— some of which were actually emitting gentle puffs of steam. Surprisingly or unsurprisingly, the farther they went into the district, the more people they saw.

There was even a little market where people were bartering food and fuel. It wasn't as glorious as bazaars from before the duskfall, but it was nice to see, nonetheless. People were slowly warming up to this new reality, finding their positions in this restructured and trimmed-down clockwork that was society.

Most factories they passed by were abandoned, and so were most of the offices. So Vern didn't hold any hopes of the relay station being in better condition than this.

Adjusting the band of his mask, he inquired, "Does the mask match my outfit?" It was his attempt at clearing the air—to repel some of the awkwardness that had crept up between them throughout the walk.

Some gave them funny looks because of their outfits. But hey, masquerade masks always look good no matter the situation. These ones especially stood out, with their long and elegant curves that covered their lower faces to some extent as well.

They had talked very little because of the increased number of people that were passing by, and it was obvious she was actively avoiding any conversations regarding observation in front of ordinary citizens.

Vern could only agree with that attitude. Another bout of panic in the masses wouldn't be any good. They already had their plates full, trying to settle down without their families and acquaintances. They didn't deserve more complications than necessary.

This reminded him. *Heh, those bystanders back at the bridge must be thinking we got real lucky with all the weapons backfiring at the last moment—*

"Ah, I think the gems on it match with your vest. But here in these surroundings, it's almost an act of rebellion," she said, interrupting his thoughts as they marched up the incline. "Though, if your eyes were glowing in the same hue, it would pull the whole look together."

Well, that seemed like it worked in getting her to talk.

"No, Miss Cera. It is very important that one doesn't reveal that they are different from others in the society. The idea is to avoid drawing undue notice to oneself. I could see commoners calling me an occultist for the matter, and it only goes downhill from there."

But instead of replying to his masterful assertion, she asked something he hadn't expected. "Vern, do you always address people with the prefixes of Miss and Mister? Is that a thing among fundamentalists?"

Huh? What?

"Uh, not really? I-I just . . . didn't want to commit a faux pas by misaddressing a noble. I am still just a lowly commoner, after all. A fundamentalist or not."

But the moment he said that, she stopped in her tracks and brought her ungloved hand to her lips, which was untouched by the mask as she chuckled. A chuckle that soon turned into laughter—her giggles like sonorous tinkling bells. The gloom that had surrounded her and broke her down in tears was nowhere to be seen.

Amid her fit of laughter, she looked at him with her crescent eyes that peeked through the elegant mask—upturned like a moon. She might be right that her eyes would look dazzling if they shone through the mask.

"A noble? Who? Where?" she said holding her hand flat over her eyebrows as she theatrically scanned the surroundings.

Vern's mind was sent reeling as his assumptions came crashing. This situation almost made him want to open his notebook and go through all the events to see where he had gone wrong. A habit of the past. One he had managed to keep in check in the recent years.

But. But that doesn't make sense. She has connections with Helena Von Arden and has always been dressed like an aristocrat. Last time, she was even in some fancy mourning dress.

But it was okay. It really looked like he had gone wrong somewhere. No matter. He wasn't some fumbling teenager anymore. Not giving in to his past introverted tendencies, he managed to eke out a few words. "Are . . . you not?"

"Hahhahhah. What gave you the idea? I can't even manage a curtsy properly. If I were a noble, I'd have been disowned the day I was born."

"I think it was your graceful mannerisms and the dignified way you present yourself that confused me. It's hard not to see something noble in that."

"Hah, I wouldn't believe that if Ephram himself came down. But please be assured. I am no noble."

However, before Vern could conjure something witty to mask his embarrassment, she resumed her strides and changed the topic. "Anyway. Now that we don't have to be as wary of the people around us, would you like to know more about observation?"

His flustered self quickly shifted gears when he heard her last words. Furrowing his brows, he asked, "Miss Cera, didn't we agree that you would give me the rest of the information later on?" He wasn't keen on looking a gift horse in the mouth, but he didn't want his earlier actions to come off as transactional in nature. He was just trying to soothe a fellow human being without expecting anything in return for it.

"Cera. Just Cera. Not a noble, right?"

Damn. It's already stuck in my mind.

He shook his head and responded, "All right. Cera. Are you sure about this? I am perfectly fine waiting until you have enlightened yourself before you divulge anything else. Please don't consider my previous actions to be something I performed in hopes of coercing you into giving me more information."

Her head swayed side to side, and her lips maintained a subtle smile as she responded, "No, it's nothing like that, Vern. Please don't worry about it. I just agree with what you said earlier. The more you understand observation, the easier it will be for me inside the station."

He sighed in relief. That was great.

"You can already render firearms impotent without having shaded your perception. Who knows what else you can do once you have a better understanding of things? I guess my earlier question of who would win if pitched against a firearm has already been answered."

He wanted to be modest, but then, she had seen it already. So he swung his arm in an elegant gesture toward his chest and bowed briefly. "Then I thank you for your generosity. I would love to hear whatever you're willing to share with me."

She nodded and looked at the ground, probably organizing her thoughts—preparing to bombard him with some complex set of information.

In the meantime, Vern observed his surroundings, not keen on repeating his earlier mistake—getting lost in a conversation only to find himself knee-deep in trouble.

It was indeed as Cera had mentioned. There were barely any people going up or down the hillside route. A few houses lined the right side of the road, but as was the usual nowadays, most looked unoccupied. With spaced out houses and somewhat dense vegetation, this area would have been the perfect hideout for gangs just a few days ago. Now they probably had castles to themselves.

Scrutinizing every nook and cranny of his surroundings, he finally noticed something odd and snapped his head backward, twisting his torso a little.

But there was nothing.

He was sure that some of the shadows that were projected on a building next to him had shifted. The greatest source of light here was the odd streetlamp that was still working. It was probably every fourth lamp or so.

A marvel of intelligent city planning and genius fundamentalists, these lamps were different than the others that preceded them. They used solar condensed fuel, which gets turned into steam when the sun is out and is stored in a chamber. At night, it's funneled into the outer section where it's ignited, illuminating the streets before condensing into its volatile form once again.

Uh, someone help me! I can't keep my thoughts straight. Banishing his meandering recollection, he focused on the matter at hand. There were only a few burning lamps behind him. So the shadow must have been generated because of something between the lamps and himself.

But then again, he was being too paranoid. For all the possibilities, it could very well be one of the cats that ran about the streets even after the duskfall. They might've ended up in the path for a second.

Anyway, even if it was something dangerous, it had to be quite some distance away according to the size of the shadow. As long as he interpreted it in his perception before it could do something untoward to him, he should be fine.

Rifles weren't much of a concern since the sun had set already. In such low light, if someone was skilled enough to shoot him down, he saw no point in hiding. He would rather not skulk around like a wraith because of figments of his imagination.

So he instead looked to his left at the gorgeous city beneath him. The sun had already sneaked away, and it was hard to make out the details. But the winding pathways were growing minuscule by the second, resembling a labyrinth with shadows obscuring many of the twists and turns.

The hint of the moon that had shown up in the purple sky alongside that disturbing rift was throwing its light down from the heavens, which reflected off the river to his north. The water shimmered like another starry sky, bisected only by the metallic bridge that connected it to some other small district.

It was the very definition of—

"Okay. So let me first ask you something else. Do you know about the whispers from beyond?" Cera interrupted.

Vern put the desolate beauty of his surroundings to the back of his mind and focused.

He weighed his words and finally ended up deciding not to mention the Ascendant Council and the madman that attributed his discovery to the whispers. She didn't need to be involved with that dangerous place. "I have experienced them myself, but no. I don't really understand their nature."

She nodded, the mask adding an air of allure to her every gesture. "Mm-hmm. So the very first thing is to not envision changes into reality recklessly. That is why we have observation records. The recorded visions are chains of thought that are considered to be safe and viable. Hundreds have succumbed to whispers trying out ideas that didn't conform with reality."

This was peculiar. It did line up with his failed attempt to mess with gravity back in the library after he'd woken up. But this puzzled him. His first voyage in the sea of observation was nothing like that. He had envisioned almost whatever came to his mind.

So he asked to confirm one of his previous conjectures. "Is that to say we can't use our viewpoints freely? That we have to follow these said paths, or we'll be putting ourselves in danger?"

"I would say you're mostly right but remember that these observation records started somewhere. Someone must have gone through a completely novel thought process to create these visions, which was further developed by later inheritors."

That was a fair point. That was to say, there was some logic over what worked and what didn't. That meant more experimentation was in order—

"But Vern, please heed my warning. Do not envision changes rashly. The warnings I received left no room for doubt that these whispers are no joke. I haven't experienced them myself, but based on how you were acting back in the library, you barely managed to survive. You were mumbling incoherently. And— And it was scary.

"Vern, you weren't yourself. Madam Helena stressed this more than anything else and made it indisputably clear. Those who succumb to the whispers don't end up pretty, and there's no coming back."

Maybe more experimentation wasn't the brightest idea.

He dispelled all foolhardy notions, soaking in her words with a more serious stance. That madman in the council was a clear example of how whispers could affect one's mind. He had no plans of giving up his greatest asset—his brain—for some vision that might not be useful.

She continued, "Secondly, Vern, there's another thing you've got to understand. Sometimes, it's better to know less than more. There are things out there, things that aren't meant to be dug into too deeply. I know it sounds onerous and pretentious, but that's exactly what the warnings say, word for word."

"I see," he said with a pensive look in his eyes.

That was another adage he would have done well to know yesterday. This whole conversation just seemed to highlight everything he had done wrong in the past few days. But he still nodded, unpacking her words.

"There are more things to keep in mind, but most of them are derivatives of these two. So, maybe I can instead tell you a little more about other things."

However, before she could start the topic, Vern waved her to stop.

The station was already in sight, just a couple lamps ahead. But that's not why he interrupted such an important conversation. Someone was standing in front of the station, hidden in the shadows, loudly tapping what seemed to be a cane.

When Vern looked over, the figure turned around and a raspy voice resounded in his ears.

"Turn back, wanderers. Turn back. These grounds aren't meant for nighttime escapades."

CHAPTER 45

STEAMSCRIPT RELAY HUB

The shadowy figure continued, "This place is haunted, and you would do well to not be around when the wretched melody plays out. It will ruin you!"

Instead of focusing on his words, Vern first tried to figure out if the man had any weapons, but he was standing in a section where light wasn't welcome at all. His cane was the only thing that shone with some luster.

Cera had stopped and was looking at the man, her eyebrows knitted together tightly. Before Vern could respond, she took the opportunity to do so. "Oh, is that so? Can you tell us more about this wretched melody? Where does it originate from, and why is it happening?"

Heh. That's one way to handle ominous-sounding declarations.

Vern looked on, waiting for a response. But maybe the man was as dumbfounded as Vern because he went completely quiet.

Then just when Vern was getting impatient, the man continued, completely ignoring Cera's question, "Don't play with fire, wanderers. You're no match for the devil that haunts the station. Begone. May you find your worth in the mundane world."

But Cera was having none of it. "How do you know about what's happening in there? Also, when did we say that we came here to go inside the station?"

Pfft. He barely held back his laughter. She was asking some real questions here.

The cane seemed to lose its balance—or maybe not? It was hard to figure out. Vern wanted to be serious and listen to the man, but even if a little unconventional, her questions were legit in their own right.

So he waited, but all the shadow did was snort, "Hmph!"

Tap. Tap. Tap.

Then the outline shifted and retreated into the alleyway that bordered the relay station's perimeter.

Cera hastily got closer and shouted, "Excuse me! Where are you going? Please answer my questions."

Vern trailed behind her, but by the time his lamp illuminated that unlit section and the alleyway, it was completely empty. Unsure of what to make of it, he glanced at the displeased Cera, who stood there, looking quite lost.

"Why can't people answer questions in good faith?"

Vern shrugged his shoulders. "Some people like to act out the role. But that aside, we should still be careful, Cera. That 'wretched melody' sounds quite like what you mentioned before."

"Right? That was the whole reason I inquired about it. That guy was just being rude."

Shaking her head, she led the way into the relay station.

Vern prepared himself one final time. He was banking on his skills as a fundamentalist to help him figure out whatever was going wrong in there. But was that enough? Hadn't Cera just cautioned him that sometimes less knowledge was beneficial? That delving too deeply could prove counterproductive?

But I guess one needs to understand when to delve into mysteries and when not to. Also, I would rather not be ungrateful to her. If it was just enlightenment, something of the order of what the man was doing in the Hotel Inkwell should be enough. Vern could easily handle that much—not including the two men he had met later on, of course.

Making up his mind, he followed Cera. The lamps around the entrance of the station were out, even the ones that reused the condensed fuel. Luckily, he had his own light source this time.

Despite some areas being shrouded in darkness, the overall structure was generously illuminated by the celestial bodies above. It stretched widely across the landscape for about twenty row houses yet was built quite low to the ground.

The metallic whistles atop the station were a feat of mechanical arts, their size likely contributing to the station's relatively low height.

Four enormous tapered cylinders, each pointing in a cardinal direction, commanded the roof. Beyond the nearest one, Vern could see pipes that connected these external mammoths to the intricate mechanisms housed within the structure.

Hmm. Is that a dent on the east whistle? He wasn't sure. But its shape was a little off compared to the others.

Well, who knew? It could just be another design choice or some defect.

Looking back down, he realized Cera was also ogling the station. *Maybe she's never been to this part of the city? That means she never used the relay station herself.*

But that didn't matter. Ignoring these idle thoughts, they crossed the perimeter surrounding the station and found a large entrance, which didn't have a gate.

As they closed in on the door to the actual building, he asked, "Are you ready?"

She shook her head. "I am not. But this is as ready as I can be. How about you?"

"Well, I still don't know what to expect, so I have a few suggestions before we head in."

"Mm-hmm."

"Let me inspect the inbound pipes to check for any faults and then survey the exterior of the building."

She agreed without hesitation.

They spent an additional thirty minutes surveying the outskirts of the building. All he discovered was a handful of pipes that surfaced briefly for pressure regulation before disappearing underground. He had unscrewed one for inspection. However, they were devoid of any signs of activity—no steam, no gas.

Everything seemed as ordinary as it could be.

There isn't much more I can deduce from the outside; going in is the only option.

Unable and unwilling to find more excuses to tarry any longer, he made his way back to the front door, Cera following closely. This much due diligence was enough. If he wanted to entertain further paranoia, he might as well just go back to the hotel.

Steeling his mind, he pushed open one of the three doors that stood in a line, giving the relay station a welcoming presence.

It was hard to make out the details due to the darkness, but this relay station was much grander than the ones he'd been to before.

The interior was an unsettling contrast of form and function, bearing the remnants of bustling life. A counter where civilians would have lined up to place and receive letter delivery orders stood abandoned, its polished wooden surface reflecting the dim light from tarnished brass sconces.

Nearby, ticketing windows and pigeonholes held an array of unclaimed messages, untouched and gathering dust. There were a couple of pews by the door, empty dresses lining their bases. The silence hung heavily in the air, broken only by the occasional creak of the wooden floor in a somber echo.

Quite the expected scene, if Vern had to be honest. Feeling more at ease, they walked in, the taps of their shoes further disturbing the silence.

"Vern, where do you suggest we begin our search?"

"Hmm, this hub's quite massive compared to the ones I've been to. Just the civilian section takes up more space than a train platform. Given that this is the capital, there must be a section for VIPs, government officials, and even royals. I remember you had looked through the architectural plan for this location. Did it mention any control hub or nexus of pipes?"

She shook her head. "The plans I found didn't outline the rooms, they only depicted the gas pipeline network in the building. From what I understand, it goes down to the basement of the structure and has nothing like a confluence you mentioned earlier."

He nodded. "Gas pipelines are different from the pipes that would transmit sound throughout the structure and channel it to the whistles up above."

He thought about it for a few more seconds before replying, "I guess we can start by checking out where the letters taken from civilians go to."

With the lamp illuminating just enough space around him, he left the main door behind and entered the chamber. It had a plaque hanging outside it that was engraved with the text MESSAGE RECEPTION HALL.

Numerous envelopes lay scattered on the floor beneath the opening of what appeared to be a sealed pneumatic tube. They were constructed from flexible glass adorned with metal joints, allowing one to see the letters whizzing by, propelled by gusts of pressurized steam. Not in this case obviously, the letters merely lay dormant, waiting for pressure to pull them in.

This design made quite a lot of sense. Since they had multiple sources of letters in the same building, it wouldn't be ideal to translate them into sound at every source.

So they must have been directed toward the nexus, where someone would retype them into a special typewriter that could record sounds. Relay stations allowed senders to type their letters themselves due to privacy concerns, but most people didn't know how to type or didn't bother. For those who did, there was an extra fee to be paid.

So, if he could trace the path of these pneumatic tubes, he should find himself nearing the core of the transmission pipes.

Cera picked up one of the envelopes and began perusing its contents. "A congratulations letter to some friend that was never delivered."

Vern didn't say anything as he shone the light inside the pneumatic tubes to see if there were any curves or changes in direction.

Both of them busied themselves for a bit.

Then Vern said, "All right. We should go farther in. There is nothing else in here that can give us any more clues."

Cera replaced the letters back on the counter, sliding them into their respective envelopes. Perturbed, he asked, "What is the point of reading them?"

"Ah, nothing. Just trying to learn more about people's intentions and thoughts."

Vern knew there was more to it, so he asked, "Is it related to your viewpoint?"

She gasped before quickly trying to hide her shock and said with some annoyance, "Sometimes you're too sharp! Please focus on the pipes. Not me. Okay? The pipes."

He chuckled and walked out of the room. Passing by a few similar rooms, which each seemed to have some sort of pneumatic tube system of their own, they followed the direction he had extrapolated the tubes to be moving in.

Navigating a narrow corridor that delved deeper into the building, they soon emerged into a grand hall adorned with thick pillars. Portraits graced each wall, adding an air of antiquity to the space.

There was a tall bronze statue in the center of the room, a motionless fountain encircling it. It was a likeness of Emperor Aldric, his arm outstretched as if offering a decree to the world.

But even though it was such an open area, the sight gave him the chills. The silent eyes of the statue and the portraits seemed to follow him as he passed by the pillars, sidestepping all the clothes that had belonged to the victims of the duskfall.

Nevertheless, he ignored his nerves and focused his attention on locating any signs of pipe fittings or markings.

It was unfortunate that the machinery was hidden within the walls with such finesse that none of it was visible. The station looked more like some government office rather than the mechanical miracle that it was.

Checking another room connected to the hall, he found one more set of pneumatic tubes. Assuming they all converged in same area, he exited the room and followed the expected trail back into the hall.

After running back and forth a few more times, he finally found a corridor where pipes were visible on the ceiling. Not hesitating too much, he followed the corridor to the end, which culminated in a vast chamber.

At last, he felt a sense of progress.

The massive hall stood eerily still. Pneumatic tubes lay motionless, gathering dust. Catwalks overhead led to a tangled mess of valves and pipes, now silent and devoid of the hissing steam that should have filled the room.

Along one wall, a row of typewriters sat abandoned at wooden desks, their keys silenced, chairs pushed askew.

He could almost hear the bustling of uniformed attendants and the whirring of gears in this mechanical wonderland, but now all that met his ears was the occasional eerie creak or distant clang resonating through the emptiness.

While this wasn't the central hub of the transmission pipes he was searching for, it was evidently a crucial part of the station. He might be able to glean some hints on where to proceed next.

But before all that, he had to burn this sight into his memory. To Vern, the room was a masterpiece. The pipes all around were arranged and directed with such careful precision that he was certain an equation must have guided their placement and spacing.

Everything was so efficiently set up that he was lamenting the fact that he hadn't come in when it had been working. Cera looked around just like him, her eyes shining with amazement.

"Vern, do you know what this place is? Are these the transmission pipes you were mentioning?"

He shook his head and said, "No, not really. I would say this is where they buffer all the letters, and those typewriters aren't exactly steamscripts, they're just normal ones. This looks to be the sorting and distribution hub instead."

Her eyes dulled for a second, but she quickly regained her energy and said, "Obviously, it can't be this straightforward. The real magic hides behind the mundane, doesn't it?"

Vern nodded, his attention focused on something else at the far end of the corridor. Something was wrong with tubes over there. There was a rush of steam in that set every few seconds, yet the envelopes inside oscillated back and forth with an abnormal fervor.

Intrigued, he moved closer to the machine, and Cera picked up on the oddity as well. It was peculiar on two fronts. First, that it worked *at all*. Second, that its behavior was leagues away from the norm.

The entire setup seemed illogical. It appeared as if a novice had tampered with everything, oblivious to the consequences of their actions. None of the configuration made any sense.

Eager to figure out why the system was still working when the whole station was out of operation and displeased by the disregard shown to this magnificent setup, Vern promptly examined the basic configuration and began adjusting the valves back to their industry standards. After turning the valve for flow control, he waited until the gauge above it read 7.13 vaporstrength.

Similar changes happened for pressure relief and the nonreturn valve. However, the moment the reading on the rotary valve hit 0.32, a screeching boom resonated throughout the hub.

WEEENNNNGGGGGG!

UNSTABLE INSTABILITY

Vern reflexively clamped his hands over his ears. Cera, almost losing her balance, followed suit, covering her ears once she found her footing.

What the hell is going on?

He had expected something to happen, but not . . . this. The sound clearly came from those colossal whistles up above. But it made no sense. There were more than a dozen configuration panels like the one he had just fiddled with. These valves couldn't have affected the working of the whistles or the whole system, no matter what.

But now wasn't the time to figure out the how. Not wasting any more precious seconds, he reached out to the panel to undo the changes. However, before he could even touch them, the piercing noise came to a halt, and the envelopes that were zooming past inside the tube stilled.

Everything calmed, and the hall became as silent as outside. He looked around in puzzlement, trying to figure out what was going on.

"Vern, was that supposed to happen?" Cera asked while looking around, seeming a little unsure of their surroundings.

"No. I don't think so." With a heavy frown, he scrutinized the tube another time before looking at the other panels.

It was as if nothing had happened.

But that's when it did.

The dust particles beneath him seemed to dance in a sporadic fashion, spinning and whirling in patterns that seemed too deliberate to be random. The valves that he had just set to industry standard began rotating on their own, steam hissing out of the pipes' joints.

The phenomenon spread to the tubes and devices around him at breakneck speed as everything began humming to life. The needles of the valves began to wobble aimlessly, their readings off by who knows how much, and he simply stood there, staring in awe.

Something gripped his hand, and he was broken out of his reverie, his heart picking up pace.

"Vern! Don't just stand there. Something's not right and we're not supposed to be caught in the middle of it. We need to leave. Now!"

Her words settled in his brain, making perfect sense. They were too close to this anomaly. Letting himself be dragged by her, he took stock of his surroundings.

His ears caught an uncanny symphony of mechanical clatters and hisses, punctuated by the sporadic thumping of a loose tube hitting the metallic wall. The age-old gears began to clank and clatter, each moving part contributing to an orchestra of discordant metallic echoes.

The keys on the typewriter began to click by themselves, and the chairs began to hobble away, steadily gaining toward Vern and Cera. The lighting fixtures flashed with bluish light, illuminating the eerie sight of the animated hall for a moment, displaying sights that didn't conform to everyday reality.

Vern and Cera rushed toward the exit, which was a short distance away, but their surroundings were changing too quickly. This sight was close to the top of the list of the most unnatural things he'd seen in his life.

"Fuck! All I did was rotate two freaking valves."

"Doesn't matter right now! Just run!"

She let go of his hand and began full-on sprinting. Vern followed, hurrying out of this bewitched room.

Ba-dum.

Ba-dum.

He first confused this sound with his own heartbeat, but that couldn't be it. His heart was racing much faster than whatever this was. On closer inspection, it was coming from his surroundings, and it wasn't the organic sound of a heartbeat.

It was something along the lines of clicks and hisses harmonizing to produce this effect. In a prolonged glance, he realized that this whole situation was more accursed than he had first thought.

All the pneumatic tubes, previously releasing steam erratically, had begun to synchronize their ventilation cycles. The pressure that pushed the envelopes now pulsed in a smooth, rhythmic fashion, echoing through the room like a heartbeat.

Whoosh.

Something whizzed past his head at a blistering pace, and his pupils constricted.

That thing could've easily fractured my skull!

"VERN, DODGE!" shouted Cera, already having stepped to one side.

Not thinking twice, he stepped to the side mid-sprint, and a small blur passed by his thigh, jamming into the wall in front of him. He looked back and noticed the source.

The fucking typewriters were shooting keys!

However, that wasn't going to be the last of his concerns. The chairs, which he initially thought were moving toward them, were actually closing in on the hall's exit instead. Drawers from a filing cabinet floated in front of the way out as other objects reached it and began congregating. They bent unnaturally and cracked into splinters, blockading the door.

All right, this is fucking it.

He hadn't been laid back at any point throughout this excursion, but some proper thought was needed if they were to make it out of this alive. Despite the ever-thickening mesh of furniture, there was still space for them to squeeze through. *But that isn't going to work. The keys are aimed straight toward the exit.*

Whoosh.

Whish.

Swing.

Cera dodged as the keys bore holes in the furniture obstructing their path. But it didn't even make a dent in the haphazard congregation of different articles that were impeding their way.

The problem was twofold—one in front of him and the other behind him. Instability inducement wouldn't help with the blockade in front. He had never tried breaking simple furniture with it, much less this amalgamation of wood and metal that was getting thicker by the second.

So he would let her deal with this.

"CERA! Charge for a wider shot, I will take care of the keys!"

She nodded with a serious look, drawing the gun from her waist as she nimbly dodged the stray keys. Luckily, the drum of the typewriters had an obvious tell with that sharp click. Alongside the angle at which they were standing, it was easy to figure out their direction of fire.

So he abandoned the exit and turned around, interpreting the typewriters in his perception, not shading it, as Cera had explained the difference.

However, something completely unexpected happened, leaving him stunned and at a loss. *Huh? What the hell?*

He tried to assign grays to the drum of all three of the typewriters that were firing away their keys, but it was as if he were trying to pour water over an oily surface. The grays refused to adhere to any component, not even the keys.

For confirmation, he tried to interpret the ground, which was the only thing that didn't seem to be affected by this whole atmosphere. As expected, it soaked up the grays like usual, straining the veins of his eyes.

So nothing was wrong with his ability to observe.

Letting go of that thought, he instead focused on the numerous pneumatic valves to test if it was just the animated objects that he couldn't shade.

And he was half right. The grays of complexity on the surface of the tube vanished in thin air, but the joints turned white, looking like the simple rings that floated in his perception.

He closed his eyes for a second.

Integrity.

But it was exactly the same situation. Changing how he perceived the balance didn't make any difference.

Fuck! There is some complex criteria on where it's working and where it isn't.

But this information didn't help him in any way. The only sections of the typewriters where a flaw could be induced were impervious to his observation. So there was no point in figuring out if there were some parts of the typewriter that he could influence.

He had to think of some other solution.

Should I just get closer and physically smash the creepy things?

But he discarded the idea the very next moment. Their aim is focused on the entrance right now, but what if they turn toward me?

Using his gun would be just as useless. Aiming precisely at the drums of the rogue typewriters seemed impossible, and shooting anywhere else would be inconsequential. At most, the bullets would shatter a key or two, but that might even draw attention to himself—something he wanted to avoid at all costs.

No. I need to change my train of thought.

If being offensive wasn't going to work, he would have to find some way to defend both of them as they made their exit.

His heart pounded wildly, each beat resonating with the urgency of the situation, while his mind whirled in a tempest of thought and fear. Time seemed to stretch, every second a restless hour, before a spark of inspiration ignited within him.

Yes! That could work.

Retrieving the compact yet heavy umbrella from his coat, he clicked the button on its handle, the bronze canopy unfolding with its mechanical movements.

He had given it a cursory look during their walk, but the examination had been nowhere detailed enough for him to understand the whole machinery inside it. And he had never gotten around to fixing the instabilities he had induced in it. He had only a few seconds to put his plan into action, or things would take a turn for the worse for them both.

Small pipes ran along the length of its shaft that connected to the hexagonal sections in the canopy. The design was probably divided into these smaller sections to allow the umbrella to be portable. Each of these hexagons had a small set of gears, and like most other devices of this style, every section was made to work independently from the rest.

He praised his prior insight to have induced instability in two of the thirteen core gears in the center where the hexagons combined their spin, or that boss would've survived even if he destabilized hundreds of gears in the outer sections.

But now he felt like condemning himself for having done so. It would be much harder to fix the core assembly in such a crunch without any proper tools.

However, his reputation as a savant wasn't just for show. With a practiced eye, he quickly identified a couple of other gears within the hexagons that could serve as suitable replacements.

Seizing every moment, he plunged his fingers right into the hexagons, wrenching gears from within them. It would reduce the overall spin since three subsections would be effectively dysfunctional, but he didn't have any other options.

Crunch. Clang.

While performing the transplant, he kept an eye on his surroundings. Getting impaled by one of those keys because he was too busy gouging gears from some contraption wasn't his idea of efficiency.

In the hall, the tubes were getting wilder by the second. The envelopes inside and the steam expelling from the joints weren't the only things that pulsed in a rhythm. The whole fucking network had begun to . . . move? It didn't make any sense. Some tubes were snaking away from their rigid postures as they changed angles and began connecting and disconnecting with different tubes.

But their actions seemed to have some logic, as the new connections were perfect in their own right while still giving off a distinct sense of being organic. What was good news, though, was that the gigantic glass snake didn't seem to care about him or Cera, as all the changes didn't look like they wanted to hamper their progress.

The lights in the room were still flashing at a haphazard pace, making every anomaly running around him a touch eerier. But he had found a solution to the current predicament, so he shoved his fears to the back of his mind. He would ponder whatever possessed these objects once he was out of this goddamned hall.

He was creating makeshift gears to replace the defective ones using multiple smaller sets, ensuring they fit the rest of the assembly. And it was quite a fast process.

First gear. Second gear. Third gear. Fourth gear. Fifth—

"VERN, I AM READY!"

This better work! He rapidly clicked three more gears into their positions before shouting back, "PERFECT! I AM DONE TOO!"

CHAPTER 47

HUNT

From the looks of it, Vern hadn't made any mistakes, and the contraption should work. So with a deep breath and grim determination, he pressed the primary switch on its shaft.

Whirrrr.

The umbrella began spinning as he fought to keep the device stable in his hands. Sparks flew out of the core assembly, and the makeshift gears began grinding away at the spokes since some were protruding where they shouldn't. This was going to stop very soon.

Fuck. If only I could've done something better with observation—

"VERN! I CAN'T HOLD ON!"

He swiveled around and noticed that the gun in her hands was starting to glow red with all that heat. Any more, and it would severely burn her hands. So he got ready and shouted, "AIM FOR THE CENTER! I'LL COVER US!"

The blaster hummed ominously as it gathered energy, the barrel glowing with an inner light. Cera took careful aim at the mass of twisted chairs, tables, and cabinets that had come to life and blocked their path. Their once-inanimate forms now shifted and creaked, moving with a wooden rigidity as if controlled by unseen strings.

She pulled the trigger.

Boom!

A searing burst of energy erupted from the blaster, a combination of heat and force that streaked across the room and struck the furniture with an earth-shattering impact, sending Cera tumbling back. The concussive shock wave ripped through the wood and fabric, the intense heat igniting the materials in a fiery explosion.

The furniture was reduced to ashes and splinters, their charred edges emitting the smell of burnt wood.

This was great! Von Industries indeed made some powerful weapons.

He didn't wait for the rest of the articles in the room to try trapping them in here again. Holding out the whirring umbrella toward his back, he threw himself into the hail of keys, skewing his sprint toward Cera. Shocks ran along the muscles of his arms as the canopy of the umbrella was pelted by one key after another.

But it held up. And that's all that mattered right now.

Still recovering from the recoil of that massive blast, Cera noticed him, and a look of realization dawned on her face. Quickly stumbling into a stride, she leapt next to him, finding cover behind the small canopy of the device.

Luckily, the typewriters weren't actively adjusting their aim, because both of them would be in big trouble if they did. He was only trying to keep their heads and torsos secure, after all.

One step after another, they closed in on the exit under the shelter of the whirring umbrella as keys were deflected in haphazard directions—sparks crackling around them.

Kicking a stool that was hobbling near to block his path, he ran right past it. In but a few seconds, they crossed the charred wooden border and found themselves back in the corridor. The pneumatic tubes out here seemed unaffected by the happenings inside, which was probably a good sign.

Whinggg.

The noises in the umbrella were getting worse. But it was okay. It had done its job for now.

His arm felt lighter as he clicked the device shut and threw it back into his pocket after having folded it mid-sprint.

He finally remembered to check up on her, and she was looking worse for wear. That shot had done a number on her hands, which were still quite red. Her breaths came in ragged gasps, and an uneasy expression covered her face.

Noticing him looking, she asked in a breathy voice, drowned by the clanks and clatter from the room behind them, "Was that not subjective enough?! Why is there still no response from my eyes?"

That was indeed a good question, and he didn't have an answer to that. Not right now, at least.

"I can't say for sure, but it was a good thing it didn't. Things could've turned for the worst if you became dazed in there, even for a second."

She closed her eyes for a second before nodding, and they quickly found themselves back in the large hall.

He looked back—nothing was following them. It didn't make sense, but he would take whatever good luck came his way in this unfathomable situation. At least the hall itself seemed tranquil. Dark but peaceful.

But neither of them stopped running. Pillar after pillar, they rushed past everything to make their way back. But the moment they got close to the narrow corridor that led to the public section, he noticed it.

In the periphery of his eyes, something moved, and his heart lurched. Skidding hard on the marble surface, he forced himself to halt and gripped Cera's arm before jerking her back.

Bam!

Stone and debris flew toward him as a gigantic metallic hand smashed into the floor, creating a crater in the ground.

"AHH!" she shrieked and looked on wide-eyed.

In front of them was the statue of Emperor Aldric. The hand that was outstretched to show care for his citizens had just clenched itself and slammed downward, perfectly angled to ground them both into meat paste.

Fuck! Fuck! FUCK!

Crunchhh.

The statue pulled its bronze leg out of the rock it had been stuck on and stomped down another crater in front of itself.

There was no way they were walking right past this thing.

Vern backed away, dragging Cera along. "This is crazy! Ephram, how could this be? What the hell is going on!?" she yelled in a hoarse voice.

She had been keeping quite a level head for someone who had never even seen visions before today, but her nerves were fraying. And he couldn't blame her.

He was barely keeping up with all the changes himself.

How the hell could this phenomenon spread everywhere?! Even Hensen could only observe things that were in his sight.

Did it really all start because he turned a few levers? Where—

No. Curse my fucking brain!

He had been standing frozen, just looking at the menace. Now wasn't the time for that. Berating himself internally, he set in motion the simplest idea that came to his mind.

"Cera. Calm down. We will have to run the other way. The pillars should make it hard for the statue to get to us instantly. We might be able to circle around and slip past it. Also, how long before you can use the gun again?"

They spun around and retraced their steps, but this time with the intent to hug the walls of the large hall along its edges, as those were the only sections studded with large pillars. Going toward the center of the hall would mean being outside the scant protection provided by the columns.

Her eyes darted rapidly as she followed his lead before replying, "I-t's . . . It's still very hot. I can feel it in the holster. It probably won't work if we try to use it right away."

That was expected but unfortunate.

Crunccch.

Having found balance on hard ground with one of its legs, the statue pulled out the other one in a very mechanical motion as the fountain beneath it crumbled into nothingness.

Smashhhh.

The whole building shuddered as the bronze statue pulled its arm back like some giant doll and then catapulted it toward another column. Vern sidestepped to avoid a big chunk of debris that burst toward him.

Cold sweat slicked Vern's brows as he stumbled around the corner, the metallic footfalls growing louder in his ears.

His heart told him to run like there was no tomorrow, but his brain knew he could do more.

So he didn't waste any time and began finding ways to use his vision to wrench some semblance of control in this mess. The bronze statue wasn't completely rigid, there were expertly crafted joints clearly visible inside. It almost seemed like an automaton, except it was impossible to make one like this with current Lennian fundamentals.

Fundamentals made miracles come true, but sentience of this degree was impossible. This thing was actively chasing them and solving problems like avoiding the pillars to get to them.

But that wasn't his concern right now. Since it had joints and sockets, it must mean there should be a few other mechanisms. Mechanisms he could destabilize.

He wasn't a puppet master or sculptor, so he didn't know the exact makeup of this thing, but if he could disbalance some joints, inertia would do the rest.

Assuming this phenomenon cared about laws of mechanics and dynamics, that is. After all, the chairs back in that sorting room didn't have any joints, but they were still hobbling around like marionettes to some tune.

No matter. It's worth a shot.

Complexity.

He tried to interpret the statue, and his heart fell yet again.

This damned thing was just like those typewriters in the sorting room—slippery like oil. He couldn't interpret its form with grays in his perception at all.

This is scrapshit! This has never happened before tonight! Why the hell does it have to happen when I need it?

Not ready to give up just yet, he continued his stride and weaved between the pillars since the statue had just started running closer to the wall, outright avoiding the pillars as it gained on them rapidly. There weren't even two pillars in between them now!

Fucking work, damn it!

He kept looking back and forth as his imagination alone couldn't keep up with the unpredictable mechanical moves of the giant. Once. Twice. Thrice. He tried to interpret section after section of the statue, but it didn't fucking work. Until . . .

Huh?

On a closer look, there was a fanciful array of teardrop designs on its waist. They were hollow, and a few of the statue's internal mechanisms peeked through the exquisite yet lethal carvings. He got a better look at the assembly inside with every movement of the emperor's figurine.

Bam!

Bam!

The statue was decimating one pillar after another. It might very well cause the whole building to collapse if left unchecked. But that was the least of his concerns right now. He was lucky to have survived this long already.

But there was no more time for random thoughts! Pushing aside the terrifying booms and the eyes of the wall paintings that seemed to glare at him with scorn and pleasure in his distress, he turned his focus to the mechanisms he'd noticed inside the statue's waist and tried to interpret them.

A series of interconnected metal rods and rough-hewn gears connected to a central axle, all crammed into the limited space within the bronze structure.

And for the love of all steam, he was able to shade the supporting rods a white for their simplicity, but only the edges of that axle took to their intended dark gray. He still didn't know the criteria of what he was able to interpret and what he was not, but he did have a few conjectures. However, he wasn't about to test anything in such a tight situation.

A plan quickly took shape in his mind, and he hurriedly asked, "Cera! How long until the gun can shoot again?"

She was already waving it in the air to cool it down and responded, "Should be just a few more seconds!"

"All right. I am about to try something. If it works, I need you to capitalize on it. Shoot where you think it'll matter the most. I am sorry for putting this on you, but that's the only option we have."

"O-okay. I'll try. I'll have to go for a concussive shot this time. There isn't enough steam or time for another charged one."

He nodded and focused back on the image of the internal mechanism he had reconstructed in his perception. From the looks of it, all this movement was already pushing far beyond the limits of what this statue was created for. The mechanism was crude and was made to be more rigid than flexible.

This somewhat simplified the situation for him. He just had to find the weak spot. A flaw. There were more than a few options. But he picked the simple one that quickly presented the notion of instability to him—warping the critical rod a little and causing it to interfere with the central axle. This was mainly because he couldn't interpret the axle wholly, so he would have to make do with this.

He really felt lucky that he had come across instability inducement. The vision allowed him to use his otherwise specialized knowledge to a great extent in this society full of contraptions. Even if they were made with techniques and designs he couldn't fathom, all he needed was to find a weakness. After all, every device was as strong as its weakest link.

Hopefully, whatever magic was puppeteering this thing wouldn't be able to bypass the Lennian laws of mechanics and work with a faulty axle.

He quickly gathered more thoughts and ideas about how this flaw could work, and the notion in his mind grew bigger. Even though it was growing at a breakneck pace within his perception, the reality became dangerous faster than that.

Bammmm.

The colossus was already upon him!

He ducked and pushed off the nearest pillar to get some distance from the trajectory of the swing, but the damned pillar itself broke at its foundation, hurling him in the wrong direction. He didn't fall, but he still lost his balance, barely catching his footing.

He managed to escape this one, but the next swing was primed right for his head.

The puppet paused for the briefest of seconds, maybe confused by both his targets being away from each other for the first time.

The pause was enough for Vern.

NOW!

He grabbed hold of the notion with ferocious desperation as it covered and shattered his perception.

"AGGHHHHHHH!" A bloodcurdling scream escaped his mouth, and his vision turned red. A horrendous pain consumed him as his crimson-streaked eyes presented—an arm.

An arm that was stretched taut, ready to smash him into a pulp before it abruptly faltered.

When it began its downward arc, the rod in its pelvis crashed right into the axle, and the very next instant, the joint gave way, causing the entire upper body of the statue to lurch awkwardly.

The limb's swing turned into a wild flail as the colossus lost its footing and toppled to the ground with a tremendous crash.

The world was turning dark as everything spun around him.

Thud.

It hurt.

It felt like a bug was eating the insides of his brain.

Like someone had punctured a hole in his eyes.

But it was okay now. Right? The vision had done a far better job than he'd thought.

Maybe that's why it hurt. IT HURT! IT HURT SO MUCH!

But then he felt it.

More pain. Physical pain. Besides the one that made him want to gouge out his eyes.

It was on his leg. Something was squeezing his right shin with a terrifying grip. Something metallic.

"AHHHHHHHH!" he let loose another scream, bracing himself for the horrific sound he feared would come next—the crunch of his bone being crushed to smithereens.

Bang!

Instead came an ear-shattering sound that seemed to echo through his head. But the force which was squeezing his shin was no more.

He tried to inject some more lucid thoughts other than pain, but all he could do was listen to the grinding of the statue as a pair of soft hands under his arms dragged him away.

But what would that do?

His bloody vision of the statue revealed a frenzied one-armed monster that wouldn't leave them alive, even if it meant crawling on one hand to do so.

Tap. Tap. Tap. Tap. Tap.

A rhythmic tapping broke the monotone sound of stone and metal crashing together, prompting him to turn his head around. Other than a distressed Cera, who exerted herself to haul him away, a silver cane shone in the dark.

CHAPTER 48

FINNESSE

The tapping of the cane got closer to them. A voice resonated from the shadows. "*Ahem!* I extended an invitation for caution, yet the melody of my warning fell upon deaf ears. Our plans did not include this stage for another week."

It was still quite dark, but the silhouette was obviously shaking his head. Vern needed to quickly assess if this was a friend or foe. He really didn't have the willpower to spare thought to all the details, but this was important. His eyes felt like needles were puncturing them, but he still held his gaze.

And that's when he noticed something.

Isn't this the cane held by that man who wanted us to turn back? But his voice is so . . . different. This person sounded like a singer rather than that scruffy badger they had met outside.

When the man tapped his cane yet again, a jolt of shock ran through Vern's mind as he saw the clean, smooth surface of the cane transform into something else—another feat of mechanical artistry.

It was actually made of segments that separated from each other. The previously hidden joints began to reveal themselves as the rigidity of the stick gave way to flexibility. The individual links unfolded in a seamless, almost organic motion, each of its pieces moving in perfect harmony with the others. The whole process was instantaneous and fluid.

Before Vern could get a better look at it, the man declared, "You two, you danced to a rhythm all your own, a rhythm that sang of trouble. Allow me to take the lead in this dance. Your efforts have been bold, too bold for them to end in silence now."

With the clack of that transformation, a refined man suddenly emerged from the shadows, his long navy blue coat fluttering behind him as he broke into a sprint.

The air stirred as the man dashed past Vern, stopping in front of the statue.

This reminded Vern of his condition and that Cera was still dragging him. He could at least try to be less of a burden. So he forced his legs to push himself, making his retreat faster.

He didn't want to leave his fate up to a total stranger, but what other choice did he have? He really wasn't in any condition to defend himself right now.

Cera settled him against a pillar and put her hands on her heart, kneeling beside him. Her eyes were glued to the man, who was standing a short distance away from the rampaging statue.

His gloved hands were held high up in the air, a serrated whip—no, a cane—in one of them. Its segments were rotated on an angle, their edges gleaming with sharpness. His coat's collar was raised so high his center-parted silver hair mingled with its frays while the golden embroidery all over the fabric gave him an exquisite touch. It was as if he were a dancer, ready to perform a piece on the stage.

Cera parted her lips as if to say something but then hesitated. She wasted a few seconds like this until she finally mumbled, "Isn't he . . . ? It's been him this whole time?"

A little confused by her words, Vern strained himself to speak, and his words came out a little staccato. "Isn't he—just the—person we saw—outside the station? Do you—know him personally?"

However, before she could say something, the man closed his eyes and loudly continued, "When I saw you in the library yesterday, poring over details of this place, a note of trouble resonated within me. Yet, I never anticipated the swiftness with which you'd take the stage, performing your daring act on the very next day."

Huh? In the library? Could it be . . .

Then, with a graceful movement, the man turned sideways, expertly avoiding the jab of the statue. Swinging the cane with a smooth motion of his hand, the distance between its segments expanded as their sharp edges gleamed and dug into the bronze hand, wrapping around it. With a twirl, he pulled the cane in a circular motion.

Clank.

The segments ripped the metal to shreds as they rushed back to the handle, sawing apart the statue's forearm, which fell on the floor with a loud clang.

His eyes still closed, the man continued his earlier discourse. "Fortuitously, I heeded the call of the rhythm and followed you out here, or the consequences might have been tragic."

Vern realized that the man wasn't talking to him at all.

Cera's face was still a perplexed painting, but she quickly found her words. "I-I. Thank you very much." It was obvious she didn't know how to feel about this.

Its lower body still out of commission, the statue pushed itself up with its stumps and rushed toward their savior with an unmatched speed, ready to crush him in a hug.

To this unexpected rally, the man opened his eyes for a second, and they glowed blue. Connecting his previous movement with the next one fluidly, he waved his free hand and—disappeared.

What?

Vern, who was wiping away the blood from his eyes, blinked repeatedly to make sure he wasn't hallucinating.

Their savior had disappeared and just now reappeared to the side of the statue instead, skidding a little.

He looked at Cera, and she did the same, a somewhat excited gleam in her eyes.

Catching the statue at an off angle, he held the rigid cane upright in his hand like a sword, slashing at the shoulder of the thing.

Shwing.

A jagged-edged crack ran down the length of its shoulder as it, too, fell to the floor with a loud thump. That attack looked smooth, but it was clear that the amount of strength it took was nothing to balk at.

The wrecked and fragmented automaton fell forward due to all that momentum and components spilled out of its truncated shoulder.

But it wasn't ready to give up just yet. Its legs, which were still pristine, kicked around haphazardly, launching chunks of stone and debris all around.

The man displayed an agility surpassing anything Vern had seen, even in the fittest of humans, avoiding all the stones flung toward him with immeasurable precision. And all this transpired with his eyes closed. Finding an opening, he slid back and swung his cane, enveloping one of the statue's feet with it.

The moment the colossus tried to pull it free, the man finally used his free hand for the first time—putting it on the cane's handle. Then, synergizing with the opposite motion of the metallic leg, he yanked it with great ferocity.

Crunch.

The bronze leg flew in the air as the silvery segments rushed back to the handle of the cane. But instead of tumbling back from recoil, the man redirected his momentum gracefully. Circling his back foot into a clean step, he turned it into a beautiful gesture.

As the man continued to chip away at the statue one chunk after another without much trouble, Vern finally relaxed enough to take his eyes away from the performance. With a blood trail still staining his right cheek, he turned to Cera with a questioning gaze and asked, "Who is he?"

Vern already had an idea from the man's words, but he asked anyway.

She looked back and forth between Vern and the man before replying with an uncertain gaze, "He's one of the persons that set the archive on fire yesterday. From the Vigil of Duskfall."

Ahh. Right.

A lot of pieces clicked in place, and he understood the chain of events. This person had been on her trail since yesterday. His faction was to deal with anomalies in the city, so when he had noticed that she was looking up one of them, he grew suspicious and followed her.

This might as well have been the person who gave him the odd feeling when they were walking up the hill. But how'd he get ahead of them on their hike to the station? Anyway, that wasn't the most pressing question right now.

Even though his brain felt heavy as a lead, he had to figure out what this meant for him. So he let his thoughts churn.

Crunch.

Clank.

Bam!

The performance continued, and he concluded that he shouldn't be in any trouble. If worse came to worst, he could just show the badge that the shaggy swordsman had given him. It was still in his coat's inner pocket.

Suddenly, his chain of thoughts was interrupted by Cera. She asked, "How are you feeling? Is your, um, eye okay? Was it because of the vision? Can I do something?"

He took a handkerchief out of another one of his pockets and wiped away the blood staining his face. He didn't want to further sully his coat with blood, after all.

It was most likely some sort of internal bleeding. Bleeding that had stopped already.

The pressure he had felt in his veins after executing that vision had been so immense he was surprised it had cauterized already. However, he didn't have any delusions of having attained fast healing or anything of the sort. His shoulder still wasn't in perfect condition from that confrontation back in the Ascendant Council.

For now, he responded, "It was indeed because of the vision. I just . . . need a minute." He closed his eyes and pondered this feeling that plagued his mind right now.

A sense of emptiness.

He had felt like this before, but it was usually much milder. The worst before today was back when he had induced instability in the Kingsman's gear at the bridge. But the pain and sense of loss had been quite moderate.

This emptiness wasn't something rare, actually. Every time he envisioned instabilities, it came like a rushing torment and made him feel sluggish. He was usually fine after a few minutes, but something was different this time.

He believed this had to be the cost of using the vision. But there was some logic to it. The instability he had induced in those gang members was much more involved than whatever he had just done, but it hadn't hurt nearly as much.

So, what was the determining factor? What was more expensive, and what was cheap? Because he'd rather not pay such a hefty price ever again. This would have been the end of him if this vigilante hadn't shown up.

Is it dependent on the size of the object influenced? Because the size of the object was larger than ever.

But after a quick thought, he found flaws in that argument. He remembered that the cost of destabilizing the wall clock in his room and that bigger one on the storefront in the Silverthread district was pretty much the same.

The clock or the gear he destabilized to show off in front of Cera was at least twice as large as the one in his room at Hotel Inkwell. But their costs were minimal and comparable, which was odd.

Then, is it something more complex like causality? The more my vision changes the reality, the higher the cost?

This seemed to fit many of the scenarios correctly. But was that to say his eyes could determine how much they could change the future? That couldn't be right. Unless . . . the cost was determined by some greater concept instead of his eyes.

But even then, won't observers be able to use this side effect to quantify how much their actions can influence the future? That would be so powerful. Each observer would be able to act like a seer to an extent.

Something else had to be going on in here.

Hmm, what if it's a more local cost rather than something grand like causality? Could it be the amount of reality that has to be viewed subjectively to achieve the effects of said vision? But not just the size of reality, but also the cascading effects caused by envisioning that change?

This was to say he would have to pay not just for breaking the rod in the waist of that statue but also for halting the functioning of the axle, even if it was an indirect result. And he would have to pay for any unnatural cascade of changes that happened during the time he kept up his vision.

In that sense, he was lucky he didn't need to maintain instability inducement for more than an instant. Or it was possible he might have burst his eyes and emptied his brain from the immense cost he'd have to pay to warp a much larger flow of reality.

If such is the case, it would be almost impossible to calculate this cost on the fly. Ahh, my brain can't handle more of this right now. I can confirm the details later.

Massaging his forehead, he opened his eyes, and the fight was ending. The statue was a ruined mess, and its components were scattered all over the ravaged floor. All that was left was a torso with a half shredded face—the perfect visage of Emperor Aldric looking like some horrifying abomination.

The vigilante also had sweat running down his face as he ran circles around the rampaging machine. He ducked, bent at awkward angles, and even did a backflip once, maintaining his poise throughout the process.

After a dozen more seconds, a serious look appeared on his face. Finding another opening in the raging mass's wide attacks, he thrust the end of his cane into its chest. Then he opened his eyes for a second, jerked the handle, and just as the blue glow reappeared in his eyes—he disappeared yet again.

Hmm, maybe *disappear* wasn't the right word. It was something akin to a very fast dash instead. A short-ranged, fast dash.

Reappearing to the side, he disappeared—no, dashed—another time. With these rapid movements, he wrapped the segments of the cane all around the statue's torso. Bringing out his free hand one more time, he wrenched the handle in a devastating jerk.

Schwing.

The sharp segments ripped through metal with deadly agility, shredding everything that came in their path, not leaving even the innards of the statue unharmed. When all the segments receded into the handle, he tapped it, and they turned completely straight, returning the cane to a smooth, glossy silver.

Flinging it a little in the air, the man caught the shaft in his palm, turned around, and executed a performer's bow. Pieces of the statue fell on the ground one after another as he looked at Vern and Cera with an amused smile and declared, "Ambrose Finnesse, at your service."

CHAPTER 49

COMPANY

Cera started clapping, and Vern felt pressure to do the same. What the hell was this situation? Just a few minutes ago, they were about to be crushed and trampled to death—now they were here, clapping like they had attended a performance.

He gave up and clapped a few times. The man deserved his thanks, and if he didn't follow Cera's lead, he'd come off as rude.

Ambrose's smile widened as he basked in the glory, but soon, his face started to turn red. He said, "Ah, my fellows usually don't give me feedback for my performances." Then he mumbled under his breath, "Twats . . ."

Vern wasn't sure if he heard it right, but Ambrose was still beaming. "Thank you for that!" Ambrose practically shouted. "Gave me some new insights."

But when he said the last sentence, he did a double take and turned to the statue's remains, looking at it in a fluster as he mumbled, "My apologies are in order. Such topics should not dance upon my lips in the company of those whose eyes have yet to open."

Before either of them could respond, he said, "Ah, no. Your eyes do perceive, so there is no need for a guarded tongue. Might I inquire if both of you share the vocation of observer?"

Vern let his hands come to a stop, and so did Cera as she responded, "I am not one. Yet. But please don't worry, I am actively seeking ways to enlighten myself, so please speak your mind."

Vern skipped over the latter half of the discourse and revisited their earlier thread. "Nice to meet you, Ambrose. My name's Vern, a fundamentalist and an observer. Thank you very much for coming to our aid."

"Oh, ah, hello. I am Cera. I-I am currently working for Von Industries. Thank you as well."

Ambrose continued picking up one thing after another from the metallic rubble, facing away from the pair. He said, "Von industries, you mention? Did you come here at their behest?"

Cera shook her head. "Not exactly. But they did indeed point to this as one of the places where I could seek enlightenment."

Vern wasn't sure if telling this guy everything was a good idea, but it wouldn't be too far-fetched to say that he held their lives in his hands. Neither of them could go against the prowess he had just displayed. Since he was being nice, reciprocating might be the right course of action.

But Vern had a burning question that he believed was worth interrupting their idle conversation. So he pushed himself off the ground with his palms and stood up with the support of the pillar and said, "I am grateful to you and would love to chat more, but I am not sure if this is the place to do that. There might be other . . . things in here that might be turning . . . sentient as we speak."

Ambrose turned to look at him, his silky hair swaying with the motion. But Vern continued, "I would rather not have to force you to fight another battle for us. Fights like the one just now are more than what we bargained for. So, should we get out of here first?"

Ambrose sighed. "We can't."

Vern's heart plummeted like a stone in his chest. It looked like there were more complications.

"Can you please elaborate?" he asked apprehensively.

Playing with the handle of his cane, Ambrose responded, "We can't go out of this building. That is why our exploration teams were waiting for more reconnaissance and divination to be completed. This is why I cautioned against your entrance and hesitated to step in myself."

A perplexed look appeared on both Vern's and Cera's faces, and she ended up asking what was on her mind. "But didn't you just come in through the doors? Why can't we go out?"

Ambrose's face turned sadder after each question. "Because the station won't let us. Our scouting instruments ventured within these walls but never returned, and our attempts at divination have yet to yield a solution."

It looked like Ambrose preferred speaking in roundabout ways, skirting the point. Paired with his archaic dialect, it made it hard for Vern to understand him.

Maybe noticing their still confused expressions, Ambrose stood up and looked around for a while before heading into one of the rooms connected to the hall.

Vern and Cera followed and were greeted by a room adorned with golden vases, a red carpet, and most of the furniture needed to seat the nobility.

His head still throbbed with lingering pain, but he removed the umbrella from his pocket and readied himself in case these articles came to life.

And he was right on the money. The filing cabinets began to shake and clatter, and Vern backed out of the room without hesitation.

Tap.

Ambrose tapped his cane, and Vern saw glowing eyes reflected in the tall dressing mirrors on one side of the room.

In but a moment, the chairs that had begun to hobble, the books that had been opening by themselves, and the cabinets that had been shaking all settled down, the room completely turning quiet.

It was as if all that noise had been nothing but an illusion.

Once there was pin-drop silence, Ambrose pointed at the window, which offered a glimpse of the world outside through its narrow frame—the sky, fence, and other buildings out in the distance. "Now look at this."

Tucking the cane under his armpit, he grabbed the window handles with both hands and tugged hard. But they wouldn't budge.

The screws holding the handles began to give way and were soon launched back in recoil, detaching from the window's frame.

He looked at them both, showing them the handles as if to say this should have explained everything.

Cera opened her mouth to say something but closed it. After Ambrose stood there, looking at them as if they were dumb. Cera finally asked, "Are you saying that since the windows won't open we can't go out?"

He shook his head and dropped the handles. "No, I am showing you that the station is actively resisting any such actions." Taking the cane in his hands yet again, he thrust it into the windowpane.

Crack.

Fragments of broken glass fell all around Ambrose, and he dodged with a smooth backstep the ones that went straight for him.

But Vern wasn't even looking at the fragments.

What?!

The wall had expanded.

Yes. Expanded.

The moment the cane was about to cross outside, past the window's borders, the wall expanded. It stretched and bent into a spiral from the seams, filling the hole made by the lack of the window.

The window frame was crushed and meshed into an unnatural shape as it was pulled into the section that filled the gap.

"This? Is this what would happen if we try to go outside?" said Cera as she gazed apprehensively at the grotesque-looking patch.

Ambrose dipped his chin in solemn acknowledgment, and Vern finally understood. Any openings in the building, be they windows or doors or ventilations, would be patched up by this mass to stop them from exiting.

This was bad.

This was supposed to be a simple exploration of the relay station, but it had expanded way out of their league. At least there was a silver lining in this dark cloud—if Ambrose hadn't followed them in here, no one would've even found their corpses.

Vern shook his head.

There was no point in moping about what had already happened. He had to figure out his next step—whether it be finding possible ways to get out of here or exploring further.

He understood that solutions came from knowledge and understanding. Trying to solve a problem without comprehending the underlying variables was akin to shooting an arrow in the dark.

If sitting here meant starving, he would instead explore as much as he could and figure out the source of the problem. Obviously, that would come after he got an opinion from his superiors.

"So what do you think should be our plan moving forward?" asked Vern with a severe gaze.

Ambrose looked left and right before pointing at himself. "I, um, might we, eh, venture to seek hidden clues, perhaps?"

Tapping his cane on the floor, he quickly walked past them and exited the room, kneeling next to the rubble again. "I typically abstain from exploratory missions, you see? My presence is more aligned with the hunts—even there, I'm seldom the conductor."

That was a little unfortunate. But then again, it didn't matter. He would just have to figure out the next step with Cera.

"I see. Then would you mind answering some of my questions?"

"I suppose."

"Just to confirm, you do not have any ideas on how we could leave the building, right?"

Ambrose shook his head.

"Then how did your, uh, team manage to figure this out? Is maybe someone else from your team stuck in here with us?"

"Oh, that? No. No one else is ensnared in here. Selena dispatched a paper avian within these confines a few days ago. Not being able to retrieve it cost her dearly in terms of representation. She still mourns the lost synergy with her month-old creation."

Ahh, so that was their scouting method? Ambrose's last sentence had many peculiarities, but he didn't want to ask unrelated questions right now.

"So, did you have any plans before coming here that could help you get out?"

"I, uh, informed Captain before I left to follow you two."

"And?"

"He might realize something's wrong and get us some reinforcements if I don't check in tonight." Then his voice almost became too low for Vern to hear. "But I don't know if even they could do something about this station."

Well. That's better than the worst case, I guess.

Vern reoriented his thoughts and asked more substantial questions. "Then do you know what is happening here? Also, how did you . . . um, suppress those articles in the room that were about to go out of control—from becoming . . . sentient?"

"Ahh, are you unfamiliar with pollution suppression? Oh right. I should have inquired sooner. What faction do you hail from? Von Industries, was it? I am surprised you managed to paralyze this thing. It simplified the encounter considerably. Usually, only a team could take on something like that unless you specialize."

Pollution suppression? Is he calling the sentience pollution? That made no sense. But other than that, it felt nice to be praised by a professional.

Vern shook his head with a bitter smile. "Indeed, I have no clue about pollution or suppression, and I am not affiliated with any faction, though I was contacted by one of your colleagues when I was roaming the city streets with an offer to join."

Vern put his hand in an inner pocket of his coat, fetched the silver badge shaped like an eye, and hung it by the chain for all to see.

Ambrose looked at it for a good five seconds before exclaiming, "Oh! Who gave you that?"

"It was a swordsman wearing, uh, shabby clothes. He looked like a foreigner too."

"Ah, your words evoke the essence of Captain Shinsei from the Third Combat Squad in the inner districts. Might this suggest you're an observer of the new generation? He reserves his ensemble for fledgling talents yet to be shaped by traditions of the past."

"New generation?"

They looked at each other, baffled, and even Cera perked up when this point came up.

Vern's brain churned as hundreds of possibilities crossed his mind, but before he could put a finger on any of them, Ambrose asked him, "How long has it been since you became an observer?"

Vern, who had been speaking his mind during the conversation, suddenly halted. This was an important question. He couldn't answer this one truthfully, or he would have to hide things or contradict himself in the future.

After Cera asked him many questions about his enlightenment, he had already made up a story. So, keeping in line with that, he answered, "It's been about two weeks." Before Ambrose could ask him further questions, he took the initiative to add more details.

"As I told you, I am a fundamentalist. I have always been fascinated by the workings of the world. When I heard rumors that a facet of reality had been hidden from me since forever, I did all I could to obtain an observation record. Alas, I only managed to get my hands on one for a brief time."

Ambrose nodded. "That confirms your status as a new-generation observer. The world swirled in chaos the month before the duskfall, with many sensing its impending arrival. You stumbling upon the subjective world wasn't a mere happenstance."

Using his cane to get back up, Ambrose continued, "Well, I guess it's a luxury to only have to wait a week or so before you could observe until your heart's content."

Vern tilted his head at this statement, and Ambrose followed suit.

"Ah, haven't you perceived the newfound ease in wielding visions post-duskfall? We can practically use our visions anywhere nowadays. I shan't miss honing my skills in forsaken chapels in some underground ruin all by myself."

Suddenly, his hand clutched the staff's handle with a white-knuckled grip, every muscle taut and veins bulging as if he were trying to crush it in his grasp. "Yet, I'd rather not have this sight at all if it meant going back. Back to the world with breath of life."

Vern was surprised. But it made sense. If observation had always been this potent, then there was no way the society would have managed to remain so peaceful. Not letting the shock creep up into his expression, he cobbled together an excuse. "Oh, that? I thought I was bad at using visions because I am not talented. Glad to hear I am not as slow as I thought."

Cera also chimed in. "Then Mr. Ambrose, how did observers enlighten themselves in the earlier times?"

Suddenly dropping his guard, he replied, "Ah, your words age me prematurely, miss. I'm merely reaching the twenty-fifth year of my long-term performance. As for the techniques of my lineage, I must plead discretion—the knowledge is closely guarded. Each method loosens the shackles of subjectivity to a certain extent, and thus, factions and families shield such insights with the utmost secrecy."

"I-I see. I didn't know that. I had no intention of prying. Sorry for bothering you," said Cera in a fluster.

"Please don't worry about it. It's usually a matter of observing something innately subjective. Some factions have places that facilitate it, while others have objects that do so. They are usually guarded with more care than generational heirlooms. However, now that the world has changed, I'd say your leaders at Von Industries have the right idea. There might indeed be an opportunity in this station."

While examining a small fragment of the statue very closely, he continued, "But we need to get out of here first for it to matter."

Vern picked up this thread and circled back to his earlier question. "Now that we have a better understanding of one another's knowledge, can you please shed some light on the specifics of this station? I would like to weigh our options."

CHAPTER 50

PLAN

Vern glanced back at the makeshift HELP sign, his gaze lingering on the impeccable eye symbol that Ambrose had etched into the hallway floor with his cane. It was Cera's idea—a way to alert Ambrose's captain if they weren't around when he arrived.

For now, Vern had settled on starting their search in the sorting room they'd narrowly escaped. The idea behind it was that it seemed like a central hub, potentially harboring a route that would bring them closer to the nexus of transmission pipes.

This plan hinged on Ambrose's ability to manage the errant articles littering the sorting room.

Vern ventured to the building's entrance alone to verify what Ambrose had said. The moment he attempted to step even one foot outside, the door through which he'd entered slammed shut on its own. When he tried to force it open, the wall itself began to constrict. However, as soon as he stepped back, everything reverted to its original state. It was an unnerving experience.

Although Ambrose seemed confident his captain would soon arrive, Vern harbored doubts. The captain would have to treat Ambrose like a lost child for him to show up just after a few hours of him going missing.

Since leaving wasn't an option, and their food search had unearthed only spoiled supplies—the thermodynamic coolers had long ago failed—they unanimously decided to focus on finding the building's central nexus.

As they walked, Cera leaned closer and whispered in his ear, "Can you ask him about that pollution suppression thing?"

Why me?

But then she had already asked Ambrose quite a lot of questions. Maybe she was just shy? Vern was slightly envious of what Ambrose did back there. He had just glanced at the objects, and as if scared stiff by his gaze, the anomalies lost all their spirit, neutralized.

"Mr. Ambrose, can I ask you something?"

Ambrose sauntered along, cane in hand. "I entertain all queries, novice. Whether I can answer them, well, only the rhythm knows."

Ignoring the euphemism, Vern went forward with his question. "Why do you call this phenomenon of sentient objects pollution? It's not the standard meaning, is it?"

Ambrose remained silent for a while as they slowly closed in on the sorting room, walking side by side. "No. It is indeed the pollution in the same sense. The difference is that it occurs when objects lose their rhythm."

Cera and Vern waited for him to continue with the rest of his explanation.

"What? Isn't it obvious?" said Ambrose, his face betraying a tinge of hurt.

Cera subtly shook her head, and Ambrose sighed. He propped up his cane and pointed at it with his other hand. "See this cane? It has a rhythm of its own. But if that rhythm is gone, anything can happen. We can't know what its cadence would be like when that happens."

"I-I . . . see."

Vern almost sighed audibly. Ambrose wasn't the best at explaining things, so he pushed him harder. "Hmm, so how does an object like this cane lose its . . . rhythm?"

"How would I know when or how the rhythm comes and goes? If I had that answer, I'd have more than two shades, wouldn't I? This cane is our workshop's treasure. I'd lose my own rhythm before letting anything happen to it. It's all that f . . ." Ambrose muttered, trailing off.

Both Vern and Cera exchanged puzzled glances. One last time, Vern tried, "So, what exactly is pollution suppression?"

"Ahh, that one's easy. When you feel those chaotic symphonies around you, just observe them with the intent to listen. Feel the unruly tempo and internalize it—it will soothe itself in no time."

Hmm, just observe them? That hasn't worked for me.

Vern proverbially threw in the towel. Ambrose's grasp of these concepts diverged too widely from his own. However, before Vern could thank him and move on to a different topic, Cera asked, "If the room's chaos is what you call pollution, does that label also apply to that metallic statue?" Cera pointed at the shattered remnants of the statue back in the hall.

Good point.

"Yes, it's rhythm was off tune. And not just by a little—it was jarring to the extreme. But there was no way I could have suppressed it just with my understanding of the rhythm. I had to fight him. But that unruly tempo did make it effortless to avoid its attacks. Unfortunately, neither of you can feel it."

Yeah, he wasn't going to glean much from Ambrose's words.

Clank.

Clatter.

As they approached the sorting room, all sorts of sounds greeted them. The atmosphere didn't differ much from Vern's expectations. The hobbling chairs circled around the room's perimeter as if they were sentinels maintaining guard.

The pneumatic tubes were still behaving oddly, their valve configurations changing every second, leading to the contents inside being dragged hitherto. Hundreds of metallic keys dotted the ground around the entrance while the typewriters lay on the ground, empty and seemingly devoid of energy.

The catwalks thrummed and creaked—

Tap.

Ambrose rapped his cane against the floor, and a blue glow shone from his eyes. As if the strings animating these puppets were cut, the moving articles fell on the ground, and the world came to a halt.

Or not. The anomalies were only suppressed within a radius. The valves and tubes on the edge of the room were still behaving oddly, but anything within a meter or so of Ambrose lost all its vigor and keeled over.

Hold on. What if . . .

Vern had an idea, and he quickly opened his perception. With haste, he tried to interpret the chair and assign it a shade.

He failed.

It was the same situation as before, but much more pronounced. His grays could not perceive anything, and his perception remained blank.

This . . .

A hypothesis formed in his mind, and he moved on and tried to interpret the ground instead. He was sure that he had been able to shade it a light gray the last time he was in this room.

Another failure.

I GET IT!

He needed to test it a few more times to be sure. So, as more and more articles succumbed to Ambrose's piercing gaze, Vern tried to interpret them.

Every one of them was elusive to his perception.

Finally, he focused back on the chair, which should now be out of Ambrose's range. The lifeless object quickly turned gray, and its relative complexity became apparent within his perception.

Yep, this is it.

This was the last nail in the coffin. It was obvious that he was unable to interpret objects already being perceived by someone else concurrently. That was to say, if Ambrose was actively observing a space, Vern wouldn't be able to do the same.

Didn't that mean he could not shade the statue or the typewriter because they were already being manipulated?

But what was the order of precedence? What would be the deciding factor if two observers were vying to manipulate the same object?

It should be the number of shades. Right?

But he had long concluded that some viewpoints were inherently better than others, so who would wrench the control when there's such a complicated power imbalance?

Also, if it was just the number of shades, did that mean Ambrose was better than whatever influenced all these objects?

Oof. This is complex. I would need a lot more data to come to a proper conclusion. But it felt great to have figured out why he had been unable to use his visions.

He initially considered asking Ambrose about it, but he quickly discarded that notion. He would be treated to another esoteric rambling that would quote rhythm and not mean anything to him.

So he kept his mouth shut, kept this new finding to himself, and searched for their path forward.

After a few minutes of searching every nook and cranny, Cera pointed behind a batch of tubes and shouted, "Look there!"

"Is that a door?"

The tubes had rearranged so much so that they covered up most of a door, almost hiding it from the view.

"Nice find!" Ambrose took the lead, as they had discussed.

He first put his cane between the tubes to push the door open, but the knob had to be turned first. After fiddling with his cane and failing, Ambrose gave up and shoved his hand between the tubes.

Vern wasn't expecting him to be so brazen. What if the tubes rearranged and crushed his hand?

Click.

But nothing so violent happened. After pushing the door open, he leapt over the tubes with poise and headed inside.

Vern breathed a sigh of relief. These tubes had been acting differently since the start. They hadn't tried to hamper him, and it was nice to see the trend continue. Jumping over the tubes with a sprinting start, he landed cleanly and extended his hand toward Cera.

She tucked a strand of her hair behind her ear and looked at the set of tubes almost stacked up to the shoulders of her petite frame. There wasn't enough space to go underneath it either.

Taking his hand, she stepped on the joint of the first tube and then the second before jumping over.

Maybe she hadn't needed my help there.

But she hadn't denied it either, so he just left it at that and looked in front of him. Two stairways presented themselves. The one on the left went up while the other one went down.

He obviously followed Ambrose and took the right, but then Ambrose suddenly halted and used his cane to bar Vern's path.

"Hold on! Something is wrong with the rhythm. We should . . . WITHDRAW!"

Both men pulled back immediately, just in the nick of time.

Hissssss.

A jet of scalding steam blasted from an overhead pipe just steps ahead. The section of the railing, which was caught in the burst, instantly began to deform and soon melted as it lost all its tension. Just looking at it sent a shiver down Vern's spine. Ambrose studied the pipe intently while Cera's grip on her revolver tightened.

The blast of steam continued to discharge from the pipe for another few seconds before it stopped. "This place really wants us dead," Ambrose said. "But do you know what that means? That we're going in the right direction. Resistance implies purpose."

Vern nodded and heightened his alertness.

Enough running away.

There was no way but forward. He was sick of fleeing and never finding the answers to all these mysteries. He would still retreat if the balance of danger tipped too much toward certain death. But now that he was in the company of someone who could deal with incidents more professionally, he felt he needed to make the best of it.

Especially considering Ambrose's recent premonition—well, rhythm-based awareness. Its utility would be nothing to balk at. Vern asked, "Is it safe to move on?"

Ambrose nodded and resumed his descent.

He also sliced through a pipe farther down, angling it away from their path. When steam vented again, it posed no real threat as long as they didn't intentionally walk into its path.

Intriguing. Vern thought of the typewriters. Like them, these pipes seemed to operate on a limited set of instructions, unable to adapt like the statue had.

After dodging more steam traps, they descended what felt like two floors. At the bottom, Ambrose pushed open the door to reveal a dark, cluttered basement—a mini-maze formed by a jumble of pipes, narrow corridors eking out their existence among them.

Yet, amid the dark, a light flickered.

Chapter 51

THE LIGHT

Not dazzling by any means, the light was still bright enough to stand out like a sore thumb in this dark vista. Despite narrow patches of pipes and fittings trying their best to keep the light contained, it offered them a clear direction.

Ambrose lifted his chin imperceptibly, and his gloved hand extended subtly with fingers pointing onward. The others caught the unspoken command, and with synchronized precision, they advanced, their footsteps echoing in the dimly lit corridor.

They stuck to their planned formation—Ambrose in the lead, Vern in the middle, and Cera in the rear.

However, just a few seconds into the corridor, the pipes around them began to churn and hum with great ferocity. The trio halted and stood with their backs to one another, forming a triangle.

The buzzing became faster, and they soon started thrumming in a rhythm. Vern reflexively looked at Ambrose, only to find a deep frown etched on his face.

Even he doesn't understand this rhythm?

Thrum.

Whirl.

"This . . ."

In just a few more seconds, the pace at which the pipes thrummed accelerated rapidly, culminating in a peak.

Wennngggg.

A muffled screeching boomed through the surroundings, almost making him want to clamp his hands over his ears due to how grating it was. Luckily, they were in the basement this time, and the piercing dissonance from the whistles atop the stations couldn't seep down here.

For a second, he thought the pipes around them had gone completely silent. But they started again. The exact same process as before—starting with slow thumps, which soon turned into rhythmic thrumming that culminated into another . . .

Wennngggg.

The steamscripts were activating nonstop. Was it because they had gotten closer to the source?

Vern quickly came to a decision and said, "We should ignore this and keep moving."

The others nodded, broke apart from their triangle, and fell back into their previous formation.

The air was thick with a tension that clung to their skin as they navigated the gloomy corridor. Shadows stretched across the walls like elongated fingers, closing in from all sides. Each step they took seemed to drown in the clamor from their surroundings in these narrow passageways, projecting a sense of confinement.

The group moved in a tight formation, eyes darting to every corner and alcove. Despite the air being cool, sweat glistened on their foreheads. Every creak from their boots, every whisper of fabric seemed to mingle with the thrumming as if the corridor was absorbing them, consuming their essence one cautious step at a time.

The path was winding, and some of the sections were caved in—large equipment blocking the most straightforward route to the light.

But they were getting closer, and the directionality of the pipes made it clear that they were indeed moving toward the nexus of the station.

Wennngggggg.

After what felt like the tenth activation of the steamscripts in less than a minute, something changed.

With a whirl of metallic clatter, their sole beacon—the inviting yellow light—dimmed and faded into nothingness. What was worse was that after every activation, the pipes became utterly silent, and this time wasn't any different.

The three of them came to a halt, and the thumping of Vern's heartbeat became all too clear. Illuminated by just the lamp on his waist, the group tried to figure out what was happening in this musty environment.

Ba-dump.

Ba-dump.

Ba-dump.

"p . . . se d . . . nt c . . . e h . . . re . . . om . . . nt h . . . dle."

Huh?

"Am . . . Ambrose, did you say something?" asked Cera.

"I? No, I believe the utterance originated from one of you."

Vern shook his head and raised his palm, signaling them to quiet.

"l . . . ve."

A sound emanated from somewhere ahead of them, and Vern strained his ears to catch it.

"le . . . ve."

". . . ve."

It was growing louder by the second.

"l . . . ave leave."

"leave."

"Leave."

A dazzling yellow light flashed ahead of them, and the sound turned into a shrill yell. "LEAVE!"

The pipes to their sides, beating to a rhythm just a few seconds ago, started to wrench free from their joints, curling in on themselves.

"LEAVE US ALONE!"

Their surroundings began to coil inward, attempting to encase the trio from both ends. Vern had no plans of waiting around, and it seemed neither did Ambrose. Planting his left foot firmly on the ground, Ambrose leaned forward and morphed his cane into a gleaming sword. With a burst of agility, he propelled himself forward, sword leading the way.

A cyan aura flickered along the blade's edge as he executed a masterful double slash, carving an elegant cross through the air. Sprinting free from the ensnaring pipes, he left only the resonant thud of collapsing metal in his wake.

Meanwhile, as Vern dashed out of the entanglement, he opened his perception. Focusing on snippets of the environment around him, he aimed to discern what he could and couldn't perceive, all while minimizing his mental expenditure.

Some of the pipes were invisible to his perception, but a big chunk of his surroundings were crystal clear.

"LEAVE US! GO AWAY!"

The shrill voice seemed to come from one of those last-generation metallic recorders. But his assumption couldn't be further from reality. When he rushed past the first entrapment, he caught a glimpse of it for a couple seconds while he turned the corner.

It was a sphere of yellow light, shards of shimmering metal orbiting around it. As if pulled by an invisible force, more fragments of their surroundings gravitated toward the mass.

A cylindrical tube perched atop the sphere, mimicking a head followed by pipes and valves that coalesced to form a makeshift arm.

Then another arm.

A leg.

Another.

Just as the mysterious construct seemed about to reach its final form, a radiant blue aura enveloped Ambrose. In a flash, he catapulted himself toward the sphere, his cane slashing through the air in a high-velocity arc aimed at its core.

However, just milliseconds before his cane could cleave through the humanoid figure, a hatch door hurtled into the path, absorbing the full force of Ambrose's assault.

"LEAVE!" it shouted, as more and more pipes around them came alive and did their best to lock them in.

Vern slipped, crouched, and jumped over one obstacle after another as he made to circle around and approach the entity from a different angle. Their group formation was already broken—might as well take advantage of it.

He didn't know what Cera was doing but was sure she could take care of herself. He had his hands full with the current situation anyway.

During his run, he found himself in another open section of the room with a clear line of sight of the fight between Ambrose and the humanoid automaton, which was getting more heated by the second—literally heated, as the automaton was releasing steam from its ad hoc arms.

He had already interpreted those pipes back in the staircase and found flaws in them, even if there were some aspects he couldn't perceive. But he had no reason to waste his vision back there.

But this? This was his chance to help.

Vern squinted and slowed down. When Ambrose lunged for another swing, the automaton brandished its right arm, ready to release a steam jet.

Now!

Executing the instability inducement, he cringed a little, and a tremor ran through his eyes, but he somehow managed to hold his gaze.

It was worth it. Instead of ejecting a jet of steam toward Ambrose, who was already poised to evade, the valve malfunctioned and backfired into the entity's own arm. A scalding burst tore through its makeshift body, warping and searing some of its assembled components.

Ambrose met Vern's eyes across the mesh of coiled conduits for a second and, with a nod, took full advantage of the opening.

Vern quickly disengaged and kicked another set of tubing that was twisting around his legs—about to lock him down.

"LEAVE! PLEASE! JUST GO!"

Everything made sense to him to an extent, except what the entity was saying. Obviously, something had been controlling the building, so pipes gaining sentience and trying to trap them wasn't anything new. Neither were the tactics applied by the entity itself.

But what was it saying? There was even a hint of pleading in its voice. It didn't make sense. It tried to kill them with deadly force, one trick after another. First the typewriters, then the statue, then the steam, and now . . . this.

But maybe it was Vern who was out of his mind for expecting logic from a mechanical entity.

Ignoring the hoarse screams, he scanned for other means to improve their situation. They had come down here with an objective, and it seemed increasingly likely that vanquishing this entity could be the key to escaping this confounding building.

His mind raced with ideas, but most seemed futile in this context. The automaton controlled most of the weapons, and if it adapted, blocking its steam release mechanisms might not even work a second time.

He could target the joints as he had with the statue, but he'd need to be more cautious. A mistake this time could lead to more than just a bleeding eye.

He easily dodged the pipes aimed to trap him. Oddly enough, their swift movements seemed almost wasted on such harmless tactics. A well-timed pipe to the side of his head could easily have given him a concussion.

It was almost as if the sole aim of these pipes was to lock him down, not hurt him. *Yeah, I am really expecting too much of a freaking machine.* Shaking his head, he ran for another minute before he jumped over a stack of pressure engines and found himself right behind the entity.

The moment he laid his eyes on their fight, it was evident that Ambrose was barely keeping up. Every time he moved in for an attack, the entity would use its new hand to release steam, pushing him into a mesh of coiled wire that tried to entangle him.

As the automaton prepared to hurl Ambrose into a web of coils yet again, Vern seized the moment. With a precisely timed vision, he destabilized the entity's makeshift joint, causing it to miss its target entirely.

Ambrose was dumbfounded for a fraction of a second before he regained his senses and dashed back out of the foe's reach, taking this brief respite to catch his breath.

"LEAVE! DON'T COME HERE!"

As the mechanical entity swiveled to face Vern, its voice rang out, tinged with a metallic resonance. Aware that his gun would be ineffective against such a construct, Vern rapidly calculated his next best course of action.

Be a bait. To give Ambrose the perfect chance. And what better way to do that than rush in precisely where the entity didn't want him to?

Determined, Vern bolted toward the area where he'd first seen the flickering light. Clearly, the automaton was guarding something vital there. By drawing its ire, he aimed to create a prime opening for Ambrose to capitalize on.

Glancing back every few seconds, he spotted a couple of weaknesses in the assortment that the abnormality's body was comprised of.

He planned to exploit them at the last moment to maximize the damage they could inflict. With a comfortable distance still separating him from the mechanical entity, he felt confident he could hold his ground for at least half a minute.

"NO! DON'T!"

Slam.

Clank.

With thunderous clangs, pipes lunged at him just as he'd anticipated. But instead of striking him, they smashed into the wall, missing their mark. If the entity was holding back this much, it wouldn't be enough to stop him.

Moreover, this section was running out of pipes to deploy. While more snaked out from the wall's edges, aiming for him, Vern deftly dodged them, slipping through the blockade to continue his sprint.

His heart pulsed with a mix of exhilaration and anxiety. The risk was high, maybe too high for his comfort, but he was convinced this strategy would pay off. That was, unless the entity decided to quit playing games and truly aimed to kill.

Banking on that, he turned once . . . twice, and then a third time. He knew he was close to the initial location of the light, but it was getting harder to persist by the second.

Hissssss.

Barely avoiding the steam from a pipe, he slid past it, breathing heavily. *Where the fuck is Ambrose?*

Why hadn't he managed to stop this steaming mammoth already? Right when he was considering his options, he noticed the improvised hand of the automaton reaching out to grab him. Steeling himself, Vern turned around and readied himself to use one of the flaws he had figured out.

Boom.

An explosion hit the machine at almost point-blank range. It took significant damage—the heat wreaked havoc on one of its sides, also gravely damaging the dimly glowing sphere in its core.

"Vern, just hold on a little longer. Ambrose is almost ready."

It was Cera! She had been charging that shot and used it for tremendous effect.

Aware that Ambrose was orchestrating something worthwhile, he stifled the dread that rose within him from being inches away from the clutches of this abomination, resisting the temptation to rely on his vision and test his luck.

Now wasn't the time. Not yet. They wouldn't have much effect by themselves anyway.

He dismissed the construct and bolted toward the section where the entity didn't want him to go, using its downtime to gain some lead.

"NO!"

"PLEASE DON'T!" it said in an animated voice, a tinge of fear clearly coloring the mechanical tones.

Vern frowned at the emotions that seemed to emerge from this entity. What could be so important that it had driven this mechanical puppet to such desperate measures?

"PLEASE! I PLEAD! DON'T GO."

Vern wasn't naive enough to blindly halt, but this sudden plea made him hesitate. Was he resorting to brute force too quickly? The entity was begging them to leave, and wasn't that ultimately their goal?

The desperation in its mechanical voice unsettled him, making him question whether their initial approach was the right one. Weren't they being too aggressive to an entity that had not killed them even when it had hundreds of opportunities to do so?

Was it really this entity that commanded those puppets upstairs?

So he halted.

"Vern! What are you doing!?" shouted Cera after he had turned around and began walking toward the humanoid.

He ignored her and asked the mechanical humanoid, its form slowly disintegrating as parts drifted away and the light within its core dimmed. "Why didn't you let us leave when we tried to go?"

The tube in place of its head seemed to look in his direction. The valves hanging by its impromptu chest began to rotate and turn as the pipes around its shoulders released a low sound.

"it was not her. it was not us. it was not—"

But then, a surge of blue light ignited behind the faltering entity. Even from a dozen meters away, separated by makeshift walls of twisted pipe, Ambrose radiated a fierce blue aura.

For a split second, Vern's eyes caught the flash of—

Crash!

Like a scorching comet, the blue blaze tore through obstacles as if they were mere paper. In the blink of an eye, the silver segments of Ambrose's cane protruded from the dimming sphere at the entity's core.

Crack.

C H A P T E R 52

NEXUS

Ambrose yanked his cane free, leaving jagged gashes in the lustrous metal shards orbiting the light. The entity's body collapsed, its components tumbling into a heap on the ground.

"Great one, fledgling. Your support was well orchestrated. Almost as if we engaged in a harmonious duet, wouldn't you agree?"

Just a performance, huh?

Vern still had his hand outstretched, the words synthesized by the entity running laps in his mind. Had they attacked someone innocent? But weren't all its abilities eerily similar to the happenings upstairs?

Cera strode toward him, ignoring the entity's crumbling form. "What were you doing, Vern?" she demanded. "That was extremely dangerous! You provoke it and then stand right in its way? Were you asking to be steamrolled?"

Um.

That was true to an extent. But he wondered what flipped her switch. He hadn't seen her lashing out like this. Even if it was in good faith.

Before Vern could formulate a response to either one of them, Ambrose continued with an even more cheerful voice than before. "Ah, my apologies. It was wrong of me to call this performance a duet. It was nothing less than a trio. You understood my intentions so quickly. If you weren't already a member of Von Industries, I'd have been happy to recommend you to the Vigil."

Cera stopped in her tracks and raised her eyebrows before replying, "Thanks for the compliment. But—"

She paused, looked at Vern, and then back at Ambrose before her tone intensified. "But I don't like the way you're handling this situation. This is not a performance! We're not on a stage!"

Her words took an edge and became sharper. "We're operating in the dark here. What do we even know about this orb? That it tried to contain us? It didn't even bother trapping me when it realized I wasn't fleeing. What does that tell us? Are we the aggressors here?"

Then she turned toward Vern and said, "And this goes for both of you. You forced my hand by pissing off the entity to such a degree. Did you really have to run in this direction and make it worse? It didn't even try to defend itself when it passed me— and I shot it. All because you were so eager to fight it."

Ambrose seemed stunned for a second before he replied, "I . . . I wasn't sure. It tried to entrap us and manipulated the surroundings—"

The flickering sphere now only had those severely damaged chunks of metal as its moons, but that's where the deterioration stopped, and it began to stabilize itself.

Soon, it even began to drift as if pulled by an invisible force. A force that multiplied by the second.

In a blink, it was hurling toward Vern. Not even thinking twice, he dodged to the side, narrowly avoiding the streak of light that shot past him.

"See. Its danger exceeds your estimations." Vern felt another gust of wind as Ambrose bolted past him, his words lingering in the air. "Let's finish this, my fellow dancers. We can't not conclude our beautiful performance now, can we?"

Gone was the hint of doubt that had crept up in his voice.

She called after him, "No. Wait— Is he, maybe, not right in his head?" Cera directed that last question to Vern, more than a little annoyed.

Vern clicked his tongue and remained silent.

"We'll discuss the recklessness of all this later." Cera sighed, her gaze now focused on the entity's remnants. "For now, let's just ensure we live long enough for that discussion to take place and hope Ambrose doesn't take beef with something beyond our control."

Cera had a point too. The same point he had realized when he tried to converse with it. Maybe a little too late.

It was frustrating to be forced into suboptimal decisions.

He moved in tow with Cera, following in Ambrose's footsteps.

The corridor they were trailing soon became wider as more paths converged into this one area. Dozens of larger-than-life pipes complimented by complex machinery peeked through in the darkness lit only by his lamp.

These were the real deal. The steamscript pipes could handle sound waves from many channels and transmit them unbothered by the surrounding noise. All kinds of machinery came together here from different paths, making it obvious where they were headed.

It was the nexus of the steamscript relay station.

Soon, the corridor tapered off into a large hall, and in the middle of it was a room. It was enclosed with great care, and multiple soundproofing solutions were implemented for tubing, piping, and the entrances.

It only made sense. Any kind of noise pollution could be detrimental to the proper encoding of the messages.

Unexpectedly, Ambrose was standing at the door of the room, looking focused. When they got close, he glanced back and said with a subtle smile, his hand stopping them from entering the room, "Please let me lead the concluding act. I want to try something special."

Peering cautiously into the room, Vern took in the peculiar setting. There were rows of tables topped with exquisite typewriters, each connected by a massive pipe that ran the length of the room. And at the end of the hall was a congregation of pipes that shot toward the ceiling, ending up in four paths.

Yet, what caught his eye was the flickering light to his left—now transformed. No longer orbiting freely, the light's metallic facets had coalesced into a sort of shield. It obscured their view of a chair positioned before one of the typewriters.

What, or who, was it shielding?

Though Vern guessed it wouldn't last for long because it looked like Ambrose was just waiting for the both of them to catch up before he took matters into his own hands. Casting a final warning glance at Cera, Ambrose stepped into the room.

Tap.

Tap.

Tap.

Tapping his cane on the floor with every step, Ambrose moseyed with a gentle gait. He seemed to become lithe, avoiding all the obstacles in the room with finesse. He circled around the shield with all these odd movements instead of heading toward it directly.

But it reacted accordingly. The metal sheets expanded spherically, barricading whatever was behind it.

Tap.

Tap.

As Ambrose spiraled closer to the shielded area, a subtle grin broke on his face, while the metallic sheets had now turned into a whole sphere, dim light shining out from its crevices.

"He's infuriating," Cera muttered under her breath. "He's playing with that thing like it's some kind of stage prop. Is this what observers do? He first forced me to shoot the entity, and now this . . . ?"

Frustration oozed out of her every word, and she moved forward, ready to barge into the room.

Vern understood her perspective, but what she was doing wouldn't fly. So he grabbed her by the shoulders and shook his head. "We are no match for him, Cera."

"But don't you see this? What is the point of this? Does he really need to disrespect a fallen foe like that? Just what is he playing at right now?"

"I see it too. But now's not the time. We're not his match. Also, keep in mind that we might have ended up doing the same thing one way or the other. This entity, or whatever it's protecting, has got to be the source of the anomaly of the station."

"It's just— I don't know. When he swooped in, I thought he was different. He looked and acted like a proper gentleman. One skirmish, and there he is, showing off how he enjoys perverse pleasures," Cera said, clutching at the doorframe in resignation as she watched the ongoing performance.

One gentle move after another, Ambrose tapped his cane on the ground, and it was as if the air itself in the room were buzzing with uncharacteristic intensity.

But the effect on the shield was quite evident. The sheets—stretched thin into a sphere—were wobbling after every strike to the floor as their cohesion worsened. It was about to come to an end.

Tap.

Tap.

Ambrose glided in a graceful circle, each step melding into the next as he inched closer. He seemed to be humming a tune to himself, wholly lost in a world of his own.

Tap.

Tap.

The shivering of metal plates grew worse by the second, and more cracks appeared on them—the distance between their crevices growing wider.

Tap.

Tap.

By the time Ambrose reached within arm's length of the shield, the plates had lost all their luster while the light shining from within flickered dangerously low.

Vern suppressed his urges and held himself back from doing what Cera wanted to do just a few seconds ago. He knew it would be a rash decision. Even if a little cruel in hindsight, Ambrose wasn't wrong. This was about survival, and it would be delusional optimism on Vern's end to want to change their plans for the sake of being nice to mechanical entities.

And that was assuming he could actually stop Ambrose. Vern wouldn't bet even a single crown on his odds of besting him.

After a brief pause, Ambrose lightly tapped his cane against the metallic shell.

Tap.

And then, as if the whole shield was made of glass, it shattered.

Piece by piece, it clattered to the floor, unveiling the once radiant light that now dimmed rapidly. The true form emerged—a simple glass bead exposed in its dullness.

A bead that didn't stop its erratic movements and gravitated toward what seemed like an exquisite headpiece adorned with many a cogs and gears, slotting itself in its front.

It was a headpiece.

Worn by a person.

Rose-colored locks were interspersed through the sections of the headpiece, which fell beyond the bounds of the table, rustled by the metallic chunks that fell all around the person.

Vern's mind quickly shifted gears as he took in the scene. His breath turned rapid, and he was unable to take his eyes away from the sight. He didn't know if it was because of her beauty or the intricate machinery on display.

A woman with striking rose-colored hair was slumped on the chair. Her head rested on the typewriter while her hand still clutched the pipe that ran across the tables.

Not heeding Ambrose's warnings anymore, Vern reflexively started walking toward her, drawn by the fascinating craftsmanship of her armor and gear. It was like nothing he'd ever seen before, an intricate blend of functionality and artistry that teetered on the line between mechanical innovation and mystic ritualism.

Her torso and arms were encased in multifaceted, angular panels that suggested an otherworldly aesthetic. Each piece was inlaid with elaborate etchings and geometric designs, shining faintly, responding to all light that shone on it.

But that was merely the prelude. Jutting out from the back of her armor was a shaft intricately crafted to blend with the rest of the ensemble. From it unfurled a pair of mechanized wings, a captivating blend of machinery and natural elegance.

These weren't just any wings—they mimicked the delicate design of butterfly wings and were structured with a lattice of metallic veins and gears, adding a sense of power and grandeur to their ethereal beauty. They were studded with micro-cogs and miniature pistons, each one a tiny masterpiece of engineering.

But something was wrong with them. They seemed . . . damaged, for the lack of a better word. He wasn't savvy enough to find flaws in such a masterful work, but some of that chipping and breaking couldn't be designed. It had to be actual damage.

But he quickly lost himself again. Just what kind of mechanical art could achieve this?

Did the wings actually work? As in, would she be able to fly in the air with them? His common sense said no, but the sheer ingenuity of the engineering at display made him doubt his understanding of fundamentals.

"AHH!"

Vern's fascinated ramblings came to an end as Ambrose suddenly lost his footing, clutched at his eyes, and screamed out of nowhere. Yet, before Vern could react, a fervent sense of drowsiness overwhelmed him, and everything went dark.

"FUCK!"

But in what felt like the next instant, he let out a curse and rested against the wall as a feeling of having been drained washed over him. The pain was then gone as soon as it had arrived.

When he looked up, he noticed that Cera was rushing toward him and Ambrose was holding his head, looking at them both with perplexity in his eyes.

"Did you also feel like—" Ambrose stopped midsentence and closed his eyes, which were scrunched up. But Vern had to ignore him. For something far more bizarre was going on with Cera.

She had been running toward him when she abruptly stopped. Her eyes drooped, and she swayed side to side. Another second, and she hobbled toward the woman on the chair instead. Vern rushed toward Cera, hoping to shake her out of it.

"Something's wrong with her rhythm! There's another . . . another rhythm around her. It was around you too. It's gone now. But it was there."

A sinking feeling appeared in Vern's mind. But even if he wasn't sure what Ambrose meant or where that feeling came from, he knew it was nothing good. So he grabbed Cera's arm and pulled her back before shaking her vigorously. "Cera. Get a hold of yourself! Cera! Cera!"

"AHH!"

She screamed and lost all strength, falling on him. Holding her upright, he looked around for any more changes.

Was something going to jump out of the corner and annihilate them? Were the women suddenly going to get up and ambush them? What was going on? First Ambrose, then him, and now Cera.

All three of them experienced something bizarre. But he couldn't put his finger on it.

What was the cause? The purpose? Was it the woman? Had all three of them had this episode because they looked at that woman?

"Vern, wh-what happened to me just now?"

He decided to give it to her straight. "You began walking toward the woman with a lifeless gaze. It was as if you weren't in control."

"I-I wasn't?"

Ambrose hurried toward them, his eyes still closed. "It's gone. It's as if it were never there. I . . . I only feel like this when I pray to the goddess during a ritual."

What was that supposed to signify about the gravity of their situation?

Vern let Cera go, and his mind began to whirl. Something had gone very wrong, and the trigger was this woman. Turning around, he walked toward her and crouched next to her table.

The glass bead, now studded in her headpiece, had screamed at them to leave her alone. And its shield form just now seemed to act more like a visual barrier than a protective one. Also, the order in which they lost control was quite peculiar.

He was done waiting for Ambrose to play his games. Something deeply unsettling had just graced their minds, and he had to figure it out before its repercussions reared its ugly head.

So he started with some preliminary questions. "Ambrose, can you describe the feeling to me? Also, what was the pattern of change in the rhythm—"

"plea . . . s . . . le . . . ve"

That's when he heard it—a faint murmuring, and his head jerked to the women. She had just said something, but it had been too low for him to hear it clearly.

Ambrose and Cera also turned silent, glancing at the woman with an apprehensive gaze.

Vern threw caution to the wind and leaned closer, putting his ear right next to her lips. She seemed seriously injured from the looks of it anyway, so there was little chance she could hurt him.

After all, the magnificent armor had more cracks running down its torso than a fractured piece of porcelain.

"esc . . . ap . . . e"

"he's . . . aw . . . are"

"it's ov . . . er"

Chapter 53

DEDUCTIONS

Vern interrupted the stranger's rambles, "What's over?"

"It's over. It's over. It's over."

The sinking feeling inside him intensified with each word. He didn't have time for this.

Thump.

Slamming his hand hard on the table with a frown, Vern asked again, "What's over?"

Her wings fluttered erratically as her body struggled with even the smallest movements as if waking from a deep sleep.

By the time her wings had multiple failed attempts at functioning properly, she finally managed to push her head up and stared into his pupils with her tired yet bewitching eyes. "Please, run. One or two of you might just make it out. You still have time."

Vern stared back at her and shook his head. "We can't go anywhere. And what exactly are we supposed to run from?"

"Please . . ." Her voice trailed off as her eyes fluttered shut, almost hitting her head on the table. But Cera was quick to steady her. Retrieving a water canteen from her bag, she gently held it to the woman's lips.

It looked like she really needed it too. She tipped her head back and drank more than half of what was in there. She must be hungry too. Unfortunately, they didn't have anything to offer her in that regard.

But he was more concerned about the chain of events that had led them here. It pointed to her being the source of the anomalies. What was he supposed to do about that? And something far more pressing was underway. He hadn't missed the warning in her words.

So the moment Cera took back her canteen, Vern asked again, "Can you please explain? What did you mean? Who's coming?"

Her gently curved eyes peeked through her bangs as she looked at him blankly. Her face looked surprisingly healthy—even beautiful for someone who had been stuck in a basement for a week.

The four dots beneath her eyes enhanced the ritualistic aura that her attire emanated, and were complemented by an aquiline nose and an impeccably sculpted countenance. She finally moved her crimson lips. "Please leave. Time's running out."

Does she not know what's going on in the building?

He shook his head with a little more force. "We cannot get out of the building. The walls seal themselves, the windows shut us in, and the doors close. Would you happen to know anything about that?"

Taken aback, she let out a soft gasp and looked down, saying, "That . . . that can't be. Has the pollution really gotten that bad?"

Vern clung to and repeated the familiar word. "Pollution?"

But she ignored him and interjected, "Which is why I tried! I tried to keep you all away! I-I would have figured it out! I just needed a few more days. It would have worked out."

Her wings seemed to match her emotional state as they flapped faster against the back of the chair. "Why . . . Why did you . . . have to come here . . . I-I."

Tap.

"Get away, fledgling. She's trying to squander our time. Listen, woman! If you don't cease your vision of this building right away, I will have to force you into it. Decide. Now."

She turned to face Ambrose, and her eyes narrowed to slits as if she could will him away with the force of her glare alone. Color seemed to return to her face, and her lethargy evaporated.

With a surprising change in the tone of her voice, she seethed. "I'm bending over backward to save you from the hell that awaits me, and yet you have the audacity to speak to me like this? It's never enough for the likes of you, is it? Nothing is ever enough."

She even began yelling. "I didn't want anyone to be harmed, but I was too naive. Really shouldn't have asked Fen to hold back. Fine, then. You shall all die with me." Leaning to one side, she touched the ground briefly. With a resounding thud, the ground beneath Ambrose hollowed out as marble hands erupted from its edges, latching on to his legs like vice grips.

"Please wait," Vern yelled.

Ambrose tried to jump away, his eyes glowing blue. Instead, he fell face-first, the arms sucking his legs into the ground. By the time he got back up, the hole had stopped deepening around his shin and had closed up, trapping him where he stood.

Ambrose looked at his legs and then at the woman as he fiercely tried to shovel himself out with his cane. But it didn't matter. Any scratches that appeared on the ground disappeared after a few seconds.

Vern surprisingly heaved a sigh of relief. This was not the worst case. It would have been a tragedy for him and Cera if a fight broke out here. And the woman's comments were starting to scare him.

What was this about sparing them? And then implying that they would die together just by being stuck in this room?

Anyway, he didn't want Ambrose's impulsiveness to worsen the situation on top of all that, and this would work wonders.

So, he instead chose to pacify her, "Please calm down, miss. We are just a little on edge. Mundane objects are doing their best to maul us to death, and we're trapped in this building, making us extra cautious. I assure you, it's nothing personal."

Vern monitored her expression, and upon noticing that her anger wasn't rising, he continued, "I apologize for his misconduct, but I think we have something much more pressing to deal with. What were you just saying about something being over?"

Her icy expression quickly melted as she ignored the struggling Ambrose and closed her eyes. After a short bout of silence, she sighed. "I was marked for extermination, and they just figured out where I am. They saw me—through you."

Cera gasped, and Vern furrowed his eyebrows as he tried to figure out the implications.

Was that what had just happened to all of them? That drowsiness and that lack of control. That had to be it. But some things still didn't make sense.

"Then, why aren't you running away? You just said we might have enough time to get out. Won't you have the same amount of time?"

She shook her head. "And do what? Anyone who notices me will become eyes for them to spy on me. Anyone and everyone. I'd rather not get chased like a dog."

"Can't you just keep moving? Hide again at a different place and fight them with your toys?" grumbled Ambrose from the back.

Thump.

She slammed her hands on the table and exclaimed, "Oh, absolutely! With my busted cogwings and visions requiring an eternity to set up, I might as well roll out the red carpet for my pursuers. Why give them so much trouble? I should just deliver myself to their doorstep, right?"

Ambrose muttered something under his breath as he continued to hack away, trying different forms of his cane to get himself out.

She was definitely pissed at him.

It sounds like her visions are better for fortification purposes. And her mobility is hampered because of the broken . . . cogwings. That indeed sounds like she's better off in this station—

But his thoughts were quickly interrupted. Cera, who was clutching at the hem of her jacket, spoke up in a quivering voice, "Then why? Why didn't you . . . just kill us?" Walking up to her table, Cera looked the woman in her eyes and continued, "If you got rid of us, you could have avoided this."

Even Ambrose slowed down his persistent scraping of the ground and looked toward them with doubt in his eyes.

The silence pervaded the room for a while as she ran her hands through her headpiece, stroking that dim gem. "I-I . . ." She interlocked her hands and rested her head in their embrace on the table's edge. Then, the whole room seemed to shudder as if letting out a breath, and she uttered, "I give up . . ."

"Give up . . . on what?" Vern pressed her, the sense of urgency within his mind growing worse. She might have given up, but he had no such plans.

"It doesn't matter. We're all soon dead anyway."

Ambrose said, "Why do you keep saying that? Who exactly is pursuing you? And what reason would they have to kill us alongside you? I am from the Finnesse household. My family knows how to hold a grudge."

"Yeah, shout out your family's name to the apostles, okay? If they can hunt me—a Lightvein—down like a dog, they surely don't give a damn about whoever the hell you are. And they obviously won't leave any witnesses like you alive."

Then she mumbled, "Only if Mother was here." Luckily, Vern picked up her words due to his proximity.

Lightvein? He couldn't recall any household named Lightvein from his limited pool of knowledge of the noble houses in Elmhurst.

But what was this about the apostles? They filled him with greater dread. Were they really so powerful that a woman who could single-handedly pollute hundreds of objects and control such a big station had lost all hope against them? That three observers won't be able to matter much at all?

But what would he know? He wasn't even a real observer yet. He hadn't shaded his perception, after all. He had wondered more than once if doing so would have changed anything.

If he had shaded his perception, he might not have fainted in front of that statue upstairs after using instability inducement. And it was possible that he might have been able to suppress the pollution too.

But how was he supposed to access this thought space where he would have to imprint a vision? He remembered Cera being unsure about it herself.

And was it really the best idea to imprint instability inducement on his thought space? A vision he picked up from a parchment that demanded one to gouge out eyes and sacrifice them? A vision of the Cryptic Constructor?

He shook his head. Now wasn't the time.

He had to figure something out right imminently. If this woman was serious, they were in deep trouble.

So he tried to push her again, injecting as much urgency as he could in his voice. "Can you please tell us a little about what you've given up? Is there any way to get out of this situation? What was your plan if we hadn't come?"

The woman twisted her head slightly to look at him past her arms and spoke softly, "I am sorry. I didn't want this to happen either. But I'd rather not let down my family in my end times and divulge details of Lightvein's legacy. They might still be watching us through one of you, after all."

Fuck this!

"How much time do we have?"

She closed her arms around her head and whispered, "I don't know."

This is scrapshit!

He turned around and somehow suppressed his urge to hit the pipes in front of him. Just what had she given up on? Why the hell did it matter if she gave away minor details about her visions?

Can I get her to somehow speak about it while being vague?

Right when he began to cook up plans to do just that, he realized something else. *No. I might be able to figure this one out myself.*

He had a lot more information about her now. It should be possible to figure out something. He paced around the room as he let his thoughts churn.

So, what do I have?

She's marked by some entity, injured, and hiding inside a relay station.

She's been here for three to seven days. Does she not need food? No, that's beside the point. I need to start from the beginning.

She was probably in some kind of battle but managed to escape it. However, someone branded her, which is why she had to hide.

He even had an idea to confirm his previous hypothesis. He remembered the dent he had seen in one of the whistles atop the building. *Hmm, given that these pipes are heading straight to the whistles, the dent should have landed here . . .*

He extrapolated the distance from the center and moved toward what should be the direction of the east whistle. Though, he quickly ran into a wall.

Ignoring the stares from everyone else, he returned to the room's entrance and circled around to continue eastward. In just a few seconds, he found it. There was a circular hole in the ceiling above and another one above it—opening into the roof. Stars shone through the hole, blocked only by the shape of the whistles.

He nodded. So she entered the building through here. But the holes are shaped too perfectly to be from a crash.

He ruled out a few inconsistent theories.

One explanation could be that her faulty wings initially led her to crash in the whistle, but after that, she somehow manipulated the building to gain entry.

That wasn't an important point on its own, but what it implied definitely was. *She chose to come here. To this station.*

But why?

He chronologically went through all the events that had occurred in the station since they entered. Knowing what he did now, he looked for a thought process behind the phenomena. She had been controlling some aspects of the station for sure.

Everything was triggered when I first configured the valves of that pneumatic tube. Back then, he had attributed it to his shitty luck and the workings of the anomaly, but now he knew there was probably a person behind some of it. That made it easier to figure things out.

The typewriters were definitely pollution. Not under her control. But the activation of whistles—that had to be her. The first things that happened when I messed with valves were the whistles. It's as if . . . Right. As if she was surprised by our presence and panicked. Maybe the fear of being discovered led her to activate the whistles.

Right! Someone mentioned that the station only activated twice a day otherwise. This was out of the norm. Not just that. The whistles activated nonstop during the fight when we finally reached the basement.

Like some kind of . . . last-ditch effort?

Perfect. He was finally getting somewhere. Not giving up this lead, he continued his deductions.

So, her main objective has been activating the whistles. But why? To send messages? But there's no way anything could have worked the way it should.

He had seen the configuration on the panels above—it was a complete mess. There was no way any kind of standard modulation could have occurred in those settings. Anything sent from here would be received as nothing but gibberish on the other end.

Not just that. There was a bigger problem. What was powering the whole system? This station was receiving no steam from the city. But the whistles did activate. So, she was supplying some sort of energy. But who knew how a lot of the components would behave if they ran on some unknown energy?

He brooded on these points for a while, and a plan took shape in his mind. A lot of it was half-baked ideas, but there was no way he was going to extend his neck to be chopped up by some apostle in a random abandoned relay station.

Taking a deep breath, he cleared his mind and walked back into the room.

Ambrose was shouting, "The rhythm! Something is changing, woman! Let me out this instant. Don't play these games anymore. We need to work together."

"Oh, what will you do? Dance around? Don't worry, I'm sure the apostles will pause their plans just to admire your dazzling footwork."

Ambrose fumed at her words, a steely glint appearing in his eyes. But before he could do anything over the top, Vern walked in between the two of them.

Keeping his words vague, he interjected loudly, "Miss Lightvein. I've grasped your intent. If we cooperate, I am sure we can execute the process flawlessly."

CHAPTER 54

THOUGHT SYNERGY

Vern made sure not to state his proposal too bluntly. It would backfire if he clearly expressed in words what she was doing. It would be leaking information she didn't want publicized, and it would piss her off.

After pondering it for quite a while outside, he had concluded that she was trying to send a message, maybe even a distress call.

His theory was simple. She was controlling the whole station as some kind of sentient entity and was ordering it to send messages. He remembered the sound of a beating heart in the sorting room upstairs, and other similar occasions bolstered the likelihood of his guess.

But this meant that she wasn't using the standard mechanical method to get the station up and running, which could conversely mean that he might be of no help at all.

Still, he wasn't going to inspire any confidence in a depressed person by telling her the complete truth. He had to at least flail before his death.

He could feel it. There was no time to slowly coax her into giving his idea a shot. Even Ambrose was babbling about the rhythm being off tune and whatnot. They had to do something. Now.

But then she replied, snark bleeding into her words, "No, you don't understand. Even if you do, what can an observer without a single shade do to help me?"

He was ready for this one. He shook his head. "An observer can't." Then he hung the hourglass badge of the Coven of Truth from his fingers for all to see and continued, "But how about a fundamentalist? A savant? This station even uses technology that I published in my own research. I know exactly how it works." He emphasized the last part.

She seemed confused for a second, but then she suddenly stood up and turned toward Cera.

"Is that true?" she asked, squinting.

Cera looked flabbergasted but still nodded rapidly.

The woman rested one hand on her forehead and swiped away her bangs and bit on the nails of her other hand as she stared into the void.

Vern wanted to hurry her up, but she was clearly debating something important.

Thump.

When his patience was about to run out, she shook her head and slammed her palms on the table as she shouted, "Grab a chair and sit next to me! Right now!"

"What, what are you guys doing? This is no time to play house."

They ignored Ambrose's pointless question, and Vern pulled a chair next to her. She settled down, and Vern made to sit himself.

Rumble.

That's when loud noises resounded from upstairs. If he had to guess from the intensity of the sound, it was akin to walls being demolished.

But there was more. He felt as if some kind of weight was lifted off his chest before another, even heavier weight was dropped right back. One eyebrow raised, he closely watched the redhead in front of him, and his heart dropped when her expression turned fearful.

"They're here."

FUCK!

Why did it have to happen when he finally managed to convince her?! He didn't know how long it would take them to do whatever she was going for.

But he couldn't give up.

Not when his only options were to either get this working or embrace death. The fact that she quickly turned so energetic at his words meant there was a chance. A possibility that her communication would give them some kind of opportunity to get out of this mess.

He was willing to put his faith in his deductions.

He wasn't naive enough to believe that his luck would let him escape murderous psychos twice in one month. He had only managed to persuade Hensen back in the library due to some atypical circumstances. This time, he had nothing to bargain for his life against these apostles. It was a death sentence if he couldn't make this plan work.

The panicking part of his brain was internally screaming at Cera and blaming her for this whole debacle. He would never be in this situation if she hadn't picked such a powder keg of a place to seek enlightenment. But he knew she couldn't have known, and he was responsible for his choices.

Yet, it still made him second-guess everything. Things he could have done differently to have not gotten ensnared in this trap, which was only entangling him further and promising a pitiful death.

Not right now. Not now. This wasn't the time. Reflection would have to come later.

So he took a deep breath and bellowed, "We might still have time. What do you want me to do? We can make it work!"

The red-haired woman bit the corner of her lip and quickly leaned to one side of her chair, briefly touching the ground.

With a fierce look, she turned to Ambrose, who had stopped manically digging himself out of the ground.

She said, "Protect us if you want to live. Whatever comes, don't let it interrupt us. If you can't do that, then get out of my sight and fuck off."

Ambrose seemed like he wanted to say something, but his face turned fearful, and he hastily freed his legs from the holes that no longer contained marble hands constricting him. With a serious nod, he turned around and flicked his cane, taking a proper stance.

It must be because he sensed danger in his rhythm, right?

Then she looked at Cera and asked, her words coming out in rapid succession, "Do you have a solid viewpoint? Would you be able to assist us right away if I helped you with your enlightenment?"

Cera was taken aback for a full three seconds before an excited, yet solemn, look spread over her face. She replied stoically, "Yes. I have been studying an observation record of Ephram—"

"Good enough. Take this." The woman clicked something on her neck and pulled out her headpiece—the red locks falling all over her face. She threw the headpiece toward Cera, who caught it promptly and wore it on her head after a nod from the woman.

Once Cera had it settled on her head, the beauty in front of him yelled, "Fen, activate the second sequence."

After having done all this, she ignored Cera's attempt at asking further questions and focused back on Vern. She extended her hand toward him, palm up, and asked, "What is your name?"

He was confused by the question. Why did his name matter in such a situation? But the urgency of the circumstances made him overrule any hesitation as he put his palm on top of hers, replying, "Vern. Vern Lockwood."

"I am Esther Lightvein. I need you to relax and let me into your thoughts . . . and I will do the same. Synergize with me and guide the . . . process. I will be there to assist you however you want."

My thoughts?! How would that—

No! Can she see my memories? What if—

I need to calm down. She clearly said thoughts. There's no way reading memories would be so simple. I should be fine as long as I don't let my thoughts wander to my secrets and stick to the business at hand.

It had to be fine. He didn't have much of a choice. Not when all their lives hung in the balance.

I just need to keep myself in line.

Should be simple.

Taking yet another deep breath, he closed his eyes and banished all unruly thoughts.

Thoughts that included him being skewered to death by some spear-wielding fanatic or of the whole basement collapsing. Or the thought where Esther peeped into his brain and exchanged the knowledge of time discrepancy and duskfall for her own life—leaving him to die at the hands of the apostles.

These were all scenarios that could happen, but their possibility was either negligible or a possible result of inaction. It was nothing but peak paranoia.

Stop.

So he did, and his thoughts became calmer than a still lake.

"Vern? Can you feel this?"

Those were not his own words or a hallucination. It was her. The words weren't conveyed as voice—instead, they were a notion. A notion that was attached to these foreign thoughts—clearly distinct from his own. They had a peculiar feeling to them. One he couldn't put a finger on. But it was a pleasant feeling, nonetheless.

So he responded in kind.

"Yes."

But something far more complicated started to populate his mind. Threads.

Hundreds— No. Thousands of threads were spreading around him . . . Or was that his perception?

No. It was her perception.

It was starkly dissimilar to his own. The more he focused on understanding it, the clearer everything became as an increasing number of threads made themselves known to him.

"What you are feeling right now are the essence strands I have weaved in objects around the station."

"I . . . see."

The more he listened to—no, sensed—her words, the richer they became. They had a vividness that was absent in vocal communication. Speech used intonation and body language to express a significant amount of meaning. But here, something else was at play, and it was making him jittery.

This synergy communicated more than just words. Each word seemed to have an emotion attached to it, while the whole sentence relayed a certain meaning right to his mind.

It was jarring. But fascinating.

"Vern, I understand that it's confusing, but I hope you're still with me. And a fair warning—if you start feeling emotionally numb, you need to let me know as soon as possible. This synergy isn't as harmless as it seems."

Well, that was the law of the world. Nothing was free.

"It's okay, Esther. I can take this much. I am with you."

He intentionally pronounced her name because she'd been doing the same. What if it was some kind of anchor to the thoughts? Better to proceed with caution wherever possible.

"All right. So tell me. What did you understand? What was I trying to achieve? Don't worry about the time. It hasn't even been a few seconds outside. Think of it as the benefits of conversing through thoughts."

Well, ideas were indeed meant to be thousands of times faster than speech. It made sense. So he put together his best pitch and let loose.

"You've been attempting to contact someone using the whole station as a conduit. But you failed. Again and again. If your vision is anything like mine, it will work far better if you have a greater understanding of the objects under influence. Which is why I offered to help. I might not know every detail, but this could be our best shot.

"However, I was expecting myself to physically rotate knobs and valves to get things in order. This . . . wasn't it."

He wondered if all his confusion, anxiety, and smugness at having figured out her problem was somehow being packed into his words and parceled to her brain for her to pick apart. Well, it was not something he could control.

"I . . . see. You're indeed worthy of being a savant. I apologize for not speaking up about it and wasting our time. It's just that my pursuers have . . . unique methods.

The branding on my body can deduce far more than what I say by matching my words with the ideas that flit through my mind. I couldn't risk that."

He felt her heaving a sigh of relief. He didn't know how that worked, but it was definitely a sigh.

"Luckily, thought synergy is completely different at a fundamental level and works outside the bounds of the physical body. It is primarily a conduit to control the essence strands, but this is another way of using it. Anyway, you're right. I was trying to contact my mother."

A sense of longing filled Vern's heart at the mention of the word *mother*, and the feeling did not amuse him. It wasn't his own. He missed his own mother, but he had long since come to terms with the fact that she was gone.

Or so he hoped.

"If I can somehow get a distress signal to her, it wouldn't take her even a second to warp here and claim the heads of these sly apostles.

"Well, maybe more than a single second. But it shouldn't take her too long to find a traveler within the family and warp here. But that's the problem. This . . . this damned station wouldn't listen to me. You have experienced it yourself already, but every time I attempt a transmission, things go out of control. They just keep getting polluted."

Vern couldn't contain his curiosity this time and interrupted.

"So pollution comes from failed visions?"

"Yes. I think. Maybe there's more, but that's not the point right now. I will need you to either explain everything about this station to me, or we need to go deeper into each other's minds. That way, you can directly take control of the essence strands, and I can assist you. But thought synergy cannot be elevated one-sidedly."

After giving him what felt like half a second, she continued.

"I would suggest the second option because I once tried to learn mechanical arts such as how my cogwings work from Master Svartlf. That was the day I realized I have as much aptitude for mechanics as a fish has for climbing trees."

That made a certain sense, but it was getting hairy. There was no way he was going to tutor a newbie about one of the most complex machines to exist on the planet as they inched toward their deaths. So he cut to the chase and asked her, *"Will you be able to read my memories?"*

He sensed something akin to a scoff as she said, *"Ha-ha, adorable. Do you really think I would open up my memories to an outsider? Do you think I can? The bindings of my observation record will turn me into a vegetable long before I willingly divulge anything in it. And what did I tell you? Thought synergy goes two ways."*

So that meant if he couldn't see her memories, she obviously couldn't see his either. That was a relief.

But he still tried to assess this proposal. Ensuring none of the stray thoughts bubbled up to the surface of his mind, he went through some of the possibilities. He didn't care if she could control his perception as well. It was a blank slate right now, anyway—

He received a notion of curiosity from her end, and he forcefully halted all such thoughts. There were possibly other dangers, but what if he thought about them, and they were transmitted straight to her mind?

That would defeat the whole purpose of being discreet. This was annoying.

So he made to nod, and he realized that the action actually sent a notion. She reacted to his nod with a . . . nod of her own?

"But what exactly am I supposed to do? How do I . . . elevate our connection?"

"It's simple. Try to reach out to the essence strands and don't resist when I try something similar."

He nodded again and visualized those thousands of glowing strands that floated all around him in the darkness. Picking one of them, he followed it.

Soon, that strand further divided itself into more strands—each leading to a different direction. Randomly selecting another one, he pursued it.

Before too long, he felt it. A sense of rigidity pervaded his mind, and an impression of some kind of goal echoed in his thoughts.

It was to stay rigid and pass along messages. The only thought looping at this essence strand's edge was to fulfill this purpose. Vern quickly realized that this had to be the result of synergizing with one of the tubes.

The feeling mesmerized him.

He was sensing what the tube felt.

How amazing was that?

But when nothing changed for a while, he retraced his steps and followed a different strand. However, before he could reach its end—

"Vern! WHAT THE FUCK?!

"WHY?!

"Why do you . . .

"Why do you have the rune of an Elden One in your mind?!"

C H A P T E R 5 5

THIRD RUNE

The moment Esther's words registered, Vern recoiled, snatching his palm away from hers—hoping to get some distance.

But those hundreds of strands that surrounded him didn't disappear, and neither did he see the nexus of the station. It didn't fucking work. He was unable to get out of this space!

"Vern! Stop! Don't strain it. We can only get out of this together. Ahh! FUCKING STOP! DAMN IT! It hurts."

He tried everything. Mentally retreated as far away as possible from the world of strands, ignored them, rejected them.

Nothing worked.

"This is bad. What should I do?!"

He stopped. The more he struggled, the more he would lose control of his thoughts, possibly divulging something far more consequential. It wasn't that bad yet. He could try and communicate. Figure out how badly he had fucked up.

"Yes, Vern, calm down. There's no point in trying to get out of this headspace. What will you do by leaving? Kill me? Just because now I know your little secret? You won't be able to. So give it a rest. And more than that, you don't need to. I can be . . . discreet."

Wow. She was digging up the darkest thoughts that had yet to even materialize in his own head. But he asked, still trying to collect his racing thoughts, *"And why exactly would you be discreet?"*

"First. Dead women tell no tales. So if we die, you don't have anything to worry about. Second, if we don't die, why would I antagonize a rune bearer? An alive and non-vegetative rune bearer!"

Did that mean that engraving runes was a risky endeavor? He didn't remember it being a challenge. But his circumstances weren't exactly ordinary, so what would he know?

After a few seconds of rest, he sighed and said, *"I-I'm sorry. It was just unexpected . . . and personal. I am not used to sharing my deepest secrets with someone I met ten minutes ago."*

Esther replied, *"Right. Don't do it again. It hurt like hell. We both have to be on board with the idea of exiting for it to work. And do you think I am not freaked out? You have access to my essence strands—the Lightvein legacy. It's a rough situation, but let's make the best of it, okay?"*

She paused, granting him a moment's grace and giving him the space to collect his thoughts.

Once he had his nerves under control, he nodded. It was almost as if they had reached a quiet understanding amid the chaos.

Her range of emotions went from admonishing to curious quickly as she said, *"Anyway, given how freaked out you were, it seems you know just how precious—or cursed—of a thing you've got in there. These have been exclusively under the control of the Institute since forever. Are you a guinea pig of the Institute? Child of some master from there? Or worse—a chosen vessel? Still can't believe you survived engraving it in your head."*

The . . . what? Institute?

A little more level-headed now, he instead rapidly assessed the current state of affairs. He knew nothing about that rune, but she seemed more than just aware of it.

This could be a chance. A chance to uncover the details surrounding this enigma in his head. He had never willingly tried to mess with it for the fear of signaling Hensen. But if he understood more . . .

So he gave her some information to get the topic started. *"No, Esther. It's more of a . . . noose around my neck. And I'd really appreciate it if you didn't pry me for its origins."*

"That I. . . . Vern, I don't want to know too much about it either. But it's the rune of the fucking Cryptic Con . . . DAMN, I almost pronounced their name. Listen, I-I just need to be sure that you're not his vessel. I don't know if you know, but it will mean a horrible death for me and you not too far down the line if you're one—worse than whatever those apostles could ever do to us."

Was there something wrong with pronouncing their name? Why?

And what was this about being its vessel? He didn't think his situation was anything like that. Hensen wasn't exactly the beacon of trust, but it was clear that he didn't have Vern engrave this rune for any such purposes.

"I don't think I am. I engraved it under dire circumstances that didn't include being some kind of vessel."

"I see."

She remained silent for a while. Just when Vern was ready to ask her more questions of his own volition, she murmured, *"Have you made contact already? What is it like?"*

Made contact? As in activating it?

He shook his head.

This time, when she spoke, her words carried an undercurrent of regret, tinged with a hint of pity. *"That's . . . wasteful. It's almost tragic, you know? Visionaries of this era—and even those long gone—would practically kill for a word of revelation from you. A chance to pry open the secrets of the Institute or this very cosmos? People have done far worse for far less. I must say, I am tempted to start pleading."*

The words sent a hint of panic coursing through him. This was why he didn't want anyone to know about these secrets. Not until he figured out their scope and volatility. But something about her last assertion didn't sit right with him.

"Beg me? Not torture or dissect me? That can't be right."

"Oh ho ho. Just what is this situation? You have engraved this rune into your mind, but you don't know what it entails? This is very suspicious." She emphasized the last part of her sentence.

Darn it. He would be blushing if someone could look at his face right now. He barely spoke. *"Dire circumstances, remember?"*

She shook her head. *"Sure. Whatever you say. Anyway, it's a miracle to have a functional human being that can make contact with the Elden Ones. As long as you don't run into religious or ideological enemies of the Constructor, the ones in the know will do anything to have you test their theories for them."*

Theories? What kind of theories? This rune was really something far more bizarre than he ever could have imagined.

However, before he could respond, she went on. *"Wow. You really have no clue? It's a pity. You haven't shaded your perception while having the rune of the Constructor! What are you? An invalid with no talent? Is your viewpoint really so useless?"*

Huh, did that mean the rune somehow assisted him in shading his perception? Combined with the fact that she said it would help him test theories, didn't it mean that—

"What?! No response? Aren't you pissed? You should be pissed. You're supposed to be very smart, aren't you? How can you have a trash viewpoint?"

". . ."

"Ahh, it hurts my brain. If we weren't on the brink of death and I didn't desperately need your help, I'd be humming 'Jibberwick's Jolly Jig' in both our heads just to scrub away the idiocy you've imparted on me."

". . ."

Wow, she really just said whatever came to her mind. He just wanted some time to process her words. Regardless, she was acting like it was all rainbows and sunshine. So he replied, *"Well, there's a cost to everything—"*

Not giving him the opportunity to finish his thought, she interjected, *"No shit, detective. Yeah, there's a cost. What about it? Is the cost not worth having your own vision? Not worth having the most flexible thought space . . . Oh, huh? Wait, wait, wait. You don't know what I am talking about, do you?"*

This was fucking mind reading. She had to be mind reading him. This made no sense.

"Frown all you want. This is when all my synergy partners start feeling like I'm in their heads. I'm not. I don't need to be. Simply analyzing the change of your emotions in reaction to my words is more than enough, you know?"

Well, she was in his head—literally. Not having the mental space to think to himself for even short bursts was annoying him to no end. He had to get back some sense of control.

So his first idea was to turn this into a back-and-forth conversation instead of being verbally abused one-sidedly.

"Esther, I'm practically a newborn observer, so your soul-crushingly technical explanations and compliments are just what the doctor ordered. Now, if I understand it right, this rune allows me to test the validity of visions without being subjected to the . . . whispers?"

"May Elysian bless the life. You actually know something! Yeah, that's what the books say. But you're missing the key point. Something that can be important to our situation right now."

He allowed himself to feel puzzled at her words, knowing she would pick it up from his thoughts.

And she did. Her previously animated speech turned solemn as she said, *"If our first plan doesn't work out, you must make contact."*

"Why? How would that help in this situation?"

"Why do you not know anything?"

". . ."

"Well. You would've if you hadn't skipped your history classes. From what I remember, this was the third rune that was discovered by the Institute after hundreds of sacrifices. Both the recorded users who successfully made contact were said to have had their 'existence deconstructed' while they were in contact. You see what I'm getting at?"

Ahh! So they disappeared while making contact. A method to hide from the apostles?

He nodded. *"I do."* Still, he asked with some apprehension, *"But what about the cost?"*

"How the heck would I know? You survived the engraving, not me. No one would have the actual details of the inner workings of an Elden rune. Except maybe the Institute. These history books I mention are just recounting from students that managed to escape long ago—interesting, but incomplete."

This made it clear that he would have to deal with more than just the risk of alerting Hensen if he decided to go this route. This was not a great idea. Not unless he was forced into it. Who knew what kind of repercussions came from making contact. The term alone had horrifying connotations.

Furthermore, make contact with what? An . . . Elden One? What was an Elden One? A concept? An entity? Was he supposed to make contact with the Cryptic Constructor? Just the thought sent shivers down his spine. So he tried to change the topic slightly. *"This is all good and well, but why are we focusing on plan B before we've even talked about plan A? Are you not confident in our chances?"*

"Well, who the hell said I have no confidence. It's just practicality. And that this time-saving, faster-than-life communication we have going on only works when we talk between ourselves. Any changes we envision in reality will take time in seconds and consume our thoughts. So once we commence plan A, we can't communicate with this ease anymore."

"Fair enough."

"Right. So yeah, plan B. If we can't send the distress signal, your best chance at survival is to make contact . . ."

She trailed off. But he realized what she was trying to nudge him toward. She wasn't giving him all this knowledge for free. So he played along with her games and inquired, *"Seeing as you are suggesting I leave you to die while I test some theories, how does this help you? Or, more like, How can I help you?"*

"Oh, you actually understand nuance? Great. Well, if things go downhill, I will try my best to lure the apostles away from you. Then if I don't come out of it alive"—suddenly her voice turned ruthless—*"I need you to contact Andrea Lightvein, my mother, in the Northern Senn Empire. She will give you more than enough*

remuneration to make it worthwhile. Incomplete records, representation, access to rare memory packets, whatever you want."

Vern replied, *"Hmm. I will have to think about it. Weigh the pros and cons."*

"If you're scared about my mother not holding up her end of the bargain, just ask around. You'll realize in no time that Lightvein's honor is famous throughout the empire. Only an ideology of honor can nurture observers of Lightvein."

Even his doubt didn't escape her, huh? But it was good to know. He would base his judgment on the validity of her statement later.

"Anyway. Now that that's out of the way. We gotta figure out the problem at hand," Esther said.

"Wait."

"Hmm?"

"Can you . . . umm. Tell me how to access thought space?"

"Huh? Come again?"

Even her facial expressions couldn't have conveyed her shock and disappointment as well as the intent packaged with her words did.

Well, that was embarrassing.

"I . . . don't know how to access my thought space."

"Yeah. What the hell kind of question is that? You don't know thought space, and you call yourself an observer? This is really befuddling. I need to get a reality check."

"I . . . had a rough enlightenment. And I don't have an observation record to follow."

"Then how did you even manage your enlightenment? Are you trying to say you synthesized a viewpoint without an observation record?"

"Kinda . . . ?"

He had long since realized that the diagram in the *Observation Record of Subjectivity* was out of the norm. Cera, Ambrose, and even Esther talked about observation records as if they presented an ideology or a viewpoint. The diagram had none of that. Actually, none of the pages he could read in that book told anything about a specific viewpoint.

"Oh, Benevolent Elysian, guide this lost soul who is dipping his toes into the cosmic cesspool of observation without a star map. I don't even know what to say, Vern." She let out a deep sigh and continued after a while, *"Well, it would be rude of this great Esther to not impart her superior teachings unto this wayward soul,"*

He sensed the curve of a grin in her emotional aura, as if she found a dark humor in their narcissistic banter. It was an odd sort of levity, especially considering they were teetering on the brink of death. In a situation so dire, finding entertainment in such cerebral sparring was both bizarre and oddly comforting.

"Thank you, oh kind Lady Esther, may your name echo through every steam engine across the realm."

"That was weirdly specific, but okay. Now listen. You got your perception, right? Interpret something in it."

Oh, she means right now.

He got to it. Since she had said to interpret something, he just imagined where the typewriter and table should be on his right. Then he began to interpret it based on complexity. He interpreted different typewriter sections as shades of gray while making the table a bright white.

"*Ooh. Interesting. So you see in shades of gray? I wonder what you can do with it. Wanna tell your master?*"

"*I doubt you need to know that.*"

"*Oops. Busted. Whatever. Something tells me you've got a boring viewpoint anyway. Now just take these thoughts that are floating in your mind—the ones that you're constantly repeating to maintain the state of your perception and imagine a shape for them.*"

"*What kind of shape?*"

"*You don't want me to tell you that. Each person has a natural inclination. If I tell you, you're going to have a harder time with it. However, you look like someone that'd shape it into tiny little cogs and gears,*" she finished, scoffing.

Ignoring her jabs, he asked, "*Does one kind of shape have any advantage over the other?*"

She remained silent for a while before shrugging. "*I don't know.*"

"*Very helpful.*"

"*My pleasure. Now get to it.*"

Well, if someone was talking about shapes, what was better than a sphere? But should it be a hollow sphere or a solid one? This sounded like an important choice. So he asked another question. "*Would I be stuck with the shape I chose right now?*"

"*Eh, I don't think so. As long as you don't imprint a vision onto it, it should be whatever. However, if it doesn't, then too bad—don't blame me. Also, lucky bastards who get to imprint a completely original vision onto their thought spaces better not whine about the little things.*"

He nodded and went ahead, imagining the perception around him to warp into a sphere. The edge of the white table became curved and bent as he envisioned this to be some kind of painting wrapped around a sphere wall.

Nothing happened.

"*Ha ha ha. You sure are dumb for a savant.*" Her words dripped with scorn, but Vern sensed something else beneath the surface—an undercurrent of insecurity that wafted through the emotional strands linking them. His newfound skill in reading emotions in this peculiar headspace had just given him a subtle clue.

She doesn't really believe I messed up. She's deflecting, maybe even a bit rattled.

"*You should reshape the thoughts, not what you perceive.*"

Oh, I took her too literally? I need to shape the ideas, not their result. That sounded simple enough. It was just another construct for mental organization. This shouldn't be too hard. Actionable feedback was always great.

Nodding, he cleared his perception of any grays and started over again. This time, when assigning a shade to the typewriter's head, he tried to imagine the idea going onto the surface of a sphere instead—long before it was interpreted into that shade of gray by his perception.

And as expected, words and ideas began to pile up as they took the shape of the sphere. But apparently, he designated the radius of the sphere to be too big, as all these thoughts barely covered a small chunk of this imaginary surface. It was akin to a small country appearing on a globe while the rest of the land and water didn't exist.

"All right. All right. Stop showing off. You got it. Happy? Pay your tuition in pieces of jewelry if we survive, okay? Can we move on now?"

Chapter 56

LIGHTVEIN

t's not like it matters before you imprint a Vision onto it."

Vern nodded in agreement. Esther was right. From what Cera had told him, his thought space would remain unstable until he imprinted a vision on it. And according to Esther's new information, he was better off imprinting an original vision than anything else.

That it would lead to the most flexible thought space. He didn't know what it meant to have a flexible thought space, but it was clearly better than the other way around.

However, there was a problem.

A big one.

Now that he knew she was just assessing him based on emotional cues and not literally reading his innermost thoughts, he let the memories of that event surface in his mind. And of that man.

Hensen Vehen.

It was like waking up from a dream only to find yourself at the edge of a cliff. Sure, all this talk about the third rune, creating original visions, and having a malleable thought space sounded enticing, almost liberating.

But what about the cost? There was a reason he hadn't dared mess with that rune up until now. He went so far as to muddle through the whispers caused by that scar in the sky head-on instead of relying on the rune to soothe his nerves.

Hensen wasn't just some abstract concept or a distant authority—he was a guillotine waiting to fall. It was already a miracle that he hadn't come knocking on Vern's door, demanding he pay the toll.

Who knew how many times Vern could trigger the rune before Hensen was alerted?

Using the rune was nothing short of a revolver's reckoning—a few chambers, but just one bullet. Maybe the next pull of the trigger would be the one that spelled his doom, alerting the madman.

But then what should I do?

What would be a good balance?

And this launched him along another tangent. How much usage could he eke out of a single trigger of the rune? If he could—

Cutting off his thoughts, Esther said, *"This much synergy should be enough. Come. Reach out to the essence strands. Let's see if the hope you gave me was worth not being depressed over."*

"Um, Esther, actually, one more question."

She glared at him. *"This conversation may not cost us time, but it costs me my representation. Can it wait?"*

Representation?

She had also used this word a while ago when she described what her mother could offer him. But given the context she just used it in, it seemed as if this was the resource that depleted when one used their visions.

But it's quite a peculiar term to use as a depletable resource. If I think about it literally in this context, representation should mean the number of things she could represent through her own viewpoint.

That felt right. It might not be the exact definition, but he had to be close. He could maybe even figure out the amount of representation he had at some point.

Taking his silence as an answer, she concluded, *"So it's not important. Now, get to it. If I end up being just a little short of the representation needed to envision all the changes in the station, I will blame you for our death."*

Ugh.

Shoving the stray thoughts to the back of his mind, he focused on the task at hand. His best shot would be to make this work so they never had to turn toward plan B and let the revolver do the reckoning.

He closed in on the world of strands, but something was different this time. In the center of the glowing blue strands was a ball of light.

No, it was . . . someone. It was Esther.

She was sitting on a bench in the empty void, a tapestry of glowing threads surrounding her. The glow around her shone so brilliantly that her body seemed almost submerged in its luminescence, casting her in an ethereal silhouette that eclipsed even the vibrant threads themselves.

She had a physical presence here. How?

Did she manifest an image of herself with the thoughts? Is it efficient?

But she must have had a reason. So, as he got closer to her, he attempted to conjure a physical form himself. Everything was just thoughts and figments of his imagination, so it was quite easy.

He willed it, and it became so. Walking over with his two legs, he stood next to her as she gracefully lifted the fallboard of the celestial piano, which turned out to be the nexus where all those glowing strands converged.

The filaments pulsed rhythmically like the arteries of some divine organism, each feeding into the diaphanous keys below. It was as if the very essence of the universe had chosen to express itself through this otherworldly instrument, and she, its virtuosa.

He looked at the display in front of him with awe. *Is this what being a Lightvein means?*

Just what exactly is happening underneath all this? What is her fundamental viewpoint? Does she perceive everything as some sort of mass of veins and then use thought synergy to assert control over them? If so, this piano has to be an artistic way to control her visions.

Ideas churned in his mind as he contrasted and compared this with his own lackluster vision. He felt like he was missing out on the flair and theatrics big time.

He couldn't even fathom being able to do something so . . . complex with balance.

If he had to perform this from his viewpoint, he would have to individually figure out a lot of basic blocks. The first would be how to achieve movement. He could probably do so by playing with gravity's balance around the object.

Then, he would have to figure out how to manipulate an object's parts with enough nuance to actually have them perform meaningful actions like release steam, shoot projectiles, or modulate speech.

He would need a special solution or vision for each kind of object. Once he had these building blocks, he would have to find a way to assemble them, and even then, it'd be a cheap imitation of what Esther could achieve with her fingertips.

He shook his head.

Some viewpoints are just not meant to be emulated.

Her viewpoint was optimal for this kind of vision, whereas balance presented itself as somewhat of a jack of all trades.

But these were all his assumptions based on how his viewpoint acted during his enlightenment in the library. Sadly, things hadn't been rainbows and sunshine after that. He couldn't even look at the sky without succumbing to the whispers.

"Are you just going to stand there, contemplating the majesty of Lightvein, or actually do something?" she said, tapping at the spot next to her on the bench.

He chuckled and sat down.

It was uncanny how this vision recreated all the sensory information. The feel of the seat on his back, the warmth of their bodies, even her scent—a curious blend of old parchment, a hint of lavender, and the unmistakable tang of freshly cut copper.

It was curious because her copper cogwings, as she dubbed them, were nowhere to be seen on her back. Heck, even her armor wasn't there. She wore a loose white dress—fitting for this casual piano performance.

Is this how she imagines herself? In her natural state of being?

"You can keep marveling later, but right now, I need you to lend me a hand. You know how to play?"

Grazing the ethereal keys of the piano with his hands, he rested them at optimal positions, looked her in the eye, and said, *"Never touched a piano in my life."*

She looked back and broke into a grin. *"Skills wouldn't have helped anyway."*

Resting her palms gently over his, she took a deep breath and spoke in a solemn tone, *"Time to get serious, Vern. You give ideas, and I help execute them. A little background if you haven't figured it out already: I perceive inanimate objects as entities. Entities with veins running through them, with personalities that are inherent to them.*

"But that's the catch. Most objects don't have personalities. So I have to assign them one. The better my guess at the personalities, the less I have to pay. Simple rule." Then she mumbled, *"Or if I am wrong, they get polluted, and we lose them to the whispers and echoes."*

So that's how the pollution started upstairs?

Before he could ponder further, she continued, *"Anyway, once that's done, I communicate with those personalities and have them perform the tasks I want. For example—I perceive this whole station as a huge entity with a complex anatomy."*

Well, his guess wasn't too off the mark.

She held his palm in her own and moved it to the rightmost key of the piano. With a gentle force, she made him press the key.

Ting.

A melody resonated in his surroundings, followed by the sensation of a pulse unlike his own.

Ba-dump.

Ba-dump.

B-dump.

As if waking up from a slumber, the beating gained momentum, rapidly picking up speed. Vern found himself faced with that feeling of rigidity and a purpose yet again. This had to be the personality she decided was a fit for the pneumatic tubes.

"These are the veins."

Then she guided his other palm to a key in the middle and pressed it.

Plunk.

He felt . . . cogs, pistons, and gears as they began to churn and thump in synergy with hundreds of others, releasing steam in huffs and puffs. This time, he got a feeling of wanting to rush to do everything, to burn as brightly as possible, to generate the most output.

This is the backup steam generator? But where is this energy coming from? Just how—

"This is the heart."

Well, that too.

Then, one after another, she guided his fingers to press other keys.

Ding.

"Whistles are the throat."

Tink.

"The nexus we're sitting in is the brain."

Ding.

"These are the muscles."

This was . . . fascinating.

He had conjectures, but he couldn't believe this vision had so much thought put into it. There was a completely rational system behind how this all worked. It wasn't some fancy hand-waving logic where everything just fit into place because of . . . magic.

There was clearly a reason for everything, from simple decisions like which part of the station was designated to what organ of the entity, to the arrangement of veins. Not just that, the personalities she designated to each object had a distinct sense of . . . correctness to them.

There was no way he could mimic this with balance. Even if he was sent back to the library with unlimited access to all visions, he doubted he would be able to build up to something so complex.

No! Not right now. I will have to pick up this train of thought later.

The time for idle thoughts was over. They were interacting with physical objects now. Every second counted.

This was it.

So Vern started, *"Obviously, you were unable to make the station send something coherent. You've got it all wrong. That's not how frequencies are encoded. Power isn't meant to be supplied rhythmically, and what the hell is this personality? Why would a pressure valve want to be free? This is dumb."*

Taking a deep breath, he lifted his fingers from the piano and looked her in the eyes.

"Here's the deal, Esther." Vern became serious. *"When you work with these strands, you see the bigger picture, like the flow of the energy, harmony between different parts, and the spirit, so to speak, of the station. That's the high-level stuff; I will leave that to you.*

"What I can do," he continued, *"is focus on the fine details—the settings, the calibration, and the sequence of operations. Handle the fundamentals. Sounds good?"*

She nodded, a solemn look in her eyes.

Shinsei nodded as he rubbed the hilt of his sword, narrowing his eyes. Today the air felt wrong. It was as if an indistinct shadow were cast across the world, not a physical one, but something intangible that nagged at the corners of his instincts.

Can't be deflected. Can't be controlled, he thought. And that made it irresistibly interesting.

It wasn't as bad as the eve of duskfall or the kid he'd seen crossing the bridge yesterday. But it was a welcome change, nonetheless. It just meant there was another phenomenon to be brought under his control.

His worn boots pounded against the uneven cobblestones as he moved through the mazelike city streets. People were merely obstacles to navigate around, their potential hostility easily deflected if it ever came to that.

His instincts led him, pulling him toward the anomaly like a moth to a flame. It wasn't recklessness that drove him but a compelling need to probe the boundaries of his own capabilities. *What can't be deflected*, he pondered, *challenges the deflector. And that's where growth happens. Or death. But it's all the same—just endpoints on a line one needs to walk every day.*

His pace quickened as the ripples of disturbance accelerated toward the outer district. Anticipation bubbled within him. Whatever it was, it was going fast. So he upped the ante and focused. It was about figuring out the path of least resistance.

He was in control. He could subconsciously feel the path that he must take. Traversing street after street lined with those somber gravestones, he reached the demarcation of the inner and outer districts.

Bothering with Kingsmen wasn't the path of least resistance, and he didn't have the time to go through their exclusive routes or take a detour to smaller gaps, so, as he reached the riverbank, he jumped with great vigor, pulling on the scarf on his neck.

It unfurled, but right as his neck was about to be greeted with the chilly air, the scarf extended and coiled tighter around his neck. It hurt, but it was within his control. He could deflect the pain, and it was worth it.

Right as the other end of the scarf dipped into the water, it turned as rigid as a bone. As Shinsei landed on it, the grip around his neck became tighter, but he paid it no heed. Sprinting at full speed, he walked along the narrow bridge created by his ever-extending and tightening scarf.

By the time he reached the outer district, his face had turned pale from the lack of air, but it was better than that time when the scarf had broken his neck.

When he clambered over the outer district's riverside parapet, the scarf began to shrink in length as it slowly handed the control back to Shinsei, deservingly so.

But he didn't have the time to deal with his unhappy scarf that wanted to throw a fit for being unable to strangle its master to death. He had an uncontrollable variable to handle.

Jumping over ledges and store signs, he quickly climbed up to the roof of a nearby building and continued his path of least resistance.

One district.

Two districts.

A hill.

An abandoned relay station? The one Akira's team was working on.

As he rounded his hundredth corner of the day, his eyes met the source of the disturbance head-on. His pulse quickened in the thrill of the unknown. *This friend sure knows how to run*, he mused as the edges of his lips upturned.

Let's see what you're made of.

CHAPTER 57

SINEWS OF REALITY

Cera's knees hit the floor as the dimly lit nexus of the station reappeared in her eyes. They were burning. They had to be. There was no other way to describe the pain.

She was doing everything she could to not scream at the top of her lungs, although the vivid memories of what she'd just experienced were working wonders at being distracting.

Everything changed when Lady Esther asked someone named Fen to activate the sequence. The world went dark before a colossal door appeared out of nowhere. It was so huge she couldn't even fathom its boundaries.

Soon, it creaked open of its own volition, revealing a hazy vista shrouded in mist. But in the center of it all was a light.

Then, the very next second, it sparked just like lightning in the sky—but contained. It shone through the mist for a fraction of a second as its glow branched into a thousand more streaks of light that traveled many meters outward in an instant before vanishing.

It was bizarre yet enthralling. An impossible wonder. Everyone knew that lightning couldn't be contained. Even fundamentalists had long given up on controlling any sort of weather phenomenon.

Yet, before she was able to make any sense of that scene, her vision came crashing down as her sight morphed into a million things her brain couldn't fathom.

The everflux.

They were the possibilities. Mostly the ones she couldn't grasp.

But knowing she had limited time, she suppressed her awe and isolated her viewpoint through the construct she had long planned. She followed the steps exactly as they were mentioned in the observation record.

Yet she was still pleasantly surprised when the Everflux listened to her and settled into her chosen vista.

The entire ordeal was a symphony of sensory delight. Now, if only she could manage to keep her eyes open, she might see it. She squeezed her eyelids harder, working through the pain for long, agonizing seconds.

Until it became bearable.

When she opened her eyes, she felt it. It was like a veil that had covered her eyes since forever was lifted. The connections became clear, and interactions turned apparent as she saw the lines. The lines that linked everything.

The sinews of reality.

Something only enlightened conductors of Ephram had the privilege to lay their eyes upon.

And now, she was one of them.

IT WORKED!

A smile spread across her face as the sinews populated her vision, connecting the typewriters with the ground, the ground with the pipes, the pipes with Vern, Vern with Esther, and many more such links.

She tucked the hair that covered her eyes behind her ears as she noticed all kinds of sinews. There were ones with various densities, tenacities, colors, and targets. Everything meant something.

This was what she had to work toward. It wouldn't be long before she would lose the guiding light of free representation.

She now had power of her own. Her eyes, though brighter, carried a quieter intensity—finally, she was no longer a burden.

Gazing at Vern's calm visage, an unpleasant thought crossed her mind. *I even managed to shove such a calm and intelligent person into the jaws of death. What am I, if not a burden?*

But not anymore.

She had to set things right. The guilt had been gnawing at her very being. The paralyzing fear and inability to do anything had made her want to scream multiple times.

It had threatened to consume her, when Lady Esther declared everything was over, and Vern left the room. She thought he was disappointed. That he wouldn't be back. And she felt it. The cold. Just like that night. She was sure that even he was out of ideas. And that it was all her fault.

Cera didn't care if she died. She was surviving on broken fragments of hope anyway. There wasn't much left for her to live for.

But the idea that others might die because of her foolish choices was disheartening. That Vern might die because she got him mixed into this whole ordeal hurt more than the idea of being left alone.

He had been nothing but understanding, adapting to every twist the situation presented. He hadn't once complained or cast blame her way, and that only intensified the guilt bubbling within her. If he had faulted her, at least this situation wouldn't be as suffocating as it was now.

He had no business coming into such a hostile district and getting almost mugged and murdered because of her. Ambrose didn't weigh on her conscience as much because he came in knowing full well the consequences. But not Vern. He couldn't have known.

She had naively believed and convinced herself that some benevolent entity or harmless item would be waiting for them in the station. That it would be a dangerous but essentially innocuous exploration.

Oh, how wrong she was.

Alistair's revolver was her only saving grace and worth. However, even that might have been better used in Vern's hands. She would've been long dead if it wasn't for him. Or worse—she could have been raped and left to rot in some alleyway.

But now there was a possibility for her to set things right, maybe even repay a little of what she owed.

The observation record of the Great Conductor had many visions, few of which she remembered by heart. She just had to get familiar with them.

Yesterday, when she had reported about the library and its oddity to Alistair at Von Industry's head station, he had rewarded her with more than just some steam and bullets to train her aim.

He had also explained some of the esoteric visions that were mentioned in the observation record. Concepts that were just a clump of words before had become ideas that took root in her mind.

And now that she was sensing all of it happening with her own two eyes and perception, those ideas turned into insights that would later become the foundation for her thought space.

UGH!

She shook her head. "Now's not the time for that."

She forced herself out of the daze. It would be unfortunate if she let some harm come to anyone in this room just because she was too busy sorting out her guilt.

"What the actual fuck?! Why am I the only motherfucker dealing with these batshit lunatics?! Why are you acting mad too? Help me already, you shit!"

These words and the voice gave Cera a pause.

Wasn't that . . . Ambrose?

She turned around and saw him dashing at sharp angles through the room with that theatrical blue flair, avoiding the attacks of the figures in white. His back and forth motions managed to keep all three of them at bay, but he was losing ground.

That's when the rest of the world and its intricacies started registering in her mind.

The apostles are already here! she thought as a chill skittered down her spine. Was she too late?

Ignoring Ambrose's vulgar speech—something she couldn't wrap her head around right now—she got up and rushed in front of Vern and Esther. One of the men in white, who had slipped past Ambrose, was running at the unconscious pair with a sword in his hand.

She didn't even think before—

Bang!

Steam rose from the chamber of her gun as she growled at the man, who had dodged it easily. "Get the hell away!" She didn't know what else to do. This was too sudden. She had never used any visions before this, and what if she couldn't manifest them in time and got Vern killed?

The man clicked his tongue and retreated with a jump, avoiding the next circling strike of Ambrose's cane whip as he shouted, "Siris, Leo, this heretic is strong. You two, focus on him, I will take care of our prince and princess alongside the nuisance that just woke up. We must wrap this up before Father Quentin shows up, or he'll be disappointed."

Father Quentin? So these weren't the apostles? That had to be the case. If Ambrose alone could hold back the apostles, there was no need for Lady Esther to fall back on such desperate measures.

The man and the woman by the door nodded as the former charged toward Ambrose at full speed with his broadsword—white cape flowing behind him.

Simultaneously, the sacred-looking woman yelled, "HERETICS MUST DIE!" Standing tall by the entrance of the nexus, she clapped her hands and closed her eyes as a golden glow overflowed from her eye sockets.

Cera backed away and tore her eyes away from the woman. She had bigger problems to address.

Their leader was doing something to the longsword in his hand. The tip of the blade began to glow resplendently as he looked at it intently with his golden eyes.

No.

She couldn't let him complete whatever he was doing. She had to shoot him down. So, she took aim—made easier by the fact that he was standing completely still. It'd be perfect if she could take down their leader like this.

But she had only practiced her aim for a few hours yesterday and wasn't confident in this shot.

Then something clicked in her mind, and she had an idea.

What if I create a connection between the man's head and the revolver?

The very next moment, a line emerged out of thin air and joined the thousands of sinews of reality that flickered in and out of her vision. It was perfect. Aiming so that the sinew was completely aligned with her line of sight, she took a quick breath.

And pulled the trigger.

Bang!

The sinew snapped instantly as she tried to keep the revolver stable from the recoil. But she was doing a bad job of it. Maybe because she was too stunned by the result of her shot. The bullet went right for his head just like she hoped, but what happened after wasn't in her plans.

The leader jerked his head back up the moment the bullet would have pierced through his skull. And then, out of nowhere, the bullet shattered.

No, that wasn't it.

The bullet exploded into golden fragments, which hovered in the air for a breath before they gravitated toward the blade of his sword, brightening its glow.

Cera was dumbfounded. She had seen Kingsmen deflect projectiles several times, but this was something beyond that. It was as if the bullet smashed against a wall, shattering at impact.

No. No! I-I need something else.

Bullets were not going to work. And she had no doubt that whatever the leader was building up to would be devastating.

I need to use a vision. There's no other way.

But the visions she had studied weren't exactly suited for combat or defense. Instead, they leaned more toward battlefield support, which might not be as bad, given Ambrose was already taking all the heat for her. She just had to figure out how to use the visions in her favor.

She remembered more than a dozen visions but only understood three well enough to give them a shot. And the free representation only made her odds more favorable.

First was the symphony of silence, where she would forcefully suppress all the sinews communicating sound. But she doubted that the visions her white-robed foes were charging needed audible chanting. It would be nothing but a waste.

The second option was discordance. It was simpler than the previous vision, but its effect could be unpredictable since she didn't fully understand all of the hundreds of classifications of the sinews she saw. It was a general type of attack that could be used to sabotage interaction between people or their environments. She had to pick the sinews connected to the target to change its properties.

Finally, the one that might be of some use right this instant was harmonic dissonance. It would disrupt the focus of the target—possibly making them fail their tasks. She didn't hesitate before she began searching for the sinews needed to make it work.

But there were hundreds of sinews.

No, thousands.

No, that wasn't right either. The more she focused, the more emerged out of nothingness, connecting to other lines, objects, and even themselves.

Dark, hollow, tangled, hazy, shiny, multicolored, vibrating, twirling. Everything that could happen to a line was happening, and she didn't know which one was which.

The observation record didn't have anything about most of these, and it didn't make sense. *Did my predecessors never voyage far enough to encounter these? Did they only show up after the duskfall?*

A trickle of sweat slid down her temple as she continued to stare at the millions of lines around her—overlaying her general sight.

"Cera, get your shit together! Don't just stand there like a useless fucking lump."

"I—am trying!" she managed to respond and looked side to side, her fingers twitching as she almost failed to keep a steady grip on the revolver.

It wasn't working.

There was no way.

It was . . . impossible.

How was she supposed to isolate the ones related to focus?

Clang.

Ambrose stumbled as the whip fell out of his hand, landing far away from him. The woman by the gate released a blazing golden ray of light from her . . . eyes. The ray was burning Ambrose's hand, but surprisingly, it didn't seem to harm his skin at all.

Then it had to be hurting him in some other way. Maybe his consciousness? That would be disastrous.

"FUCK! Goddamn it!"

Ambrose dashed one thrust after another as the man with the broadsword slashed at him frantically.

To top all this, the blade in the leader's hand had turned completely golden while the woman clapped and closed her eyes yet again.

Cera's heart beat frantically as things began going out of her control. Why did the observation record not explain how to deal with such a situation?

What if it did exist, but Madam Helena had never given her the sections describing how to handle herself in free representation?

Maybe she thought it wouldn't matter since Cera would never again have the privilege of observing an overwhelming number of sinews in her perception.

Every sinew she would experience in the future would need to be perceived based on her own insights of the topic, after all.

Only if Vern could tell me what to do, she thought. He'd been doing that for the past few hours, and everything just worked.

What would he do?

She hadn't known him long enough to come up with a wholly accurate answer, but it was obvious what his first action would've been.

To take a deep breath and think it over. She did that—just like Vern.

Was it the shiny ones? They looked like what the record had described.

But what if it wasn't? She didn't have the luxury to second-guess herself. One wrong move and that could spell her end alongside Vern's. And Esther's.

Is it the gray one, then. Aghhh!

She might be overthinking this.

Her perception wasn't a picture where she would have to find the required sinews with her eyes.

What if she just . . . thought about it?

Or maybe she could do something even better. She could try forming a focus sinew of her own and use that as a reference to identify others of the same nature.

Yes! That could work.

That was a great idea. She broke out of her focused state and noticed that some sinews snapped and transformed during her exit. And the moment she focused on these oddities, she noticed a few new sinews in her perception.

This is the one!

She quickly realized the kind and looked back up at the leader with newfound vigor. But he was staring right back at her with a crooked grin—glowing blade in his hand as he yelled, "I have shown you courtesy enough. Now die!"

Was she too late!?

No!

She still had a chance.

In no time at all, she singled out all the sinews around the leader that had the same feeling to them as the ones she had just noticed, and she waited for him to make a move.

Where he stood, the leader held out the glowing sword in one hand and, with a flick of his wrist, made to slash it in a wave.

"No! Stop!" shouted Ambrose as he weaved through the broadsword's attacks to try to defend them.

But Cera was ready.

Now!

She snapped the strands that represented the leader's focus, and an acute pain surged in her eyes as she held on to the table next to her to keep from falling.

"AHHHHHHHH!"

What was it?!

Cera tried and tried, but her eyes just wouldn't open due to the assault on her faculties. So she focused on her other senses. The smell of burning flesh tainted the air as it was complemented by shrieks from the leader.

"HELP!"

That was a good sign.

She had yet to feel any other pain, so she was physically safe. Hopefully, Vern and Esther had managed too.

"Ha ha ha! What the fuck? Is your leader fucking blind or something?" shouted Ambrose, followed by unbridled laughter. She would recognize that arrogant voice anywhere. She still didn't understand what happened to the polite and awkward Ambrose, but it was a great relief to hear those words just now.

"HELP ME, YOU MORONS! I'M BURNING! AGHH!"

"Leo, keep attacking, or we won't have a chance! We just need to take this heretic down. We can help Captain after that," shouted the woman as the glow around her eyes burned even hotter.

"AAAHH! I will never let this slight go; I will get you all expelled for heresy! Come help me!"

This was a positive development too.

When Cera finally managed to open her weary eyes this time, she saw golden flames. Flames that were burning everything within a radius of where the leader had been standing just a few seconds ago. He was ferociously rolling around on the ground to extinguish the licks of flames that latched onto his body and refused to leave.

The woman named Siris let out another ray of light from her eyes, which Ambrose dodged by the skin of his teeth with a sidestep and a backflip.

But Cera focused on the situation at hand instead. This was far better than she could have ever hoped.

She had done it. Made a tangible change in the direction of fate.

But she didn't want to stop there. She could obviously do more.

She looked around and zoned in on the sinews of focus around the man with the broadsword as he continued to slash vehemently. But they were snapping and reforming at a ridiculous pace.

Which meant that he wasn't focusing at all.

Her vision wouldn't do anything to him, even if she gave her it all. It just wasn't suited for someone like him.

So she quickly moved on to the woman.

The woman was still squeezing her eyes tightly as a golden glow spilled out of them, and the sinews of focus around her piled up in droves.

She is the perfect target!

Cera didn't waste any time, and the moment she felt herself reach the limits of the sinews she could isolate and manipulate simultaneously, she snapped them.

"AHH!"

"AHHHHH!"

Two screams resounded—one muffled, while the other hysteric—followed by thuds as Cera fell on her knees. But apparently, she had managed to disrupt the woman's vision, possibly even forcing some sort of backlash since the other tumbling sound had come from that woman.

This was good enough for now. Had to be. She could feel it. If she tried messing with another one of the sinews, she might snap a vein in her eye instead.

She didn't feel like moving, at least for a while. Amid the cacophony of screams, she fought to stifle her own pain as she lay grounded.

Ambrose should be able to handle the rest.

"Whoa, that was you, huh? You really did it?" said Ambrose, followed by the clank of his cane's transformation. He had probably picked it back up. And she knew what was about to come.

Splat.

Gasp.

Crack.

She wouldn't be their killer, but her actions undoubtedly led to their deaths. Vern's consoling words from that theater resurfaced in her mind as the sounds painted a bloody picture of the situation.

Hiss.

Snap.

Thud.

Within a minute, the screams died down alongside the constant clatter of the fight. The room became silent again except for the whirring of the pipes around them. Vern and Esther were already on the move.

When the pain finally became manageable, Cera opened her eyes again and was greeted by Vern and Esther, their palms still connected to each other.

Would he—

Her thoughts were interrupted by a booming sound that resounded all around them. "Foolish child, yield now or face your inevitable demise."

C H A P T E R **58**

DISTRESS SIGNAL

I t was hard.

In Vern's last few years as a professional, he had handled large projects with hundreds of variables. But this was a monster far beyond any of those. It was like he was doing the jobs of dozens of departments and fundamentalists all by himself.

He had completed the tasks of a tubular fundamentalist, whistlemeister, steamwright, valve keeper, fuse handler, calibration clerk, coolant chemist, bellows operator, pressure regulator, modulation maestro, and maybe a few more—all concurrently.

Initially, he meticulously fine-tuned each alteration down to the smallest detail. That was, until Esther's impatient shout forced him to pick up the pace. As he gained a bit of familiarity, he soon discovered a rhythm—a cadence that allowed him to engage multiple keys on that otherworldly piano simultaneously without many missteps.

He started with domains he was expert in, but the blue sand in the hourglass she had imagined on top of the piano trickled down a little too fast for his liking. So he branched out and tuned whatever he encountered.

There was no way he was proficient at all the aforementioned tasks, so he did what he was best at: finding a balance. He fixed and created changes in the settings of the station to the point where it was a good enough estimation.

When he became of his depth, he guessed, assigning whatever made the most sense. And to be fair, this vision that Esther was operating was far more magical than he gave it credit for. Some of his changes made no physical sense, but she always managed to find a personality for the devices such that the contraptions themselves agreed with the change.

Esther knew what she was doing. She guided his fingers to the keys that represented the desired part of the station and smoothed his jumbled orders into something that made sense to the entity—adapting to everything he managed to throw at it.

However, it wasn't all smooth sailing.

The whole station mimicked and radiated Esther's nervousness, and it didn't help. He was already feeling it through their direct connection—heightened anxiety from the personalities in the station only served to crack him down further.

He had never even met this apostle, but a dreadful picture had taken root in his mind.

However, besides the nervousness, there was hope in those same strands. Hope that everything would work out.

Vern could feel it too. The process was on the brink of completion. They had already finished modifying the station for their specific needs. On Esther's demands, he had ensured the output sound would be modulated to cover maximum distance, not to be more coherent.

Apparently, her mother wasn't a walking decoder of steamscript sounds. Who could've guessed? That was to say, they didn't need their message to make sense. It just had to reach its destination. Esther was confident that her mother could easily trace back the source of the sound stream from that.

This was great news. He had been worried about the time it'd take the station clerks of the Northern Senn Empire to forward the message to her mother. This completely solved that problem.

To make it easier for their recipient to find the source, he had gone above and beyond, setting up the whistles so that they relayed the message as a continuously emitting stream—not something sent in one short burst.

He had done the math.

The Northern Senn Empire was about an overnight train trip away, which equated to something around five hundred kilometers. With the speed of sound accelerated by the steamscript, paired with its concentration and specifically chosen height in the air, it shouldn't take more than a minute for their message to reach its destination.

So he had ensured to let the backup generator churn just enough power to keep up the whistle for that long with a little to spare in case of unexpected delays.

If only there was actual steam coming into the station instead of this makeshift energy generated out of forced mechanical movements, he thought. He could have overloaded the whistles to transmit the message even faster.

But he shook his head. These were the limitations he had to work with. No amount of hoping or pleading would change that. So he continued to perform a piece on the piano with Esther's palms on top of his, the melody giving this all a passionate atmosphere.

The preparations were almost complete. The pressure in some of the chambers just had to reach a threshold before they were ready to send off the signal. He had taken care of most things.

"*Just a little more*," she said, her voice lethargic.

He interrupted her with a shake of his head and said, "*Shh.*"

She was getting wearier by the second, and any kind of communication was detrimental. This had taken a toll on her. She almost seemed as tired as she was when he had first met her—worse even.

With another press of the key on the piano, he synergized with one of the type-writers. Its purpose was to write *Help, Mother* onto the recording pipes. Its personality was adamant too. Even if Esther's mother could not decode the text, they still had to initiate the transmission of the message somewhere.

Soon he felt the pneumatic tubes record these keystrokes and forward them to the encoder that warped it into something illegible before it coursed through one of the channels in the pipes. Cogs spun into life, gears meshed and unmeshed, directing airflow through convoluted pipes. Here, a series of modulators received the obscure sequence in a chamber arrayed with dials and meters.

Vern couldn't see it, but he sensed it—the ethereal tangle of air, steam, and signal twisting together, guided by the invisible hands of calibrated machinery. Each turn of a gear and each flick of a valve seemed a purposeful gesture, steering the chaos toward order.

The hum of energy generators pulsed in the background, a heartbeat that gave life to the entire system. As the message moved, a choir of steamscript whistles began to warm, the steam within them simmering, poised for utterance. Gauges marked the climb of pressure, needles dancing in anticipation.

The message, now a coded symphony of sound, erupted through vents, ascending into a labyrinthine network of bronze pipes that stretched across the station's height. Finally, with a release as controlled as it was powerful, the northern steamscript whistle unleashed with purpose.

Wengggg.

It was out there—born upon the wind, carried by the ether, awaiting a listening ear.

The palms that were gently guiding him until now clutched his hands harder than ever as she shouted with unmarked joy in her voice, *"Vern! WE DID IT! It actually worked! How long—"*

But her words were cut short as he felt a weight settle down on his shoulder.

Even her mental image had collapsed on him. She really had overdone herself.

"Yes, we did," he murmured back.

He was still doubtful about their chances, but it was starting to look promising. If Esther's confidence wasn't unfounded, they just had to survive the next few minutes, and all their problems would soon solve themselves. The corner of his lips curled upward as he looked at her beautiful face in his peripheral vision.

The blue glow reflecting off her red hair cast her face in a complex shade that suited her soft features. A little too beautiful. A little too—

Tangg.

Esther jolted awake as a pained expression quickly overshadowed her surprise.

This wasn't a sound from one of the station's components. It was from the piano. The piano, of which one of its strings had snapped.

Tanggg.

Before he could react, the discordant sound rang again, matched by the snapping of another string.

He inhaled a sharp breath, suppressing the acute pain that emerged from nowhere.

"Ahh," A groan escaped her mouth as she leaned onto the piano, gasping for breath.

This was getting worse. Something was wrong with the piano.

No. Not the piano. It is the essence strands. Did she lose control of them due to fatigue?

But her face was visibly perplexed while being in equal parts pain. She wasn't expecting this at all. Then what was going on?

Tanggg.

Another strand flew out of the piano and rebounded with great strength as it soon disintegrated into nothingness. That vein was lost.

He barely controlled himself and managed to not squeeze her palms back from the pain that erupted out of nowhere in his head.

Something was wrong.

More and more strands began to wobble as another one bit the dust, almost making him see dark with the sharp stabbing ache it brought him.

Esther wasn't doing any better. Her groans were only getting worse, and she began to convulse.

Fuck. Blast it all. Why now?

He had to do something.

Patting her back like he had seen some doctors do to their patients, he urged, *"Esther, we need to leave!"*

She responded violently, *"No! If I—we—don't defend these strands, we're doomed. Someone is envisioning changes in the station, and most strands are only holding up because we're observing them actively. We— AHHH!"*

"UGH!"

Tanggg.

Tang.

Tangg.

Another bunch of strands fractured abruptly as they both screamed.

No. This wasn't sustainable.

"Esther. If we stay in here, we'll die from the pain alone. Please, let's just exit. We have already sent the message. It's time to go. These strands don't need to persist."

"No! You don't understand. They're attacking the station, and we'll be buried alive if it collapses on us. Holding on to these strands is our best bet at avoiding that. We're— UHH! AHH!" Her hoarse screams were soon drowned out by the dissonant snaps as, one after another, the keys on the piano dimmed—losing their blue glow.

"Esther, shut up! I might be able to handle it for a while, but you're in no condition. Let's get out."

"But—"

"Esther! Trust me. We have bigger problems outside than handling this."

"..."

Willing for the imaginary world to fade, he waited. Just when he was ready to switch his approach and try coaxing her instead, the piano disappeared, and he felt all his senses turn empty for a second.

In the next instant, he felt warmth on his hand. The real kind.

Opening his eyes, he first settled the enervated Esther to the back of her chair. She took deep breaths, massaging her forehead.

But Vern was already on to his next move. He quickly surveyed his surroundings and wasn't surprised to see the battered and disarrayed state of the room. What did surprise him, however, were the three bloody or charred bodies scattered around the room.

Holding his hand over his nose, he thought, *Were these the apostles?*

No, that can't be. There is no way Ambrose alone, or even with Cera—with or without her new powers—could have taken down someone even Esther was afraid of.

They had to be the apostle's underlings or something. It was great that Ambrose and Cera handled them, or he wouldn't have even been able to flinch before his neck was chopped off cleanly.

But then he noticed something weird. Neither of his two companions were looking at him. They were facing away, focused on something above them.

"Cera, Ambrose, what is happening?"

When they didn't respond, Vern followed their gazes and looked up at the maze of gears, his eyes narrowing on a strange atmospheric disturbance above him. In the dark ceiling, a golden glow had appeared.

The glowing machinery's constant clanking and hissing slowed, then gradually quieted to a surreal silence. Even the air felt still, as if the very particles had ceased their restless dance.

A golden light began to pierce through the station's thick concrete and metal layers—a light that didn't obey the laws of architecture or material. It was a concentrated beam, a cylinder of illumination that broke through the floors and the walls.

The light expanded, and for a moment, Vern felt as though he was standing at the bottom of an impossibly long well, the walls of which were vanishing in slow spirals.

The machinery in this newly carved tunnel didn't just break or shatter; it seemed to unravel, its constituent parts drifting away like dandelion seeds in the wind. Steel turned to mist, bolts, and nuts floating upward like wayward balloons. The destructive process was eerily quiet, leaving a straight line of emptiness that connected Vern directly to the source of the light above.

Hovering at the other end of this emptiness was a figure, majestic in a way Vern had never before witnessed. An intricately designed clergy robe framed his form, punctuated by ethereal runes. A soft halo hovered above his head, its radiant glow contrasting sharply with the absolute, unsettling quiet he had imposed on their world.

Vern felt his breath catch in his throat. It was as if the man's presence alone emanated some kind of pressure, denying Vern free thought.

What was he supposed to do now? It hadn't been enough time for Esther's mother to receive their message, and Esther herself was still out cold.

That's when a booming voice resounded, "Foolish child. No one is coming to save you. Surrender yourself, or I'll unravel your very essence. A shattered vessel has its uses too, you know?"

Vern's heart sank as he sensed the meaning of his words. *Did the trans—*

The radiant man waved his hand, and multiple golden lights appeared on the ceiling. To Vern's chagrin, one of the lights was directly above the insensate Esther.

Hastily dragging her chair away from the path of the light, he witnessed the same process yet again. The steel beams creaked under the forced yet natural transformation as everything gave way for the holes, and Esther convulsed out of nowhere, pain clear in her unconscious visage as her body shook with light tremors.

This process is destroying her strands and somehow causing a backlash. Is she connected to the strands even outside thought synergy?

This . . .

He didn't understand. He couldn't fathom how these two completely disparate schools of thought interacted—Lightvein and this golden unraveling.

Above, the station peeled away like wet paper, layer by layer, revealing a sky he didn't recognize. There, a golden hemispherical canopy blocked out the stars beyond.

But there was a peculiar point in the golden dome. Radiant particles congregated around it as golden ripples exploded out of the center continuously.

This . . .

The hollow echo of his heartbeat drowned out Esther's soft moans of pain as he clenched his fists so hard his nails dug into the flesh. They were doomed.

This golden dome was . . . blocking their distress signal.

CHAPTER 59

PRESERVATION

This was it.

They had failed.

Their only hope—the distress signal—was being contained like some water in a cup, while the apostle loomed over them like some deity ready to mete out punishment.

Was this really it? Were all of them about to be wiped out? But his soul—if such a thing existed after death—would be discontent if he didn't at least try. What if there was some kind of instability he could induce?

He is floating in the air. If I can figure out how, maybe I can do something? Make him fall.

Sweat trickling down his forehead, Vern tapped into his perception and homed in on the radiant man across one of the artificial chasms he had created.

Alas, it wasn't meant to be.

It was exactly what he was afraid of. The apostle eluded the grays. His entire form failed to register in Vern's perception at all. And now that Vern mulled it over, it made perfect sense. How would the apostle float if he wasn't observing himself?

Vern's heart sank further as the implications became clearer. He would have to run away like a coward. Let them die.

No! There has to be something else!

He fidgeted as he emptily stared at the wannabe god. What if Esther was exaggerating, and the man wasn't going to hunt all of them?

But he promptly splashed water over his own delusions.

He was accustomed to a life of meritocracy, where brains mattered more than brawn. *But this isn't going to play out like that. This man wouldn't even deign to listen to us—much less negotiate.*

However, before he could come to a decision, the apostle, high in the sky, shook his head and spoke in a voice that was calm yet resounded all around them. "Foolish indeed."

Then he made the motion of plucking something from the air, and a golden mote appeared before him. This was followed by a huge chunk of the radiant dome disintegrating into particles, which soon converged into a golden ball somewhere new up in the sky.

Vern didn't know what the hell was going on, but whatever it was, it wasn't good. He shook Esther intensely. "Get up, Esther! You need to run. Attack. Use the station. Block him. Talk to him. Anything! Don't just sit here!"

But she was unresponsive. She held her head in her hands and screamed silently. *What the hell is going on with her?!*

He didn't know what to do. Everything was falling apart.

"It seems my previous leniency was a disservice to both of us. My actions were imbued with a kindness that has failed to bring forth any worth in you, making you unworthy of preservation." Then he repeated his previous actions and plucked at the air once more as a small mote appeared in front of him.

"This time, let's call it tough love, shall we? A more stringent lesson is clearly required for you to understand the true gravitas of what it means to be preserved."

Another chunk of particles separated from the golden dome and flew in a direction—appearing and disappearing from Vern's view through the holes within this station. Soon, they fused into a dense golden mass that floated opposite to the previous one.

"You misunderstand the essence of preservation. You see, it isn't merely a matter of abstaining from destruction. Preservation is an act that can only follow creation—meaningful creation. What you have built here—this fragile simulacrum—is garbage unworthy of even observation."

Another plucking gesture and one more golden ball appeared far away from the previous two. The dome had now shrunk by quite a margin, but it still blocked the leftover signals from the station without a problem.

"Neither are you, I'm afraid, worthy of preservation. To bring forth something that merits the act, I must first eradicate the flawed foundation. Only then can true preservation commence. Do you understand?"

He reenacted his earlier actions, and Vern finally figured out where this was going. Four points floated before the man, mirrored by four identical masses of golden light that soared in the sky, forming the same shape—a square.

This had to be his elaborate way of getting rid of them.

"Ah, you take pride in those veins of yours, pulsing with untamed potential. How misplaced that pride is. Let me offer you a lesson in humility and divine purpose. I'll annihilate that which you hold dear, reducing it to mere ash. From that point, we'll have a foundation truly worth preserving."

The golden masses began to shimmer and soon melted into a giant plane that hung higher than the tallest tower in the empire. The apostle was barely a dot standing beneath its translucent glow.

"Trust me, by the time this process is complete, even your mother would deem you unworthy of her love—but perfectly worthy of preservation."

This was unhinged.

"Shut up!" Ambrose interjected. "You fucking phony preacher. Don't ignore me. You really think you can do whatever you want in Elmhurst? You want this bitch? Take her. But if you fuck with me and my people, I'll burn your godforsaken church to ashes and scatter your deluded flock. Elmhurst will be purged of your damnation, mark my words.

"If not by me, then my family—"

"Ambrose! STOP!" Vern barked. "Now's not the time to provoke him."

He hated the apostle too. But speaking up like this wouldn't make the least of the difference—not to a person like him. He knew far too many people with such a demeanor—his own master, for one—to give them the benefit of the doubt.

He knew how they justified it. They loved to disregard any minor variables for the greater good. Their lousy excuses about divine plans were nothing but sad attempts at denying their own hypocrisy.

Even though it confirmed Vern's assumptions regarding the apostle's attitude, what the hell was Ambrose doing? He wasn't always so foolhardy. Not ten minutes ago.

But as expected, the apostle didn't even look at Ambrose. He just drew something akin to a line in the air with his other hand—

Damn!

Vern instinctively rushed toward Ambrose, not sure how that would help. Yet before he could even halve the distance—*clank*—the cane fell from Ambrose's hand, and he froze where he stood.

A golden line skewered Ambrose. It entered at his head and pierced through his back. But there was no blood. Nor were there any signs of pain. Yet, it was as if the time itself had stopped for Ambrose.

Vern's skin tingled as goose bumps rose all over his body, and a sense of uncanny serenity threatened to consume him the closer he got to Ambrose.

Fuck! This is preservation?

He backpedaled, barely getting out of the influence of whatever afflicted Ambrose. This was . . . unsettling.

He tried to rationalize this ability—this godly display. But he knew it was a waste of time. There was nothing he could do for Ambrose.

Nothing he could do for any of them. Nothing.

This feeling of helplessness. It was—disgusting.

That's when Cera, who had been staring at the sky with a hollow expression, turned toward Ambrose, her eyes drooping over.

She was in the range of that vision!

"Cera, get out of there!"

But she was one step ahead of him.

"AHH!" A muffled scream leaked out of her mouth before she fell to the ground—blood streaming down from her eyes like tears. Yet, the glow of the arrow had dimmed a notch.

It seemed like she had managed to become an observer. But that didn't mean she should pit herself against an apostle's vision. That was unnecessarily dangerous.

Yet it was more than he could manage. How did she even do this? Wasn't it impossible to perceive something already being observed?

Ignoring that, he ran toward her. Doing something was better than nothing. Even if it was just to make himself feel better. To deny it better.

But as he closed the gap, his pupils constricted, and his heart pounded so fiercely he feared it would rupture.

There was no denying it anymore.

It's coming.

The dark nexus began to light up as the distorted pipes reflected a golden haze. It was like the sun had risen in the sky, dyeing the world a bright gold. Radiance flitted down into the hub through those narrow gaps, and the light became the norm.

The apostle in the sky pushed at the square in front of him with both hands, one after another. And the mirror image—the golden ceiling that was larger than the whole station—began its manic descent with a disturbing droning sound.

Wenggggg.

"In the face of true preservation, all imperfections must be eradicated!"

This self-righteous piece of shit!

The falling canopy gained momentum, its edges almost seeming to blur. Maybe this was the reason the apostle had started it so high in the sky.

So that it would have enough force to crush anything.

Vern had to make a choice.

Right now.

This golden sky was going to crush the station into a crater, and none of them were going to survive the collapse.

So this is the end?

Vern looked around him one more time. Ambrose was frozen stiff, looking at the heavens with a defiant gaze. He was a little misguided in his actions. But it was nothing that couldn't be fixed by staying away from his family. He obviously had goals, aspirations, and hopes.

All of which will never come to fruition now.

Esther was even worse. Her cogwings flapped erratically as she shivered—her lovely features twisted into a grimace. It pained him to see her like this, knowing what must have been going through her mind.

Maybe he should apologize. Everything was happening because they had to go into the station and pry out the truth. Was there time for that? Could she hear him? Would she?

Cera had warned him that secrets were secrets for a reason. She couldn't be blamed for her misjudgment because she had no experience. But he did. He had been to the Ascendant Council. He knew what could happen.

He failed to figure out the right balance to maintain. A grave imbalance—even fatal.

And then there was Cera. Her short hair covered her eyes, but the blood still flew freely as she pushed herself back up, one step at a time. He wanted to deny it. Deny what was coming. Deny what would happen to his first friend in this godforsaken city.

First friend in this dying world.

He didn't know if the feeling was mutual, but he hoped.

Yet, instead of congratulating her on her enlightenment or helping her up, he stood there, finding reasons to justify his cowardice. To deny it.

He had leaned too far toward recklessness on the spectrum of caution, and this was his comeuppance.

One he would have to live with. The price was that every person he had connected with since after duskfall would . . . die.

It disgusted him.

He had a few more tricks and ideas up his sleeve, but simply twisting a rod in a puppet had caused him to become insensate. How would he pay the representation cost needed to manipulate anything that would bar the path of this larger-than-life sky—descending onto them like a meteor?

There's no other choice.

Clenching his teeth so hard they felt like shattering, he began to withdraw. He closed his eyes and called for his rationality. It was better than sticking to the pathetic hope. It wasn't like back in the library.

He just didn't have the tools necessary to deal with this.

So he focused. The third rune, as Esther had dubbed it, was an ephemeral concept in his mind. But he wasn't worried that he'd be unable to activate it.

It was omnipresent. Just thinking about it caused his mind to hallucinate impossible triangles.

Soon, the triangles began to coalesce, their edges getting sharper and the details more pronounced.

This was the rune he dreaded more than anything. It reminded him of everything that was wrong with the world and how it all came to be. That he was living on borrowed time. The more he used it, the tighter the noose around his neck became.

Finally, all the shapes merged into two inverted triangles—impossibly looping around each other. He could feel it now. He just had to make contact with it through his thoughts, and whatever the activation of this rune entailed would begin.

But his trip to this dark void of disturbing triangles was interrupted by a low sound.

"r . . . mbr pr . . . ms . . ."

It was Esther.

Ensuring this gateway of contact remained open, he focused on her low mutterings.

"Remember . . ."

". . . the promise."

She had to make it hard for him, didn't she? He'd been trying not to think about it.

Back at his master's lab, he had colleagues—even friends. But no real connections. His life had been quite dull in the emotional connections department—instead filled with competition and sleepless nights spent figuring out the next big problem.

Maybe it was more apt to say he never even reached out—he never felt the urge or had the time. Yet, just now, he had created a connection. They had been in each other's minds.

Her feelings, opinions, insecurities—all were laid bare, and so were his. It was a connection. One he hadn't even known could exist.

It is too soon.

Why did it have to end like this?

He opened his eyes and watched the golden sky that was hurling toward them at a breakneck pace. It went from being a small shape far off in the sky to a heaven-spanning plane of destruction that would soon crush them into nothingness.

So he ceased his useless emotional pandering and replied to Esther with two simple words, "I will."

It was time to let his rationality wash over him and do what must be done. He needed it . . .

That's when two arms wrapped around him, and a tremor ran through his spine. Cera rested her face on his shoulder. Again. And spoke through choked sobs, "I . . . am . . . sorry. Vern, I am so sorry. It's all my fault. I am sorry. You shouldn't have been here. I am . . ."

She broke down, blood and tears soaking his shoulder as he stood there.

Why were they making it so hard?

He knew he hadn't known them long enough to care. But he did. And that was not okay. Not right now. Not in this situation. He still hadn't reunited with Ariane. He couldn't die here.

I guess I, too, am a hypocrite, he thought as he pulled her closer and embraced her.

Clenching his eyes tight, he held the tears at bay and whispered, "It was not your fault."

But it wasn't working. He needed to get out of here. This warmth almost made him want to give up. To die a martyr. To let the end come.

Almost.

The droning sound coming from that golden calamity rushing toward them only grew louder.

Rumble.

Crash.

It had begun.

It was time.

The gap between the two inverted triangles in his mind glowed brightly, inviting him in. He took a final deep breath, firmed up his resolve . . .

And made contact.

The inverted triangles burst apart at the seams, and the white spilled all over his mind, consuming him. Before he lost all senses and Cera's warmth, he whispered one final time, "I am sorry."

A flash in the sky caught Shinsei's eyes, manifesting as a golden square of sheer divinity. For a moment, the world seemed to pause, its glow a haunting precursor to something catastrophic. Even from this distance, he could sense the pressure it exuded, a force of annihilation ripping through the air.

The other uncontrollable friend is inside too. Can't let it end like this.

Without a second thought, Shinsei's feet left the rooftop, propelling him skyward as if he'd broken the chains of gravity itself. His hand tightened around the hilt of his sword, its blade shimmering with a light of its own, almost in response to the golden calamity hurtling toward the earth.

Time to get you under control.

His eyes took in the descending golden sky, not as a looming threat but as a test of his mastery. In his world of control, things were simple—there were the things that bent and those that didn't. This golden phenomenon, for all its divine might, had a pattern, a structure, and a will that propelled it—things he could interact with.

The essence of control isn't to clash but to guide, to find that moment where force becomes merely a suggestion that can be renegotiated.

Force is an object moving at a speed. Disrupt the speed, and you control the force. A gold-colored divine sky was no exception.

The world around him blurred into streaks of color, yet his focus remained unwavering, zeroing in on the golden square. He was a tempest, a force of nature, and his sword was the eye of the storm.

It wasn't going to be his usual deflection, but a little bending of semantics was fine. Swinging to deflect was still deflection.

His body aligned, his blade positioned—he swung. It wasn't a swing born merely of physical strength but one driven by purpose, by conviction. In the split second that felt like an eternity, his blade met the golden surface.

Clanggg.

A resounding clash echoed through the heavens, the shock wave dispersing clouds and ripples of displaced air spreading outward. For a moment, the world held its breath.

The golden square splintered, its form fragmenting into shards of light that dissipated into nothingness. Shinsei's sword hummed, its resonance quieting as he landed back on a rooftop, his eyes never leaving the spot where the sky had nearly fallen.

As if recognizing his authority, the world resumed its course, no longer paused in the face of impending doom. A small grin stretched across Shinsei's lips, stained by a trickle of blood seeping from one corner of his mouth.

That was insightful. I could do better.

But then he turned around, perplexed.

He had deflected the calamity that befell the kid, hadn't he? Then where did he go? His uncontrollable aura just . . . disappeared.

CHAPTER 60

THE LAND OF DARK SUN

One hundred ninety.
One hundred ninety-one.
One hundred ninety-two.
One hundred ninety-three.
One hundred nin—

Vern finally stopped counting as the numbness that draped over his senses began to wane and feeling returned. His heart began pumping, followed by his arms, legs, back, and every other part of his body heating up.

He still had no control over his eyelids, so he pondered instead. Now that he no longer needed to count the number of seconds it took for death or something even more bizarre to claim him, he let the misery rush in.

It had been over three minutes already.

They are dead. All dead.

And here he was, counting the number of seconds for the sake of distracting himself during that nonexistential silence. But it did do him some good, since he managed to rationalize it.

It was a tough pill to swallow, but it was over.

It was great while it lasted. Even if all he experienced was danger, adrenaline, and bittersweet emotions—it was worth it. It had been fun to masquerade as just another human being in whatever was left of the society.

But maybe he wasn't suited for simple joys like these. Things never ended well. Not today, not the last three times.

He had hoped things would be different this time. They were more capable than him in some respects, after all. Not like his previous attempts, where he tried to make friends with a street urchin or that new apprentice.

It was a skewed balance.

All he needed was knowledge and proper information to advance and progress with his observation. But that was one thing he had the greatest trouble with.

Every piece of intel came with a death sentence attached to it. He wondered if it'd have been better to take up Shinsei on his offer yesterday. Maybe he'd have known what to do right now instead of running away like a coward.

Things would be so different.

And now I think in ifs *and* buts *too?*

He shook his head. What happened was already set in stone. He didn't know how to process this guilt right now. Letting it fester was a tempting offer that he jumped at, without any hesitation.

This reminded him that he was able to shake his head. So, he was already in control of his body.

Alongside the plethora of emotions coursing through his brain, another one reared its head—excitement. And maybe fear too.

What was it going to be? What did it mean to make contact with the Cryptic Constructor's rune?

One part of him was dying to open his eyes, while the other wanted to find ways to make it safer. That he could just lie down here and spend a long time before going back out.

He obviously managed to convince himself to do the former.

Blinking his eyelids, he finally opened them fully and took in the sight.

Good heavens!

It was really the heavens that awestruck him.

He was lying on his back somewhere, but he didn't have the mind to care about that. The sky was dominated by a celestial body that defied explanation—an orb of utter darkness at the center, surrounded by a blazing ring of warm, golden light.

This ring had an almost liquid luminosity, bending around the dark core in an enigmatic dance. The effect was disconcerting, yet oddly comforting—a dark sun that cast its unique radiance upon the world below, turning the sky a dark, hazy red.

He kept staring at the marvel for who knew how long. He'd have missed the counting now, even if he had kept up with it. The sight actually gave him a twisted sense of peace—of life and death.

But after a while, he felt it.

A sense of loss. It was like someone ripped a piece of his flesh—a very small piece.

He frowned and thought, *Is it the sky again?*

Were skies always this dangerous? The gash up in the Elmhurst's sky had done something to him, and now this? So he tore his gaze away from the celestial marvel and focused on his surroundings.

He pushed up and supported himself with his arms as he surveyed the lands.

What in the name of steam is . . . this?

The sight made him question his eyes. So he brought one of his hands to his face for closer inspection, grabbing a fistful of ash from the ground while at it.

It was everywhere.

Not just the ash but the layers upon layers of fallen structures. A sprawling landscape of crumbled edifices assaulted his sight, all stacked haphazardly like a mountain range made of ruins.

Bringing the ash close to his nose, he inhaled with a deep waft.

Hmm, there's no smell in the ash.

That was odd. Whatever burned had either no inherent smell or had been sitting here for a very long time.

Vern preferred to believe in the second theory, given the state of affairs all around him. These structures had definitely been left untouched for an eternity. He wondered what would happen if he got too close to them. What if they crumbled and buried him alive on a touch?

The thought alone was disturbing.

However, something still wasn't right.

He had stopped looking at the astronomical spectacle above. Yet, that feeling or erosion within himself didn't go away. On a mental level, it felt more like something was forcing him to change himself. As in to fit more within this world.

However, this didn't incite a sense of urgency within him. Whatever was happening was slow. In fact, it was so slow he guessed it would take dozens of hours before he would feel any significant change.

Obviously, the other reason was that he couldn't leave. Not that he couldn't, but it'd be dumb to jump back into that one-sided battlefield. The inverted triangles within his mind had reforged themselves—his thoughts flowing to the conduit within the triangles naturally.

He guessed it would be as simple as redirecting his thoughts elsewhere, and this sight would end. This world of ash, ruin, and cosmic wonders would be gone in the blink of an eye.

So he flitted through the possibilities of what could be happening.

It isn't sapping away my representation.

He knew how it felt to lose representation when using visions. This wasn't it. This was something far beyond that. He was being deprived of something permanently—an essential part of him.

This had to be the cost of staying in this . . . whatever this place was.

But what cost exactly?

My thoughts?

That was as likely as it was unlikely.

So he unclenched his fist, and the ash seeped through the gaps of his fingers before he shoved his hand into his coat pocket.

Luckily, he hadn't lost his outfit this time, or it'd have been a mess next time he woke up . . .

Next to the bodies of Cera and Ambrose.

Ugh.

He would get nothing done if he kept circling back to them. This was an opportunity, and he had to make the most of it. He was going to lose more than just this unknown part of himself if he couldn't handle Hensen whenever he came.

And he didn't want to feel helpless. Not anymore.

It had happened far too often for his liking, just within a week. He even entertained the thought that he wasn't suited for a dangerous life like this. He was a scholar and pretending otherwise had parted him from things he liked, one after another. First his life, then Ari, then everyone else.

So he sat straighter on the ashen ground and leafed through his notes—the light of his lamp dissipating enough darkness to let him read. There was nothing else in his sight other than rubble, so it was probably fine to sit and read.

Take his mind off saddening matters.

It was a waste.

Mostly.

He hadn't written anything about the eve of duskfall in the notepad for obvious reasons. And nothing else was of much help. Not even the details of that parchment that described instability inducement.

However, perusing the chain of events did set him up for an interesting discovery. It started with some choice words by Hensen and Ambrose. Hensen had said something along the lines of, *And you just happened to break all your shackles of subjectivity during your enlightenment?*

Whereas Ambrose had mentioned, *Each method of enlightenment loosens the shackles of subjectivity to a certain extent.*

At first glance, it didn't seem all that connected. But if one looked at the underlying meaning of shackles of subjectivity, there was a connection to his current situation.

According to Vern's short analysis of semantics, shackles of subjectivity were literal shackles on one's viewpoint. As in, one with a tighter shackle would have difficulty observing something that doesn't align with their viewpoint or thinking.

So Esther would have had a hard time reconciling with how Vern perceived or understood things.

However, there was another possibility. This one felt like a better match from his understanding of observation and its related concepts.

It was that there was something akin to a unified perspective of the masses and the society, and living under this unified perspective for extended periods placed shackles on the very mind itself.

Then breaking these shackles is a measure of how much an observer can distinguish themselves from this unified perspective and immerse themselves into their own.

The looser the shackles, the better of an observer one can be.

However, he wasn't excited about having figured out this little semantic puzzle for the sake of it. It held significance right this moment.

What if this gnawing feeling at his being was just a manifestation of the shackles being put back on or getting tighter? According to Hensen, Vern had broken the shackles at their limit.

But now, by sitting here in this realm of the Cryptic Constructor, he was being shackled again. Forced into the unified perspective.

No. Not the unified perspective. What if it's related to the Cryptic Constructor?

That staying in this realm forced his perspective to subtly shift in favor of the Constructor's perspective.

This has to be it!

Jotting down the details of his findings and thought process in the notepad in a somewhat obscure fashion, he shoved it back into his coat.

He let out a deep breath and finally loosened up a little.

This small step forward felt like bathing in steam in snowy weather. Something finally worked his way. Knowing that he was essentially giving away his future potential just by being here, he sprang to his feet.

Taking off his coat to bear the hot weather, he picked the only direction available to him and started moving. The path behind him was blocked by the piece of some exotic-looking structure—with dozens of openings for what seemed to be windows. But overall, he couldn't put a finger on what exactly the inspirations were.

He knew he wasn't here to sightsee, but he considered it essential to figure out his surroundings. Especially in such a marvelous setting.

This seemed to be the ruin of some former city wrecked by something ten times worse than the worst earthquakes. It was almost as if the buildings were dropped from the skies.

His eyes still found it hard to not wander upward and marvel at this dark sun.

Is there a name for this kind of phenomenon? Ari would know . . .

Only he didn't know where she was.

That's when a spark ran through his mind, and he stopped walking.

What were those three bodies in the nexus?

They were wearing white robes too. Didn't that mean Ari was taken away or coaxed by the members of this religion? It was not to say that there could only be one organization with such an outfit, but it was a lead.

A lead to finally find Ari.

But.

One step at a time.

Filing away this information in the notepad, he continued wandering this desolate land. He passed by many foreign and outlandish constructions—all broken, twisted, or contorted beyond any sense.

The materials that comprised these structures didn't resemble wood, stone, or metal. Instead, they were an amalgamation of substances that defied categorization, shimmering in the unique light of the dark sun overhead.

Once, he even passed between two chunks of what seemed like a singular building. But their insides were . . . bizarre, uncanny even. It was as if the interior space didn't adhere to the logic of conventional architecture. The walls, or what should have been walls, appeared almost porous, filled with cavities.

Cavities that looked like they could either be rooms or tunnels of sorts, lined with fibrous material resembling a cross between mineral and organic matter. The whole experience was disorienting, and yet it felt like an eerie sort of order reigned over the chaos.

The irony of the Cryptic Constructor's realm being filled with a hodgepodge of shoddily constructed structures didn't go unnoticed by Vern, and it tickled his fancy for dark humor.

Luckily, there was no one else to share this feeling with. He wouldn't wish any unwanted company to spring up to him in this desolate land. He couldn't deal with anything that could survive and thrive in this atmosphere.

This landscape continued for about half an hour before the vista finally had a real change. And it was a jarring one.

What is this . . . ?

A gigantic shadow stretched ahead of him—an oddity since the warm ambient light from the dark sun was already so dim. So he looked up and just stared for a while.

It was something akin to a pyramid, made of the same shiny material, patched together in an inconsistent manner. What was peculiar, however, was that it pointed downward instead of up. Its peak was floating a couple hundred meters high with nary a movement.

It hadn't been visible beforehand because of how tall some of the rubble in his path had gotten, but now that he was here, he was awed by it.

Until he moved on and walked into its shadow.

However, Just as he was about to delve deeper into this shadowy land, a niggling caution held him back. The sense of his subjectivity eroding—or shackles tightening—intensified the closer he got to this shadow.

And it wasn't a gradual increase. Just within a few steps, he was losing his subjectivity twice as fast as before.

No. This is not worth it.

He quickly acted on his thoughts and ran back in the direction from where he came. As expected, the erosion slowed down to its earlier pace.

It seems the more I progress, the worse it'll get?

Unless there was a way to reduce this loss, he couldn't go any farther. Vern had no problems with that.

He was getting tired from all the walking anyway. He had seen enough to feel safe and let himself wander off in his conscious, trying to figure out a new vision.

So he picked a structure that seemed to jut out at a horizontal angle the same as the ground and perched atop it.

Now comfortable, he began with the vision he'd been hoping to get his hands on the most.

Gravity.

CHAPTER 61

LINK

It was the most practical concept he could think of for theorizing a vision. It had given him a fighting chance against someone of Hensen's caliber.

So he closed his eyes and tapped into his perception, waiting for some kind of change.

And as expected, nothing happened.

He was taking it slow. Even though he believed Esther, he wasn't gonna let that cloud his judgment and throw caution to the wind. What if something had changed since the time she had learned about this rune, and those whispers were just waiting for him to make a mistake?

His perception was a blank slate right now, but it was fair to assume he was primed to observe the balance of gravity, not complexity or integrity.

Given that I don't feel much lighter or heavier out here, the gravity should be the same as usual. Its intensity should be higher close to the ground while gradually decreasing as I observe skyward.

Nodding, he let these thoughts slowly bleed into his perception, ensuring things remained in control as he progressed in measured steps.

Yet the darkness persisted.

He focused harder and bombarded his perception with these thoughts as if it were a wall that would break with more pressure.

There was no response. It remained as dark as a void.

He analyzed this anomaly. This in itself was unusual. He had already tried something similar outside. Attempting this in Elmhurst would invite the whispers to assault him relentlessly, slaughtering his psyche in no time.

Here, however, all he felt was a little strain on his eyes.

This is good.

It wasn't the same free lunch as back in the library, but it was more . . . real. That phenomenon of the world following his whims and bending however he wanted was more of a guided tutorial. He could test the limits, but the insights didn't carry over to his life after.

He remembered that he just had to think of a possible balance, and his perception would be populated with grays by itself. This threw him for a loop.

Didn't that mean I wasn't using my own understanding of the balance of those concepts to interpret the world?

In other words, the balance he saw was actually determined by something else. Maybe it even had something to do with the Unified Perspective theory. His eyes were determining how to distribute the grays in his perception based on the under-standing of the whole planet.

Well, that means it was faking my perspective.

That was ironic. It was showing him a subjective world he wanted to see based on an objective consensus of others.

He shook his head. He was getting off track. It was good to add to his understanding of these concepts, but he had a goal to achieve here.

So he resumed his earlier train of thought and dug deeper into his own insights regarding the matter while keeping in mind his previous experience in the library.

What exactly is gravity?

In terms of fundamentals, gravity was generally considered to belong to the upper southeastern octant of the insight sphere. Most of the theories around forces—including the steam force theory, combustion art vector, gravitational uplift, and many others originated from this octant alone.

However, some fundamentalists liked to group it with the octant next to it because it also behaved like a fundamental of relations. Essentially, gravity was a concept that weakly linked two objects together, attracting them to each other.

The former set of fundamentalists would die on that hill where they proclaimed it was just a force between two objects. The bigger the mass, the greater its pulling capability. On the other hand, the second group of synergy fundamentalists had filed hundreds of petitions to fix the definition of gravity in records and books of empires all around the planet.

To them, the gravitational pull of Prima meant a binding connection between every object. A sympathetic link whose strength was determined based on the affinities between certain kinds of ideas.

It was an otherwise naive idea that would have long been buried under a mountain of practical evidence from the opposition if they hadn't managed to come up with some of their own.

The synergy fundamentalists had performed a few controlled experiments demonstrating lighter objects pulling heavier objects toward themselves. And to this day, no one had managed to find a better theory to explain the phenomenon.

But that's when Vern was jerked out of his deep trance, and the corner of his lips was raised in an obvious grin. His introspection had finally managed to color his perception.

To his delight, he finally saw that beautiful gradient once again. Just like he had imagined—a black fog surrounded him, gradually fading into a lighter gray as he tilted his head upward.

Until . . .

Ahh! Damn!

He snapped his eyes shut along with his perception as he realized his mistake.

The gravity here wasn't as simple as he interpreted it to be. That pyramid high in the sky wasn't floating out of hate for the land. And when he tried to forcefully interpret that as a decreasing amount of gravity, a fatal sense of incongruity filled him.

Luckily, he had realized it quickly, or he would be in for some painful times.

But something worthy of note was happening here. He was sure that he hadn't assigned the gradient of gravity everywhere else perfectly either. He couldn't have, as that would require measurement. So it should have made him feel incongruous too.

But it didn't. It only became a problem if he was completely off the mark in perceiving something.

Interesting. I wonder what's the tolerance.

This whole chain of events raised even more questions, and his curious mind-set hungered for answers. After trivially addressing the simple ones and discarding the low-priority ones, he narrowed it down to one final question that stuck out like a sore thumb.

Why was it harder to perceive gravity compared to complexity or integrity?

He could easily assign grays within his perception when he tried to interpret and manipulate the balance of complexity, but he couldn't say the same for gravity. One simple explanation for this was that it was because of instability inducement. That learning the vision had somehow boosted him in that regard.

But he didn't buy it.

He had come up with the idea to use the balance of complexity to induce instabilities on his own, and the same was true for integrity. He either had an affinity for a whole bunch of similar ideas, or this wouldn't make sense. Why could he induce instabilities in complexity but not gravity?

There's something deeper at play here.

The silent world remained utterly motionless—not changing one bit as he sat there pondering this question. Sometimes, he scribbled something in his notepad before quickly scratching it away and starting anew.

But fortunately, or unfortunately, he never lost track of time. His shackles of subjectivity were getting oh so tighter every other minute, keeping him alert. Yet the loss didn't help in giving him more ideas.

It felt good to forget everything and just ponder the mysteries of the universe.

But he was on a leash. Not a short one, but a leash nonetheless.

So he decided to cheat.

He pulled out an iridescent fist-sized sphere from the second of the eight pockets in his coat. His insight sphere. Well, not technically his—but hey, finders keepers. It was the one he had brought back from the Ascendant Council.

Luckily, insight spheres were one of the hardest materials to grace their civilization, or he doubted any other glass would have survived the chain of events he had faced today. Some said the spheres came from the ruins of the old world, whereas most others believed they were the gifts of Lady Lennix herself and rained from the heavens—hence the name Lennian fundamentals.

Not that it mattered right now. He was going to make use of those foreign thoughts inside the sphere once again to accelerate his rationalization prowess.

He would generally hoard it and shy away from using it unless he encountered a dire situation, but this situation was dangerous in its own right. He had a conjecture that his nonexistent shackles of subjectivity was the reason he had resisted turning into a vegetable after carving the third rune into his mind.

So if he let the shackles tighten too much, he might just start drooling here—never to get back up.

Holding the sphere in both hands, he leaned in and peered into the depths of this sphere of infinite knowledge, interpreting it into his perception.

In no time, his mind was at the void of initiation—surrounded by the most abstract fundamentals. Not wasting any time, he linked the thoughts needed to reach that cloud of foreign ideas that had invigorated him last time. It had shrunk considerably, but it was enough for what he needed.

It was the same routine as last time.

From nothingness, particles coalesce. Particles form matter. Matter, by nature, adheres to conservation . . . Inheritance implies perpetuity. Perpetuity intertwines with preservation. Preservation, a dance eternally enshrined within existence.

The irony of the situation wasn't lost on him. He had tucked his tail and fled from someone who preached all about preservation only to come back and seek help from some foreign thoughts related to the same idea of preservation.

However, the moment he came in contact with those foreign thoughts, it was as if someone had shoveled ten times the coal needed to keep the engine running, overclocking it beyond limit. Even drinking fifty cups of coffee wouldn't do this to someone. It was like his thoughts were on crack.

He was sure that if anything really moved around in this world, he would see it in slow motion as he perceived their every little detail. Alas, he had better things to do.

Like figuring out why it was easier to interpret one concept in his perception but not the other. Why complexity and not gravity? What was common between complexity and integrity? What was the link between both kinds of preservations he had just encountered?

He quickly theorized a ruled set of tests to glean necessary information, and not even a moment passed before he put them into action.

He was going to measure the difference in the time it would take him to interpret the balance of a small piece of the ground under different concepts. He would test complexity, integrity, gravity, height, breathable air—all the balances he remembered using back in the library.

He wasn't going to try to induce instabilities in them. He just wanted to plot his perception's speed.

In this maddening frenzy, it didn't take him long to finish the first set of comparisons. But he considered this one a trial and repeated it a few more times before an obvious pattern emerged.

Complexity and integrity only took him around a tenth of a second, height needed three-tenths, gravity unsurprisingly spanned over two seconds, whereas breathable air took him over five seconds.

This . . .

It was very intriguing, and it spurred his thoughts into an obsessive momentum. He was getting close to an answer. There was a larger pattern to all this.

Using these numbers, he began to theorize the possible reasons as to why some came easier to him while others didn't. What was the relation between those that were easy?

This almost drug-induced lucidity and comprehension began to take a toll on his mind as he mapped out hundreds of possibilities.

And finally, he found an answer that seemed to fit. It would answer everything.

Are they really connected?!

His heart was beating with intense thumping as nausea threatened to overwhelm him.

But he needed confirmation!

Suppressing the sickness from overusing his brain, he resumed the tireless contemplation. He needed a few other keywords, like integrity, to confirm his hypothesis. He didn't want to sit around for hours to slowly figure them out with his dulled brain. So he charged on, ignoring his overheating brain.

He remembered that the essence of an instability inducement was actually composition. What else could be a good keyword for this?

After a couple of agonizing seconds, he found one—refinement.

Not letting this stop him, he continued his brainstorming and stumbled upon a whole range of them—firmness, resilience, sturdiness, and reliability.

These are enough.

Cough. Cough!

Wiping away what seemed to be blood from his lips, he repeated the previous experiment, but this time with the new keywords he had figured out.

And it was exactly as he had theorized.

I knew it!

All these keywords took less than half a second for him to perceive.

He was proficient in perceiving ideas that originated from the upper northwestern octant, or from the school of order fundamentalists. They governed the concepts that pertained to the structure of reality.

That was to say, observation and Lennian fundamentals shared a common link. A very practical link.

He was sure that he was probably one of few observers to have figured out this relationship.

And he was going to exploit it.

C HAPTER 62

ANALYZING THE OBSERVATION

There was a simple explanation to why he thought that only a few observers grasped the nuanced link between fundamentals and observation.

Lennian fundamentals had only emerged as a legitimate study thirty years ago—before that, they were dismissed as witchcraft or folklore. Coupled with Ambrose's hint that observers had been limited pre-duskfall, and further constrained by the deadly whispers, the odds were slim that many had reached the same conclusion as him.

The primary contributors, in this case, would be the third rune and this disconnected land. Despite being an observer for just a few days, Vern possessed insights that eluded even seasoned observers—yet he also remained ignorant of basic concepts.

But there was a silver lining in all this. He might have had a much better understanding of mundane aspects of observation if he had stuck to the slow and safe route of carefully digging out the information throughout the city. But then who knew how long it would have taken him to learn about such an important connection between fundamentals and observation? About the uses of the third rune? Even though he wouldn't have activated it, given the threat of Hensen.

However, he shook off these boastful thoughts to focus on how this information could be useful.

At first glance, it might seem insignificant, but this insight provided him with a systematic approach to observation. It could be an analytical lens to decode the underpinning variables that influenced how observation worked.

It was like the particle doctrine of reality—a tool that enabled fundamentalists to analyze and explain more sophisticated phenomena.

It still can't explain the bizarre limitations on the theorized motion in the negative particles though.

The subtlety of these insights wasn't meant to be underestimated. They might not seem groundbreaking, but often it's the overlooked details that made the difference. With cautious optimism, he wondered if his unique, ground-up approach to solving these problems might offer a subtle edge over existing standards in observer society. If so, the mental effort he'd invested would be well justified.

Anyway . . .

He tucked the insight sphere into his coat pocket and cradled his head in his hands, kneading his temples. His brain demanded a break, and the next experiments he had in mind would take more than a dozen seconds, so it didn't warrant melting his brain prematurely. Only a few foreign thoughts lingered in the sphere, just enough for maybe a couple more seconds.

He now had to figure out a few more things, like what vision to imprint on his thought space, and more importantly, what was stopping him from repeatedly imprinting it, shading his perception more than once.

What was the measure of progress between each shade? He had a few conjectures, but he would need to confirm their validity within his own thought space. Until then, they were just that—theories. This was what he had hoped to ask Esther when she had shut him up.

He smiled wryly at the thought. Well, he couldn't even begrudge her for that now. That'd be a luxury.

This all funneled down to a single question. What vision should he forge? Gravity-related ideas were a no go. To be exact, straying from the structure domain in fundamentals wouldn't be ideal.

He realized the visions could be far more intricate than merely altering one value within the viewpoint. In fact, he might be selling his own visions short if it only tipped a specific balance one way or the other.

Instability inducement, for example, worked primarily on the composition of objects, but its essence was catalyzing instabilities in them. It worked with his balance, and he didn't doubt for one second that many other viewpoints could adapt and use instability inducement but with a completely different underlying concept and achieve a similar result.

He needed a vision flexible enough to go beyond just tipping the balance yet focused enough to be personally effective. It was a fine line he'd have to navigate blindly. But at least he had a safety net in this land.

Another complex problem.

He almost instinctively reached out for the insight sphere again but then stopped. Over-reliance on anything was never a good idea. Extremism lacked rationale, and he would stick to balancing his mundane choices whenever possible.

Once his head stopped throbbing, he wiped the blood that leaked out of his nose and looked back out at the red world again.

He considered another subproblem. *How are my manipulation abilities affected by my affinity to structural fundamentals?*

Observing objects within his perception was only one part of the equation—manipulation was the key to producing tangible outcomes.

So, he wanted to try something simple for a start.

Height.

His affinity to height wasn't bad, and it was easy to understand. Even though height couldn't be exclusively contained within fundamentals of structure, a lot of discoveries surrounding it could be linked to that octant.

In his perception, he lumped the pebble on the ground with a black haze around it that slowly thinned out and turned brighter the higher he perceived—just like gravity, even though their underlying meanings were quite different.

He would start simple.

In one sense, couldn't gravity and height achieve the same results? He focused on the outline of that dark pebble on the ground and lightened it a notch.

In less than a heartbeat, he pulled back, his perception shattering.

Ugh.

Predictable, yet still deflating. Well, at least he didn't bleed out of his eyes.

So I just did something wrong, huh? Something that would have unleashed the wrath of whispers in full force were I to have tried this in Elmhurst.

But there was something to rejoice about here—there appeared to be no consequences for fucking up. The lack of catastrophic outcomes spurred him on as he jotted down his observations and repeatedly entered his perceptive world, trying out one thing after another.

This round, he zeroed in on the gray area above the black pebble, imagining it to be darker.

In an instant, his vision crumbled.

Okay, something's off.

The intended result had been . . . *Wait. What should happen?*

What exactly had he anticipated when he tried to alter the height of that patch above the pebble? Did he expect it to simply lower itself? To carve out and relocate a piece of reality? Compress and displace the air within? Substitute its height with something else?

It didn't make sense.

Upon reflection, he realized he wasn't even clear on what height really meant. Was it the measure of distance from the ground? Or perhaps an attribute of an object's elevation? And if he intended to raise the rock's height, did that mean elongating it to reach the height he envisioned?

Yeah. It didn't make sense.

It was the confusion. It had to be. There were far too many possibilities, and he wasn't sure exactly what he wanted. If he didn't know what he wanted, how could that lens in his eye interpret it?

He nodded to himself and adjusted his perception once more.

All right. I want that pebble to rise.

Focused, he lightened the rock's hue in his mind.

And his thoughts rang true. The rock began its slow ascent, casting a faint, elongated shadow beneath itself. But Vern quickly identified a problem. It was . . . slow.

Far too slow. As slow as it was to observe the gravity in his perception. Then it clicked.

That was it. He probably wasn't manipulating height at all. His focus had shifted to more basic elements like position and gravity. And because these fell outside the structural domain, the pace was sluggish—like a train inching along an outdated track.

Yet the moment this realization dawned on him, the rock's ascent quickened. Not by much, but it was perceptible.

Fascinating. Acknowledging the underlying mechanics made the manipulation smoother . . .

There were too many variables at play here. His viewpoint, the object under observation, his intent, and his understanding of the concept he was manipulating. They all affected the outcome, and he had to figure out which aspect did what. Where he had more leeway and what was a strict rule.

For now, ambiguity could be tolerated, but confusion was a hard no. Will took precedence over vague intentions, as it unconsciously shifted the focus of his observation to different concepts.

Moreover, his level of understanding was a significant influencer. Zero comprehension led to a stalemate—partial understanding made things possible, while deeper insight ramped up the efficiency.

Did that also mean he was more proficient at observing and manipulating concepts under structure domain because he better understood them? That seemed like a logical conclusion.

Then could he get better at gravity too? Maybe other concepts? The idea was worth testing out—so he did.

The outcome, however, was tepid at best. Repeating the same action of lifting the pebble with his vague intentions helped for a while, as the speed of ascent increased a little. Yet, despite his best analytical efforts, the law of diminishing returns kicked in, and the improvements plateaued.

It wasn't a terrible idea by any means, but it hardly seemed like the most efficient use of his time in this whisper-free realm. He would need to think more about this when he wasn't spending his precious subjectivity.

What else?

He scanned his notepad again before pivoting to a new angle. Rather than fiddling with balance like it was a simple dial, he wondered what it would be like to see it as a means to achieving something more articulate—not singular in nature, just like instability inducement.

Rumble.

But that's when the world shuddered, and he almost tumbled down the little beam he was sitting on. This could only be an earthquake. A few of the tall, iridescent buildings already on the verge of ruin took the fall and crumpled like a house of cards, kicking up dust and debris around him.

He scrambled away from the disintegrating structures into an open clearing as everything around him began to collapse and fragment, their foreign designs distorted and damaged irrecoverably.

This isn't good.

However, he quickly realized he was secure in this clearing. Nothing actively tried to get to him—even the cracks in the ground were leagues away. So he finally turned his eyes to the inverted pyramid in the sky and understood what just happened.

The rumbling and shaking slowly subsided as he gazed at the gigantic peak of the pyramid, which had now ruinously plunged itself into the ground far out in the distance.

He had thought he was right at the boundary of where the pyramid would have been if it had been on the ground, but apparently not. The vast distance between the point of impact and the cracks reoriented his sense of distance.

Like a bullet shattering glass, the land had splintered from the impact point. Strangely, he had not seen the pyramid's peak fall. The whole structure still floated in the sky, now sheared and its center hollowed out.

But when did it fall?

He had been looking in the same direction, and the pyramid never moved an inch until its peak had somehow broken off and impaled the land.

Bizarre.

Yet he was more interested in returning to his experimentation. There was already so much wrong with this place. This wasn't going to stop him from doing what he intended to do. Who cared about a little natural disaster if he could always make a swift exit? Not like it—

Wait. No.

It had changed. The speed at which his subjectivity was being sapped away changed.

He closed his eyes and focused within himself for a second, only to realize that the rate had increased significantly.

Well, time to pick up the pace.

He didn't waste any more seconds and dove back into his previous line of thinking. What if he became a little more articulate about what he wanted to achieve with the vision? Then he simply had to supplement the idea with his understanding of the underlying concepts to make it more efficient.

And he had an idea. A good one too.

He pulled out the beefy yet small umbrella from another one of his pockets and unfurled its canopy. A few sprockets and gears fell out just from this action as his patchwork began to show its seams.

Given the circumstances, he hadn't done a terrible job fixing it, but it was far from ideal. It was destructive, and he would need a whole slew of new parts to get it back to its prime.

But what if I could repair it? Reverse what I did to it? Un-induce the instabilities. Or, more accurately, induce stability?

The thought excited him, and he quickly broke down what he had to do to shape this into actionable steps based on his recent experimentation. observe the gears, will some articulate changes to them, and then finally supplement the process with his understanding of the concept—vaguely relating it to his underlying viewpoint.

So, for the keyword, he could probably look at its balance under complexity like he had done while destabilizing this umbrella, but he wanted to try something else. Something that might just work better.

Stability.

It wasn't an exact keyword, but it had a concrete meaning in his mind, and he understood it well enough to not be confused about what should happen. He guessed the shades of gray for the faulty gears and sprockets should be dark cloudy-gray while he left the rest of the umbrella neutral.

Now came the time to impose his intentions.

I want these flawed components to become stable.

And as if on cue, the sprocket in his hand began to wobble before adapting to the shape of his palm while others that were still rolling around on the ground from their initial momentum stopped dead in their tracks.

Well, I guess I need to narrow it down further.

Stability was slightly too vague, leading to the gears becoming stable in his hands and on the ground instead. Not exactly what he had wanted, but it was definitely working. He wasn't confused this time—he just had too many valid ideas going through his mind. So he concentrated and imagined the abrased gears growing their grooves back—becoming more balanced in the sense of stability within the contraption.

And it worked. In the name of blasted fucking steam, it actually worked!

His heart raced as the potential of this new vision crystallized in his mind, each implication amplifying his excitement. The immediate advantage was clear—it shared the same foundational elements as his existing vision, instability inducement. This similarity promised that his affinity for this new concept would be at least as robust.

Moreover, the two visions could work in synergy. Just as instability inducement leveraged his deep understanding of fundamentals to offer him an edge in high-stakes situations, this new vision held similar promise.

But what truly thrilled him was its untapped potential. Could he apply this to biological structures, like the human body? If so, the possibility of healing wounds would make him remarkably self-sufficient, adding another layer of utility to his abilities.

Beyond that, the ability to make on-the-fly repairs would be invaluable, particularly in a city where so many systems had broken down.

Yet every choice came with trade-offs. The major downside here was opportunity cost. Was he missing out on something even more groundbreaking by sticking close to familiar territory? While he was carving out his own path, how much was it diverging from the known routes?

What if he was wasting his possibly only opportunity within this land of the third rune on an ordinarily available vision? He didn't have too many frames of reference to compare the utility or potency.

But hey, he had to be realistic too. With limited time and gaps in his foundational knowledge, he couldn't afford to aim for an ideal he didn't fully understand. With this concept, he at least had a measure of confidence—it was, after all, an extension of his already potent instability inducement.

Glancing over his hastily compiled list of pros and cons, he considered the scale that tipped decisively in one direction. That's when—

Rumble.

He cast a quick look ahead and saw that another massive chunk had vanished from the floating pyramid's corner. What were once mere cracks in the ground had widened into ravines, spreading across the landscape at an alarming rate.

The gravity of the moment settled on him. Any further hesitation could cost him dearly, leaving him with no visions of his own.

Taking a deep breath, he made his choice audible. "Stability inducement it is."

Chapter 63

RHYTHM OF WAR

The rhythm had played Ambrose today. First, it lured him into helping those lost newbies, telling him it'd be worth it. But ever since the moment he laid his eyes on that girl with the off rhythm, it changed its tune completely, whispering that it was over. That he wasn't going to survive, no matter what. A bunch of mixed signals, if someone asked him.

Not to say he didn't have fun. Being able to fight without Captain Akira breathing down his neck and controlling his every move like some pawn on the chessboard was a breath of fresh air. On top of that, he didn't have to worry about looking like a hypocrite. These were new people, so it was easy to respect the rhythm and act politely around them.

He wasn't big on being polite. Heck, fuck being polite, but such was his legacy. Finnesse were masters of the rhythm, and rhythm demanded a modicum of respect. Respect for everything. Whenever he let the anger consume him, the rhythm became . . . constant. He couldn't glean anything new about it, and his growth stagnated.

So it was nice to be in the element. He had even slightly improved at rhythm disruption today. Akira rarely gave him the chance to use it, and his colleagues would despise him for even trying it. But that's where the fun ended.

Because, fuck that guy.

Ambrose had held it in for as long as he could, but that bastard wouldn't stop spouting bullshit. Religious suckers already made him want to beat them up, but this guy was on another level.

He acted like he was a big fucking deal. Well, guess what? He was just an old piece of trash that fed on the faith of others and bullied those weaker than himself. He was showing off in front of the newbies and that girl whose rhythm was off. Like, why? Yeah, you got more shades, but anyone can have that if they suck insights from innocent believers for decades on end. What was there to gloat about in that?

Grandpa could also play me like a fiddle. Doesn't mean he's better than me.

It was like pumping your ego for being able to beat a toddler. And he was sure that his grandpa alone could give this asshole a run for his money. These suckers of faith always had flashy bullshit that would shatter by carving a simple seam in their rhythm.

But oh well, Grandpa wasn't here, and he had fucked up. It was bound to happen one day. But who knew it wouldn't be his own fault? Mother always said he'd step on the toes of some great personage one day and die a stupid death. Well, he proved her wrong.

No, really. This wasn't his fault. That sucker would have killed all of them anyway. He knew the likes of him. It was better to go out like this—abusing the fuck out of him.

And again, it wasn't his fault. Rhythm had guided him here. Father would be proud that he had died in pursuit of the rhythm.

Is this death? Do I really want to know?

Not really. He didn't want to feel this . . . It was— It was that fucker's fault!

The scammer had wrapped him in some type of material, cutting off all his senses. He could still think simply because of the shades in his perception, which detached his personality from his physicality and blended with the rhythm. His brain might already be dying due to the lack of air. He had better odds than many in this situation because his body was part rhythm, but there were limits to that.

Only if he could synchronize his body with the rhythm. But it didn't fucking work in here. He had tried. Tried everything.

This was where he'd usually synchronize his breathing with a flow in the rhythm and ruminate over Father's teachings, but even that seemed like a pipe dream now.

Well, if death wasn't going to claim him right away, he might as well listen to the rhythm instead. Moping around too much wasn't his style. It'd be better than just . . . disappearing.

So, he discarded the unnecessary thoughts and focused.

To him, rhythm wasn't some abstract concept. It was a visceral, lived experience. He'd always felt it in the steady beating of his heart, the pulse of the blood in his veins, the flap of a bird's wings, the death throes of a beggar, and every little change that transpired around him. Even right now, he felt something, and he wanted to move. To synchronize with the rhythm.

Yes, this is the feeling.

Rhythm wasn't just about the timbre, the colors, or the flowing visuals. It was more than any of that. It was everywhere.

However, right now, the rhythm felt . . . constricted. Like someone was strangling it, cutting it off from the outside world—mirroring his own situation. Nevertheless, it was there. Muffled, yes, but there. That was enough for him.

Maybe it was the rhythm of whatever trapped him in here. Or maybe it was something else. Who knew? Rhythm was unpredictable like that. Whenever there was no rhythm around him, it pulsed to the beat of his memories, while at other times, it flowed to the ebb of echoes.

No one knew what it'd be this time.

So he calmed himself further and gave up on the anger, distress, and bitterness. Soon, the stagnated rhythm livened up, and he let it wash over him.

It pulsed with a maddening frenzy, fervor, and heat. Fire?

But there was a flow to it. Lava?

Then there was the calmness amid this zealous pulse. Very calm. Just like his own situation. Death?

That's when the rhythm suddenly amplified, and an acute pain shot through his body, leaving him gasping for breath in an unsteady beat.

UGH!

His head swam, and he felt light. It was as if someone had sapped him of all his energy.

What the fuck is going on?

However, even amid this, his perception remained active. Heck, it was instead saturated to the nth degree.

In this vertigo-inducing mess, he felt it pulse.

The flow of the rhythm distorted and cracked, parting way for something. Something terrifying. A gaze.

A shuddering jolt went down his spine, and his brain finally caught up. His eyes flashed open, throbbing intensely, and his perception shattered.

But he was back.

He didn't know how, but he wasn't trapped anymore. He could see everything.

And he was falling.

Usually, it wouldn't matter, but the rhythm had just cracked a second ago. He'd need at least a few moments to reconnect. That meant he'd have to take this fall. Bracing for impact, he sucked in large mouthfuls of air.

With his brain having not died of asphyxiation, his memory caught up soon too.

Bam.

The pain of landing on his hands was utterly dwarfed by the terror of that sight. That gaze.

"Fuck me!" he yelped amid his heavy breaths.

Goddamn, it hurt. What the fuck just happened? He was back alive in the ruined basement of the station, and out of pure habit, he reached out for his cane. His precious cane.

That's when he heard a voice say, "Get up, my dancer friend. We need you to perform for a while longer. Akira would throw me into the Brass Harbor if I let you kick the bucket here."

Captain Shinsei? That was his voice! When did he get here?

Not my concern. He's here now.

Well, wasn't this just beautiful? He wasn't gonna die. Sounded like a *fuck you* to that old shithead.

Good. Good.

He closed his eyes briefly and reached out to the rhythm. In no time, his perception livened up once again with all its myriad facets—colors, sounds, and ideas.

That terrifying gaze had disappeared, but his skin still tingled with goose bumps. The doctrine of rhythm proved itself right at times like this. He had to be respectful. He usually didn't bow down to unknowable entities, but whatever that was, it deserved respect.

So he set aside his crass, vulgar mind-set and opened his eyes. He had to get in the zone now. He couldn't waste this second chance.

Clutching his cane in hand, he found himself an anchor and pushed up. Rest was simple. The movement was simple. Getting up was simple. He was the rhythm now. He just had to follow the minute pulses of the rhythm, and everything became a dance.

Thump.

Tapping the cane loudly on the floor, he reveled in the waves of the new rhythm it generated. *Ahh, what beauty indeed!* The process invigorated him and helped him leave behind the fear and terror that had begun to creep up a while ago.

Ting.

Clang.

That's when earth-shattering sounds snatched his attention, and he cast his gaze skyward, breathing in an upbeat rhythm. There he beheld an unusual performance. Captain Shinsei was locked in close combat with that religious bastard—no—uh, preacher. Actually, no, fuck that.

He didn't want to call this scammer a preacher either. That would be disrespectful to the real preachers worthy of his adoration. However, he couldn't keep repeating hateful thoughts. So . . . uh, Quentin. Yes, that was his name.

It was hard to see, but the rhythm told Ambrose his obvious features. He was, unfortunately, a man of style. Only, if clothes could choose their master, they would never pick him. For even though they suited him, he disrespected the attire by simply existing.

Beneath a mane of wild snow-white hair—that shouldn't have graced one such as him—were his piercing blue eyes glinting with hostility. His face, chiseled and stern, bore an air of regal disdain. The celestial jacket he wore shimmered in silvery hues, adorned with gilded epaulets that hinted at a divine arrogance. Despite the elegance of his garb, there was an undeniable darkness in his rhythm, a stark contrast to the brilliance that wrapped around him.

But if Ambrose ignored the golden disgrace, it was an electrifying scene. Quentin maneuvered gracefully midair, brandishing a lance formed of golden particulates. Meanwhile, the captain engaged him back in a dance of the most unconventional form.

Occasionally, Captain Shinsei would alight upon the station's roof only to vault back into the air, sprinting along a path formed by his . . . scarf.

Yes, scarf. It was a perceptual artifact originating from the captain's homeland. If memory served Ambrose right, Captain once revealed that this unique item materialized when an observer of cartographer shade sequence had fallen prey to the seductive calls of the whispers.

Anyway, their back and forth fascinated him. Every other bout, Quentin brandished his glowing lance with intense ferocity, dodging and weaving through sharp slashes of Captain's swords, backing away after every hit. However, even though it looked like Captain had the upper hand, Ambrose could feel the rhythm of war. It wasn't in Captain's favor.

It was that Captain was just too good at deflecting. Nothing could touch him.

Each of the lance's thrusts shot beams of golden light that cleaved through the air like celestial arrows, leaving a scalding trail of divine fire in their wake, searing the very fabric of the rhythm.

Quentin raged. "What an insolent agent of dissolution! Get out of my way! You're making enemies of the Eternal Directorate. This will not end well!"

But Captain was in his element.

Clang.

It was as if he were directing the rhythm itself. The celestial arrows that blazed their trail toward him hit the edge of his infinitely sharp sword—the rhythm was far too condensed there—and deflected into arbitrary directions. Some were even sent right back toward the man as if his sword were a mirror.

One perfectly calculated swing after another, Captain stood amid the field of glowing arrows that slowly disintegrated whatever they touched. Then the captain chortled and said, "My friend, I'm not afraid of that piece of god you killed and hid in your basement. Why the hell would I fear you, a bunch of sinners?"

Quentin's rhythm became disharmonious at these words, and his expression scrunched up as he spoke through gritted teeth, "You know nothing of our burden! Give me the girl and get out of here. I can be benevolent and let this slide."

Captain remained in his perfect stance and spoke with a haughty tone, "My friend, I didn't know you were incompetent on top of being a sinner. It would have been fine if you dealt with her before I got here. But now? You want me to be an accomplice in the kidnapping of the Lightvein heiress? Get my whole organization turned into puppets and vessels? Drinking all that blood of your god has really made you stupid, eh? Who would've thought?"

"YOU DARE DISRESPECT MOTHER ASEA!" shouted Quentin, hate oozing from his every word.

The rhythm around him emblazoned like flame, and his cape shone bright as he flew higher, disengaging from this battle of attrition. In less than a second, he was already outside the bounds of the rhythm.

Ambrose put his free hand on his heart and regulated his wildly thumping heart. That was exhilarating! Worthy of his respect. Worthy of being a captain—on the same level as Captain Akira.

Quentin was still cooking something, but Ambrose had yet to reply to the captain's words. So he thundered with a booming voice, "My gratitude extends to you, Captain. Do you have further directives for my course?"

But Captain was doing something enigmatic yet again. He swung his sword in fluid arcs, going from one angle to another with a momentum that increased by the second. Then Captain glanced back for a brief second and signaled with his free hand to wait as he shouted loudly toward Quentin, "Come, my sinner friend. Show me what you can do. Show me your best!"

Ambrose nodded. Captain was busy. He wasn't having as easy of a time as he had made it seem. Ambrose had to figure something out on his own. Find some way to help the cause.

He surveyed his surroundings to figure out what had changed. It appeared as though the station had endured yet another series of hardships in his absence and was peppered with hundreds of holes.

The animated pollution upstairs was getting worse too. Objects morphed and shifted into uncanny things with a discordant rhythm. Pollution gave him the creeps. Not this one here in the building—this was nothing. But let it fester and grow, and that's when one was faced with the most unspeakable horrors.

One such product still lurked in their ancestral castle. He had been forced to experience its presence for his enlightenment—left alone in there with that . . . thing. Luckily, he had heard the rhythm just in time and managed to escape. He didn't dare think what could have happened.

But that was in the past. This station wasn't even close to that level of awful, and it wasn't his concern. Someone would take care of the pollution if they survived this.

Or even if they didn't. For now, he would just follow the rhythm until the captain had orders for him.

The rhythm chimed for survival. He could get all of them to a safer place.

Wait. Huh?

Something was missing.

He turned around frantically. There were only five bodies in his vicinity. Two of them had some rhythm to them, while the rest didn't. The newbie girl looked exhausted, while the woman whose rhythm was off seemed pained beyond measure. But where was the newbie guy?

He focused harder and let the rhythm wash all over him.

Nothing.

There should be a lingering rhythm here, even if he was dead. Where'd he go? Did he run away?

With a frown, Ambrose trotted toward the newbie girl before kneeling to check her breath. He didn't need to, but it was the polite thing to do. She had helped him a while ago.

He quickly realized through her breathing rhythm that she was just unconscious. It was probably post-enlightenment exhaustion.

Yeah. She's breathing all right.

That's when he felt it. A subtle change in the rhythm.

It was already disgusting that he had missed this hidden rhythm until it had gotten so close. Not wasting any time, he let the rhythm of traversal wash over him and synchronized with it.

When he was in tandem with the world, it was a rush. Everything became a blur, and in an instant, he was already there, in front of the sneaky fuck—no, the man— his cane's sharp edge extended toward his neck.

The sneaky . . . man reacted poorly to Ambrose's actions, retreating like a scared rat while throwing something toward that off-rhythm woman. Ambrose felt it long before it left the man's hand and intercepted it with the hilt of his cane. Following this up with his smooth footwork, he kept up with the ratlike movements of the man.

What was funny, however, was that whatever Quentin was doing up in the air was helping him. It was too damned bright—it was like the sun had risen at night.

He didn't care about the woman's life, but it looked like Captain knew who she was, and it'd be a bad idea to let her die or be nabbed on their watch. And who said he needed a reason to fight these religious fucks.

Damn, it was hard to remain respectful to people like this. But now that one of them wanted to hamper Captain's plan, he knew what to do. Maybe Captain expected this and woke him up for this exact reason. He wasn't going to make the Vigil look stupid when Captain was performing so beautifully himself.

He took a quick glance back, only to see not a sun but a golden spiral of majestic proportions that churned with what seemed like unlimited energy.

What a backdrop!

The corners of his lips lifted, and he spoke to the sneaky religious rat with immaculate grace, "Let's have a dance, shall we?"

Chapter 64

CREATING A VISION

On the 28th of the month of Winterveil, Year 731, I will construct my own vision and imprint it into my thought space. While I have not yet comprehensively grasped all the governing parameters that distinguish a vision from mere manipulative acts of the viewpoint, I believe my foundational understanding of surrounding concepts is solid enough to proceed. I currently possess several conjectures that require further scrutiny, and I will record them here as I go.

This is what Vern would have written in his notepad had he a little less common sense. He ripped one page after another from the pad and shredded them into countless pieces.

He had already gone too far by recording the details of what happened in this land on paper. His justification for doing so until now was that he had an easier time linking his thoughts if he saw them laid out with ink.

But that wouldn't do in this case. They had to go. He wasn't going to bring a record of anything that had transpired in here to Elmhurst. If observers can locate Esther from the eyes of others, who was to say they couldn't find ways to read his notes?

This wasn't to say he was completely giving up on jotting down his thoughts because of the paranoia, but the risks and benefits had to be balanced.

The risk that came with the leak of the secrets he had gleaned in here would set him back too much. He had to pile up his advantages, not make them public for anyone to benefit from.

Once he removed all the evidence of his endeavors from the notepad, he scattered the paper around him like confetti and settled the pad next to his coat on the ground.

Every once in a while, the world shook, and another fragment of the suspended pyramid disappeared. Blisters appeared on the ground, and particulates of ash in the air began to coagulate.

But he couldn't be bothered with analyzing it. As long as there was no immediate danger to himself, he had better things to do.

Let's start simple and figure out how a vision is different from plain old manipulation of the viewpoint like I had done in the library. Why and how is instability inducement different from changing the balance a little.

He had a conjecture. It came from his experiences with instability inducement. Every time he executed that vision, he felt like he went through a chain of specific thoughts, and they somehow brought to life the changes he envisioned.

Keywords being chain of thoughts. So, the real question here was how to build one such chain for stability inducement. One idea would be to divide the process into steps and link them together, creating a chain. However, it seemed a little far-fetched. If that's all it took to create visions, it wouldn't be as big of a deal as everyone made it out to be.

But it was worth a shot.

With a perfectly shaped gear from the umbrella in his hand, he first went ahead and induced an instability into it. Its teeth became dull and lost their shape, morphing from perfectly usable in any machinery to utter junk in mere moments.

The next step was to stabilize it back. He had done it just a while ago, so that shouldn't be too hard. His plan was to repeat it a bunch of times and see which parts of the vision could be further divided into steps for the chain.

So he considered a balance of stability in his mind and imagined the teeth going from being dull and abrased to perfectly angled and sharp—the way they had been before instability. And as if on cue, the gear reshaped into a perfect sample in the very next moment, its curved edges stretching to become straighter. The process was actually far faster than inducing the instability.

Hmm, wait . . .

That hadn't happened last time. Previously, It had taken him quite a while longer to fix the sprockets and gears. Had he just gotten so much better in one stroke? Or maybe it happened because he was only focusing on a singular item? The latter made more sense.

Anyway, it was easy to confirm with a simple test. So he perceived ten of the sprockets that spilled from the umbrella under complexity and induced an instability within them. It took about double the time compared to destabilizing a single sprocket. That was to say, the time or representation cost didn't exactly depend on the number or volume of items he perceived. If it did, it should have taken him ten times longer to achieve this result.

Still, specifications of instability didn't matter right now. Stability inducement was what he had to focus on.

So he emptied his perception and started again with stability in mind. He mentally shifted the balance of everything to become lighter and imagined the gear in his hand turning back to its unharmed state.

And something interesting happened. The gear morphed into perfection almost instantly, but the other sprockets on the ground took more than a second. It was still faster than instability inducement for all of them, but he didn't expect this odd spread.

So he reflected on his actions and quickly rushed through possible reasons for this uneven distribution of time it took to stabilize items. It wasn't the distance. He had measured the potency of his visions based on distance before; it never produced a similar result.

Oh. Damn. It's so obvious!

He had gotten so lost in analyzing everything in terms of the underlying details that he forgot one of the earliest observations he had made about manipulating reality. The more comprehensively he imagined the results of his manipulation, the better and closer they would be to his ideal.

He had been applying this concept to the balance aspect of his visions ever since the library, but today, he stumbled into this situation by pure coincidence. He wasn't focusing on the exact steps like usual and also just happened to be deeply pondering what changes should occur to the chosen object in reality.

Well, it was easy to test whether imagining in both types of realities made any difference at all. He could compare the times with and without considering the objective reality.

He cracked his neck and induced instability in all the sprockets yet again. But this time, when he reached the next step and considered stability, he went ahead and only visualized how the balance should be affected to make the teeth of the gears angular and neglected to visualize it happening in reality—like he had always done.

The vision still worked—the sprockets became useful, but it took about two seconds. Far longer than the instant it had taken last time.

That confirmed it. His imagination and visualization in terms of subjective reality, as well as objective reality, played an important role in determining the cost of the vision.

But then he nodded to himself and suppressed his bubbling excitement at all these findings. He had to take these results with a grain of salt. This wasn't the most rigorous set of tests, and he only had one measure of success or failure—the time it took to bring the visions to life. Generally, he would have another factor to figure out if he was doing the right thing, which was the amount of representation used.

However, in this land of the dark sun, not once was he pinched for representation, nor were his eyes ever exhausted. In Elmhurst, doing what he had done in this past hour would've been impossible. That feeling of emptiness would have permeated his body long ago, followed by the veins around his eyes bursting into a bloody mess.

So, in one sense, it was a boon that he didn't have to worry about representation here, but on the flip side, he had one less variable to observe and measure the correctness of his approach.

Of course, it was far too big of an edge to trade it for some extra experimental value. This was a great balance between usability and practicality.

Anyway. That was an insightful detour, but I should be figuring out how to partition the manipulation process into more steps, not this.

However, the very next moment, a pensive look overtook his face, and he ran his fingers through his hair as he stood there, staring at nothing in particular.

Yeah. That can't be right.

He found a big hole in his previous logic about dividing the process into steps. How could the chain of thoughts needed to stabilize one object be the same as a wholly dissimilar one? For example, one wouldn't follow the same steps to fix a gear as one would follow to . . . uh . . . patch up shredded paper? Or any other kind of stabilization, for that matter?

Then did he need to subdivide his vision into very general and common steps that didn't assume the behavior of the object under influence?

He ruffled his hair and threw the sprocket down as he groaned internally. *Wow, this is too fucking complex.*

If someone told him that observation just happened to work like this, then he was going to get into a very heated argument that day. There was clearly a system and set of rules behind all this. Rules that didn't seem to be born of nature.

One could argue that human life itself and the fundamentals of physics were products of cosmic coincidence, but who was to say they weren't? Maybe there was no true creator, maybe fundamentals were always the way of the world, maybe subjectivity was the nature of reality, but there was also the possibility that it was all engineered.

The truth of creation has always been one of the most heated yet futile debates at the annual Symposium. But add these Elden Ones to the equation, and all the previous arguments became flimsy. What was their hand in the creation? The evolution of intelligent species? The planet? The solar system and beyond?

He let out a deep breath and set aside these existential queries. They weren't going to help him in any way right now.

He knelt and picked up the torn bits of paper. Could he consider these bits and pieces as some sort of instability in the paper's structure and patch it back up?

He nodded and tried just that—observing it under the lens of stability. After wasting a couple minutes getting the grays just right for the paper, he considered how things should change. The dull darkness of each bit of paper should come together to form a more stable and bright structure. And in terms of reality, the pieces should fly toward each other and connect.

That sounded reasonable.

He executed these thoughts . . . and the pieces moved. But only for a brief second. In a flash, everything lost momentum, and his perception shattered into nothingness, jerking him out of his world of grays.

Uh . . .

Damn! Right, that's not how it works for structural fundamentals.

Distractions really were the bane of good ideas. That was stupid of him. How could stability inducement do the work of gravity or force? His imagination there had combined more than what the fundamentals of structure would be able to encompass on their own. The structure didn't involve any concepts that'd help papers fly toward one another.

He should isolate the problem to primarily be a structural one. So he took a bunch of pieces of paper and put them next to each other, assembling them into a rough shape of paper on the ground.

Doubt gnawed at the edge of his thoughts, but if he was right about his previous idea not working because of mixing fundamentals, then this should be promising.

He repeated his earlier set of actions, populating the pieces in his perception with grays. But the moment he envisioned the changes—pieces of paper combining together, something happened. Something unexpected. It was like dots connected in his mind, and he skipped a few steps.

When he came to in the next instant, three of the twenty or so torn bits had lost the seam between them—fused together as if they had never been apart.

He let out a breath he didn't realize he'd been holding, his heart pounding like a drum. *Did I just . . . ?* He couldn't finish the sentence, his mind racing ahead, already contemplating the possibilities this revelation had flung open before him.

That had felt similar to when he used instability inducement. It was like he went through checkpoints in his mind, and his thoughts automatically guided him in the right direction.

But it wasn't the same experience either. It was . . . incomplete.

Many hypotheses whirled in his mind, and he rejected the ridiculous ones outright while setting up the grays of the papers in his perception once more. He had to experience that again. He had to be sure that it wasn't a random fluke, that he didn't just get lucky again. Because luck was very hard to factor into his calculations.

So he assigned a light gray to the row of bits that were now fused together and a dark gray to the completely separate pieces, all of them hugging one another. Then he imagined them fusing into a singular entity both in terms of balance and in terms of reality.

Stabilize.

The moment the thought crossed his mind—it happened. His thoughts became transient, and something steered them through particular notions, delving into the concept of stability. He observed the process closely this time, not missing a single detail.

The gaps between each of the torn pieces became finer and finer, and the curl on their edges straightened out. It was like watching a film in reverse.

Crack.

He didn't hear that sound, but his brain had already come to associate it with his perception shattering. It happened again.

Damn!

At least it wasn't a fluke.

So the vision was executed like a chain of thoughts—yes, but it halted midway. Which could mean this chain wasn't complete.

No, that's what it has to be.

One of his myriad hypotheses seemed more and more likely by the second. It conjectured that visions didn't need to be subdivided into steps, rather, he just needed to provide a lot of thoughts relating to that vision.

In simpler terms, he needed more experience with inducing stability to mature it into a proper vision.

However, the fundamental reasoning he theorized for it was far more intriguing. He believed that he needed a plethora of thoughts related to inducing stability, so when he tried to envision something similar, his lens would automatically pick and choose some of his previous insights to infer what should happen in this new scenario.

It made sense. And again, there was a simple test to confirm it.

He emptied his perception of the papers and induced instability in the sprockets instead. Dozens of dull and abrased gears dotted his perception, which he now switched to stability.

His heart pounded faster, almost matching the rate at which the ground around him shook, and the pyramid disintegrated. If this worked, then he would have figured out the core secret to making one's own vision.

With a deep breath, he shifted the balance of stability in the cogs.

And there it was. Unlike the last time, where he had to envision the whole process himself, his thoughts rushed through a series of notions on their own before interrupting abruptly.

But the sprockets had changed. That meant simply knowing how to induce stability in another situation—patching up the bits of paper—had boosted his ability to do the same in this scenario.

It didn't finish the process, sure. But that could be easily remedied by practicing to induce stability in more such scenarios. And it would only grow from there until it could accommodate any situation.

This . . .

This was fascinating.

C H A P T E R 65

COLLECTING INSIGHTS

After his newfound discovery, he spent a short while contemplating the nature of visions and soon found a more succinct and appropriate explanation for them.

He believed visions were actually a cluster of ideas and insights into one's viewpoint biased to perform a certain action. So, when an observer executed a vision, a chain of ideas and insights was chosen from that cluster to approximate the vision's effects in a new situation to produce the intended result.

However, as he sat there and solidified his understanding of these ideas, he suddenly felt something. A distinct sense of loss. It didn't make any sense, so he checked himself all over.

Then a possibility crossed his mind, and his heart fell. He interpreted the cogs in his perception, then repeated the new vision he had theorized a while ago. And to his horror, some of the nodes that he was consistently going through in the previous rush of thoughts . . . were missing.

They were gone.

He slumped back on the quaking ground as he came to a realization. *It's my memory, isn't it?*

That was the only explanation. He didn't have a thought space, and that probably meant any new insights would only be useful as long as he remembered them down to the smallest detail. It would be one thing if they were words or pictures, but these were ideas and abstract concepts. How did one force their subconscious to remember such constructs?

I can't. It's just not possible.

But who had said that was the only solution to this problem?

I just have to be quick.

Yes. He would have to consolidate the thought space and shade his perception soon after he had accumulated a bunch of insights in his memory. That was the only option. He couldn't and wouldn't spend days here trying to get familiar with every one of those insights.

That method worked for others because they couldn't accumulate insights regarding a vision at his pace, but if he did that, he'd be wasting the opportunity. Given how much the ground was shaking, he was sure he didn't have much time left in here.

Knowing that he'd have to go into a no-nonsense focused state after this, he pondered this from all angles to ensure he didn't waste time later.

He nodded. *But I can't imprint it right away either. All I know how to do is stick some paper together and fix some cogs.*

That would be an utter waste. This was an optimization problem. He would have to cram as many important ideas into his memory before he made that leap.

What if the cluster of thoughts became unchangeable once he imprinted them onto his thought space? He would be left with a weak-ass vision that could barely manage to stitch three pieces of paper together.

That would be tragic.

On that note, why can I use instability inducement at all without a thought space?

Cera had told him that it didn't make sense for someone like him, who hadn't shaded his perception, to be flinging out visions. Did that mean the vision had found some way to embed itself into his scattered thought space?

However, that's when an idea crossed his mind. *No, that's too simple. What if it was something far more involved, something related to the rune in my head? Could the vision have . . . imprinted itself to the rune?*

Yes! That would answer a lot of questions brewing in his mind. Like why he was able to gain a vision just by reading a few words off a parchment or why he could use it as a shadeless observer. If the vision and the rune had some kind of affinity, it was possible that the rune acted as a thought space for the vision.

Though that did lead to a question in and of itself. Could he use the rune as a thought space for himself?

He had been nodding in agreement with everything until now, but this time, he shook his head. *I won't try to use it as my personal thought space even if it's ten times better than whatever I can cobble together. It's just not worth it.*

What if one day, Hensen came along and stripped him of the rune? Vern would be helpless, left completely to the madman's mercy. He had to build up strength to resist the lunatic, not hand his hard work to him on a silver platter.

Before getting started with this, he massaged his head a little. It was becoming increasingly more difficult for him to keep his focus. Even though representation wasn't a problem right now, his brain was still paying the toll. This whole day had been exhausting physically, mentally, and emotionally. On top of that, repeatedly using foreign thoughts to accelerate his thinking only exacerbated the situation.

Clap.

He slapped his cheeks as hard as he could and felt a surge of blood rush to his brain. Whining was for those who had the luxury. He didn't. He was always on a clock. So he would act like it.

Time to get it done!

This was the final stretch. He could almost see the light at the end of this tunnel.

He sat back up and cleared his mind before he started. *Right. So, I need to induce stability in more objects around me.*

There were quite a few things that could be stabilized. His attire, for one, but he didn't want to become the most notorious seamster in the city. He wanted the limited insights his brain could manage to be inherently practical.

Well, for that, there were also the fissures in the ground, which could do with some stabilizing. But he hadn't forgotten what had happened to him when he messed with that polluted statue in the relay station. Any manipulation that could cause too many cascading changes would suck him dry in no time.

Yes, it seemed like he had infinite representation, but he wouldn't bet his life on having enough to mend the fissure in the ground all the way to its center by the pyramid's peak.

He wasn't suicidal yet, and even if it didn't kill him, what if it made him unconscious, causing him to miss the opportunity to shade his perception? All in all, a bad idea.

So, after some careful consideration, he settled on a few objects available to him in this ruin of a world. The list included: a cracked pillar in the building closest to him, his umbrella, pen, mechanisms of his gun, and finally, himself.

He would start with these options and monitor his memories at all times to see if he missed something. He tried to keep the sample biased toward more realistic scenarios he might face in the future so that insights related to these could always come in handy.

With a plan at hand, he didn't waste even a moment and began the mad rush. He shifted his focus to the large pillar-like object that lay there in the ruin, a crack running down its length. He didn't dare move too close to the building, he could perceive it just fine from right here.

This was the perfect target because even though the column was split down the middle, one chunk was still on top of the other, meaning he wouldn't need to move the two parts closer together.

In his perception, he assigned a dark gray to both halves and considered how the balance would shift to accommodate them combining together. Then, he visualized how the seam between them would slowly mend itself and fade away. Once he felt he was sure enough about the details, he let his eyes do the rest.

Stabilize.

Another rush of thoughts claimed him, tunneling him through a bunch of ideas, and the border between the two chunks of the pillar began to disappear from its edges, moving toward the center.

When he was about 50 percent done, it stopped. But Vern was ready this time. He wasn't going to wait for his perception to shatter and leave the vision half complete. The instant the automated guidance within his thoughts halted, he took over and directed the process himself.

In reality, the recovery of the pillar did suspend for a split second, but it picked right back up, and in another few breaths, it was finished. He had stabilized—no, repaired—an architectural object just with his thoughts.

How cool was that?

At least he considered it impressive. But he wasn't done. He had to cram in more experience as soon as possible. So he moved onto the umbrella that was sitting on the ground. He had repaired the tiny gears that made up the device, but the whole contraption itself was still out of order.

He wanted to take this chance to further test a theory. If it worked, he wouldn't mind losing some insights from his useless memory. He wanted to know just how much matter his vision could create in the name of stability.

Because when things break, some of their particles were lost to the wind or get turned into a different kind of energy. Like when they repaired those bits of paper or shaped the cogs, it was creating matter out of nothing. He wanted to know the limit of that.

So he picked up the contraption and looked at its rotation mechanism, which was missing more than a dozen gears. He perceived the whole lattice as a dark gray, with the missing gears as gaping black holes in the machinery.

Now instead of using the cogs he already had, he visualized new ones materializing out of thin air within the mechanism, plugging the holes as he shifted the balance of those dark hollows to a bright white.

Stabilize.

Another rush of thoughts claimed him . . .

Crack.

But his perception shattered the very next instant, and he was jerked out of it. Expecting this to happen, he picked up the original cogs while eyeing the results of this short burst of manipulation and was pleasantly surprised.

Pitter-patter.

Small pieces of metal dropped on the ground from the umbrella, and on closer scrutiny, they all looked like half-cut gears and cogs. So his vision could indeed create matter out of nothing! But it was severely limited. All these components were practically useless.

And he quickly figured out the rationale behind it.

Creation and structure are two separate fundamentals, after all. Can't expect one to do the job of the other too well. Creation-related fundamentals were grouped in the lower southwestern octant of the insight sphere, whereas structural ideas resided within the upper northwestern octant.

He was glad he had made the connection between fundamentals and observations. It was helping him comprehend why observation worked the way it did.

Vern didn't linger on this discovery and moved on. *Let's do it correctly this time.*

He first made sure all the original cogs were in proper shape, then he loosely plugged them into their desired positions and induced stability to the whole contraption. This time, the cascade of thoughts pushed the 70 percent threshold, almost stabilizing the whole thing on its own.

Once that was done, he picked up the umbrella and clicked the primary switch on its shaft.

Whirrrr.

A smile appeared on his face as the intense grinding of the umbrella drowned out the noises of the crumbling world around him. After basking in the soothing sound for another moment, he closed the canopy and placed it inside a pocket of his coat on the ground.

While doing that, he pulled out the revolver and picked up the pen. These were his next experimental apparatus.

He first emptied the chamber of the gun, then induced a minor instability into it. After fiddling with the grays in his perception for a while, he visualized both realities only to be swept up into the whirlwind of thoughts that piloted the vision almost to completion. Closer to 80 percent—the rest he finished on his own.

Putting back the bullets into the chamber, he cocked the gun and—

Bangg!

Still working, huh?

This was good. No, this was great. A little more push and he would be ready.

However, after performing the two-step routine of instability-stability on the pen, he groaned. He had just begun to feel optimistic about his memory not being a problem, but his fears were not unfounded. He felt it. Some of the thought nodes which his mind always went through at the start of the vision were missing this time.

It was clear what was happening. He had reached the limit. But he had to go through this last trial no matter what. He would trade other insights in his limited short-term memory for this one any day—hence the reason he left it for the end.

This last trial required him to be prepared. Mentally and physically.

He wiped the pen's nib clean off any residual ink and held it against his thumb. With a focused gaze and a hint of levity in his voice, he declared, "For Science!" and then drove the sharpened point into his thumb. The sharp tip ripped through the epidermis like butter and punctured it—blood leaking out in a constant stream.

He winced, acknowledging the acute sting, but he refused to yield to the discomfort. Instead, he narrowed his perception on the wound. In his perception, it became a dark hollow surrounded by a blurry gray that became lighter the farther he observed from the point of impact.

With an internal command, he envisioned a wave of restorative light sweeping over the darkness, its luminosity snuffing out the shadows and knitting the torn flesh together, cell by cell, layer by layer, restoring its previous unblemished state.

"Stabilize," he whispered with gritted teeth as a cascade of rapid-fire insights danced through his consciousness. When the flow of ideas ebbed, he took the cue and completed the procedure. The puncture on his thumb receded as if drawn back through time, leaving behind blood that now seemed misplaced—a random splotch almost.

"YESSS!" he shouted, throwing his fist up in the air.

It worked! It really worked. He still felt some pain in his thumb, but the wound was closed. He didn't know human anatomy well enough to understand exactly what was going on underneath such that he still felt the pain, but this was good enough for him. The ability to close wounds would be nothing to balk at.

But he didn't give himself more than a couple seconds to celebrate. He had to imprint all this into his thought space. Right now. Missing out on embedding them in the thought space would be the tragedy of the ages.

He sat up straight and placed the pocket watch in front of him.

It was time to shade his perception.

CHAPTER 66

SHADING THE PERCEPTION

Vern sat up straight and placed the pocket watch in front of him to check the time as he pondered Esther's words—ruthlessly suppressing any lingering emotions that made him want to mourn. There would be a specific time for those emotions, and this wasn't it.

Vern remembered she had said, *Take these thoughts that are floating in your mind—the ones that you're constantly repeating to maintain the state of your perception and imagine a shape for them.*

Now, one way to go about doing that would be to slowly go through the thoughts in his mind one by one, shaping them—even repeating some of the procedures to ensure he didn't miss out on any important details. All this while also forcing his thoughts into a mental construct. Or, he could be smarter about it and make use of the resources available to him.

He obviously chose the latter. Leaning over, he grabbed the insight sphere and closed his eyes. He had left that final cloud of foreign thoughts within the sphere precisely for this moment.

Whenever he used those thoughts, his mind went into overdrive—his memory became perfect, and his reasoning abilities soared. That was exactly what he needed right now. He had about four seconds' worth of enhancing foreign thoughts in there.

He quickly rushed from the void of initiation to the lower northwestern octant. The moment he came in contact with the foreign notions, he let them wash over him.

And clarity became the norm.

Every node of thought in his brain became distinct, and fuzzy ideas became solid. Without wasting even a fraction of a second, he followed Esther's words. He just had to mold the thoughts into his desired shape.

He had considered this question beforehand and knew exactly what he wanted. It wasn't just a simple sphere. He had a better idea. Something marvelous.

An insight sphere.

So he began. First, he took all his general thoughts and molded them into a sphere. But this was just the start. Next, he picked each thought node related to stability inducement and decided which fundamental it primarily belonged to.

Notions associated with structural fundamentals were pushed into a section of this newly created hollow sphere—the upper northwestern octant. This was the same area where structure was defined in an insight sphere. Whenever he came across ideas of varied fundamentals like creation or force, he aligned them in their respective octants.

He knew that this might not matter in the grand scheme of things, that this extra effort might just be a waste of time, but if there was a perfect shape for a thought space, it was an insight sphere. Every one of these spheres embodied the mysteries of the universe in the most efficient and saturated manner.

Positioning each concept within an Insight Sphere meant something. It was like someone with nigh infinite thought and care deliberately put them there to make it easy to understand. Some believed it was Lady Lennix. Regardless, every idea complemented those surrounding them, while those on the borders of the octants embodied multiple schools of thought.

Right now, he predominantly had thoughts related to structure, so it wouldn't make much of a difference, but who knew about the future? If he could progress on paths other than just structure, he would have the most scalable foundation. He was quite proud of having thought of it.

As he perused the shelves of his mind, seconds felt like minutes, and the arduous process of segregation soon turned tedious. But he wasn't about to stop now. This was it!

This current scenario far exceeded his expectations. He would never have guessed that he would be shading his perception like this. It was neither generic nor immeasurably groundbreaking; it was . . . balanced.

Apart from imprinting the ideas of vision onto his thought space, he only let one other thing distract him—the ticking of his pocket watch.

Tick.

Tock.

Tick.

To—

Done!

It didn't even take him the full four seconds, and he was finished. It was over! He could sense it . . . within himself.

Scattered thoughts were transient; one could barely grasp or engage with them. But this was different—it was substantial, like a steadfast planet rotating in the core of his consciousness. A planet whose one section was covered with innumerable small lights, roughly forming the boundary of an octant, and the rest of it was emptiness, interrupted only by a tiny island of thoughts of varied nature.

Clink.

The insight sphere slipped from his shaking hands as he let out a sharp breath. His head throbbed, and exhaustion seemed to claim him, but beyond all that was relief.

Now what?

He waited. Instants turned into seconds, and seconds soon turned into minutes. Nothing happened.

Vern paced frantically. Things were going downhill. His perception was supposed to populate on its own once he had a thought space—it didn't. Instead, the image of the pseudo-insight sphere in his mind began to deform and distort.

He was about to lose all his progress.

The fuck was he missing?!

His fingers clawed through his hair, grasping at the strands with a weary desperation. "I shouldn't panic. I shouldn't panic," he muttered to himself, each repetition of the chant a feeble attempt to stave off the rising tide of dread over imminent regression. "I need to try something. Anything!"

He grabbed a handful of paper confetti from the ground and manually perceived it like usual, deciding on the grays based on how big they were. Then, without a moment of respite, he visualized them merging into one.

Stabilize.

Crack.

His mind blanked, and a profound silence enveloped his consciousness.

That actually worked?!

He didn't know if this was the right step forward or what to expect, but it was better than sitting there twiddling his thumbs.

In that fleeting instant, he drifted in an abyss—a realm stripped of thought, sense, and perception. Suddenly, a constellation of luminescent streams emerged, cascading in unison toward a particular direction.

He traced the luminous path, and there it was—his thought space. He mentally heaved a sigh. *This has to be the right step. It feels . . . correct.*

The sphere had a dark surface that shone under the incoming lights. Millions of white illumination sources sparsely populated one specific section of this otherwise barren and unlit construct. Soon, the fresh cascade of light from above weaved into the existing ones, each beam settling among the stars, intensifying the collective gleam.

But soon, he noticed something.

The pulsation of each of the lights—which probably represented ideas—had a pattern to it. In an instant, they flared with intense brightness momentarily, then, the next moment, their darkness seemed to devour the surrounding light.

They were the two extremes.

And just looking at them birthed a sense of disharmony within himself. Extremes were not in his nature. At least not in the same sense that everyone understood them. Being extreme could have its advantages, but if one was always extreme, that's where things inevitably would start to fall apart.

Consequently, he felt compelled to find a balance for each one of them. He knew, almost instinctively, that the intensity of the lights represented how prominent that particular idea would be in deciding the results of his vision or maybe even his perspective.

So, he immersed himself in the process. It was quite similar to what he had done to shape his thoughts a while ago. But this time, he was in control. Anything he wished, his thought space would obey.

The ideas whose prominence he manipulated were basic in nature. Like the concept of complexity versus simplicity, where one light shone too aggressively, advocating for elaborate frameworks and multifaceted approaches, while its counterpart suffused a subdued glow, promoting the elegance of simplicity and minimalism.

Vern worked to balance these extremes, allowing for systems that were robust yet not unnecessarily convoluted, where each component served a purpose without contributing to entropy.

Another set of lights represented change versus stability. One flared with the intense glow of constant, uncontrolled change, while its opposite was a faint glimmer, signifying rigid stagnation.

Here, too, Vern sought equilibrium, enhancing the dim light of stability just enough to temper the brightness of change, seeking a dynamic yet controlled progression.

Moving forward, Vern discovered the interplay of form and function in the architectural and organic structures, where one light dazzled with aesthetic beauty but risked impracticality, and the other, too dim, signified purely utilitarian constructs devoid of inspiration.

He sought aesthetic functionality, a synergy where beauty enhances utility and structures serve their purpose while elevating the space they occupy.

As Vern adjusted hundreds of such fundamental aspects of his vision, he felt a profound sense of alignment. His thought space no longer seemed like a chaotic collection of ideas but more like a well-orchestrated symphony, each note playing its part to create a harmonious whole.

It was a perspective that embraced the complexity of life, acknowledging that there were no absolute answers, only balanced approaches tailored to each unique scenario.

It was an intriguing process, if someone asked him. It was like introspection but tangible. Some concepts that he used to think of as contradictory in nature when given an opportunity to fiddle with like this didn't seem so mutually exclusive anymore.

The more he repeated this routine, the foggier his recollection of the events became. Moment to moment, he knew what he was doing, but the monotony of the task dulled his consciousness.

When he came to, a cluster of innumerable lights of varying intensities greeted him. And in a single glance, he felt at peace. It was the perfect equilibrium.

In that moment of clarity, the rush of thoughts and the weight of uncertainties that had plagued Vern stilled. There was no sudden revelation, no cascade of knowledge—it was simply a quiet certainty, a knowing that seeped into his bones.

He had crossed a threshold, his mind now moving in sync with a deeper set of rules that had always been present yet just beyond reach.

It was as if he had been squinting all along and now, for the first time, he opened his eyes to their fullest, seeing everything in sharp relief. But he knew that was a relative concept. Maybe he was still squinting and just didn't know yet.

But that didn't matter right now.

This was the moment of breakthrough, marked not by the dramatic, but by the profoundly simple. The balance he had long sought in his new life didn't arrive with a flourish—it was a silent accord, a natural alignment of his perceptions with the world as it truly was.

His senses, now keen and attuned, picked up the transformation. The dark expanse that was his thought space began to coalesce into distinct shapes and shades. With each steady breath, the shadows receded, revealing the intricate tapestry of his newfound sight.

His dreamlike encounter was cut short as he registered a change in the darkness beyond this tiny sphere of lights. Grays seeped into his vision, and soon, the blurry vista had details breathed into it.

Outlines became apparent as curves—smooth and jagged—and combined to form silhouettes of the quirkiest objects one could imagine. Soon, he noticed the similarity of the shapes of his physical surroundings to that of the land of dark sun.

That meant he was waking back up to the reality.

However, his vision—a world of grays—was getting wilder by the second. A lot was happening inside, and he couldn't figure out half of it. There were gradients, a lot of them. It wasn't a single puny gradient that he was so used to manifesting all the time.

Some were even overlapping with one another, confusing him further as to what was happening there. So, instead of trying to comprehend the meaning of unknown structures out in the world, he turned to himself. He brought his hand up—which felt awkward for a second—opening and closing his fist repeatedly.

Vern gazed at his hand, marveling at the array of grayscale tones that now illustrated the once-familiar landscape of his skin and bones. The grays danced in a spectrum from the palest of silvers to the deepest charcoals, each hue shifting subtly with the motion of his muscles and sinews.

As he clenched and unclenched his fist, certain shades deepened, mirroring what seemed like the natural tension within. It was an intricate play of light and shadow, reflecting a balance between the exertion and relaxation of his muscles. The gradations of gray provided a visual symphony of movement. He hadn't expected this.

But this wasn't even close to the end of it. Each time his pulse throbbed, a corresponding ribbon of lighter gray pulsed along his wrist, a visual echo of his heartbeat. He recognized the synchronization between the visual cues and his own biological rhythms, a perfect balance that was momentarily disrupted by an out-of-place streak of darkness—a signal, perhaps, of an imbalance he could not yet interpret.

Fascinated, he continued to explore, noting how the grays aligned with the known structure of his hand. Yet among the familiar, anomalies surfaced. A stress line of gray in the webbing of his fingers seemed to stretch too far. When he moved his hands, it abruptly changed its direction and followed no pattern in particular.

This . . .

The grays blurred yet again as he stared beyond his hand into nothingness and pondered on the meaning of all this.

It seems like multiple types of balances are currently overlapping in my perception. One of them portrays something akin to harmony-disharmony with its shades, while another depicts energy flows. And that line—it seems . . . off.

And if he thought more about it, it made sense. He was a mechanical artist himself—he understood a good deal about structure and energy flows, but he didn't grasp all the nuances of these topics. Since his perception was directly related to his understanding of the world, he obviously was making some guesses that didn't fully make any sense—like that line that reached out to nothing in particular.

There were many more subtle aspects of balance that he could almost notice—but he was unable to put his finger on what exactly they represented. The information overload was real.

But he would take nothing less than this. It was blowing him away, just looking at his hand. There was the whole world yet to be observed with this lens.

Shaking his head, he focused back on his hand and tried to identify the more intricate facets that were taking place here, like that unusual glow on some of the joints of his wrist or that darkening trail that seemed to follow the shape of his hand.

It was surreal. He didn't want to wake up.

Letting out a deep breath, he deliberated. *If I had to guess, these are all the various types of balances I could observe in structures. But they're more specific in nature than simple instability or stability.*

They were like complexity and integrity—two different kinds of balance for exactly the same scenario. But these weren't as limited in nature. He would have to take some time and figure out what each one of them did.

And he surmised it was best he tried this in here, in this land of dark sun. Who knew what representation cost was attached to viewing the world in so many shades?

So he dropped his hand and shifted his focus to the whole world beyond. Time to see the fruits of his labor.

He soon discovered he expected too much of himself. There was so much going on in the grays that he could barely make out all the edges of the world, but he didn't want to open his physical eyes and distract himself from this life-changing experience.

So he decided to compromise. He wasn't going to be able to see anything with all the facets of balances overlaying one another. Thus, he focused.

He focused on the gradients that seemed to belong to the same art style and willed for one to take over his perception—and it did. He wanted to call this one pathway balance sight because of how it allowed him to see clear functional pathways running—

But that's when he noticed something out of the norm. Something that didn't make sense in this vision.

Circles.

There were circles everywhere. Be that next to the dormant outline of his coat on the ground or by the pillar he had repaired. What was even more disturbing, however, was that each of these circles had some energy moving to and fro almost constantly.

He spent a minute or so contemplating the nature of these circles or what they could mean, but he couldn't arrive at a satisfactory answer. So he gave up on this particular kind of sight and switched to another one of the many options.

This time, it seemed like he picked a simpler kind of sight. It depicted everything in a bunch of gradients, but there was clearly a pattern. However, he couldn't figure out what it was because his attention was entirely concentrated on those fucking circles.

They showed up in this one too. Not exactly as circles but instead as spheres that seemed to embody a gradient that was lighter around the surface and became darker around the center.

He frowned. *What the hell is this?*

An uneasy feeling began to creep up his spine, so he stopped playing around and snapped open his physical eyes. And his breath caught in his throat.

He had been facing that dark sun when he began shaping his thought space. But that voluminous celestial body surrounded by the ring with liquid luminosity was . . . staring back at him.

CHAPTER 67

RESURGENCE

A horizontal crease appeared in the middle of that star of nothingness, and the seam widened as an even darker pupil stared back from within. A shudder went down his spine as he stood there, frozen stiff.

It was a sun—the fucking sun! Maybe not the one he was used to, but a star of planetary proportions had parted itself in half, peering through the endless void to gaze at him.

What had he done to warrant this?

But then he shook his head frantically. *No. I am giving myself too much credit.* That pupil was so ginormous that even if it was looking at anything within thousands of kilometers around this area, it would still seem like it was staring at him.

"Right. Right," he muttered as he tore his gaze away from that thing. This rationalization, even if flimsy—gave him some hope, and he soon found wits enough to survey his surroundings and gather his belongings.

The air around him had taken on a quality of stillness that felt unnatural, as if the very atmosphere were holding its breath. The usual sounds of this place—the quaking of the ground, crumbling of the structures, the disintegration of that pyramid—had all but vanished, replaced by a silence so complete it buzzed in his ears.

His breathing seemed loud, ragged intrusions in the quiet, and he found himself holding his breath, afraid to make any noise. Because sound wasn't the only thing that had disappeared, the physical structures and half of that pyramid in the sky were missing too.

When he noticed what had appeared in their place, his blood ran cold. Eyes. Hundreds—no, thousands of eyes.

It seemed like the world was closing in around him—those pebble-sized eyes enlarging, impossibly fixating on him with unsettling precision. The vast eye that had replaced the soaring pyramid loomed, eclipsing his vision in its entirety.

From tracking his every minute shiver with a disturbing oscillation to trailing his shaking head—some of which elicited the pupils to escape out of their irises, they observed him with an apathetic distaste.

Yeah, this wasn't going to work. He had to get the fuck out of here.

It was all in his head. He knew it. Obviously, he knew it. Still, it didn't do scrapshit to steady his wobbling knees or slow his heart that hammered against his ribcage in a maddening frenzy.

For his sanity, he had chosen to believe that the eye up there wasn't focused on him, but what rationalization could he conjure for these? They were everywhere.

These were the circles he had noticed in the grays of his perception, and beyond any shadow of a doubt, each one of them was staring at him with an unflinching and indifferent gaze.

The oppressive atmosphere was like nothing he had ever faced. Maybe that shadow of the entity he had seen during the enlightenment could compare, but his memory of that event was quite faded—he was only happy for the fact.

He would rather not have these beings show up in his dreams and destroy his scarce moments of relaxation. Though he was sure this sight had the potential to keep him awake for more than a couple nights.

He had to get the hell out of here.

That link within his mind was the only thing keeping him from breaking down right here, right now. He just had to stop the channeling of thoughts into the rune, and this nightmare would stop.

Huff.

Somehow, that thought gave him some measure of control, and he managed a deep breath as he looked at the surroundings one final time. He wasn't going to stick around. He had some reservations about going back, but he still had to go. Because otherwise, this land would ruin his mind, if not also his body.

There was a risk in returning to Elmhurst, but more than an hour and a half had passed. So, he would have to hope that the dangerous elements had left the scene and he wasn't being hasty in getting out of here.

If that priest or whatever was still waiting for him, Vern might as well go down in a last-ditch effort with his newfound visions and sights. At least there was a chance of survival out there.

Here? It was hopeless.

That thing beyond the horizon was a star greater than his whole planet for fuck's sake, and who knew if something even more profound was at play here? Where did all these eyes come from? Was some central entity controlling them? He didn't want to know.

However, now that he had managed to calm down a little, he noticed something peculiar about his environment. Other than the eyes, obviously.

There was a pattern. A spiral. And when he followed it to its ends, he realized that he was in the center of that spiral. Its one end was quite a distance away, ceasing at the tip of that pyramid's peak, which was now half-disintegrated.

What does this mean? He felt like there should be a simple explanation for this, but that gaze from the sky was always in the back of his mind. He had a hard time thinking with such a—

Wait. He had an idea. A good one too. Maybe he was not that scared, after all. *Those notions that poured into my thought space . . . Where did they come from?*

Surely, they had a source, right? Then was this the aftermath of that? Had he assimilated all those buildings and the pyramid into his thought space? Maybe not their physical aspects, but their representation? Is that how one shaded their perception?

It felt like a logical assumption. How could one evolve and surpass their human selves—gaining extraordinary command over the world without consuming some sort of resource? Surely, observation worked on some kind of law of conservation.

If everyone could shade their perception without a cost to the world, it would imply infinite energy. That was not the case. Never. At least he hadn't seen it happen.

Could this be the reason this eye had awakened? To punish him for his transgressions in consuming this land's resource? But he disregarded that thought the very next moment. He really wasn't important enough in the grand scheme of things. Something else—

And then, in his peripheral vision—he saw it. The horrifying scene. The sun blinked. Just once, a slow, deliberate motion that sent a fresh wave of terror crashing over him. It was a confirmation of his worst fears—that this was no illusion, no trick of the mind, but a sentient being of immeasurable power and inscrutable intent.

The blink shattered the fragile veneer of calm he had clung to. It was not just the sight of that cosmic eye but the feeling that came with it—a sense of insignificance so profound that it threatened to erase his very sense of self.

He was an ant under the magnifying glass of a child, an infinitesimal speck about to be burned into nothingness by a curiosity without empathy.

Not wanting to push his luck any more, he did it. He ceased the trickle of thoughts that consciously connected him to the rune in his mind. He would deal with whatever was in Elmhurst as it came. This was so far beyond him, it wasn't even a joke.

Why is it taking so long? He was definitely exiting this realm, maybe even turning immaterial this very second.

But it wasn't fast enough!

Then the eye in the sky blinked again, and a pulse of unseen energy radiated outward. It was not a dramatic flare—no thunderous declaration of its might—it was subtle, almost a whisper, yet it carried the force to unmake worlds.

The ground beneath him didn't just shake—it disintegrated, grains of reality coming undone like sand against an unrelenting tide. The plethora of eyes around him bent, their shapes warping as if reality itself were a reflection in a funhouse mirror.

It wasn't destruction with intent. It was destruction as a consequence. The eye's gaze, indifferent and sweeping, was like a laser passing over delicate film, leaving only a void in its wake. The world didn't scream—it simply ceased to be, piece by piece, an unmaking of existence that paid no heed to what was caught in its view.

As his consciousness finally slipped away, the last thing he saw was the horizon itself peeling back, the sky and earth curling away like the pages of a burning book, consumed by knowledge too vast to be contained.

Huff.
  Puff.
  Huff.
  Puff.

The moment he felt sensible enough to breathe, he inhaled large mouthfuls of air, his heart still ramming against his chest—almost seeming to want to escape it. *What the hell happened there . . . ?*

In a couple more breaths, his body keeled over on its own, and he shivered intensely, trying his best to regain his faculties.

But his body didn't listen to him.

Vern had felt that destructive energy pass by him. One second. If he had hesitated for even one more second, he would've been nothing more than ash swept up in unfelt winds in that desolate world. His very existence would've been wiped clean.

He had long since accepted that he was nothing but a speck of dust in this unfeeling cosmos, but a reminder like that didn't feel good. It—

"What the fuck, newbie?! Where'd you come from? Nah, never mind, just RUN! Forget the chicks and get out of there. Captain can't contain this one completely. You'll be buried alive."

The words sent another jolt through him, and his mind reeled. *That . . . ? Is he not dead?* That was Ambrose's voice, wasn't it? But that can't be right.

Nevertheless, the content of those words was too significant for him to pass up as a hallucination. Gritting his teeth hard, he stabilized himself and stood up. *No rest for the wicked.*

And when he looked up, that sentiment was only further solidified. *Back to square one, huh?* He chuckled, almost with a dark amusement.

When he had escaped, an impossible attack was looming over them like a reaper. Now that he was back and expecting safety, another, even more destructive attack was hurling toward him.

A gigantic spiral bursting with golden radiance drilled toward them from the heavens with a ferocious momentum. It was like one of those depictions of dragons, but very real and very lethal. It distorted the air wherever it passed through—its destructive might clear for all to see. But in its path stood a man on a . . . cloth. *Isn't that . . .*

But now wasn't the time to question what that shaggy swordsman was doing here. Ambrose had insinuated that Cera and Esther were alive. A simple look at his surroundings confirmed the fact—Cera was lying unconscious next to some rubble, whereas Esther held her head and was curled into a ball.

His brain almost failed to process it. *How could this be? There's no way they survived this onslaught for over an hour. Did the fight shift to another battlefield before the radiant man managed to pull it back here?*

Many conjectures clashed with one another in his mind, but he ruthlessly quashed all the unnecessary questions. Cera and Esther weren't dead, but they would be in a few seconds if he didn't do something about it.

Carrying them out of the building wasn't an option, given how that golden spiral was closing in at an alarming pace. Maybe Ambrose could have done it with his dashes, but a look at him told Vern that he was busy in his own battle—chasing a white-robed man out of the building.

This only firmed Vern's resolve. He would have to take charge this time. He was done escaping this fight—no one was going to be buried in this damned station. He had just shaded his perception with a vision related to stability, for fuck's sake. It'd weigh down his conscience too much if he didn't give it his best shot.

So, he rapidly analyzed the attack and its possible effects. Ambrose said the swordsman would try to contain *this one* but might be unable to do so thoroughly. The phrasing suggested that the previous attack, which had elicited Vern to flee into the third rune, was thwarted by the swordsman too.

And given how the station was mostly unharmed except for some of the holes from before, he must have had a formidable defense. Compared to the previous attack, it wouldn't be a stretch to assume that the swordsman could handle the brunt of this attack.

Because if that spiral came for them, there was nothing he could do about it. He didn't understand what the spiral was, much less its structure or weakness, to induce instability in it. So, countering it outright was out of the question.

His new sight might help, but he didn't think it was a great idea to pit himself against someone who probably had far more representation than himself. There was also the problem of it being hard to observe when something was already being manipulated by another observer.

Left with only one option of holding his ground, he peered into his perception with nothing in particular as the keyword.

That was a mistake, and he shut it back down right away.

Because in that short instant, his blindingly bright thought space dimmed a little, and he managed to glean almost nothing from the mess of grays—wasting the sight. But this made him wonder, *Could the brightness of my thought space be a measure of my representation?*

It sure looked like it. But then he shook his head and instead worked out the specifics of what had to be done.

A plan soon took shape in his mind, factoring in all the extraordinary visions and sights at his disposal. He had long imagined the possible uses of stability induce-ment, and now was the time to be creative.

Once he filled in the gaps in his plan with all the details, he felt ready to exploit the heck out of his perception. And it was about damn time too.

Harmony and disharmony.

His surroundings fractured into a tapestry of grays and silvers—the harmony and disharmony of the structure around him becoming as clear as day and night. Intact sections of the ceiling glowed with a resolute silver sheen, indicative of their unyielding strength, while the cracked pillars bled with darker shades, signaling their desperate need for stability.

So, his conjectures were indeed right. His thought space was a tool of permanence, immortalizing the insights he had gleaned in the past. He didn't need to assign the gray to everything by himself anymore—though he felt like he could still do it if he wanted to. Just as it should be.

Mentally noting the current state of the building, he moved on.

Fulcrums.

His focus narrowed, and the world seemed to lose shape. Each beam, each stone, now sported a directional gradient that pointed toward the sections that held the building aloft. The fulcrums, the critical points that bore the weight of architecture, shone brightly like stars in a dark space. These were the key points that needed to be protected when push came to shove. Because if they broke, a collapse would be imminent.

What else? The intense beating of his heart resounded in his ears alongside the shrieks generated by the traversal of that golden spiral. It was almost upon them. The swordsman's silhouette cut a lean figure against the chaos, hand poised on the hilt of his blade, ready to draw from its sheath in a swift, defining move.

Time to maintain balance. He had deduced the critical points that had to be stabilized to maintain an equilibrium. He still had to extrapolate the balance in the rest of the building, but he would wait till the last moment to do that—making optimal use of his representation.

So, this was all he could do to prepare in the limited time available to him, and hopefully, it would be enough.

"Newbie . . . no, Vern! Get out of there, man! Don't be stupid."

Unfazed, Vern focused harder, eyes narrowing on the advancing threat. "Trust me," he thundered, voice steady as an oak tree, "I have a plan."

CHAPTER 68

DEFENSE

Clang!

An earth-shattering collision resounded as the swordsman executed the smoothest quick draw Vern had ever seen. The spinning spiral of radiant light seemed to bend, drawn to the edge of the swordsman's blade, altering its course to collide directly.

This must be his vision, right? Deflecting light isn't physically possible. That seemed like the only reasonable explanation.

Yet Vern's job remained unchanged. The spiral drilled toward them, whirling with terrifying momentum. A single deflection wouldn't suffice against a continuous stream of light like this one that was poised to obliterate everything in its path.

Vern watched the spiral intently, aware that even a stray fragment from it could devastate the entire station.

Clang!

Ring!

Metal clashed upon metal as the swordsman sliced the energy into segments, flinging them aside to where they dissipated quickly. All the while, he laughed. "Hahhahhaha, my friend. You had me waiting eagerly for . . . this? I expected more. I know you have more. Show me what you've got! Unleash the sins your Asea so desired. Reveal your true strength!"

A thundering voice retorted, "STOP SULLYING HER NAME WITH YOUR VILE TONGUE!"

And as if reacting to the swordsman's provocation, the lighting arrangement changed. A single giant spiral multiplied—first to five, then ten, and finally, an overwhelming barrage of a hundred spirals spun menacingly above.

"Ugh," Vern groaned under his breath. Madness seemed to be a common trait among everyone fighting in here.

He wanted to scold the swordsman for his reckless taunts as the weaker party, yet he couldn't deny the strategy's cunning. Forcing an enemy to play their hand prematurely was indeed clever. Handling this barrage would have been impossible if it had appeared when the massive spiral was closer to the station.

With a smirk, the swordsman moved with the speed of lightning, darting through the barrage and reflecting spirals into the void. He leapt from the cloth platform, defying gravity to stand at another similar platform suspended in midair—an odd yet seamless maneuver that helped him clear the spirals.

However, Vern, observing with a mix of awe and anxiety, knew it wouldn't be enough. The swordsman's speed was unmatched, but the spirals were relentless and far too numerous.

He observed the spectacle with bated breath, and it didn't take long before his fears materialized. A cluster of a dozen or so spirals advanced together, heading straight for one of the whistles atop the station.

The swordsman intercepted them just in time, deflecting nine before he had to pivot to the next wave, allowing three to slip through his guard, lest it cause relatively more damage.

A white gleam sparked in Vern's eyes as he braced himself. Leaning against a pillar, he exuded calm, a stark contrast to his racing mind. *Now's the time.*

He couldn't see most of the upper floor clearly because his only window to the outer world was this gigantic hole that ran through all the floors of the station. To preserve the building's integrity, he had to extend his perception to its entirety.

His perception that was now observing the balance of stability only assigned grays to the world in his line of sight. Anything beyond that, he only had one option—interpret it manually.

He recalled the upper floor's layout—the rooms, the piping network, the roofs, the pillars, and its structure in general. For their stability, he guessed at their current condition, inferring it by drawing parallels between similar structures down here.

He assigned darker shades of gray to the rooms and pillars that should be on the verge of collapse and lighter shades to those unharmed. And surprisingly, his perception was like a sponge that absorbed his ideas liberally, even assisting him in the process.

He was hoping this mental map of grays, even if just an estimation of reality right now, would update and reflect the effect those radiant whorls would have on the whole structure. That way, he would have a far easier time reacting to the changes in the situation.

This whole process seemed like something he could have set up beforehand, but this increased range came at a cost he didn't want to pay unless necessary. Who knew how long this fight would take?

He could feel the intensity of his thoughts within the thought space wane. It was a gradual drain right now, but he knew it would accumulate, possibly leading to his usual affliction—bleeding from the eyes.

He didn't want that.

Boom.

And here it comes. One of the spirals drilled through the roof of the station. From its trajectory, it was evident that it would hit one of the pillars in the hall upstairs, causing massive damage. The other two would be crashing through mostly unimportant sections of the building.

Vern had resigned himself to the sacrifice of the roof and other nonessential structures. They were expendable. His focus had to be the fulcrums—the true supports of the station. With this in mind, he concentrated on the imperiled pillar, currently represented by a silver-gray shade in his mind, indicating its stability.

Krrrrr.

The spirals pierced the roof effortlessly, their lengths diminishing as they penetrated deeper. Vern braced for the imminent change in the pillar's condition.

The moment the tip of the spiral touched the pillar, a dark aura spread around the point of impact, which soon turned into a sickening darkness. If left unchecked, it would break and shatter the whole thing in a second.

Narrowing his eyes, he whispered, "Stability inducement."

For the first time, he understood what happened under the hood when his mind raced through ideas on the execution of a vision. A particular thought in his thought space ignited, followed by another, then hundreds more, a chain reaction like lightning streaking across a nocturnal cityscape.

In his perception, however, the darkness that spread on the surface of the pillar like some plague retreated—replaced by a healthy white glow. Though, it didn't last long.

Because this was a continuous battle. He would have to defend against the spiral until it expended all its fuel. So a path of lightning shone in his thought space, repeatedly activating all those thought nodes that could induce stability in a pillar.

Whirrrr.

The once fierce golden drill faded as its energy was consumed fruitlessly.

Krr.

As the spiral's energy was finally depleted, Vern exhaled and allowed himself a moment of respite. The pillar stood mostly whole, save for a small section that had been eroded too swiftly for his power to restore.

But by all means, this was a win in his books.

"Hahhahha, my sinner friend, what's this? You can't breach the defenses of a literal child?" the swordsman taunted while effortlessly nullifying another spiral.

"You've yet to leave a mark on me, heathen. Your only skill is cowering, like a turtle in its shell. We'll see who has the last laugh," Quentin retorted.

Amid their caustic exchange, Ambrose added fuel to the fire with a taunt of his own. "Hahaha, mad because bad, eh? Sweet religious fool."

Vern pressed a hand to his forehead, fighting the urge to demand silence from both belligerents. Taunting the enemy seemed pointless—any psychological edge gained was not worth the risk of provoking a reckless and potentially devastating response. Fortunately, the enemy appeared preoccupied with the spirals, or they would have seized the opportunity for a deadly counterattack.

Tuning out the unhelpful jibes of his allies, Vern focused on the spirals' trajectories, relieved that the next wave was still some distance away. This gave him a moment to evaluate the damage caused by the other drills.

One had already punctured the basement ceiling and was now gouging the earth below—no mystery there. And, as he had hoped, even the areas outside his line of sight shifted in response to external forces turning grayer where there was more damage.

He checked the stability of the mail storage room's cabinets—they were a mess, but none of it compromised the structural fulcrums. To confirm, he visualized the fulcrums yet again.

This time, the upper floor was also included, and once he confirmed the tension points were unaffected, he swiftly dismissed the unnecessary visual aids.

The third spiral had unexpectedly met its end against a container of cranksteel. *Unsurprising,* Vern thought, *nothing gets through cranksteel—not without a hell of a fight.*

Nevertheless, this was great. This small victory quelled some of his daylong insecurities and guilt. His new vision had proved itself, and though they weren't out of danger yet, he'd contributed to their survival.

It helped him assuage some of that built-up regret and gain some much-needed confidence. He didn't understand how everyone had managed to survive the initial onslaught, but they had, and that's all that mattered right now.

Just then, the swordsman missed a pair of spirals, calling out, "Heads up, buddy! I'm passing these to you—no free meals on our watch, eh?"

Vern didn't respond. He wasn't going to participate in the taunting of their enemy, though he did appreciate the humor. It went a long way in calming him down.

The first will strike the arch, which could collapse the entire room if destroyed. The second . . . it won't impact anything above but will shatter the basement's retaining wall.

Standing taller, Vern drew a deep breath and prepared himself for the simultaneous onslaught. The archway was struck first, the darkness of instability spreading like spiderwebs, threatening collapse. But a single pulse of his stability inducement denied any such events from coming to pass.

Luckily, he just had to use the vision in bursts, not continuously, or he would have faced immense trouble stabilizing multiple impact points.

However, something changed when the other spiral penetrated the basement ceiling. It shifted its course—heading straight for Vern. *He's controlling them,* he realized.

While repeatedly inducing stability in the archway upstairs, he dodged the divine attack with a wide leap—the spiral unable to change its course in time.

However, before he could revel in his own deftness, he noticed its trajectory. It didn't need to change its course, he now understood as his heart sunk at the realization, *Esther is the true target.*

"Fuck!" He cursed out aloud and ran toward her with all his might. He knew it would be futile. Regardless, he didn't stop. He might still be able to get her out of there alive, even if it meant a lost hand or a foot for her.

But that's when a mirthful bellow added itself to the mix from Vern's left. "Not so fast, you old fuck," yelled Ambrose with a hearty chuckle, whizzing past Vern in a blue flash, halting right in front of Esther.

There he tapped his cane on the ground, which led to the emergence of subtle waves even in Vern's stability sight. But that was just a side effect. As if utterly disrupted, the vigorously spinning spiral rushing toward Esther lost all its momentum and dissipated into nothingness.

Vern nodded solemnly at Ambrose and went back to ensuring that the other drill didn't play any tricks on them. He was delighted when Ambrose jumped back in to help them, though he was still irked by the unnecessary taunting.

Fortunately, that gigantic singular spiral hadn't been under the radiant man's direct control, or it would have been a disaster. Or maybe the limitation was different in nature. Maybe it was even possible that he could only control a few at a time, and the rest had to be left to their own devices.

However, Vern soon found his assumptions challenged. Their enemy was adapting to the swordsman's tactic, and all the spirals moved closer to one another. Just enough so that the swordsman couldn't handle them with a single deflect, but it made his job relatively harder.

So their foe could indeed move them, but there had to be limitations, or the first spiral wouldn't have stupidly continued drilling an impossible pillar.

However, he had a bigger problem than that right now. The swordsman tried his best, moving so fast it made it seem like he was disappearing and reappearing at other spirals up in the sky. But there were too many this time.

Five of the spirals managed to sneak past the swordsman, and he chortled. "Get them, boys. I trust you." He moved on to another cluster. Vern didn't understand where the swordsman's confidence in them came from, but he had no intentions of failing anyway.

"By that, he meant you. I still have a rat to deal with. He's too fucking slippery, if you ask me." Ambrose let these words hang in the air as he dashed back to where he'd come from.

Vern grunted and focused on the incoming barrage. It was going to be tough to stabilize five spots all at once, even when the spirals weren't actively finding targets. Now that there was a chance they could move? He would have to hope that he was better at adapting to changes than their foe in the air.

The first one was going to barrel through one end of the station and out the other, but it would hit multiple beams in the process. He would have to stop this one no matter what.

Two were gunning for the odd edges of some random rooms. The fourth seemed like it wouldn't hit anything critical.

The last one, however, was primed to drill a hole in the engine room. That one was too risky to not be nullified preemptively. A little bit of friction on some odd chemicals could lead to a massive explosion in no time. *Yeah, I will have to hold that one down earlier in its path.*

Just as Vern prepared to act, an anomaly in his perception caught his attention. It was very minor, even negligible—two ripples of a slightly darker shade in an otherwise uniform silver-gray patch of the floor above him. But he wouldn't have noticed it if that's all it was.

That pair of ripples . . . moved. Every moment that passed, they inched forward, almost as if step-by-step—heading straight toward Vern. There was no sound or any other clue, but he was more than sure his perception wasn't deceiving him.

A sharp glint appeared in his eyes as he arrived at the only logical conclusion. *Someone's trying to sneak up on me.*

They like to surprise people, eh? Hope they like getting surprised too.

CHAPTER 69

COOPERATION

A*surprise attack?*

It couldn't have happened at a worse time. Five of those spirals were on their way to decimate the station, one wall at a time.

Vern had to pick his battles. Either he could nullify this assassination by changing positions while keeping the station perfectly secure, or he could go on the offensive and risk losing some of the essential structures.

The latter seemed like the better option. *An intelligent human is far more dangerous than predictable attacks.* This realization settled it. After a short deliberation, he figured out how to approach his offense.

Closing his eyes, he emptied his perception, and the grayscale view of the station's stability floating in his mind fizzled, giving way to complete darkness. For offense, he only had one option.

Complexity.

Instability might have been another keyword that could work well, but he hadn't practiced with it beforehand. This wasn't a situation where he could risk trying out new concepts, so he stuck to his tried and tested methods.

The sight of complexity was interesting. Because of the sophisticated encoding devices in his line of sight that burned too bright, the roof above him was almost as dark as every other wall in the room.

But he didn't have the time to tease out and comprehend every little nuance of the observation right now. He had an assassin to deal with.

And deal he would. There was no room for mercy or pity. Not here, not right now. Even a little compassion in this situation could spell everyone's doom.

Less than a second passed before his perception stopped changing, and he focused above himself, a little to the left. There, he envisioned a shift in the balance and a large flaw in the structure.

He couldn't sense the shuffle of his steps anymore, but he was sure the assassin would be right there according to his walking speed. Ensuring he had envisioned all the details correctly, he gripped his revolver tight and decreed to himself, *instability inducement.*

A rectangular seam appeared in the balance of the roof, and the seam grew larger and larger until—

Crash!

A torrent of dust and debris came hurtling down, but he stood his ground and stared at the plummeting wreckage with an unwavering gaze. The moment a white cloth entered his sight, he steadied his shoulder, extended his arm straight forward, and—

Bang!

Crimson blood spurted out of the falling body, dying his vision red. Everything was happening too fast, so, to be entirely certain, he resolved to be liberal with the bullets and pulled the trigger—

Bang!

The revolver's chamber rotated once more—

Bang!

But this was where balance demanded he stop. Overcommitting would do more harm than good. If the station was destroyed beyond repair because he wasted time shooting a corpse, then that would be utterly stupid.

So, he chose not to inspect the aftermath of his ruthless assault and moved away from the body. He didn't have the time to contemplate murder right now anyway.

With a single thought, he wiped his perception clean of instability and observed stability once again. This time, the population of grays was instant. He didn't even need to manually assign the shades to the floor above—it just remembered.

However, a solemn expression overtook his face as he surveyed the current state of affairs. *It's only been a dozen seconds. How the hell—*

Whirrrrrr.

The whole building shook, and the foundation quivered violently, sending shivers through the concrete and steel. Overhead, timbers groaned, a cacophony of snaps and cracks heralding their demise.

The grayscale view of the whole building had turned a shade darker, while some of its structures were well on their way to turning pitch black.

Simultaneously, two of the drills lit up his physical sight, radiating with their ghastly golden glow, wreckage trailing behind. Anything they touched turned to ashes in no time.

Fuck me.

This wasn't done. He had to stop this. Right now.

Taking a deep breath, he anchored himself in the moment and focused on all the vital points that were in bad shape. If not entirely stable, he could at least stop them from causing cascading changes that could bring down the whole station.

The first order of action was stabilizing that tanker in the engine room. If given even another few seconds, the last spiral from the batch would spark a disastrous explosion in there.

Without a moment's delay, he channeled pulses of stability inducement toward the tanker, reinforcing the structure where a disastrous puncture was imminent.

Fortunately, it took to his efforts and soon turned stable enough for him to focus elsewhere.

Next, he surmised it was better to patch up the vital points rather than prevent the third drill from destroying some medium-priority structures.

Right. He nodded to himself, making one snap decision after another.

With methodical precision, he turned his thoughts to the building's skeleton, infusing the beams and pillars teetering on the verge of collapse with pulses of stability.

Soon, he found himself cycling between six or seven key points. Some were in pretty bad condition, losing their brilliance even though he stabilized them consistently.

Gravity and tension were a bitch for damaged key points, deteriorating their condition almost as fast as he fixed them. But he did have the upper hand. He would just need to keep this up for a while.

Beads of sweat formed on his forehead as he pushed his mind to its limits, ensuring nothing went wrong. Then, suddenly, he heard something—

Crunch.

Crackle.

That pile of debris, which was supposed to house his murder victim . . . shifted. Vern snapped toward it involuntarily, his brows furrowed. He somehow kept up those pulses of stability, but his mind was already wandering elsewhere.

What is this? He couldn't wrap his head around this situation. *How can someone survive that?*

The blood pooling around the wreckage was enough to fill half a man. There was no way someone should be alive after losing that much blood. But logic wasn't prevailing.

Thud.

The slab of concrete was thrown away with an intense force as a figure sat up in the rubble.

"Mother . . ." came a whisper. Regardless of Vern's conjectures, the figure slowly stood up, blood flowing out of his shin, exposed intestines, and . . . neck. *That should've ended him, no?*

But then Vern noticed something peculiar. The figure was tightly clutching a small vial to his mouth, gulping down its contents with intense fervor.

Suddenly, it happened. A disturbingly familiar scene unfolded before him, reminiscent of an experience he had encountered under vastly different circumstances.

Last time, it was a devotee on stage, surrounded by hundreds of onlookers, weeping and singing hymns in praise of Mother Asea while drinking what they claimed were her tears. The macabre spectacle of limbs regrowing had etched itself indelibly in his memory. He was sure this was the same.

The figure's body, just seconds ago riddled with see-through holes, began a rapid transformation. Red tissues swarmed the gaps, weaving and fusing in a chaotic dance. Skin stitched itself together right before Vern's eyes, sealing the wounds. Blood flow slowed to a stop, and the figure's ghostly pallor blossomed into a healthy, flushed glow.

Fuck! Vern cursed as he stared at this hellish sight and contemplated its implications. Even more unfortunate was the fact that he could do nothing but stand here as his foe recovered to full health.

He didn't have the luxury to divert his attention too much. A single slipup and a huge explosion would be the outcome. He just had to hold on for a while longer until that spiral ran itself dry.

For now, he couldn't even shoot the fucking ghoul. He would mess up his stability cycle, and something would come crashing and burning down by the time he would reload his revolver and aim it at the man.

Not that it would have done much either, with his poor aim and this guy's healing capabilities.

"AH, MOTHER ASEA! Your sorrow won't be wasted! I shall preserve your decree! DIE, HEATHEN!" exclaimed the assassin as he sprinted toward Vern, throwing the vial to the side, completely empty.

Fucking lunatics, one and all.

Vern couldn't deal with this guy, at least not while keeping the building stabilized. So he chose the only sensible approach—call for backup. "Ambrose! I could use some help right about now," he shouted.

A blue light flared from another room, followed by Ambrose's voice. "Another one of these rat-arsed bastards? How the hell are they hiding from my rhythm so effectively? They are nothing like regular humans, man."

Almost immediately, a bloodcurdling scream echoed from the same room. Over it, Ambrose yelled, "You've got to come up with something, Vern. I am all out of ideas. These rat-fucks are too resilient. Every time I think I've taken him down, the cunt gets right back up."

And then another blue flash later, Ambrose stood in front of the assassin, thrusting his cane into the man's head.

Clang.

But a golden dagger appeared in the assassin's hand out of nowhere as he deflected Ambrose's thrust and backed away, joining the other zealot. He had walked over from the other room, the hole in his chest healing rapidly.

"In the name of MOTHER ASEA!" shouted both in unison, their eyes bloodshot and faces contorted.

"I told you, didn't I, newbie? These cunts are undying fucks. Think of something, I'll keep 'em busy."

Well, that was a lot of responsibility to offload to a *newbie*. But what other choice did Vern have? As if he didn't have enough problems already.

His dimming thought space was the worst of them. Having a thought space exponentially increased his maximum representation capacity, but sending those pulses of stability so frequently was squeezing him dry.

Then there were all these unstable fulcrums—*Huh?*

But just then, the rapidly spreading instability in the wall of the tanker began to slow, and that could only mean one thing—the spiral drilling it was on its last legs!

One second.

Two seconds.

The third—

And it was over. *Phew . . .* Vern exhaled sharply, relieved. He still continued stabilizing a few other vital points, but they were improving too and didn't demand as much concentration.

Now, with a moment to think, he could focus on the problem at hand. *I have my gun, umbrella, and the stability-instability inducement.* How could he leverage these tools to permanently deal with those men?

For starters, Vern tried to observe the white-robed figures directly. If he could cause some grave instability within their bodies, dealing with them should be a walk in the park.

However, his efforts hit an unexpected roadblock—they were a complete failure. *Huh?*

The resistance he encountered was astonishing. It had been easier to try to observe the golden spirals than these people. And he soon had a conjecture of why this was the case.

Because he was trying to observe an observer.

An observer transcends objective reality, embodying a unique, subjective representation of the world. They weren't like humans in the way he perceived them to be. It made sense then—since Vern didn't fully understand them, he couldn't effectively observe them.

This also meant it would be nigh impossible for him to directly manipulate an observer. But this would have to go both ways, meaning he would be safe from being turned into a golden spiral or something along those lines as long as they didn't understand his viewpoint.

Anyway, what else? He looked around him in search of ideas. If he couldn't harm them directly, he would have to find indirect ways to do so. *Burst a pipe in front of them? Collapse the roof? Or maybe . . .* a spark of inspiration flickered in his mind.

"Ambrose, lend me your ear for a second."

The cane wielder glanced back with an incredulous look. Vern met his gaze, his expression grave and unwavering.

Tap.

Ambrose drove his cane into the thigh of a zealot and, in a flash of blue, appeared next to Vern, facing the opposite direction. "This better be good, newbie. I can appreciate humor, but don't mistake that for a free pass to order me around."

Vern sighed inwardly. It was hard for him to even move without fucking something up; humor was the furthest thing from his mind.

So, in a tone devoid of emotion, he replied, "It's serious. Do you think you can redirect those spiral drills in a particular direction? You did something along those lines back when Esther was inside the shield, right?"

"Esther? Who?"

Why was that the first thing that came to his mind in this situation? Vern gestured toward the red-haired beauty who was lying in a fetal position, and a look of realization dawned on Ambrose.

"You really think I am that stupid, huh? Do you think I didn't try? Uh . . . I mean, I tried with the big one. It was—too big. Oh fuck, you're right. These small ones, I might—" He stammered a little before he tapped his cane, and a blue aura rose around him. "Well, you handle the rat-fucks, okay? I need some time to set up the disruption field."

Vern nodded, a hint of smirk on his face as he left a few final words with Ambrose. "Let me know when you're ready. I will try to get them to stand under that biggest hole right there."

Ambrose nodded, followed by a tap of his cane.

That was acknowledgment enough. Vern took a deep breath and gave up on stabilizing the building. Most drills had already done the damage, and his efforts of stabilizing damaged key points had already reached the limits of their effectiveness.

On top of that, he would need everything in his arsenal to fend off these zealots.

Without hesitation, he dashed toward Cera. Still engaged in his peculiar tap dance, Ambrose shot him a perplexed look but didn't stop.

Why Cera? Well, because she possessed a better weapon. His revolver was out of bullets. *Why reload when you can upgrade?*

Luckily, the vapor blaster was still in her hands, so he didn't have to touch her inappropriately to look for it. Snatching it out of her hands, he switched it to concussive shots since they had the highest rate of fire.

"Preserve their souls! Let them unite with the Mother!" The white-robed zealots' chant echoed as they charged toward Ambrose.

"Preserve them!" they bellowed in unison.

As the cries for preservation filled the air, Vern felt a surge of adrenaline mixed with a twinge of nerves. Clutching the vapor blaster, he knew it was his moment.

Now's the chance to balance the scale—no more sitting by the sidelines.

CHAPTER 70

ART OF BALANCED COMBAT

Both zealots rushed toward Ambrose with twisted smiles since he was closer to them. Vern couldn't let that happen. If direct attacks were out of the question, he would stick with indirect ones.

He observed the network of pipes running through the basement. Some were connected to the ceiling, while others stood tall, even if broken and battered.

Regardless, this was more than enough for him to work with. Picking one of the largest standing pipes on the path of the fanatics, he envisioned—

Instability inducement.

Bam!

A pipe thicker than his whole body and probably a dozen times heavier lost its support as the bolts holding it down came loose. The metallic behemoth plummeted, ramming directly into the shoulder of one of the zealots—almost crushing him.

The second attacker dodged in time, twisting midair to face Vern and hurling a golden dagger at him.

Vern, grounded in a stable stance, yanked back his right leg and arched his upper body, barely dodging the golden streak that zipped past him, sending his heart into overdrive.

Luckily, the adrenaline or something was keeping him sharp, and there was enough distance between them. Or this would've been the end of the line.

I really need to get my shit together. My physical strength and hand-eye coordination is piss-poor.

Extrapolating from his experiences of the last few days, he would be dead sooner or later if he didn't change his ways in this department.

Jumping from cover to cover, he resolved to himself, *If I survive today, I have to get myself in shape.* For now, he would have to deal with it.

Leaving no room for his enemies to breathe, he destabilized one pipe after another, even releasing some of the valves on them as steam came gushing in bursts.

It singed their flesh and charred the skin, but all they shouted was, "MOTHER ASEA! Preserve thy flesh, for ye shalt preserve this heathen," and the burns scabbed in no time and fell off, smooth skin visible beneath them.

The fuck is inside those tears? he wondered with morbid curiosity. Both zealots had firmly turned their attention to him, ignoring Ambrose entirely. Just the way he wanted it to be.

One of them charged toward him like a mad bull while the other recovered from the earlier shock and knelt. Clasping his hands together, he chanted something, and a golden glow soon enveloped him.

It seemed like Vern had been underestimating them. They did know how to use strategies and visions. It was weird that they hadn't bombarded Ambrose already. *Or Ambrose never gave them a chance.* This, however, definitely looked like preparation for some vision.

So Vern switched his perception back to stability and prepared to defend himself from anything that might come.

However, just at that moment, the eyes of the attacker charging at him glowed golden, and a similar aura surrounded his foot.

In an instant, his next step covered ten, and he was almost upon Vern—a twisted smile on his face and a dagger in hand.

Fuck.

A golden sheen appeared on the man's forearm, and he swung the dagger in what seemed like a blur.

Swish.

The dagger sliced through the entire pillar Vern had taken as cover, and he narrowly escaped being cut himself.

The situation was escalating rapidly.

He had to do something. Right now. Using a gun was hardly feasible without a proper opening. It was impossible for him to shoot them from afar because of his trashy aim, whereas up close, the man's speed surpassed Vern's reaction time.

So, if no opportunity to strike presented itself, I'll have to create one, he thought, his eyes narrowing at the zealot, who swung in a full circle and propelled himself toward Vern with increased momentum.

A plan quickly formed in Vern's mind, and he hid behind another similar pillar. The man flashed a toothy grin and, utilizing another golden step, repeated the previous attack.

Exactly the same movements and pattern. *Foolish.*

Stability Inducement.

Clank.

The dagger, which had previously cut through the pillar like a hot knife through butter, was forced to a halt mere moments after it began its intended cut.

Vern stabilized the pillar so rapidly that the dagger didn't budge even when the man almost dislocated his shoulder. Soon, the crevice created by the slash filled in, firmly trapping the dagger within the pillar.

"Ugh," grunted the man, channeling more power into the dagger as it glowed brighter.

Got you.

A smile spread across Vern's face as he aimed his vapor blaster directly at the man's head. The man, straining to retrieve his dagger from the pillar, was oblivious. Then, without a flicker of hesitation, Vern fired the gun at point-blank range.

Bang!

A hole ripped through the man's skull, and his eyes rolled as he slumped down to the ground. But Vern didn't have the time to confirm the kill or press his advantage.

A stream of what could only be called golden stars was rushing toward him, ripping through everything in its path. This must be the vision of the other zealot, who had stopped to pray.

Vern was ready. Retreating farther, he found himself a neat little enclosure, a cabin of sorts. The health of the walls in terms of stability was perfect. It was just what he needed to defend against something like this.

When those stars attacked from all over, he focused on the perfectly white and stable walls in his perception and ensured they didn't change their shade even a little.

Each one of those stars ground against the walls, but they barely managed to nick it before they fizzled away into nothingness. These were . . . weak. Compared to the spirals he had dealt with, these were nothing.

Unfortunately, the stream was relentless, and the first zealot soon stood back up—the hole in his head nothing but a small mark now. It almost looked like some divine sigil rather than a bullet wound.

Vern needed another strategy for the ranged guy. If he continued to hide in here, the melee zealot would mow him down sooner or later.

So he wondered if there was some way for him to use a mobile shield. But nothing in here would work. The only reason he managed to exhaust the energy within these projectiles was because of the thickness of the walls.

If the object was thin enough to be pierced in a single strike, there was nothing stability inducement could do about it. Its fundamental capability to create wasn't as good as maintaining structure.

What else? His mind raced anxiously. He could maybe run in a direction where the walls would always shield him? *But no, he can just curve them around the obstructions. That wouldn't work.*

Nonetheless, something out of the norm happened. The melee fanatic growled at Vern from afar, extended his palms, and clawed at the ground. Vern was perplexed beyond measure. *What the fuck is he doing?*

Wham!

But he realized in the next moment. A tremor ran through the ground, and sharp golden blades jutted out of it, rushing toward his legs like some grinder.

The walls could do nothing to protect him this time. The blades had appeared mere inches away from his foot. By the time his brain registered it, he didn't know what the fuck to do.

In a panic, he jumped and managed to dodge two of the sliding blades, but the last one was going to chop his leg right down the middle. *Fuck! Fuck! Fuck!* This was too damned sudden.

But his brain churned, and an idea he had fiddled with previously crossed his mind. Observing the stability of his leg's skin, he envisioned it to remain as bright as possible. But before he could imagine all the details, it came.

"AHHH!"

He let out a scream and keeled over, slumping against the wall, blood pouring out of his sliced shin. His stabilized foot had exhausted most of the blade's momentum, but he couldn't manage to protect his shin in time.

It left a deep wound in his shin, ripping through the skin, flesh, and even a bit of the bone. But he counted himself lucky it ended there.

His head felt light, and it hurt like hell, but stopping the bleeding was his priority. Gritting his teeth, he wiped the sweat from his forehead and observed the gash on his shin under the lens of stability.

A thin black line of instability in his otherwise gray leg.

Stabilize.

"AHHHH!"

Clutching his wounded leg tightly, he unleashed a bloodcurdling scream. The vision realized his imagination by stretching the skin around the wound to seal it. His sight blurred, and pain threatened to overwhelm him, yet he persevered through the agony.

When the bleeding stopped, he smacked the wall and stood back up. He couldn't rest. Not yet. In the pain, he had lost control of the walls, and a couple of golden stars managed to cut through them, whizzing past his head and coming out the opposite wall.

But that wasn't the end. There was a whole wave of projectiles right behind them.

This cabin was compromised already, so stability wasn't an option, but he had another solution. Heat wouldn't have worked so well on the fanatics because of their broken regeneration, but these stars were constructs of finite energy.

Switching the vapor blaster's mode to the heat wave, he aimed in their general direction and let it rip. And like ice melting under the hot sun, the energy lost its shape and burst before dispersing uselessly.

This gave him a breather from the assault. Not missing the opening, he escaped the room and ran in the direction with the most obstacles. His wound was closed, but it was as if his leg were on fire. The bone chafed against his skin, and sprinting felt like someone was peeling his flesh.

Nevertheless, enduring pain was preferable to facing death. A death that seemed inevitable if he allowed both enemies to attack him simultaneously. He needed to isolate and confront them one by one.

So he glanced at the network of tubes running overhead and made up his mind. It was a risky idea, but it was the only good one he had.

The reason he was hesitating was that the tubes were connected to one another a little too well. A single instability in the network would cause the whole thing to come crashing down.

Under the theory of cascading changes, it would cause an instantaneous immense strain on his eyes and thought space. But he would have to risk it. There was no other choice.

Instability inducement.

Bammm.

Crunch.

"AGHHH! MOTHER, HELP!"

The whole room shook when sections of pneumatic tubes all around the basement fell and shattered. One of them crashed right on the head of the zealot who was kneeling with his hands clasped—splitting it open with all its weight, staining the tube's glass red.

Vern's eyes flared with as much pain as his leg, but he simply pressed his palms against his eyes and kept running.

"Ye shan't escape preservation!" shouted the melee zealot, sidestepping the falling hazards as he tailed Vern at an alarming pace.

Vern himself dodged and weaved through the final wave of stars until they lost their source, and soon, he was free from the annoying scrapshit.

And that's when the words he'd been desperately waiting for tolled in his ears. "Vern, I am ready!"

Finally! At last, Ambrose was done with his preparations.

Vern turned around, switched his gun to concussion mode, and fired in the general direction of the melee guy. The man dodged it and rushed toward him like a ferocious beast. And that was the plan.

Vern had been inching closer to the hole in the roof, and now that it was time, he gritted his teeth, ignored the pain, and accelerated.

Two daggers of pure light appeared in the man's hands as he took a golden step toward Vern. Vern didn't have a pillar as cover this time, so he induced an instability within a generator in the man's path.

It was supposed to simply send another jet of steam in the man's face, but maybe luck was finally in Vern's favor because the odd component he destabilized caused the tanker to explode.

Boom!

The man slammed into the wall beside the generator, hitting it with such force that Vern heard bones crack. Yet, the violent impact seemed to have no lasting effect on him—he stood back up, grin unwavering.

But everything was now in place, and Vern wasn't going to fuck it up. He slowed down, limping with each step before turning to face the man. Vern's expression was a vivid display of fear, alarm, and despair, his arms trembling as he aimed the gun.

"The hour of preservation is nigh! May the mother of all preserve ye, oh heathen."

One second, the zealot was leaning against the wall, his skin undulating as protruding bones realigned themselves. In the next, he had covered half the distance between them, moving with startling speed.

Another blink, and he was right upon Vern, but Vern simply looked on, terrified and shaken to the core.

The zealot lunged at Vern, his hands crossed, each clutching a dagger of light and poised for a lethal swipe aimed to decapitate Vern with a single, swift strike.

"PRESERVE!" he bellowed, his face bursting with an unsettling amount of glee.

Vern fired his shot, but his trembling hand sent the bullet off course, missing its target. This misfire only served to broaden the man's sinister smile.

However, despite his missed shots, injured leg, and expression marred by terror, Vern's gaze never wavered from the man. Unflinching and steadfast, he locked eyes with his adversary, peering into what he knew were the eyes of a soon-to-be corpse.

For he was certain this was the last light those eyes would ever reflect.

Whirrrrl.

An overwhelming cascade of golden light flooded the basement, heralding the sudden appearance of a spiral drill right above the man's head. A look of shock swept across his face. He attempted to adjust his stance, desperate to evade, but he was caught midair, his movements proving futile.

"May you find peace in the embrace of fundamentals," whispered Vern, a common saying among the fundamentalists for the departed. He stood taller, that terrified expression and quivering demeanor nowhere to be seen. In its place was his usual solemn and calm self.

It started with the man's neck, drilling through it in a mere second. The sinews of his muscles came alive and wriggled toward one another to reattach themselves, but they didn't stand a chance against the might of that radiant drill.

Next was his tilted head, his chest, his ribcage, his waist. Nothing mattered, for the drill impaled him into the floor and grounded him down until nothing was left. Of neither the man nor the spiral.

Blood spilled all over Vern's outfit, his half-sliced shoe, his face, and his conscience. But he turned around, wiped away the stains, and limped toward Ambrose. The pain in his leg was no act.

It was time to end this.

One final plan.

CHAPTER 71

WAKING HER UP

His plan was an iteration of a previous one. But this time, the conditions were right. And he had to do something radical to solve this situation.

Just killing one of these vermin had taken so much effort from the two of them. What if there were more? And who was to say the swordsman wouldn't lose?

Were they supposed to hang around here like coal waiting to be dumped in the furnace? No, not after all this. He shook his head repeatedly, limping toward Ambrose.

All the golden spirals were already spent, and Ambrose seemed worse for wear already. "Newbie, that's all I got for now," he shouted with less spark in his voice.

Vern nodded and gazed at the second zealot, whose head was already patching itself up. The man would be back in the fight soon.

Then he gazed up, peering past the opening that connected this hellhole to the night sky. Whatever was left of the spiral barrage had changed its collective shape to surround the swordsman from all angles.

It seemed their foe had changed his priorities and was determined to kill the swordsman no matter what.

Not something Vern could help with, but this settled it. Only one enemy was left in the basement, so Vern didn't need to be involved in the fighting anymore.

He would instead enact his plan. Up until now, they were reacting to all the surprises thrown at them, playing right in the hands of the enemy, barely coping with their tactics.

"Ambrose, I have an idea, but I will need your help to keep the enemies busy," said Vern, trying his best not to sound authoritative. He didn't want his ally going against him at such a critical juncture just because he couldn't be more polite.

"What've you got?"

Vern signaled toward Esther with his eyes, and a look of realization dawned on Ambrose's face. "Second time's the charm, eh?" he chortled, rushing toward the zealot that slowly stood back up, "Go for it. I got your back, newbie."

Perfect.

Indeed, that was his plan. That dome blocking their transmission signal was no more, and the swordsman was keeping their foe busy enough.

However, this time, Vern knew how to optimally use different parts of the station to send that distress signal with the least amount of preparation and cost.

In his stability vision, he had been taking extra care to not let any of the essential components come in harm's way. They were needed to start the steamscript again, after all.

The only problem was . . . Esther and her lack of representation.

But he had an idea.

As he hurried back to where she was lying, his surroundings continued to be abused unceasingly. It was the fusion of utter darkness and golden radiance sprinkled with sparks of blue.

Sometimes, it echoed the sound of metal hitting metal. At other times, it replayed the bloodcurdling screams followed by maddened chanting.

As surreal as it was, he kept moving. He was a fucking bookworm, for steam's sake. What was he doing fighting these religious fanatics?

But he instantly banished the insecure ramblings of the imposter inside him and knelt next to Esther.

She lay there in a fetal position, her vivid red locks falling over her metallic cogwings. The wings fluttered with little strength as they moved to retract into their sheath, only to be disrupted by the broken mechanism and shattered pieces.

Her otherwise graceful countenance was scrunched up, marked by an unhealthy paleness. Her lips opened every other second, only to close inaudibly, and her arms that held her head shivered.

Looking at her in such a defenseless and distressed state, a sense of pity gushed within him.

So he gently gripped her shoulder and shook her body. "Esther. Esther, can you hear me?"

"Esther. It'll be all right. I have a plan to end this once and for all, but I will need your help."

Her breathing grew rapid, and she mumbled something. "i . . . a."

Vern closed in, his unruly hair hanging above her face as he strained to hear her words. ". . . via . . . Livia."

Livia?

Why did it feel like he had heard that name before?

She continued, her voice growing louder and anxious, ". . . please don't take her. No. No. NO. NO!" And that's when her eyes snapped open, and she stared back at Vern from mere inches away.

His mind was still repeating that name, trying to figure out why it felt familiar. This was why he liked his notepad. He should—

"Vern, we only just met. Isn't it a little too early and a little too unromantic to force yourself on a dying girl?"

Uh. Um. Fuck!

He jerked back instantly, and his cheeks flushed red. Taking a deep breath, he rushed to clear the misunderstanding, "Esther, no. It's nothing like that. I was just trying to listen to what you were saying. You were in so much pain—" That's when he noticed her weak smile and paused.

She looked at him with what could only be interpreted as an amused smile. After staring at each other in silence for a couple seconds, she shifted her gaze and looked at the sky through the station's only opening before focusing back on him.

"So it didn't work, huh?"

It? Does she mean the third rune? He pondered before replying, "It did—"

She interrupted him with a weak voice, looking slightly offended, "Then why are you here?!"

Vern found himself stumped by the question. He himself didn't understand why he was back before the fight was over, even though he'd spent over an hour in there.

Misinterpreting his silence, she continued, her eyes drooping, "I am sorry. I . . . am sorry, Vern." She paused, then spoke right as Vern was about to, "I should've done more. But I know how . . ."

Cough-cough.

Her body trembled with each of her coughs, but she persisted in speaking. "I know how this ends. They'll change me. Just like my sister . . . I don't . . ."

Cough-cough.

Blood trickled down her lips as Vern tried interrupting her again, only to be shut down by her glare. How could the glare of such a weak person be so persuasive?

"End it, Vern. Before they turn me. Please kill me—"

"Okay. Shut up, Esther. Calm down and listen to me. I have a plan," he interjected, not letting her ramble on anymore.

Her expression looked like she wanted to protest, but her body relaxed in his grip. Not flaming her fancies anymore, he started, "That priest or whatever isn't blocking the skies anymore. If we send another signal right now, it will reach its destination without any trouble."

Her expression, which had turned hopeful for a second, became utterly downcast as she curled into herself farther and closed her eyes. "Thanks for trying, Vern. But sometimes, we need to accept when we've lost the bet."

Vern's expression crumbled. She didn't have one iota of trust in him, eh? That hurt a little. Not letting his unnecessary feelings color his words, he continued, "Esther, do you really think I would waste our time with stupid endeavors? I said I have a plan. Not just an idea."

"Vern, you don't get it. I don't have enough representation, and most of the station isn't even working anymore. You're not even a real observer—"

"I can't see you in my perception. Did you . . . ?" she murmured, staring at his kneeling figure.

He nodded. "You didn't let me explain. I shaded my perception according—"

"Nuh-uh," she interjected, light returning to her eyes. She tried and failed to push herself up as she continued, "Hah. Don't waste time going over all that right now. I can see we don't have time. If you've got something good, just shoot."

Vern nodded after he cushioned her fall and assisted her back up, "Sure."

Soon he managed to help her sit against a wall—rotated to her side because her wings made it hard to sit straight. Right as he was about to pull back, however, she grabbed his collar feebly and whispered in a trembling voice, "You're not giving me false hope . . . right?"

This . . .

This was a conundrum. He didn't like setting false expectations. His plan had accounted for how to solve each potential roadblock, but nothing could be said for sure. He didn't . . . but then he stopped overthinking it and sighed before replying, "Trust me."

He caved in, and she let him go. It just meant he had to make it work no matter what. Vern quickly masked his uncertainty with a veneer of calm and extended his hand toward her.

She looked back with a dubious expression but still extended her palm nonetheless. "What are you doing?"

He shook his head. "Not me. You. You have to initiate thought synergy."

She bit her lip, deep in thought, and then replied after a couple seconds, "Are you sure? You want me to spend the last vestiges of my representation just so you can get into my head? Because if I run out of representation, it's . . . it's not going to be pretty."

"I don't know what you mean by that." Her expression faltered before he could even finish, but he gripped her palm with his own and quashed her bubbling concerns. "but it won't come to that. I have a solution to restore your representation."

Now she was just plain confused. Her face said it all. Not keeping her in the dark anymore, he pulled out the insight sphere from his pocket and placed it atop their conjoined palms.

She stared at the glassy sphere, then back at him before her brows furrowed, and she said, "Vern, I don't know how to use these spheres. Only fundamentalists like you can use this to store or collect representation. I just . . . can't. All those concepts and images inside it mean nothing to me."

Vern smirked at her words, and a perfect response came to him. He knew it wasn't the time to joke around, but he couldn't hold himself back from throwing her own words back at her.

So he grinned and chortled, "Oh ho ho. Just what is this situation? You have this special vision to synergize thoughts, but you don't know what it entails? This is very suspicious."

A deadpan expression overtook her face, and she replied, "Very funny." But when Vern continued to stare at her unflinchingly with that smirk, her lips twitched, and she let out a short laugh before caving in. "Just tell me. I don't have the mind to solve riddles right now."

He shrugged. "Well if I traverse and retrieve the representation from within the insight sphere while our thoughts are already synergized, what do you think will happen?"

Her expression went from being slightly amused to confused to one of realization in a quick succession. She parted her lips to say something but held back and instead closed her eyes.

Vern smiled and soon felt a tug on his consciousness.

Before heading into her thoughts, he took quick stock of the current situation. Ambrose was playing with the zealot, whereas the swordsman was holding his own against the barrage of spirals.

Not intending to waste any of her precious representation, he let those thoughts pull him away.

One moment, it was the ruined basement of the station. Next, it was darkness. There was a light, yes, but it was unusually faint. Willing to move closer, he soon reached the source of the light and saw that piano again.

It was in utter disrepair. Tangled, lusterless, and broken strings fed into its back, while the piano itself seemed worse for wear. This actually helped him realize what he was looking at. It was a manifestation of her thought space, and it was unremarkably dim, signifying how spent she already was.

Depressing thoughts arose in his mind from just looking at the instrument—surely her feelings were bleeding over to him. So he didn't waste another moment and engaged his own perception.

Focusing on the whirling sphere of grays in their hands, he found himself in that special place yet again. The void of initiation. He wondered how his consciousness was handling so much abuse.

He was already in a different mental space—of Esther's making. Then from there, he jumped to the one within the insight sphere.

Well, who the hell knows? He had to progress in a new direction this time. It was a risk, hence the reason he didn't want to make any promises to Esther, but here he was.

His goal was that specific cloud of representation that he never touched before. When he found this sphere back at the Ascendant Council, there were two foreign clouds stored inside it. One belonged to the preservation fundamental, which he had fully consumed already like some enhancement drug.

Then there was another cloud he hadn't yet had a chance to explore. He even regretted it a little because if he had tested it already, he would've known if this cloud of representation was worth pinning their hopes on.

It is what it is.

This foreign cloud was in the direction directly opposite to where his own representation was stored—the lower southeastern octant. From his experience, that octant usually held ideas related to growth and creation, so hopefully, it wouldn't be anything nefarious.

Clearing his mind of unnecessary thoughts, he began.

From nothingness, particles coalesce. Particles form matter. Matter, by nature, adheres to conservation . . .

Creativity, in its essence, is a whisper of possibility. Possibility suggests infinity. Infinity coalesces into form. Form, in its final act, blossoms into creation.

This was his usual traversal of the fundamentals, but it was the first time he had an audience. She tried her best not to disturb him, but her awe and amazement at all the sights that whirled past them were clear for him to see.

But he was here, at his destination—a glowing patch of incandescent lights bundled together. Taking the mental equivalent of a deep breath, he forged ahead on the path and soon made contact with the foreign cloud of thoughts.

Usually, it was this invigorating rush of ideas in his mind, but not this time. Instead, something completely out of his expectations transpired.

A soul-crushing headache assaulted him for a short moment, and his whole world seemed to turn upside down.

Then before he could scream or make heads or tails of the situation, the scenery changed yet another time, and a voice boomed in his head like a thunderclap. "Speak, insignificant one. By what means didst thou dare to engage with mine own representation?" A metallic clang of deafening proportion followed.

CHAPTER 72

WHY ME?

*C*lang.

Tang.

The words registered in Vern's mind, but the sight stunned him too much to conjure any response. In what could only be called a dimly lit environment, he saw the back of a man—no, a humanoid.

The entity wasn't wearing anything except a thin cloth around his waist. Sleek circular patterns of silver ran along his aqua skin, glowing faintly in the dark, while cyan specks of dust glittered all over his lean muscles.

Clang.

With every hammer of his tool, his dazzling long silver hair billowed with a ferocious intensity as silver glyphs of some sort emerged from the item resting on the anvil. Stretching those impossibly lean tendons taut above its head, he hammered down at the anvil in a crushing blow—

Tang.

This . . .

This . . . this is no human.

But then, what was he? A new species? Or a very old one?

His face, deeply mired by shadows, lit up every other second as glowing glyphs came bursting out of whatever was taking that savage hammering. The weapon itself was a construct of an unknown quantity, silver particles streaming behind it as it streaked through the air like a blur—hit after hit.

Bang.

Clang.

In stunned curiosity, Vern finally managed to tear his eyes away from the entity to look at the object being forged, only to feel his brain throb with intense pulsations.

A chill ran down his spine as that dead eye on the anvil stared right back at him.

Fuck!

Fuck! Fuck! What the hell is all this? What is going on? This entity looked exactly like what many imagined gods to be. But was he really a god?

Vern had contradicting views on the matter, and there had to be a better explanation.

But that's when the entity suddenly stopped, his muscles flexed to an unimaginable degree, and his voice boomed in Vern's ears and permeated his very being. "I demand. Speak, insignificant one. I shan't repeat myself."

Clang.

Crunch.

Wave after wave of silver glyphs exploded from the eye on the anvil, but Vern found himself utterly incapable of action or speech.

But he had to answer. He had to answer. This was no mere threat. This was a promise—a promise of destruction and annihilation if the command was not obeyed.

This situation wasn't like when he faced that eye in the sky. There, he had a retreat at hand. Here? He didn't even bother thinking about running away. He had no clue how this was going to play out.

So he did his best to rationalize this impossibility. First thing at hand was to give an answer.

Mustering courage he didn't know he had, he spoke, using this time to theorize what the fuck was going on. "I recently acquired an insight sphere from the Ascendant Council in the city of Elmhurst within the Calidian Empire. A few moments ago, I attempted to retrieve one of the representation clouds stored within it. That's all I really did."

But even after stating the facts so clearly, his nervousness didn't subside. Instead, the entity's lack of reaction only scared him more.

No. Think. Think, goddamn it.

The Ascendant Council.

Was it possible that him coming here had something to do with that cursed place? But he never encountered such a situation when he accessed that other cloud of representation in the insight sphere.

Can this be the person that came down the stairs in the Ascendant Council when I ran away?

But he quickly found a loophole in that argument. That being in the council was a woman, nothing like this entity in front of him.

But when he followed this train of thought and eliminated some random conjectures, an insane yet hopeful possibility crossed his mind. As much as it was a leap of faith, it was also logical to an extent.

Could this be . . . Yharl Ballin?

His benefactor. The one that had gifted him that book, the *Observation Record of Subjectivity*, allowing him to survive the nightmare that was the duskfall of sorrows.

But Vern remembered what the butler Beaumont at Hotel Inkwell had told him. That there was no administrator named Yharl Ballin. That the Ascendant Council was run by some other guy.

There was no trace of Yharl Ballin's existence. At least not after the duskfall.

Clang.

"Hah." The entity sighed, almost like a human. "A blunder on mine avatar's part, I presume. Then, I hath better erase thine memory of this happenstance, and let thee go. For knowledge is a burden too great."

"Uh, um, no. Please wait . . ."

The entity didn't seem to hear him as he deposited the hammer into the air, and the weapon didn't dare move an inch—defying gravity as if it didn't exist. The silver sparks on the entity's hands grew shinier as he plunged them ahead of him and tore open the air.

No. I can't waste this chance. I need to at least try!

Not letting the entity complete whatever it was doing, Vern shouted, "Benefactor Yharl Ballin, please wait!"

The god-entity suddenly stopped. The air stilled, and breathing became a chore. The world seized up, and even the shine of the glyphs faded into nothingness.

Did that mean he had guessed correctly?

In this suffocating atmosphere, the entity turned his head a little. Barely lit by the glow of the patterns from his own skin, the being had immaculately handsome features beset by the glowing orbs that were his eyes.

They shone like a beacon in the dark sea, a plethora of glyphs visible within their infinite depth. And then something churned within them.

Vern felt naked. Nothing could be hidden. It was as if every fiber of his being was dismantled before being placed back. The same was true for his mind and his every cell.

He was being scanned in some unknown capacity. The process almost dazed him into nothingness, but then he finally heard a voice say, "I understand." All the crushing pressure that had been boring down on him vaporized like it had never existed.

The voice that had been utterly impassive up until now seemed to be mixed with some kind of emotion as it echoed all around him. "Thou art of passing skill, for thee survived the rebellion of radiance. Perchance, the sole seed to have done so out o' all I hath scattered in the realm of mortals. I commend thee, for thou hath achieved great deeds in a mere speck of time."

But then he squinted and uttered, "Yet know that architect of reality, the Constructor of Cryptic realms doth watch over thee. Tis a burden thou art not yet fit to bear."

Then, the god-entity turned around and walked over in Vern's direction, glyphs pouring out of the ground from his every step. Vern had misunderstood the height of the entity. By the time he was right in front of him, Vern had to crane his neck to look him in the eyes.

A fresh change for him since he rarely had to look up to anyone.

The azure being put his hand on Vern's head, and not one inch of his being dared protest. But he had to!

Is he still trying to erase my memories? But why?! Vern didn't want to forget. Yharl Ballin had been a mystery always on his mind. The question of who had assisted him back then, and why, had been one of his innermost motivations to survive.

Every cell in his body was clearly aware that he was not the one in control. One squeeze of that arm resting on his head would end it here, once and for all.

However, before he managed to gather his courage, a silver shape appeared in his mind. Avoiding his thought space altogether, it headed toward the third rune. Wrapping those two inverted triangles in what seemed like a bubble made of glyphs, the entity removed his hand and turned around, walking back to his ethereal smithy.

Vern stood there speechless. What was this? Was erasure of memories a slow process? Or had the entity given him something instead?

He had a million questions, but he couldn't bring himself to speak out of turn, for the sheer presence of this entity made him ashamed of his own existence.

But then he spoke, his deep voice seeming a little . . . reluctant, "Depart thou hence. For each fleeting moment within this domain doth betray thy presence. The viewpoint of a primal visionary is a temptation too alluring, even for them. I have bestowed upon thee a chance to elude the doom of Elden descent. Once. Employ it with great sagacity."

That was . . . incredible. He couldn't even begin to fathom the value of this gift. Yet, there was a louder voice in his mind that urged him to ask questions. Surely this entity had the answers, and it was all but confirmed that the being had no intentions of harming him.

Afraid he might be kicked out before he had a chance, Vern let loose, "Benefactor, forgive me for asking, but could I request another gift? A gift of knowledge? What is this rebellion of radiance? What caused a third of our planet's lives to be culled? What—"

"Inquire not further, for knowledge is a burden most heavy," interrupted the entity with a serious tone. "There abide observers with visions beyond thy ken. Thy awareness of their existence might verily lead to their cognizance of thine own. A burden thou art not yet fit to bear."

However, before Vern could protest any further, the being waved his hand, and Vern's vision began to fade. He was being expelled!

"Nevertheless, I shall impart unto thee one truth. Objectivity is shattered and those from beyond the veil seek to claim the ownerless representation, while the pollution spreads unchecked. Be aware that thy world can't escape the doom, and on this occasion, it won't turn back."

Is that what all this is? He even knows about the reversal of time. This . . .

Even more questions flitted past his mind, but none of them seemed like something he would get an answer for in this short time. So before he lost this opportunity, he decided to ask that one question that was buried so deep down in his own conscience that no one but his insecure imposter self could dig it out.

"Why me?" he blurted, unsure what he wanted to hear in response.

What had he ever done to deserve this opportunity? Why help him? Neither was he a member of some peerless heritage nor was he born with limitless talent. Everything he had in this life required untold sacrifices on his part.

The world turned dark, but those eyes still shone brilliantly as he replied, "Why not? Life experience and choices shape one's viewpoint, not merely the circumstances of one's birth. Thine own journey, akin to many others, merited an opportunity. An opportunity to struggle.

"To peer into the shades of reality."

Then the entity picked up his hammer, and—

Clang.

Everything shattered.

"   "
. . .

"   "
. . .

"*. . . e . . . n.*"

"*Vern.*"

"*Vern! Where are you?!*"

"Vern! Stop scaring me. I can't do this alone!"

". . . Um . . . should I force him out of here . . . No, that could leave him as a vegetable."

"Should I try to send the distress signal myself? But I don't fucking understand how any of this works . . . This f—"

"Huh? Is this a feeling of . . . awe? And . . . dread?"

"Vern? Vern. That's you, right? I am not feeling any of that scrapshit. It has to be you! Come out here."

When he finally came to, Esther, garbed in that long white dress without her wings, paced in front of her dazzling piano. The instrument looked as beautiful as herself, and it wasn't broken or tattered one bit.

So, the insight sphere really worked? It restored her representation.

"Damn right, it worked! Now show yourself, you selfish creep. Where the hell have you been?!"

Well, apparently, she could still read his thoughts or something like it.

Still perplexed about his recent experience, Vern distractedly conjured a physical form in her thought space. She seemed to prefer to communicate like humans in here instead of two formless voices screaming at each other.

He didn't mind it.

Pulling him by his arm, she guided him to the bench in front of her piano. Once seated beside him, she stared down with a suspicious look.

When she didn't budge, Vern gave in and sated her curiosity, *"I don't know."*

At his words, she took a deep breath and chanted with a zealous fervor, *"I am nice. I am nice. I am nice. I shouldn't read your thoughts. I shouldn't read your thoughts. I don't need to know. I don't need to know.*

"Um, Esther, didn't you swear that you can't read my thoughts?"

"Swear? Me? Hmph. If it wasn't in the name of the great Elysian, it doesn't count."

However, before he could protest any further, she placed a finger in front of her lips and shushed him.

"I will deal with you later. Right now, I want to introduce my mother to you and that cunt up there in the sky. Can we focus on that, please?"

His mind still whirled with all he'd heard and seen, but soon, the urgency of the situation settled on him once again. If they delayed too much, the swordsman might slip up. And that would be it.

He couldn't let that happen. That swordsman was the reason he could even talk to Esther right now. That Cera and Ambrose were alive and kicking. That his shaky conscience wasn't burdened by their deaths.

So, with a deep breath, he rested his palms on the keys of the piano and waited for her to guide him.

She rested her palms on his and asked, *"Are you sure the station can still send another signal? I can only control this meager amount of essence strands."*

It was a valid question. Many of the strands feeding into the piano were either outright missing or severely damaged. These represented the shattered and decimated objects within the station itself.

Nonetheless, the objects that mattered weren't beyond help. He could even fix the malfunctioning ones with his vision working in conjunction with hers. So he replied with a firm voice, *"Trust me."*

She nodded imperceptibly and began the final piece.

Quentin couldn't believe he was being held off by a mere plebeian, a disgusting foreigner at that. The wretched thing had the gall to disrespect Mother Asea and question his burden.

His kin's burden!

Mother had ordained her own death, and as her most beloved children, his kin had carried out her wish. Killed her.

But she wasn't gone. Such a world wouldn't be worth living in. No, no, she was merely finding herself suitable vessels. For her rebirth. For a new beginning!

And this hateful peasant was barring him from presenting Mother with a vessel of immense potential. A specimen that had finally ripened. She was a fruit they had been waiting to pluck and preserve since forever.

Her sister had changed the whole world when she accepted the gods within her. Now, it was time for the younger sister to follow in the footsteps of the elder.

However, he did recently hear that another candidate of immense potential was procured. But Mother had many avatars—the more the merrier.

Only Mother could realize the true potential of these simpleminded fools. These unworthy rabble didn't realize what they were running away from.

"Tch."

It was time to finish this. He had seen enough. He would end it once and for all. He would sacrifice his past month's insights to Mother. This was dragging on for too long, and his pride couldn't allow him to be toyed with by these pests anymore.

A smile of pure bliss blossomed on his face, further enhancing his already perfect visage as he visualized Mother's effigy, her infinite love, and—

Wengggg.

But that's when something completely unexpected happened. It was those ignorant imbeciles, playing with that machine in hopes of calling for reinforcements.

But this can't be!

More than half that machine had been ground down to smoke. How was it still working?! He hastily conjured a plane of preservation, placing it in the path of that thing, but . . .

No!

All his preservation aura was currently grinding that foreigner bastard to death. That . . . that . . . was to say, his absolute plane of preservation wouldn't be ready in time.

It just wouldn't.

Well, fuck it! I need to wrap this up. NOW!

His voice booming throughout this pathetic land, he proclaimed, "You've done it now, you meddling fools. You've called upon my wrath. I will end every one of you miscreants before any help arrives!"

He would blow it all. Mother's tears can then heal that ignorant girl, priming her for descent.

It was perfect!

Sacrificing a chunk of his thoughts to Mother, he felt a surge of energy boil within him.

"BEHOLD, FOR I AM THE ARCHITECT OF YOUR DEMISE. ARIA OF DOOM!" he declared, his voice echoing through the station as he drew a sphere around its edges, orchestrating an implosion that would grind everything within to dust.

However, just as he was about to unleash his final act, a flash of brilliant red lightning streaked down from the heavens, stealing all his thunder.

The ground trembled, dust billowed, and smoke swirled into the air, revealing the silhouette of a formidable figure emerging from the lightning's heart. A shudder went down his spine as he realized who it was. And the voice that came next only confirmed his worst fears—

"Grandiose words for a flying corpse. Let me offer you a reality check."

Chapter 73

EXECUTION

The she-devil was garbed in brass armor, fitting that terrible gauntlet in her hand.

Quentin knew her. Not personally, but through the words of his kin, prayers of his worshippers, and news from his sources. They all pointed to one fact—she was a devil.

When her elder daughter was chosen, she eradicated three monasteries of the Aetheric Collective in a single night in her search. That tallied more than a dozen observers with three shades and at least a hundred of the lesser kind.

And this was all before the duskfall. So she managed all that in the enemy's territory, where they had the advantage in terms of perspective domain. That's to say, they weren't suppressed by the objectivity of the world, but she was.

Even with everything going against her, she still came out victorious. If that wasn't a devil, he didn't know who else could be.

The only reason she didn't get her daughter back was her inability to defeat her own child. No one could stand against that monster after the false god descended into her.

Anyhow, their plan didn't account for this worst case. How could it? The fact that the vessel had managed to run this far and hide for so long was already outside their initial plan.

His orders for today were straightforward—extract the vessel. What he couldn't grasp was how she had managed to call for help in barely twenty minutes. And to have contacted her mother, of all people.

It was all disheartening news, sure. But Quentin was no pushover. He was this close to mastering the fifth vision in the shade sequence of the observation record imparted to his kin by the Mother—templars of preservation.

The fifth shade in this sequence, justiciar, represented a watershed in terms of difficulty. The sheer amount of preservation essence one needed to accumulate from their followers was mind-boggling, and only years of unwavering perseverance had brought him to this point.

And now was his chance to reach higher. To earn himself the fame needed to establish his own temple. His feat of shutting down the Puppeteer of Crimson Court, followed by an ascension to the justiciar, would cement his position in the kin.

What if she killed a bunch of third-shade trash? He was a literal god who had gained the adoration of tens of thousands. A peak fourth-shade high templar.

He had survived a spar against Father Oras, a fifth-shade justiciar, a kin of the Mother. She was just that, a fifth-shade observer. On top of that, different viewpoints of the same shade weren't always comparable in strength.

He was confident that his prowess of preservation could overpower this puppeteer devil any day. Not everyone was as good of a turtle as that foreigner bastard. He knew enough about the Lightveins to judge that she didn't counter him well.

So he retracted all the preservation essence he had been spending on that turtle and redistributed it within his own body. He had to take this seriously.

Soon, the building with the vessel began shaking, and a staircase emerged out of it. It had to be that devil's doing. That disrespectful filth, a sheeple, and the vessel ascended the stairs with an unconscious mundane one floating behind them.

Those useless fools! More than five templar initiates were sent alongside him, each with two shades in their perception, to handle the situation. How, then, had they failed to defeat such pathetic rabble?

DISGRACEFUL! I shall fix that now! he resolved to himself. Such a stain on Mother's dignity couldn't stand!

And time was nigh. The she-devil was done equipping her hallmark gauntlets. One can only be so strong if they have to use outside help to fight. This only bolstered his confidence.

Quentin assumed a square stance high in the air, gazing down at the rabble below. He was prepared for anything. Having sacrificed the past month's insight to Mother, he felt more ready than ever for the confrontation ahead.

But he was going to be smart about the fight. Preservation as a concept was more suited toward defense, so he would first gauge her power and wait out a couple attacks before going in with his own.

It was a perfect plan.

"COME, devil! I shall end your legacy today."

But then he felt something decay around him. The antithesis of preservation. The air shifted, and a whirlwind began to form around him. Smoke churned out of nothingness, and the air dried.

Out of an abundance of caution, he drew three spheres of absolute preservation around him.

The she-devil had her hands spread wide apart, looking up at him like the god he was. Puppet strings reeled out of those gauntlets on her arms, attaching to one thing after another. Surely, she was going to hurl all those objects at him.

He could dodge such a slow attack a million times before it could ever reach him. The nerve of this woman! Was she treating him like a child?

Quentin looked at the cattle beneath him, unsure if this was a joke. The devil was staring right back at him with those glowing red eyes.

It was coming. His own pupils shone a brilliant golden as he prepared to fight with a small-scale aria of dooms. He would launch it right after her attack.

But then he heard that devilish voice. "This is for the despair you wrought."

Clap.

A rush of smoke surged around him, and an inconceivable amount of pressure attacked him from all sides, threatening to squeeze his very being. Yet this was only the beginning.

Quentin instantly realized he had landed himself in a trap. She hadn't been wasting time putting on those gauntlets—she had been preparing this since the start!

Pouring his essence into the cape on his back—a gift from his kin—he charged forward while his spheres followed behind him, nothing but a blur given his speed. But that's when the pressure increased, and he realized what was trapping him.

Odd objects floated in the air around him, all of them connected to form what could only be called a towering bony hand. Each of the fingers was made up of countless items, a thread sewing everything together.

But Quentin didn't care about their form. All he saw was an opportunity to gain the upper hand.

He didn't need to fly straight out of this monstrosity. He could just pass between its fingers. A smile extended on his face, and he swerved mid-flight, rushing through the useless imitation.

Not even two seconds had passed since she started her offense, and he had already found a way to nullify it. She might be some devil, but he was the son of a goddess herself!

However, right that instant, the pressure increased a couple notches, and his flight faltered. And before he could catch his breath, a bone-chilling scene played out in front of him.

The smoke swirling aimlessly became coherent out of nowhere, and like flesh wrapping around bones, the formless smoke created a palm centered around all those fake fingers.

A sinking feeling surged from within. This wasn't good. He involuntarily looked back, and what he saw horrified him.

It was another one of these gigantic palms, made out of nothing but random machine parts and air itself. And it was hurtling toward him with an unprecedented momentum.

Out of sheer panic and a will to save himself, he conjured however many spheres of absolute preservation he could manage around him and braced.

The pressure alone seemed enough to squeeze him to death. It was only gonna get worse.

And then, without any mercy, it came.

Crack.

Boom.

"Father Oras! I . . . I come with a message from the Omniscient Gazebinder," shouted the devotee, his voice shaking intensely.

Kneeling in front of the largest statue of Asea in the realm, Oras looked back at the quivering devotee. Sparing the child some terror, Oras replied in a soothing voice, "Tell me, child, what does Ruppert have for me?"

The devotee's knees only grew weaker at the mention of the Gazebinder's name. Still, he persisted and spoke with a stammer, "Father Quentin has failed to procure the vessel in time, and . . . now the Puppeteer of Crimson Court, Andrea Lightvein, has arrived to rescue her daughter. Father Quentin has chosen to pit himself against the devil, and . . . and at this rate, the temple will lose the vessel as well as Father himself."

"By thy grace, Mother, kin shall rise," muttered Oras—a final prayer before he got up and walked toward the devotee, his celestial robe dragging behind him on the floor. Once out of the sight of Mother's statue, his eyes turned sharp, and he held the shoulder of the devotee that had been following behind him meekly.

Looking him in the eyes, Oras said, "Go and ask High Templar Siris to wake up Mother's new avatar. Ask him to tell her that it pains me to put such a burden on her so soon, but we can't afford to lose kin and a vessel on the same day."

"Ye-yes. Yes, Father!"

"Also . . ." Oras smiled as he swirled his finger in the air, and in no time, a droplet floated in between them. The moment the devotee laid his eyes on it, a hungry look flashed in his eyes, and he pounced at it without regard for his station.

Oras didn't mind it; instead, he encouraged it. After all, Mother's tears were perfect to reward a concerned devotee. At least until they couldn't live without it.

"Thank you, Father! THANK YOU, FATHER! I will, I will . . . never forget this grace!" replied the devotee with a zealous fervor in his eyes as he watched his fingers elongate and arms shrivel—breaking out of their mortal shell.

"Now go, child."

"YES, FATHER!"

Vern stared at the sky, stupefied by the marvel Esther's mother had conjured. In mere moments, two colossal palms, each towering higher than the tallest clock towers he'd seen, materialized out of thin air and crushed the priest into oblivion.

But Vern saw more than just that. One moment, everything was stable. Next, the whole station was uprooted from the ground, its components floating in the air as they formed the skeleton of titanic hands.

Ethereal strings erupted from the gauntlets in her grasp, spearing through the objects with the precision of a seamstress's needle, binding the trembling objects into a macabre unity mirroring that of human bones. Whirlwinds of air encircled each of those bony fingers, the flow so rapid that it almost acted like solid skin.

And then before anyone could react, the colossal constructs clashed with a thunderous, bone-jarring impact.

His blood boiled simply looking at this spectacle from the sidelines. *This is the power of a real observer.* The capability of someone who knew what they were doing with their eyes.

He wasn't one to yearn for more power, but this was . . . fascinating. And soon, he would have to shift his mindset in this regard anyway. Yharl Ballin had put it clearly for him. The world was never going back to the way it had been before this disaster.

The whole planet was on a one-way trip to doom, and it would be stupid to think he could survive that without power. Power that he had already tasted. It felt great to finally have some sense of control and balance in his life.

This was the first step, and he would keep moving forward until he could decide the balance of all factors in his life. For now, he just had to get good enough to find Ariane, ensure her safety, and overcome Hensen.

That was a great balance to strive for, at least according to him. But his musings ended abruptly as Esther's mother turned her crimson eyes toward him for a second and ordered, "Take good care of her. I'll be right back."

"I am fine, Mom!" She wasn't. She looked paler than ever, barely managing to remain standing even when she was being supported by Vern's shoulder.

Who knows how many days she had been down there in that deserted and almost haunted basement? There was no food, no water. She couldn't go out, for that risked being discovered by her watchers.

There was no one to help, no one she could trust. Nothing was working out for her down there. She was doomed to either die there alone or in the grasp of her enemies. Just that thought alone terrified him.

He nodded solemnly, but her mother was already gone. Reeling those unnaturally long strings, she propelled herself into the air. Her rose pink hair fluttered behind her, each of her moves naturally domineering and graceful.

"Hey, friend. Small world, eh?" hollered the swordsman as he landed, using his scarf on the uprooted ruins of the station with those gigantic palms in the backdrop. Sheathing his blade into an ornamental scabbard, he joined their group of four.

Cera was still unconscious. Esther's mother had done something to the headpiece Esther liked to call Fen, and it was now carrying Cera. Pretty neat, if someone asked him.

Trying and failing to execute a bow because of Esther, he settled for lowering his head, replying, "Thank you very much for coming to our aid—"

Before he could finish, however, Esther chimed in, seeming quite lovely, "Uh, right! Thank you very much, master swordsman. If it weren't for you, I'd be a puppet just like the ones my mother controls."

"Where's my gratitude?" grumbled Ambrose, playing with his cane.

Her eyes instantly narrowed, and she strained forward to look past Vern's face at Ambrose. "You are twenty rescues away from being absolved for what you did to Fen!"

"Rude," he replied in a meek voice, looking away from them.

This unnecessary banter went a long way in anchoring Vern and calming him down. They had succeeded. This was it. It was over. There was no question that Esther's mother had it all under control.

Even if that priest wasn't dead yet, he would be in no time. This situation was already resolved as far as he was concerned.

It took a million unexpected turns, but the net result was great. He shaded his perception, saved a beautiful human from a terrifying fate, met new people, made some friends, learned far too many secrets, and had a couple directions for what to work on next.

So, with a light heart, he listened to the swordsman speak. "My friends, you don't have to thank me. I didn't help you so much because of the kindness in my heart, but to save my own skin and the Vigil's. I couldn't let the whole of Elmhurst down by offending Lightveins as a member of the Vigil. The Vigil shouldn't be eradicated just because I couldn't hold back a sinner."

Esther quieted down, turning her gaze toward that valiant figure in the sky. "She's not as bad as everyone makes her out to be . . ."

Just then, a golden explosion burst from the center of those gigantic palms, and a radiant figure emerged out of the hollow of those colossal hands, fleeing in the opposite direction with a frenzied pace.

"I WILL REMEMBER THIS DISGRACE!"

But Esther's mother wasn't having any of it. A single wave of her hand and all the objects forming the skeleton of one arm rearranged, even higher in the sky, coalescing into a single fist.

"This is for the pain you inflicted."

Crash!

Like a fly being swatted, the fist pummeled the radiant priest into the ground, the resulting tremors making it hard for Vern to stand straight.

She extended her hands, those fingers dancing with deliberate grace, just like a puppet master controlling her puppet's fate.

"MY KIN WILL REMEMBER THIS DISGRACE!"

Strings wrapped around the limbs of the priest, pulling his limp body back up. The man tried to protest, but they only constricted around his appendages farther, digging into his skin.

The strings pulled him into the air and laid him down on a platform made of rapidly flowing air. It burned and scraped his back, but that was the least of his worries.

"AGHHHHHH!"

A needle hundreds of meters tall, shining with a deadly gleam, hung above him in the sky, its infinitely sharp tip pointed at him.

"This is for daring to take another one of my daughters!" she shouted, letting go of the strings, an unmistakable fury fueling her words.

Like the guillotine's decisive drop, the needle plunged from the heavens, a metallic comet streaking toward its inevitable target.

"MOTHER WILL REMEMBER THIS DISGRACE!"

Vern, Ambrose, Esther, and Shinsei all watched the execution with rapt attention, not one of them flinching at those disgusting pleas.

This is the end.

However . . .

"Don't worry, child, for I am here," came a voice that sent shivers down Vern's spine, and the whole world stilled.

CHAPTER 74

WILL AND A VESSEL

A disturbing pressure settled all around Vern, and the descent of that ungodly needle halted, its tip already having pierced through the man's heart.

Breathing became a chore, and it felt like he was locked in a room made of his own shape. All movement became nothing but a luxury. Heck, his body didn't even fall under gravity. It was as if everything were frozen in time in its own twisted way.

And he wasn't the only one. From his limited view, everyone was immobilized—even Esther's mother. Yet, strings soon reeled out of her mechanical gauntlets, their ends wrapping around her limbs.

And like a puppet moving alone on a stage full of props, her figure became a blur, falling straight down. When close to the ground, she decelerated with the help of another few strings, her movements mechanical and stiff. Once stable, she beelined toward Vern—or actually Esther.

In the periphery of Vern's vision, however, burned a white glow so bright it heated his irises just looking at it. This had to be the source of this anomaly.

A figure of a woman, enveloped by a dazzling glow, made its way toward the skewered man on that platform made of air.

Vern didn't understand how the situation could have reversed so thoroughly in just a few seconds.

What is happening? Who is this? Her words had painted the picture of a mother talking to her child. Was that how the higher-ups addressed their underlings in this Eternal Directorate? Just a convention of hierarchy?

Or was it . . .

That can't be.

There was no way a real goddess would show up for such a meager matter. Did she come running every time one of her so-called children was in trouble? It just didn't make sense. There was no way to make it make sense.

No. This is happening. I need to figure it out!

It was possible that Esther was too precious, and their organization wasn't keen on giving her up. But if they already had a goddess at hand, what did they need to find vessels for? Maybe this one was a vessel too.

But wasn't this too strong? He kept reasoning through this logic, but nothing he came up with proved useful. His lack of understanding of how this Elden descent business worked only made it worse.

"Rise, child," came a soothing voice from inside that brilliant glow. And as if listening to that heartfelt plea, the colossal needle turned ethereal and continued its descent, harmlessly passing through the man's heart. It soon impaled itself into the ground and stayed there, motionless.

This . . .

Vern sensed something wrong with this situation, but he couldn't put his finger on it. Something about that voice felt off. The next scene, however, didn't surprise him.

The goddess's vessel knelt by the priest and lifted his head, making him drink something. And just like those uncanny bastards that Vern fought a while ago, the hole in that priest's chest began closing by itself.

How? It was stupid and broke all the conventions of medicine. Surely, there were some limitations or drawbacks to this method. There's no way something so potent could exist without repercussions. It would be against the natural balance.

But that was the least of his problems. The situation was about to turn dire.

It was one thing after another. They had just cleared an impossible hurdle, barely managing to summon someone who could handle that priest. Now, an even stronger player had entered the stage—one that might very well be a piece of god.

What the hell were they supposed to do? Call a god of their own as backup? Yeah, life didn't work like that.

Not wanting to be at the mercy of this goddess, he made an attempt to observe the balance of stability.

But he was no Puppeteer of Crimson Court as the man had dubbed Esther's mother. He couldn't overcome the insane amount of resistance that his surroundings presented his perception.

Everything was rigid to an unimaginable degree. He had hoped things would be different, but they weren't. Every particle in his vicinity was actively being observed and manipulated by that goddess's vessel. There was no way Vern could become the primary observer under such circumstances.

This was disheartening. He had made some questionable choices to get where he was, though he still didn't have a consistent logic that would have made him choose otherwise.

Here's hoping Esther's mother can do something about it. Because if not, his only hope was to enter the third rune again. That was it. Those were all the cards he had left to play.

Even that wasn't a surefire method of survival. Last he knew, that land of dark sun was disintegrated into nothingness. What if that eye in the sky was still there? It would end him in no time. He would be leaving this plane only to be killed in another.

And going inside another time so soon might very well be the catalyst that forced Hensen to put an end to what he started.

Contacting Yharl Ballin was not an option either, not that there was any guarantee he would have helped him anyway. His insight sphere was empty, and Vern didn't know of other ways to reach him. The gift Vern had received from him was supposed to help him escape Elden descent, not cheat death.

Hmm, maybe there is another possibility. Maybe this "Mother" was a kind goddess, and she wouldn't bother killing mortals for the sake of it. Maybe she would be content with rescuing her "child."

But he knew the chances of that. They were slim.

Nothing boded well.

So, it was time to . . . let go.

When he had no way of influencing the outcome of an event, he had a simple way to go about it. He let go. It was leagues better than believing in the delusional hope that his thoughts alone would change the world.

It would be great if Esther's mother had a plan and even simpler if the goddess chose to act like a benevolent one. But if she didn't, and death was inevitable, he would escape to the third rune. And if, even there, he was served death, he would accept it.

That was all there was to it.

Such was the simplicity of his life. Would he be discontent and crestfallen? Yes. Would it matter? No.

It was just like he had told Ari on the eve of duskfall. She had asked if this was the end. If this was really it for them and the world. He had the same thoughts on the matter right now as he did back then—

If I die in such circumstances, there's not much I can do.

With all the contingencies and possibilities predicted ahead of time, Vern settled down and relaxed his anxious mind. In doing so, he even realized that his brain wasn't asphyxiated, something that was the norm for humans who hadn't breathed for a couple dozen seconds.

Wonder how this works.

But he instead chuckled internally at the absurdity of his thought. Emptying his mind of all unnecessary thoughts, he watched the events play out with the detachment of an observer. There was a twisted sense of amusement in simply watching the chaos ensue.

So when the pink-haired puppeteer came rushing toward him with those stiff movements and extricated her daughter from his grip, he didn't feel hurt. When she powered that Fen entity and cocooned herself and Esther inside it, he didn't feel betrayed.

It was par for the course. Everyone had limited capabilities, and one really had to ask oneself how much they could accomplish given those limitations. Especially when they were up against a literal god.

Vern couldn't expect her to save everyone only to end up sacrificing herself and maybe even her own daughter in the process. That would be stupid. And the puppeteer didn't seem the kind. She did exactly what he would've done had he the choice.

Soon, the priest gained back his voice and yelled, "Oh, MOTHER! I beg thee. I beseech thee, Eradicate these heathens and take back what's rightfully yours. This one has failed you and dare not make demands, but even in death, I hope to see your name flourish! To let your fame be the guiding light."

Unable to elicit any reaction from the figure within the light, the sore loser began another tirade. "These infidels have not only slain your children but also obstructed our sacred quest to find another vessel for your divine essence. They defy your will, disrupt your plans. Unleash your fury upon them, great MOTHER! Let your righteous anger purge this place of their sacrilege and restore the sanctity of your abode!" The man continued to pour venom, yet Vern felt nothing.

And as expected of life, there were no happy endings. Even a "Mother" wasn't impervious to inciteful bullshit, it seemed. The outline of the figure within the white brilliance stood up and declared, "Indeed. Children that don't listen must be . . . punished."

And the very fabric of existence shifted.

The world, which had been frozen in a near-perfect state for the last minute, underwent a drastic transformation. All brightness vanished as if snuffed out by an unseen hand.

Darkness engulfed everything, and reality faded from Vern's sight. Even the brilliance that surrounded the goddess was nothing but a lost cause. All that was left in this void were those eyes.

Those apathetic black eyes.

It was his first time seeing black pupils shine, and it was . . . disturbing. They stared at all of them like one would stare at ants. A comparison that probably wasn't too far from the truth.

Ready to flip the switch in his head at a moment's notice, Vern continued to watch another show of humanity's insignificance against the uncaring cosmos.

Soon, a dot of light emerged before those indifferent eyes, gradually expanding. Growing steadily, it cast a glow that pierced the void-like darkness. Vern watched as this orb of light, a beacon in the blackness, formed around the goddess's finger.

It was coming. He could feel it. Everything he had done was about to be proved futile.

So when she uttered, "Now sl . . . eep, children," her voice strained and erratic, he took the abnormality in stride and sighed to himself. *It's over.*

Directing his thoughts to that rune wrapped by silver glyphs in his mind, he felt the brightness that had started to eke out a corner in this world fade again. This time, however, it was his consciousness giving way.

He braced for the inevitable, to be whisked away into oblivion. Yet, in this odd moment, they changed.

Those uncaring eyes lost their rigid shape, and the ball of light expanded, casting a soft glow that faintly illuminated her face. That single sight sent a shudder down his spine, and he screamed without voice.

NO!

He forcefully snapped the tether that linked him to that foreign world, and his consciousness anchored back in this illogical reality with a slicing pain.

It doesn't make sense!

It did.

This can't be!

But it was happening.

Why?!

He inferred.

This is a fucking joke!

It had to be.

His rational mind made the links in no time, but it was nothing short of a cruel prank by this disgusting cosmos.

It was her.

His sister.

Ariane.

Ari.

He had been thinking about her since the second he woke up in the library one way or another and even had a few leads on how to go about finding her. Leads that helped him extrapolate and understand the twisted reality of this sight his eyes showed him.

She was the goddess—no, the vessel of some fucking outsider sent to clean up this mess.

How did this happen in two days?

Did that matter though?

It didn't. It had happened, and now he was on the other side, watching her struggle, unable to even move.

The pain from that failed contact with the rune was nothing compared to what came from looking at her expression.

Ari had her other hand pushing down on the outstretched one with all her might, a terrified grimace contorting his baby sister's face. Those eyes, which he had assumed to belong to some uncaring entity a moment ago, shimmered, gushing with tears as they stared right at him.

She had surely noticed him.

He had hoped he would meet her in better circumstances than this. At least then he would be able to explain his "death." That was the only assumption she could have made.

Mom and Dad's death had crushed her. He didn't want to imagine what his own had done to her.

It wasn't right!

The raw power coursing through her was like a tempest she could barely contain, her outstretched finger trembling intensely. She was clearly fighting an internal battle against that thing from beyond.

This should never have happened. Maybe. Maybe. If he had handled the situation in the library better . . . He should have burned that fucking observation record or something.

They chose her because of that book, right? He had hoped it would help her find a footing in this new world. But reality had a twisted sense of bringing wishes to life.

If he had woken up from his unconsciousness sooner. Just one day. No, even a few hours would've been enough. They could have left this city, for fuck's sake.

How had they even managed to find her? Why did they find her!?

Yet the time didn't pause for his fruitless justifications. The air around her crackled with energy, a tangible manifestation of the chaos within that distorted ball of light.

She was trying.

At this moment, however, that despicable fucker shouted, "You pathetic mortal dare to obstruct Mother's divine verdict? Who do you think you are to challenge her will? Father Oras has indulged you far too much, you insignificant little bitch!"

"Oh, revered Mother, to you I offer my profound insights, unwavering faith, and my very essence. Dominate the will of this ignorant imposter, I beseech thee, and assertively demonstrate to her the reality of her insignificance."

The scourge knelt where he stood, and a radiant aura flared out of his body, almost as if he were on fire. The aura turned into thin strands that burrowed into Ari's skin, and soon her hand that was holding back the other one turned limp.

AAAAAAGHH.

The cadence of Vern's thought space became a turbulent mess, a seething fury burning inside him as he glared at the insufferable vermin. This bastard had done it. Vern's conscience had a scale, and this scum had tipped it.

I.

WILL.

KILL.

YOU!

He had always been one to stay in control, but this . . . This disgusting fuck was actively wiping away the consciousness of his sister.

HIS SISTER!

ARI!

GODDAMN IT!

Her eyes, which had been wide with fear, now flattened, mirroring the sudden stability in the sphere of light that enveloped them.

Her trembling hand stilled, and her breaths evened out. The chaotic energy that had been crackling around her dissipated, replaced by a steady, pulsing glow, and the rate at which the orb grew accelerated.

I WILL END YOU!

I WILL KILL YOU!

I WILL END YOU!

I WILL KILL YOU!

A fiery fury claimed him, and he turned to his perception, seeing red rather than black as he forced shades of white into it.

When that didn't work, he pushed harder.

When the air proved impossible to shade, he moved on to that platform. It didn't work, so he forced his thoughts upon some of the objects that floated in the air—grasping, hoping he would find something to stop this madness.

Stability, instability, complexity, integrity, firmness, resilience, sturdiness, reliability, refinement. He exhausted all possibilities and attempted all combinations. Arcs of lightning struck throughout his thought space ceaselessly, yet he barely managed to force a white in his perception before being pushed back mercilessly.

When all else failed, he focused on the vermin himself.

One failure.

Two.

Three.

Ten.

He didn't know how many times he failed before he literally saw red, and his eyesight threatened to shut down on him.

It didn't matter.

Nothing he did mattered at all.

His weakness disgusted him.

Yet regardless of how much he burned, seethed, or thrashed around in rage—it was futile.

There was no god for him. He wasn't even supposed to be alive—Hensen should have ended him long ago. He was nothing but a grain of sand that slipped through the cracks.

A speck of dust that could do nothing when it mattered.

Nothing.

Yet reality always managed to calm him down. ALWAYS.

He loathed to think of anything that didn't result in burning all to hell, but the world denied bending to his will. He understood the logic, the chances, and the possibilities. He knew it all. Yet there was nothing. Nothing he could do.

His mind felt like it was being sliced apart from all the various pains, but he did it. He guided his thought to that abominable third rune and made contact.

He would run away. Again.

Even if he died in that land of dark sun, at least he wouldn't burden Ari's conscience. She would never be able to forgive herself if she became the cause of his death.

If nothing else, he could at least do that much for her.

Yet before he could justify it further as something like living another day to fight, his mind buzzed, and the thoughts directed toward the rune scattered.

He tried again, and the rune buzzed harder.

He went again, and this time, the rune dimmed entirely.

It seemed like his act of forcibly cutting off his previous attempt at making contact had set off a cooldown or something. Those inverted triangles had lost all their glow.

Hahhahhahhahhah . . . hah He barked a mirthful laugh at his own expense.

This was pathetic.

He was pathetic.

He couldn't speak. He couldn't move. He couldn't use any visions. Now, he couldn't even give her some peace of mind. And unfortunately, he only had himself to blame for the fact.

If he hadn't forcefully terminated his earlier attempt at making contact, things wouldn't have come to this. If he had remained calm and predicted the outcome, she wouldn't have had to carry his murder on her mind.

All this knowledge, the veneer of logic, but not one thing he could do to help his sister. Not one.

Not a single thing.

No.

No, no, no. FUCK THIS!

He would, at the very least, convey what he couldn't last time. She might not remember any of it, but their last conversation was an argument.

Ever since they were young, he was the one who had to back down. No matter if it was for something as small as taking apart her toys or as serious as snitching about her sugar addiction to their mom.

Didn't matter if they lived together or hundreds of cities apart, whether they were young or adults, joking or dead serious, he had been the one to step back.

She was prideful like that. And he wouldn't change that for the life of him. However much of it he still had left.

So when the stilled winds began to twirl and warp toward that ball of light, he strained against the pressure that constricted him in his place, pushing so hard his very thought space began to dim.

He knew it. This vision that froze everyone was more of a perceived preservation than a physical one, or Esther's mother couldn't have moved, no matter what.

So he detached his mind from his body and focused on moving his lips. There was no way he could let out a sound, but lips would be enough. Hopefully.

She would notice it. In there, somewhere, she would see it. There was no way some outsider had managed to vanquish her completely just because this trash of a human decided to sacrifice some of his insights.

If it was that easy, they would have wiped her away long ago.

He didn't believe that this stupid message of his would bring about a change or something in the situation. It was just . . . just . . .

A farewell. And an apology for all the years he hadn't been there.

She had been living by herself ever since she was fifteen. His master didn't allow any visitations from family members, and Nvoria wasn't suited for her education.

So, just two years after Mom and Dad died, she had been surviving on her own. He would send her letters and whatever money he could scrape together, but he knew.

Letters couldn't fill in for a family. She always complained about minor things but never asked for anything that would compromise his career. When he had left her all the way back then, she hadn't even shed a single tear as he got on the train, but her swollen eyes were all he remembered.

He had never been a proper big brother to her. So when he managed to keep her alive back in that library, he thought he had finally done something worthy of that title.

So based on that one account, he deserved to ask for forgiveness, right? She might not find it in her heart to pardon him. But he would ask. The cosmos wouldn't take that opportunity away from him as well, would it?

A hint of darkness appeared in the center of that ball of white, and Vern knew it was time. So when his efforts began to bear fruit, he carved the final image in his mind and mouthed it, his final words to her.

I.

Am.

Sorry.

All he managed to glimpse was the tear that rolled off her cheek before the brightness overwhelmed him and the black spark exploded.

CHAPTER 75

IN SEARCH OF A BALANCE

Boom.

The ground peeled and curled in on itself, disintegrating in mere moments as the tidal wave of pure destruction headed toward them at a disturbing pace.

He felt the shock wave before he heard it, a deep rumble that tore through the air. Dust and debris shot up, blinding him momentarily. His ears rang, the noise echoing in his skull like a siren.

The end was nigh.

"AGHHHH!" roared Ari with a gut-wrenching scream, but the wave of death approached relentlessly.

He couldn't take this anymore. If only she knew when to let it go. But she wouldn't. And as much as he loathed this situation, he still felt a little proud of his baby sister.

With every fiber of her being, she screamed, "I WILL NOT BE YOUR PAWN!" Her voice, fueled by pain and steely determination, pierced the chaos around her. In response to her resolute defiance, the ruinous tempest didn't just slow—it ceased entirely, its searing white heat emitting a smoldering smoke that scorched the air itself!

Lines of brilliant white ran along Ari's arms as this pure light of devastation found purchase within her body. Two whirling tempests formed around her hands, sucking the destructive aura within them, singeing her skin to unrecognition.

"AGHHHH!" With a fierce cry, she persisted, her voice unwavering even as blood trickled from her mouth. Despite faltering midair, her determination remained unbroken, and she continued to hold back the tempest.

Vern gritted his teeth so hard that another hot surge of pain washed over him. Apparently, his scope of movements was expanding. But what did it matter if he could gnash his teeth or flail around? It was too little, too late.

She shouldn't have to tolerate this agony.

Not for him.

But there was also the fact that she was a better human being than himself. She wouldn't harm a fly if she had a choice, much less six people alongside an unknown number by association. She was probably trying just as hard to spare the others around him.

If he could, he would've advised her to run away from all this and find some way to dump the goddess out of her head while staying safe. Not that she ever listened to him on important matters.

Bit after bit, chunk after chunk, that light of obliteration found itself absorbed into her arms, and the sight horrified him. One part of him badly wanted to close his eyes and just escape to his thoughts. He couldn't bear to see it.

But that realization of what could go wrong if he stopped using his brain was still fresh in his mind. One fumble in a couple minutes was more than enough. So he watched.

And etched it into his memory.

If he survived this, he would have to get someone to account for all the hell that she was going through right now.

EVERY IOTA OF IT!

It didn't matter if her body had undergone a change or if she could regenerate herself using that liquid. Someone would have to answer.

Tears streaked down his baby sister's face, and her body trembled as those white lines shone under her charred skin and kept creeping higher.

Yet, despite all that, her lips slowly curled upward, and she looked him in the eyes, speaking one word after another through all that misery.

"Where . . . were . . ."

Vern knew what she was going to say. She was asking where he had been all this time. So he pushed harder against the bindings of his surroundings, hoping to at least say something in return.

"Y—"

But her words were ruthlessly cut short as a golden aura flared behind her, and that fucker lashed out. "Traitor to the kin! YOU SHALL BE PUNISHED!" He held her shoulders and injected a pulsing energy into her body. And as if on cue, Ari's hands went limp, and her eyes closed as she started plummeting to the ground.

No. No no no no no no.

How did that weak bastard manage to render her unconscious? Wasn't he worse than even Esther's mother?

Was it the vision? It had to be. She just used such a potent attack and then tried to retract it. How could there be no cost to such a thing?

"May Mother's light judge your sins. The vessel will be ours, one way or the other." That piece of garbage chuckled, schadenfreude clear in his tone.

However, both of them were soon covered by the wave of deadly light as it surged with a terrifying aura again, its unwieldy momentum and devastating potency eroding whatever it touched to oblivion.

This was when Vern felt a surge of fresh breath enter his body—even if it was hotter than steam itself. It was back. He was back in control. The state of preservation forced upon everyone was dispelled alongside Ari's fall. That motherfucker dared hit Ari. He would bury that cunt so deep underground—

Crrrrrankk.

A rapid noise resounded from Vern's side, and out came the rose-haired puppeteer and Esther, a sharp look in the former's eyes. In a tone that brook no discussion, she declared, "Use everything you have! We can defend against this! This isn't the full might of the eternal annihilation. Don't let that girl's efforts go to waste!"

"Fen, make the first layer of defense. Esa and I will power you. Swordsman, you take the second and don't hold back. You two, do whatever you can. Also, keep that girl behind you alive."

Flashes of blue, red, and gray erupted around Vern, but he stood there, unmoving. Yet before anyone had to remind him of the gravity of the situation, he bit his tongue even harder and moved.

He wasn't about to throw all of Ari's efforts into the garbage by blindly rushing into that wall of radiating light. A balanced and well-thought-out reaction was the right way to go about it. Balance demanded that of him.

The fucking balance demanded that he be rational!

The device called Fen assumed the shape of a dome while the swordsman knelt in its center, his sword stabbed into the ground. Ambrose launched into a whirlwind of dance steps, tapping his cane in a specific rhythm.

Esther held her mother's hands, puppet strings steaming out of the gauntlets worn on them, spreading through the dome like a network of veins. No one talked as they finished the preparation in mere moments.

Vern rushed back into the dome, carrying Cera in his arms, and it closed shut the moment he entered. Now, the insides were lit only by the fires that burned in the eyes of everyone.

Laying Cera on the ground in a hurry, he sat beside the swordsman and shouted, "Please don't resist my vision. I can reinforce the dome."

There was no time for niceties.

Esther's mother gave him a suspicious look, but the winged angel tugged at the puppeteer's arm and nodded gently.

Sensing the dome appearing in his perception, he focused on the world of grays. In the darkness cut only by blue, red, and gray cinders, a pair of pure white ones joined the fray.

Stability inducement.

Zhishhh.

The scorching wave of radiance came like a tide of pure energy, bombarding the dome with its boundless heat and potency that would melt away even a block of cranksteel.

He felt every inch of this disastrous annihilation in his perception as it uniformly decayed, withered, and dissolved whatever it touched. He would enforce the dome to be a bright white in his perception, only for it to be eroded back to pure black almost instantly.

But like a thin rope along the edge of a cliff, it held on. This was surely the doing of the mother-daughter pair. They were somehow supplying energy to this device. He didn't understand it, and for once, he didn't feel like bothering to comprehend.

It took all his mental faculties to not scream and destroy everything here out of the pure rage that bubbled within him. But these few seconds of forced calm gave him reason to hold strong.

No one had realized he and Ari were siblings because of the specific circumstances of the situation, and Vern hoped to keep it that way. Because if he didn't, his existence would boil down to being a tool used by those fanatics to blackmail Ari.

As unreal as it sounded, that's what would happen if he dared to mess with the Eternal Directorate in his current state—a low-shade observer who would die from a single flick of their leaders. Who knew what she would agree to for them just to keep him alive?

Yeah, he would rather kill himself than let things come to that. He wasn't about to make Ari's life harder than it needed to be.

So he kept quiet while the apocalypse outside continued to take its toll on their sole bastion. Cracks appeared in abundance, but just as many sword arcs erupted from the kneeling swordsman, creating another invisible dome around them. It blocked whatever managed to pass through the primary one.

Stability inducement.

Stability inducement.

Stability inducement.

Stability inducement.

One after another, and another, and another, he executed the vision he had forged, becoming familiar with it to a new degree. After the first couple of times, it became a mindless task, giving him a chance to collect his thoughts and sort out his emotions.

This world was a little too fucked for him to not have a goal. To not yearn for and seize every ounce of power that was available to him. He was by no means slacking, but he had certainly lacked the ambition other than wanting to know the secrets of the world.

Now, however, he had one.

He realized it wasn't just about maintaining or finding a balance, for things weren't that simple. How could he strike a balance if the scale didn't even have a counterbalance? How was he to define an equilibrium if the spectrum only had one end?

Events and phenomena, when broken down into their fundamental components, revealed multiple balances—control versus freedom, logic against emotion, knowledge opposing ignorance, selfishness contrasted with altruism, tradition against innovation, experience versus intuition, ethics versus expediency, chaos versus order, and many more. A truly balanced world would minimize situations that force one to the extremes of these spectrums.

In such a world, Ari wouldn't have been forced to murder her own brother without having any say in the matter. A bookworm like himself wouldn't have been thinking so hard about life and death. Cera, that timid girl, wouldn't have had to thrust herself into danger just to eke out a meaningful life. Children wouldn't have had to sleep on the graves of their parents.

Billions wouldn't have had to die simply because of the whim of some outsider.

He understood that such an uncaring world was reality—has almost always been—but he didn't like it, and never did. Even before duskfall, one was forced to make extreme decisions out of necessity almost daily.

So he would have to create it. Create it with his own two eyes. A system that would achieve a world that's far more balanced than whatever it was right now. At least around himself. If his conjectures about observation in the long term were right, this wasn't just some delusional fantasy but an achievable goal.

He wasn't some knight of justice, nor did he plan on becoming one. He wasn't even talking about forcing his idea of balance on the rest of humanity. Instead, he firmly believed that a balanced world would allow sentient beings to have the highest freedom of expression without being inherently ruinous to those around them.

Like how black and white were only two colors, but there were infinite shades in between. Why stick to the extremes? The smaller the number of people that chose extremes, the better the world became for others.

Actions would have more consistent repercussions, be they good or bad. In one sense, it was like the idea of karma but far more comprehensive and not something regulated by supernatural forces. Instead, things would fall into place as a result of the culmination of hundreds of other minor systems being balanced properly.

It would be an inherent property of reality. And for that, he would have to work toward a level of power that would allow him to observe a wider world and more nuanced balances.

But that's when his deep introspection abruptly ended. "That girl was extraordinary," started the puppeteer with a low whisper, the tempest of eradication outside already at its tail end. "Livia couldn't do it and lost herself to the power," she added, a clear hint of melancholy coloring her tone.

It was that name again. Livia.

Brushing her daughter's cheeks with a light touch, she continued, "I am glad you're safe, Esa. If something happened to you as well . . ."

"I . . ."

Esther looked away from all of them, replying with a shaky voice, "Mom, don't call me by that name in front of everyone."

But then Ambrose chimed in, "Anyone that rebels against the religion already has my respect. But she went ahead and fought the very goddess herself. I would propose to her if I could."

Vern, who had been smiling at their words, suddenly found himself coughing. Ari and Ambrose . . . ? That was never going to happen. She would sooner die than let a nobleman court her.

Though he wondered how her current state would change her and how bad her situation could become. So Vern moved away from those who had secondhand experience and asked, "What exactly is the status quo of Elden descent? Does the host slowly lose themselves over time to the Elden will?"

The pink-haired woman turned to Vern and looked at him intently for a couple seconds before responding, "Not exactly. There's a reason the higher beings chose to descend into an observer and not just create a body out of thin air." Brushing Esther's hair gently, she continued, "They wish to make use of the specific viewpoint of their vessels. As the scholars of the Institute stated in the first axiom of observation— viewpoints are unique and cannot be replicated."

That was . . . relieving to hear. And from her words, it seemed that this Institute had multiple axioms. He would look into that at some point in time. Inferring from his previous knowledge, he guessed, "Is that to say the host doesn't lose their personality even after cohabiting with those beings?"

"In theory, yes. It's in the parasite's best interest to ensure the host doesn't deviate too far from their initial perspective. However, most lose themselves within a couple years."

Embracing Esther into her bosom, she combed her hair and added, "No one knows what the Elden Ones are, but we do know that a human's mind is too fragile to accommodate their very notion."

She didn't say a word beyond that, and Vern didn't ask either, for silent sobs filled the room. The puppeteer simply held the distressed angel, stroking her hair with utmost care.

The swordsman, or Captain Shinsei, as he had reminded the group, fell to one side, heaving roughly as blood ran down his eyes. The man had overused his eyes. Three observers held the physical dome together while he alone had taken care of every gap.

And it was finally over. It took over a minute before the stability of the dome turned dark enough to warrant his attention. According to Mrs. Lightvein, this place was polluted, and it would be a long while before it would be safe again for regular humans.

Observers polluted reality by simply existing, it seemed.

Others, Vern included, weren't faring much better either. It had been a battle of attrition, but they had won. Everyone was exhausted—physically and mentally. That bombardment of disrupting light had gone on for almost half an hour.

Esther sulked in the corner, still mad at everyone for watching her become a crybaby as a grown woman, her eyes swollen beyond measure. On the other hand, Mrs. Lightvein was fiddling around with her gauntlets while Vern looked on with annoyance and jealousy.

She told him it was a masterpiece created by the fusion of the mechanical arts of fundamentalism and the perceptual artifact forgery of observers. And that it was off-limits for him to look at its interiors even after the sacrifices he had made to save her Esa.

Ambrose was standing there, looking suave, leaning on his cane, proclaiming he was hearing the rhythm better than ever and that no one should disturb him.

"My friend Vern, care to answer a query of mine?"

Not minding the interruption of his aimless thoughts, Vern turned toward the captain and gave him a tired nod.

"Where did you disappear to during the fight? It was like you were completely gone. I couldn't feel your otherwise wild aura at all," the swordsman asked with a nonchalant bearing.

But Vern's mind jolted awake at the seemingly harmless inquiry. This was a loaded question that could very well spell his doom if handled without care. He wasn't going to share details about the third rune unless forced. It was too much of an unknown quantity and a risk.

Nodding, he made a show of settling into a better position while his mind whirled to come up with a plausible excuse. He hadn't had a chance to conjure something solid, so he would have to make do with a half-baked idea. He had no clue how well it would fare under close scrutiny.

"Right, so it was this—"

"Ahh, lemme explain that to you!" interrupted Esther with too much vigor. Vern didn't know what she had in mind. Hopefully, she wasn't rude enough to divulge his secret. Using this time to solidify his own idea, he listened in on what she had to say.

"I entrusted him my cracked ring of evanescence. It can hide one's perception in the Everflux for a while."

Vern had no clue what she was talking about. Mrs. Lightvein looked back with a dubious look while Shinsei appeared awed, and she only seemed proud to have got all of them thinking like that.

But it seemed Captain was a curious one, for he asked a follow-up question. "Why not use it on yourself?"

She shook her head, seeming disappointed by the captain's theory. "I am not shortsighted like that. Sure, I could have used it myself, but for how long? Ten seconds? Twenty? It barely managed to keep Vern, a "newbie," hidden for ten minutes. There's no way it could've proved useful to me at all. My perception would be too heavy for it to hide." She sighed melodramatically. "Well, someone has to think long term, right?"

Wow, that was . . . well thought out. He didn't expect that. Did she make up these excuses preemptively to ensure his secret didn't get out? How did that align with her interests?

Wiping away the blood from his eyes, the captain continued, "You're indeed correct, my friend. But I wonder if giving him a trip to who knows where for a few minutes was worth wasting such a precious artifact."

"Nah, nah nah, that's where you're wrong, sword master. This man right here was already on the verge of shading his perception, and those ten minutes of peace and quiet were all he needed to become a real observer. And you know how that went. We managed to contact Mom because of that—"

"Esa. That reminds me," Mrs. Lightvein interrupted her daughter. Reaching into the sack on her belt, she pulled out a decrepit-looking notebook. Lightly smacking Esther on the head with it, she said with a smile, "For you."

Esther's eyes brightened when she looked at the item, and she grabbed it with great zeal. "It's the real thing?! Just for me?"

Mrs. Lightvein nodded. "Just for you."

Vern didn't understand what all the fuss was about. He also had a notepad. Pulling his treasured record out, he parsed through it out of habit. It obviously didn't have his records from the land of the dark sun, so he would have to make sure he didn't forget any important details.

Yet, when he passed through his recollection of events at the library that he had written down like a report of some mundane experiment, his eyes fell on a name, and his pupils dilated.

Mistress Livia.

It was dated for the night of duskfall itself, and it all came back to him. Every time that name was mentioned, it sounded so familiar, and now he understood why. This was the mistress that Hensen Vehen had been rambling about!

She was connected to Hensen! And the Lightveins! Mrs. Lightvein's other daughter, who had an Elden One descend into her, was called Livia too.

Can it be a coincidence? Only the first names match. I don't even know the last names.

Still, this was big.

He might finally have a lead linking back to Hensen. If he could gather intel on the man, he might be able to prepare for his threat beforehand. This was great!

He could—

"... give Vern." The mention of his name interrupted his eureka moment, and he strained to patch together what was being talked about.

"But Esa, I acquired it for you, and I don't know how long it'll be before I can get my hands on another one! I can't have you getting stranded like this again. Ever. This decision is not up for debate," declared Mrs. Lightvein with a menacing look.

"Mum, I am not saying I don't want it. Heck, I want to talk to my academy friends every day too, but he deserves it more. We owe him this much, Mom. He's done far too much for me and received nothing but suffering in return. If we go back without a way to contact him, how will he tell us what he wants?"

A conflicted look appeared on Mrs. Lightvein's mature face as she looked back and forth between Vern and Esther.

Maybe to push her mother a little further, she added, "Also, I want to stay in touch with him." A red blush crept up her cheeks.

Vern stared at her, a little dumbfounded by that sweet smile and pure look. Yet, his paranoid mind found a plausible excuse. *Is she doing this so she can talk to me regarding the third rune later?* He couldn't tell. She was too good at acting.

Finally, after staring daggers at him for a while, Mrs. Lightvein sighed. "Okay, but you must always carry the family's convergence note on your person. Also, you will devote three hours every day in the accounting hall to facilitate the messages that still need to be sent."

"Mommmm! Three hours is tooo longgg."

"Four until I find another one."

"Uh, no, three. I will take three."

Still unsure what was going on, Vern stared at them in puzzlement. Esther made her way toward him and presented him with that decrepit-looking notebook, complementing it with that sweet smile. "A gift. You can now say thank you."

Not sure what to make of this, he accepted the notebook and replied hesitatingly, "Thank ... you? Can you tell me exactly what this is?"

With a smug grin, she began, "This right here is a convergence note. Had I had one before all this started, things would have never come to this. It allows one to write to anyone as long as they also have a convergence note of their own."

He was starting to get an idea of what she meant, but he had to be sure, so he asked, "From anywhere?"

She nodded, her bangs waving energetically.

"To anyone?"

She shook her head, her locks falling to and fro around her shoulders.

Vern tilted his head in confusion, and she smirked. "Really a newbie with no common sense." Opening the notebook to some pages filled to the brim with weird symbols and glyphs, she continued, "Just think about the person you want to send a message to, the uniqueness of their viewpoint, and start writing."

Interesting.

That made sense. Especially considering he had just learned that viewpoints were unique. Even if someone followed the same observation record, a mental image of the exact recipient and viewpoint should be enough to identify anyone on the planet.

But was she teasing him? "What do you mean blank page?" he asked.

She looked at him like he was some stupid simpleton. She gripped his shoulder, almost as if encouraging a child. "It will be all right, Vern. Someone can tell you what blank pages are if you go back to preparatory school. Let me know if you can't get in and need a recommendation, okay?"

Her sweet smile became a grin as she continued, "There's a hundred-something empty pages. If you use it judiciously, it should last you a couple years."

Vern questioned his sanity as he held the book by the edge and leafed through the whole thing, glancing at each page briefly. Not one page was empty. Not a single one.

This was either a joke. Or . . .

Or he was seeing things that others couldn't, like that gash in the sky.

Myriads of glyphs presented themselves, and Vern's mind began to churn as he tried to figure out what this could mean.

"Are you . . . not happy?" asked Esther, her voice on the verge of disappointment.

"Hey, no. Thank you very much. I just don't know what to feel about this. I clearly don't understand the value of this gift, but I am sure I'll come to appreciate it in time. Thank you, Esther. Thank you, Mrs. Lightvein."

Knock knock.

Before Esther could reply, someone had knocked on the shell of the dome, and in came a voice. "Master Shinsei, Master Akira has asked me to tell you to stop being a turtle."

Ambrose, who had been acting like he was having some out-of-world experience, suddenly jerked and shouted, "Butler De Flanc! Does Captain have some orders for me?"

"Yes, young master. He asked me to relay these words: 'Don't follow women into dark alleys next time.'"

Ambrose halted in his tracks, dumbfounded. Shinsei got up and said to Mrs. Lightvein and her daughter, "Please come, my friends. My colleagues can set you both up with a traveler that can send you back to the Northern Senn Empire."

The dome soon retracted itself, growing smaller and smaller, as the mass disappeared into thin air and the starry night revealed itself, hiding horrors unknown.

Vern looked all around him, trying to catch a glimpse of Ari. And obviously, she wasn't here. That bastard had run away and taken her along with him. He was sure that the disgusting filth probably waited to see if they would fail in their defense so he could scoop Esther away.

But the end result was still the same. Ari was gone. Again.

Sigh.

After taking a deep breath in and admiring the clear sky, Mrs. Lightvein held her daughter's hand and addressed everyone. Then in a wide gesture that combined their beauty with their otherworldly charm, they curtsied. "Thank you very much, gentlemen."

Just as thankful, if not more, Vern displayed his own gratitude with a half bow, and so did others—each in their own style. She continued, "You men have done the Lightveins a favor of life, and we owe you a debt of gratitude. I hope the choices I made during our time of distress didn't offend anyone. I would like to compensate you all for your efforts, so please don't hesitate to ask for whatever comes to your mind. Lightveins will do their best to fulfill any sensible requests you might have."

Captain pondered his response as everyone began to move out. Ambrose leaned in and whispered in Vern's ear, "Heh, you thought you were the only one that got to shill these rich women? Captain knew what their family's reputation was like and hence waited for them to offer it themselves."

Vern didn't reply and simply shook his head.

Fen carried Cera as they walked down the steep slope of the ruin. A vast donut-shaped crater had carved itself around them, extending almost halfway down this hill. It was a sickening aftermath. Not just the station but most of the hillside neighborhood had been evaporated into nothingness.

Everyone looked around with poignant looks in their eyes, but no one spoke on the matter. So Vern also let it be and marched on.

"Glad to hear that, my friends. The Vigil will suffer a loss since we've made enemies with a prominent religion in the city, so your help would be very welcome. Anyway, I am not the one to talk business on behalf of the Vigil. A colleague of mine will do that if that's okay with you?"

"Sure."

Ambrose whispered again, "Hahhah, they're gone, newbie, they're gone. He just offloaded negotiations to Captain Akira. And when that man is called, it's never pretty for the other side."

This Akira person really seemed like someone important from all the tidbits he'd heard. Hopefully, he will get a chance to meet him sometime soon.

On that note . . .

"Captain Shinsei."

"Yes, my friend?"

It was time to seize all the power and knowledge he could get his hands on and search for the balance. A better balance.

"Does the offer to join the Vigil of Duskfall still stand?"

DUSKFALL OF SORROWS

Cera awoke with a start as she reached out for something, and words spilled out of her mouth involuntarily. "I am sorry!"

"I . . . am . . ."

But then the sight registered in her mind, and the serenity of this somewhat familiar environment calmed her down. Muffled sounds of thumping and grinding rang in her ears while that routine metallic smell assailed her nose.

Then there were the gadgets and contraptions that lined the wall, all overshadowed by that giant clock, which continued its mechanical march, one tick at a time.

Withdrawing her hand, she shielded her eyes. The opulence of this room was too dazzling for her still groggy mind.

But what was this situation? Why was she here? Wasn't she . . . ? Was that a dream? Then, did she not become an observer? No. No. That can't be.

The image of that terrifying wall of gold disintegrating everything in its path was still vivid in her mind. But what had happened to everyone else? To Vern? Last she remembered, he . . . disappeared.

Did he come back?

Did he survive?

"How're you feeling, Miss Cera?" came a calm and serene voice from somewhere, and Cera almost jumped off the couch she was lying on. A mature woman with burgundy hair had her elbows planted on a table made of cogs and gears as she stared at Cera with an impassive expression.

Cera's brain churned, and she quickly realized what was going on. She had her inhibitions, but her heart didn't listen to her brain, and words came out of her lips in rapid fire. "Good morning, Madam Helena. I-I am great, and I am sorry for asking, but do you know what happened to Vern? To everyone else? What happened after I . . . passed out?"

Madam turned toward the large clock for a second, and when Cera followed her gaze, her cheeks heated up, and a surge of embarrassment washed over her.

It was seven o'clock. In the evening. Not morning. But Madam turned back and continued to stare at her silently.

This couldn't be right. Was Madam mad at her for getting the time wrong?

Her amber eyes continued to peer through Cera, unblinking. When the silence grew too much to bear, Cera began fidgeting, hundreds of bleak scenarios crossing her mind.

Did he really . . .

But before her overthinking led to destructive thoughts, Madam replied, "Vern who?"

Oh. That. Wow. I am stupid. Obviously, she doesn't know him by name.

"He . . . he was the Lennian fundamentalist in the group."

This elicited a minor reaction in Madam's impassive face, and she replied, "Oh, him? I see. Alistair didn't report any names when he dropped you off last night. But yes, he did say that the fundamentalist is doing well. He's joined the Vigil of Duskfall too, if I remember correctly."

As if a boulder had been lifted off her body, Cera sighed with relief, and her body deflated as she sagged back on the couch.

"Anyway, Miss Cera, are you ready?"

These words, however, instantly snapped Cera back to reality. Her spine straightened as the gravity of the current situation dawned on her. She was in the presence of Helena Von Arden. A magnate of unimaginable wealth, political power, and maybe even . . . tangible power.

Didn't matter if she had just survived hell. This woman had handled far worse. Cera forced her hair straight in one stroke of her fingers, rested her hands on her knees, and stared back with a serious gaze.

Madam asked again, "Ready to conduct in this city of death?"

"YES, MA'AM!"

"Master, Lady Fily's team just reported back. Fifteen new incidents have cropped up in the city, seven of them in the Athenaeum district, while the rest are distributed all over the city. I've penned the summaries in here," reported Butler De Flanc to Shinsei in his servile yet monotonous voice that was followed by a rustle of papers.

Not expecting any affirmation, he continued, "We also have news from Master Arthur's team. They're done suppressing the pollution in Starfall Heights. They've publicized the explosion to have been caused by an unstable fundamentalist device that was left unchecked." They had to maintain the veneer of objectivity, after all.

"The numbers are thirty-seven dead, one hundred and twenty injured, and an unknown number missing. Everything within a two-kilometer radius of the steamscript station was evaporated—except, of course, for Master Shinsei and others. Shock waves were felt all the way up to Westerleigh borough. And now the nobles and by extension, the crown, are demanding an explanation."

Thump.

"Hah. That's enough, Akira. If it goes on like this, they'll be expecting us to carry around their bags in a few weeks. We can't follow their every whim," interjected Shinsei, more annoyed than usual. He squinted hard, trying to figure out what outfit the butler was wearing, but obviously, his eyes couldn't see through the dark. That wasn't his blessing.

This was the reason he avoided Akira whenever he could. The man clung to darkness like moths clung to light. Shinsei considered himself somewhat of an eccentric, but this one was on another level.

T-T-Tap.

The man rapped his fingers on the table, surely cooking something up in that intelligent head of his. So Shinsei addressed the butler instead, "My friend, we don't work for the Crown. Let those paper pushers know we're here to make sure humanity lives to see another day. If they want an explanation, they can investigate themselves. Our blessings are not to be wasted to give them gossip for their tea tables."

T-T-Tap.

"Hold it, Zephyr," came the enigmatic whisper, a voice that threaded the air like silk yet held the weight of ancient tomes. He was probably one of the two or three people who knew Shinsei's first name and dared use it.

Shinsei clicked his tongue, calmed down, and waited.

"De Flanc, get someone from the unenlightened staff to pen a report with that information but ask them to spread it out across as many pages as possible. Let them know we'll cooperate, but only to an extent."

"Yes, Master."

"But Akira, my friend—"

Tap.

"Zephyr," cut in the mysterious voice, and the intensity of sounds in the room matched that of the lights.

The silence lasted for a couple seconds before the voice continued, "As you said, we have a job to do. We already have the Crown's permission to act in the city, but we're far from having our roots all over it.

"In your own words, we need to take the path of least resistance, and I am telling you this is it. I will take care of the nobles if they overstep their boundaries. Until then, can you tell me what you have on the new vessel that's harboring the result of the Directorate's sin?"

Shinsei gently rubbed the handle of his sword as the texture helped him calm down. Knowing the man spoke reason, he let it be for now and started on the matter he was here for. "We have . . . nothing. Just by the nature of her current existence, every kind of scrying has failed. As for her facial features, our seers and Kingsmen have found nothing over the past couple of days. So it's possible she's from a different city."

T-T-Tap.

"As expected. Well, it's unfortunate that we can't guess her viewpoint based on her personal history. De Flanc, look into shade sequences related to the Eternal Directorate that also support light-based visions like that explosion. That combination doesn't make sense."

"Yes, Master. Other than that, we have a couple more things. Kingsmen have requested our assistance on one of the matters that's been getting out of hand."

" . . . "

When no response came, De Flanc started again, "It's apparently a serial murder case where twenty people of different stations were found dead. They say that the victims had died while flailing around and babbling incoherently, very much mirroring what observers go through when they succumb to the whispers.'"

"But unenlightened can't hear the whispers," countered Shinsei.

"Interesting . . ."

When he heard that phrase, a chill crept up Shinsei's spine. This was his cue to get the hell out of here. He had no interest in listening in as the madman grilled his butler for every little detail. His finding something interesting was a bad omen.

Shinsei stood and began ambling in the direction from where he had come, letting the path of least resistance guide him in the darkness.

"Zephyr."

Shinsei stopped and looked back. Not that it helped, for everything was a little too dark.

"How is the new kid?"

"Well, he doesn't have the blessing of some evil god. His vision pollution quotient is instead quite low, even lower than mine. And I am supposed to be the turtle."

"Motives for joining?"

"Why the heck would I want to know that?"

"Viewpoint?"

"He kept mum."

"Smart."

"Don't worry. I'll keep an eye on him. May the clarity guide your path, my friend." Shinsei left those words in the air before leaving the darkness for good.

"Who are you writing to, Master Vern?" asked De Flanc with a curious gaze as the scenery outside the carriage window faded past them.

Vern finished penning *aaaaaaaaa* on the convergence note as he closely scrutinized the glyphs, which began glowing. They moved and transformed in a pattern, a pattern Vern couldn't understand for the life of him.

But he still replied with his official excuse, "It's just a test to figure out how much representation it costs me based on the length of the message." It was true too.

He was trying to figure out if the complexity of the message changed the cost or the way the glyphs moved. He had sent more than fifty different kinds of messages over the past few days.

"Ahh, that's very astute of you, Master Vern. I believe there might be some papers in the Vigil's library that try to answer similar queries. However, I wager their study won't be as rigorous as a fundamentalist's like yourself."

"You flatter me, De Flanc. Anyway, do you know anything about convergence notes in general?"

"Not much, Master Vern, but some have theorized it links fates. They say if you don't think of someone's name and viewpoint in particular when writing a message, one bearing the same fate as yours will end up being the recipient of your message."

"Fate, huh?"

But their conversation came to an end as their carriage halted abruptly on a deserted market road in front of a bridge. De Flanc rushed out of the carriage and opened the door for him. Vern didn't like it, but the man wouldn't listen.

"We'll have to stop here, Master Vern."

When Vern got out, he saw a group of twenty or so men standing on the other end of the bridge, guns, cleavers, knives, and whatnot in their hands as they eyed the lone figure atop the arch of the bridge.

"Since you wanted to hone your melee combat, Master Akira has temporarily assigned you under Lady Amelia, the Eclipsed Reaper, a Kingsman squadron commander that's cooperating with Vigil."

As the men clamored harder and began pushing forward on the bridge, the figure draped in black gripped the handle of the oddly shaped blade attached to her back. In a swift jerk of her hand, it opened, transforming into a scythe, its edge gleaming with a deadly sharpness.

One of the men raised his hand high before dropping it in a chopping motion.

Bang.

Bang.

Bang.

But that black figure disappeared from everyone's sight, and all Vern saw were heads flying one after another, a fog of blood soon permeated the environment.

When one received a message through a convergence note, a notion would grow in one's mind. But it was transient, and if one didn't pen it down quickly, the message would be lost.

If they tried to use any other surface to release the message, all they would write was some gibberish going through their heads. The note helped one channel that notion into words—without it, the message would be lost.

This was the reason Illeana always kept the convergence note she had stolen from her uncle's manor on her person. How could she know what was going on in Karthain from hundreds of kilometers away if she didn't get all the intel?

But something weird had been going on for a couple of days. Every few hours, she would feel a notion birthing in her mind, begging to be released on a convergence note. In hopes of not missing out on some important information, she would make some alone time from her busy schedule only to be greeted with some stupid message.

Someone was playing pranks on her. That had to be it. Either someone had figured out her viewpoint's trace and identity, which would be disastrous, or that rumor was true, and she was very unlucky.

Messages on the convergence note had to go somewhere even if there was no destination, but they were almost never linked to a real human. Then what had she done to be so damn unlucky?

It would be one thing if she was receiving anything legible. At least she could assess the emotions of the sender through the words, but this?

What were *wwww* and *bbbbbbb* supposed to mean?

It was driving her mad. And that was a big deal. It was making her lose control of her emotions.

But could she really blame herself? It had cost her so much time, tension, and anxiety. She'd had to excuse herself more than a few dozen times just to read what turned out to be stupid messages.

"Miss Ella, you're up next," shouted the handler from across the hall.

Illeana responded with a nod, already accustomed to her fake name. Dropping the silk gauze down her face, she picked up the violin and stepped out, ready for another performance.

Apparently, the new third prince of Karthain was going to be here at this ball, and she wasn't going to miss this chance to assess the emotional state, fears, and personality of her enemies.

But when she was only halfway across the hall, a notion birthed in her mind, and she halted. Pulling out a folded piece of paper and her rouge pot from the small silk pouch on her dress, she held the paper against a wall. Dipping her finger in the pot, she let the notion guide her hands.

aaaaaaaaa

She closed her eyes and gripped the violin's bow tighter. And tighter. Her arms trembled, and right as the wooden bow was about to give way, she let out a deep breath.

This was it.

She had lost enough sleep and opportunities because of this stupid prank. Dipping her fingers in the rouge another time, she penned these four words in the most disturbing fonts she could manage.

SHUT THE FUCK UP!

"The fate of our planet rests upon this vote. Members, declare your stance."

"Elysian Circle stands in favor."

"Aetheric Collective firmly opposes this blasphemy."

"Astral Conclave, aligned in favor."

"Coven of Truth echoes approval."

"Transcendent Circle, resolutely opposed."

"Veiled Sovereigns cast their favor."

"Twilight Society shadows agree."

"The scales have tipped in favor. As decreed, the Third Confluence of Visionaries shall be invoked under the Luminar sky of Year 732. Each faction must bear the sacred cost of summoning the era's visionaries. Beware, for those who falter in their duty shall find no sanctuary among us."

"May the clarity guide your path."

As the assembly dissolved into whispers, two figures lingered in the shadows, the former's eyes glinting with an unreadable emotion. The latter, on his knees, chimed in, "Mistress, the Coven of Truth voted in the favor of this motion. Should I go and knock some sense into Ruppert?"

"Not necessary. Our talks with the coven have broken down. This was expected."

"I see. It shall be as you say, Mistress."

"How's your rune?"

"I . . . I—"

"Speak!" interjected the cold voice.

"I . . . I can't maintain contact."

The figure stood up from the seat, turned around, and left as her words lingered in the air, "Sort it out or pass it on to a more worthy candidate. That rune is the only reason the Collective is paying the cost to keep you sane."

"Yes . . . Mistress."

About the Author

FiniteVoid writes computer science concepts disguised as epic progression fantasy. Also, Void is actually just 13m^3. Trust him.